# VOICE FOR THE VOICELESS

Thorsons
An imprint of HarperCollins*Publishers*
1 London Bridge Street
London SE1 9GF

www.harpercollins.co.uk

HarperCollins*Publishers*
Macken House, 39/40 Mayor Street Upper
Dublin 1, D01 C9W8, Ireland

First published by HarperCollins*Publishers* 2025

2 4 6 8 10 9 7 5 3



Designed by Nancy Singer
Map by Alexis Seabrook
Title page illustration @ 心灵艺坊/stock.adobe.com
All photographs in the photo insert are courtesy of Tibet Museum, Dharamsala

A catalogue record of this book is available from the British Library

ISBN 978-0-00-877409-7
NON FICTION

Printed and bound in India by Thomson Press India Ltd

# VOICE FOR THE VOICELESS

## OVER SEVEN DECADES OF STRUGGLE WITH CHINA FOR MY LAND AND MY PEOPLE

HIS HOLINESS THE

DALAI LAMA

Thorsons

# Contents

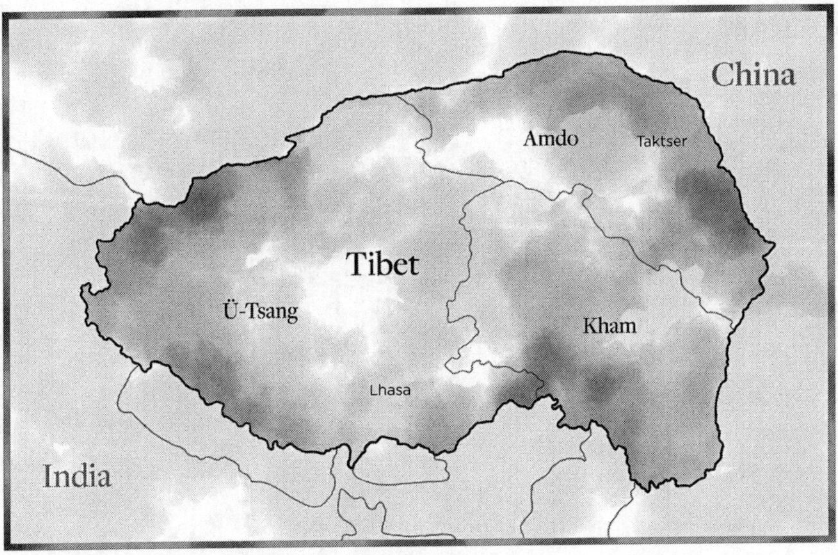


Historical Tibet traditionally comprised the regions of Ü-Tsang, Kham, and Amdo.

Disclaimer: This map is not to scale and is for illustrative purposes only. The boundaries shown are neither authenticated nor intended to reflect the official position of any government. For official boundaries, please refer to the Survey of India or the relevant authoritative sources.

# Preface

On March 17, 1959, in the darkness and frozen air of the night, I slipped out of the main gate of the Norbulingka Palace disguised and wearing a *chuba*, an everyday layman's form of clothing. That began what turned out to be more than six decades of life in exile away from my homeland of Tibet. Although the seed that grew into my need to flee was sown by the Communist Chinese invasion of my country in 1950, the immediate trigger was the tension that had been building up in the Tibetan capital city of Lhasa, exploding into a people's uprising on March 10, 1959. For nearly nine years, after the invasion, I had tried to come to some kind of accommodation with the Communist Chinese for the sake of my people's well-being, but it was an impossible task. A few days after my departure, China's People's Liberation Army bombarded the city. In this way, the tragic tale of my homeland and people over the second half of the twentieth century and into the twenty-first unfolded.

Ever since first being forced into exile in India in 1959, my primary task has been the cause of Tibet and its people. I am now approaching my ninth decade. The issue of Tibet remains unresolved, while my homeland is still in the grip of repressive Communist Chinese rule. Tibetans inside Tibet continue to be deprived of their dignity as a people and their freedom to live their lives according to their own wishes and their culture, as they did for more than a millennium before 1950. Since any expression of Tibetan identity is seen today as a threat by Tibet's new rulers, there is the danger that in the name of "stability" and "territorial integrity" attempts might be made to erase our civilization.

This book is, primarily, an account of more than seven decades of my dealing with successive leaders of Communist China on behalf of Tibet and its people. It is also an appeal to the conscience of the Chinese people—many of whom share with us a spiritual heritage in Mahayana Buddhism (which I refer to as the Sanskrit tradition)—as well as the broader international community, to care for the plight of the Tibetan people. Ours is an existential crisis: the very survival of an ancient people and their culture, language, and religion is at stake. Drawing on the lessons learned from my long period of engagement with Beijing, the book also aims to offer some suggestions on what might be the path forward. Given that ours is the struggle of a people with a long history of distinct civilization, it will, if necessary, continue beyond my lifetime. The right of the Tibetan people to be the custodians of their own homeland cannot be indefinitely denied, nor can their aspiration for freedom be crushed forever through oppression. One clear lesson we know from history is this: if you keep people permanently unhappy, you cannot have a stable society.

# Introduction

Unlike all my other missions, which I have chosen for myself, the responsibility for the nation and people of Tibet was placed upon me the moment I was recognized as the Dalai Lama at the age of two. It was formalized in 1950, when I became Tibet's temporal leader at the age of sixteen.* Since that time, I have carried the duty of protecting Tibet and its people as well as our culture at the center of my heart and will do so as long as I am alive.

This principal commitment is in addition to the other commitments that I have taken on as part of my life's mission, including promoting fundamental human values based on a universal or secular approach to ethics, fostering interreligious understanding and harmony, and encouraging a deeper appreciation of India's ancient wisdom and knowledge. In these other domains, I feel happy that I have been able to make some tangible contributions, through

* This is according to the Tibetan system of counting; according to the non-Tibetan system, the Dalai Lama's age at the time was fifteen. All annotations, as well as the Selected Bibliography, were prepared by the editor, the Dalai Lama's longtime English translator Thupten Jinpa, to help offer the reader key sources and necessary further explanations.

wide-ranging conversations, the writing of books, and extensive international visits.

In the case of Tibet, my first and most intimate charge, it has been much more difficult. I have tried my best, ceaselessly, to make openings for a negotiated settlement with the Chinese Communists, who invaded my country in 1950. There have been three periods of intense dialogue: in the 1950s, when I was resident in Tibet as a young leader; in the 1980s, when the Chinese leader Deng Xiaoping opened up China; and in the first decade of this century. In all other aspects of my life and in all other domains of my work, I have engaged with people who have shown a commitment to shared vision, an openness to trust, the honesty to express one's thoughts even in disagreement, and the willingness to truly engage and learn. With the Chinese Communist leadership, from Chairman Mao Zedong to President Xi Jinping in the current era, sadly, the situation has been very different. I have often complained that the Chinese Communist leaders have only a mouth to speak but no ear to listen.

Take, for example, the white paper on Tibet issued by the Chinese government in May 2021. The document began with the statement that, after the Chinese invasion of 1950, the people of Tibet "broke free from the fetters of invading imperialism for good, embarking on a bright road of unity," and today Tibetans enjoy "a stable social environment, economic and cultural prosperity." According to this narrative, ever since Communist China's "peaceful liberation" of Tibet, the Tibetan nation and people have been on a continuous upward trajectory to freedom, prosperity, and contentment within the family of the People's Republic of China (PRC). Had this been true, at any period since the invasion, how does one explain more than seven decades of continued resistance and resentment of China's presence on the part of the Tibetans? It seems that Communist China has a simple answer: it's because of "the splittist activity of the Dalai clique." What they are referring to here is our long nonviolent campaign for the freedom of our people, and our efforts to save our unique language, culture, ecology, and religion. We Tibetans are the people who have traditionally inhabited the Tibetan plateau for millennia, and have every right to continue to be the custodians in our own homeland. The issue of Tibet is not about the matter of economic development, which we acknowledge as having improved significantly since the economic liberalization of the People's Republic of China. The issue is about a people's need and right to exist with their distinct language, culture, and religious heritage. Since the people inside Tibet have no freedom to speak out, it has fallen to me especially, since I came into exile in 1959, to be the voice of the voiceless.

While our goal remains to find a mutually agreeable negotiated solution, that aim would require in the end that the Tibetans and the Chinese sit down together and talk. Until such a negotiated solution is found, we Tibetans who are in the free world have the moral responsibility to continue to speak on behalf of our brothers and sisters inside Tibet. Doing so is neither anti-China nor "splittist." Indeed, far from splitting, being honest and open is the only way to create the basis on which each side can understand and accommodate the needs of the other. Only when we have created an atmosphere where both sides can speak and negotiate freely can there be a lasting settlement.

We have been fortunate to have so many friends around the world who have stood in solidarity with us and our cause. Governments, especially at the parliamentary level, and international organizations across the free world have strongly supported our approach, which seeks genuine autonomy for Tibet—a middle way between the independence cherished by the Tibetans, on the one hand, and, on the other, the current reality on the ground that denies agency or any meaningful self-rule for the Tibetan people in their own homeland. A series of resolutions has been passed by the United Nations, by the European Parliament, and in many countries, including especially the United States, where, in addition to resolutions, important acts have been adopted.

We have been particularly fortunate in having received such a generous welcome and such continuing support from India and its people, including successive governments since I arrived in India as a refugee. From India's first prime minister, Pandit Jawaharlal Nehru, to the present prime minister, Narendra Modi, India has never wavered in its hospitality, generosity, and support to me, the Tibetan refugees, and our efforts at educating our youth and the rebuilding of our culture and institutions in exile. For me personally, this has been deeply heartwarming.

Ever since the seventh century, when the Buddhist texts were first translated from Sanskrit into Tibetan, we Tibetans have looked up to India as "the land of the noble ones" (Aryavarta). Our Buddhist tradition, which we cherish so deeply, came from India. Our written script was invented in the seventh century, taking the Indian Devanagari as its model. Our philosophies, psychology, logic, and cosmology are the gifts of the Indian Nalanda school. Our astro-sciences and calendar system are deeply enriched by the Indian Kalachakra tantra. Our medical science and practice have been influenced by Indian Ayurveda. So, to have found India as my second home has offered me a powerful anchor.

I have spent the greater part of my life in India. And I sometimes describe myself as a son of India. My mind has been nourished by India's rich philosophical tradition, while my body has been fed by Indian rice and dal. When I used to travel internationally, I often stated that I am a messenger of two great gifts from India to humanity—religious pluralism and the teaching of ahimsa, the principle of nonviolence.

I have had more than seven decades of engagement with the People's Republic of China since 1950. During this long period, we have seen at least five different eras within the leadership of the country. First, under Chairman Mao, ideology was prominent amid vast and constant social upheaval, culminating in the disastrous Cultural Revolution. Millions died and many more suffered tremendously. Then, in the era of Deng Xiaoping, ideology became less important and the stress was on wealth creation. Deng, in fact, became famous for his slogan "To get rich is glorious." This was followed by the age of Jiang Zemin, during which Communist Party membership expanded to embrace other sectors of Chinese society, under the slogan "Three Represents."* Next came the period of Hu Jintao and his slogan "socialist harmonious society," where, at least on the surface, there was a focus on closing the growing wealth gap that had developed since the era of Deng. Today, China is under the leadership of Xi Jinping, who proclaimed the slogan of "New Era of Socialism with Chinese Characteristics." Judging by Xi's last decade in office, when it comes to individual freedom and everyday life, China seems to be reverting to the oppressive policies of Mao's time, but now enforced through state-of-the-art digital technologies of surveillance and control. What we have in China is, in essence, market capitalism tied to a Leninist obsession with state control. This is a fundamental paradox—profoundly unstable because essential to capitalism is the opening up of the economy, which ultimately requires the opening up of society, while the fixation on control at every level by the Party requires the closing of society. These two polar forces are pulling in opposite directions. The question is, how long can this last?

Even within a history of approximately seventy-five years, there has been tremendous change hidden beneath the apparent continuity of a single governing Communist Party. Specifically, between the eras of Mao and Deng, change was fundamental and astonishingly swift. Those who are old enough to remember the Cold War might recall how the Soviet Union seemed so stable and enduring. But when change came, it did so with extraordinary speed and in ways very few Kremlinologists had predicted. One thing is for sure: no totalitarian regime, whether headed by an individual or a party, can last forever, because

* Jiang articulated this theory to define a new relationship between the Chinese Communist Party and the people, with the need for the Party to represent what he called: (1) the development trend of China's advance productive forces; (2) the orientation of China's advance culture; and (3) the fundamental interests of the majority of the Chinese people.

they abuse the very people they claim to speak for, and also yearning for freedom is a powerful force within human nature. Furthermore, the very nature of their rule—paranoid, suspicious, and afraid of ordinary citizens—makes totalitarian regimes inherently unstable, even if the gun may prevail in the short term. In the case of Communist China, the popular movement of students in 1989 in Tiananmen Square demonstrated the deep aspiration of the people for individual freedom and a real opening. Regardless of how China might look today from the outside, the simple fact remains that this aspiration for greater freedom has not gone away.

Thanks to Deng's turn to capitalism and his opening up of China to the outside world, it is undeniable that today China is a major economic power. And of course, with economic power comes military might and international political influence. How the country exercises these newfound powers over the next decade or two will define its course for the foreseeable future. Will it choose the path of dominance and aggression, both internally and externally? Or will it choose the path of responsibility and embrace a constructive leading role on the world stage in meeting the collective challenges of humanity, such as peace, climate change, and the alleviation of poverty? Today, China stands at a crossroads. That it chooses the latter path is in the interest not only of the whole world but of the Chinese people themselves. In essence, this is a matter of the very heart of China as a country and its people. Here, I believe that resolving the long-standing problem of Tibet through dialogue would be a powerful signal, both to its own people and to the world, that China is choosing the second of these two paths. What is required on the part of their leadership are long-term vision, courage, and magnanimity.

CHAPTER 1

# The Invasion and Our New Master

On October 7, 1950, some forty thousand soldiers of the People's Liberation Army crossed the Drichu (Yangtze) River in Kham (eastern Tibet). By the nineteenth of the month, they had taken Chamdo as well as the governor of eastern Tibet, Ngabö Ngawang Jigme, who had been recently appointed to the post. Thus began Communist China's invasion of my country. The newly independent India protested to the People's Republic of China, stating that the invasion was not in the interest of peace in the region. I was only sixteen years old at the time, according to the Tibetan system of counting age. By then, I already had a suspicion that something terrible was looming, for I had once, snooping, seen a sign of disbelief on the face of Regent Tadrak Rinpoche as he read a letter presented to him.* I later discovered that the letter was in fact a telegram from Ngabö, the governor of eastern Tibet, reporting a raid on a Tibetan post by Chinese soldiers.

* Tadrak Rinpoche was, at the time, both the regent for the young Dalai Lama as well as his senior tutor, responsible for overseeing the latter's formal education.

A few minutes later, the regent walked out of his room and gave orders to summon the Kashag (cabinet). On November 11, the Tibetan government appealed to the United Nations:

> To the Secretary General of the United Nations,
>
> The attention of the world is riveted on Korea where aggression is being resisted by an international force. Similar happenings in remote Tibet are passing without notice. It is in the belief that aggression will not go unchecked and freedom unprotected in any part of the world that we have assumed the responsibility of reporting through you recent happenings in the border area of Tibet. . . .
>
> . . . The conquest of Tibet by China will only enlarge the area of conflict and increase the threat to the independence and stability of other Asian countries.

Only El Salvador attempted to place Tibet on the agenda of the General Assembly of the United Nations. Sadly, none of the great powers supported the move. One would have hoped, given Great Britain's historical involvement in Tibet, including the signing of bilateral agreements, such as the Lhasa and the Simla Conventions (respectively of 1904 and 1914), that it would have had greater sympathy and might have stood by us, especially at this crucial moment in Tibet's history. The world seemed to have abandoned us.

Great Britain and the other powers asserted there was a lack of clarity about Tibet's exact status. Yet they knew very well that in 1950 Tibet was an independent nation. The status of Tibet's independence according to international law was confirmed later by the International Commission of Jurists in 1959, following my escape into exile. The tragic irony is that it was, in fact, Great Britain and Russia, the two empires competing for power in Central Asia in what came to be called the Great Game, who were among those responsible for muddying the waters of Tibet's international status. Great Britain, in particular, had dealt with Tibet directly as an independent nation capable of making decisions on its own. It had even supplied weapons so Tibet could protect its eastern border against the Chinese. Yet it had also conducted bi-party negotiations with Nationalist China as if the latter had some claim over Tibet, invoking the obscure concept of suzerainty* and distinguishing it from sovereignty. If you will allow me to provide some historical context, Britain chose not to appreciate the crucial difference between the Qing empire and the modern nation-state of China: The former was a Manchu empire that had, at various times, different nations under its protectorate. Modern China, on the other hand, was claiming to be an anti-imperialist multi-nation state, not an empire. So the basic logic behind China's claim over Tibet, even in terms of suzerainty rather than sovereignty, was flawed. The failure (or political unwillingness) to see through this flawed logic and the refusal to accept the actual facts on the ground that showed Tibet's independence, as well as the various moves already made in the Great Game, are what had created the fog obscuring Tibet's "legal status" from the international point of view.

Communist China's invasion impacted me personally in a profound way. I remember hearing from the sweepers at the Potala Palace that posters had been put up around the Tibetan capital city, Lhasa, asking that I be given full temporal power. I was told that street songs were being sung by people demanding that the Dalai Lama be given his majority. The opinion on what to do, however, was divided—with one side saying that the Dalai Lama was too young, while others asserted that the time had indeed come to empower me. In the end,

* *Cambridge Dictionary* defines "suzerainty" as "the right of a country to partly control another."

the Tibetan cabinet headed by the regent decided to consult the State Oracles.*

At a certain point in the ceremony, whose tense atmosphere was unmistakable given the stakes, one of the oracles, while in a trance, laid a *kata* (ceremonial white scarf) on my lap and shouted, "*Dü la bab*" (The time has come). So, on November 17, 1950, I was enthroned as Tibet's temporal leader, two years before the traditional age in normal circumstances. To mark the occasion, I granted a general amnesty across Tibet and asked that all prisoners be freed.

Communist China's forcible invasion thrust me into this leadership role. With a single stroke, it turned a carefree young boy into someone with the heavy responsibility of leading a nation under attack. This is why I often say that at age sixteen I lost my freedom. My country too suffered the same fate: by the end of November, about seven weeks after the invasion, Kham (eastern Tibet) had effectively fallen.

As the new leader of a people faced with the threat of full-scale war, toward the end of the year I decided in consultation with my cabinet to send delegations to India, the United States, Great Britain, and Nepal, hoping to persuade these countries to intervene on our behalf. I also sent a delegation to Chamdo in eastern Tibet with the hope that we could negotiate a withdrawal of China's army from our territory. With the Communist Chinese forces consolidating in eastern Tibet, it was decided that I should move with the cabinet from Lhasa to Yadong (Yatung) near the Indian border, in case we needed to flee the country. Strangely, one of my first major acts as Tibet's ruler turned out to be the escape toward the Indian border. My mother took this opportunity to go to India on a pilgrimage, and she left accompanied by my youngest brother, Tenzin Choegyal.

---

* The practice of consulting oracles is common in Tibetan Buddhism, and the State Oracles here refer principally to Nechung and Gadong, who are associated especially with the lineage of the Dalai Lamas.

The People's Liberation Army meanwhile paused at Gyamda, near the western borders of Kham. The road to Lhasa was open, but they wanted to take the rest of the country without the use of force. We had no option but to authorize a delegation to go to Beijing to conduct a negotiation forced upon us. It was the same governor of eastern Tibet, Ngabö, who was chosen to lead this delegation. We told Ngabö that he could open negotiations with my authority on the condition that the Chinese advance no farther. In April 1951, my delegation arrived in Beijing and formal discussions began.

Although there was sporadic communication with the team by wire at the beginning, thereafter there was silence while I waited at the monastery in Yadong. Then, on May 23, 1951, while listening to my old Bush radio, I heard on the Tibetan-language broadcast from Radio Peking that a Seventeen-Point Agreement for the Peaceful Liberation of Tibet had been signed that day by the People's Republic of China and what was described as "the local government of Tibet." You can imagine my shock. The broadcast went on to say Tibet had been occupied for the last hundred years by aggressive imperial forces who had carried out all kinds of deceptions and provocations, plunging the people into the depths of enslavement and suffering. I felt physically sickened by this cocktail of lies and insults.

Only after my delegation returned to Lhasa did I discover what had actually happened during the negotiations. My representatives were coerced, insulted, abused, and threatened with personal violence against themselves as well as military action against the people of Tibet. As the delegation sat down to negotiate, they were presented with the already prepared text of a ten-point draft agreement. My delegation argued that Tibet is an independent country, and produced evidence to support the case. The Chinese side, of course, dismissed this. They then revised the original ten-point draft into a seventeen-point document and presented this as a final ultimatum. Under duress, the Tibetan delegation had no choice but to yield. In the absence of any communication with me or my government, Ngabö and his colleagues had no authority to sign any agreement on behalf of Tibet. Still, the Chinese asked if Ngabö had brought the official seal of the Tibetan government, and although he had the seal of the governor of eastern Tibet with him, he denied possessing any seal. Undeterred, the Chinese then forged new seals for each delegate and had the document signed on May 23, 1951, effectively in the individual names of the five Tibetan delegates.

On July 14, I received a delegation from China bearing a letter to me from Chairman Mao. I told Chinese General Chang Ching-wu that I would reply to Mao on the issue of the Seventeen-Point Agreement after I'd returned to Lhasa from Yadong and was able to consult with other Tibetan officials. Understandably, there was an intense debate within the Tibetan National Assembly in Lhasa as to whether I should return to the capital. I decided against fleeing to India from Yadong then, and turned down also an offer from the United States to broker a place of refuge. In the end, I decided that it was best to return to Lhasa, and in September 1951, the Tibetan National Assembly held a special session. Ngabö made a formal presentation of the supposed agreement. After a long debate, it was felt that we had no choice given the massive numbers of Communist Chinese troops at our door. At the time, the entire Tibetan army consisted of approximately 8,500 soldiers, while more than 80,000 battle-hardened soldiers of the People's Liberation Army stood ready to march into Tibet. Tibet's small force was armed mostly with old British Enfield rifles, machine guns, and mortars.

The Seventeen-Point Agreement opens with a preamble that presents a fanciful revision of the history of Tibet in relation to China—"the Tibetan nationality is one of the nationalities with a long history within the boundaries of China, . . . our great Motherland." Let me quote the following key provisions:

- "The Tibetan people shall return to the big family of the Motherland—the People's Republic of China."

- "The local government of Tibet shall actively assist the People's Liberation Army to enter Tibet and consolidate the national defense."
- "The Tibetan people have the right of exercising national regional autonomy under the leadership of the Central People's Government."
- "The Central Government will make no change with regard to the existing political system in Tibet. The central authorities will not alter the established status, functions and powers of the Dalai Lama."
- "The religious beliefs, customs, and habits of the Tibetan people shall be respected, and lama monasteries shall be protected."
- "The spoken and written language and school education of the Tibetan nationality will be developed step by step in accordance with the actual conditions in Tibet."*

Although the agreement was forced upon us, the text of the document clearly commits the People's Republic of China to guaranteeing regional autonomy and self-government to Tibet, including freedom of religion, protection of language, custodianship of our land and its ecology, and our right to exist as a distinct people with its unique culture and heritage. This agreement became the basis of my government's relationship with China until 1959, when I escaped. It also appeared to have become the basis for the position of some in the international community on the status of Tibet. There seems to be a strange contradiction here. Regardless of the geopolitical situation at the time, the fact remains that consideration of Tibet as having become part of the People's Republic of China after 1950 accepts the justification

* The full text of the Seventeen-Point Agreement can be found in International Commission of Jurists, *Question of Tibet*, 139–42; Tsering Shakya, *Dragon in the Land of Snows*, appendix 1.

of the rightness of conquest and the validity of an agreement signed under duress. On the part of Tibet, the Seventeen-Point Agreement was imposed on a coerced delegation and at the threat of a conqueror's massed army at the door.

Even though Beijing would later justify its forcible invasion on historical claims of ownership of Tibet, it seems clear that, for Mao at least, at the time of the invasion of Tibet it was a blatant land grab of an independent nation by force. His view of Tibet as independent is reflected in a statement I was told he once made to the American journalist and author Edgar Snow. Referring to the foraging for food committed by his Red Army in Tibetan areas during the Long March, Mao said that this was the Chinese Communists' only foreign debt, which would need to be repaid one day. Today we also know, from archival records, that in January 1950, Mao asked Joseph Stalin if the Soviet Union would lend China military transport planes to ferry Chinese troops in a plan to invade Tibet.

I am told that some geopolitical scholars and historians suggest two primary motives behind Mao's invasion of Tibet, in the immediate aftermath of establishing a Communist government in Beijing. One relates to what Mao and his Communist colleagues saw as the need to restore China's "national honor," especially in the wake of what they refer to as the "hundred years of national humiliation." An important part of this, according to their view, was the reclaiming of territories that had once been part of the Manchu Qing empire. In this regard, Mao may have felt that Tibet's independence represented a visible "loss" or contradiction, given Communist China's claim to all territories once portrayed as part of the Qing empire.

The second reason, the experts suggest, pertains to Tibet's strategic geography with its borders touching East Turkistan (Xinjiang), India, Nepal, and Bhutan, and, of course, China to the east. In 1954, the Panchen Lama, three years my junior in age, whose institution is one of the most prominent in Tibetan Buddhism and closely associated with the Dalai Lamas, joined me on a trip to Beijing. Mao told him the following: "Now that the Tibetans are cooperating with the Han, our national defense line is not the Upper Yangtse River but the Himalaya Mountains."* Regardless of their motivations, we found ourselves under Communist China's boot.

* What Mao said to the Panchen Lama then is cited (in English translation) in Melvyn C. Goldstein, *A History of Modern Tibet*, vol. 2, *The Calm Before the Storm: 1951–1955* (Berkeley: University of California, 2007), 22. "Han" refers to ethnic Chinese who constitute the overwhelming majority within the People's Republic of China.

## CHAPTER 2

# Meeting Chairman Mao

In my role as the Dalai Lama, I was trying to mitigate the disaster for my people. On October 26, 1951, approximately three thousand troops from the People's Liberation Army's Eighteenth Route Army entered Lhasa. Soon after, a further large detachment of soldiers arrived, and combined with a large influx of horses, this led to a serious food shortage. Lhasa in 1951 had a local population of just over thirty thousand, so one can imagine the impact of such a massive influx of Chinese troops in the city. This situation came to worsen further as thousands of Tibetans came as refugees from eastern Tibet.

The period between 1951 and 1959 proved to be one of the most challenging times of my life. In part, I was still studying intensively for my final Geshe Lharam degree. Geshe Lharam is the highest academic degree one can obtain within the formal scholarly training of the great monastic universities of the Geluk school, analogous to a doctorate in divinity, which would culminate in February 1959. In part, I was going through a massive learning curve as a young man in the complexities of politics, having received no formal training in any of these matters.

Of course, the rigorous education I was receiving in Buddhist philosophy and psychology did help me immensely in maintaining my sanity against the complex political challenges I had no choice but to face as the leader of the Tibetan people. And my on-the-job education meant dealing with the very real disagreements between my government and the Chinese generals who were stationed in Lhasa and had all the guns. I was often caught between the extremely reluctant and at times confrontational Tibetan officials, on the one hand, and the increasing heavy-handedness and haughty attitudes of the Chinese generals, on the other. Ultimately, in 1952, my two prime ministers (one lay and one monastic) were forced to resign by the Chinese. I made the decision not to appoint replacements to these posts since they would simply be scapegoats, and it was better that I accept the responsibilities myself. The situation in Lhasa was getting more tense by the day.

I also still had to govern, and one of my priorities was to improve our system and society. I set up a reform committee to help create a more equitable system with explicit attention paid to the needs of the ordinary people and the poor. As a child growing up, I learned a lot from sweepers at my residence, who were often my playmates, about the problem of injustice and abuse by the powerful. But I faced major obstacles from the Chinese since they wanted reforms according to their own system, along lines introduced in mainland China. They probably felt that if changes were initiated by the Tibetans themselves, it might hinder their own agenda.

So, when in 1954 the Chinese government invited me to Beijing, I felt it was the only option left to me to attempt to improve my people's deteriorating situation. In June, I received a telegram from Deng Xiaoping, then the senior figure responsible for Tibetan affairs in the Chinese leadership, inviting me to attend the inaugural National People's Congress in Beijing in September 1954. The same invitation was extended to the Panchen Lama. Although the Tibetans in Lhasa were deeply concerned about my trip to Beijing, I decided that it was best that I go for the sake of my people. To assuage their fear, during a large gathering of Tibetans at a religious ceremony at Norbulingka, my summer residence, I reassured them and promised to be back within a year.

To this day, I remember when I left Lhasa for Beijing, there were so many people crying. I heard some of the older women shouting, "Please don't go! It would be not good!" As there was no bridge over the Kyichu River at the time, we had to cross it in the traditional Tibetan coracles, made out of yak hide stretched over a willow frame. On the sides of the river there were so many people crying; some even seemed they might jump into the river. Later I heard that some fainted and even died.

On September 4, 1954, Panchen Lama and I, with our delegations, finally arrived in Beijing by train from Xi'an. We were received at the station by Prime Minister Zhou Enlai; Vice Chairman Zhu De, who was also the commander-in-chief of the People's Liberation Army and a member of the Standing Committee of the Politburo; and other Chinese officials. A few days later, I met Chairman Mao Zedong himself for the first time. He was sixty-one years old to my nineteen. He was warm and welcoming.

This meeting, joined by other top leaders, including Zhao Enlai and Liu Shaoqi, took place at the house of reception, a former imperial garden adjacent to the Forbidden City and later transformed into a compound that houses government offices as well as residences for senior leadership. The setting of this meeting was quite majestic with its opulent imperial legacy unmistakable. Here we were, myself only nineteen years old and the Panchen Lama sixteen years old, in a formal meeting with Chairman Mao himself, flanked by Communist China's most senior leaders. That we felt awed and somewhat nervous would be an understatement. At this first meeting, only Chairman Mao and I spoke. Mao said that he and the Central Government were very happy about my first visit to Beijing, and that the relationship between Chinese and Tibetans was very important. He also assured me that in the future the Central Government would make great efforts to help develop Tibet. On my part, I responded to Mao, saying I was very happy to have the opportunity to meet him and other leaders of the Chinese Communist Party.

The meeting lasted about an hour. As we left, Mao and other leaders accompanied us out of the house, and Mao himself opened the car door for me. As I was getting into the car, Mao shook my hand and said, "Your coming to Beijing is coming back to your own home. Whenever you come to Beijing, you can call on me. . . . Don't be shy; if you need anything, just tell me directly."

I came out of that meeting impressed with Mao and encouraged at the possibility that things could improve in Tibet. With me in the car was Phuntsok Wangyal, a rare Tibetan Communist, who was my official interpreter during my stay in Beijing. I was so relieved that this first meeting with Mao and other Chinese leaders went well—in fact, I hugged Phuntsok Wangyal and told him that Mao was truly unlike anyone I had met. The success of this first meeting also reassured my Tibetan entourage, including especially my senior tutor, Ling Rinpoche, who had been feeling quite worried about me. Phuntsok Wangyal was a true believer in Communism in its original Marxist internationalist sense. And at the time he believed, later to his disappointment, that the Chinese Communists also shared this internationalist vision of Marxism. (Decades later, when Phuntsok Wangyal was allowed to visit Europe, I was able to speak with him by phone. I asked him, "What happened to your dream of true socialism?" He just laughed.)

On September 16, I addressed the first National People's Congress, noting that the draft constitution of the People's Republic of China states, in particular, that all nationalities may draw up their rules governing the exercise of autonomy and separate regulations in accordance with the special features of the development so that they can exercise full autonomy. By then, I had been made a vice president of the steering committee of the People's Republic of China.

During my stay in Beijing, I had several meetings with Mao and other leaders, including Zhou Enlai and Deng Xiaoping. In Beijing, I was introduced to a number of senior international leaders as well, including the Indian Prime Minister Jawaharlal Nehru, the Soviet leader Nikita Khrushchev, and the Burmese Prime Minister U Nu. Whenever I had some free time, I also took classes from my senior tutor Ling Rinpoche on the philosophically dense "insight" section of Tsongkhapa's *Great Treatise on the Stages of the Path to Enlightenment*. Technically, I was still a student, studying for my Geshe Lharam exams. One memorable experience of my stay in Beijing included the conducting of a formal Buddhist teaching—in fact, an important initiation ceremony of a meditation practice known as Vajrabhairava—to an assembly of Chinese Buddhists who were followers of Tibetan Buddhism. My translator at this teaching was the Chinese monk Fa-Tsun, who informed me that he was working on a Tibetan translation of a major Buddhist philosophical text, *Great Treatise on Differentiation* (*Mahavibhasha*)—a second-century work extant only in Chinese translation. By then Fa-Tsun had already translated a major Tibetan work, entitled *The Great Treatise on the Stages of the Path to Enlightenment*, by the fourteenth-century master Tsongkhapa.

Then I went on an arranged tour of cities within China, such as Tianjin, to see the way in which the Communist government had industrially developed the country. Phuntsok Wangyal was assigned as my translator during this tour, and I was accompanied also by another Communist cadre by the name of Liu Geping, a member of the ethnic Hui (Muslim) minority. I met many party members of different ranks, some veterans of the revolution and many very sincere Communists. Incidentally, one of these was Xi Zhongxun, father of the current Chinese leader Xi Jinping. He had an affable personality and seemed quite broad-minded. I really liked him. (I was told that he treasured all his life a wristwatch I had given him at the time.)

I was impressed by the sense of purpose and dedication displayed by many of these first-generation revolutionaries, as well as their obvious successes in their attempt to create a more egalitarian society. I learned much about Marxism-Leninism, and was particularly struck by the emphasis in Marxist economic theory on equal distribution of resources rather than pure profit-making. The idea of taking care of the less privileged people, of the working class, is wonderful. To oppose all exploitation, and to strive for a society without national boundaries—these are excellent ideals. As I was exposed to all this in my youth, these aspects of socialist thinking left a strong impression such that I sometimes describe myself as half-Buddhist and half-Marxist. However, as I have thought about it over the years, what is lacking in Marxism is compassion. Its greatest flaw is the total neglect of basic human values, and the deliberate promotion of hate through class struggle. Furthermore, as time went on, in the case of Communist China, Marxism seemed to have given way to Leninism, with state control of the people by the Party as the primary objective.

During this tour around China, I had the rare opportunity to cross into Inner Mongolia for a brief visit.* It was a moving experience given the long and close association between Tibetans and Mongols spiritually. Although for me this tour of Chinese cities was educational and enjoyable, most of my officials, including my two tutors, were completely uninterested. So when it was announced that there was going to be no more sightseeing, there was a collective sigh of relief. My mother, in particular, did not enjoy her stay in China, especially the hectic sightseeing schedule. At one point she even got ill with a serious case of flu. Since my return to Beijing from the tour was close to Losar (Tibetan New Year), I decided to host a banquet and extend invitations to Chairman Mao and the other three senior Chinese leaders—Zhou Enlai, Zhu De, and Liu Shaoqi. They all accepted and we had a memorable celebration.

---

* "Inner Mongolia" refers to a historical part of Mongolia that is today the Inner Mongolia Autonomous Region within the People's Republic of China. Today's independent Mongolian People's Republic contains the bulk of the territory that was at one point known as Outer Mongolia.

One day Chairman Mao paid an unannounced visit to my lodgings. During this meeting, he unexpectedly asked if Tibet had a national flag. Somewhat nervously, I replied that we did, and he said that it would be fine for us to keep it. Mao's surprising response implied that, at that time at least, he had in mind a model of the diverse nations within the People's Republic along the lines of the republics within the Soviet Union. In fact, I know Mao gave orders to senior Chinese officials stationed in Tibet at the time—Zhan Jingwu, Zhang Guohua, and Fan Ming—to display the Tibetan flag alongside China's red star and also my photo alongside his own. So later, in exile, when Tibetans and international Tibetan supporters would display our national flag in public, especially when greeting me during international travels, I used to tell them that Mao himself had given permission to keep our flag. Today, sadly, the Tibetan flag is illegal in Tibet, and anyone caught in possession of it will go to prison.

Before I left Beijing, I had a final meeting with Mao. He looked very happy and told me to communicate directly with him through the telegraph, saying I should train some trusted Tibetans to do this. He then came close to me and said, "Your mind is scientific, and that is very good. I have watched your thinking and activities all these months. Your mind is a very revolutionary mind." He gave me excellent practical advice about government and I took notes.

As the meeting came to a close, Mao told me, "Your attitude is good, you know. Religion is poison. It reduces the population because the monks and nuns must stay celibate and it neglects material progress." I was shaken and attempted to hide my feelings by leaning forward as if to write something. It was then I knew despite all the hints of positive dialogue that he was the destroyer of Buddha Dharma.

As I prepared for my journey back home to Lhasa in March 1955, despite Mao's last disconcerting comment about religion, I still had hopes of saving my people from the worst consequences of the Chinese occupation. I thought my six-month visit to China had helped in two ways. It had shown me exactly what we were up against and had appeared to have persuaded the Chinese leaders not to go ahead with their original plan of governing Tibet directly from Beijing through a military and political committee: we seemed to have a firm promise of autonomy. In fact, on the way back to Tibet I met the Chinese General Zhang Guohua, who was stationed in Lhasa but was en route to Beijing. I told him that on my way to China I was full of anxiety, but now on my way back home I felt more hopeful and confident. So I had some faith that we could work with the Chinese. Tibet could be modernized and its people would live on some kind of equal terms with the Chinese majority within the People's Republic of China.

I worked earnestly to seek a lasting accommodation that would save my nation and people within the constraints of the Seventeen-Point Agreement. I tried to institute some reforms—notably to establish an independent judiciary, to encourage proposals for the development of a program of modern education, and to build modern roads. It proved to be a hopeless task, constantly undermined by the Chinese Communist military and civil officials stationed in Tibet, with rising resentment of repression and the risk of spontaneous revolt from the Tibetan people. My efforts were blocked at every stage by the Chinese officials and military. The Preparatory Committee for the Autonomous Region of Tibet (PCART), which was meant to give the Tibetans autonomy over the process of reform and of which I was the chair, turned out to be just a show, with all actual power in the hands of the Chinese.

The promises and assurances received in Beijing turned out to be empty; my messages to Mao elicited no response. During the many disasters and unspeakable acts against Tibetans that were to follow, I wrote three times to Chairman Mao, the third time ensuring that my letter was personally delivered. There was never an answer. Whatever little hope I had in Mao and the Communist leadership was shattered. The commitments that the Communist Party of China had made in the agreement it had forced upon us turned out to have no real meaning at all.

CHAPTER 3

# A Visit to India

In late 1955, I received a formal invitation from the crown prince of Sikkim in his capacity as the president of the Maha Bodhi Society of India to participate in the celebrations of the 2,500th anniversary of Buddha Jayanti (the birth of the Buddha). Initially, Fan Ming, a senior political officer in the People's Liberation Army stationed in Lhasa, urged me to refuse the invitation. He told me that the crown prince was not high enough in rank for me to be accepting such a formal invitation. So I quietly sent a message to the Indian Mission in Lhasa to explain the situation, which led to the arrival of a second invitation, this time from the vice president of India, Sarvepalli Radhakrishnan. After several months, I was told that Beijing had okayed my trip to India.

Before I left, General Chang Ching-wu warned me, "Be careful. There are many reactionary elements and spies in India. If you try to do anything with them, I want you to realize that what has happened in Hungary and Poland will happen in Tibet." He was referring to the suppression of the Poznan protests in Poland in June 1956, when tanks and troops fired on protesting civilians, and the brutal crushing of the people's uprising in Hungary by Soviet tanks and troops on November 4, 1956, a few weeks before my trip. Despite his warnings, I was thrilled at the chance to visit the holy land of India and the sites associated with the life of the Buddha.

At the same time, however, I was acutely aware of the worsening situation in Tibet, especially the growing arrogance and belligerence of the Chinese authorities in Lhasa. For example, by 1956, when Chinese interpreters came to see me, they would wear pistols under their coats, unlike before. One day, I clearly saw the mouth of the gun jutting out. The situation in Lhasa also continued to deteriorate, with tension rising due to the presence of the large number of People's Liberation Army soldiers as well as the growing number of refugees who escaped frightening conditions in eastern Tibet. In March 1956, for example, the People's Liberation Army attacked Lithang Monastery in eastern Tibet—an important foundation associated with the Third Dalai Lama—bombing the monastery, killing several hundred people, and capturing its abbot.

In November 1956, I was finally able to visit India. My Dharma brother, the Panchen Lama, had also been officially invited and joined me as well. My two elder brothers, Taktser Rinpoche and Gyalo Thondup, both of whom were then living outside Tibet, met me at the border of Sikkim. The first words they said, before any kind of greeting, were, "You must not go back." Their urgency really shook me, and I knew there was good reason based on what I described earlier. I found myself in profound doubt about whether I should return after the celebration. For now, though, we continued on, flying to Delhi on November 25, to be met by Prime Minister Jawaharlal Nehru, Vice President Radhakrishnan, and the speaker of the Indian Parliament, M. A. Ayyangar. We were then driven to the president's official residence to meet Rajendra Prasad. After this, the following morning, the first event in my program was to pay homage at Raj Ghat, the place where Mahatma Gandhi—perhaps the greatest being of our age, who applied India's ancient philosophy of ahimsa (nonviolence) into an effective political movement for the freedom of his people from British colonial rule—was cremated. At that site, I affirmed more strongly than ever that I could never involve myself with any acts of violence.

The formal celebrations of Buddha Jayanti took place in Bodh Gaya, the most sacred place for Buddhists everywhere. The Mahabodhi Stupa in Bodh Gaya marks the site where the Buddha attained enlightenment under a pipal tree, which later came to be known as the Bodhi tree. The tree that stands there today is a continuation of the very same tree—by way of a sapling brought from Sri Lanka in the nineteenth century that in turn was a sapling of the original tree—under which the Buddha sat, more than 2,600 years ago. How I felt when I came face-to-face for the first time with the sacred Bodhi tree, I described in my autobiography of 1962:

> Every devout Buddhist would always associate Bodh Gaya with all that is noblest and loftiest in his religious and cultural inheritance. From my very early youth, I had thought and dreamed about this visit. Now I stood in the presence of the holy spirit who had attained enlightenment in this sacred place and found for all mankind the path to salvation. As I stood there a feeling of religious fervor filled my heart, and left me awestruck with the knowledge and impact of the divine power which is in all of us.

In my address at the celebration, I touched upon the long history of Buddhism in India, how it came to Tibet from India, and the long historical and spiritual ties that lie at the heart of this transmission, as I highlighted earlier. I particularly emphasized the Buddha's teaching of nonviolence and how this teaching could contribute to ushering in a new era of peace in the world. I expressed my deep admiration of the adoption of Ashoka's Dharma Chakra (Wheel of Law) as the nation's symbol of India at independence, indicating the country's deep admiration of the universal values promoted by Buddhism. When the formal celebrations were over, I took the opportunity to go on a pilgrimage to other sacred sites around Bodh Gaya and Sarnath in Central India associated with the life of the Buddha: the ruins of Nalanda in Bihar, the greatest Indian Buddhist monastic university, as well as the ancient Buddhist monuments at Sanchi and Ajanta.

Prime Minister Nehru accompanying me on my visit to Rajgir, a site associated with the Buddha's life and especially sacred to Mahayana Buddhism because it was where the *Perfection of Wisdom* scriptures were delivered, was particularly unforgettable. A memorial for the seventh-century Chinese traveler Xuanzang was formally inaugurated at Rajgir, at which Premiere Zhou Enlai was supposed to represent the People's Republic of China. In the end, Zhou could not come so I was asked to present the check representing a gift from the Chinese government. These visits to the sacred Buddhist sites offered some of the most joyful and memorable moments—rare beams of sunlight amid the dark clouds surrounding me and my homeland.

During my time in India, a number of prominent Tibetans living there came to urge me not to go back home. They expressed very strong views against the signing of the Seventeen-Point Agreement. I also had important meetings with Prime Minister Nehru, who was then in his sixties and was the first prime minister since his country's independence. At my first meeting I took the opportunity to explain in detail the full story of the Chinese invasion, how unprepared we were and how hard I had tried to accommodate the Communists as soon as I became aware that no one in the outside world was prepared to acknowledge our rightful claim to independence. I then told him how desperate things had become by now in eastern Tibet, following the bombing of Lithang Monastery, and that I feared that the Chinese really meant to destroy our religion and customs forever. I explained that I wanted to stay in India until we could win back our freedom by peaceful means.

Nehru agreed with me that it was useless to fight against the Chinese. He was emphatic, however, that India could not support us, and said that I should go back to my country and try to work with the Chinese on the basis of the Seventeen-Point Agreement. When I protested that the Chinese authorities had broken my trust and that I did not believe that the agreement was workable any longer, he said he would speak personally to the Chinese Premier Zhou Enlai. At one of my meetings with Nehru, he actually brought a copy of the agreement in his hand. Going through it point by point, he demonstrated how it could be the basis for a genuine model of autonomy and self-rule. Nehru reported on his own conversations with Zhou Enlai and especially the unambiguous assurance Zhou had given him with respect to the autonomy of Tibet within the People's Republic of China.

The trip to India was also the occasion for several meetings with the Chinese premier. Zhou Enlai, in his late fifties then, was full of smiles and charm, a courteous man with a swift intellect—in brief, clever and smooth-talking. At my first meeting in November in Delhi, I told him straightforwardly of my concerns about eastern Tibet, how the Chinese authorities were behaving, and especially of the brutal repression and murder of innocent people following the Lithang bombing. I also asked Zhou what happened during their reforms there and in northeastern Tibet (Amdo) that had forced so many thousands to flee as refugees to central Tibet.

Zhou made a serious attempt to reassure me, admitting that major mistakes were made in eastern Tibet by the local cadres and that the leaders at the top too had to accept responsibility since they should have intervened sooner. He told me that reforms in Tibet would not occur until my government thought the conditions were appropriate. I also shared with him my observation of the contrast between the Indian Parliament and the Chinese Communist People's Congress. In India, the parliament members are free to express themselves as they really feel and criticize the government when they think necessary. In Beijing, I had observed that most of the members in the assembly barely dared to speak. Even if they did make a point, it was mostly about small corrections in wording, but nothing of substance. Zhou responded that I had only been at the first assembly in Beijing and that things had changed immeasurably for the better at the second assembly. Zhou also took the trouble to meet with my brothers and key cabinet ministers of my government, including Ngabö, who had been forced to sign the Seventeen-Point Agreement in Beijing on behalf of my government.

The last time I met with Zhou in Delhi was after his return from a trip to Pakistan. On December 30, 1956, I received a message from the Chinese Embassy that Zhou was back in India and wanted to see me. I rushed to Delhi by train to find the Chinese Ambassador Pan Zili waiting for me at the station. He insisted that I ride with him in his car. With the help of Indian protocol officials and security, we drove straight to the Chinese Embassy, where I met with the ambassador, Zhou Enlai, and Marshal He Long. By the time my staff reached the embassy I was already in the meeting, with my staff not knowing if I was inside or not, and some even wondering if I had been abducted! At some point someone brought a warm shawl for me, saying that my staff wanted to make sure that I was not cold. Later they told me that they were worried and wanted to let me know that they too had arrived at the Chinese Embassy.

I must admit I found that meeting intimidating: three seasoned Chinese political and military men—a premier, a marshal, and an ambassador—surrounding one inexperienced young Tibetan monk. The fact that we were in Delhi and not Beijing made me at least feel safe. I stood firm and expressed my fear that the Communist Party might force unacceptable reforms in Tibet. By this time, it appeared that Zhou Enlai had clearly consulted with Mao Zedong. So he repeated all the reassurances he had given me earlier, about dealing with the excesses of repression in eastern Tibet and about postponing reform. He conveyed to me Mao's pledge that the plan for Communist reform in Tibet would be delayed at least for six years, and, even after that, it would be up to me to decide whether or not to implement the reforms. He added that the Chinese government would not tolerate any outbreak of armed insurrection in Tibet, and stressed that I needed to return to Lhasa at the earliest possible moment. He concluded by telling me not to visit Kalimpong, an Indian town near the border of

Tibet where there was a community of Tibetans, some of whom had already fled into exile.

To this last point, I told Zhou that I would think about his suggestion. The morning after this meeting, Marshal He Long came to see me. He repeated Zhou's advice that I return to Lhasa. He then quoted the saying "The snow lion looks dignified if he stays in the snows, but if he descends to the plains he would be treated like a dog." He was, of course, issuing me a serious warning.

All of this added up to real pressure from many sides about whether I should go back to Tibet or remain in India. Certainly, among the Tibetan officials with me there were conflicting views. It also appears that Beijing was trying to influence matters behind the scenes. Zhou had even dangled before Nehru the possible offer of China abiding by the boundaries determined between India and Tibet known as the McMahon Line, if India would refuse asylum to me at the time. I realized in the end I myself would have to make the decision on whether to return to Tibet or not. There is a Tibetan saying, "Ask others for opinions, but make the decision yourself." So in my next meeting with Prime Minister Nehru, I told him that I had made up my mind to go back to Tibet for two reasons. "Because you have advised me to do so, and because Zhou Enlai has given definite promises to me and my brothers." As it would prove, Nehru was sincere but idealistic in his belief about the Chinese pledges; Zhou was simply lying.

In January 1957, ignoring Premier Zhou's advice, I left for Kalimpong from Calcutta. On my way back home, I stopped in Gangtok, where I was able to meet with many devout Buddhists and give formal religious teachings and blessing ceremonies, and also laid the foundation stone for the Namgyal Institute of Tibetology, at the invitation of the maharaja of Sikkim.

I had planned to stop in Gangtok for only a few days. However, due to a heavy snowstorm, the Nathu-la Pass had become impassable, which meant I was happily stuck in Gangtok for a few extra weeks. While there, I also extended a formal invitation to Nehru to visit Lhasa. I wanted to reciprocate his generous hospitality during my stay in India, and, more important, offer him an opportunity to acquire a firsthand impression of what was actually happening in Tibet. Although Nehru accepted my invitation and the Chinese initially did not object, later they pulled back by saying that they could not guarantee Nehru's personal safety in Tibet. This was sad, for I would have benefited immensely from his counsel if he had visited Lhasa.

Even though Nehru had not been able to come to the capital, he did end up putting a foot on Tibetan soil on his way to and back from Bhutan, which he visited in September 1958. He spent a night at Yadong, the very town where I had fled in 1950 when the Chinese Communist army invaded from eastern Tibet. A high-level Tibetan delegation was sent to formally welcome the prime minister and his daughter Indira Gandhi when they arrived. It was during this visit to Bhutan that Nehru gave a strong assurance that it was India's wish to see Bhutan remain an independent country, with its own people choosing their own way of life and taking a path of progress according to their own will. This contrast between how Bhutan's giant neighbor India was treating it and how Tibet was being treated at that very moment by our giant neighbor to the east was, of course, too painfully striking to miss.

Finally, as the weather improved and the way became open toward the end of February, we crossed the Nathu-la Pass and reached Tibetan soil. The farewell, especially to my immediately elder brother Lobsang Samten, before crossing the pass was a sad moment. Among all my siblings, he and I had been the closest since, as children, we shared the ten-week-long journey from Amdo to central Tibet, and immediately after my formal recognition as the Dalai Lama, we also went through early monastic tutorials at the same time. Lobsang Samten was not well at the time and was feeling quite weak. So I suggested we sit together quietly in the car for a while. He was crying and I was myself feeling sad, and all of this caused some delay, irritating the Chinese officials accompanying me back to Tibet.

CHAPTER 4

# Fleeing Home

On my way back to Lhasa from Gangtok, I stopped in many places trying to reassure my countrymen only to receive increasingly disquieting reports. I arrived in the capital on April 1, 1957, knowing that the situation was slipping out of control—due to the Chinese government's actions and from my own inability to have any meaningful influence. By midsummer, it had become clear that virtually everything I had been told by Zhou himself and by him on behalf of Mao had been falsehoods and dissimulations. There continued to be open conflict in Kham and Amdo (eastern and northeastern Tibet). The People's Liberation Army showed no restraint—bombing more towns and committing such atrocities that I found difficult to believe for their levels of depravity but were later confirmed by the International Commission of Jurists in 1959: forced sterilization, crucifixion, vivisection, disemboweling, dismemberment, beheading, burning, beating to death, burying alive, dragging people behind galloping horses, hanging them upside down, and other horrors. Thousands more refugees from Kham and Amdo fled to Lhasa and camped outside the city.

Through 1958 and early 1959, the situation worsened further, with growing numbers joining an active Tibetan resistance that came to be based in southern Tibet, called the Volunteer Force for the Protection of the Faith (*tensung danglang magmi*), led by the energetic leader Adruk Gompo Tashi. To defuse tension, I had several meetings with the People's Liberation Army's senior-most generals in Lhasa, including especially General Tan Guansan, the head of the Chinese military in Tibet, known for his bad temper. Through these generals, the Chinese government insisted that the Tibetan government use our own Tibetan soldiers against the Tibetan guerrillas. It was unthinkable to send Tibetan troops against our own people, especially when they were fighting to safeguard our land and culture. At the same time, I received an intimation from the Americans that if I solicited assistance for the resistance movement, they would provide it. Of course, as a student of the Buddha and a deep admirer of Mahatma Gandhi's nonviolence philosophy, I could not imagine myself making such a request.

Part of me at the time, I must admit, admired the guerrilla fighters. They were brave Tibetans who were putting their lives at risk for the sake of our nation and Buddhist faith. I also knew that many of them saw themselves as fighting out of loyalty to me as the Dalai Lama. I wondered what advice Mahatma Gandhi would have given me in this charged situation. Would he have condoned violence here? I could not believe that he would. Practically speaking too, I was convinced that using force against the Chinese would be not only useless but actually suicidal. It would give the Chinese army the perfect excuse to crush Tibetans with maximum force.

In the midst of all this, I was preparing for my final Geshe Lharam exams, scheduled at the Great Prayer Festival of 1959. February 22, 1959, when I formally sat for my examination debates at the great Jokhang Temple in Lhasa, was a rare break from the incessant and challenging politics. The day I completed my formal Geshe debates was, perhaps, the happiest day of my life. It was the culmination of a series of debates I had participated in at the "three great seats of learning"—Sera, Drepung, and Ganden—the three largest monastic universities of the Geluk school in central Tibet, all established at the beginning of the fifteenth century. I was both excited and nervous about the debates at Tibet's great centers of learning. Later I found out that those who had been chosen to question me at these debates too were quite nervous, if not more so than me!

Following my final Geshe exams in Lhasa, over the next two weeks the crisis in the country reached a boiling point. The people's anxiety about my own safety and the presence of Chinese troops in Lhasa led to an explosive situation in the capital. With so many people gathered in one place—several thousand Tibetans from other parts of Tibet in addition to the local residents—and with such a large number of People's Liberation Army soldiers stationed in the city, there was a pervasive sense of nervousness and unease. Many felt something untoward was about to happen.

On March 10, I was supposed to attend a cultural show at the Chinese garrison in Lhasa, with the worrisome suggestion that my bodyguards should not accompany me. Word had gotten out, and thousands of people crowded the city to prevent me from leaving my residence at Norbulingka. The crowd grew through the day, with people shouting anti-Chinese slogans and saying that they would not allow the Dalai Lama to leave. It was soon out of control and became a massive popular uprising. Over the next few days, the situation became increasingly tense and chaotic with the crowd refusing to disperse. On the twelfth, thousands of Tibetan women took to the streets and assembled in front of the Potala Palace. They burned the Chinese flag, as well as photos and effigies of Mao, Zhou Enlai, and Zhu De, and shouted, "Tibet has always been free! Tibet for the Tibetans! Long live the Dalai Lama! Long live Gaden Phodrang," the last being the name of the Tibetan government under the Dalai Lamas. The leader of this women's protest, Gurteng Kunsang, and some of her colleagues would be later executed by firing squad. On March 14, I met with approximately seventy representatives chosen by the people in the hope that I could help defuse the situation. However, tension kept building, with the Tibetan crowds growing day by day.

From the tenth to the seventeenth of March, the Chinese army remained in its barracks while I exchanged messages with the short-tempered General Tan Guansan, which may have helped to buy time. My last letter to him was on March 16. It might also have been the case that the Chinese army was awaiting instructions from Beijing. We had information that they were planning to attack the crowd and shell the Norbulingka Palace. Within my own immediate circle, many were urging me to seriously consider leaving Lhasa for the time being. But I kept hoping that if we could find a way to reassure the mass of ordinary Tibetans gathered outside who were worried about my safety, we could somehow defuse the situation and avert an immediate explosion.

On the seventeenth, around 4 p.m., two heavy mortars landed just outside the north side of the Norbulingka, which, fortunately, did not cause any harm. Everyone thought that an attack was imminent. Earlier on that day, the State Oracle Nechung,* in a trance, had in fact urged me to leave, saying, "Leave! Leave! Go tonight!" This instruction was consistent with the outcome of a few divinations I had performed myself on the question of whether to stay or leave.† So the landing of those two mortars came as a reinforcement of what the State Oracle had instructed me to do—namely, to leave immediately. Not only was my own life in danger, but the lives of thousands of my people now seemed certain to be lost as well. With everyone around me urging the path of escape as well, I took the decision to flee Lhasa. I went to the

* Nechung (known also as Dorje Drakden) is an important oracle, historically connected with the Dalai Lamas, who communicates through a medium in a trance. The practice of consulting oracles is common in Tibetan Buddhism.

† "Divination" (*mo* in Tibetan), typically involving the throwing of dices and interpreting the result of the throw, refers to a method of examining the pros and cons of a particular course of action.

chapel of Mahakala, an important protector in Tibetan Buddhism, a chapel where I had always gone to say good-bye before embarking on a long journey. The monks there must have been a little surprised when I offered a long white scarf to the image, but they did not show it. Then, having changed my monastic robe into layman's clothing, I went to my prayer room to sit down for a quiet moment.

I opened the text that was lying on the small table in front of the throne, which turned out to be the *Eight Thousand Lines on the Perfection of Wisdom*, a scripture sacred to Mahayana Buddhism. I randomly picked up a page and read from the top, ending at the sentence "Have courage and confidence." Energized, I closed the book, blessed the room, and turned off the lights. One precious item I took with me was an old *thangka* (a traditional Tibetan painting on canvas framed with silk brocades that could be rolled into a scroll) that had belonged to the Second Dalai Lama.*

As I walked out of my room, a blanket of silence enveloped me, where I could feel every step I took and the ticking of the clock on the wall. I took the rifle of one of the bodyguards who was standing outside my room. And so, at 10 p.m. on March 17, I put my glasses into my pocket and stepped out of the Norbulingka Palace disguised as a layman with a rifle over my shoulder. This was a truly eerie experience. I was afraid, but also had a more immediate practical thing to worry about: how not to trip as I walked without my glasses. As I stepped out of the gate, I felt the presence of a great mass of people gathered outside the Norbulingka. Thinking of them, I prayed—worrying what fate lay in store for these thousands of innocent Tibetans.

After I left, the Tibetan government in Lhasa continued as if I were still in residence. Once we were away from the immediate threat

* The *thangka* is of Palden Lhamo, an important female protector deity connected with the Dalai Lamas since the period of the Second Dalai Lama, Gendun Gyatso, in the fifteenth century.

of being captured by the People's Liberation Army, personally, the most powerful thing I felt was a sense of relief. Alongside this was the acute awareness that I was now free to speak my mind and openly criticize the policies of the Communist Chinese government. This feeling of freedom was so vivid and strong. The nine years of working with the Communist Chinese in Tibet and Beijing, during which I had to carefully consider every phrase I uttered, had placed a heavy weight in my heart. And I was now able to breathe the air of freedom.

Early the next morning, as we were crossing the Chela Pass, one of the guides leading my horse told me that this was the last point from where we could still see the Potala Palace, with its striking white-and-red fortresslike structures covering the entire face of a rocky mountain overlooking Lhasa. He then helped turn my horse around so I could take a last glimpse. With a heavy heart, I said good-bye to Lhasa, Tibet's capital city, where I had grown up since age four. I prayed that I would be able to return there one day.

A few days later, on March 20, the Chinese army shelled the Norbulingka and the crowd, killing many. By that time, the People's Liberation Army had a well-integrated plan of attack. When I heard this news, from a messenger during my escape, I prayed for my people. Nobody knows exactly how many were killed in Lhasa—I was told that thousands of bodies were seen inside and outside the Norbulingka. What took place in Norbulingka, Lhasa, Chokpori (a hill opposite Lhasa and the site of the Tibetan medical school), and Sera Monastery over two days of relentless bombing was a massacre.

We made for Lhuntse Dzong in Lhoka (in the south), which is just on the Tibetan side of the border from India. Our original intention was not to go directly into exile to India. My idea was to negotiate with the Chinese from a place of safety to see if I could return to continue to lead the Tibetan government. However, as the news of what took place in the immediate aftermath of my flight and what was continuing to happen reached us, we became convinced that there was no point in talking with the People's Republic of China. Furthermore, the Chinese authorities in Lhasa had announced the dissolution of the Tibetan government.

I later heard that when Mao was informed of my escape, he reacted, "We have lost!"* Mao probably realized that with me gone out of Tibet, China would struggle with the question of legitimacy both of their authority and their presence in Tibet. He was right. This question of legitimacy still remains at the very heart of China's presence in Tibet, even after seven decades of occupation.

At Lhuntse Dzong we paused and took stock. Looking back at more than eight years since the Seventeen-Point Agreement was signed, and notably after my return from visiting China in 1954–1955 and India in 1956–1957, despite all the efforts I made to find an accommodation, it was clear to me that the task was simply impossible. There is an old Tibetan saying that captures the essence of the relationship between the Tibetans and the Chinese: "Tibetans are let down by their hopes; the Chinese are let down by their suspicions."

At Lhuntse Dzong, on March 26, 1959, I formally repudiated the Seventeen-Point Agreement and announced the reconstitution of our own government of Tibet as the only legally constituted authority for the country. More than a thousand people attended this ceremony, where Surkhang, one of the ministers in my cabinet, read the document aloud to the gathering. At the opening of this document, announcing the formation of Tibet's legitimate government, the text stated:

> In the past, for several thousand years, this snow land of Tibet was widely known as an independent country that was ruled by

---

* Jung Chang and Jon Halliday, *Mao: The Unknown Story* (New York: Alfred A. Knopf, 2005), 447, reports that, according to a source, Mao is said to have sent a telegram to the Chinese General Tan Guansan ordering the Chinese army to let the Dalai Lama escape and not to kill him. He was concerned that killing the Dalai Lama could inflame world opinion, especially in India and the Buddhist countries in Asia, which Mao was courting at the time.

> a system that combines the religious and the secular. . . . Except for the differences between a big and a small country, we have identical attributes, greatness, and qualifications for being an independent country in the world.

The concluding part of the text makes the call that "as soon as people see this edict, which contains the good news about setting up a new state called Gaden Phodrang, you should publicize it to all the monks and lay people in your area and make sure they have heard it." Copies of the proclamation of Tibet's independent government with my signature were dispatched across Tibet, with one sent to the Panchen Lama.

At this point, reports of Chinese troops nearby precipitated the decision to cross the border into India. I had the difficult task of bidding farewell to the Tibetan soldiers and resistance fighters who had so faithfully escorted me from Lhasa and who were now about to turn back to face the Chinese army. I knew that some were returning to certain death. They were going back to rejoin the Volunteer Force for the Protection of the Faith. As part of the US government's overall strategy to prevent the spread of Communism in Asia, as later I came to know, the Tibetan resistance movement led by Gompo Tashi did actually receive some support from the CIA, including a handful of them getting communication and combat training.

From Lhuntse Dzong we decided to head toward the Indian border. After two days of hard riding, we reached Mangmang, which is the last Tibetan village before the border of India. There, to my delight, was one of the officials I had sent earlier to inquire if India would receive me and my entourage. He brought the good news that the government of India was willing to grant asylum to me and my people. That night at Mangmang, I felt quite safe for the first time in many days. There was only one track leading to this place and that route was well guarded by several hundred Tibetan resistance fighters. So unless the Chinese army bombed us from the air, I knew we were safe.

But the weather wasn't so kind—it rained heavily and my tent was leaking pretty much everywhere. I was forced to sit up the entire night, with the result that I caught a cold the next day. With me being ill, we had to postpone our remaining trek to the border for two days. Still too sick to ride a horse, when we did move finally, I was placed on a *dzo* (a cross between a yak and cow). In this way, I left the last stretch of my own homeland. On March 31, 1959, my party entered India. I have not been able to go back to my homeland since.

CHAPTER 5

# A Geopolitical Reflection

Here I was at age twenty-five, a refugee in a new country. As the Tibetan saying goes, as a refugee, the only thing that was familiar to us was the earth and the sky. At that time, it was impossible to grasp the full significance of what had happened to my homeland in a global historical context. Predictably, the first and foremost experience for me and my fellow Tibetans was the shock of displacement. The immediate task, in the wake of my escape, was the very opposite of deep reflection—the urgent work of looking after the growing and desperate community of tens of thousands of refugees who managed to follow me over the course of several months into exile. Only later, with the benefit of time and hindsight, did it become possible for me to come to some more general reflections on the meaning of what has happened to Tibet.

Tibet, my homeland I had been forced to flee, is a landlocked country with the huge Himalayan mountain range to the south, beyond which are India, Nepal, and Bhutan; the deserts of Central Asia to the north, past which lie East Turkistan* (Xinjiang) and Mongolia; and to the east the lowlands and rice fields inhabited by the Chinese. We Tibetans, the inhabitants of the vast Tibetan plateau, are seminomadic eaters of *tsampa* (roasted barley flour), occupying a vast high-altitude plateau rimmed to the south by the mighty Himalayas beneath a deep blue sky. Ancient texts describe the land in terms of "high peaks and pure earth" and trace the origin of "the meat-eating red-faced race of Tibetans" to the union of a monkey and a rock-dwelling ogress to which were born six children. From these sprang the Tibetan people, according to this story of origin. I first heard this story as a child after my arrival in Lhasa. A monk told it to me, explaining a mural inside the Potala Palace showing the monkey. Tibetan histories identify Tibet's first king as Nyatri Tsenpo, whose reign began in 127 BCE. In fact, one traditional Tibetan calendar system, bö gyalo (Tibetan royal year), takes this to be year 1—making 1950, when Communist China invaded Tibet, year 2077 on the Tibetan calendar. An early chronicle says that this king descended from heaven and "went of his own accord to become the lord of all under heaven . . . to the center of the earth, in the heart of the continent, in the enclosure of snow mountains, at the head of all rivers, where the mountains were high, the earth pure, the country fine, . . . a place where swift horses flourished."

Given the Tibetan plateau's exceptional geography, which we often refer to as "the roof of the world" (*zamling sayi yangthok*), the Tibetans developed a lifestyle and culture over millennia that was uniquely adapted to the high-altitude environment and ecology. We Tibetans recognize the seventh-century Emperor Songtsen Gampo to be our greatest king, crediting his reign with a series of landmark achieve-

* Although Xinjiang (literally "New Frontier") is the name most recognizable in current international literature for East Turkistan, it is, in fact, a colonial name invented by China. The Uyghur people themselves refer to the geographic region that is their home as East Turkistan.

ments that enriched Tibetan civilization. It was during his rule that the current Tibetan writing system was invented and that the first Buddhist texts were brought from India to be translated from Sanskrit. The emperor established a universal legal system, standardized forms of measurements across the Tibetan plateau, and brought about many innovations to agriculture and craftsmanship. It was also during his reign that two of Tibet's oldest temples—the Jokhang and Ramoche—were built to house two sacred statues of the Buddha brought from Nepal and China by the two princesses whom Emperor Songtsen married. Even as a child, I knew the tale of the ancient marriage between Songtsen Gampo and the Chinese Princess Wencheng, given as a bride by the Tang Emperor Taizong. Every summer, I would look forward to the Shotön Festival in Lhasa, during which Tibetan operas were performed in the garden outside the Norbulingka Palace. One of the famous operas tells the story of Songtsen's marriage to this Chinese princess and also to a Nepalese princess called Bhrikuti. Like many ancient neighbors with a long history, there have been ups and downs in the engagement between Tibet and China, periods of friendship, periods of cool tolerance, periods of bickering, and times of outright conflict. However, Communist China's forcible invasion of Tibet marked an unprecedented tragedy for the Tibetan people.

Looking back, I have come to understand the ways Tibet and its people were the victims of tragic circumstances of history. The major powers that had historic connections with Tibet were all preoccupied in very particular ways during the crucial period. Great Britain, which had, after all, invaded Tibet in 1903–1904, had just given up India and had no stomach for the politics of South and Inner Asia. India had become independent on August 15, 1947, in the midst of a most traumatic partition, and almost immediately in October of that year was caught up in war with the newly partitioned Pakistan, lasting till January 1, 1949. There was no appetite for further conflict with another neighbor right next to the arena of the former war. The United States had become interested in Tibet as part of its concern to stop the spread of Communism after the end of the Second World War. The last thing it wanted to see was a repeat in Asia of what had happened in Eastern Europe in the immediate aftermath of that war. During the civil war in China from 1946–1949, for example, the United States gave significant support to the losing Nationalist government of Chiang Kai-shek. In the 1950–1953 Korean War, the United States committed troops on the ground to help defend South Korea from the Communist invasion from the north, the latter backed by the Soviet Union and Communist China. What little support the United States extended to the Tibetan resistance was largely motivated by the broader policy to stem the tide of Communism in Asia.

What happened to Mongolia around the same period is a profoundly interesting historical point of contrast. When the Manchu Qing dynasty fell in 1911, the political status enjoyed by Mongolia was exactly parallel to that of Tibet. Just as Nationalist China was claiming Tibet to be part of its territory, so too did it claim Mongolia. It is no coincidence that Mongolia and Tibet made a bilateral treaty reiterating each other's independence in 1913. Because the Soviet Union backed Mongolia's independence from China—following a referendum in 1945—the world powers persuaded Chiang Kai-shek to accept the result of that vote. As a consequence, although reduced in size, Mongolia is now an independent country and a member of the United Nations.

We Tibetans were not so lucky. To some extent, we have ourselves to blame. While the rest of the world was waking up to the significance of global understanding about the place of nations, especially in the wake of the First World War, we Tibetans had buried our heads in the sand. Significant mistakes were made during this period. For example, too few systematic initiatives were taken during this crucial period to express Tibet's status as an independent country at the international level. The Thirteenth Dalai Lama's measures for reform, especially in education and defense, were largely thwarted by various sectional interests and elites. After his death in 1933, efforts could have been made to join international forums, such as the League of Nations and later the United Nations. The crucial point that Tibet's ruling elite, with the exception of the Thirteenth Dalai Lama, simply did not grasp was that in the new political reality of the twentieth century it was not adequate for a country to enjoy independence. It had to make a series of international gestures to prove its presence on the world stage as one among many sovereign states. It was particularly unfortunate that, while the storm was gathering around Tibet, the ruling elite, including my two successive regents, were largely preoccupied with political infighting, which came to a climax in 1947 with the death of my first regent, Reting Rinpoche. So, by the time the People's Liberation Army was at the door in 1950, Tibet was completely unprepared, and it was too late.

When I think about the political life of my immediate predecessor, the Thirteenth Dalai Lama, there is a striking parallel with my own karma. Twice he was forced to flee into exile due to foreign invasion—first when the British forces under the command of Colonel Francis Younghusband invaded Tibet in 1903, returning only in 1909, and then again in 1910 when the armies of the Manchu Qing dynasty attacked Tibet from the east. The British certainly hadn't come to stay, but it is very likely that conquest was the intention of the imperial Manchu forces. However, the Qing itself collapsed in 1911, and with the last emperor's abdication in 1912, the Qing *amban* (the imperial representative) in Lhasa surrendered. It was after his return in 1913, as already stated, that the Thirteenth Dalai Lama tried to assert Tibet's independence internationally, with acts such as the signing of a treaty with Mongolia in 1913, in which both states mutually affirmed each other's independence. This independence was the status of Tibet when Communist China invaded in 1950. If we Tibetans had read the signs correctly in those years, we might have seen that another invasion was likely. This strongly suggests that we missed our opportunities during the crucial period between the death of the Thirteenth Dalai Lama in

1933 and the birth of Communist China in 1949, especially amid the chaos of an unstable government and civil war in China.

In fact, shortly before he died, the Thirteenth Dalai Lama left an extraordinary and prophetic final testament. I read this text when I was young. Let me quote from it at length since it shows both his foresight and the extent of the failure on the part of the Tibetan government to heed his very clear warnings. He wrote:

> I am now almost fifty-eight years old, and soon it will be impossible for me to serve you any longer. Everyone should realize this fact, and begin to look to what you will do in the future when I am gone. Between me and the next incarnation there will be a period in which you will have to fend for yourselves.
>
> Our two most powerful neighbors are India and China, both of whom have very powerful armies. Therefore, we must try to establish stable relations with both of them. There are also a number of small countries near our borders which maintain a strong military. Because of this, it is important that we too maintain an efficient army of young and well-trained soldiers that is able to establish the security of the country. . . . If we do not make preparations to defend ourselves from the overflow of violence, we will have very little hope of survival.
>
> In particular, we must guard ourselves against the barbaric red communists who carry terror and destruction with them wherever they go. They are the worst of the worst. Already they have consumed much of Mongolia. . . . They have robbed and destroyed the monasteries, forcing the monks to join their armies, or else killing them outright. They have destroyed religion wherever they have encountered it. . . .
>
> It will not be long before we find the red onslaught at our own front door. It is only a matter of time before we come into a direct confrontation with it. . . .
>
> And when that happens, we must be ready to defend our-

> selves. Otherwise, our spiritual and cultural traditions will be completely eradicated. . . . The monasteries will be looted and destroyed, the monks and nuns will be killed or chased away, the great works of the noble Dharma kings of old will be undone, and all of our cultural and spiritual institutions persecuted, destroyed, and forgotten. The birth rights and the property of the people will be stolen; we will become like slaves to our conquerors, and will be made to wander helplessly like beggars. Everyone will be forced to live in misery, and the days and nights will pass slowly, and with great suffering and terror.
>
> Therefore, when the strength of peace and happiness is with us, while the power to do something about the situation is still in our hands, we should make every effort to safeguard ourselves against this impending disaster. Use peaceful methods where they are appropriate; but where they are not appropriate, do not hesitate to resort to more forceful means. Work diligently now, while there is still time. Then there will be no regret.

Tragically, the regency and the Tibetan leadership, following the Thirteenth Dalai Lama's death, failed to grasp the urgency and seriousness of his warning. Pretty much every aspect has proven to be precisely correct.

When we think of the tragedy of Tibet in the wider global context, we see an extraordinary irony. Immediately after the Second World War, the imperial nations of the world were giving up their colonies everywhere—one thinks of the end of the British and French mandates in the Middle East in the late 1940s and, of course, above all, of Indian independence in 1947. When all other imperial powers were divesting themselves of former colonies, Communist China was acquiring its own. The new Communist China chose to invade an independent country, Tibet, and make a colony out of it. In any case, the forcible inclusion of Tibet into Mao's new People's Republic of China has been disastrous not only for us Tibetans. It has also been problematic, to say the least, for China itself. For the imposition of a single Chinese nationhood over multiple nationalities, including Tibetans—each with its distinct language, culture, history, and people who have never viewed themselves as Chinese—created an inherently unstable modern state with a chronic threat of ethnic tension that perpetually requires brutal colonialist subjugation from Beijing.

There is a second irony, which might be characterized as ethical and moral. In December 1948, the United Nations adopted the Universal Declaration of Human Rights, a fundamental document that lays the foundation upon which civilized societies in the modern world must treat their citizens and those of other countries. This declaration acquired a legal basis in 1976 as the International Covenant on Civil and Political Rights, reaffirmed again in 2022. Communist China, in contrast, moved in the opposite direction. Almost immediately after the Universal Declaration of Human Rights was adopted, China began what has been more than seventy years of systematic abuse of the human rights of the Tibetan people.

Around the fiftieth anniversary of the UN declaration, a few countries led by Communist China contended that the standards of human rights laid down in the Universal Declaration are not truly universal and do not apply to Asia because of the differences in culture, society, and economy. They argued that the concept of universal human rights needed to be revisited to accommodate what they referred to as "Asian values." I stated that I do not share this view and argued that if any aspects of a culture or traditional customs were to conflict with respect for basic human rights, it is the traditional customs that need to be modified, not the other way around. I said that the majority of people in Asia would agree with me on this point.

To be candid, I find the idea that somehow people in Asia do not value basic human rights, such as individual freedom and dignity, or that they do not need them, to be disrespectful toward the peoples of Asia. Anyway, worried by this attempt to dilute the spirit of what is a seminal document in human history, I repeatedly argued that basic human rights are truly universal, for they pertain to the inherent nature of all human beings to yearn for freedom, equality, and dignity, and their right to achieve them. There is nothing West or East, North or South about this. I deeply believe that the principles laid down in the Universal Declaration of Human Rights constitute something like a natural law that ought to be followed by all peoples and governments.

The cost of the conquest of Tibet for the Tibetan nation and its people is obvious. But it is worth thinking more broadly about the geopolitical effects in the region. To begin with, for the first time in history, the world's two most populated nations had a long border that had to be increasingly militarized. Up until this invasion of Tibet, there was only an Indo-Tibetan border, and no such thing as an Indo-Chinese border. In his letter to Prime Minister Nehru of November 7, 1950, shortly before his death, India's Deputy Prime Minister Sardar Vallabhbhai Patel lamented the "expansion of China almost up to our gates. Throughout history, we have seldom worried about our north-east frontier. The Himalayas have been regarded as an impenetrable barrier against any threat from the north. We had friendly Tibet which gave us no trouble."

Just as Patel worried, there was a Sino-Indian war in 1962, followed by another conflict in 1967. Patel was more of a realist and pragmatist; by contrast, Nehru was more of an idealist and a visionary. The latter was worried about the world becoming too polarized between the North Atlantic Treaty Organization (NATO) and the Warsaw Pact and, economically, between the north and the south. His dream of a nonaligned collaboration led to the signing of the Panchsheel Agreement (literally, "Five Principles Agreement") between India and China in 1954—which set out a plan for mutual respect for each other's territorial integrity, mutual nonaggression, noninterference in each other's internal affairs, equality and mutual benefit, and peaceful coexistence. In brief, the invasion and forcible occupation of Tibet has created long-term instability on the Tibetan plateau affecting a host of nations that traditionally relied on peace at their northern border—India, Nepal,

Bhutan, and Myanmar. It is with this concern for peace and security in Asia in mind that I later made the suggestion, in my Five Point Peace Plan of September 1987, that the Tibetan plateau be turned into a demilitarized buffer zone between Asia's two largest military powers.

Ecologically speaking, the Tibetan plateau houses the source of many of Asia's greatest rivers—including Yarlung Tsangpo (Brahmaputra) and Senge Khabab (Indus), which flow southward, and Dzachu (Mekong), Machu (Yellow River), and Drichu (Yangtze), which run east. The Communist Chinese occupation of Tibet has had a devasting effect on the health of these rivers, with significant environmental consequences to many countries in Asia. In the future too, unless responsible custodianship of the sources of these major rivers is ensured, there may be significant conflicts in connection with access to water, indispensable for the survival of hundreds of millions of people in India, Pakistan, Bangladesh, Myanmar, Laos, Thailand, Vietnam, and Cambodia. Some environmental specialists refer to the Tibetan plateau as "the Third Pole," to add to the North and South Poles, for reasons including it being the largest repository of fresh water. In addition, the ecosystem of the plateau plays a crucial role in the regulation of the monsoon across South Asia.

China's mass deforestation in the Tibetan plateau, aggressively carried out especially in the 1980s, is reported to have destroyed more than 50 percent of forests in Kham (eastern Tibet), for example. Environmentalists are deeply concerned about the long-term negative impact of such extensive deforestation in the plateau, especially in relation to temperature increase and flooding during the monsoon in the lower regions. With respect to climate change, many years ago, an environmental scientist told me that, given Tibet's high altitude and dry climate, any ecological damage done on the plateau will take much longer to recover. The same scientist also told me about how Tibet's vast northern plains, Jangthang, plays a crucial role in cooling the temperature through reflecting the sun's light instead of absorbing it.

One of the greatest sources of concern is the construction of megadams such as the one at Yamdrok Lake and the Zangmu Dam in the Lhoka region close to the border of Bhutan. Today, we know from environmental science that there is a connection between earthquakes and the construction of dams in the high-altitude Tibetan plateau, given that the region is one of the most seismically active areas in the world. The Tibetan plateau is also known for its vast mineral deposits. According to China's own Geological Survey bureau, the plateau is understood to have reserves of thirty to forty million tons of copper, more than forty million tons of zinc, and billions of tons of iron, including especially large deposits of rare minerals, such as lithium and uranium. In fact, the Chinese word for Tibet, Xizang, literally means "western treasure house." If mining is done at all in the Tibetan plateau, it has to be conducted in accord with the highest sensitivity to environmental impact. In the end, a careless, instrumental, or mercantile approach to extraction will lead to long-term consequences, which will be experienced way beyond the boundaries of the Tibetan plateau.

Lastly, there has been a large-scale forced migration of nomads from their traditional grasslands in different parts of the Tibetan plateau. Historically, Tibet's nomadic communities have lived in the vast open plains, including the grasslands, and have developed a symbiotic relationship with their environment such that their presence on the vast open space has served as the best form of caretaking for the ecology. Displacements of these traditional nomadic communities have not only been devastating for the nomads, but also they have created a new cycle of imbalance in the environment.

I had hoped, given that ecological health is a concern common to Tibetans as well as the Chinese, that the protection of Tibet's fragile environment would be one area where one could see systematic and sustained joint efforts. If the Chinese authorities were to allow environmental scientists, including especially Chinese scientists, to work hand in hand with local Tibetans who know their environment best, there is the possibility of creating an effective approach to reducing unnecessary ecological damage on the plateau. I was told that a noted

Chinese environmental scientist who had spent many years in Tibet has commented that where religious tradition is strongest, the environment is well protected, and this is something that should give us pause for thought.

Historically, with our cultural and religious practices that emphasize living in harmony with nature, Tibet's natural environment—including flora and fauna—had never suffered excessive abuse at the hands of the human inhabitants of the vast plateau. Very worryingly, there are many reports that Communist China has installed nuclear missiles in the high altitude of the Tibetan plateau. Setting aside the implications for regional and international stability, the risk of leaks or mistakes carries a devastating threat to the fragile ecology. Were the waters of the rivers to be polluted, the destructive impact on the lives of many millions dependent on these rivers cannot be calculated.

When you take all these issues together—the militarization of the Tibetan plateau, which includes the stationing of nuclear weapons; an increasing security face-off between two of Asia's largest armies across more than three thousand kilometers of border, of which some crucial parts remain disputed; and ecological destruction of the plateau through deforestation and extensive mining, as well as unpredictable management of the sources of some of Asia's greatest rivers, on whom the livelihoods of hundreds of millions depend—the invasion of Tibet has been truly tragic, not just for the Tibetans but for the whole of humanity too. It is a tragedy of historic proportions whose destructive fallout will continue to reverberate through the centuries.

Had Tibet been able to remain free, these geopolitical and ecological problems would not exist. This is the plain truth.

CHAPTER 6

# Devastation at Home and Rebuilding in Exile

On March 31, 1959, around 3 p.m. Indian Standard Time, my party arrived in the Indian border village of Kenzamane, near Tawang. The moment I crossed into India I felt a tremendous sense of relief. It didn't matter that we might have been a pitiful sight to the handful of Indian soldiers guarding the border—approximately eighty of us physically exhausted by the ordeal of hard travel. Even my mother said we no longer had to be afraid of the Chinese and could say what we thought. Obviously, my mother too had been carrying a heavy burden of having to weigh every word she uttered and every action she engaged in.

We were met with an extraordinarily warm welcome from the local people and a cordial telegram from Prime Minister Nehru:

> My colleagues and I welcome you and send you greetings on your safe arrival in India. We shall be happy to afford the necessary facilities for you, your family, and entourage to reside in India.

> The people of India, who hold you in great veneration, will no doubt accord their traditional respect to your personage. Kind regards to you. Nehru

We were formally received on behalf of the government of India by a familiar face, P. N. Menon, an Indian foreign ministry official who had previously been stationed at the Indian Mission in Lhasa. Waiting there was also another familiar face, Kazi Sonam Topgyal, who had helped translate for me during my 1956–1957 visit to India. From the Indian border we traveled to the town of Tawang, in what was then known as the North East Frontier Agency (NEFA), today as Arunachal Pradesh. On April 18, I was taken by jeep to the town of Tezpur, where the international media were waiting. At the railway station I felt overwhelmed to find thousands of telegrams of good wishes waiting for me, and approximately a hundred journalists and photographers from across the world who had come to cover what they called "the story of the year." I took the opportunity to issue a statement to the world, giving a full account of the circumstances that led to my escape—the spontaneous people's uprising in Lhasa and our long, peaceful approach to seeking accommodation with the Chinese Communists—and announcing that I was in India to oppose Chinese Communist occupation of my country and to appeal to the free countries of the world. I concluded by saying that I hoped fervently that the crisis in Tibet would be over soon without any more bloodshed. Two days later, Beijing issued a statement asserting that the "so-called statement of the Dalai Lama . . . is a crude document, lame in reasoning, full of lies and loopholes." It then went on to claim that I had been abducted by rebels from Lhasa!

Understandably, there were heated debates in the Indian Parliament, the Lok Sabha, on what had just happened to Tibet, India's historic neighbor to the north. What the veteran politician and freedom fighter Jaya Prakash Narayan said captured the sense of frustration and moral dilemma felt by many Indian leaders at the time:

> No one expects India to go to war with China for the sake of Tibet. But every upright person, every freedom loving individual should be ready to call a spade a spade. We are not serving the cause of peace by slurring over acts of aggression. We cannot physically prevent the Chinese from annexing Tibet and subduing that peaceful and brave people, but we at least can put on record our clear verdict that aggression has been committed and the freedom of a weak nation has been snuffed out by a powerful neighbour. Let us too not waver to tear the veil from the face of communism, which under the visage of the gentle Panchsheel hides the savage countenance of imperialism. For in Tibet we see at this moment the workings of a new imperialism, which is far more dangerous than the old because it marches under the banner of a so-called revolutionary ideology.

From Tezpur we traveled to Mussoorie, a beautiful British-era hill station in the foothills of the Himalayas north of Delhi. At every major train stop thousands of Indians came to welcome me, shouting, "*Dalai Lama ki Jai*" (Hail to the Dalai Lama) and "*Dalai Lama Zindabad*" (Long live the Dalai Lama). In Mussoorie, the government of India had established my first residence in exile. Here, on April 24, Nehru came to meet me and welcome me in person to India. We spoke for over four hours. Since Nehru was one of the powerful voices that had urged me to return to Lhasa in 1957, I reported how, despite all my best attempts to deal fairly and honestly with the Chinese according to the terms of the Seventeen-Point Agreement, they had been impossible to work with. On June 20, 1959, I gave my first formal press conference. I declared that Tibet had been independent, enjoying and exercising all rights of sovereignty, whether internal or external, and that by invading Tibet, Communist China's army had committed a flagrant act of aggression. This is something any objective person would agree with. In any case, I said at this press conference that since the Chinese side had violated key terms of the agreement, effectively it had become invalid.

If a treaty is violated by one of the parties to it, then it can legally be repudiated by the other party, at which point it is no longer in force. I also stated that, as far as Tibetans everywhere are concerned, where my cabinet and my person are present, there will exist the legitimate government of Tibet.

In the wake of my escape, many thousands of Tibetans managed to follow me into exile. At home in Tibet, the oppression had become intolerable. Listening to the accounts of the new arrivals, in the face of the destruction of my people and all that they live for, I devoted myself in exile to the only courses of action left to me—to remind the world of what happened and what was still happening in Tibet and to care for the Tibetans who escaped with me to freedom. All that we had heard from the accounts of refugees—and more—was confirmed by the report of the International Commission of Jurists' Legal Inquiry Committee on Tibet at Geneva in July 1959, entitled *The Question of Tibet and the Rule of Law*. What gives weight to this report is that it was commissioned and conducted by an independent judicial body beholden to no government or interested party. It was, in effect, totally impartial. The report concluded that "the evidence points at least to a prima facie case of Genocide against the People's Republic of China" and "Genocide is the gravest crime known to the law of nations." The Genocide Convention of 1948 condemns "acts committed with intent to destroy, in whole or in part, a national, ethnical, racial or religious group as such." In the second report from the International Commission of Jurists, *Tibet and the Chinese People's Republic*, published in 1960, "The Committee found that acts of genocide had been committed in Tibet in an attempt to destroy the Tibetans as a religious group, and that such acts are acts of genocide independent of any conventional obligation."

On September 4, 1959, I made an important trip to Delhi. There, in addition to crucial meetings with Prime Minister Nehru as well as other important leaders, including especially the president and the vice president of India, I also met with ambassadors from various countries.

Personally, the most moving part of this visit was the engagement I had with a gathering of several thousand Indians organized by Bharat Tibet Sangh (India Tibet Fraternity) and chaired by Acharya Kripalani, a noted Gandhian and social activist. (Acharya remained a staunch supporter of the Tibetan cause and a dear personal friend until his death in 1982.)

Now that I was in a free country, I also set about consulting with international experts about taking the case of Tibet to the General Assembly of the United Nations. So while in Delhi that September 1959, I wrote to the secretary-general of the United Nations, Dag Hammarskjöld: "In view of the inhumane treatment and crimes against humanity and religion to which the people of Tibet are being subjected, I solicit immediate intervention of the United Nations." On October 21, 1959, the General Assembly adopted a resolution sponsored by Ireland and Malaysia that called "for respect for the fundamental human rights of the Tibetan people and for their distinctive cultural and religious life," and acknowledged that "the fundamental human rights and freedoms to which the Tibetan people, like all others, are entitled include the right to civil and religious liberty for all without distinction." I continued in my appeals to the UN secretary-general and to many governments, updating them on the worsening situation inside Tibet. Notably, in 1960, the United States government announced its support for Tibet's self-determination. In fact, I received two letters from Secretary of State Christian A. Herter—one in February 1960 and the second in October of that same year—assuring me that the United States' position remained "that the principle of self-determination should apply to the people of Tibet and that they should have the determining voice in their own political destiny." In 1961, at the sixteenth session of the UN General Assembly, a further resolution was adopted, sponsored by Malaya, Ireland, El Salvador, and Thailand. This resolution solemnly renewed the UN's "call for the cessation of practices which deprive the Tibetan people of their fundamental human rights and freedoms, including their right to self-determination." One more resolution on

Tibet was passed at the UN, on December 18, 1965, at its plenary session, reaffirming the earlier resolutions and the UN General Assembly's grave concerns "at the continued violation of the fundamental rights and freedoms of the people."

In January 1960, I took the opportunity to visit Bodh Gaya and Sarnath, to pay homage, respectively, to Mahabodhi Stupa with the sacred Bodhi tree and the site of the Buddha's First Turning of the Wheel of Dharma—this time with my mind in a more settled state. (The last time I visited the sacred Buddhist site of Bodh Gaya in 1956, my mind had been racing with the question of whether to return to Tibet or seek asylum in India.) In Sarnath, near Varanasi, I officiated for the first time at a ceremony for the full ordination of monks. Tradition demands that the monk officiating at a full ordination ceremony be someone who has himself received full ordination vows for ten years, or at least five years earlier in the case of someone with exceptional qualifications. My two tutors insisted that I met the required qualifications and should conduct my first ordination ceremony for others at the site of the Buddha's first public discourse. I was then twenty-six years old. As someone to whom the identity of monkhood is close to his heart, this was both a profound honor and joy. I reflected on how fortunate I was to be able to perform such an ordination ceremony at the very place where the Buddha gave his first public sermon following his enlightenment, known as the First Turning of the Wheel of Dharma. Among those who took ordination in Sarnath was Dagyab Rinpoche, a high-ranking reincarnate lama in the Geluk tradition.

In Bodh Gaya too, I conducted an ordination ceremony, and among those who took full ordination there was Samdhong Rinpoche, who would later become the first directly elected political leader of our exiled Tibetan community. There in Bodh Gaya, in January 1960, we also had what was effectively the first formal gathering of the Tibetan people in the free world. Key constituencies—including representatives from the three Tibetan provinces of Ü-Tsang, Kham, and Amdo; senior members of Tibet's major Buddhist traditions; abbots of the great monasteries; and delegations from various parts of India—came together to host a long-life ceremony for my good health. At this ceremony, representing the Tibetan people in exile, they all took what was called the "Great Oath of Unity" (*Na-gan Thunmoche*). Those present pledged that from now on, they would strive for the unity of Tibetans from all three provinces and shoulder the responsibility to work for the common welfare of Tibet, under the Dalai Lama's leadership. It was in Bodh Gaya, also, where we decided that we would strive to establish a representative form of government for future Tibet and, of course, for our exile community.

Returning to Mussoorie, we commemorated the first anniversary of the Tibetan People's National Uprising of March 10, 1959. In this way, we began the tradition of a major address to the Tibetan people on March 10 every year, marking this tragic anniversary. On that first anniversary, I stressed the need on our part to adopt a long-term view of the situation of Tibet. I said that for those of us in exile in a free country, our priority must be ensuring the survival of our civilization, especially through the protection of our distinct language and cultural traditions. I assured my people that truth, justice, and courage would be our weapons and that we would eventually prevail in our struggle for freedom. While in Mussoorie, we began our plans to educate our younger generation. To this end, we set up the first Tibetan school in India with an initial number of fifty mature students. Within a year, we were able to send some from this first batch to various parts of India, as well as remote areas in Nepalese border regions like Khumbu Valley, to teach Tibetan refugee children, including the teaching of English language as well.

On April 30, 1960, I arrived in Dharamsala, which was to become my permanent residence in exile. There, we reconstituted what was, in effect, a Tibetan government in exile, called at the time the Central Tibetan Secretariat, later renamed the Central Tibetan Administration (CTA). With the help of my colleagues, I initiated a two-pronged strategy. There was first and foremost, after caring for the immediate necessities of more than eighty thousand Tibetan refugees, the need to establish resettlements for the Tibetans in a way that would enable us to preserve our culture and identity while in exile. The second was to reach out to the governments around the world, the United Nations, and the international community to help resolve the Tibetan issue. An important part of this strategy was to draw international attention to the plight of the Tibetan people and China's unjust occupation of our country. At that time, my hope and efforts in this regard were directed toward the ultimate goal of restoring Tibet's independence.

In my March 10 address of 1961 at my new residence in Dharamsala, I undertook to prepare a draft of the constitutional and economic structure to which I aspired for our country and said that I would place it shortly before the representatives of the Tibetan people in India and neighboring countries for their consideration. Ever since my first visit to India in 1956, especially witnessing democracy in action by contrast with what I saw in Beijing, I have been a deep believer that democracy really is the most appropriate form of government. So, once I was resident in a free country, I strove to initiate a process of democratizing the Tibetan political system. It took me and my officials two years, following consultations with various experts, studying a number of constitutions around the free world, as well as many internal debates, to finalize a draft, which we proclaimed on March 10, 1963. This constitution envisions a future Tibet as "a unitary democratic State founded upon the principles laid down by the Lord Buddha." Key provisions included an independent judiciary, an elected national assembly, prohibition of "discrimination on any ground such as sex, race, language, religion, social origin, property, birth or other status," as well as "the right to freedom of thought, conscience and religion." The document also includes, as Article 36, section (e), a clause for the possible abolition of the Dalai Lama's authority by two-thirds of the majority of the National Assembly. Over the course of years, this document has been revised into a fully democratic model governing the norms of the Tibetan people, at least in the exile community.

In November 1963, at my residence in Dharamsala, most memorably, we held the first summit representing all Tibetan Buddhist schools attended by, in addition to the heads of the lineages, senior lamas, reincarnate *tulku*s, *geshe*s (equivalent to holders of a doctorate in divinity), and scholars, as well as senior members of the Tibetan administration. This four-day meeting offered an excellent opportunity to create the basis for a strong sense of unity across the diverse traditions of Tibetan Buddhism as well as to encourage a united effort to preserve Tibet's rich religious traditions.

One of the important topics that Prime Minister Nehru and I discussed in the early days of my exile was the education of the refugee children. Nehru emphasized that in order to preserve Tibetan culture and identity it would be necessary to have separate schools for the Tibetans. He thus undertook to establish an autonomous body within the Indian Ministry of Education, with the government of India bearing the costs. Furthermore, Nehru advised that while it was very important for our children to have a thorough knowledge of their history and culture, it was vital that they be conversant with the modern world, and hence that we use English as our medium of education. From this emerged a network of Central Schools for Tibetans (CST), producing generations of modern-educated young Tibetans.

During the sixties, we reestablished in exile many of the historically important cultural and religious institutions of Tibet, including especially the monasteries and monastic universities belonging to the major schools of Tibetan Buddhism. New establishments founded in Dharamsala included the Thekchen Choeling Temple, the Tibetan Children's Village (TCV), the Tibetan Medical and Astro. Institute, the Tibetan Institute of Performing Arts (TIPA), and the Library of Tibetan Works and Archives. During this crucial decade, many of the refugees found work in the great effort of building roads at high altitude. I personally visited some of these road construction sites to encourage and give comfort to those many Tibetans who were engaged in such hard labor. A most unusual but memorable experience at one road construction camp took place when I visited Chamba, in northern India. There was a substantial number of monks among the road workers, and since my visit coincided with the day of a required bimonthly confession ceremony, I led the monks through the confession ceremony. Since the monks only had trousers and shirts, they had no choice but to participate in the ceremony in lay clothes. Recognizing that employment such as road construction would only be temporary, efforts were made to seek more long-term forms of livelihood for the refugees. Thanks to the generosity of several Indian states, we were able to establish more than twenty Tibetan settlements during the 1960s and early 1970s, especially in southern India. In this way, we ensured that, even in exile, we could live as a distinct community so that we could preserve our language and culture. We were also the beneficiaries of the generous support of many international aid agencies and nongovernmental organizations (NGOs). Two countries—Switzerland in the early 1960s and Canada in the 1970s—offered asylum to several hundred Tibetan refugees. We were also able to send many Tibetan children and young adults for education to the United Kingdom, France, Germany, Switzerland, Sweden, Denmark, Norway, and Iran, as well as Japan, many of whom were later able to serve in various capacities in our offices in exile. Throughout this period, there was no contact with the People's Republic of China, principally because Tibet was, just as China proper, engulfed in the chaotic period of the Cultural Revolution.

On May 27, 1964, sadly, Prime Minister Nehru passed away. He had been the constant face in all my international political dealings since I'd met him in Beijing in 1954, during my first trip to India, and then in my exile. And, of course, he had been so supportive and generous to our initiatives for the Tibetan refugees. His successor, Prime Minister Lal Bahadur Shastri, continued Nehru's policy of supporting the exile community, thus establishing an enduring position on the part of the Indian government in its support of the Tibetans in India. Shastri adopted a more robust position in relation to China, which was reflected in India's support of the UN resolution on Tibet of 1965.

Sadly, Prime Minister Shastri died in 1966, while visiting Tashkent in Uzbekistan. He was succeeded as the prime minister by Nehru's daughter, Indira Gandhi, whom I had known because of my long friendship with her father. Indira was familiar with the Tibetan situation and the Tibetan refugees in India; in fact, she once sat on the board of trustees of the Tibetan Homes Foundation in Mussoorie.

Meanwhile, inside Tibet, things were disastrous and grim. The response to my flight had been brutal, and the repression terrible, as if people were being punished for my escape. The most powerful account of what happened in this period is given in the seventy-thousand-character petition written in Chinese by the Panchen Lama in 1962, which Mao Zedong described as "a poisoned arrow shot at the heart of the Party." The petition, submitted to the Chinese Premier Zhou Enlai but seen by the outside world only years later, was entitled "A Report on the Sufferings of the Masses in Tibet and Other Tibetan Regions and Suggestions for Future Work to the Central Authorities Through the Respected Premier Zhou." Unlike me, the Panchen Lama had stayed behind in occupied Tibet, at his monastic base Tashi Lhunpo in Shigatse. Following a tour of parts of Tibet, he wrote:

> Because of many errors of mistakes . . . serious harm was done to agriculture and animal herding production. . . . Because the anguish of such severe hunger had never before been experienced in Tibetan history, and was such that people could not imagine it even in their dreams, the masses could not resist this kind of cruel torment, and their condition declined daily. Therefore, in some places, colds and other such minor infectious diseases caused a percentage of people to die easily. In some places many people directly starved to death because the food ran out; in some places, there was a phenomenon of whole families dying out. . . .
>
> No matter whether they were men or women, old or young, as soon as they saw me, people thought of the bitterness of that

> period and were unable to prevent tears flowing from their eyes. A few brave people among them said through their tears, "Do not let all living creatures starve! Do not destroy Buddhism! Do not extinguish the people of our snowy land! These are our wishes and our prayers!" These are the hopes, concise but comprehensive and profound, more urgent than wanting water when you are thirsty, of the broad masses of the monastic and secular people, produced by bitterness resulting from what has happened and from the existing situation in Tibetan areas.

One of the key concerns raised by the Panchen Lama in his petition relates to the issue of protecting Tibetan nationality and cultural identity within the People's Republic of China. Clearly, this concern came from the fear of Han chauvinism.* He writes:

> Once a nationality's language, costumes, customs, and other important characteristics have disappeared, then the nationality itself has disappeared too.

In relation to the destruction of religion, the Panchen Lama declares:

> Before democratic reform, there were more than 2500 large, medium, and small monasteries in Tibet. After democratic reform, only 70 or so monasteries were kept in existence by the government. This was a reduction of more than 97%. . . . In the whole of Tibet in the past, there was a total of about 110,000 monks and nuns. . . . After democratic reform was concluded,

* By "Han chauvinism," the Panchen Lama is referring here to the ideology that the Han race is superior compared to the other ethnic members within the People's Republic of China and that other cultures need to be assimilated into the Han culture, an ideology that Mao explicitly attacked.

the number of monks and nuns living in the monasteries was about 7,000 people, which is a reduction of 93%.

The Panchen Lama's courage in writing in the above manner in the midst of the cruelest totalitarian oppression deserves the deepest admiration. It was written on the basis of his visiting many Tibetan areas, including Amdo, as well as East Turkistan (Xinjiang). In personal terms, he paid a terrible price. The petition confirmed my worst nightmare of what might have happened in the wake of the Tibetan People's Uprising of March 1959 and my own escape. In 1964, the Panchen Lama was declared an enemy of the Tibetan people and publicly humiliated through the ritual of what came to be called "struggle sessions,"* which would later become a hallmark of the Cultural Revolution. He was arrested and remained in prison until 1977, and then kept under house arrest until 1979.

After his release, the Panchen Lama spoke out forcefully on behalf of the Tibetan people and criticized Chinese policies in Tibet. Particularly, in March 1987, he spoke candidly at the Tibet Autonomous Region's Standing Committee meeting in Beijing, during the National People's Congress, criticizing Communist Chinese policies inside Tibet, including especially the language policies, as well as Han chauvinism. My heart goes out to the memory of this heroic figure who did so much to protect the Tibetan people in their darkest hour, especially after his release in 1979 and until his sudden death under suspicious circumstances in January 1989.

Five days before his death, I understood that he made the following statement:

* "Struggle session" (*thamzing* in Tibetan) was a public humiliation ritual where the target is made to wear a dunce hat and, with their head bowed, subjected to insults, shouts, and spitting from the "ordinary" public.

> Since liberation, there has certainly been development, but the price paid for this development has been greater than the gains.

I was fortunate to have phone conversations with him during his trips outside the People's Republic of China. This gave me a chance to express my thanks and admiration personally. The Panchen Lama was three years younger than me and had been my companion on the trips to China in 1954–1955 and to India in 1956–1957. Not a man of patience for diplomatic niceties—for the Panchen Lama what mattered was honesty and integrity. Over the years, the Chinese Communists tried to create and exploit conflict between us on the old colonial principle of divide and conquer. Yet even though we were unable to have contact for a long time, I advocated awareness of the fate of Tibet to the outside world, while, with immense courage, he presented the truth to the leaders of the oppressors themselves.

The Panchen Lama's petition describes the situation before the Cultural Revolution, which Mao unleashed in May 1966 and which lasted until his death in 1976. Recognizing that China as a whole suffered immensely during this decade of turbulence, it was a terrible time, especially for Tibet. It began in Lhasa with Red Guards invading the Jokhang Temple—destroying ancient frescoes and images and burning scriptures in the courtyard in the name of abolishing "the four olds," which were old ideology, old culture, old habits, and old customs. As I noted in my March 10 Statement of 1967, among the countless images destroyed was one of Avalokiteshvara made in the seventh century and considered one of the most sacred icons of Tibet. The destruction spread to the Norbulingka and across the city, and ultimately there would be street battles in Lhasa and other cities between rival factions.

In this chaotic period, not only did many thousands die, but numerous historic monuments were destroyed, such as Ganden Monastery, founded by Tibet's great philosopher-saint Tsongkhapa in 1409. In essence, everything Tibetan was attacked: the practice of the Buddhist faith was outlawed; incense burning, ceremonies, and festivals were banned; traditional songs and dances were prohibited. Struggle sessions and public humiliations were meted out to monks and "class enemies." In brief, Tibet experienced a large-scale and systematic attempt to erase its cultural identity and collective memory.

If any of my colleagues who fled with me into exile in 1959 ever had any doubts about the correctness of our course of action, then the Cultural Revolution utterly dispelled them. Had I stayed in Tibet, I wouldn't have been able to do anything meaningful in the face of this insane and systematic onslaught.

In January 1976, the Chinese Premier Zhou Enlai died, followed by Marshal Zhu De in July and Chairman Mao himself on September 9. Mao's legacy includes the deaths of more than forty million people, especially during the famine of his Great Leap Forward in 1958–1962. On the geopolitical side, instead of decolonizing as the great empires were doing at the time, Mao's China chose a policy of colonialist imperialism in relation to Tibet, Mongolia, and East Turkistan, couched ironically in strident anticolonial rhetoric. What this has created for Mao's successors is a legacy of perpetual instability, paranoia, and repression, especially against the non-Chinese nationalities. As a result, today, even after more than seven decades of occupation, any expression of Tibetan identity is seen as a threat questioning Chinese legitimacy in Tibet.

The death of Mao was the beginning of an intense power struggle in which Mao's wife Jiang Qing, who had been one of the instigators of the Cultural Revolution and the Gang of Four, lost power to the faction headed by Hua Guofeng. While this was happening, I was watching events from India with interest and some hope.

Among the noticeable changes was the visit of the former American Defense Secretary James Schlesinger for a three-day tour of Tibet soon after Mao's death. Schlesinger's visit was the beginning of a chance to obtain a clearer picture of the conditions inside Tibet. I was told that he described the Communist Chinese presence there as oppressive, even by colonial standards, since it aimed at total domination.

Until then, the People's Republic of China had only allowed foreign visits to Tibet from among their close allies. Shortly after, Beijing began to allow sympathetic Western journalists and writers into Tibet. For nearly two decades since my flight into exile in 1959, the entire Tibetan plateau had been run like one giant prison. No one was allowed to communicate with the outside world, which meant that, except for a few messages received through secret channels, the Tibetans living in exile were totally cut off from their compatriots and families back in our homeland. Back home, Tibetans had been told that those in exile were living in abject poverty, since it was only the socialist countries that had successfully achieved economic prosperity.

When the dust settled from the power struggle in the Chinese Communist Party in the aftermath of Chairman Mao's death, it was my old acquaintance Deng Xiaoping who emerged as the paramount leader of China in 1978.

CHAPTER 7

# Overtures Toward a Dialogue

I had met Deng Xiaoping, now the paramount leader of China, several times during my visit to Beijing in 1954–1955 and knew that he was one of the senior Chinese figures who had been most involved in matters related to Tibet. In an overture to this new regime in China, in my official March 10 Statement of 1978, I said:

> If the six million Tibetans in Tibet are really happy and prosperous as never before there is no reason for us to argue otherwise. If the Tibetans are really happy the Chinese should allow every interested foreigner to visit Tibet without restricting their movements or meetings with the Tibetan people. This would enable the visitors to really know the true conditions in Tibet. Furthermore, the Chinese should allow the Tibetans in Tibet to visit their parents and relatives now in exile. These Tibetans can then study the conditions of those of us in exile living in free countries. Similar opportunity should be given to the Tibetans in exile.

Quite unexpectedly, at the end of 1978, my brother Gyalo Thondup, who was then living in Hong Kong, received an invitation to meet with Deng Xiaoping in Beijing. This was clearly an overture and Gyalo Thondup consulted me about what to do. In November of that year, thirty-four members of my former government in Tibet were released from prison with great public ceremony: clearly a hopeful message was being sent. On February 1, 1979, the Panchen Lama made his first public appearance after fourteen years and called for my return to Tibet. At the same time, the United States established formal diplomatic relations with the People's Republic of China, signaling the possibility for a fundamental shift taking place in China vis-à-vis the international community.

I told my brother that he should accept the invitation but at this stage to do so in a personal capacity, rather than as my formal representative. On March 12, 1979, he met Deng Xiaoping in the Great Hall of the People. Deng opened the meeting by asking how my health was, and he asked how long it had been since my brother was last in Beijing. He answered that it was in 1949, thirty years ago. As their conversation progressed, Deng told my brother that complete independence of Tibet was nonnegotiable. "But except for independence, everything is negotiable. Everything can be discussed," he said. Deng was extraordinarily open and indeed positive about a series of questions Gyalo Thondup raised, even though my brother had made it clear that he was speaking in a personal capacity. Deng agreed to open up the border between Tibet and India so family members who had been cut off for two decades could see each other. He accepted that we send from our exile community Tibetan language teachers into Tibetan areas, and even agreed to the opening of a liaison office in Beijing to begin the process of a conversation. Deng assured him that China's new leadership was committed to fundamental and lasting change, and if the Dalai Lama had doubts, then we should send people to investigate the situation inside Tibet. He said that it is better to see things with one's own eyes than hear something a hundred times from other people.

By the early 1970s, after careful and deep contemplation, I had come to some important realizations on the nature of our struggle and what might be the best means to move forward. One thing I realized was that if our side insisted on our goal of restoring Tibet's independence, this would mean the Tibetans might even have to consider the possibility of a prolonged armed struggle against Communist China, which would be not just impractical but, in fact, suicidal. I vividly remember what Prime Minister Nehru said about the unrealistic nature of our quest for restoring Tibet's independence—that the United States is not going to go to war with China for the sake of Tibet.

Of course, as someone categorically opposed to violence, I could no longer lead the freedom movement if the Tibetan struggle were to choose violence as its path. Furthermore, I came to recognize that what mattered most to us Tibetans was the protection of a people with a unique language, culture, and religion, who are historically connected with the unique geography that is the Tibetan plateau. Finally, there was the crucial understanding that to resolve the Tibetan issue we would have to eventually sit down and talk with the Chinese. And for that, despite the historical truth of our independence and the Tibetan people's deep attachment to this ideal as well as their right, we recognized that to call for Tibet's independence would be a nonstarter for the Chinese side. Now, if our problem was to be solved through a peaceful process of negotiation, this required us to take into account seriously the perspective of the Chinese side. I understood that what mattered most to the People's Republic of China was stability and territorial integrity, while on our part, what mattered most for us Tibetans was the ability to survive and thrive as a distinct people with our own unique language and cultural heritage. The seed was sown for what later came to be known as the Middle Way Approach—seeking not independence but genuine autonomy within the framework of the People's Republic of China.

So, even before we received the overture from Deng, by 1974 I had shared my thoughts with a small circle of key leaders within our

Tibetan community in exile. We discussed in a candid manner the pros and cons of continuing to seek the restoration of Tibet's independence versus the new perspective I had come to formulate. We also discussed and debated how and when we might bring this new approach to the broader Tibetan exile community as well as to our international supporters. After a series of serious discussions, the key members of our exile administration, including the cabinet, were all on the same page as me. So when Gyalo Thondup brought the message from Deng that except for independence everything could be discussed, I was convinced that there was indeed a scope for a meaningful conversation within a framework acceptable to both sides.

Deng was as good as his word, at least with respect to sending delegations to Tibet. Between August 1979 and June 1985, we were able to send four fact-finding missions to Tibet. Remarkably, the Chinese government agreed that they could visit all Tibetan areas, not just what the Chinese call the "Tibet Autonomous Region."* I don't know what impression the Chinese leadership expected from our delegation, or how they supposed the Tibetans inside Tibet would react to their presence. In fact, fearing that our delegates might be attacked physically by "right-thinking" local people, the Chinese authorities actually briefed the locals to show courtesy to the visiting delegates.

When the five members of our first delegation, led by Juchen Thupten Namgyal (then a senior minister in my cabinet in Dharam-

* "Tibet Autonomous Region" (TAR) is a modern construct created by the People's Republic of China, following its invasion of Tibetan in 1950 and formally established in 1965. The region, containing the historical Tibetan province of Ü-Tsang and western Kham, roughly corresponds to the territory under the rule of the Dalai Lama government of Lhasa at the time of the Communist Chinese invasion of Tibet in 1950. Historically, Tibet consists of Chol-kha-gsum, the three provinces of Ü-Tsang (central, southern, and western Tibet), Kham (eastern Tibet), and Amdo (northeastern Tibet).

sala), arrived in Amdo, my birthplace, they were mobbed in adulation by thousands of people, especially the young. This alarmed their Chinese minders, who signaled ahead to warn the authorities in Lhasa. The reply came back saying that people in Amdo and Kham were simple nomads without class consciousness, but thanks to the standard of Marxist training in the capital, there was no possibility of embarrassment there. Yet in Lhasa, the crowds were immense and ecstatic. One of the delegates overheard a senior Chinese cadre's remark: "The efforts of the last twenty years have been wasted in a single day!" In fact, everywhere the delegates were mobbed by people crying and recounting the terrible tragedies they had suffered. There was a horrific litany of human rights abuses, and cultural destruction was graphically illustrated by many photographs of monasteries and nunneries reduced to rubble.

Despite the Chinese leadership's evident surprise and embarrassment at the Tibetan reaction to our first delegation, I should acknowledge that it was magnanimous of Deng to allow the planned second, third, and fourth delegations to go ahead, although in the end the second delegation, led by Tenzin Namgyal Tethong (at the time my representative at the Office of Tibet, New York) and consisting of young Tibetan leaders, was sent back early. (The third delegation was led by Jetsun Pema, my younger sister, and the fourth led by the former senior Tibetan official Kundeling Woeser Gyaltsen.) Perhaps Beijing interpreted the outpouring of grief on the part of the Tibetans as an immediate expression of anguish at the excesses of the Cultural Revolution rather than reflecting deeper feelings against Communist Chinese occupation. What these visits demonstrated to us was the massive support within Tibet for the struggles we were undertaking for them in exile and my own leadership.

One of the immediate results of our delegation visits was the unprecedented fact-finding mission of the new Party Secretary Hu Yaobang and Vice Premier Wan Li, who went to Lhasa in May 1980. They were dismayed by what they saw and subjected the local Chinese leadership to a severe dressing-down. Hu declared:

> We feel that our party has let the Tibetan people down. We feel very bad! The sole purpose of our Communist Party is to work for the happiness of the people, to do good things for them. We have worked for nearly thirty years, but the life of the Tibetan people has not notably improved. Are we not to blame?*

Hu is said to have compared the situation in Tibet to colonialism. He announced a six-point policy, including full rights for Tibetans to exercise regional autonomy, the development of Tibetan culture, language, and education in accord with socialist orientation, and an increase in the number of Tibetan officials. This new, more liberal policy led to the reappearance of individual religious practices, the reopening and rebuilding of monasteries, permission for new young monks, and reprinting of classical Tibetan texts in modern book format. The Communist Party made good on Deng's promise to my brother Gyalo Thondup, allowing both exiled Tibetans to return for visits and resident Tibetans to go abroad, especially to India to meet their relatives.

Among those able to leave Tibet in the early 1980s was Lopon-la, a senior monk at Namgyal Monastery in the Potala Palace complex, whose monks are traditionally responsible for assisting the Dalai Lama in rituals and official ceremonies. Following my departure from Lhasa in 1959, Lopon-la had spent eighteen years in Chinese prisons. After

* Hu Yaobang's critical statement to the local Chinese leadership in Tibet is cited in Wang Yao's "Hu Yaobang's Visit to Tibet, May 22–31, 1980: An Important Development in the Chinese Government Tibet Policy," in Robert Barnett and Shirin Akiner, eds., *Resistance and Reform in Tibet* (London: Hurst & Company, 1994). Wang Yao was a member of the delegation accompanying the Chinese leader Hu Yaobang on the latter's visit to Tibet.

he rejoined his old monastery, now reestablished in Dharamsala, his tall and somewhat stooped posture became a recognizable presence.

Since I had known Lopon-la in Tibet and liked him a lot, I met with him on many occasions. During one such meeting, when we were having tea together, he casually remarked that during his prison time there were two or three occasions when he felt real danger. Thinking that he was speaking of some kind of threat to his life, I asked, "What kind of danger?" He replied, "The danger of losing my compassion toward the Chinese." When I heard what he said, I just bowed to him. Later I learned of similar stories from other Tibetans, especially monks and nuns, who took extreme care not to lose sight of the humanity of the Chinese, even those who were inflicting such harm and hardship on them.

In my efforts to deal directly with the Chinese leadership in the spirit of what Deng Xiaoping had said to my brother in 1979, I wrote a letter to Deng in March 1981. I expressed my appreciation of Hu Yaobang's trip to Tibet and his efforts to right the wrongs and for frankly admitting past mistakes. I acknowledged the invitation through my brother that Deng and I should keep in contact with each other, and I thanked him for allowing us to send delegations to the Tibetan areas. I wrote:

> If the Tibetan people's identity is preserved and if they are genuinely happy, there is no reason to complain. However, in reality, over 90 percent of the Tibetans are suffering both mentally and physically, and are living in deep sorrow. These sad conditions have not been brought about by natural disasters, but by human action. Therefore, genuine efforts must be made to resolve the problems in accordance with the existing realities in a reasonable way.
>
> In order to do this, we must improve the relationship between China and Tibet as well as between Tibetans in and outside Tibet. With truth and equality as our foundation, we must try to develop friendship between Tibetans and Chinese through better

understanding in the future. The time has come to apply our common wisdom in a spirit of tolerance and broadmindedness to achieve genuine happiness for the Tibetan people with a sense of urgency.

The Chinese response came swiftly, through a private meeting between my brother Gyalo Thondup and Hu Yaobang in July 1981. Hu articulated a five-point basis according to which a rapprochement would be possible from the Chinese point of view.* This was disappointing because the focus in that proposal was entirely on my personal position and my return to Tibet, rather than on the much bigger question of the well-being of the six million Tibetan people. Effectively, nothing of substance was on offer, and whatever Deng Xiaoping had said to my brother in 1979, it was clear, at least from this proposal, it was not true that except for independence everything was negotiable.

In any case, following the opening of direct conversations with China, both formal and informal, and the opening up of China itself, as

* Hu Yaobang's five points were, as later published in the *Beijing Review*, December 3, 1984: (1) The Dalai Lama should be confident that China has entered a new stage of long-term political stability, steady economic growth, and mutual help among nationalities; (2) the Dalai Lama and his representatives should be frank and sincere with the Central Government, not beat around the bush. There should be no more quibbling over the events in 1959; (3) the central authorities sincerely welcome the Dalai Lama and his followers to come back to live. This is based on the hope that they will contribute to upholding China's unity and promoting solidarity between the Han and Tibetan nationalities, among all nationalities, and modernization program; (4) the Dalai Lama will enjoy the same political status and living conditions as he had before 1959. It is suggested that he not go to live in Tibet or hold local posts there. His followers need not worry about their jobs and living conditions. These will only be better than before; and (5) when the Dalai Lama wishes to come back, he can issue a brief statement to the press. It is up to him to decide what he would like to say in the statement.

well as some opening in Tibet, it became clear that we were in a much more complex phase with respect to our advocacy for Tibet compared to before. Previously, our role was to bring attention to the crimes and destruction taking place and to make the case for freedom and human rights. Now we needed to bring substantive proposals from our side that might lead to a mutually acceptable agreement. So, in my official March 10 Statement of 1981, I noted that past history had disappeared into the past, and what was more relevant was that in the future there actually must be real peace and happiness through developing friendly and meaningful relations between China and Tibet. For this to be realized, I said, it was important for both sides to work hard to have tolerant understanding and be open-minded.

I decided to send a high-level delegation to Beijing, and in April 1982 my three-member exploratory delegation, consisting of two of my *kalon*s (cabinet ministers)—Juchen Thupten and Phuntsok Tashi Takla—and the speaker of our Assembly of Tibetan People's Deputies, Lodi Gyari, left for Beijing. They were briefed on my thoughts and ideas for a possible resolution. We were eager to find out if there had been a real shift in the Chinese Communist position, and what Deng Xiaoping's statement "except for independence, everything is negotiable" meant in concrete terms. For example, one of our negotiators asked whether Tibetans, in view of our different race and history, should not have the same rights as the ones being offered by the People's Republic of China to Taiwan. He was told that Tibetans could not expect to get what they were willing to give to Taiwan, because Taiwan was, unlike Tibet, not yet liberated.

When my exploratory delegation arrived in Beijing, however, the Chinese side was expecting a reply to the five-point proposal Hu Yaobang had given to my brother during his visit. This led to some initial confusion. The members of my delegation and their Chinese counterparts were talking at cross-purposes. The Chinese side then provided a copy of the proposal and shared the official transcript of my brother's meeting with Deng Xiaoping in 1979. In the end, the Chinese simply reiterated their position. Clearly, there was no space yet for a substantive conversation.

That said, I was feeling quite positive about the changes taking place on the ground in Tibet. For example, at a formal Buddhist teaching in Bodh Gaya in 1983, hundreds of monks and laypeople from Tibet itself were able to come on a pilgrimage. As such, I publicly expressed my wish to visit Tibet, possibly in two years' time. I proposed to send an advance party to prepare for it, but unfortunately, they did not respond positively.

In May 1984, we held a special meeting in Dharamsala, attended by my cabinet and representatives from the Assembly of Tibetan People's Deputies and other key constituencies, such as the Tibetan Women's Association and the Tibetan Youth Congress, to discuss my ongoing engagement with Beijing. And in October of that year, I sent the same exploratory delegation for further talks in Beijing. There, our delegation pointed out that the five points proposed by the Chinese government concerned only the status and return of the Dalai Lama. We reminded the Chinese that the issue was Tibet and its people, and the delegation again conveyed my wish to visit my home country.

One substantive suggestion we made was the idea of a demilitarized Tibet (including Kham and Amdo) that would have internal autonomy within the People's Republic of China. The Chinese rejected any discussion of these proposals, denying that there was such a thing as "the Tibetan issue," and claimed that the only matter to be discussed was the position of the Dalai Lama. They reiterated Hu Yaobang's five points of 1981, making them public for the first time soon after my representatives returned to India from Beijing.* After what seemed to be progress, we were again at an impasse.

* As noted earlier, these five points were made public by the Chinese government through the *Beijing Review*, December 3, 1984.

CHAPTER 8

# Reaching Out to Our Fourth Refuge

While no substantive progress was made with China, the facts on the ground in Tibet were now beginning to change in a worrying direction. On the one hand, it is true that Tibet had opened up to some extent, and that things were better compared to the period of the Cultural Revolution. On the other, contrary to Hu Yaobang's pledge to reduce the number of Chinese officials and cadres, a massive Chinese migration into Tibet had begun in the name of "development." This was profoundly concerning because, if left unchecked, it would fundamentally alter the demographics of the region, turning the Tibetan plateau into just another Chinese province with Tibetans marginalized in their own homeland.

The historical evidence of what China had done in the regions of other nationalities was clearly a source of deep anxiety. From a sociocultural point of view, this influx of Chinese in Tibet could signal the beginning of a process that had the potential to change the very character of places dear to us Tibetans, including especially the holy city of Lhasa. At the same time, politically speaking, the picture coming out of Tibet was getting confusing, to say the least. Under the Party leadership of

Wu Jinghua in Tibet, there seemed to be a newly liberal policy toward religious practice, exemplified, for example, by the permission given for the revival of the Great Prayer Festival in Lhasa in February 1986, for the first time since 1967. Yet from the senior Beijing leadership side, there seemed to be nothing but intransigence.

We needed to reassess our strategy. We made the decision to make our proposals more systematic and present them at international forums. Our discussions with Beijing left us no choice but to use some international stage to make our proposals. This strategy also allowed us to offer our supporters across the world, who had been patiently waiting to hear the results of our discussions, an opportunity to learn about what our deeper aspirations were. I often describe the international community as our "Fourth Refuge," in addition to the traditional Buddhist refuge of the Three Jewels—the Buddha, dharma, and *sangha* (community).

Some of our efforts had an effect. In July 1985, ninety-one members of the United States Congress signed a letter addressed to the president of the People's Republic of China. The letter expressed support for direct talks and urged the Chinese "to grant the very reasonable and justified aspirations of His Holiness the Dalai Lama and his people every consideration." The Chinese, concerned about the growing international attention to Tibet, invited the former US President Jimmy Carter to visit Lhasa in June 1987, followed by the German Chancellor Helmut Kohl in July of that same year.

In June 1987, the House of Representatives in the United States adopted a bill condemning human rights abuses in Tibet and urged China to establish a constructive dialogue. On September 21 of that year, the United States Congressional Human Rights Caucus invited me to address them. I opened with the following:

> The world is increasingly interdependent, so that lasting peace—national, regional and global—can only be achieved if we think in terms of broader interest rather than parochial needs. At this

time, it is crucial that all of us, the strong and the weak, contribute in our own way. I speak to you today as the leader of the Tibetan people and as a Buddhist monk devoted to the principles of a religion based on love and compassion.

Then I proceeded to lay out a five-point peace plan, as the basis for a potential negotiation with China. They were:

1. Transformation of the whole of Tibet into a zone of peace, demilitarized so that there could be a buffer between the armies of Asia's two most populous countries, India and China;
2. Abandonment of China's population transfer policy, which threatens the very existence of the Tibetans as a people;
3. Respect for the Tibetan people's fundamental human rights and democratic freedoms;
4. Restoration and protection of Tibet's natural environment and the abandonment of China's use of Tibet for the production of nuclear weapons and dumping of nuclear waste;
5. Commencement of earnest negotiations on the future status of Tibet and of relations between the Tibetan and Chinese peoples.

Shortly after, in October, the United States Senate passed the congressional bill that had previously been adopted by the House of Representatives. And in December of that year, President Reagan signed into law the Foreign Relations Authorization Act, which declared that the United States would take the treatment of the Tibetan people into account in its relations with the People's Republic of China—encouraging the Chinese government to respect human rights in Tibet, to reciprocate the Dalai Lama's efforts in establishing a constructive dialogue, and calling for the release of political prisoners.

The Chinese state media strongly criticized the Five Point Peace Plan. This criticism, especially of me personally, deeply hurt many Tibetans. Less than a week after my speech in Washington, on

September 27, monks from Drepung Monastery protested, carrying a Tibetan national flag and calling for independence. They were arrested. When I heard about the news, I was deeply concerned. Then, on October 1, monks from Sera Monastery staged a second demonstration, joined by large crowds demanding the prisoners' release, and a major disturbance began. The police station was burned down and Chinese police opened fire, killing several people. This was followed by a further protest on October 6. After a lull, on the last day of the Great Prayer Festival on March 5, 1988, another protest erupted by the monks from Ganden Monastery. This led to spontaneous protests across the country, and martial law was imposed on March 8, 1988, in Lhasa. All this amply demonstrated that the aspirations of the Tibetan people inside Tibet went way beyond mere economic improvement, not to mention a profound discontent.

In the meantime, as I had been invited to address the European Parliament in mid-June, I wanted to take this opportunity to formally elaborate on the Five Point Peace Plan. To prepare, I convened a special meeting in Dharamsala to discuss the key points of what I was planning to present in Strasbourg. For three days, June 6–9, presided by my Kashag (cabinet) and attended by the members of the Assembly of Tibetan People's Deputies, public servants, NGOs, selected newly arrived Tibetans, as well as special invitees and others representing Tibetan communities in diaspora, I discussed at length the key points of my proposal. Following this in-depth discussion as well as debates, the participants of this special meeting unanimously endorsed the proposal.

On June 15, 1988, I addressed the European Parliament in Strasbourg, including these key additional points:

> The whole of Tibet known as Cholka-Sum (Ü-Tsang, Kham and Amdo) should become a self-governing democratic political entity founded on law by agreement of the people for the common

> good and the protection of themselves and their environment, in association with the People's Republic of China.
>
> The Government of the People's Republic of China could remain responsible for Tibet's foreign policy. The Government of Tibet should, however, develop and maintain relations, through its own foreign affairs bureau, in the field of commerce, education, culture, religion, tourism, science, sports and other non-political activities. Tibet should join international organizations concerned with such activities.
>
> The Government of Tibet should be founded on a constitution or basic law. The basic law should provide for a democratic system of government entrusted with the task of ensuring economic equality, social justice, and protection of the environment. This means that the Government of Tibet will have the rights to decide on all affairs relating to Tibet and the Tibetans.

We were effectively stating that we were not going to seek independence; we were expressing our willingness to remain part of the People's Republic of China but only with a guarantee of genuine autonomy. This position I later came to call the Middle Way Approach—a middle way between independence and the present reality that was threatening the survival of the Tibetan people and culture. In essence, what I was offering to Beijing leadership was this: since, with the invasion of 1950 and the subsequent signing of the Seventeen-Point Agreement, Communist China had chosen to force Tibet into a union with the People's Republic of China, I was proposing that we work together, with sincerity and dedication on both sides, to make this union truly viable. I was trying to find a way for both sides to make the Tibetans feel truly at home within the family of the People's Republic of China. I was not seeking to turn back the historical clock somehow. I was looking to the future, based on a hard-nosed awareness of the present reality of Tibet forcibly occupied by China. At the same time, I was seriously taking into account

Beijing's key concern, namely territorial integrity and stability. My proposal was aimed at mutual benefit and seeking a mutually agreeable solution. Sadly, Beijing chose not to appreciate the historic significance of what we were offering. I do not think this is due to their failure to grasp what was being offered; my own sense is that it is simply due to the lack of political will on the part of the Chinese leadership to seriously address the issue of Tibet. I still remain convinced that given political will and vision on the part of the Chinese leadership, it would not be that difficult for China to satisfy the needs of the Tibetans.

I admitted that, when I first presented it, many Tibetans, both inside Tibet and in exile, would be disappointed by the moderate stance the Strasbourg Proposal represented. But I insisted that the thoughts outlined in my Strasbourg speech represented the most realistic means by which to reestablish Tibet's separate identity and restore the fundamental rights of the Tibetan people while accommodating China's own interests. I also stated that it was my wish not to take any active part in any future government of Tibet, but would continue to work as much as needed for the well-being and happiness of the Tibetan people. In fact, the core of what was presented in the Strasbourg Proposal had already been shared with the Chinese leadership through my exploratory delegation who met their Chinese counterparts. In Strasbourg, we were bringing these ideas to wider international attention.

After my speech at Strasbourg, I visited Switzerland and met with a large gathering of Tibetans there, and I took the opportunity to share my thinking. I knew the moderate stance outlined in the Strasbourg Proposal entailed ceasing our advocacy for full independence, which could cause unhappiness among many Tibetans. I stressed at this gathering of Tibetans that the essence of what we aspired to—the ability to protect our language, culture, religion, and our identity as a people—could be achieved within the framework of the People's Republic of China. I also pointed out that, given Tibet's status as a landlocked country, from the economic development perspective, we Tibetans might actually stand to gain by such an arrangement. I also stated that, in the end, it is the Tibetan people who will have to decide their own destiny.

While I understand people's emotional attachment to ideas of sovereignty and independence, personally, I have always been more of a pragmatist. I am a huge admirer of the ideals behind the European Union. Today, nations like France and Germany, which traditionally saw each other as enemies, join together and cede part of their cherished sovereignty to a collective European body so that the citizens within the individual countries have a greater chance of flourishing. It is a historical fact that sometimes, due to geopolitical conditions, what were previously independent nations come together to form a composite entity. Yet at other times, again because of changed political situations, some nations newly obtain their freedom, such as Timor-Leste.* For me, at least, what matters is the presence of an adequate structure and framework that ensures the continued survival and thriving of a people with their unique language, culture, and identity.

In the immediate aftermath of my Strasbourg Proposal, not only was there disappointment among some Tibetans, there were, in fact, some sharp criticisms of this stance. For example, my own eldest brother, Taktser Rinpoche, sent a letter to prominent Tibetans in the diaspora criticizing the decision to relinquish the demand for Tibetan independence. He went so far as to characterize our proposal as a sell-out. At the same time, the reaction from key Tibetan figures inside Tibet and China was encouraging. In the words of Phuntsok Wangyal, the Tibetan Communist who was my official translator during my visit to Beijing in 1954–1955, "the Dalai Lama's 'Middle Way Approach' of 'seeking only a meaningful autonomy for Tibet rather than

* Timor-Leste is a small Southeast Asian nation occupying one-half of the island of Timor, with the other half being part of Indonesia. Formerly a colony of Portugal and later under the occupation of Indonesia, Timor-Leste gained independence in 2002.

independence,' in the present historical context, is an expression of the great responsibility he takes in giving serious thought over the fundamental issues." Similarly, another prominent Tibetan scholar inside Tibet stated that because the Middle Way Approach was "mutually beneficial" to both Tibetans and Chinese, it was "the only way . . . to resolve the issue of Tibet once and for all."

Let me pause here to address an important question. Sometimes, Chinese authorities criticize me for "allowing" Tibetans inside as well as outside to speak about Tibetan independence. This criticism is premised on the strange idea that, somehow, I must or should have the power to ban any Tibetan from even mentioning the phrase "Tibetan independence." It's one thing for an authoritarian regime to ban free speech and use force when it deems someone has violated the ban. It is something else when it comes to a free and open society, such as the Tibetan community in exile. One of the defining marks of a democratic system is freedom of expression. Even though I disagree with those Tibetans who argue that advocating for Tibetan independence is the best way forward for our freedom struggle, I have the greatest respect for these people. The Tibetan Youth Congress, for example, has as part of its mission "to struggle for the total independence of Tibet."

My own aim, however, has been to ensure that the formal leadership of the Tibetan movement as well as the majority of Tibetans living in the free world are convinced of the correctness of our Middle Way Approach, seeking a genuine autonomy rather than separation from the People's Republic of China.

Despite my explicit public announcement that we were not seeking independence, when the Chinese Embassy in New Delhi issued a formal response on September 23, 1988, they stated, "The new proposal put forward by the Dalai Lama in Strasbourg cannot be considered as the basis for talks with the Central Government because it has not at all relinquished the concept of the 'independence of Tibet.'" Nonetheless, Beijing did accept our suggestion to engage in a series of talks to start in Geneva in January 1989. In the end, though, Chinese officials put forward a number of pretexts for not starting the talks; one of the reasons, it seemed, was they were upset that we had made public the composition of our team as well as the venue of the talks. We had even proposed that a pre-meeting be held in Hong Kong in April to resolve any issues and concerns they may have had in mind, but to no avail. It is possible that further demonstrations in Lhasa in December 1988, in commemoration of international Human Rights Day, might have been another reason why the meeting did not take place.

On January 28, 1989, the Panchen Lama died suddenly at his monastic base of Tashi Lhunpo. We mourned his death with a heavy heart, recognizing that we had lost a heroic Tibetan leader who had suffered much on behalf of his people. While he was alive, I felt that his efforts inside Tibet, especially on the front of the protection of Tibetan language, culture, and identity, and my own efforts to be a free spokesperson for the Tibetans in the outside world really complemented each other well. So his sudden death deeply saddened me, with the acute awareness that I had lost a truly powerful and courageous ally on the ground inside Tibet. We held memorial prayers for the Panchen Lama at the Thekchen Choeling Temple in Dharamsala, and similar religious ceremonies in many monasteries, including especially at Tashi Lhunpo, the Panchen Lama's traditional monastery reestablished in southern India. As is the custom, I composed a prayer for his quick return (*nyurjön söldeb*) consisting of nine verses, which contained the following lines:

> *Even under a canopy of dense clouds of constant threat,*
> *with no control and freedom at all, you shouldered*
> *the great burden of Buddha's doctrine and beings' welfare.*
> *Alas! Sad indeed is your sudden departure into peace.*
> *In accord with your aspiration cultivated for so long,*
> *may the new moon of your unmistaken reincarnation*
> *shine from the eastern snowy peaks, of the good fortune of the people of the Land of Snows—*
> *May we soon find the joy to cherish this resplendent new moon.*

The Buddhist Association of China, obviously acting with full knowledge of the government, invited me to participate in his memorial service. We took this invitation with great seriousness. However, Beijing had just canceled the planned Geneva talks, the relatively moderate Party leader in Tibet Wu Jinghua had been dismissed at the end of 1988, and the invitation was only to Beijing, rather than to Tibet. There was no clarity on whether I would be able to meet any of the senior Chinese leaders or any important Tibetan figures. With much uncertainty and no adequate time to evaluate carefully the implications, in the end we made the decision that I would not go. Afterward, events rapidly went out of control.

On March 5, 1989, in the run-up to the anniversary of March 10, the largest demonstration against the Communist Chinese rule since the Lhasa uprising of 1959 broke out. For three days, the Chinese police cracked down viciously on the Tibetan people, leaving several hundred dead. On March 8, the Chinese imposed martial law in Lhasa. The issue of Tibet was now being raised also in the parliaments of many European countries, with the first international hearing on human rights abuses in Tibet organized in Germany in that same year.

On April 15 of that year, Hu Yaobang, who had been dismissed from the Party leadership in 1987, died. A series of student-led protests began from that day continuing to June 4 in Tiananmen Square in Beijing. The students called for greater accountability, democracy, freedom of the press, and freedom of speech. At their height, more than a million people assembled, constituting the most significant challenge to the Chinese Communist Party since it rose to power. Like the rest of the world, I was transfixed by these events, following them with a mixture of admiration, anxiety, and hope. On May 14, I stated:

> I am watching with great interest the current movement in China for democracy and freedom. The Chinese people, particularly the youth and the intellectuals, are trying to convey their real feelings. . . . I support their movements and admire their courage.

> These developments will benefit China. . . . It seems that at least a section of the leadership of China is trying to adopt a more positive approach to these developments [in spite of] tremendous pressure from within the system. I urge upon the Chinese leadership to have the courage to accept the reality and comprehend the aspirations of their people.

On May 20, martial law was declared in Beijing and some three hundred thousand troops mobilized in the city. As tension was building and the dramatic events were unfolding across the world's televisions, I felt that I must express my solidarity with the protesting students and their aspirations. Many within my circle advised me not to do so, for it could offend Beijing, with whom we were, after all, trying to negotiate. On June 3, 1989, as we all know, the Chinese leadership unleashed the People's Liberation Army on its own people, using live ammunition. On the fourth, they sent armored personnel carriers and tanks into Tiananmen Square. To this day, we do not know how many were killed. I was shocked—the sight of the Chinese army killing its own people simply because they were asking for more freedom and a better life was horrifying.

I called my secretary, Tenzin Geyche Tethong, and Lodi Gyari, then in charge of Information and International Relations, to come to see me at once. I asked them to work on a statement expressing strong opposition to the Chinese government's crackdown and my solidarity with the young Chinese people gathered in Tiananmen Square. They were understandably concerned that such a public statement from me would negatively impact our ongoing discussion with the Chinese leadership. But I said that if I did not speak out now, what moral right would I ever have to speak for freedom and democracy? I reminded them that those young Chinese in the square were asking for nothing more than greater freedom.

There are moments in time, especially in which fundamental issues of humanity are concerned, when one cannot remain silent out of expediency or self-interest. So I issued a statement, expressing my opposition in the strongest terms against the military actions of the Chinese leadership; I expressed my deep disappointment at the Chinese government's failure to appreciate the true feelings of its people. And mourning the loss of so many innocent lives, I said how I shared in the sorrow of those families, relatives, and friends who had lost their loved ones. I can say with confidence that on that day of June 4, 1989, Tibetans everywhere, both inside Tibet as well as outside it, stood in solidarity with the Chinese people.

Later, when I formally accepted the Nobel Peace Prize in Oslo, on December 10, 1989, I began by saying:

> I accept the prize with profound gratitude on behalf of the oppressed everywhere and for all those who struggle for freedom and work for world peace. I accept it as a tribute to the man who founded the modern tradition of nonviolent action for change—Mahatma Gandhi—whose life taught and inspired me.

Since I felt it was essential to include a statement about the events of Tiananmen Square in my acceptance speech, I said:

> In China the popular movement for democracy was crushed by brutal force in June this year. But I do not believe the demonstrations were in vain, because the spirit of freedom was rekindled among the Chinese people and China cannot escape the impact of this spirit of freedom sweeping many parts of the world. The brave students and their supporters showed the Chinese leadership and the world the human face of that great nation.

While popular movements for freedom in the former Soviet Union and Eastern Europe succeeded, bringing down the Berlin Wall and freeing so many from Communist totalitarianism, the student-led freedom movement in Tiananmen did not succeed in bringing down

Communist China's bamboo curtain. Needless to say, historians and geopolitical experts will seek to understand fully what might explain this contrast. At the risk of sounding simplistic, two things come to mind. One is that Communist China's People's Liberation Army, despite its name, was willing to shoot its own people, which was not the case with Eastern Europe. Second, in Eastern Europe, when the challenge to power came in the form of popular movements for freedom, the momentum had the backing of pretty much the entire population. In the case of Tiananmen Square, even though protests supporting the student-led movement did spread to several hundred towns and cities in China, it did not seem to have reached a critical mass that could have made a real difference. But I do not believe, even for a second, that Tiananmen Square marks the end of the Chinese people's quest for greater freedom, dignity, and democracy.

It is not surprising that Tiananmen Square, though not related directly to Tibet, had a significant impact on our attempts to come to a negotiation with the Chinese. The process that had begun in 1979, with Deng Xiaoping's statement to my brother Gyalo Thondup that apart from independence everything could be discussed, had come to an end. Deng's leadership, which had promised so much, in the end proved capable of as much brutality as that of Mao's.

Martial law was imposed in Lhasa on March 8, 1989, and was only lifted on May 1 of the following year.

CHAPTER 9

# In the Aftermath of Tiananmen

One immediate side effect of the tragedy of Tiananmen was that for the first time a large segment of the Chinese population—especially the many intellectuals and dissidents who had escaped China after the crackdown—began to have more empathy for the plight of the Tibetan people. In the years following 1989, I have had many meetings with Chinese involved in the pro-democracy movement who had fled to the outside world—Paris, London, Switzerland, Germany, the United States, Canada, Australia, and Japan as well.

Several key members of the Tiananmen Square protest movement formed an organization in Paris in September 1989 called the Federation for Democratic China (FDC). At their request, I had a moving meeting with their leadership in Paris in December 1989. Among the dissidents I met was Yan Jiaqi (once a political adviser to the Chinese Premier Zhao Ziyang and later a prominent advocate for a democratic China). I applauded them for their courage and commitment to bringing greater democracy in China. Given the size of China's population, the mission of a democratic China is truly a noble work, and they need perseverance and unflagging determination if they are to succeed. I shared with them our own struggle for Tibetan freedom and dignity and said that we would remain undaunted and totally committed to our cause, no matter how long it might take. I took the opportunity to stress to them that, with respect to our own struggle, we made the decision to pursue the Middle Way Approach to not seek independence; rather to seek genuine autonomy that would enable us to survive and thrive as a people with our own distinct language, culture, and religion. I reminded them that, in comparison to our struggle for freedom, their struggle for a democratic China had only just begun.

Later I also met other senior figures among Chinese dissidents, including especially Wei Jingsheng, the well-known human rights activist famed for his 1978 essay "The Fifth Modernization" posted on the Democracy Wall in Beijing, and Harry Wu, who was instrumental in exposing the horrors of China's gulag system. The latter, in fact, urged me on a few occasions to reconsider my stance and instead campaign for the full independence of Tibet.

In 1991, at a conference on human rights at Columbia University in New York, I had the honor to share the platform with the distinguished Chinese astrophysicist Fang Lizhi, who by then had also been living in exile. I met the remarkable Chinese writer Wang Ruowang as well, who famously wrote a letter to Deng Xiaoping supporting the student-led demonstrations at Tiananmen and helped lead a march to the Shanghai City Hall. What these great Chinese intellectuals as well as the hundreds of student leaders who fled China in the wake of Tiananmen were fighting for was greater freedom, dignity, and democracy in China. Regardless of how they were portrayed by the Communist Party, all of these individuals—who paid a heavy personal price for their conscience—were true patriots that cared deeply for the future of China and its place in the world.

I have always maintained that our struggle is not against the Chinese people but against an oppressive regime and for the rights of the Tibetan people. So logically, I have deep empathy for others oppressed by the Communist Chinese regime, which include the Chinese people themselves, the Mongols of Inner Mongolia, and the Uyghur people of East Turkistan (Xinjiang). I have met with a number of Uyghurs in exile, notably Isa Alptekin and his son Erkin Alptekin, and later Rebiya Kadeer and Dolkun Isa, respectively the former and current presidents of the World Uyghur Congress. I shared with them the importance of embracing strict nonviolence in one's just struggle for freedom and my enduring belief that only through nonviolence and consideration of the needs and concerns of both sides can there be a truly lasting solution to any conflict. And adopting an approach that is mutually beneficial is key to finding solutions through the nonviolence method. Speaking to them about our own Tibetan struggle, I repeated what I often tell our supporters in the international community: that I consider them neither anti-Chinese nor pro-Tibetan but pro-freedom and pro-truth.

The awarding of the Nobel Peace Prize to me in October 1989 and the subsequent ceremony in Oslo brought extensive international attention to the Tibetan cause. For Tibetans across the world, this prize was an important recognition of our steadfast commitment to a nonviolent struggle to regain our freedom and dignity. For me personally, one of the most moving aspects of the experience was to see the joyful and celebratory faces of so many Tibetans and our international supporters who have worked tirelessly over decades. To this day, I remember vividly the beautiful and joyful energy of the presence of so many who had come to Oslo to be part of the celebration. I took the opportunity to thank many of them in person. Back home in Tibet too, I learned that many Tibetans celebrated, despite the obvious dangers they faced for doing such a thing. If anything, the situation inside continued to worsen.

In July 1990, the Chinese Communist Party leader Jiang Zemin and the head of the People's Liberation Army General Staff Department Chi Haotian visited Tibet. By now, as in China, a much more hard-line faction was in control in Tibet. The Chinese authorities emphasized loyalty to "the motherland" and "the struggle against splittism"—that is, the struggle against me and the exile community. They greatly increased incentives for Chinese migration into Tibet, such that a newly arrived worker from China stood to gain a substantial increase in salary. This growing migration caused much resentment among the Tibetans, including Tibetan Communist Party cadres. This hardening inside Tibet was such a sad and strange development in comparison to what was happening in the wider world. For this was the period when the tide of freedom was sweeping across the world, including the ending of dictatorships in the Philippines in 1986 and in Chile in 1990 and, of course, the fall of the Berlin Wall in 1989. It was also a moment of genuine détente and significant nuclear disarmament between the Soviet Union and the United States. Yet in China, and in Tibet especially, this was the beginning of a new era of repression. My own efforts for seeking a solution through dialogue continually hit a wall of rejection.

On the international front, in May 1991, the US legislature passed a congressional concurrent resolution recognizing Tibet as an illegally occupied country and reaffirmed the United States' position on Tibet, as stated by the US ambassador to the United Nations in 1961, which is that the United States believes its objectives must include the restoration of human rights of the Tibetan people and their natural right of self-determination. The resolution concluded:

> [It] is the sense of the Congress that Tibet, including those areas incorporated into the Chinese provinces of Sichuan, Yunnan, Gansu, and Qinghai, is an occupied country under established principles of international law whose true representatives are the Dalai Lama and the Tibetan Government in Exile as recognized by the Tibetan people.

A few years later, in 1997, the US government established the Office of the US Special Coordinator for Tibetan Issues within the State Department. Today this office coordinates the US policies and programs related to Tibetan issues in accord with the Tibetan Policy Act of 2002, which was amended with the Tibetan Policy and Support

Act of 2020. I have had the pleasure to meet with every holder of the position since its inception.

Deeply concerned by the worsening situation inside Tibet in 1991 and, in particular, China's outlier status as an active agent of repression, that year I accepted an invitation to speak at Yale University. I began by recognizing the momentous era we were living through, and how the world had changed dramatically in the last few years. I reflected on how the fall of the Berlin Wall and the Soviet Union after seventy years of Communist control signaled the aspirations of people and nations for freedom and democracy. I spoke of how I felt deeply inspired during my recent visits to Mongolia and the Baltic states and Bulgaria, seeing millions of human beings enjoying the freedom they had been denied for so many decades. I particularly noted how this amazing transition took place without resorting to violence.

Emphasizing the need for the international community to continue to engage with China, I said that I was a firm believer that relations between people and between nations must be based on human understanding. The world should engage China whenever it is willing to take part in the international community in a constructive manner. But when it persists in violating fundamental norms of civilized behavior it should not be indulged like a spoiled child. China must be made accountable for its actions as a responsible member of the international community. With respect to our ongoing attempt to negotiate with China, I observed that the Chinese government's refusal to reciprocate my efforts to start negotiations had increased the impatience of many Tibetans inside Tibet, especially among the youth, with the nonviolent path we were following. Tension was increasing as China encouraged demographic aggression in Tibet, threatening to reduce Tibetans to a second-class minority in our own country. I was extremely anxious that, in this explosive situation, violence could break out. I said that I wanted to do what I could to help prevent this.

I then expressed my wish to be able to visit Tibet so I could communicate directly with my people and urge them not to abandon our path of nonviolence. My visit would offer the possibility for the senior Chinese leadership to understand the true feelings of the Tibetan people.

Since there had been no constructive response from Beijing to both my Five Point Peace Plan and the subsequent Strasbourg Proposal of 1988, in September 1991, I stated that I no longer considered myself bound by them. Yet I stressed that we remained fully committed to the path of negotiation. Of course, we continued with our efforts to keep lines of communication open with China. When, in December 1991, the Chinese Premier Li Peng visited Delhi, I sought unsuccessfully to meet with him. In June 1992, my brother Gyalo Thondup met Ding Guangen, a Politburo member, who carried a message from the Chinese government offering resumption of dialogue on the condition that I publicly renounce the idea of Tibetan independence. This was odd since we had already stated unequivocally and repeatedly that we were willing to cease our demand for independence as part of a negotiated settlement. Nonetheless, on September 11, 1992, I wrote formally to both the paramount leader Deng Xiaoping and General Secretary Jiang Zemin. I expressed my openness to talks and, by way of setting things in a broader context, included a supplemental note summarizing the history of our conversations thus far, since 1951. The letter was delivered to the Chinese ambassador in Delhi alongside a suggestion for regular monthly meetings at the Chinese Embassy to build confidence. However, it took until July 1993 before the Chinese government allowed my representatives to present this letter in person.

The letter, addressed to Jiang Zemin, conveyed my basic belief in the process of negotiation as the only viable means to solve the issue of Tibet. I wrote:

> I am pleased that direct contact has once again been established between us. I hope that this will lead to an improvement of relations and the development of mutual understanding and trust.
>
> I have been informed of the discussions Mr. Ding Guangen had with Gyalo Thondup on June 22, 1992, and the position of

the Government of China concerning negotiations for a solution to the Tibetan question. I am disappointed with the hard and inflexible position conveyed by Mr. Ding Guangen, particularly the emphasis on pre-conditions for negotiations.

However, I remain committed to the belief that our problems can be solved only through negotiations, held in an atmosphere of sincerity and openness, for the benefit of both the Tibetan and Chinese people. To make this possible, neither side should put up obstacles, and neither side should, therefore, state pre-conditions.

For meaningful negotiations to take place it is essential to have mutual trust. Therefore, in order to create trust, I believe it is important for the leaders and people of China to know of the endeavours I have made so far. My three representatives carry with them a letter from me, accompanied by a detailed note of my views and my efforts through the years to promote negotiations in the best interests of the Tibetan and Chinese people. They will answer and discuss any questions and points you wish to raise. It is my hope that through these renewed discussions we will find a way that will lead us to negotiations.

On my part, I have put forward many ideas to solve our problem. I believe that it is now time for the Chinese government to make a genuinely meaningful proposal if you wish to see Tibet and China live together in peace. I, therefore, sincerely hope that you will respond in a spirit of openness and friendship.

Accompanying this letter was a detailed note I prepared for the Chinese leadership outlining succinctly the history of my approach to the issue of Tibet and the thinking behind it, and my proposal for a discussion to move toward a substantive dialogue. In the conclusion of that note, I stated:

If China wants Tibet to stay with China, then China must create the necessary conditions for this. The time has come now for the

> Chinese to show the way for Tibet and China to live together in friendship. A detailed step by step outline regarding Tibet's basic status should be spelt out. If such a clear outline is given, regardless of the possibility of an agreement or not, we Tibetans can then make a decision whether to live with China or not. If we Tibetans obtain our basic rights to our satisfaction then we are not incapable of seeing the possible advantages of living with the Chinese.

I concluded with an expression of hope, saying that I trusted in the farsightedness and wisdom of China's leaders and hoped that they would take into consideration the current global political changes and the need to resolve the Tibetan problem peacefully, promoting genuine lasting friendship between our two peoples.

In the meantime, the Chinese government published a white paper in September 1992 entitled *Tibet: Its Ownership and Human Rights Situation*. Misleadingly, the document dwells long on a history of Tibet presented as if it had always been part of China, indicating a defensiveness on the part of China's leadership on the legitimacy of China's presence in Tibet. The document presents a series of arguments against Tibetan independence, claiming that "the so-called Tibetan independence which the Dalai clique and overseas anti-China forces propagate is nothing but a fiction of the imperialists who committed aggression against China in modern history." Shockingly, the document further asserts, "Another lie is the claim that a large number of Hans have migrated to Tibet, turning the ethnic Tibetans into a minority," flatly denying a fact acknowledged by every independent observer and recognized as a major source of resentment for the Tibetan people.

Back home in Tibet, protests by more than a thousand laypeople erupted in Lhasa on May 23, 1993, initially over rising costs but swiftly becoming about independence. These demonstrations resulted in brutal suppression and mass arrests. One of the causes was clearly the increasing influx of Chinese migrants into Lhasa. In 1994, when the Third

Tibet Work Forum was convened by the Party Central Committee in Beijing, a set of new repressive policies was imposed. Among these was increased spending on security mechanisms of control, and a newly vitriolic attack on me personally. For example, one of their official statements contained the allegation that "although sometimes Dalai speaks softly and says nice things to deceive the masses, he has never ceased his splittist activities." It then went on to assert: "The focus-point in our region's fight to oppose splittism is to oppose the Dalai clique. As the saying goes, to kill a serpent, we must first cut off its head." This same document then urged the monastic community inside Tibet to renounce the Dalai Lama. It stated that "we must firmly stop the Dalai clique influencing lamas and nuns in Tibet in any way." The issuing of this statement was accompanied by a complete ban on any photographs or portraits of me, both in public spaces and private homes in Tibet. Effectively, a form of ideological indoctrination (especially in the area of education) that had not been seen since the Cultural Revolution was being imposed on Tibet. The Party leadership in Lhasa asserted:

> Ethnic education cannot be regarded successful if it successfully maintains the old culture and traditions. . . . The essence of educational work is to cultivate qualified constructors and successors for the socialist cause, and this is the sole basic mission in ethnic education.

Official statements such as this and the repressive policies on the ground targeting Tibetan identity, culture, and traditions, as well as the large-scale demographic change taking place on the Tibetan plateau caused me great alarm, compelling me to say that what was happening inside Tibet was either willingly or unwillingly, a form of cultural genocide.

CHAPTER 10

# Practices I Find Helpful in the Face of Suffering

Let me pause here and offer a reflection on how we can sustain our determination in the face of situations that seem daunting, even hopeless. It is human to feel discouraged when confronted with terrible suffering with no perceivable end in sight. This is the experience for those in Tibet, and for so many who have aspired for freedom under oppressive regimes. This must have been the overwhelming feeling for those many thousands of students in Beijing in 1989, in the wake of the cruel crackdown. Many a time, in the years since 1950, I too have been confronted with such feelings and have had to sustain my sense of hope.

Here are some practices I have found helpful in my own life. First and foremost, I remind myself that in any important journey we will face difficulties, so it is crucial to adopt a stance of being prepared right from the start. This way, when we meet adversities, they do not come as a shock out of the blue and catch us unaware. As a Tibetan saying goes, "Hope for the best, and prepare for the worst."

Suffering and problems are an inevitable part of human life; the question is how we respond. When we face suffering caused by natural disasters, despite the devastation and the loss of human life, generally, we are able to cope with the pain without giving in to defeatism or bitterness. These tragedies also bring out the best in humanity, and people respond spontaneously with compassion. There is, however, man-made suffering, for which we humans ourselves are the direct cause. It is this class of suffering that is harder to bear and requires more strength on our part to deal with. There is the risk of giving in to despair and hatred, or responding to violence with violence. Unfortunately, we humans tend to keep repeating this cycle. The key here is never to lose sight of our shared humanity, common to perpetrator, victim, and ourselves. It is exactly for this reason I have always urged my fellow Tibetans to guard against hatred toward the Chinese.

I once told my fellow Tibetans when marking the first anniversary of the uprising in 1959 that in spite of the fact that we have to oppose Communist China's actions, I can never bring myself to hate its people. I said that, especially from the perspective of our struggle for freedom, hatred of an entire people will be a weakness, not a strength. I also reminded them that when the Buddha spoke of hatred leading only to further hatred, he was not just giving a spiritual teaching; he was also giving practical advice. I truly believe that a movement rooted in hatred, however noble the cause, will destroy the basis for a lasting future resolution. In Buddhist teachings there is, in fact, a special emphasis on viewing one's adversaries—those who are creating trouble for you—as spiritual teachers. Regardless of their intention, they provide you with the opportunity to practice patience and compassion. Our adversaries are our most valuable teachers. This is a demonstrable fact of life. While our friends can help us in many ways, it is our adversaries who provide us the challenge to develop the virtues essential for cultivating peace of mind and bringing us true happiness.

Personally speaking, as a follower of Mahayana (a system of Buddhism that I personally refer to as the Sanskrit tradition, which we Tibetan Buddhists share with Chinese Buddhism), I have a deep appreciation for the ancient nation of China in preserving the Buddhist tradition. Buddhism came to China about four centuries before it arrived in Tibet. Many texts that are lost in their original Indian language today survive in Chinese translation, such as the famous fifth-century Buddhist logician Dignāga's work, *Hetumukha*. Within the two Tibetan canonical collections of *Kangyur* (translation of scriptures) and *Tengyur* (translation of treatises), there are several important texts translated from Chinese. The Chinese commentary on the famed Mahayana scripture *Samdhinirmocana Sutra* (*Unraveling the Intent*) by the Korean monk Woncheuk is highly admired in the Tibetan monasteries. Numerous schools of Mahayana Buddhism emerged, developed, and flourished in China—for example, Tiantai, Huayen, San-lun, Pure Land, and Chan. Admirably, it is only in the Chinese tradition that the lineage of full ordination for women as *bhikshuni* (fully ordained nuns) has survived, traceable all the way back to the time of the Buddha. The continued existence of this women's full ordination tradition gives me great joy. Among the numerous Chinese monastics I have met over the years—in Taiwan and in the West—two who inspired me most in the richness of the Chinese Buddhist tradition were the revered Chan master Sheng Yen and the great Chinese Vinaya master Dao-hai. I have had the opportunity to engage in formal dialogues with both, on our two Buddhist traditions—Tibetan and Chinese—with the latter once also in New York. I even had the aspiration to visit the sacred Buddhist site of Mount Wutai Shan with master Dao-hai so that we could conduct a reading in Chinese, Tibetan, and Sanskrit of Nagarjuna's famed *Treatise on the Middle Way*, which is dear to both Tibetan and Chinese Buddhism.

Needless to say, the courage and spirit of the indefatigable Chinese pilgrims who traveled to India in search of Buddhist texts and practice traditions has been a profound and continuing inspiration for me. From Faxian at the end of the fourth century to Xuanzang in the mid-seventh century, and Yijing in the later seventh century, these extraordinary monks risked everything for the sake of the dharma. One remarkable thing about these Chinese monks is the meticulous records they kept of their journeys. Of these pilgrims, Xuanzang's enduring contribution is universally recognized today. His story is the inspiration behind the famous fable of Monkey in the Chinese literary tradition. It was thanks largely to Xuanzang's *Records of the Western Regions*—a massive account of his travels formally prepared for the Tang emperor on his return—that many of the important sites associated with the life of the Buddha and with the history of Buddhism in India, such as Nalanda University, were later rediscovered. Today, millions of Buddhists from all over the world are able to make pilgrimages and honor these sites. So I have always been someone with a deep reverence and respect for the ancient nation of China and its people.

Second, I find it helpful to adopt a wider perspective, since our sense of being overwhelmed or powerless often arises from viewing a problem too closely. If you look at your palm up close, you can't see your hand properly. By looking too closely, we get fixated and our perspectives narrow. In contrast, if we can situate the given problem in a larger context, we are then able to appreciate its complexity—its causes, effects, and interconnections—allowing us to choose a course of action that is more in tune with reality and has greater likelihood of success. The wider perspective also allows us to see any issue within its right proportions, making what previously seemed insurmountable possible to manage, and to recognize any positive aspects there might be despite what has happened. The embracing of this kind of wider perspective also makes it possible for us to see the opportunities a specific adversity might bring. As I have often stated, becoming a stateless person brought me closer to reality. When you are a refugee, there is no room left for ceremony or pretension. Had I remained in Lhasa as the theocratic ruler of an independent Tibet, imprisoned in what might be called a "golden cage" as the holy Dalai Lama, today I might be quite a different person. Being outside my homeland as a refugee has allowed me to meet with people from so many diverse backgrounds and walks of life—from fellow spiritual seekers to scientists, from activists to political leaders, and from artists to engineers. I particularly cherish the privilege I have had to establish friendships and engage in deep conversations with scientists. I would argue that my own Tibetan Buddhist tradition too has gained a lot from my being in exile. Today, we have successfully instituted the Geshema degree (highest monastic academic accomplishment) for the nuns; introduced formal science education in the monasteries; and initiated ongoing dialogues and collaborations with scientists on the study of the mind and possible applications of mind-based tools for greater mental well-being. The point is that if, instead of adopting a wider perspective, we had chosen to remain fixated on our loss, we would have never had the will or inclination to explore the opportunities that opened up in the wake of our tragedy.

Third, it is essential to choose optimism as a basic standpoint, however bad things may seem. The problem with its opposite, pessimism, is that one has already chosen to give up, even before trying. Of course, optimism must be based on an appreciation of reality and a clear-eyed approach to seeking the best way forward. In the case of Tibet, for example, the issue is existential and we don't have the luxury of giving up. That is what pessimism is.

Fourth, it is important to recognize and appreciate past successes, no matter how small. This is vital for encouraging ourselves and recharging our motivation to keep on going. We must never lose hope and must always maintain it if we are to meet with success in the challenges we face. With hope, we have the courage to care and the courage to act.

Finally, regardless of whatever happens, we must never lose faith in humanity. Here the key is to remain in touch with our own natural capacity to care for others, and never become divorced from our shared humanity, even in relation to those who might have done us harm. Personally, I find this basic altruistic orientation of the heart to be the source of my greatest strength and courage. Every morning when I get up, I remind myself I am just another human being, one among the billions on this earth. We are all the same, each and every one of us wishing to be happy and not wanting suffering. As social beings, we seek connection with others and find joy through them. There is no such thing as my own independent interest separate from others', because our well-being is interconnected with the well-being of others. With this in mind, I chant these verses from the eighth-century master Shantideva:

*All those who are happy in the world*
*Are so because they desire happiness for others;*
*All those unhappy in the world*
*Are so because they desire only their own happiness.*
*Therefore, if one does not switch the outlook*
*Of self-centeredness to other-centeredness,*
*Let alone the attainment of enlightenment,*
*Even in this life there can be no joy.*
*As long as space endures,*
*As long as sentient beings remain,*
*Until then, may I too remain,*
*And dispel the miseries of the world.*

Chanting these verses gives me deep inspiration and reinforces my determination on a daily basis.

We are all the same human beings sharing this small planet. We all happen to have been born here at this time in the long history of humankind. At most, we have a life span of about a hundred years. This is but a blip in the great age of our planet. What matters most is what we do with our short life. If we live our life divorced from our shared humanity, embroiled in discord and division, and causing harm, what a waste of our precious life! If we choose to live our life caring for others—our human family and fragile planet—we will have made our life meaningful. So, when the final day comes, we will look back without regret and feel that our life on this earth has been worthwhile.

CHAPTER 11

# As the Millennium Came to an End

One of the consequences of this hardening of Chinese policy inside Tibet—quite apart from its terrible effects on ordinary Tibetan people—was the tragedy that took place over the selection of the new Panchen Lama. I had genuinely hoped that I could help with the search for the Panchen Lama's reincarnation by working with the Tashi Lhunpo Monastery in Tibet and, through it, with the Chinese authorities. The recognition of the reincarnation of the Panchen Lama is, like in the case of important Tibetan lamas, a matter of great spiritual significance in Tibetan Buddhism, though the "official selection" of the Panchen Lama might have political significance from the perspective of Chinese authorities. In February 1991, on the third day of the Tibetan New Year, I conducted a divination on the question of whether the reincarnation had been born inside Tibet or outside, and the result indicated that he had been born within. So in March 1991, I conveyed a message to Beijing through the Chinese Embassy in New Delhi indicating that I would like to offer assistance in the process of the search for the new Panchen Lama. Ever since the Fourth Panchen Lama Lobsang Chökyi Gyaltsen's recognition of the Fifth Dalai Lama in the seventeenth century, the Dalai Lamas and the Panchen Lamas have played key roles in recognizing each other's reincarnations. Given this historical tradition, Tibetans everywhere, as well as the communities of Tibetan Buddhists in the Himalayan regions that have a historical connection with the Panchen Lama institution, reached out to me, asking that I recognize the new Panchen Lama. It was thus my responsibility, both historical and moral, to help in the search.

On July 17, 1993, Jadrel Rinpoche, the abbot of Tashi Lhunpo, in charge of the search process, met with my brother Gyalo Thondup in Beijing and handed him a scroll asking me to assist in the process. Naturally, I assumed that Jadrel Rinpoche was acting with full permission of the Chinese leadership, and consequently I invited him to Dharamsala for consultation. Although he could not come, at the end of 1994, I received a carefully selected list of more than twenty candidates from Jadrel Rinpoche. He also conveyed to me that he and his search team considered one of these candidates, Gendun Choekyi Nyima, to be the true incarnation. On the basis of this information, I performed a series of divinations and other traditional procedures, such as consultations with oracles, and was pleased to come to the same conclusion.

This information was passed confidentially to Jadrel Rinpoche in February 1995, with the text of a prayer for the long life of the young Eleventh Panchen Lama. I hoped he would be able to navigate the politics in Beijing. Given that the reincarnation of a lama is a religious matter in Tibetan Buddhism and since the chosen candidate would be within the territory under Chinese control, my hope was that Jadrel Rinpoche and his team's choice would be acceptable to the Chinese leadership. I also wrote confidentially to Geshe Yeshe Wangchuk, a senior monk at Sera Monastery at the time in Tibet, informing him that I was really happy with how my own observations confirmed the candidate the search committee had recommended. Sending a copy of the long-life prayer I had composed for the new Panchen Lama, I requested that Geshe use his influence to help assure the Chinese authorities that the parents of the new Panchen Lama had no contact with me whatsoever. I also informed him that, for the time being, I would keep the result of my observation confidential.

Unfortunately, in March 1995, the Chinese government insisted that three to five names be placed in a golden urn for selection by lot,* rather than approve the correct reincarnation. This put me in an impossible position. They were likely to choose a wrong candidate. So, after a series of divinations, I came to the conclusion that I needed to share with the Tibetan Buddhists around the world the result of my own divinations on the reincarnation of the Panchen Lama. Thus, on May 14, 1995 (the full-moon day of the fifteenth of the fourth month in the Tibetan calendar), having sent a day's advance notice to the Chinese government that was conveyed through my brother Gyalo Thondup, I formally announced that I had accepted Gendun Choekyi Nyima as the Eleventh Panchen Lama. I chose this day for this important announcement since it was an auspicious day connected with an important system of Buddhist teaching known as the Kalachakra tantra, a set of teachings and practice with special association with the Panchen Lamas. I also

* This use of a golden urn was probably an attempt on the part of Beijing leadership to invoke the "authority" of a custom first introduced by the Qing Emperor Qianlong toward the end of the eighteenth century. There are two important historical facts about the issue of the "Golden Urn" to keep in mind: First, it was introduced by Qianlong, a devout Tibetan Buddhist, to be used in the presence of sacred icons with the names of the candidates rolled inside dough balls and placed within the urn. The urn, on its own, has no meaning. An important part of Qianlong's motivation was to help prevent corruption or unnecessary factional disputes in the process of recognizing the new reincarnation of prominent Tibetan lamas. Second, even in instances when it was used in connection with the Panchen Lama and the Dalai Lama—that is, the selection of the eighth and ninth Panchen Lamas and the tenth to the twelfth Dalai Lamas—it was more ceremonial than actual. The real recognitions were made through traditional Tibetan systems of divination and other methods, especially consultations with oracles. In any case, it was illogical for Communist China, an avowedly atheistic state, to be invoking this custom for the recognition of the Panchen Lama.

made sure that a copy of my formal announcement was presented to the Chinese Embassy in New Delhi, with also a request to have a copy forwarded to Jadrel Rinpoche and his search team at the Panchen Lama's Tashi Lhunpo Monastery in Tibet. For me, this confirmation of the Panchen Lama's reincarnation was, first and foremost, a matter of integrity of Tibetan Buddhist tradition. Once I was convinced of the authenticity of the new Panchen Lama, the very person selected by the official search party set up by his own monastery, it was unthinkable that any other candidate could be endorsed.

Unfortunately, the fallout was terrible. Jadrel Rinpoche was imprisoned for six years, and Tashi Lhunpo Monastery was subjected to serious harassment, including the arrest of more than thirty monks. To this day, I have not heard any reliable news about Jadrel Rinpoche or his whereabouts, even though he is supposed to have been released from prison. Not only did he serve the previous Panchen Lama with dedication, but also he worked hard to ensure that the Panchen Lama's new reincarnation would be recognized in accordance with Tibetan Buddhist tradition. Furthermore, he tried his best to have the Beijing leadership approve the work of the search committee he was leading, and to that end, he kept Beijing abreast of all the stages in the search process. So to see him suffer so much for his sincere efforts was painful indeed. Gendun Choekyi Nyima, a boy of only six years old, and his family were detained, making the new Panchen Lama the youngest political prisoner in the world at the time. To this day, his whereabouts remain unknown, perhaps making this one of the best kept secrets in the history of the Chinese Communist Party. I have been told by some Chinese, one of them in fact quite a knowledgeable person, that Gendun Choekyi Nyima has been living under a form of house arrest within the compound of a military base somewhere in mainland China. The Chinese authorities proceeded to select a different candidate, Gyaltsen Norbu, whose parents were both members of the Communist Party, and thrust him upon Tashi Lhunpo Monastery as the new Panchen Lama. This act was accompanied by the stationing of a large number of Chinese soldiers in Shigatse, where the monastery is located. I feel deeply sad for the two boys caught up in this tragic situation. We know that the true Panchen Lama is missing, while the boy chosen by the Chinese Communist Leadership and enthroned at Tashi Lhunpo is referred to by Tibetans as well as some Chinese Buddhists as the "false Panchen Lama" or the "Chinese Panchen Lama." To this day, the photo of Gendun Choekyi Nyima remains banned.

In November 1996, the Chinese President Jiang Zemin came to India on an official visit for eight days. I recognized it was not possible to meet him, but I took the opportunity of this visit to appeal to him, through a statement, to reverse China's repressive policy inside Tibet. On February 19, 1997, China's paramount leader Deng Xiaoping died. In my statement on that day, I expressed my regret that serious negotiations on the issue of Tibet did not take place during Deng's lifetime and also my hope that there were now new opportunities to reset the clock. In my letter of condolence to Jiang Zemin, I wrote:

> It is very regrettable that serious negotiations on the issue of Tibet could not take place during Mr. Deng's lifetime. However, I firmly believe that the absence of Mr. Deng provides new opportunities and challenges for both Tibetans and the Chinese. I very much hope that under your leadership the Government of China will realize the wisdom of resolving the issue of Tibet through negotiations in a spirit of reconciliation and compromise. For my part, I remain committed to the belief that our problem can be solved only through negotiations, held in an atmosphere of sincerity and openness.

Given Deng's initial overture with the statement to my brother that "except for independence, everything is negotiable," I had hoped that we could achieve some breakthrough during his leadership. Sadly, this was not to be.

Deng's death marked the end of an era—he was the last of the old

Communist revolutionaries to rule China and also the last of its senior leaders whom I knew personally. He had been responsible for the opening up of China, and, under his leadership, very significant headway was made in economic development, resulting in lifting millions of people out of poverty, especially the poverty caused by the famines of the Great Leap Forward and the suffering of the Cultural Revolution. At the same time, it was under Deng's watch that China's People's Liberation Army fired on its own people in Tiananmen Square.

In March 1997, I had the good fortune to visit Taiwan for the first time. My official host was the Buddhist Association of China (Taiwan), and the government, ruled by the Nationalist Party (known also as Kuomintang) originally founded by Chiang Kai-shek, who, following Mao's Communist takeover of mainland China in 1949, fled to this island. Given that Kuomintang (KMT) saw itself as a continuation of the government of the Republic of China, albeit away from the mainland, at the time it was still formally asserting sovereignty over all of mainland China, as well as Tibet. I was received officially by the Taiwanese President Lee Teng-hui, which indicated that there was a softening of Taiwan's "official" position on the status of Tibet. Needless to say, my visit to Taiwan, including especially my meeting with the Taiwanese president, angered Beijing, which accused me of colluding with Taiwan to undermine China. For me personally, the most memorable and valuable aspect of the visit was the chance to meet with so many Chinese Buddhists who were sincere in their devotion to Buddhism and were free to practice their faith without interference from the state. In 2001, I visited Taiwan for the second time at the official invitation from President Chen Shui-bian. At that time, I also had the opportunity to meet with Tsai Ing-wen, who would later become the president of Taiwan. This was the beginning of Taiwan's relinquishing of their claim to sovereignty over Tibet, resulting in the issuing of visas to stateless Tibetans from India on their Indian travel documents and the eventual closing of the United Front Office (known formally as the Mongolian and Tibetan Affairs Commission), originally established for dealing with the affairs of non-Chinese peoples like the Tibetans and the Mongols in Inner Mongolia.* Finally, in 2009, in response to an invitation, I visited the southern part of Taiwan to pray at the sites of a massive typhoon that had caused much suffering and loss of life.

As part of my usual approach of consulting the Tibetan people on an ongoing basis, an important gathering took place in September 1997, aimed at reviewing our position in relation to dialogue with the Chinese government. In the end, as I have often stated, it is the Tibetan people who must choose their destiny, not the Dalai Lama or the Communist Chinese government. At the conclusion of this meeting, the Assembly of Tibetan People's Deputies adopted a formal articulation of what I have described as the Middle Way Approach. The key points were:

- Without seeking independence for Tibet, the Central Tibetan Administration strives for the creation of a political entity comprising the three traditional provinces of Tibet;
- Such an entity should enjoy a status of genuine national regional autonomy;
- This autonomy should be governed by the popularly-elected legislature and executive through a democratic process and should have an independent judicial system;
- As soon as the above status is agreed upon by the Chinese government, Tibet would not seek separation from, and remain within, the People's Republic of China;
- The Central Government of the People's Republic of China has the responsibility for the political aspects of Tibet's international relations and defense, whereas the Tibetan people should manage

* The reference here is to the closing of the United Front Office in Taiwan, which was set up as a continuation of the same office in Beijing under the Nationalist government of Kuomintang (KMT) in China.

all other affairs pertaining to Tibet, such as religion and culture, education, economy, health, ecological and environmental protection;

- To resolve the issue of Tibet, His Holiness the Dalai Lama shall take the main responsibility of sincerely pursuing negotiations and reconciliation with the Chinese government.

On the Chinese side, one presumes in response, in February 1998, the State Council Information Office of the People's Republic of China issued a white paper entitled *New Progress in Human Rights in the Tibet Autonomous Region*, indicating an aggressive public strategy. The document concluded that "the exiled Dalai Lama has tried by every means to cover it up and vilify and attack the development of progress in new Tibet." It went on to say, "The Dalai Lama's wanton fabrication of lies and his violation and trampling of this commandment serve only to expose him in all his true colors: He is waving the banner of religion to conduct activities aimed at splitting the motherland."

In the meantime, on my part, I strove to encourage China's entry into the mainstream of the world community. My deep belief was then, as it is now, that the opening up of China was in the best interests of the Chinese people. So, when discussions and debates were taking place as to whether or not the United States should grant most-favored-nation trading status to China, I expressed my support for doing so. In fact, I wrote to the chair of the US Senate Foreign Relations Committee expressing my personal encouragement for granting this status. As far as our direct contact with the Beijing leadership was concerned, after 1989 nothing of substance happened for many years. That said, there were indeed a few meetings in Hong Kong and Chiang Mai, Thailand, confidential at the time, between my envoys Lodi Gyari and Kelsang Gyaltsen and an emissary from the Chinese President Jiang Zemin. Also, on September 28, 1997, when Senator Dianne Feinstein and her husband, the American businessman Richard Blum, met with the Chinese president, they were kind enough to deliver by hand a letter from me to Jiang Zemin. This was several months before the summit in Beijing between President Bill Clinton and Jiang.

At the press conference in Beijing, Clinton revealed that the question of Tibet had been discussed, and he urged the resumption of dialogue. Jiang commented:

> Actually, as long as the Dalai Lama can publicly make a statement and a commitment that Tibet is an inalienable part of China and that he must also recognize Taiwan as a province of China, then the door to dialogue and negotiation is open. Actually, we are having several channels of communications with the Dalai Lama. So I hope the Dalai Lama will make positive response in this regard.

This was the first time that the head of the People's Republic of China had publicly addressed the question of Tibet and spoken of the possibility for a genuine dialogue. Of course, as to Jiang's first condition, he knew that I had already made public statements relinquishing the call for independence, ever since my speech to the European Parliament in Strasbourg in 1988. With respect to the second condition, frankly, the question of Taiwan is totally unconnected to Tibet and our cause. Jiang may have been sincere in reaching out to my envoy, but it was unclear to what extent he had support within the Chinese Politburo.

As the eventful decade of the 1990s drew to an end, there was one pleasant surprise. The fourteen-year-old Karmapa, head of the Karma Kagyu lineage of Tibetan Buddhism, escaped into India from Tibet, arriving suddenly in Dharamsala on January 5, 2000. I knew his predecessor, the Sixteenth Karmapa, who had been an important lama among senior Tibetan spiritual leaders that came into exile in 1959. So, I was very happy to welcome the new Karmapa, Ogyen Trinley Dorje, and offered to assist him and his entourage in whatever ways I could, especially in relation to his education.

CHAPTER 12

# The Final Series of Dialogues

In 2001, when I was sixty-six years of age, I took a major step within the political structure of the Tibetan exile community by choosing to go into semiretirement and devolve the executive aspect of Tibetan political leadership. For the first time, the executive in charge of the Tibetan exile administration would be directly elected by the people, and this leader would then nominate his or her own cabinet. Having already established an Assembly of Tibetan People's Deputies (equivalent of an elected parliament), I felt this was another milestone in moving toward full democracy of our own administration. To institutionalize these changes, we revised the Charter of Tibetans-in-Exile, and this amendment was adopted by the Assembly of Tibetan People's Deputies on June 14, 2001. Within this new structure, Professor Samdhong Rinpoche became the first directly elected leader of the administration, taking the title of Kalon Tripa (chief of the cabinet).

The thinking behind this was that were the issue of Tibet not to be resolved in my lifetime, we would need to institutionalize the movement for the freedom of our people so that it could remain vibrant for a long time to come. As long as I am alive, of course, I remain fully committed to doing all I can. However, I have always believed that overreliance on any single individual, especially in the case of the fate of an entire people, is unstable. To be honest, I feel that sometimes Tibetans rely on me too much.

On October 22, 2002, at the initiative of Beijing, my envoy Lodi Gyari met with an important official from the United Front Work Department (the body within the Chinese Communist Party charged with relations with, among others, peoples that the People's Republic of China considers "national minorities"), in Ottawa, Canada. This would open a new phase in our talks with Beijing, leading altogether to nine rounds of formal discussions, the last one ending in January 2010. Throughout this process, our representatives worked closely with me as well as with Samdhong Rinpoche, the Kalon Tripa.

We knew that the first few meetings would have to be devoted to establishing personal relationships and trust between my delegation, composed of four members and headed by my two envoys, Lodi Gyari and Kelsang Gyaltsen, and their Chinese counterparts from the United Front assigned with the task. Since by then the Summer Olympics of 2008 had already been awarded to Beijing, understandably a key concern on the part of the representatives of Beijing at our meetings seemed to be about ensuring a successful hosting of the Olympics. During the fourth meeting, which took place at the Chinese Embassy in Bern in 2005, my envoys made a serious effort to persuade their Chinese counterparts to consider a proposed visit to China by me on a pilgrimage, especially to the sacred site of Mount Wutai Shan, which I have always wanted to visit.

One important reason they shared was that, according to Tibetan tradition, I was soon approaching what is called a *kag* year (literally, "an obstacle year"), and the custom is to go on an important pilgrimage to ward off any potential obstacles.* They also made the request that permission be granted for a low-key visit by a small group of monks from the Tibetan exile community in India, who would make offerings at the presence of the sacred images in the Jokhang Temple in Lhasa, as well as various monasteries and sacred sites in Tibet, praying for my good health. The envoys also presented the idea that such a private visit from me might offer an opportunity to share with the Beijing leadership directly my aspirations for the Tibetan people. The Chinese delegation responded that this was a matter of national importance and that they themselves were not in a position to make any decision. They told my envoys that they would pass this suggestion on to the Beijing leadership. Sadly, nothing came of this suggestion.

While these dialogues did offer an opportunity for frank exchanges, including presenting a formal document that outlined what we meant by a genuine autonomy for the Tibetan people within the People's Republic of China, we were never able to engage substantively at a level higher than the leadership of the United Front. This meant that it was impossible to get to the point where we could negotiate with someone or a body empowered to make actual decisions. Between the seventh and the eighth meetings, the Beijing Olympics of 2008 took place. With the world's attention on China, especially that of the international media throughout the run-up, many Tibetans and sympathizers in various parts of the free world seized the opportunity to protest against what was happening inside Tibet and that no visible progress was being made from our dialogues with Beijing.

During that year's anniversary of the Lhasa uprising of March 10, 1959, spontaneous protests erupted in Lhasa as well, and rapidly spread across the Tibetan plateau. In fact, on March 10, 2008, when I first

---

* There is the belief in the Tibetan tradition that, depending on one's birth year, there are specific ages when one might be more susceptible to illness and other adversities.

The Dalai Lama was called upon to assume temporal leadership of Tibet and its people in November 1950, when he was barely sixteen.

The Fourteenth Dalai Lama with his family. *From left to right:* his mother, Dekyi Tsering; elder sister, Tsering Dolma; brothers, Gyalo Thondup, Taktser Rinpoche, and Lobsang Samten; His Holiness; his younger sister, Jetsun Pema; and youngest brother, Tenzin Choegyal.

Being greeted by Chairman Mao Zedong at the inaugural National People's Congress in Beijing, September 1954.

With the Panchen Lama, accompanied by Vice Premier Deng Xiaoping, walking past well-wishers at a railway station in Beijing, 1954.

With the Panchen Lama (who was sixteen years of age to the Dalai Lama's nineteen) in Beijing, 1954.

Hosting a banquet to celebrate Losar (Tibetan New Year) in Beijing. *From left to right:* Premier Zhou Enlai, the Panchen Lama, Mao Zedong, the Dalai Lama, and Lui Shaoqi (who would go on to succeed Mao as chairman).

With Indian Prime Minister Jawaharlal Nehru and Premier Zhou Enlai at an official function in India, 1956.

In February 1959, while tensions were building in Lhasa, Tibet's capital city—which would erupt in the Tibetan People's Uprising of March 10—the Dalai Lama, still a student, had to undertake his rigorous Geshe Lharam final exams.

The Dalai Lama being escorted by Tibetan soldiers and resistance fighters as he escaped into exile in March 1959.

With his entourage after fleeing from the Tibetan capital city of Lhasa, March 1959.

With his youngest brother, Tenzin Choegyal, walking down a pass during the long journey to freedom, March 1959.

Large parts of Drepung Monastery (founded near Lhasa in 1416), still in ruins in 1993, were completely destroyed by the People's Liberation Army during the Cultural Revolution.

Spontaneous uprising of the Tibetan people in Lhasa on March 10, 1959.

Adruk Gompo Tashi, the leader of the Tibetan resistance, called the Volunteer Force for the Protection of the Faith (*tensung danglang magmi*).

Tibetan refugees arriving in India, following the Dalai Lama's escape into exile in March 1959. Altogether, up to 80,000 Tibetan refugees would manage to flee into exile from 1959 to the early 1960s.

Tibetan refugees working in road construction in northern India. The fall of Tibet to China meant that India now needed to militarily guard their more than 3,000 kilometers of border with Tibet.

Nehru visits the Dalai Lama in April 1959, in Mussoorie, where His Holiness was first hosted after his arrival in India.

Visiting the site of a new Tibetan settlement being established in southern India in the early 1960s.

Visiting another site of a new Tibetan settlement in southern India. The monk official on the far left was the Dalai Lama's senior secretary, Tara Tenzin Choenyi.

Greeting some of the Tibetan refugee children in the early 1960s, at the Dalai Lama's first residence in Dharamsala, Swarg Ashram.

With young Tibetan students at a makeshift school in northern India in the early 1960s.

With young refugee children in the early 1960s.

With Indira Gandhi, Nehru's daughter, who would later become India's third prime minister.

Conducting the Kalachakra Empowerment Ceremony (a major multi-day religious event connected with peace in Tibetan Buddhism) in Dharamsala, 1970.

Receiving the Nobel Peace Prize in 1989 in Oslo, Norway.

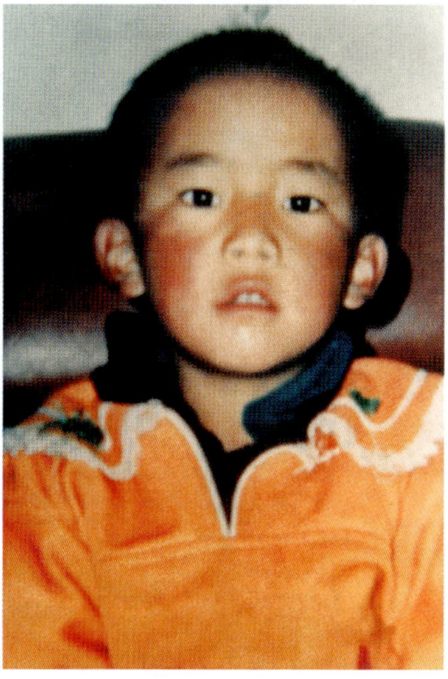

The Eleventh Panchen Lama, Gendun Choekyi Nyima, photographed at age six. To date, there is no reliable information on his whereabouts, and this photograph remains banned inside Tibet.

Receiving the Congressional Gold Medal from President Bush at the United States Capitol, October 27, 2017.

heard through a message from Lhasa that a group of several hundred monks from Drepung Monastery were walking toward the city center demanding religious freedom, I was deeply worried and immediately prayed for their safety. The next day, several monks from Sera marched to protest, demanding the release of many monks detained the previous day. Then monks and nuns from other monasteries, including Ganden Monastery, began marching to Lhasa to join the protests. The police reacted brutally and arrested many. This cruel treatment of the monks and nuns was the spark that lit a fuse long laid by Chinese oppressive rule in Tibet. On March 14, there was a massive protest, demanding the release of the monks and nuns. When the police regrouped on that day, they were joined by the army, with tear gas, machine guns, and armored personnel carriers. From March 14, spontaneous protests spread to Amdo and Kham (the northeastern and eastern parts of Tibet) and lasted through much of April.

There were international demonstrations across many countries during the Olympic torch relays, expressing solidarity with the Tibetan people. This began with a disruption of the speech by the head of the Beijing organizing committee at the inaugural torch ceremony in Athens on March 24, 2008. A number of world leaders called on the Chinese authorities to exercise restraint and reiterated their support for the dialogue process we had begun. On the part of Beijing, however, instead of taking stock and reflecting on why the Tibetans should be reacting this way, the Chinese propaganda machine responded to the crisis by blaming me personally. They accused me of instigating these protests inside Tibet. On March 18, 2008, the leader of the Communist Party in Tibet said, "The Dalai is a wolf in monk's robes, a devil with a human face but the heart of a beast. . . . We are now engaged in a fierce blood-and-fire battle with the Dalai clique, a life-and-death battle between us and the enemy."

During his state visit to Laos, the Chinese Premier Wen Jiabao urged me (while speaking to international media) to calm the situation inside Tibet. In response, I offered to speak directly with the Chinese leader Hu Jintao. I did not hear back. Meanwhile, Communist China's state television broadcast across the mainland, portraying the Tibetan protests as an attack against the Chinese, with the propaganda having the tragic consequence of racism against Tibetans living in the Chinese mainland. I heard stories of discrimination against Tibetans, involving refusal by hotels to rent rooms, public transportation such as trains and airlines refusing to sell tickets, and Tibetans being spat upon in parks. Unwittingly, what the Chinese state media have succeeded in creating is a generation of deeply resentful Tibetans, who will never forget their experience of overt racism.

While the official Chinese government response to the spontaneous Tibetan protests was harsh, encouragingly, many Chinese, including intellectuals and writers in mainland China, showed unprecedented support and sympathy. More than a thousand articles appeared in the Chinese language from both within and outside the People's Republic of China expressing their support for the Tibetan cause, urging the government to engage in substantive dialogue with me. Liu Xiaobo, one of the architects of Charter 08 (a manifesto for human rights in China issued in December 2008) and who would later receive the Nobel Peace Prize in 2010 for his long and nonviolent struggle for fundamental human rights in China, was among those who wrote. A glimpse at the titles of some of these publications from Chinese authors—"Federalism Is the Best Way to Resolve the Issue of Tibet," "The Middle Way Approach Is the Panacea for Curing the Disease of Ethnic Animosity," "The Dalai Lama's Middle Way Approach Is the Right Way of Resolving the Issue of Tibet"—unmistakably demonstrates their support for our approach to resolve the issue of Tibet.

Meanwhile, I issued a series of appeals. I urged the Tibetans to practice nonviolence and not to waver from this path, however dire the situation might be. I also reminded them that, right from the beginning, I had supported the hosting of the Summer Olympics in Beijing, and I urged the Tibetans not to hinder the games, because I understood that the hosting of the Olympics was a matter of great pride to the world's most populous nation. (In fact, when I was invited to speak at the US Congressional Gold Medal Ceremony in October 2007, I spoke of how I have always encouraged world leaders to engage with China, and that I have supported China's entry into the World Trade Organization [WTO] as well as the awarding of the Summer Olympics to Beijing.) I emphasized again that our struggle is with the leadership of the People's Republic of China, and not with the Chinese people. We should never cause misunderstanding or do something that would hurt the Chinese people.

To the Chinese brothers and sisters across the world, I made appeals asking them to support my call for the end of the brutal crackdown inside Tibet, and to help dispel the misunderstandings between our two communities. I emphasized that the Chinese and Tibetan people share a common spiritual heritage in Mahayana Buddhism, that we worship the Buddha of compassion and cherish compassion for all suffering beings as one of the highest spiritual ideals. Concerned about the danger of rising enmity between Tibetans and Chinese, I also suggested to Tibetans living in different parts of the world to establish Sino-Tibetan Friendship Associations. Such associations could extend invitations to Chinese living in the same city to Tibetan festivals and celebrations and to share meals together.

Meanwhile, I instructed my envoys to yet again contact their Chinese counterparts and seek a meeting. It was a matter of urgency to defuse the situation inside Tibet, and to urge the Chinese leadership to investigate the real causes for these widespread protests and take seriously the genuine grievances of the Tibetan people. Our initiative led to an informal meeting between my two envoys and their Chinese counterparts in Shenzhen in May 2008. At that meeting, both sides agreed to hold the seventh round of formal dialogues in Beijing in July 2008. Soon after, on May 12, 2008, a massive earthquake struck the province of Sichuan, including the Tibetan area of Ngawa (Ngaba). When we heard the news, large-scale prayers were held for the victims of the earthquake across the Tibetan communities in the diaspora, including at the Thekchen Choeling Temple here in Dharamsala. I also made a personal donation to the relief fund through the International Federation of Red Cross and Red Crescent Societies. Later, in the same month, when I was visiting London, the Chinese Embassy there was gracious enough to permit my secretary to sign on my behalf the condolence book at the embassy, expressing my solidarity with the victims.

With respect to our dialogue, by the end of the sixth meeting, I was feeling frustrated that we had gone round in circles, having talks about talks. There is a Tibetan saying, "Your steps should contribute to your journey." So, after the sixth meeting, I asked my team to present me with an analysis of the conversation thus far. At that stage, they remained hopeful. They felt that, after all the hard work of listening to each side's complaints and concerns, perhaps a space had been created now to get into actual discussions.

Thus, the seventh round of meetings took place in Beijing in July 2008. At the start of this round, my envoys expressed to their counterparts that by now our discussions should touch upon substantive issues. They also shared my and the Tibetan community's rising frustration and impatience. We were asked for a formal statement of our views on the degree or form of autonomy we sought for our next meeting.

While our position had been clear for years, we prepared a formal document entitled "Memorandum on Genuine Autonomy for the Tibetan People," and presented this at the eighth round of talks on October 31, 2008. We reiterated our commitment not to pursue separation or independence but instead a solution to the Tibetan issue through seeking genuine autonomy compatible with the principles of autonomy in the Constitution of the People's Republic of China. Given that our foundational objective was (and remains) the protection of Tibetans as a people with our unique culture, language, and religion, a key point of our proposal was to seek a framework within which all Tibetan areas could enjoy the same form of protection and governance. We also stressed that if our autonomy was to be genuine, it needed to include the right, within the People's Republic of China, to self-government on the local level.

This document was in a format and language that carefully respected the Constitution of the People's Republic of China as well as the Law on Regional National Autonomy. We wanted to assure Beijing that we truly believed that our goals could be realized within the existing framework of the People's Republic of China and, to our understanding, fully compatible with its constitution.

Even though the Chinese knew the "Memorandum on Genuine Autonomy for the Tibetan People" represented our sincere attempt to present a formal basis for discussions, Beijing chose to react negatively, including making a public statement on November 10, less than a fortnight after our meeting. They accused us of "ethnic splitting" and "seeking a legal basis for so-called Tibetan independence or semi-independence or covert independence." They stated emphatically that "the doorway to Tibetan independence, semi-independence, or covert independence will never be open." (This same line of criticism was repeated later in China's white paper of 2009, issued to mark the fiftieth year since 1959, entitled *Fifty Years of Democratic Reform in Tibet*, in which it was declared that "There is no way for the Dalai clique to uphold 'Tibetan independence,' neither will it succeed in its attempt to seek semi-independence or covert independence under the banner of 'a high degree of autonomy.'") But the autonomy we were asking for was not, as claimed by the Chinese side, some kind of "high degree of autonomy" that is outside the Law of National Autonomy of the People's Republic of China.

In view of Beijing's initial negative response, and in accord with our Charter of Tibetans-in-Exile, a five-day special meeting was held November 17–22, 2008, to discuss our ongoing dialogue with Beijing. Nearly six hundred delegates representing Tibetan communities from different parts of the world as well as key sectors deliberated and, once again, overwhelmingly supported our Middle Way Approach.

A month later, addressing the European Parliament in Brussels on

December 4, 2008, I responded to the Chinese critique by underlining that our intention had never been to expel non-Tibetans from the Tibetan plateau, but rather to express our concern about the induced mass movement of primarily Han, but also some other nationalities, into many Tibetan areas, which in turn had marginalized the native Tibetan population and threatened Tibet's fragile environment. Confronted with such unreasonable and excessively negative responses to our proposal, I could not help sharing my frustration, saying that although my faith in the Chinese people remained unshaken, my faith in the Chinese government was becoming thinner by the day.

Beijing's official response to the memorandum was deeply disappointing. Throughout these rounds of negotiation, which began in 2002, at no point did the Chinese side present any substantive proposal. Despite their immediate and willful attack on our proposal, we nonetheless prepared a note on the memorandum responding to their reactions and claims, on the assumption that the issues may have been misunderstood. In this clarification note, we also addressed what the Chinese side referred to as "the three adherences," forming a kind of boundary line that could not be crossed. They are (1) the adherence to the leadership of the country by the Chinese Communist Party, (2) the adherence to socialism with Chinese characteristics, and (3) the adherence to the Law on Regional National Autonomy. Our clarification document was presented at the ninth round of discussions in January 2010. It turned out to be the end of the conversation. Formal dialogue has not resumed since.

On March 19, 2011, when I was seventy-five years old, I made a public announcement that I had decided to go into full retirement, thereby completing the process of devolution of political authority that began in 2001, when we had our first directly elected full political leader within the exiled Tibetan community. I said that rule by kings and religious figures was outdated, and we had to follow the trend of the free world, which is toward democracy. Furthermore, it was most appropriate for me as the fourteenth in the line of the Dalai Lamas to voluntarily, happily, and proudly end the temporal authority of the Dalai Lama so that a democratically elected leadership could take on the role. On May 29 of that year, we were able to make the necessary preparations, including the amendment of the Charter of Tibetans-in-Exile, to institutionalize this fundamental change. This amendment of the charter was preceded by a special assembly of the Tibetan people, and my final executive act was formally signing this revised charter; with that, I went into full retirement, devolving all secular authority to the elected Tibetan leadership. In August 2011, having won the election, Lobsang Sangay assumed the office of Kalon Tripa (chief of the cabinet) and later took on the title of Sikyong (president of the Central Tibetan Administration), and after serving two five-year terms, in 2021, Penpa Tsering, the current Sikyong, was elected.

In announcing this full retirement from my political position in May 2011, I reassured the Tibetan people both within Tibet and in exile that my decision to devolve political authority did not in any way reflect a loss of interest or determination, or a giving up of my involvement in the Tibetan struggle for truth and freedom. As a Tibetan, and as someone karmically connected with the lineage of the Dalai Lamas, there is simply no way that I could abandon the cause of Tibet and its people. My motivation was solely that of what I believed to be best for the Tibetan people, especially with respect to ensuring the long-term sustainability of our struggle for freedom. If the Tibetan issue were to remain unresolved for several more decades, then we all knew that a time would come when I would be no longer able to lead the movement. If, instead, we instituted a system while I am alive whereby the Central Tibetan Administration took on the full responsibility of political leadership, our administration would have the time to acquire the necessary skills and experience to function without the need for my leadership. And, if during this period of transition, challenges were to arise, of course I would be there to assist in whatever way I was able. Also, this act of devolution would demonstrate to the world, and especially to Beijing, that our struggle pertains to the well-being of an entire people, not to that of the Dalai Lama or his institution. I was ending the Dalai Lama's political leadership of the Tibetan people not only voluntarily but also happily and proudly. This full devolution of power not only was a decision pertaining to my person, but it also marked the ending of the temporal authority of the Dalai Lamas, which had been established in the seventeenth century in the era of one of my predecessors, the Fifth Dalai Lama.

As it was becoming clear that our discussions with Beijing were not leading to any meaningful outcome, many Tibetan people grew desperate. One tragic expression of this was the wave of self-immolations that occurred inside Tibet, beginning on February 27, 2009, when a young monk, Tapey, from Kirti Monastery in the Ngawa county (in northeastern Tibet) set fire to himself in the marketplace. Since then, more than 160 monks, nuns, and laypeople—most of them young—have resorted to this form of protest, mainly in Tibet, but a few also in India and Nepal. One of the more recent instances took place on February 24, 2022. Tsewang Norbu, a famous singer with a large following both in Tibet as well as in mainland China, self-immolated in front of the Potala Palace. He was twenty-five years old. I am told that his songs were removed from music platforms in China, and all news relating to his death has been suppressed. In fact, his entire online presence, including any biographical information, has been erased such that no trace of his existence is to be found online in any resources available to people in China and Tibet. I am told that Norbu's father took his own life in May, after being repeatedly harassed by the Chinese police. This latest example powerfully demonstrates that the grievances of the Tibetan people transcend socioeconomic status and reside much deeper in their very psyche. These acts of self-immolation express the depth of desperation, hopelessness, and unhappiness Tibetan people fundamentally feel in the face of Communist China's rule in their homeland.

The first known instance of Tibetan self-immolation actually took place in New Delhi, in 1998. I personally went to see Thupten Ngodup as he lay dying in a burn unit in a hospital in the Indian capital. One of the first times I spoke publicly about my feelings on this very painful issue was at a press meeting during a visit to Tokyo in June 2010. It was about a year after that young monk at Kirti Monastery in northeastern Tibet had self-immolated. In response to a question from a journalist, I shared three things as part of my response: first, that I feel deep sadness and pain every time I hear about such an incident; second, that I cannot encourage such drastic acts because I do not believe it will have any real effect on the Chinese authorities; and third, that it is my hope that these tragic acts on the part of the Tibetans will make the Chinese authorities ask what is motivating these young Tibetans. To this day, I feel conflicted about this issue of self-immolation. On the one hand, I can empathize with the profound helplessness Tibetans feel about what is happening inside their homeland. On the other hand, the loss of every life is a loss too many. This act is undoubtedly extreme, but the fact remains that those who have committed it chose not to kill others, only to sacrifice their own lives.

## CHAPTER 13

# Taking Stock

As I've shared, since I came into exile in 1959, we have had only two substantial periods of discussions with Beijing. Neither of these have led to a stage where real substantive negotiation at the highest level could take place. Naturally, I have asked myself why these rounds of dialogue did not lead to a negotiated solution to the issue of Tibet.

Looking back, when we had our first series of conversations, spurred by Deng's overture to my brother in March 1979, and the latter's subsequent meeting with Hu Yaobang, we thought there was a real potential opening. On our part, we had placed much hope in the possibility of really getting to the specifics of how, within the framework of Deng Xiaoping's original statement—"except for independence, everything is negotiable"—a lasting solution could be found that was mutually acceptable. The aim was that these dialogues would culminate in an agreement formally signed by the Chinese leader and me. At least we knew that, at the very highest level of the Chinese leadership, there was an expressed willingness to talk. Moreover, it seemed clear that the Chinese government was genuinely open to serious discussions about unresolved international issues that remained at the heart of the

People's Republic of China's formation as a modern country. For in the same month, March 1979, Deng invited the governor of Hong Kong for discussions about the future of what was then a British colony, which was followed by a series of international negotiations, concluding in 1984 with the agreement to hand over the colony to China in 1997.

During one of the earlier rounds of meetings in 1982, the Chinese side shared with our delegation a copy of the text of the Special Administrative Region (SAR) being proposed that could be applied to the status of Hong Kong, which was later adopted as Article 31 of the Constitution of the People's Republic of China, and suggested that we study it, since the proposed Special Administrative Region could have relevance for Tibet. My delegation understood this to mean that crafting a solution along the lines of Article 31 could be possible, which would conform to the basic principle enunciated by Deng. In the end, though, as we've seen, the Chinese side showed no serious interest.

With regard to the second period of dialogues, 2002–2010, looking back with the benefit of hindsight, I wonder if there was ever a genuine intention on the part of the Chinese leadership for substantive discussion. Our conversations never went beyond the level of that wing of the United Front within the Chinese Communist Party charged with dealing with national minorities. One might ask why we persisted in this context. The answer is simple. In the end, the problem of Tibet should be and can only be solved by the Tibetan people and the Chinese people themselves sitting down and talking. There is no other viable option. By virtue of having become the Dalai Lama, it has been my responsibility and my role in life to speak and to keep on speaking on behalf of the Tibetan people.

One explicit response from Beijing to our "Memorandum on Genuine Autonomy for the Tibetan People" came in 2013 in the form of China's white paper on Tibet entitled *Development and Progress of Tibet*. It accused us of having "put forward the so-called concepts of 'Greater Tibet' and 'a high degree of autonomy,' which in fact go against China's actual conditions, and violate the Constitution and relevant laws." Perhaps the accusation about "Greater Tibet" was a reference to our proposal that all Tibetan areas—composed of the three provinces of Ü-Tsang, Kham, and Amdo—be governed under a single administration to ensure a uniform policy across the Tibetan plateau. This is, in fact, not a new idea. Before his death in 1989, the Panchen Lama, acting in his capacity as the vice chairman of the National People's Congress within the People's Republic of China, stated that the desire for the establishment of an autonomous region for a unified Tibetan nationality was appropriate and in accordance with the legal rules. By "legal rules," the Panchen Lama was referring to the Chinese Communist Party's own nationalities doctrine. This states that autonomous territorial units should correspond to places where nationalities live in compact and contiguous areas. According to this doctrine, the entire Tibetan plateau—composed of the three provinces of Ü-Tsang, Kham, and Amdo—should be within a single autonomous region. Also, earlier in 1956, a special committee was set up by the Chinese Central Government that included the senior Communist Party member Sangye Yeshe (known also as Tien Bao)—a rare early Tibetan Communist who had the confidence of Chairman Mao—to draft a detailed plan for the integration of the Tibetan areas into a single autonomous region. This initiative was thwarted by ultra-leftist elements within the Chinese Communist Party. There is also a precedent in the People's Republic of China's dealings with other nationalities where districts once split into separate areas were later brought under a single administration. In 1979, for example, the breakaway areas of Inner Mongolia were brought back within the autonomous region of Inner Mongolia. The heart of the matter is really about what might be the best way to protect the Tibetan people with their distinct language, culture, and spiritual heritage.

In our dealings with Beijing, on our side, there was indeed a clarity of purpose and a recognizable line of command by which my envoys were reporting directly to me and I, in turn, was speaking on behalf of the Tibetan people, both within Tibet and in exile. Especially when the second series of dialogues began, the leaders of the team were explicitly designated as my envoys. This meant that the Chinese side would always know who they were talking to. But for us as outsiders, it was difficult to know whom exactly one was dealing with on the Chinese side. First of all, when leadership change takes place in the Chinese Communist Party, what that means can be opaque: in retrospect, there was a radical shift between the era of Mao and that of Deng; yet the nuances of change between Deng and Jiang Zemin, between Jiang and Hu Jintao, and between Hu and Xi Jinping were extremely difficult to gauge and navigate in real time. Moreover, in dealing with any Chinese leader, it is not clear if one is speaking to an empowered individual or someone who is caught in the complex web of power relations with other members of the Politburo. For example, the overtures of Jiang Zemin in 1998 may have been sincere, but they seemed to have been thwarted within the leadership. In view of this point, since Xi Jinping has emerged as the most powerful Chinese leader since Deng Xiaoping, I had hoped that he would seize the opportunity for a bold vision to solve the issue of Tibet. I was aware that President Xi had made positive remarks about the importance of Buddhism, such as in China's struggle against a moral void that has manifested in widespread corruption. This view would later be confirmed when he visited the headquarters of the United Nations Educational, Scientific and Cultural Organization (UNESCO) in Paris, where he made a remark about how Buddhism had made a deep impact on the religious belief, philosophy, literature, and customs of the Chinese people. Some people also told me that Xi's mother was a practicing Buddhist. And, of course, as mentioned earlier, I had personally known Xi Jinping's father, having met him during my visit to Beijing in 1954–1955. Xi's father, who had suffered during the Cultural Revolution, even though he was an ally of Deng Xiaoping, had opposed the brutal crackdown against the students' protest of Tiananmen. So I had hopes that President Xi would have more personal empathy for the Tibetan people. In fact, when it was announced that Xi Jinping would visit Delhi in 2014, I even communicated my wish to meet him in person. Unfortunately, nothing came of this gesture.

Two important questions come to mind: Were the Chinese ever serious about substantive negotiations on Tibet? What lessons should we learn from our history of dealing with the People's Republic of China thus far for the future of our struggle for freedom?

Some of our international supporters have made the point that the Chinese side was never sincere in their intention to resolve the situation. They say that what mattered to China was to be seen talking, rather than to actually talk. Its motives for this in the 1980s would have been to facilitate the negotiations about Hong Kong and Macau (which were, of course, a huge international triumph for Deng Xiaoping), later to enable China to open its economy internationally, and then to attract international acceptance of its coming of age on the world stage, such as the hosting of the Summer Olympic Games in 2008.

I knew Deng Xiaoping personally in the 1950s, and when I received his overture, I genuinely believed that he was serious. This belief was strengthened further when Hu Yaobang visited Tibet and publicly acknowledged some of the mistakes the Chinese Communist Party had made in relation to the Tibetan people, followed by Hu Yaobang's meeting with my brother Gyalo Thondup. Yet the discussions that ensued led nowhere, their proposals never going beyond the issue of my personal status and return.

Let me turn to the second question: What lessons should we learn from our experience in these dialogues? First and foremost, once both sides have made the commitment to the path of negotiation, there needs to be genuine trust in each other's good intention. This is crucial so that events in the world—there will always be events during a long period of dialogue—do not derail the ongoing dialogue. Second, as part of the protection of mutual trust, there needs to be an open line of communication so there is a mechanism to immediately allay any possible suspicions or doubt that could arise for whatever reasons, including especially public statements from either party. Third, in any negotiation where there is enormous power disparity, as was the case with our dialogue, the stronger side needs to demonstrate greater magnanimity and respect to its dialogue partner.

I am told that in a negotiation there will be a give and take on both sides, and my approach has always been to state honestly what I think the solution we are striving to obtain should look like. As my two envoys as well as their colleagues who joined them in the various rounds of talk know, my approach in our dialogues has been sincere and simple. As a monk, honesty matters to me deeply. So I told my envoys that I wanted to present in clear and candid terms what my actual objectives were, rather than starting with some initial "negotiating position" that could then be pared down to what I was actually seeking. Hence, the proposals I have made represent, as I have already stated, major departures from a demand for a restoration of Tibetan independence. They entail significant accommodation on our part. As a people of an occupied country, we Tibetans have the right to the restoration of our independence; but for reasons I have explained above, I believe that it is possible for us Tibetans to find a way to live within the family of the People's Republic of China provided there is a genuine respect for our rights, dignity, and needs as a people with unique linguistic, cultural, religious, and historical heritage.

To date, I do not believe Beijing has succeeded in creating a multination state within which the Tibetan people could truly feel that they have a home. In other words, it has failed to realize what was envisioned in the important part of its name, "People's Republic of China," whose Chinese equivalence contains the word "*gunghe*" (Tibetan, *chithun*), which connotes a "harmonious union." I often cite the example of the Soviet Union (formally known as the Union of Soviet Socialist Republics), before its collapse, as an example at least of a serious attempt at creating a modern multi-nation state. Unlike the name "People's Republic of China," the words "Russia" or "Russian" do not figure anywhere in the name of the modern composite state. This simple fact made it easier for non-Russians to identify with the new state, and made it possible also for even non-Russians like Stalin and Brezhnev to become leaders of the Soviet Union. Communist China, on the other hand, has not yet succeeded in creating an inclusive modern multi-nation state within which the Tibetans could feel at home. The simple truth is no Tibetan will ever say, "I am a Chinese."

My stance on how best to resolve the issue of Tibet has been consistent since direct discussions with Beijing began in 1979. I have called this the Middle Way Approach. At the core of this approach was the search for a robust framework that would offer the ability for the Tibetans to continue to survive as a distinct people with dignity, with their unique language, culture, ecology, and Buddhist faith. Furthermore, in my approach I have always striven to respect the principle that it is important to take seriously the perspectives and interests of both sides. What matters most to China seems to be territorial integrity and stability, while what matters most to us is a genuine autonomy that guarantees self-governance in the arena of language, culture, ecology, and religion. Even if and when a mutually acceptable agreement is found through negotiation, a robust compliance mechanism is essential to ensure that both sides abide by the terms agreed upon. I say this from my own personal experience and from observing the situation of Hong Kong in the last decade.

While our formal dialogue with Beijing came to an end in 2010, up until 2019, I did maintain informal and at the time confidential contacts with Beijing leadership through individual Chinese. Among those who came to see me and speak with me were a few who did seem to have access to important leaders in Beijing. Some of those who came to speak with me had a singular aim: to persuade me to return "home." At these meetings, I made it clear that at present such discussion was quite premature. I said that we should instead work toward paving the way for me to visit China and Tibet, especially on a pilgrimage. Perhaps Beijing felt that, given my age, I might be more amenable now to going back home. Behind this informal invitation might also have been the belief that once the Dalai Lama "returned," the issue of Tibet would be "resolved," with the question answered in the form of my permanent return. If this is the case, this would mean that after several leadership changes over four decades, and despite two series of dialogues (1979–1989 and 2002–2010), Beijing has not moved beyond the five points Hu Yaobang presented, all pertaining exclusively to my own status, with no attempt at addressing the real issue—the well-being of the Tibetan people.

It is most unfortunate that Beijing did not seize on the opportunity I had offered to resolve the issue of Tibet in a manner that is mutually beneficial. I do not believe that Beijing failed to understand what I was offering. The only rational conclusion I can draw is simply this: *Although there might have been at one point a genuine wish and desire to resolve the issue of Tibet through negotiation, there was neither the courage nor the necessary political will to do so on the part of Chinese leadership.* It is my sincere hope that Beijing will find the necessary courage to resolve the long-standing issue of Tibet through peaceful means before it is too late.

CHAPTER 14

# What Gives Me Hope

Although to date there has been no meaningful breakthrough with the Beijing government, what gives me hope is that the relationship between the two peoples—Tibetans and Chinese—has not been irreparably damaged. As more and more ordinary Chinese come to understand the issue of Tibet, they are coming to understand and sympathize with our just struggle. On my part too, I have cherished whatever opportunities I have had to engage with Chinese people, especially those who are from mainland China. For example, through the auspices of the Brookings Institution, I have had a series of dialogues with prominent Chinese scholars who deeply care about the future of China. These conversations, which were quite open and candid, took place in Washington, DC, at the Aspen Institute and, memorably, in Ladakh, India. At one such meeting in Washington, DC, an important focus of the conversation turned to the issue of moral crisis in light of the aggressive "get rich" culture sweeping across China. Personally, I have found these conversations deeply helpful in understanding current China and its challenges and opportunities. I have also had similar dialogues with Chinese scholars in other places like Berlin, Geneva, and Hamburg.

Thanks to the noted Chinese intellectual Wang Lixiong, who is married to the amazingly brave Tibetan poet and activist Tsering Woeser, in 2010 I also had the rare opportunity to engage in a live Q and A with Chinese from inside China. Announcing this live internet dialogue a few days earlier, Wang had asked for internet users in China to pose questions to me. Web users were then asked to rank these questions according to their preference, and through this democratic process, eight questions were selected. The questions I was asked I took to be representative of what many people in China truly wanted to know about and from me. So let me briefly share here this exchange of questions and answers.

One question was in relation to my view on the future role of religious leaders in Tibet, and in particular the status of the Dalai Lama and the Panchen Lama. Here, I replied that as early as 1969 I had issued a formal statement that the question of whether the Dalai Lama institution should continue or not is for the Tibetan people to decide. I also told them that as soon as Tibet attains genuine autonomy I would hold no official position in any future Tibetan government.

There was a question about how Chinese and Tibetans can nurture and sustain good relations as two peoples. I stressed that if Chinese and Tibetans were to approach one another on the basis of equality and recognition of each other's shared humanity, there would be no barriers for communication. On this basis, many problems could be solved easily. I said that, in my own personal approach, no matter what country I visit, I always emphasize the importance of our common humanity. I said that even when we meet to discuss some difficult problem, it is crucial for the two sides to first connect with each other at the human level. This is the level where we are all exactly the same. Only when this fact is recognized and mutually honored can the parties address the more challenging issues that might have arisen through differences of race, religion, culture, language, or politics.

I was then asked why the various meetings between the Tibetans and the Chinese government have always proved to be fruitless. What were the exact questions that had been so intractable over the decades? I said that the main problem was that the Chinese government kept on insisting that there is no such thing as a Tibetan issue; there is only the Dalai Lama problem. But the simple truth is that I have no demands of my own. The issue pertains to the fate of the Tibetan people, their culture, language, religion, and fragile ecology. I said that if and when the day comes that the Chinese leadership is ready to face the Tibet question and work for its solution, I will lend my full support, because our objective is to seek a meaningful place for Tibet and its people within the family of the People's Republic of China. I also said that the Beijing government keeps stressing stability in Tibet, but true stability can come only from trust, which cannot be achieved through force and repression.

Personally, I found this live internet dialogue truly memorable. The fact that I could have a live conversation with Chinese brothers and sisters from inside China was almost unbelievable. What I took home from this dialogue was that many thoughtful Chinese, who care about the future of their country, understand the situation of Tibet and recognize that a lasting solution has to be found that can ensure the survival of the Tibetans as a people. This live exchange with Chinese brothers and sisters gave me hope and reinforced my belief, regardless of the status of our relationship at the governmental and "official" level, that so long as Tibetans and Chinese avoid the path of mutual hatred, there will always be a basis for finding a genuine understanding between our two peoples.

In 2013, during a visit to New York, I had the delightful opportunity to engage with the Chinese artist and activist Ai Weiwei. One question he asked me was if I hoped to return to my native land. "Yes, I am hopeful," I said. It is indeed human to miss one's home, even though we Tibetans often say, "Where you are happy, that is your home." I had hoped that I would be able to go back at least once before I die.

Now, with my age approaching ninety, this is looking increasingly unlikely.

During my trips to North America, Europe, Japan, and Australia, Chinese from various backgrounds came to see me—ordinary Chinese, intellectuals, writers, artists, business leaders, individuals with access to senior Beijing leadership, former government and military officials. I also met with some high-level Tibetan lamas and Tibetan officials within the Chinese system who had managed to come to see me. So I have had good opportunities to explain to them the need to resolve the issue of Tibet through a path of strict nonviolence and an approach that is mutually beneficial. One of the most moving and emotional meetings with a Chinese I had was that with the wife of the Chinese Nobel Laureate Liu Xiaobo. I met Liu Xia during a trip to Sweden in 2018. The instant she saw me, Liu Xia burst into tears. I consoled her and expressed my deep admiration of Lui Xiaobo's courageous efforts for human rights in China and also her own courage and support of her husband's mission. She said that she wanted to tell me how her husband had a deep respect for me and truly believed that my Middle Way Approach offered a real basis for resolving the long-standing issue of Tibet. She then gave me a copy of a poetry book by her late husband, and, on my part, I gave her Chinese translations of two of my books.

Anyway, this kind of human-to-human contact between Chinese and Tibetans, at the personal level, should really be nurtured and enhanced. And on the part of the Tibetans, it is crucially important to remember that the Chinese people too have suffered under the oppressive rule of the Communist Party. We must also never forget that nations and countries belong to their peoples, not to their governments. No matter how enduring or powerful they might seem at any given time, governments will come and go, but the peoples will always remain. This is a simple truth.

Also, given the large number of Buddhists in China, at the request of relevant organizations, I had the joy of conducting formal teachings in India specifically for Chinese Buddhists, especially since

2009, when the annual tradition was established to offer teachings for them. Among the attendees were also many monastic members, including some from the monasteries at Mount Wutai Shan. On a few occasions, when individual Chinese from the mainland came to see me privately, some of them would weep in my presence and apologize for the sufferings the Tibetan people had experienced under the Communist Chinese rule. And they expressed their deep gratitude that what Beijing had done to the Tibetans had failed in planting seeds of hatred in Tibetans' hearts for the Chinese people. They said that they felt totally at ease when walking around in Dharamsala (where I live) or Bodh Gaya, where thousands of Tibetan Buddhists converge during winter for pilgrimages and Buddhist teachings.

During one of my visits to Paris, I had a meeting with a group of Chinese that I shall never forget. One young man—a student from Inner Mongolia—stood up and said that he had an important message for me from his grandfather. He explained that his grandfather had been part of the cavalry in the People's Liberation Army that attacked Tibet in 1950. All these years later, he asked his grandson to apologize to me on his behalf. I was touched by the depth of sincerity with which the grandson conveyed this apology on behalf of his grandfather.

CHAPTER 15

# Situation Today and the Path Forward

Sadly, at present the situation inside Tibet looks grim. The policies of Xi Jinping, who visited Tibet in 2021 (the first visit of a Chinese leader in more than thirty years), seem to be focused on the tightening of control and intensification of measures aimed at assimilation. For example, on the language front, Chinese is being enforced as the primary medium in education, aimed at creating a generation of Tibetans whose first language will be Chinese, not Tibetan. There are worrying reports of children—according to some sources, up to a million—being taken away from their families and placed in Mandarin-only boarding schools, suggesting that the Chinese government is adopting a totally discredited colonial practice. Alarmed by this new development, in December 2023 the European Parliament passed a resolution condemning this kind of forced assimilation of Tibetan children in Chinese state-run boarding schools and called for immediate cessation of the practice. Similar concerns were raised by the United Nations Human Rights Council as well as the United States Congress. This practice, in fact, contradicts China's own constitution, which guarantees that "all nationalities have the freedom to use and develop their own language."

It is also in direct violation of the Law on Regional National Autonomy, which stipulates that schools and other educational institutions with "ethnic minority students may use their own language for teaching." I am deeply concerned by this situation.

On the religious front, there is a new policy of direct control by the Party over monasteries and nunneries, imposing intensified surveillance and control over the monastic communities. I am told that today there are police stations within the compounds of many monasteries. The Tibetan monasteries are also being forced to have Communist Chinese officials within the administration of the monasteries' management. This tightening around the Tibetan people's religious life, including especially the monasteries, began in 2017 with a specific policy adopted by China's State Council's Regulation on Religious Affairs. In brief, various new regulations are being introduced, all aimed at what the Chinese authorities call promoting "Tibetan Buddhism with Chinese characteristics." One of these new regulations states that the monastic curriculum must include courses on politics, laws, regulations, policies, Chinese language, and the history of the relationship between Tibet and the "motherland."

With respect to the general Tibetan populace, I am informed that in Lhasa and elsewhere, there has been a significant increase in pervasive surveillance of both everyday life and internet use. Community leaders, environmental campaigners, philanthropists, and social activists are especially targeted. There is still no news on the fate of the Panchen Lama, while any display of the Tibetan national flag or my portrait remains banned. In effect, a new social experiment is being conducted through intimidation and forced assimilation, amplified by the apparatus of new technology and digital media. Increasingly, the Tibetans inside Tibet are being made to feel that what is wrong with them from the Chinese authorities' perspective is simply that they are Tibetans.

If Beijing were to look at past history, it would see that policies of repression and forced assimilation do not actually work. It is, in fact, counterproductive, with the main result being the creation of generations deeply resentful of Communist China's presence on the Tibetan plateau. If the Chinese leadership truly cares about a stable and harmonious country wherein the Tibetan people could feel at home, its policies need to be grounded in respect for the dignity of Tibetans and to take serious note of their fundamental aspiration to thrive as a people with a distinct language, culture, and religion.

If, in the end, Beijing deems our foundational objective to be incompatible within the framework of the People's Republic of China, then the issue of Tibet will remain intractable for generations. I have always stated that, in the end, it is the Tibetan people who should decide their own fate. Not the Dalai Lama or, for that matter, the Beijing leadership. The simple fact is no one likes their home being taken over by uninvited guests with guns. This is nothing but human nature.

I, for one, do not believe it would be so difficult for the Chinese government to make the Tibetans feel welcome and happy within the family of the People's Republic of China. Like all people, Tibetans would like to be respected, have agency within their own home, and have the freedom to be who they are. The aspirations and the needs of the Tibetan people cannot be met simply through economic development. At its core, the issue is not about bread and butter. It is about the very survival of Tibetans as a people. Finding a resolution of the Tibetan issue would undoubtedly have great benefits for the People's Republic of China. First and foremost, it would confer legitimacy to China's presence on the Tibetan plateau, essential for the status and stability of the People's Republic of China as a modern country composed of multiple nationalities willingly joined in a single family.

In the case of Tibet, for instance, it has now been more than seventy years since Communist China's invasion in 1950. Despite the physical control of the country, through brutal force as well as economic inducements, the Tibetan people's resentment, persistent resistance in various forms, and moments of significant uprising have never gone away. Even though generations and economic conditions have changed, very little has changed when it comes to the Tibetan people's perception and attitude toward those they still view as occupiers. The simple fact is that insofar as the Tibetans on the ground are concerned, the Communist Chinese rule in Tibet remains that of a foreign, unwanted, and oppressive occupying power.

The Tibetan people have lost so much. Their homeland has been forcibly invaded and remains under a suffocating rule. The Tibetan language, culture, and religion are under systematic attack through coercive policies of assimilation. Even the very expression of Tibetaness is increasingly being perceived as a threat "to the unity of the motherland." The only leverage the Tibetan people have left is the moral rightness of their cause and the power of truth. The simple fact is Tibet today remains an occupied territory, and it is only the Tibetan people who can confer or deny legitimacy to the presence of China on the Tibetan plateau.

All my life I have advocated for nonviolence. I have done my utmost to restrain the understandable impulses of frustrated Tibetans, both within and outside Tibet. Especially, ever since our direct conversations after my exile began with Beijing in 1979, I have used all my moral authority and leverage with the Tibetan people, persuading them to seek a realistic solution in the form of a genuine autonomy within the framework of the People's Republic of China. I must admit I remain deeply disappointed that Beijing has chosen not to acknowledge this huge accommodation on the part of the Tibetans, and has failed to capitalize on the genuine potential it offered to come to a lasting solution. At the time of publishing this book, I will be approaching my ninetieth year. If no resolution is found while I am alive, the Tibetan people, especially those inside Tibet, will blame the Chinese leadership and the Communist Party for its failure to reach a settlement with me; many Chinese too, especially Buddhists—some people told me that there are more than two hundred million in mainland China who self-identify as Buddhists—will be disappointed with their government for its failure to solve a problem whose solution has been staring at them for so long.

Given my age, understandably many Tibetans are concerned about what will happen when I am no more. On the political front of our campaign for the freedom of the Tibetan people, we now have a substantial population of Tibetans outside in the free world, so our struggle will go on, no matter what. Furthermore, as far as the day-to-day leadership of our movement is concerned, we now have both an elected executive in the office of the Sikyong (president of the Central Tibetan Administration) and a well-established Tibetan Parliament-in-Exile.

People have often asked me if there will be a next Dalai Lama. As early as the 1960s, I have expressed that whether the Dalai Lama institution should continue or not is a matter for the Tibetan people. So if the Tibetan people feel that the institution has served its purpose and there is now no longer any need for a Dalai Lama, then the institution will cease. In which case, I would be the last Dalai Lama, I have stated. I have also said that if there is continued need, then there will be the Fifteenth Dalai Lama. In particular, in 2011, I convened a gathering of the leaders of all major Tibetan religious traditions, and at the conclusion of this meeting, I issued a formal statement in which I stated that when I turn ninety, I will consult the high lamas of the Tibetan religious traditions as well as the Tibetan public, and if there is a consensus that the Dalai Lama institution should continue, then formal responsibility for the recognition of the Fifteenth Dalai Lama should rest with the Gaden Phodrang Trust (the Office of the Dalai Lama). The Gaden Phodrang Trust should follow the procedures of search and recognition in accordance with past Tibetan Buddhist tradition, including, especially, consulting the oath-bound Dharma protectors* historically connected with the lineage of the Dalai Lamas, as was followed carefully in my own case. On my part, I stated that I will also

* *Damden chos skyong* in Tibetan, "oath-bound Dharma protectors," connected with the Dalai Lamas include especially Palden Lhamo and Dorje Drakden (known also as Nechung).

leave clear written instructions on this. For more than a decade now, I have received numerous petitions and letters from a wide spectrum of Tibetan people—senior lamas from the various Tibetan traditions, abbots of monasteries, diaspora Tibetan communities across the world, and many prominent and ordinary Tibetans inside Tibet—as well as Tibetan Buddhist communities from the Himalayan region and Mongolia, uniformly asking me to ensure that the Dalai Lama lineage be continued.

In the official statement I issued in 2011, I also pointed out that it is totally inappropriate for Chinese Communists, who explicitly reject religion, including the idea of past and future lives, to meddle in the system of reincarnation of lamas, let alone that of the Dalai Lama. Such meddling, I pointed out, contradicts their own political ideology and only reveals their double standards. Elsewhere, half joking, I have remarked that before Communist China gets involved in the business of recognizing the reincarnation of lamas, including the Dalai Lama, it should first recognize the reincarnations of its past leaders Mao Zedong and Deng Xiaoping! In summing up my thoughts on the question of the reincarnation of the Dalai Lama in that 2011 official statement, I urged that unless the recognition of the next Dalai Lama is done through traditional Tibetan Buddhist methods, no acceptance should be given by the Tibetan people and Tibetan Buddhists across the world to a candidate chosen for political ends by anyone, including those in the People's Republic of China. Now, since the purpose of a reincarnation is to carry on the work of the predecessor, the new Dalai Lama will be born in the free world so that the traditional mission of the Dalai Lama—that is, to be the voice for universal compassion, the spiritual leader of Tibetan Buddhism, and the symbol of Tibet embodying the aspirations of the Tibetan people—will continue.

CHAPTER 16

# Appeal

As I end this book, let me take the opportunity to make some appeals as well as share personal expressions of gratitude.

To my fellow Tibetans: Never lose hope, however dark the sky may become. As our saying goes, "If you fall nine times, you get up nine times." Always remember that a bright sun awaits behind the clouds. We are an ancient people with a long history of resilience. For millennia we *tsampa*-eaters have been the custodians of the expansive Tibetan plateau known as the "roof of the world." Throughout our history of more than two millennia, we have navigated through all sorts of ups and downs, always sure of our identity as a people with our distinct language, culture, and religion, and the core values that define us. Today's dark period of Communist Chinese occupation may seem endless, but in our long history, it is but a brief nightmare. As our Buddhist faith teaches us, nothing is immune to the law of impermanence.

Some might think, given my age and Communist China's position as a global power today, that time is not on our side. I disagree. Yes, the Dalai Lama institution plays today an important role in unifying Tibetans everywhere, but let us not forget that while the Dalai Lama institution is only five hundred years old, Tibet's history is older by more than a millennium and a half. So, I have no doubt that our struggle for freedom will go on, for it pertains to the fate of an ancient nation and its people. As an inherently unstable system, totalitarianism definitely does not have time on its side. Time is on the side of the people, Tibetans as well as Chinese, who aspire for freedom.

What we need is patience, unflagging determination, unity, and courage rooted in the clarity of our goal. Today, after more than six decades of being in exile, the issue of Tibet remains strong in the world's consciousness: this is thanks to our unflagging determination and steadfast commitment to our just cause for the freedom of a people. Saving Tibet is a noble work; it is the work of the dharma, which, as Buddhists, we believe to be the true source of happiness for all beings. Therefore, regardless of the provocation and the understandable human urge to respond to violence with violence, I appeal to you never to give in to this impulse. See the humanity even in our oppressors, because, ultimately, it will be with their humanity that we come to some kind of settlement. But this does not mean that we should allow abuse and the violation of our human dignity to go unchallenged. In whatever ways we can, we must stand up against injustice. Nonviolence does not preclude taking a firm stand and expressing our opposition in a forceful way. Mahatma Gandhi has taught the world the enduring power of what a robust and effective nonviolent struggle means. Especially to my fellow Tibetans who are living in free countries, I say, never forget our brothers and sisters who are oppressed in our own homeland. They look to us as their hope in dark times, and expect us to keep bright the flame of our aspiration for a free way of life.

To the great nation of India and our Indian dharma brothers and sisters: You have been my host and my home since 1959. I have spent more of my life in India than in my own homeland of Tibet. I will never forget the amazing and long generosity you have offered to me and my people in exile. The fact that India gave us a new home, a base, is what enabled us, more than anything else, to reestablish our civilization in exile and to keep the torch of justice for Tibet alight for so many decades. We Tibetans have always looked to India as the source and teacher of wisdom, knowledge, and spirituality in our Buddhist tradition that was received from you many centuries ago. Throughout our long religious and cultural history, India (*arya-bhumi*, "the land of the noble ones") has been our guru, and we Tibetans the *chela* (student). I thank you for your unflagging support of me and my people, and I request of you to continue to extend the same as long as we need it.

To Chinese brothers and sisters: I appeal to you to open your hearts to the ongoing plight of the people of Tibet. The Chinese and Tibetan peoples share a common spiritual heritage in Mahayana Buddhism, and cherish compassion for all suffering beings. I assure you that through the long history of my struggle on behalf of the Tibetan people, I have never harbored enmity against the people of China. I have always urged Tibetans not to give in to hatred due to the injustices inflicted by a cruel government in the name of the Chinese people. I ask you to be vigilant against any attempts to promote racial hatred against the Tibetans, through state propaganda aimed at splitting the long history of good feeling, neighborliness, and friendship between our peoples. I appeal to you to make efforts to understand that the Tibetan struggle for freedom is not only just; it is also not anti-Chinese. Help us find a peaceful, lasting solution to the issue of Tibet through dialogue in the spirit of understanding and accommodation. Over the years, many Chinese scholars and intellectuals have spoken out. I believe many Chinese who know the truth about Tibet, its culture, and its people will come out when they are able to express their true feelings without fear of reprisals. Protecting Tibet is a matter important also to the very heart of China itself. I want to share with you that for me, like for so many across the world, one sad thing is that the amazing economic liberalization of China was not matched with progress in respect for human rights and democratic freedom for your people.

To the nations and peoples of the world, especially those who have stood in solidarity with the Tibetan people: Your expressions of concern and support, as well as the attention of the international media on Tibet, continue to encourage us and give us comfort. I thank you and ask you not to forget Tibet at this critical and challenging time in our people's long history.

Over the long course of my efforts to save Tibet and its people, quite early on I came to recognize that the survival of Tibet—as a civilization with its distinctive language and Buddhist tradition—is a matter of great importance not only to us Tibetans. Of course, with our cultural heritage that emphasizes harmony with nature, if we Tibetans are empowered, the fragile ecology of the Tibetan plateau can also be safeguarded, especially against unrestrained exploitation. Beyond this, the protection of Tibet is also about the survival and flourishing of a culture that is rooted in compassion and has the potential to be of benefit to humanity. The Tibetan tradition represents today the only surviving custodian of the full spectrum of the rich heritage of the great Nalanda school of Indian Buddhism, from philosophy to logic and linguistics, and from psychology to diverse spiritual practices. At the heart of our tradition is the emphasis on the principle of the interdependence of all things, and also the understanding that compassion grounded in the recognition of shared humanity forms the basis of an ethical way of life leading to happiness for all. As our world becomes more interconnected, all human beings need to learn to rise above narrow self-interest for the sake of each other and for the sake of our fragile planet.

In more than five decades of traveling around the world, a key message I have shared from my culture is the importance of embracing the more compassionate parts of human nature, and how doing so will enable us to promote peace and happiness both at the individual as well as societal levels. One of my deeply held convictions is that if each one of us could embrace what I call "the oneness of humanity"—a visceral sense of our shared human condition that acknowledges the simple fact that just like me everyone else wishes to be happy and does not want suffering—our world would be a better and kinder place for all. As social creatures, each one of us came from a mother's womb and survived thanks to someone else's care, especially our parents', in our most vulnerable period of infancy. This total dependence on another's care and the inborn appreciation of others' care that comes with it are what have imprinted in us the natural capacity to care for others, even for strangers. I sometimes describe this as the human quality of "warmheartedness." This is our basic nature. I truly believe that even as the world becomes ever more complex, any solutions we bring to address our challenges—both at the individual as well as at the societal levels—must take into account this basic nature of who we are. I deeply believe that Tibetan knowledge and our culture of compassion have the potential to offer a rich resource to promote inner peace and happiness for all. So the survival of Tibet and the Tibetan people is in the larger interest of humanity itself.

Let me end this book by sharing the following verses from the eighth-century Buddhist teacher Shantideva, whose writings have remained an enduring source of deep inspiration for me:

*The sages who have contemplated for many eons*
*See this [altruism] alone to be of greatest benefit.*
*Through it, immeasurable beings can obtain,*
*With ease, the highest state of happiness.*
*Those who wish to undo hundreds of miseries of existence,*
*And those who seek to relieve creatures of their sorrows,*
*Also those who long to enjoy many hundreds of joys,*
*They must never abandon the altruistic awakening mind.*
*My I be the protector to those without protector;*
*May I be the guide to those traveling on the road;*
*May I become a boat, a causeway, and a bridge*

*For those who long to reach the further shore.*
*Just like the great elements such as earth,*
*As well as like space, at all times,*
*May I be a sustenance of many kinds*
*For an immeasurable number of beings.*
*Likewise, for beings whose expanse*
*Reaches to the furthermost edges of space,*
*At all times and until they all attain nirvana,*
*May I remain a source of sustenance for all.*
*For as long as space endures,*
*For as long as sentient beings remain,*
*Until then, may I too remain,*
*And dispel the miseries of the world.*

# Acknowledgments

I would like to thank first and foremost India, its people and its leaders, for their kind hospitality, boundless generosity in support of me and the Tibetan refugees, and unwavering concern for the fate of the Tibetan people. Let me also express my thanks to all the individuals, organizations, and governments who have stood in solidarity with our just cause and whenever necessary have spoken out. In particular, I thank so many across the world who have lent their voice and sympathy through joining the network of various Tibet support groups. I convey my deep admiration for my fellow Tibetans, inside as well as outside Tibet, for their unflagging steadfastness in standing up for their rights and freedom. This has always been a major source of encouragement and vitality for me in my work on behalf of the Tibetan people. In relation to this book, I thank my longtime English translator, Thupten Jinpa, for assisting me in the process of writing; Jaś Elsner for working closely with Jinpa; those who have helped read the manuscript and offered critical comments; my staff for making all necessary arrangements; my agent for this book, Stephanie Tade, for organizing the publication; and William Morrow for publishing the book.

APPENDIX A

# Tibet: A Historical Overview

Let me address a point that kept being brought up in the various rounds of discussions by the Chinese counterparts: that there must be a consensus on the historical status of Tibet along the lines Beijing claims. For example, at times a demand had been made that I issue a formal statement affirming their claim that Tibet has been an "inalienable part of China since ancient times." It is unclear to what extent they view this to be a precondition for serious negotiation, or if the Chinese delegates have been constantly instructed by their superiors to reiterate this as a face-saving device to avoid delving into any substantive negotiation.

My position on this point of past history has been simple and consistent. I have stated that as a Buddhist monk, it is against my vows to tell a lie, and that includes saying that Tibet has been an "inalienable part of China since ancient times," when I do not believe this to be true. Through my envoys, we have made it clear to Beijing that just as it may have its own version of history, we Tibetans also have our own view of history. Similarly, contemporary historians who are studying the long history of the relationship between Tibet and China will have their own understanding of the long and complex history of the two nations. If Beijing insists on our acceptance of its version of history to be a pre-condition for any substantive negotiation, then what is being asked for is total submission, including even of our own narrative of our history!

Here is a brief overview of our history as I understand it. From the seventh to the end of the ninth century, Tibet was a powerful nation under its Purgyal empire, whose army at one point even raided the Tang capital Chang'an (present day Xi'an), forcing the Tang emperor to flee. The most notable testament of the equal and independent status of the two empires at this time is the treaty of 821–822, inscribed on a pillar in Lhasa in both Tibetan and Chinese, with identical copies set up in the Tang capital Chang'an and at the agreed border of the two countries. This treaty was established between the Tibetan Emperor Tri Ralpachen and the Tang Emperor Muzong. Its text contains the following:

> Both Tibet and China shall keep the country and frontiers of which they are now in possession. The whole region to the east of that being the country of Great China, and the whole region to the west being assuredly the country of Great Tibet. From either side of that frontier there shall be no warfare, no hostile invasions, no seizure of territory. . . .
>
> . . . Between the two countries no smoke or dust shall appear. Not even a word of sudden alarm or of enmity shall be spoken, and from those who guard the frontier upwards, all shall live at ease without suspicion or fear, their land being their land, and their bed, their bed. Dwelling in peace they shall win the blessing of happiness for ten thousand generations. The sound of praise shall extend to every place reached by the sun and moon. And in order that this agreement, establishing a great era when Tibetans shall be happy in Tibet and Chinese shall be happy in China shall never be changed, the Three Jewels, the body of saints, the sun and moon, planets and stars have been invoked as witnesses.

In the second half of the ninth century the Tibetan empire splintered into multiple smaller kingdoms. Soon after, China's Tang dynasty too came to an end, and China also split into multiple kingdoms and dynasties. Finally, in the latter half of the tenth century, the Chinese Song dynasty emerged, reigning over a territory much reduced from that of the Tang empire. During this period after the end of Tibet's imperial age and the Tang dynasty, there was very little contact between Tibet and China. Then, in the early thirteenth century, vast parts of central, inner, and eastern Asia fell to the Mongol armies of Genghis Khan. In 1260, one of Genghis's grandsons, Kublai Khan, emerged as the great khan of the Mongols. Thereupon Kublai named Drogon Chogyal Phagpa (known also as Phagpa Lama, a nephew of the great Tibetan master Sakya Pandita) the national preceptor (*kou-shih*), effectively the head of Buddhism within Kublai's domain. Thus began what we Tibetans call the "priest-patron" (*chöyon*) relationship, whereby the Mongol khan offered patronage to senior Tibetan lamas. In 1271, when Kublai proclaimed the Yuan dynasty as Mongol rulers of China, he appointed Phagpa Lama to be the imperial preceptor (*ti-shih*), with his religious leadership extending across the territories of China. The founding of the Yuan dynasty in 1271 and the final defeat of the Song dynasty in southern China later marked the Mongols' full control over China itself as part of Kublai's imperial realm.* The Mongol overlordship of Tibet through Phagpa Lama's Sakya school came to an end in 1354, when the Phagmo Drupa dynasty established its rule in Tibet. In China, the Mongol Yuan rule came to an end in 1368,

---

* After careful study, the noted specialist on the Yuan dynasty Herbert Franke concludes (in "Tibetans in Yuan China," 301) that "most of Tibet proper remained outside the direct control of the Sino-Mongol bureaucracy and that even the border regions were throughout the Yuan dynasty an unruly and troubled region." Unlike China, according to historians such as Franke, Tibet was actually never under the direct rule or full control of the Mongols.

with the emergence of the native Chinese Ming dynasty. During the Ming dynasty (1368–1644), the relations between Tibet and China were largely spiritual and ceremonial.* As a native Chinese dynasty, the Ming saw itself as having regained independence for China from Mongol control—that is, from foreign rule, just as Tibet achieved independence from the Mongols more than a decade earlier.

In the first half of the seventeenth century, the militarily ascendant Manchuria proclaimed the new Qing dynasty and, following the seizure of Beijing from the Ming, began its rule over China as well. During the reign of the Manchu Qing Emperor Shunzhi, the Fifth Dalai Lama established diplomatic relations with the Qing court and in 1653 visited Beijing, where he was greeted as a fellow sovereign by the Qing emperor. This visit by the Dalai Lama strengthened the relationship between the Manchu emperor and Tibet, ushering in a very rich period of interaction between the Qing rulers and important Tibetan lamas, especially the Dalai Lama, on the priest-patron model. Manchu Qing emperors, being devout followers of Tibetan Buddhism, took their role as patrons seriously. In accordance with the Manchu emperor's status as a protecting patron, at the request of the Tibetans, the Qing sent an army to repel the several thousand Dzungar soldiers who had entered central Tibet in 1717, helped restore the Seventh Dalai Lama to his throne in 1720, and established the tradition of *amban*s, resident imperial representatives of the Manchu court. Later, toward the end of the

* Interestingly, the new Ming dynasty chose to continue the practice of conferring formal titles or honors on important Tibetan figures, including high lamas. That the Ming emperor had no influence in Tibet is demonstrated by the fact that the fourteenth-century Tibetan master Tsongkhapa declined the Yongle emperor's invitation to visit Beijing on at least two known occasions (Thupten Jinpa, *Tsongkhapa: A Buddha in the Land of Snows*, Boulder: Shambhala Publications, 2019, 226–30), and later both the Third and the Fourth Dalai Lamas declined similar invitations from China's Ming emperor.

eighteenth century, again at the request of the Tibetans, the Manchu emperor sent troops to help defeat Nepalese invaders.* In essence, the Qing was a Manchu empire whose imperial family were devout Tibetan Buddhists and whose domain contained both the nations of Tibet and China alongside other nations.† The primary Manchu identity of the Qing is illustrated by the fact that the Qing emperor's senior representative in Lhasa was normally an ethnic Manchu or a Mongol. The end

---

* Judging by historical records, the Qing emperors never seemed to have physically controlled Tibet, and the Tibetans, at least in central Tibet, never paid taxes to the Qing's representative, the *amban*. Even in the case of around fifteen hundred troops stationed at one point in central Tibet, their primary role seems to have been that of protection rather than as a colonial ruling force. This primarily protective role of the Manchu emperor, his *amban*s, and the Qing troops in Tibet can be discerned in a letter to the Eighth Dalai Lama. There, the Manchu general in charge of the Qing garrison in Tibet writes: "This demonstrates the emperor's concern that Tibet comes to no harm and that welfare be ensured in perpetuity. . . . The emperor will withdraw the Ambans and the garrison. . . . Moreover, if similar situations occur in future the emperor will have nothing to do with them. The Tibetans may therefore, decide for themselves as to what is in their favor and what is not or what is heavy and what is light, and make a choice of their own." English translation of this citation is from Smith, *Tibetan Nation*, 136.

† On the exact nature of the relationship between the Qing and Tibet, the modern Tibetan studies scholar Gray Tuttle writes in *Tibetan Buddhists in the Making of Modern China* (New York: Columbia University Press, 2007), 63, "Qing relations with Tibet had always been directly handled by the Manchu dynasty (mediated by the Imperial Household Department and the Court of Managing the Frontiers) with the assistance of a handful of Mongolian, Mongour, and Tibetan Buddhist religious leaders and the Tibetan nobility." In a similar vein, the international relations scholar Warren Smith concludes (*Tibetan Nation*, 137): "The nature of the Ch'ing relationship with Tibet remained one between states, or an empire and a semi-autonomous peripheral state, not a relationship between a central government and an outlying part of the same state."

of Manchu Qing dynasty, just after the first decade of the twentieth century, marked also the end of Tibet's priest-patron relationship with the Qing.

In brief, when Communist China's forcible invasion took place, Tibet had its own national government, currency, passports, postal service, military, foreign relations—for instance, Tibet refused the Allies permission to transport weapons across its territory to supply China against Japan during the Second World War. In other words, Tibet had the key attributes of an independent country. This position of independence remained the status quo until the Communist Chinese invasion of 1950.

The above, in brief, is what I believe to be the history of my country. In fact, an eminent Chinese scholar, Professor Hon-Shiang Lau, whom I first met in 2016 in Brussels, told me that his own careful research into Chinese sources reveals no evidence at all that Tibet had ever been part of China. He said that he was at the time writing a book presenting the results of his multi-year research.

The resolution of the issue of Tibet *is not* and *should not be* contingent on the two sides having a consensus on past history. I have always stated that as to the exact historical status of Tibet at any particular time, this is a matter for historians looking dispassionately at the past, on the basis of available evidence. No one can change past history, certainly not me. History is not a political decision to be made in the present. As to the course of the future, this is indeed within the remit of political decision-making now. I truly believe that if both sides are genuinely committed to establishing a future together based on a mutually beneficial relationship, there is no need to insist that the two parties agree on exactly the same version of the past.

## APPENDIX B

# Treaty Between Tibet and China AD 821–822

### TRANSLATION FROM THE TIBETAN TEXT*

The Great King of Tibet, the Miraculous Divine Lord, and the Great King of China, the Chinese Ruler Huangdi, being in the relationship of nephew and uncle, have conferred together for the alliance of their kingdoms. They have made and ratified a great agreement. Gods and men all know it and bear witness so that it may never be changed; and an account of the agreement has been engraved on this stone pillar to inform future ages and generations. The Miraculous

---

* The English translation of the treaty presented here is the version available at https://www.claudearpi.net/wp-content/uploads/2016/11/821822Treatybetween TibetanChina-1.pdf; reproduced here with permission from Claude Arpi. For an earlier translation of the treaty by H. E. Richardson, see "The Sino-Tibetan Treaty Inscription of AD 821–823 at Lhasa," *Journal of Royal Asiatic Society* 2 (1978), 153–54.

Divine Lord Trisong Detsen and the Chinese King Wen Wu Hsiao-te Wang-ti, nephew and uncle, seeking in their far-reaching wisdom to prevent all causes of harm to the welfare of their countries now or in the future, have extended their benevolence impartially over all. With the single desire of acting for the peace and benefit of all their subjects, they have agreed on the high purpose of ensuring lasting good; and they have made this great treaty in order to fulfill their decision to restore the former ancient friendship and mutual regard and the old relationship of friendly neighbourliness.

Tibet and China shall abide by the frontiers of which they are now in occupation. All to the east is the country of Great China; and all to the west is, without question, the country of Great Tibet. Henceforth on neither side shall there be waging of war nor seizing of territory. If any person incurs suspicion he shall be arrested; his business shall be inquired into and he shall be escorted back.

Now that the two kingdoms have been allied by this great treaty, it is necessary that messengers should once again be sent by the old route to maintain communications and carry the exchange of friendly messages regarding the harmonious relations between the Nephew and Uncle.

According to the old custom, horses shall be changed at the foot of the Chiang Chun pass, the frontier between Tibet and China. At the Suiyung barrier the Chinese shall meet Tibetan envoys and provide them with all facilities from there onwards. At Ch'ing-shui the Tibetans shall meet Chinese envoys and provide all facilities. On both sides they shall be treated with customary honour and respect in conformity with the friendly relations between Nephew and Uncle.

Between the two countries no smoke nor dust shall be seen. There shall be no sudden alarms and the very word 'enemy' shall not be spoken. Even the frontier guards shall have no anxiety, nor fear and shall enjoy land and bed at their ease. All shall live in peace and share the blessing of happiness for ten thousand years. The fame of this shall extend to all places reached by the sun and the moon. This solemn agreement has established a great epoch when Tibetans shall be happy in the land of Tibet, and Chinese in the land of China. So that it may never be changed, the Three Precious Jewels of Religion, the Assembly of Saints, the Sun and Moon, Planets and Stars have been invoked as witnesses. An oath has been taken with solemn words and with the sacrifice of animals; and title agreement has been ratified.

If the parties do not act in accordance with this agreement or if they Violate it, whichever it be, Tibet or China, nothing that the other party may do by way of retaliation shall be considered a breach of the treaty on their part. The Kings and Ministers of Tibet and China have taken the prescribed oaths to this effect and the agreement has been written in detail. The two Kings have affixed their seals. The Ministers specially empowered to execute the agreement have inscribed their signatures and copies have been deposited in the royal records of each party.

*The treaty is carved in Tibetan and Chinese on one side of a stone pillar near the Jo-Khang, Cathedral of Lhasa. On another side is a historical introduction in Tibetan only; and on the other two sides are bilingual lists of the names of the ministers who witnessed it. The texts have been edited in H. E. Richardson,* Ancient Historical Edicts at Lhasa, *vol. 19 of the* Prize Publication Edicts of the Royal Asiatic Society.

# APPENDIX C

# Letters to Chinese Leaders Deng Xiaoping and Jiang Zemin

## LETTER TO DENG XIAOPING, MARCH 23, 1981

Your Excellency:

I agree with and believe in the Communist ideology which seeks the well-being of human beings in general and the proletariat in particular, and in Lenin's policy of the equality of nationalities. Similarly, I was pleased with the discussions I had with Chairman Mao on ideology and the policy towards nationalities.

If that same ideology and policy were implemented it would have brought much admiration and happiness. However, if one is to make a general comment on the developments during the past two decades, there has been a lapse in economic and educational progress, the basis of human happiness. Moreover, on account of the hardships caused by the unbearable disruptions, there has been a loss of trust between the

Party and the masses, between the officials and the masses, among the officials themselves, and also among the masses themselves.

By deceiving one another through false assumptions and misrepresentations there has been, in reality, a great lapse and delay in achieving the real goals. Now, signs of dissatisfaction are naturally emerging from all directions and are clear indications that the objectives have not been fulfilled.

To take the case of the situation in Tibet, it is regrettable that some Tibetan officials, who lack the wisdom and competence required for promoting basic human happiness and the short- and long-term welfare of their own people, indulge in flattering Chinese officials and collaborate with these Chinese officials who know nothing about Tibetans and work simply for their temporary fame, indulging in fabricating impressive reports. In reality, the Tibetan people have not only undergone immeasurable sufferings, but large numbers have also unnecessarily lost their lives. Besides, during the Cultural Revolution, there has been immense destruction of Tibet's ancient cultural heritage. All these regrettable events present a brief impression of the past.

Now, taking into account the experiences of the past mistakes, there is a new policy of Seeking Truth from Facts and a policy of modernisation. With regard to the Tibetan issue, I am pleased and applaud Comrade Hu Yaobang's efforts to make every possible attempt to right the wrongs by frankly admitting the past mistakes after his visit to Lhasa.

As you are aware, during the past 20 years, we Tibetans abroad, apart from trying to preserve our national identity and traditional values, have been educating our youth to enable them to decide their future through a knowledge of right conduct, justice, and democratic principles towards a better Tibetan community.

In brief, considering the fact that we are living in alien countries other than our own, we can be proud of our achievements in the history of the refugees in the world. On the political front, we have always pursued the path of truth and justice in our struggle for the legitimate rights of the Tibetan people. We have never indulged in distortions, exaggerations and criticism of the Chinese people. Neither have we harboured any ill will towards them. Above all, we have always held to our position of truth and justice without siding with any of the international political power blocks.

In early 1979, at your invitation, Gyalo Thondup visited China. Through him you had sent a message saying that we should keep in contact with each other. You had also invited us to send fact-finding delegations to Tibet. Thereafter, three fact-finding delegations were able to find out both the positive and negative aspects of the situation in Tibet. If the Tibetan people's identity is preserved and if they are genuinely happy, there is no reason to complain. However, in reality, over 90 percent of the Tibetans are suffering both mentally and physically, and are living in deep sorrow. These sad conditions have not been brought about by natural disasters, but by human actions. Therefore, genuine efforts must be made to resolve the problems in accordance with the existing realities in a reasonable way.

In order to do this, we must improve the relationship between China and Tibet as well as between Tibetans in and outside Tibet. With truth and equality as our foundation, we must try to develop friendship between Tibetans and Chinese through better understanding in the future. The time has come to apply our common wisdom in a spirit of tolerance and broadmindedness to achieve genuine happiness for the Tibetan people with a sense of urgency.

On my part, I remain committed to contribute my efforts for the welfare of all human beings, and in particular the poor and the weak, to the best of my ability without any distinction based on national boundaries. As the Tibetan people have great trust and hope in me, I would like to convey to you their wishes and aspirations for their immediate and future well-being.

I hope you will let me know your views on the foregoing points.

With the assurance of my highest
regard and esteem,
The Dalai Lama

### *Note Accompanying the March 23, 1981, Letter to Deng Xiaoping*

In recent times, in accordance with the contacts made by Beijing through Gyalo Thondup, three fact-finding delegations have already visited Tibet. The fourth one is scheduled to leave in April this year. Although Beijing had already agreed to the deputation of 50 teachers from India to different schools in Tibet for a period of two years and the opening of a liaison office in Lhasa to facilitate mutual contacts, recently Gyalo Thondup received the following message from Beijing through the Xinhua News Agency in Hong Kong:

- As regard the fourth fact-finding delegation, nothing has been confirmed so far. A response will be given later either through Hong Kong or the Chinese embassy in New Delhi.

- Although we have agreed in principle to the opening of a liaison office in Lhasa and the deputation of teachers, it would be better to defer the opening of the liaison office and instead more contact should be made through Hong Kong and the Chinese embassy in Delhi.

- The teachers having been brought up in India with all good facilities would find it difficult to live in Tibet where facilities are lacking at the moment. This could harm their morale. It is therefore suggested that the sending of teachers to Tibet be deferred. For the time being some teachers may be deputed to the nationalities schools inside China from where they could gradually be sent to Tibet. (Subsequently, a message received through the Chinese embassy in Delhi conveyed that the fourth delegation should be postponed for this year.)

The following is our response to the above matters:

- We agree to the postponement of the fourth delegation for this year, as well as the opening of the liaison office in Lhasa for the time being.

- On the matter of sending teachers to Tibet, since the teachers are already aware of the difficult conditions in the schools in Tibet, this will neither lower their morale nor come in the way of carrying out their tasks. Above all, the main reason for sending the teachers is to uplift the standard of education of the students living in difficult conditions. We hope you will reconsider this matter. The teachers will be concerned solely with educational matters and will not indulge in any political activities. There is, therefore, no need to worry on this point.

## LETTER TO DENG XIAOPING, SEPTEMBER 11, 1992

Dear Mr. Deng Xiaoping,

I am pleased that direct contact has once again been established between us. I hope that this will lead to an improvement of relations and the development of mutual understanding and trust.

I have been informed of the discussions Mr. Ding Guangen had with Gyalo Thondup on June 22, 1992, and the position of the Government of China concerning negotiations for a solution to the Tibetan question. I am disappointed with the hard and inflexible position conveyed by Mr. Ding Guangen, particularly the emphasis on pre-conditions for negotiations. However, I remain committed to the belief that our problems can be solved only through negotiations, held in an atmosphere of sincerity and openness, for the benefit of both the Tibetan and Chinese people. To make this possible, neither side should put up obstacles, and neither side should, therefore, state pre-conditions.

For meaningful negotiations to take place it is essential to have mutual trust. Therefore, in order to create trust I believe it is important for the leaders and people of China to know of the endeavours I have made so far. My three representatives carry with them a letter from me, accompanied by a detailed note of my views and my efforts through the years to promote negotiations in the best interests of the Tibetan and Chinese people. They will answer and discuss any questions and points you wish to raise. It is my hope that through these renewed discussions we will find a way that will lead us to negotiations.

On my part, I have put forward many ideas to solve our problem. I believe that it is now time for the Chinese government to make a genuinely meaningful proposal if you wish to see Tibet and China live together in peace. I, therefore, sincerely hope that you will respond in a spirit of openness and friendship.

Yours sincerely,
The Dalai Lama

## LETTER TO JIANG ZEMIN, SEPTEMBER 11, 1992

Dear Mr. Zemin,

I am pleased that direct contact has once again been established between us. I hope that this will lead to an improvement of relations and the development of mutual understanding and trust.

I have been informed of the discussions Mr. Ding Guangen had with Gyalo Thondup on June 22, 1992, and the position of the Government of China concerning negotiations for a solution to the Tibetan question. I am disappointed with the hard and inflexible position conveyed by Mr. Ding Guangen, particularly the emphasis on pre-conditions for negotiations.

However, I remain committed to the belief that our problems can be solved only through negotiations, held in an atmosphere of sincerity and openness, for the benefit of both the Tibetan and Chinese people. To make this possible, neither side should put up obstacles, and neither side should, therefore, state pre-conditions.

For meaningful negotiations to take place it is essential to have mutual trust. Therefore, in order to create trust, I believe it is important for the leaders and people of China to know of the endeavours I have made so far. My three representatives carry with them a letter from me, accompanied by a detailed note of my views and my efforts through the years to promote negotiations in the best interests of the Tibetan and Chinese people. They will answer and discuss any questions and points you wish to raise. It is my hope that through these renewed discussions we will find a way that will lead us to negotiations.

On my part, I have put forward many ideas to solve our problem. I believe that it is now time for the Chinese government to make a genuinely meaningful proposal if you wish to see Tibet and China live together in peace. I, therefore, sincerely hope that you will respond in a spirit of openness and friendship.

Yours sincerely,
The Dalai Lama

### *Note Accompanying the September 11, 1992, Letters to Deng Xiaoping and Jiang Zemin*

On June 22, 1992, Mr. Ding Guangen, head of the United Front Works Department of CCP Central Committee, met with Mr. Gyalo Thondup in Beijing and restated the assurance given by Mr. Deng Xiaoping to Mr. Gyalo Thondup in 1979 that the Chinese government was willing to discuss and resolve any issue with us except total independence. Mr. Ding Guangen also said that, in the Chinese government's view, "the Dalai Lama is continuing with independence activities," but the Chinese government was willing to immediately start negotiations as soon as I give up the independence of Tibet. This position, repeatedly stated in the past by the Chinese government, shows that the Chinese leadership still does not understand my ideas regarding the Tibetan-

Chinese relationship. Therefore, I take this opportunity to clarify my position through this note.

1. It is an established fact that Tibet and China existed as separate countries in the past. However, as a result of misrepresentations of Tibet's unique relations with the Mongol and the Manchu Emperors, disputes arose between Tibet and the Kuomintang and the present Chinese government. The fact that the Chinese government found it necessary to conclude a "17-Point Agreement" with the Tibetan government in 1951 clearly shows the Chinese government's acknowledgement of Tibet's unique position.

2. When I visited Beijing in 1954, I had the impression that most of the Communist party leaders I met there were honest, straightforward and open-minded. Chairman Mao Zedong, in particular, told me on several occasions that the Chinese were in Tibet only to help Tibet harness its natural resources and use them for the development of the country; General Zhang Jingwu and General Fan Ming were in Tibet to help me and the people of Tibet, and not to rule the Tibetan government and people, and that all Chinese officials in Tibet were there to help us and to be withdrawn when Tibet had progressed. Any Chinese official who did not act accordingly would be sent back to China. Chairman Mao went on to say that it had now been decided to establish a "Preparatory Committee for the Establishment of the Tibet Autonomous Region" instead of the earlier plan to put Tibet under the direct control of the Chinese government through a "Military-Political Commission."

   At my last meeting with Chairman Mao, before I left China, he gave me a long explanation about democracy. He said that I must provide leadership and advised me on how to keep in touch with the views of the people. He spoke in a gentle and compassionate manner which was moving and inspiring.

While in Beijing, I told Premier Zhou Enlai that we Tibetans were fully aware of our need to develop politically, socially and economically and that in fact I had already taken steps towards this.

On my way back to Tibet, I told General Zhang Guohua that I had gone to China with doubts and anxiety about the future of my people and country, but had now returned with great hope and optimism and a very positive impression of the Chinese leaders. My innate desire to serve my people, especially the poor and the weak, and the prospect of mutual cooperation and friendship between Tibet and China made me feel hopeful and optimistic about Tibet's future development. This was how I felt at that time about the Tibetan-Chinese relationship.

3. When the "Tibet Autonomous Region Preparatory Committee" was set up in Lhasa in 1956, there was no alternative but to work sincerely with it for the interest and benefit of both parties. However, by then the Chinese authorities had already started to use unthinkable brutal force to impose Communism on the Tibetan people of the Kham and Amdo areas, particularly in Lithang. This increased the resentment of the Tibetans against Chinese policies, leading to open resistance.

I could not believe that Chairman Mao would have approved of such repressive policy because of the promises he had made to me when I was in China. I, therefore, wrote three letters to him explaining the situation and seeking an end to the repression. Regrettably, there was no reply to my letters.

In late 1956, I visited India to attend Buddha Jayanti, the anniversary of the birth of Buddha. At that time, many Tibetans advised me not to return to Tibet, and to continue talks with China from India. I also felt that I should stay in India for the time being. While in India, I met Premier Zhou Enlai and told him how deeply saddened I was by the military repression inflicted upon Tibetans in Kham and Amdo in the name of "reforms." Premier Zhou Enlai said that he regarded these matters as mistakes committed by Chinese officials and that "reforms" in Tibet would be carried out only in accordance with the wishes of the Tibetan people, and that in fact the Chinese government had already decided to postpone the "reforms" in Tibet by six years. He then urged me to return to Tibet as soon as possible in order to prevent further outbreaks of unrest.

According to the Indian Prime Minister, Jawaharlal Nehru, Premier Zhou Enlai told him that the Chinese government "did not consider Tibet as a province of China. The people were different from the people of China proper. Therefore, they (the Chinese) considered Tibet as an autonomous region which could enjoy autonomy." Prime Minister Nehru told me that he had assurances from Premier Zhou Enlai that Tibet's autonomy would be respected and, therefore, advised me to make efforts to safeguard it and cooperate with China in bringing about reforms.

By then, the situation in Tibet had become extremely dangerous and desperate. Nevertheless, I decided to return to Tibet to give the Chinese government another opportunity to be able to implement their promises. On my return to Lhasa through Dromo, Gyangtse and Shigatse, I had many meetings with Tibetan and Chinese officials; I told them that the Chinese were not in Tibet to rule the Tibetans, that the Tibetans were not subjects of China, and that since the Chinese leaders had promised to establish Tibet as an autonomous region with full internal freedoms, we all had to work to make it succeed. I emphasised the point that the leaders of China had assured me that all Chinese personnel in Tibet were there to help us, and that if they behaved otherwise, they would be going against the order of their own government. I believe, I was once again doing my best to promote cooperation between Tibet and China.

4. However, because of the harsh military repression in the Kham and Amdo parts of eastern Tibet, thousands of young and old Tibetans,

unable to live under such circumstances, began to arrive in Lhasa as refugees. As a result of these Chinese actions the Tibetan people felt great anxiety and began to lose faith in the promises made by China. This led to greater resentment and a worsening of the situation. Nevertheless, I continued to counsel my people to seek a peaceful solution and to show restraint. At the risk of losing the trust of the Tibetan people I did my best to prevent a breakdown of the communications with the Chinese officials in Lhasa. But the situation continued to deteriorate and finally exploded in the tragic events of 1959 which forced me to leave Tibet.

Faced with such a desperate situation, I had no alternative but to appeal to the United Nations. The United Nations, in turn, passed three resolutions on Tibet in 1959, 1961 and 1965, wherein it called for the "cessation of practices which deprived Tibetan people of their fundamental human rights and freedoms including their right to self-determination" and asked member States to make all possible efforts towards achieving that purpose.

The Chinese government did not respect the United Nations resolutions. In the meantime, the Cultural Revolution started and there was absolutely no opportunity for solving the Tibetan-Chinese problems. It was, in fact, not even possible to identify a leader with whom we could talk.

5. In spite of my unfulfilled hopes and disappointments in dealing with the Chinese government, and since Tibet and China will always remain as neighbours, I am convinced that we must strive to find a way to coexist in peace and help each other. This, I believe, is possible and worthy of our efforts. With this conviction I said in my statement to the Tibetan people on March 10, 1971: "In spite of the fact that we Tibetans have to oppose Communist China, I can never bring myself to hate her people. Hatred is not a sign of strength, but of weakness. When Lord Buddha said that hatred cannot be overcome by hatred, he was not only being spiritual. But

his words reflect the practical reality of life. Whatever one achieves through hatred will not last long. On the other hand, hatred will only generate more problems. And for the Tibetan people who are faced with such a tragic situation, hatred will only bring additional depression. Moreover, how can we hate a people who do not know what they are doing? How can we hate millions of Chinese, who have no power and are helplessly led by their leaders? We cannot even hate the Chinese leaders for they have suffered tremendously for their nation and the cause which they believe to be right. I do not believe in hatred, but I do believe, as I have always done, that one day truth and justice will triumph."

In my March 10 statement of 1973, referring to the Chinese claim of Tibetans being made the "masters of the country" after being "liberated from the three big feudal lords" and enjoying "unprecedented progress and happiness," I stated: "The aim of the struggle of the Tibetans outside Tibet is the attainment of the happiness of the Tibetan people. If the Tibetans in Tibet are truly happy under Chinese rule then there is no reason for us here in exile to argue otherwise."

Again in my 1979 March 10 statement, I welcomed Mr. Deng Xiaoping's statement "to seek truth from facts," to give the Chinese people their long-cherished rights, and of the need to acknowledge one's own mistakes and shortcomings. While commending these signs of honesty, progress and openness, I said: "The present Chinese leaders should give up the past dogmatic narrow-mindedness and fear of losing face and recognise the present world situation. They should accept their mistakes, the realities, and the right of all peoples of the human race to equality and happiness. Acceptance of this should not be merely on paper; it should be put into practice. If these are accepted and strictly followed, all problems can be solved with honesty and justice." With this conviction I renewed my efforts to promote reconciliation and friendship between China and Tibet.

6. In 1979, Mr. Deng Xiaoping invited Mr. Gyalo Thondup to Beijing and told him that apart from the question of total independence all other issues could be discussed and all problems can be resolved. Mr. Deng further told Mr. Thondup that we must keep in contact with each other and that we could send fact-finding delegations to Tibet. This naturally gave us great hopes of resolving our problem peacefully and we started sending delegations to Tibet.

   On March 23, 1981, I sent a letter to Mr. Deng Xiaoping, in which I said, "The three fact-finding delegations have been able to find out both the positive and negative aspects of the situation in Tibet. If the Tibetan people's identity is preserved and if they are genuinely happy, there is no reason to complain. However, in reality over 90 percent of the Tibetans are suffering both mentally and physically, and are living in deep sorrow. These sad conditions had not been brought about by natural disasters, but by human actions. Therefore, genuine efforts must be made to solve the problem in accordance with the existing realities in a reasonable way.

   "In order to do this, we must improve the relationship between China and Tibet as well as between Tibetans in and outside Tibet. With truth and equality as our foundation, we must try to develop friendship between Tibetans and Chinese through better understanding in the future. The time has come to apply our common wisdom in a spirit of tolerance and broadmindedness to achieve genuine happiness for the Tibetan people with a sense of urgency.

   "On my part, I remain committed to contribute my efforts to the welfare of all human beings, and in particular the poor and the weak, to the best of my ability without making any distinction based on national boundaries. . .

   "I hope you will let me know your views on the foregoing points."

   There was no reply to my letter. Instead, on July 28, 1981, General Secretary Hu Yaobang gave Mr. Gyalo Thondup a document, entitled "Five Point Policy Towards the Dalai Lama."

This was a surprise and a great disappointment. The reason for our consistent efforts to deal with the Chinese government is to achieve lasting and genuine happiness for six million Tibetans who must live as neighbours of China from generation to generation. However, the Chinese leadership chose to ignore this and, instead, attempted to reduce the whole issue to that of my personal status and the conditions for my return without any willingness to address the real underlying issues.

Nevertheless, I continued to place hope in Mr. Deng Xiaoping's statement "seeking truth from facts" and his policy of liberalisation. Therefore, I sent several delegations to Tibet and China and wherever there was an opportunity we explained our views to promote understanding through discussion and dialogue. As initially suggested by Mr. Deng Xiaoping I agreed to send Tibetan teachers from India to improve the education of Tibetans in Tibet. But for one reason or the other the Chinese government did not accept this.

These contacts resulted in four fact-finding delegations to Tibet, two delegations to Beijing, and the start of family visitations between the Tibetans in Tibet and in exile. However, these steps did not lead to any substantial progress in resolving the problems between us owing to the rigidity of the Chinese leaders' positions which, I believe, failed to reflect Mr. Deng Xiaoping's policies.

7. Once again, I did not give up hope. This was reflected in my annual March 10 statements to the Tibetan people in 1981, 1983, 1984 and 1985, wherein I said the following:

"... past history has disappeared in the past. What is more relevant is that in the future there actually must be real peace and happiness through developing friendly and meaningful relations between China and Tibet. For this to be realised, it is important for both sides to work hard to have tolerant understanding and be open-minded" (1981).

"The right to express one's ideas and to make every effort to implement them enables people everywhere to become creative and progressive. This engenders human society to make rapid progress and experience genuine harmony. . . . The deprivation of freedom to express one's views, either by force or by other means, is absolutely anachronistic and a brutal form of oppression. . . . The people of the world will not only oppose it, but will condemn it. Hence, the six million Tibetan people must have the right to preserve and enhance their cultural identity and religious freedom, the right to determine their own destiny and manage their own affairs, and find fulfillment of their free self-expression, without interference from any quarters. This is reasonable and just" (1983).

"Irrespective of varying degrees of development and economic disparities, continents, nations, communities, families, in fact, all individuals are dependent on one another for their existence and well-beings. Every human being wishes for happiness and does not want suffering. By clearly realising this, we must develop mutual compassion, love, and a fundamental sense of justice. In such an atmosphere there is hope that problems between nations and problems within families can be gradually overcome and that people can live in peace and harmony. Instead, if people adopt an attitude of selfishness, domination and jealousy, the world at large, as well as individuals, will never enjoy peace and harmony. Therefore, I believe that human relations based on mutual compassion and love is fundamentally important to human happiness" (1984).

". . . in order to achieve genuine happiness in any human society, freedom of thought is extremely important. This freedom of thought can only be achieved from mutual trust, mutual understanding and the absence of fear. . . . In the case of Tibet and China too, unless we can remove the state of mutual fear and mistrust, unless we can develop a genuine sense of friendship and goodwill the problems that we face today will continue to exist.

"It is important for both of us to learn about one another. . . .

It is now for the Chinese to act according to the enlightened ideals and principles of the modern times; to come forward with an open mind and make a serious attempt to know and understand the Tibetan people's viewpoint and their true feelings and aspirations. . . . It is wrong to react with suspicion or offence to the opinions that are contrary to one's own way of thinking. It is essential that differences of opinion be examined and discussed openly. When differing viewpoints are frankly stated and sensibly discussed on an equal footing, the decisions or agreements reached as a result will be genuine and beneficial to all concerned. But so long as there is a contradiction between thought and action, there can never be genuine and meaningful agreements.

"So, at this time, I feel the most important thing for us is to keep in close contact, to express our views frankly and to make sincere efforts to understand each other. And, through eventual improvement in human relationship, I am confident that our problems can be solved to our mutual satisfaction" (1985).

In these and other ways I expressed my views clearly. But, there was no reciprocity to my conciliatory approaches.

8. Since all the exchanges between Tibetans and Chinese yielded no results, I felt compelled to make public my views on the steps necessary for an agreeable solution to the fundamental issues. On September 21, 1987, I announced a Five Point Peace Plan in the United States of America. In its introduction, I said that in the hope of real reconciliation and a lasting solution to the problem, it was my desire to take the first step with this initiative. This plan, I hoped, would in the future contribute to the friendship and cooperation among all the neighbouring countries including the Chinese people for their good and benefit. The basic elements were:

   i. Transformation of the whole of Tibet into a zone of ahimsa (peace and nonviolence);

ii. Abandonment of China's population transfer policy which threatens the very existence of the Tibetans as a people;
iii. Respect for the Tibetan people's fundamental human rights and democratic freedoms;
iv. Restoration and protection of Tibet's natural environment and the abandonment of China's use of Tibet for the production of nuclear weapons and dumping of nuclear waste;
v. Commencement of earnest negotiations on the future status of Tibet and relations between the Tibetan and the Chinese peoples.

As a response to this initiative, Mr. Yan Mingfu met Mr. Gyalo Thondup on October 17, 1987, and delivered a message containing five points criticising me for my above peace initiative and accusing me of having instigated the demonstrations in Lhasa of September 27, 1987, and of having worked against the interests of Tibetan people.

This response, far from giving a serious thought to my sincere proposal for reconciliation, was disappointing and demeaning.

Despite this, I tried once again to clarify our views in a detailed 14-point response on December 17, 1987.

9. On June 15, 1988, at the European Parliament in Strasbourg, I once again elaborated on the Five Point Peace Plan. I proposed as a framework for negotiations to secure the basic rights of the Tibetan people, China could remain responsible for Tibet's foreign policy and maintain a restricted number of military installations in Tibet for defence until a regional peace conference is convened and Tibet is transformed into a neutral peace sanctuary. I was criticised by many Tibetans for this proposal. My idea was to make it possible for China and Tibet to stay together in lasting friendship and to secure the right for Tibetans to govern their own country. I sincerely believe that in the future a demilitarised Tibet as a zone

of ahimsa will contribute to harmony and peace not only between Tibetans and Chinese, but to all the neighbouring countries and the entire region.

10. On September 23, 1988, the Chinese government issued a statement that China was willing to begin negotiations with us. The announcement stated that the date and venue for the negotiations would be left to the Dalai Lama. We welcomed this announcement from Beijing and responded on October 25, 1988, proposing January 1989 as the time and Geneva, an internationally recognized neutral venue, as our choices. We announced that we had a negotiating team ready and named the members of the team.

    The Chinese government responded on November 18, 1988, rejecting Geneva and expressing preference for Beijing or else Hong Kong as the venue. They further stated that my negotiating team could not include "a foreigner" and consist only of "younger people," and that it should have older people, including Mr. Gyalo Thondup. We explained that the foreigner was only a legal advisor and not an actual member of the negotiating team and that Mr. Gyalo Thondup would also be included as an advisor to the team.

    With a flexible and open attitude we accommodated the Chinese government's requests and agreed to send representatives to Hong Kong to hold preliminary meetings with representatives of the Chinese government. Unfortunately, when both sides had finally agreed on Hong Kong as the site for preliminary discussions the Chinese government refused to communicate any further and failed to live up to their own suggestion.

11. Although I championed this proposal for over two years there was no evidence of consideration or even an acknowledgement from the Chinese government.

    Therefore, in my March 10 statement in 1991, I was compelled to state that unless the Chinese government responded in the near future I would consider myself free from any obligation to abide by the proposal I made in France.

Since there appears to be no benefit from the many solutions I had advocated concerning Tibet and China, I had to find a new way. Therefore, in a speech at Yale University on October 9, 1991, I said:

". . . I am considering the possibility of a visit to Tibet as early as possible. I have in mind two purposes for such a visit.

"First, I want to ascertain the situation in Tibet myself on the spot and communicate directly with my people. By doing so, I also hope to help the Chinese leadership to understand the true feelings of Tibetans. It would be important, therefore, for senior Chinese leaders to accompany me on such a visit, and that outside observers, including the press, be present to see and report their findings.

"Second, I wish to advise and persuade my people not to abandon nonviolence as the appropriate form of struggle. My ability to talk to my people can be a key factor in bringing about a peaceful solution. My visit could be a new opportunity to promote understanding and create a basis for a negotiated solution."

Unfortunately this overture was immediately opposed by the Chinese government. At that time, I was asked on many occasions by the press whether I was renewing the call for Tibetan independence since I had declared that the Strasbourg proposal was no longer valid. To these questions, I stated that I did not want to comment.

12. The Chinese government has, with great doubt and suspicion, described our struggle as a movement to restore the "old society" and that it was not in the interest of the Tibetan people but for the personal status and interest of the Dalai Lama. Since my youth, I was aware of the many faults of the existing system in Tibet and wanted to improve it. At that time I started the process of reform in Tibet. Soon after our flight to India we introduced democracy in our exile community, step by step. I repeatedly urged my people to follow this path. As a result, our exiled community now implements a sys-

tem in full accordance with universal democratic principles. It is impossible for Tibet to ever revert to the old system of government. Whether my efforts for the Tibetan cause are as charged by the Chinese for my personal position and benefit or not is clear from my repeated statements that in a future Tibet, I will not assume any governmental responsibility or hold any political position. Furthermore, this is reflected clearly in the Charter which governs the Tibetan Administration in Exile and in the "Guidelines for Future Tibet's Polity and the Basic Features of Its Constitution," which I announced on February 26, 1992.

In the conclusion of these guidelines, I suggested that "Tibet shall not be influenced or swayed by the policies and ideologies of other countries but remain a neutral state in the true sense of the term. It shall maintain a harmonious relationship with its neighbours on equal terms and for mutual benefits. It shall maintain a cordial and fraternal relationship with all nations, without any sense of hostility and enmity."

Similarly, in my statement of March 10, 1992, I stated, "When a genuinely cordial relationship is established between the Tibetans and the Chinese, it will enable us not only to resolve the disputes between our two nations in this century, but will also enable the Tibetans to make a significant contribution through our rich cultural tradition for mental peace among the millions of young Chinese."

My endeavours to establish a personal relationship with Chinese leaders include my offer, presented through your Embassy in New Delhi in the latter part of 1980, for a meeting with General Secretary Hu Yaobang during one of his visits abroad at any convenient place. Again in December 1991, when Premier Li Peng visited New Delhi, I proposed to meet him there. These overtures were to no avail.

13. An impartial review of the above points will clearly show that my ideas and successive efforts have consistently sought solutions that will allow Tibet and China to live together in peace. In the light of these facts it

is difficult to understand the purpose of the Chinese government's position that Mr. Deng Xiaoping's statement on Tibet of 1979 still stands and that as soon as "the Dalai Lama gives up his splittist activities," negotiations could start. This position has been repeated over and over again with no specific responses to my many initiatives.

If China wants Tibet to stay with China, then China must create the necessary conditions for this. The time has come now for the Chinese to show the way for Tibet and China to live together in friendship. A detailed step-by-step outline regarding Tibet's basic status should be spelt out. If such a clear outline is given, regardless of the possibility of an agreement or not, we Tibetans can then make a decision whether to live with China or not. If we Tibetans obtain our basic rights to our satisfaction, then we are not incapable of seeing the possible advantages of living with the Chinese.

I trust in the farsightedness and wisdom of China's leaders and hope that they will take into consideration the current global political changes and the need to resolve the Tibetan problem peacefully, promoting genuine lasting friendship between our two neighbouring peoples.

## LETTER OF CONDOLENCE TO JIANG ZEMIN, 1997

Your Excellency,

On the passing away of Mr. Deng Xiaoping, I wish to express my condolence to members of his family and to the people and government of the People's Republic of China. The demise of Mr. Deng Xiaoping is a great loss for China.

I met Mr. Deng Xiaoping when I visited China in 1954. He was a revolutionary and a great leader of China, with an exceptional courage, perseverance, capability and leadership ability.

In the case of Tibet in 1979, Mr. Deng Xiaoping invited my elder brother Mr. Gyalo Thondup to Beijing and stated to him that apart from the question of total independence of Tibet, all other issues could be discussed and resolved. Encouraged by the overall changes in China and the new pragmatic attitude towards the issue of Tibet, I have, since then, consistently and sincerely made attempts to engage the Chinese government in earnest negotiations over the future of Tibet. Sadly, the Chinese government has not responded positively to my proposals and initiatives over the past 18 years for a negotiated resolution of our problem within the framework stated by Mr. Deng Xiaoping.

It is very regrettable that serious negotiations on the issue of Tibet could not take place during Mr. Deng's lifetime. However, I firmly believe that the absence of Mr. Deng provides new opportunities and challenges for both Tibetans and the Chinese. I very much hope that under your leadership the Government of China will realise the wisdom of resolving the issue of Tibet through negotiations in a spirit of reconciliation and compromise. For my part, I remain committed to the belief that our problem can be solved only through negotiations, held in an atmosphere of sincerity and openness.

With prayers and good wishes,
Yours sincerely,
The Dalai Lama

## LETTER TO JIANG ZEMIN, 1997*

Your Excellency,

As you and other members of the Chinese leadership prepare for the crucial forthcoming Party Congress, I would like to make yet another effort to press the need for an early solution to the issue of Tibet.

---

* This letter was hand delivered by US Senator Dianne Feinstein and her husband, Richard Blum, when they met with President Jiang Zemin in Beijing on September 8, 1997.

Since nearly five decades, the Tibetan problem has resulted in much suffering to the Tibetan people, physically and emotionally. Moreover, the inability to resolve the Tibetan problem has been tarnishing increasingly the international image and reputation of the great nation of China.

I have great personal respect and admiration for China and sincerely wish it to be a leading member of the comity of nations. The earlier we can find a mutually acceptable solution to the Tibetan issue, the better it will be for Tibetans and the Chinese peoples. I continue to believe that, given earnest efforts from both sides, we can find such a solution. On my part, I have taken every opportunity to clarify some of the misgivings that the Chinese leaders seem to have concerning my position.

It is my belief that it is more important to look forward to the future than dwell in the past. The important thing is the maximum benefit for the concerned people. With this conviction, I have been proposing a solution to the Tibet issue that does not require the separation of Tibet from China. If you examine my proposal, as I had outlined it in 1988, you will find that it is consistent with the policy China is adopting on issues like Hong Kong and Taiwan. My proposal is no different from this "one country, two systems" political concept and is clearly within the framework formulated by Mr. Deng Xiaoping on the issue of Tibet.

In past recent years, lack of direct contact between our two sides has increased misunderstanding and distrust, resulting in a deepened sense of alienation from each other. This is very unfortunate and does neither serve the interest of the Tibetans nor that of your Government. For centuries Tibetans and Chinese have lived side by side. In future, too, we will continue to do so. Despite the growing international support for Tibet, ultimately it is for Tibetans and Chinese to find a mutually acceptable solution.

It is, therefore, the time for all of us to act with courage, vision and wisdom. I remain willing to dedicate my remaining life to the service of reconciliation, mutual respect and friendship between the Tibetan and

Chinese peoples. I would like to assure you that you will find in me a committed partner in searching for a mutually acceptable and beneficial resolution of the Tibetan problem.

I would, therefore, like to propose meetings at the earliest possible time, between my representatives and officials of the Chinese leadership, which will provide the opportunity for us to understand each other's thinking. There is a need to initiate new openings, conducive to building confidence and trust. It is my hope that the Government under your leadership will act wisely and pragmatically and give us a favourable response at an early date.

With my prayers and best wishes,
Yours sincerely,
The Dalai Lama

## APPENDIX D

# Memorandum on Genuine Autonomy for the Tibetan People

### I. INTRODUCTION

Since the renewal of direct contact with the Central Government of the People's Republic of China (PRC) in 2002, extensive discussions have been held between the envoys of His Holiness the 14th Dalai Lama and representatives of the Central Government. In these discussions we have put forth clearly the aspirations of Tibetans. The essence of the Middle Way Approach is to secure genuine autonomy for the Tibetan people within the scope of the Constitution of the PRC. This is of mutual benefit and based on the long-term interest of both the Tibetan and Chinese peoples. We remain firmly committed not to seek separation or independence. We are seeking a solution to the Tibetan problem through genuine autonomy, which is compatible with the principles on autonomy in the Constitution of the People's Republic of China (PRC). The protection and development of the unique Tibetan identity in all its aspects serves the larger interest of humanity in general and those of the Tibetan and Chinese people in particular.

During the seventh round of talks in Beijing on 1 and 2 July 2008, the Vice Chairman of the Chinese People's Political Consultative Conference and the Minister of the Central United Front Work Department, Mr. Du Qinglin, explicitly invited suggestions from His Holiness the Dalai Lama for the stability and development of Tibet. The Executive Vice Minister of the Central United Front Work Department, Mr. Zhu Weiqun, further said they would like to hear our views on the degree or form of autonomy we are seeking as well as on all aspects of regional autonomy within the scope of the Constitution of the PRC. Accordingly, this memorandum puts forth our position on genuine autonomy and how the specific needs of the Tibetan nationality for autonomy and self-government can be met through application of the principles on autonomy of the Constitution of the People's Republic of China, as we understand them. On this basis, His Holiness the Dalai Lama is confident that the basic needs of the Tibetan nationality can be met through genuine autonomy within the PRC. The PRC is a multi-national state, and as in many other parts of the world, it seeks to resolve the nationality question through autonomy and the self-government of the minority nationalities. The Constitution of the PRC contains fundamental principles on autonomy and self-government whose objectives are compatible with the needs and aspirations of the Tibetans. Regional national autonomy is aimed at opposing both the oppression and the separation of nationalities by rejecting both Han Chauvinism and local nationalism. It is intended to ensure the protection of the culture and the identity of minority nationalities by empowering them to become masters of their own affairs. To a very considerable extent Tibetan needs can be met within the constitutional principles on autonomy, as we understand them. On several points, the Constitution gives significant discretionary powers to state organs in the decision-making and on the operation of the system of autonomy. These discretionary powers can be exercised to facilitate genuine autonomy for Tibetans in ways that would respond to the uniqueness of the Tibetan situation. In implementing these principles, legislation relevant to autonomy may consequently need to be reviewed or amended to respond to the specific characteristics and needs of the Tibetan nationality. Given goodwill on both sides, outstanding problems can be resolved within the constitutional principles on autonomy. In this way national unity and stability and harmonious relations between the Tibetan and other nationalities will be established.

## II. RESPECT FOR THE INTEGRITY OF THE TIBETAN NATIONALITY

Tibetans belong to one minority nationality regardless of the current administrative division. The integrity of the Tibetan nationality must be respected. That is the spirit, the intent and the principle underlying the constitutional concept of national regional autonomy as well as the principle of equality of nationalities. There is no dispute about the fact that Tibetans share the same language, culture, spiritual tradition, core values and customs, that they belong to the same ethnic group and that they have a strong sense of common identity. Tibetans share a common history and despite periods of political or administrative divisions, Tibetans continuously remained united by their religion, culture, education, language, way of life and by their unique high-plateau environment. The Tibetan nationality lives in one contiguous area on the Tibetan plateau, which they have inhabited for millennia and to which they are therefore indigenous. For purposes of the constitutional principles of national regional autonomy Tibetans in the PRC in fact live as a single nationality all over the Tibetan plateau. On account of the above reasons, the PRC has recognised the Tibetan nationality as one of the 55 minority nationalities.

## III. TIBETAN ASPIRATIONS

Tibetans have a rich and distinct history, culture and spiritual tradition, all of which form valuable parts of the heritage of humanity. Not only do Tibetans wish to preserve their own heritage, which they cherish, but equally they wish to further develop their culture and spiritual life and knowledge in ways that are particularly suited to the needs and conditions of humanity in the 21st century.

As a part of the multi-national state of the PRC, Tibetans can benefit greatly from the rapid economic and scientific development the country is experiencing. While wanting to actively participate and contribute to this development, we want to ensure that this happens without the people losing their Tibetan identity, culture and core values and without putting the distinct and fragile environment of the Tibetan plateau, to which Tibetans are indigenous, at risk.

The uniqueness of the Tibetan situation has consistently been recognised within the PRC and has been reflected in the terms of the "17-Point Agreement" and in statements and policies of successive leaders of the PRC since then, and should remain the basis for defining the scope and structure of the specific autonomy to be exercised by the Tibetan nationality within the PRC. The Constitution reflects a fundamental principle of flexibility to accommodate special situations, including the special characteristics and needs of minority nationalities.

His Holiness the Dalai Lama's commitment to seek a solution for the Tibetan people within the PRC is clear and unambiguous. This position is in full compliance and agreement with paramount leader Deng Xiaoping's statement in which he emphasised that except for independence all other issues could be resolved through dialogue. Whereas, we are committed, therefore, to fully respect the territorial integrity of the PRC, we expect the Central Government to recognise and fully respect the integrity of the Tibetan nationality and its right to exercise genuine autonomy within the PRC. We believe that this is the basis for resolving the differences between us and promoting unity, stability and harmony among nationalities.

For Tibetans to advance as a distinct nationality within the PRC, they need to continue to progress and develop economically, socially and politically in ways that correspond to the development of the PRC and the world as a whole while respecting and nurturing the Tibetan characteristics of such development. For this to happen, it is imperative that the right of Tibetans to govern themselves be recognised and implemented throughout the region where they live in compact communities in the PRC, in accordance with the Tibetan nationality's own needs, priorities and characteristics.

The Tibetan people's culture and identity can only be preserved and promoted by the Tibetans themselves and not by any others. Therefore, Tibetans should be capable of self-help, self-development and self-government, and an optimal balance needs to be found between this and the necessary and welcome guidance and assistance for Tibet from the Central Government and other provinces and regions of the PRC.

## IV. BASIC NEEDS OF TIBETANS: SUBJECT MATTERS OF SELF-GOVERNMENT

### 1) Language

Language is the most important attribute of the Tibetan people's identity. Tibetan is the primary means of communication, the language in which their literature, their spiritual texts and historical as well as scientific works are written. The Tibetan language is not only at the same high level as that of Sanskrit in terms of grammar, but is also the only one that has the capability of translating from Sanskrit without an iota of error. Therefore, Tibetan language has not only the richest and best-translated literatures, many scholars even contend that it has also the richest and largest number of literary compositions.

The Constitution of the PRC, in Article 4, guarantees the freedom of all nationalities "to use and develop their own spoken and written languages . . ."

In order for Tibetans to use and develop their own language, Tibetan must be respected as the main spoken and written language. Similarly, the principal language of the Tibetan autonomous areas needs to be Tibetan.

This principle is broadly recognised in the Constitution in Article 121, which states, "the organs of self-government of the national autonomous areas employ the spoken and written language or language in common use in the locality." Article 10 of the Law on Regional National Autonomy (LRNA) provides that these organs "shall guarantee the freedom of the nationalities in these areas to use and develop their own spoken and written languages. . . ."

Consistent with the principle of recognition of Tibetan as the main language in Tibetan areas, the LRNA (Article 36) also allows the autonomous government authorities to decide on "the language used in instruction and enrollment procedures" with regard to education. This implies recognition of the principle that the principal medium of education be Tibetan.

### 2) Culture

The concept of national regional autonomy is primarily for the purpose of preservation of the culture of minority nationalities. Consequently, the Constitution of PRC contains references to cultural preservation in Articles 22, 47 and 119 and also in Article 38 of the LRNA. To Tibetans, Tibetan culture is closely connected to our religion, tradition, language and identity, which are facing threats at various levels. Since Tibetans live within the multi-national state of the PRC, this distinct Tibetan cultural heritage needs protection through appropriate constitutional provisions.

### 3) Religion

Religion is fundamental to Tibetans and Buddhism is closely linked to their identity. We recognise the importance of separation of church and state, but this should not affect the freedom and practice of believers. It is impossible for Tibetans to imagine personal or community freedom without the freedom of belief, conscience and religion. The Constitution recognises the importance of religion and protects the right to profess it. Article 36 guarantees all citizens the right to the freedom of religious belief. No one can compel another to believe in or not to believe in any religion. Discrimination on the basis of religion is forbidden.

An interpretation of the constitutional principle in light of international standard would also cover the freedom of the manner of belief or worship. The freedom covers the right of monasteries to be organised and run according to Buddhist monastic tradition, to engage in teachings and studies, and to enroll any number of monks and nuns or age group in accordance with these rules. The normal practice to hold public teachings and the empowerment of large gatherings is covered by this freedom and the state should not interfere in religious practices and traditions, such as the relationship between a teacher and his disciple, management of monastic institutions, and the recognition of reincarnations.

### 4) Education

The desire of Tibetans to develop and administer their own education system in cooperation and in coordination with the central government's ministry of education is supported by the principles contained in the Constitution with regard to education. So is the aspiration to engage in and contribute to the development of science and technology. We note the increasing recognition in international scientific development of the contribution which Buddhist psychology, metaphysics, cosmology and the understanding of the mind is making to modern science.

Whereas, under Article 19 of the Constitution the state takes on the overall responsibility to provide education for its citizens, Article 119 recognises the principle that "[T]he organs of self-government of the national autonomous areas independently administer educational . . . affairs in their respective areas . . ." This principle is also reflected in Article 36 of the LRNA.

Since the degree of autonomy in decision-making is unclear, the point to be emphasised is that the Tibetan need to exercise genuine autonomy with regard to its own nationality's education and this is supported by the principles of the Constitution on autonomy.

As for the aspiration to engage in and contribute to the development of scientific knowledge and technology, the Constitution (Article 119) and the LRNA (Article 39) clearly recognise the right of autonomous areas to develop scientific knowledge and technology.

### 5) Environment Protection

Tibet is the prime source of Asia's great rivers. It also has the earth's loftiest mountains as well as the world's most extensive and highest plateau, rich in mineral resources, ancient forests, and many deep valleys untouched by human disturbances.

This environmental protection practice was enhanced by the Tibetan people's traditional respect for all forms of life, which prohibits the harming of all sentient beings, whether human or animal. Tibet used to be an unspoiled wilderness sanctuary in a unique natural environment.

Today, Tibet's traditional environment is suffering irreparable damage. The effects of this are especially notable on the grasslands, the croplands, the forests, the water resources and the wildlife.

In view of this, according to Articles 45 and 66 of the LNRA, the Tibetan people should be given the right over the environment and allow them to follow their traditional conservation practices.

## 6) Utilisation of Natural Resources

With respect to the protection and management of the natural environment and the utilisation of natural resources the Constitution and the LRNA only acknowledge a limited role for the organs of self-government of the autonomous areas (see LRNA Articles 27, 28, 45, 66, and Article 118 of the Constitution, which pledges that the state "shall give due consideration to the interests of [the national autonomous areas]"). The LRNA recognises the importance for the autonomous areas to protect and develop forests and grasslands (Article 27) and to "give priority to the rational exploitation and utilization of the natural resources that the local authorities are entitled to develop," but only within the limits of state plans and legal stipulations. In fact, the central role of the State in these matters is reflected in the Constitution (Article 9).

The principles of autonomy enunciated in the Constitution cannot, in our view, truly lead to Tibetans becoming masters of their own destiny if they are not sufficiently involved in decision-making on utilisation of natural resources such as mineral resources, waters, forests, mountains, grasslands, etc.

The ownership of land is the foundation on which the development of natural resources, taxes and revenues of an economy are based. Therefore, it is essential that only the nationality of the autonomous region shall have the legal authority to transfer or lease land, except land owned by the state. In the same manner, the autonomous region must have the independent authority to formulate and implement developmental plans concurrent to the state plans.

## 7) Economic Development and Trade

Economic development in Tibet is welcome and much needed. The Tibetan people remain one of the most economically backward regions within the PRC.

The Constitution recognises the principle that the autonomous authorities have an important role to play in the economic development of their areas in view of local characteristics and needs (Article 118 of the Constitution, also reflected in LRNA Article 25). The Constitution also recognises the principle of autonomy in the administration and management of finances (Article 117, and LRNA Article 32). At the same time, the Constitution also recognises the importance of providing State funding and assistance to the autonomous areas to accelerate development (Article 122, LRNA Article 22).

Similarly, Article 31 of the LRNA recognises the competence of autonomous areas, especially those such as Tibet, adjoining foreign countries, to conduct border trade as well as trade with foreign countries. The recognition of these principles is important to the Tibetan nationality given the region's proximity to foreign countries with which the people have cultural, religious, ethnic and economic affinities.

The assistance rendered by the Central Government and the provinces has temporary benefits, but in the long run if the Tibetan people are not self-reliant and become dependent on others it has greater harm. Therefore, an important objective of autonomy is to make the Tibetan people economically self-reliant.

### 8) Public Health

The Constitution enunciates the responsibility of the State to provide health and medical services (Article 21). Article 119 recognises that this is an area of responsibility of the autonomous areas. The LRNA (Article 40) also recognises the right of organs of self-government of the autonomous areas to "make independent decisions on plans for developing local medical and health services and for advancing both modern and the traditional medicine of the nationalities."

The existing health system fails to adequately cover the needs of the rural Tibetan population. According to the principles of the above-mentioned laws, the regional autonomous organs need to have the competencies and resources to cover the health need of the entire Tibetan population. They also need the competencies to promote the traditional Tibetan medical and astro system strictly according to traditional practice.

### 9) Public Security

In matters of public security it is important that the majority of security personnel consists of members of the local nationality who understand and respect local customs and traditions.

What is lacking in Tibetan areas is absence of decision-making authority in the hands of local Tibetan officials.

An important aspect of autonomy and self-government is the responsibility for the internal public order and security of the autonomous areas. The Constitution (Article 120) and LRNA (Article 24) recognise the importance of local involvement and authorise autonomous areas to organise their security within "the military system of the State and practical needs and with the approval of the State Council."

### 10) Regulation on Population Migration

The fundamental objective of national regional autonomy and self-government is the preservation of the identity, culture, language and so forth of the minority nationality and to ensure that it is the master of its own affairs. When applied to a particular territory in which the minority nationality lives in a concentrated community or communities, the very principle and purpose of national regional autonomy is disregarded if large-scale migration and settlement of the majority Han nationality and other nationalities is encouraged and allowed. Major demographic changes that result from such migration will have the effect of assimilating rather than integrating the Tibetan nationality into the Han nationality and gradually extinguishing the distinct culture and identity of the Tibetan nationality. Also, the influx of large numbers of Han and other nationalities into Tibetan areas will fundamentally change the conditions necessary for the exercise of regional autonomy since the constitutional criteria for the exercise of autonomy, namely that the minority nationality "live in compact communities" in a particular territory is changed and undermined by the population movements and transfers. If such migrations and settlements continue uncontrolled, Tibetans will no longer live in a compact community or communities and will consequently no longer be entitled, under the Constitution, to national regional autonomy. This would effectively violate the very principles of the Constitution in its approach to the nationalities issue.

There is precedent in the PRC for restriction on the movement or residence of citizens. There is only a very limited recognition of the right of autonomous areas to work out measures to control "the transient population" in those areas. To us it would be vital that the autonomous organs of self-government have the authority to regulate the residence, settlement and employment or economic activities of persons who wish to move to Tibetan areas from other parts of the PRC in order to ensure respect for and the realisation of the objectives of the principle of autonomy.

It is not our intention to expel the non-Tibetans who have permanently settled in Tibet and have lived there and grown up there for a considerable time. Our concern is the induced massive movement of primarily Han but also some other nationalities into many areas of Tibet, upsetting existing communities, marginalising the Tibetan population there and threatening the fragile natural environment.

### 11) Cultural, Educational and Religious Exchanges with Other Countries

Besides the importance of exchanges and cooperation between the Tibetan nationality and other nationalities, provinces, and regions of the PRC in the subject matters of autonomy, such as culture, art, education, science, public health, sports, religion, environment, economy and so forth, the power of autonomous areas to conduct such exchanges with foreign countries in these areas is also recognised in the LRNA (Article 42).

## V. APPLICATION OF A SINGLE ADMINISTRATION FOR THE TIBETAN NATIONALITY IN THE PRC

In order for the Tibetan nationality to develop and flourish with its distinct identity, culture and spiritual tradition through the exercise of self-government on the above-mentioned basic Tibetan needs, the entire community, comprising all the areas currently designated by the PRC as Tibetan autonomous areas, should be under one single administrative entity. The current administrative divisions, by which Tibetan communities are ruled and administered under different provinces and regions of the PRC, foments fragmentation, promotes unequal development, and weakens the ability of the Tibetan nationality to protect and promote its common cultural, spiritual and ethnic identity. Rather than respecting the integrity of the nationality, this policy promotes its fragmentation and disregards the spirit of autonomy. Whereas the other major minority nationalities such as the Uyghurs and Mongols govern themselves almost entirely within their respective single autonomous regions, Tibetans remain as if they were several minority nationalities instead of one.

Bringing all the Tibetans currently living in designated Tibetan autonomous areas within a single autonomous administrative unit is entirely in accordance with the constitutional principle contained in Article 4, also reflected in the LRNA (Article 2), that "regional autonomy is practiced in areas where people of minority nationalities live in concentrated communities." The LRNA describes regional national autonomy as the "basic policy adopted by the Communist Party of China for the solution of the national question in China" and explains its meaning and intent in its Preface:

> the minority nationalities, under unified state leadership, practice regional autonomy in areas where they live in concentrated communities and set up organs of self-government for the exercise of the power of autonomy. Regional national autonomy embodies the state's full respect for and guarantee of the right of the minority nationalities to administer their internal affairs and its adherence to the principle of equality, unity and common prosperity of all nationalities.

It is clear that the Tibetan nationality within the PRC will be able to exercise its right to govern itself and administer its internal affairs effectively only once it can do so through an organ of self-government that has jurisdiction over the Tibetan nationality as a whole.

The LRNA recognises the principle that boundaries of national autonomous areas may need to be modified. The need for the application of the fundamental principles of the Constitution on regional autonomy through respect of the integrity of the Tibetan nationality is not only totally legitimate, but the administrative changes that may be required to achieve this in no way violate constitutional principles. There are several precedents where this has been actually done.

## VI. THE NATURE AND STRUCTURE OF THE AUTONOMY

The extent to which the right to self-government and self-administration can be exercised on the preceding subject matters largely determines the genuine character of Tibetan autonomy. The task at hand is therefore to look into the manner in which autonomy can be regulated and exercised for it to effectively respond to the unique situation and basic needs of the Tibetan nationality.

The exercise of genuine autonomy would include the right of Tibetans to create their own regional government and government institutions and processes that are best suited to their needs and characteristics.

It would require that the People's Congress of the autonomous region have the power to legislate on all matters within the competencies of the region (that is, the subject matters referred to above) and that other organs of the autonomous government have the power to execute and administer decisions autonomously. Autonomy also entails representation and meaningful participation in national decision-making in the Central Government. Processes for effective consultation and close co-operation or joint decision-making between the Central Government and the regional government on areas of common interest also need to be in place for the autonomy to be effective.

A crucial element of genuine autonomy is the guarantee the Constitution or other laws provide that powers and responsibilities allocated to the autonomous region cannot be unilaterally abrogated or changed. This means that neither the Central Government nor the autonomous region's government should be able, without the consent of the other, to change the basic features of the autonomy.

The parameters and specifics of such genuine autonomy for Tibet that respond to the unique needs and conditions of the Tibetan people and region should be set out in some detail in regulations on the exercise of autonomy, as provided for in Article 116 of the Constitution (enacted in LRNA Article 19) or, if it is found to be more appropriate, in a separate set of laws or regulations adopted for that purpose. The Constitution, including Article 31, provides the flexibility to adopt special laws to respond to unique situations such as the Tibetan one, while respecting the established social, economic and political system of the country.

The Constitution in Section VI provides for organs of self-government of national autonomous regions and acknowledges their power to legislate. Thus Article 116 (enacted in Article 19 of the LRNA) refers to their power to enact "separate regulations in light of the political, economic and cultural characteristics of the nationality or nationalities in the areas concerned." Similarly, the Constitution recognises the power of autonomous administration in a number of areas

(Article 117–120) as well as the power of autonomous governments to apply flexibility in implementing the laws and policies of the Central Government and higher state organs to suit the conditions of the autonomous area concerned (Article 115).

The above-mentioned legal provisions do contain significant limitations to the decision-making authority of the autonomous organs of government. But the Constitution nevertheless recognises the principle that organs of self-government make laws and policy decisions that address local needs and that these may be different from those adopted elsewhere, including by the Central Government.

Although the needs of the Tibetans are broadly consistent with the principles on autonomy contained in the Constitution, as we have shown, their realisation is impeded because of the existence of a number of problems, which makes the implementation of those principles today difficult or ineffective.

Implementation of genuine autonomy, for example, requires clear divisions of powers and responsibilities between the Central Government and the government of the autonomous region with respect to subject matter competency. Currently there is no such clarity and the scope of legislative powers of autonomous regions is both uncertain and severely restricted. Thus, whereas the Constitution intends to recognise the special need for autonomous regions to legislate on many matters that affect them, the requirements of Article 116 for prior approval at the highest level of the Central Government—by the Standing Committee of National People's Congress (NPC)—inhibit the implementation of this principle of autonomy. In reality, it is only autonomous regional congresses that expressly require such approval, while the congresses of ordinary (not autonomous) provinces of the PRC do not need prior permission and merely report the passage of regulations to the Standing Committee of the NPC "for the record" (Article 100).

The exercise of autonomy is further subject to a considerable number of laws and regulations, according to Article 115 of the Constitution. Certain laws effectively restrict the autonomy of the autonomous region, while others are not always consistent with one another. The result is that the exact scope of the autonomy is unclear and is not fixed, since it is unilaterally changed with the enactment of laws and regulations at higher levels of the state, and even by changes in policy. There is also no adequate process for consultation or for settling differences that arise between the organs of the Central Government and of the regional government with respect to the scope and exercise of autonomy. In practice, the resulting uncertainty limits the initiative of regional authorities and impedes the exercise of genuine autonomy by Tibetans today.

We do not at this stage wish to enter into details regarding these and other impediments to the exercise of genuine autonomy today by Tibetans, but mention them by way of example so that these may be addressed in the appropriate manner in our dialogue in the future. We will continue to study the Constitution and other relevant legal provisions and, when appropriate, will be pleased to provide further analysis of these issues, as we understand them.

## VII. THE WAY FORWARD

As stated at the beginning of this memorandum, our intention is to explore how the needs of the Tibetan nationality can be met within the framework of PRC since we believe these needs are consistent with the principles of the Constitution on autonomy. As His Holiness the Dalai Lama stated on a number of occasions, we have no hidden agenda. We have no intention at all of using any agreement on genuine autonomy as stepping stone for separation from the PRC.

The objective of the Tibetan Government in Exile is to represent the interests of the Tibetan people and to speak on their behalf. Therefore, it will no longer be needed and will be dissolved once an agreement is reached between us. In fact, His Holiness has reiterated his decision not to accept any political office in Tibet at any time in the future. His Holiness the Dalai Lama, nevertheless, plans to use all his personal influence to ensure such an agreement would have the legitimacy necessary to obtain the support of the Tibetan people.

Given these strong commitments, we propose that the next step in this process be the agreement to start serious discussions on the points raised in this memorandum. For this purpose we propose that we discuss and agree on a mutually agreeable mechanism or mechanisms and a timetable to do so effectively.

APPENDIX E

# A Note on the "Memorandum on Genuine Autonomy for the Tibetan People"

## INTRODUCTION

This Note addresses the principal concerns and objections raised by the Chinese Central Government regarding the substance of the "Memorandum on Genuine Autonomy for the Tibetan People" (hereinafter "the Memorandum") which was presented to the Government of the People's Republic of China (PRC) on October 31, 2008, at the eighth round of talks in Beijing.

Having carefully studied the responses and reactions of Minister Du Qinglin and Executive Vice Minister Zhu Weiqun conveyed during the talks, including the written Note, and in statements made by the Chinese Central Government following the talks, it seems that some issues raised in the Memorandum may have been misunderstood, while others appear to have not been understood by the Chinese Central Government.

The Chinese Central Government maintains that the Memorandum contravenes the Constitution of the PRC as well as the "three adherences."* The Tibetan side believes that the Tibetan people's needs, as set out in the Memorandum, can be met within the framework and spirit of the Constitution and its principles on autonomy and that these proposals do not contravene or conflict with the "three adherences." We believe that the present Note will help to clarify this.

His Holiness the Dalai Lama started internal discussions, as early as in 1974, to find ways to resolve the future status of Tibet through an autonomy arrangement instead of seeking independence. In 1979 Chinese leader Deng Xiaoping expressed willingness to discuss and resolve all issues except the independence of Tibet. Since then His Holiness the Dalai Lama has taken numerous initiatives to bring about a mutually acceptable negotiated solution to the question of Tibet. In doing so His Holiness the Dalai Lama has steadfastly followed the Middle Way Approach, which means the pursuit of a mutually acceptable and mutually beneficial solution through negotiations, in the spirit of reconciliation and compromise. The Five Point Peace Plan and the Strasbourg Proposal were presented in this spirit. With the failure to elicit any positive response from the Chinese Central Government to these initiatives, along with the imposition of martial law in March 1989 and the deterioration of the situation in Tibet, His Holiness the Dalai Lama felt compelled to state in 1991 that his Strasbourg Proposal had become ineffectual. His Holiness the Dalai Lama nevertheless maintained his commitment to the Middle Way Approach.

The re-establishment of a dialogue process between the Chinese Central Government and representatives of His Holiness the Dalai Lama in 2002 provided the opportunity for each side to explain their positions and to gain a better understanding of the concerns, needs

* The "three adherences" as stipulated by the Central Government are: (1) the leadership of the Chinese Communist Party; (2) socialism with Chinese characteristics; and (3) the Regional National Autonomy system.

and interests of the other side. Moreover, taking into consideration the Chinese Central Government's real concerns, needs and interests, His Holiness the Dalai Lama has given much thought with due consideration to the reality of the situation. This reflects His Holiness the Dalai Lama's flexibility, openness and pragmatism and, above all, sincerity and determination to seek a mutually beneficial solution.

The "Memorandum on Genuine Autonomy for the Tibetan People" was prepared in response to the suggestion from the Chinese Central Government made at the seventh round of talks in July 2008. However, the Chinese Central Government's reactions and main criticisms of the Memorandum appear to be based not on the merits of that proposal which was officially presented to it, but on earlier proposals that were made public as well as other statements made at different times and contexts.

The Memorandum and the present Note strongly reemphasise that His Holiness the Dalai Lama is not seeking independence or separation but a solution within the framework of the Constitution and its principles on autonomy as reiterated many times in the past.

The Special General Meeting of the Tibetans in Diaspora held in November 2008 in Dharamsala reconfirmed for the time being the mandate for the continuation of the dialogue process with the PRC on the basis of the Middle Way Approach. On their part, members of the international community urged both sides to return to the talks. A number of them expressed the opinion that the Memorandum can form a good basis for discussion.

## 1. RESPECTING THE SOVEREIGNTY AND TERRITORIAL INTEGRITY OF THE PRC

His Holiness the Dalai Lama has repeatedly stated that he is not seeking separation of Tibet from the People's Republic of China, and that he is not seeking independence for Tibet. He seeks a sustainable solution within the PRC. This position is stated unambiguously in the Memorandum.

The Memorandum calls for the exercise of genuine autonomy, not for independence, "semi-independence," or "independence in disguised form." The substance of the Memorandum, which explains what is meant by genuine autonomy, makes this unambiguously clear. The form and degree of autonomy proposed in the Memorandum is consistent with the principles on autonomy in the Constitution of the PRC. Autonomous regions in different parts of the world exercise the kind of self-governance that is proposed in the Memorandum, without thereby challenging or threatening the sovereignty and unity of the state of which they are a part. This is true of autonomous regions within unitary states as well as those with federal characteristics. Observers of the situation, including unbiased political leaders and scholars in the international community, have also acknowledged that the Memorandum is a call for autonomy *within* the PRC and not for independence or separation *from* the PRC.

The Chinese government's viewpoint on the history of Tibet is different from that held by Tibetans and His Holiness the Dalai Lama is fully aware that Tibetans cannot agree to it. History is a past event and it cannot be altered. However, His Holiness the Dalai Lama's position is forward-looking, not backward grasping. He does not wish to make this difference on history to be an obstacle in seeking a mutually beneficial common future within the PRC.

The Chinese Central Government's responses to the Memorandum reveal a persistent suspicion on its part that His Holiness's proposals are tactical initiatives to advance the hidden agenda of independence. His Holiness the Dalai Lama is aware of the PRC's concerns and sensitivities with regard to the legitimacy of the present situation in Tibet. For this reason His Holiness the Dalai Lama has conveyed through his Envoys and publicly stated that he stands ready to lend his moral authority to endow an autonomy agreement, once reached, with the legitimacy it will need to gain the support of the people and to be properly implemented.

## 2. RESPECTING THE CONSTITUTION OF THE PRC

The Memorandum explicitly states that the genuine autonomy sought by His Holiness the Dalai Lama for the Tibetan people is to be accommodated within the framework of the Constitution and its principles on autonomy, not outside of it.

The fundamental principle underlying the concept of national regional autonomy is to preserve and protect a minority nationality's identity, language, custom, tradition and culture in a multi-national state based on equality and cooperation. The Constitution provides for the establishment of organs of self-government where the national minorities live in concentrated communities in order for them to exercise the power of autonomy. In conformity with this principle, the White Paper on *Regional Ethnic Autonomy in Tibet* (May 2004) states that minority nationalities are "arbiters of their own destiny and masters of their own affairs."

Within the parameters of its underlying principles, a Constitution needs to be responsive to the needs of the times and adapt to new or changed circumstances. The leaders of the PRC have demonstrated the flexibility of the Constitution of the PRC in their interpretation and implementation of it, and have also enacted modifications and amendments in response to changing circumstances. If applied to the Tibetan situation, such flexibility would, as is stated in the Memorandum, indeed permit the accommodation of the Tibetan needs within the framework of the Constitution and its principles on autonomy.

## 3. RESPECTING THE "THREE ADHERENCES"

The position of His Holiness the Dalai Lama, as presented in the Memorandum, in no way challenges or brings into question the leadership of the Chinese Communist Party in the PRC. At the same time, it is reasonable to expect that, in order to promote unity, stability and a harmonious society, the Party would change its attitude of treating Tibetan culture, religion and identity as a threat.

The Memorandum also does not challenge the socialist system of the PRC. Nothing in it suggests a demand for a change to this system or for its exclusion from Tibetan areas. As for His Holiness the Dalai Lama's views on socialism, it is well known that he has always favoured a socialist economy and ideology that promotes equality and benefits to uplift the poorer sections of society.

His Holiness the Dalai Lama's call for genuine autonomy within the PRC recognises the principles on autonomy for minority nationalities contained in the Constitution of the PRC and is in line with the declared intent of those principles. As pointed out in the Memorandum, the current implementation of the provisions on autonomy, however, effectively results in the denial of genuine autonomy to the Tibetans and fails to provide for the exercise of the right of Tibetans to govern themselves and to be "masters of their own affairs." Today, important decisions pertaining to the welfare of Tibetans are not being made by Tibetans. Implementing the proposed genuine autonomy explained in the Memorandum would ensure for the Tibetans the ability to exercise the right to true autonomy and therefore to become masters of their own affairs, in line with the Constitutional principles on autonomy.

Thus, the Memorandum for genuine autonomy does not oppose the "three adherences."

## 4. RESPECTING THE HIERARCHY AND AUTHORITY OF THE CHINESE CENTRAL GOVERNMENT

The proposals contained in the Memorandum in no way imply a denial of the authority of the National People's Congress (NPC) and other organs of the Chinese Central Government. As stated in the Memorandum, the proposal fully respects the hierarchical differences between the Central Government and its organs, including the NPC, and the autonomous government of Tibet.

Any form of genuine autonomy entails a division and allocation of powers and responsibilities, including that of making laws and regulations, between the central and the autonomous local government. Of course, the power to adopt laws and regulations is limited to the areas of competency of the autonomous region. This is true in unitary states as well as in federal systems.

This principle is also recognised in the Constitution. The spirit of the Constitutional provisions on autonomy is to give autonomous regions *broader* decision-making authority over and above that enjoyed by ordinary provinces. But today, the requirement for prior approval by the Standing Committee of the NPC for all laws and regulations of the autonomous regions (Article 116 of the Constitution) is exercised in a way that in fact leaves the autonomous regions with much less authority to make decisions that suit local conditions than that of the ordinary (not autonomous) provinces of China.

Whenever there is a division and allocation of decision-making power between different levels of government (between the Central Government and the autonomous government), it is important to have processes in place for consultation and cooperation. This helps to improve mutual understanding and to ensure that contradictions and possible inconsistencies in policies, laws and regulations are minimised. It also reduces the chances of disputes arising regarding the exercise of the powers allocated to these different organs of government. Such processes and mechanisms do not put the Central and autonomous governments on equal footing, nor do they imply the rejection of the leadership of the Central Government.

The important feature of entrenchment of autonomy arrangements in the Constitution or in other appropriate ways also does not imply equality of status between the Central and local government nor does it restrict or weaken the authority of the former. The measure is intended to provide (legal) security to both the autonomous and the central authorities that neither can unilaterally change the basic features of the autonomy they have set up, and that a process of consultation must take place at least for fundamental changes to be enacted.

## 5. CONCERNS RAISED BY THE CHINESE CENTRAL GOVERNMENT ON SPECIFIC COMPETENCIES REFERRED TO IN THE MEMORANDUM

### a) Public Security

Concern was raised over the inclusion of public security aspects in the package of competencies allocated to the autonomous region in the Memorandum because the government apparently interpreted this to mean defence matters. National defence and public security are two different matters. His Holiness the Dalai Lama is clear on the point that the responsibility for national defence of the PRC is and should remain with the Central Government. This is not a competency to be exercised by the autonomous region. This is indeed the case in most autonomy arrangements. The Memorandum in fact refers specifically to "internal public order and security," and makes the important point that the majority of the security personnel should be Tibetans, because they understand the local customs and traditions. It also helps to curb local incidents leading to disharmony among the nationalities. The Memorandum in this respect is consistent with the principle enunciated in Article 120 of the Constitution (reflected also in Article 24 of the LRNA), which states:

> The organs of self-government of the national autonomous areas may, in accordance with the military system of the state and practical local needs and with approval of the State Council, organise local public security forces for the maintenance of public order.

It should also be emphasised in this context that the Memorandum at no point proposes the withdrawal of People's Liberation Army (PLA) from Tibetan areas.

### b) Language

The protection, use, and development of the Tibetan language are one of the crucial issues for the exercise of genuine autonomy by Tibetans. The emphasis on the need to respect Tibetan as the main or principal language in the Tibetan areas is not controversial, since a similar position is expressed in the Chinese Central Government's White Paper on *Regional Ethnic Autonomy in Tibet*, where it is stated that regulations adopted by the Tibet regional government prescribe that "equal attention be given to Tibetan and Han-Chinese languages in the Tibetan Autonomous region, *with the Tibetan language as the major one* . . ." (emphasis added). Moreover, the very usage of "main language" in the Memorandum clearly implies the use of other languages, too.

The absence of a demand in the Memorandum that Chinese should also be used and taught should not be interpreted as an "exclusion" of this language, which is the principal and common language in the PRC as a whole. It should also be noted in this context that the leadership in exile has taken steps to encourage Tibetans in exile to learn Chinese.

Tibetan proposal which emphasises the study of the Tibetan people's own language should therefore not be interpreted as being a "separatist view."

### c) Regulation of Population Migration

The Memorandum proposes that the local government of the autonomous region should have the competency to regulate the residence, settlement and employment or economic activities of persons who wish to move to Tibetan areas from elsewhere. This is a common feature of autonomy and is certainly not without precedent in the PRC.

A number of countries have instituted systems or adopted laws to protect vulnerable regions or indigenous and minority peoples from excessive immigration from other parts of the country. The Memorandum explicitly states that it is *not* suggesting the expulsion of non-

Tibetans who have lived in Tibetan areas for years. His Holiness the Dalai Lama and the Kashag also made this clear in earlier statements, as did the Envoys in their discussions with their Chinese counterparts. In an address to the European Parliament on December 4, 2008, His Holiness the Dalai Lama reiterated that "our intention is not to expel non-Tibetans. Our concern is the induced mass movement of primarily Han, but also some other nationalities, into many Tibetan areas, which in turn marginalises the native Tibetan population and threatens Tibet's fragile environment." From this it is clear that His Holiness is not at all suggesting that Tibet be inhabited by only Tibetans, with other nationalities not being able to do so. The issue concerns the appropriate division of powers regarding the regulation of transient, seasonal workers and new settlers so as to protect the vulnerable population indigenous to Tibetan areas.

In responding to the Memorandum the Chinese Central Government rejected the proposition that the autonomous authorities would regulate the entrance and economic activities of persons from other parts of the PRC in part because "in the Constitution and the Law on Regional National Autonomy there are no provisions to restrict transient population." In fact, the Law on Regional National Autonomy, in its Article 43, explicitly mandates such a regulation:

> In accordance with legal stipulations, the organs of self-government of national autonomous areas shall work out measures for control of the transient population.

Thus, the Tibetan proposal contained in the Memorandum in this regard is not incompatible with the Constitution.

### d) Religion

The point made in the Memorandum, that Tibetans be free to practice their religion according to their own beliefs, is entirely consistent with the principles of religious freedom contained in the Constitution of the PRC. It is also consistent with the principle of separation of religion and polity adopted in many countries of the world.

Article 36 of the Constitution guarantees that no one can "compel citizens to believe in or not to believe in any religion." We endorse this principle but observe that today the government authorities do interfere in important ways in the ability of Tibetans to practice their religion.

The spiritual relationship between master and student and the giving of religious teachings, etc., are essential components of the Dharma practice. Restricting these is a violation of religious freedom. Similarly, the interference and direct involvement by the state and its institutions in matters of recognition of reincarnated lamas, as provided in the regulation on the management of reincarnated lamas adopted by the State on July 18, 2007, is a grave violation of the freedom of religious belief enshrined in the Constitution.

The practice of religion is widespread and fundamental to the Tibetan people. Rather than seeing Buddhist practice as a threat, concerned authorities should respect it. Traditionally or historically Buddhism has always been a major unifying and positive factor between the Tibetan and Chinese peoples.

### e) Single Administration

The desire of Tibetans to be governed within one autonomous region is fully in keeping with the principles on autonomy of the Constitution. The rationale for the need to respect the integrity of the Tibetan nationality is clearly stated in the Memorandum and does not mean "Greater or Smaller Tibet." In fact, as pointed out in the Memorandum, the Law on Regional National Autonomy itself allows for this kind of modification of administrative boundaries if proper procedures are followed. Thus the proposal in no way violates the Constitution.

As the Envoys pointed out in earlier rounds of talks, many Chinese leaders, including Premier Zhou Enlai, Vice Premier Chen Yi and

Party Secretary Hu Yaobang, supported the consideration of bringing all Tibetan areas under a single administration. Some of the most senior Tibetan leaders in the PRC, including the 10th Panchen Lama, Ngabö Ngawang Jigme and Bapa Phuntsok Wangyal have also called for this and affirming that doing so would be in accordance with the PRC's Constitution and its laws. In 1956 a special committee, which included senior Communist Party member Sangye Yeshi (Tian Bao), was appointed by the Chinese Central Government to make a detailed plan for the integration of the Tibetan areas into a single autonomous region, but the work was later stopped on account of ultra-leftist elements.

The fundamental reason for the need to integrate the Tibetan areas under one administrative region is to address the deeply felt desire of Tibetans to exercise their autonomy as a people and to protect and develop their culture and spiritual values in this context. This is also the fundamental premise and purpose of the Constitutional principles on regional national autonomy as reflected in Article 4 of the Constitution. Tibetans are concerned about the integrity of the Tibetan nationality, which the proposal respects and which the continuation of the present system does not. Their common historical heritage, spiritual and cultural identity, language and even their particular affinity to the unique Tibetan plateau environment is what binds Tibetans as one nationality. Within the PRC, Tibetans are recognized as one nationality and not several nationalities. Those Tibetans presently living in Tibet autonomous prefectures and counties incorporated into other provinces also belong to the same Tibetan nationality. Tibetans, including His Holiness the Dalai Lama, are primarily concerned about the protection and development of Tibetan culture, spiritual values, national identity and the environment. Tibetans are not asking for the expansion of Tibetan autonomous areas. They are only demanding that those areas already recognised as Tibetan autonomous areas come under a single administration, as is the case in the other autonomous regions of the PRC. So long as Tibetans do not have the opportunity to govern themselves under a single administration, preservation of Tibetan culture and way of life cannot be done effectively. Today more than half of the Tibetan population is subjected to the priorities and interests first and foremost of different provincial governments in which they have no significant role.

As explained in the Memorandum, the Tibetan people can only genuinely exercise regional national autonomy if they can have their own autonomous government, people's congress and other organs of self-government with jurisdiction over the Tibetan nationality as a whole. This principle is reflected in the Constitution, which recognises the right of minority nationalities to practice regional autonomy "in areas where they live in concentrated communities" and to "set up organs of self-government for the exercise of the power of autonomy" (Article 4). If the "state's full respect for and guarantee of the right of the minority nationalities to administer their internal affairs" solemnly declared in the preamble of the Law on Regional National Autonomy is interpreted not to include the right to choose to form an autonomous region that encompasses the whole people in the contiguous areas where its members live in concentrated communities, the Constitutional principles on autonomy are themselves undermined.

Keeping Tibetans divided and subject to different laws and regulations denies the people the exercise of genuine autonomy and makes it difficult for them to maintain their distinct cultural identity. It is not impossible for the Central Government to make the necessary administrative adjustment when elsewhere in the PRC, notably in the case of Inner Mongolia, Ningxia and Guangxi Autonomous Regions, it has done just that.

### f) Political, Social and Economic System

His Holiness the Dalai Lama has repeatedly and consistently stated that no one, least of all he, has any intention to restore the old political, social and economic system that existed in Tibet prior to 1959. It would be the intention of a future autonomous Tibet to further improve the social, economic and political situation of Tibetans, not to return to the past. It is disturbing and puzzling that the Chinese government persists, despite all evidence to the contrary, to accuse His Holiness the Dalai Lama and his Administration of the intention to restore the old system.

All countries and societies in the world, including China, have had political systems in the past that would be entirely unacceptable today. The old Tibetan system is no exception. The world has evolved socially and politically and has made enormous strides in terms of the recognition of human rights and standards of living. Tibetans in exile have developed their own modern democratic system as well as education and health systems and institutions. In this way, Tibetans have become citizens of the world at par with those of other countries. It is obvious that Tibetans in the PRC have also advanced under Chinese rule and improved their social, education, health and economic situation. However, the standard of living of the Tibetan people remains the most backward in the PRC and Tibetan human rights are not being respected.

## 6. RECOGNISING THE CORE ISSUE

His Holiness the Dalai Lama and other members of the exiled leadership have no personal demands to make. His Holiness the Dalai Lama's concern is with the rights and welfare of the Tibetan people. Therefore, the fundamental issue that needs to be resolved is the faithful implementation of genuine autonomy that will enable the Tibetan people to govern themselves in accordance with their own genius and needs.

His Holiness the Dalai Lama speaks on behalf of the Tibetan people, with whom he has a deep and historical relationship and one based on full trust. In fact, on no issue are Tibetans as completely in agreement as on their demand for the return of His Holiness the Dalai Lama to Tibet. It cannot be disputed that His Holiness the Dalai Lama legitimately represents the Tibetan people, and he is certainly viewed as their true representative and spokesperson by them. It is indeed only by means of dialogue with His Holiness the Dalai Lama that the Tibetan issue can be resolved. The recognition of this reality is important.

This emphasises the point, often made by His Holiness the Dalai Lama, that his engagement for the cause of Tibet is not for the purpose of claiming certain personal rights or political position for him, nor attempting to stake claims for the Tibetan administration in exile. Once an agreement is reached, the Tibetan Government-in-Exile will be dissolved and the Tibetans working in Tibet should carry on the main responsibility of administering Tibet. His Holiness the Dalai Lama made it clear on numerous occasions that he will not hold any political position in Tibet.

## 7. HIS HOLINESS THE DALAI LAMA'S COOPERATION

His Holiness the Dalai Lama has offered, and remains prepared, to formally issue a statement that would serve to allay the Chinese Central Government's doubts and concerns as to his position and intentions on matters that have been identified above.

The formulation of the statement should be done after ample consultations between representatives of His Holiness the Dalai Lama and the Chinese Central Government, respectively, to ensure that such a statement would satisfy the fundamental needs of the Chinese Central Government as well as those of the Tibetan people.

It is important that both parties address any concern directly with their counterparts, and not use those issues as ways to block the dialogue process as has occurred in the past.

His Holiness the Dalai Lama is taking this initiative in the belief that it is possible to find common ground with the People's Republic of China consistent with the principles on autonomy contained in PRC's Constitution and with the interests of the Tibetan people. In that spirit, it is the expectation and hope of His Holiness the Dalai Lama that the representatives of the PRC will use the opportunity presented by the Memorandum and this Note to deepen discussion and make substantive progress in order to develop mutual understanding.

# Notes

## Introduction

xii *The document began with the statement: Tibet Since 1951: Liberation, Development and Prosperity* (The State Council Information Office of the People's Republic of China, May 2021), 3–4. http://english.www.gov.cn/archive/whitepaper/202105/21/content_WS60a724e7c6d0df57f98d9da2.html.

xiii *A series of resolutions has been passed:* On the important international resolutions passed on Tibet, see https://tibet.net/international-resolutions-and-recognitions-on-tibet-1959-to-2021/.

## Chapter 1: The Invasion and Our New Master

2 *To the Secretary General:* Full text in Dalai Lama, *My Land and My People* (New York: Grand Central Publishing, 1997), appendix II. Reacting to the Chinese invasion of Tibet, on December 7, 1950, Prime Minister Jawaharlal Nehru made a statement to the Indian Parliament in which he declared, "Since Tibet is not the same as China, it should ultimately be the wishes of the people of Tibet that should prevail."

8 *Referring to the foraging for food:* This statement is reported in Edgar Snow, *Red Star Over China* (New York: Random House, 1938), 193.

## Chapter 3: A Visit to India

19 *bombing the monastery:* For a detailed account of the bombing of Lithang Monastery in March 1956 and the massacre of Tibetans in other parts of eastern Tibet around this time, see Jianglin Li, *When the Iron Bird Flies: China's Secret War in Tibet* (California: Stanford University Press, 2022), especially chapters 3–6.

20 *Every devout Buddhist:* Dalai Lama, *My Land and My People* (New York: Grand Central Publishing, 1997), 121.

20 *I expressed my deep admiration:* The full text of an English translation of the Dalai Lama's address is available in W. D. Shakabpa, *Tibet: A Political History* (New Haven: Yale University Press, 1967), 329–31.

22 *The trip to India was also:* Jianglin Li's *Agony in Tibet: Lhasa 1959*, trans. Susan Wilf (Cambridge: Harvard University Press, 2016), chap. 2, contains a detailed account of the Dalai Lama's meetings with Zhou and the latter's meetings with Nehru during the Dalai Lama's visit to India in 1956.

24 *Zhou had even dangled:* This is attested to in Jawaharlal Nehru, *Selected Works of Jawaharlal Nehru*, series 2, vol. 36 (New Delhi: Jawaharlal Memorial Fund, 2005), 600.

## Chapter 4: Fleeing Home

27 *Of course, as a student of the Buddha:* The Dalai Lama's refusal is reported in John Kenneth Knaus, *Orphans of the Cold War: America and the Tibetan Struggle for Survival* (New York: Public Affairs, 1999), 141.

32 *In the past, for several thousand years:* An English translation of this pronouncement as well as a Wylie (transliteration) version of the Tibetan text can be found in Melvyn C. Goldstein, *A History of Modern Tibet*, vol. 4, *In the Eye of the Storm* (Berkeley: University of California, 2019), 473, appendix B.

33 *As part of the US government's overall strategy:* This Tibetan resistance movement later regrouped and came to be based in Mustang, Nepal. Eventually, it was a taped message from the Dalai Lama himself, brought by a delegation from Dharamsala, headed by Phuntsok Tashi Takla, the Dalai Lama's brother-in-law and chief security officer, which persuaded the Tibetan resistance force to disarm. For a detailed account of the history of US support for Tibet, especially its support of the Tibetan resistance fighters, see Knaus, *Orphans of the Cold War* (New York: Public Affairs, 1999).

## Chapter 5: A Geopolitical Reflection

36 *An early chronicle says that this king: The Old Tibetan Chronicle*, Pelliot Tibétain MS 1286; English translation of the excerpts from Matthew T. Kapstein, *The Tibetans* (Oxford: Blackwell, 2006), 35.

40 *I am now almost fifty-eight years old:* English translation of the excerpts from Glenn H. Mullin, *The Fourteen Dalai Lamas: A Sacred Legacy of Reincarnation* (Santa Fe: Clear Light Publishers, 2001), 437–39.

43 *expansion of China almost up to our gates:* The full text of Sardar Patel's letter

to Prime Minister Jawaharlal Nehru can be found in *Indian Leaders on Tibet*, 5–11. https://tibet.net/indian-leaders-on-Tibet/.

45 *In the end, a careless, instrumental:* On why Tibet matters, especially from an ecological perspective, and for an account of Communist China's destruction of Tibet's ecosystems, see Michael Buckley, *Meltdown in Tibet: China's Reckless Destruction of Ecosystems from the Highlands of Tibet to the Delta of Asia* (New York: Palgrave Macmillan, 2014).

45 *a noted Chinese environmental scientist:* This is cited in He Huaihong, *Social Ethics in a Changing China: Moral Decay or Ethical Awakening?* (Washington, DC: Brooking Institution Press, 2015).

## Chapter 6: Devastation at Home and Rebuilding in Exile

48 *I concluded by saying that I hoped:* The full text of this first press statement from the Dalai Lama can be found in *Facts About the 17-Point "Agreement" Between Tibet and China* (Dharamsala: Department of Information and International Relations, 2022), 110–13. https://tibet.net/facts-about-17-point-agreement-between-tibet-and-china-2001/.

49 *No one expects India to go to war:* The full text of this statement can be found in *Indian Leaders on Tibet*, 18–19. https://tibet.net/indian-leaders-on-Tibet/.

50 *If a treaty is violated by one:* The full text of this press statement is available in *Facts About the 17-Point "Agreement,"* 114–17. https://tibet.net/facts-about-17-point-agreement-between-tibet-and-china-2001/.

50 *All that we had heard:* International Commission of Jurists, *The Question of Tibet and the Rule of Law* (Geneva: International Commission of Jurists, 1959), iv, 17, 18, 68.

50 *In the second report:* International Commission of Jurists, *Tibet and the Chinese People's Republic: A Report to the International Commission of Jurists by Its Legal Inquiry Committee on Tibet* (Geneva: International Commission of Jurists, 1960), 13.

51 *So while in Delhi that September:* The full text of this letter to the UN secretary-general can be found in Dalai Lama, *My Land and My People* (New York: Grand Central Publishing, 1997), 218–20.

51 *On October 21, 1959, the General Assembly:* The full text of this and other subsequent UN resolutions on Tibet can be found in Central Tibetan Administration, *International Resolutions and Recognitions on Tibet (1959 to 2021)*, 6th ed. (Dharamsala: Department of Information and International Relations, 2021).

51 *two letters from the Secretary of State Christian A. Herter:* The full text of the October 1960 letter from the secretary of state to the Dalai Lama is available at https://history.state.gov/historicaldocuments/frus1958-60v19/d402.

53 *At this ceremony, representing the Tibetan people:* The original Tibetan text and

an English translation of this great oath are found in Lodi Gyaltsen Gyari, *The Dalai Lama's Special Envoy: Memoirs of a Lifetime in Pursuit of a Reunited Tibet* (New York: Columbia University Press, 2022), appendix A.

54 *The document also includes, as Article 36:* An English translation of the entire text of this Constitution of Tibet promulgated on March 10, 1963, can be found at https://www.tibetjustice.org/materials/tibet/tibet2.html.

54 *Over the course of years, this document:* This constitution, in the wake of the Dalai Lama's semiretirement in 1991 and full devolution of political authority to an elected leadership in 2011, has been revised and the full text of this revised document can be found at https://tibet.net/about-cta/constitution.

57 *Because of many errors of mistakes:* The Tibet Information Network (TIN) in the United Kingdom was able to obtain a copy of this lengthy petition, whose English translation was published under the title *A Poisoned Arrow: The Secret Report of the 10th Panchen Lama* (London: Tibetan Information Network, 1997), 113–14.

58 *Once a nationality's language, costumes, customs: Poisoned Arrow*, 69.

58 *Before democratic reform, there were more than 2500: Poisoned Arrow*, 52.

59 *in March 1987, he spoke candidly:* The full text of the English translation of the Panchen Lama's speech to the Tibet Autonomous Region's Standing Committee in Beijing during the People's Congress of 1987 can be found in Central Tibetan Administration, *The Panchen Lama Speaks* (Dharamsala: Department of Information and International Relations, 1991).

60 *Since liberation, there has certainly been:* As reported in the *China Daily*, January 25, 1989, and cited in Isabel Hilton, *The Search for the Panchen Lama* (London: Viking, 1999).

61 *I was told that he described the Communist Chinese:* Secretary Schlesinger's actual statements are cited in Warren Smith, *Tibetan Nation* (Boulder: Westview Press, 1996), 560n58.

## Chapter 7: Overtures Toward a Dialogue

63 *If the six million Tibetans in Tibet are really happy:* The full text of the statement is available at https://www.dalailama.com/messages/tibet/10th-march-archive/1978.

64 *"But except for independence":* The Dalai Lama's brother provides a detailed account of this first meeting with Deng Xiaoping in his memoir, Gyalo Thondup and Anne F. Thurston, *The Noodle Maker of Kalimpong* (New York: Public Affairs, 2015), 258–62.

69 *If the Tibetan people's identity is preserved:* The full text of the Dalai Lama's letter to Deng Xiaoping can be found at https://tibet.net/important-issues/sino-tibetan-dialogue/important-statements-of-his-holiness-the-dalai-lama/his-holiness-letter-to-deng-xiaoping/.

71 *For this to be realized, I said, it was important:* The full text of this March 10 Statement of 1981 can be found at https://www.dalailama.com/messages/tibet/10th-march-archive/1981.

## Chapter 8: Reaching Out to Our Fourth Refuge

74 *The letter expressed support for direct talks:* Point 14 of Sec. 1243 of Foreign Relations Authorization Act, Fiscal Years 1988 and 1989, H.R. 1777, 100th Cong. (1987) (enacted).

74 *The world is increasingly interdependent:* The full text of the Dalai Lama's Five Point Peace Plan presented at the United States Congressional Human Rights Caucus can be found at https://www.dalailama.com/messages/tibet/five-point-peace-plan.

76 *The whole of Tibet known as Cholka-Sum:* The full text of the Strasbourg Proposal is found at https://www.dalailama.com/messages/tibet/strasbourg-proposal-1988.

80 *Despite my explicit public announcement:* The text of the New Delhi Chinese Embassy's press statement, as it appeared in *News from China*, no. 40 (September 28, 1990), is cited in Dawa Norbu, "China's Dialogue with the Dalai Lama 1978–90: Prenegotiation Stage or Dead End?," *Public Affairs* 64, no. 3 (Autumn 1991): 351–72.

84 *I accept the prize with profound gratitude:* The full text of the Dalai Lama's formal acceptance speech at the Nobel Peace Prize ceremony can be found at https://www.nobelprize.org/prizes/peace/1989/lama/acceptance-speech/#:~:text=I%20accept%20the%20prize%20with,life%20taught%20and%20inspired%20me.

## Chapter 9: In the Aftermath of Tiananmen

89 *[It] is the sense of the Congress that Tibet:* The full text of the resolution is available at https://www.congress.gov/bill/102nd-congress/house-concurrent-resolution/145/text.

90 *I have had the pleasure to meet with every holder:* On July 12, 2024, President Joe Biden signed into law the Promotion of a Resolution to the Tibet-China Dispute Act, which states "that U.S. government statements and documents counter, as appropriate, disinformation about Tibet by China's government and the Chinese Communist Party, including disinformation about Tibet's history and institutions." https://www.congress.gov/bill/118th-congress/senate-bill/138.

90 *I particularly noted how this amazing transition:* The full text of this speech can be found at https://tibet.net/important-issues/sino-tibetan-dialogue/important-statements-of-his-holiness-the-dalai-lama/embracing-the-enemy/.

92 *If China wants Tibet to stay with China:* The full text of this detailed note

accompanying the Dalai Lama's letter to Jiang Zemin is presented in appendix C and can also be found at https://tibet.net/important-issues/sino-tibetan-dialogue/important-statements-of-his-holiness-the-dalai-lama/note-accompanying-his-holiness-letters-to-deng-xiaoping-and-jiang-zemin-dated-september-11-1992/.

93 *The document presents a series of arguments:* https://en.humanrights.cn/1992/09/30/9ed6ff95f0ce4c2099928bafef562f98.html.

94 *For example, one of their official statements:* English translation as cited in Robert Barnett, ed., *Cutting Off the Serpent's Head: Tightening Control in Tibet, 1994–1995* (London: Human Rights Watch, Tibet Information Network, 1996), 32.

94 *This same document then urged the monastic community:* Barnett, *Cutting Off the Serpent's Head*, 33.

94 *Ethnic education cannot be regarded successful:* Barnett, *Cutting Off the Serpent's Head*, 42.

## Chapter 10: Practices I Find Helpful in the Face of Suffering

96 *I truly believe that a movement rooted in hatred:* The full text of this March 10 Statement is found at https://www.dalailama.com/messages/tibet/10th-march-archive/1976.

## Chapter 11: As the Millennium Came to an End

107 *Without seeking independence for Tibet:* The full text of this statement can be found at https://tibet.net/important-issues/sino-tibetan-dialogue/the-middle-way-approach-a-framework-for-resolving-the-issue-of-tibet-2/.

108 *The document concluded that "the exiled Dalai Lama":* http://un.china-mission.gov.cn/eng/gyzg/bp/199802/t19980201_8410934.htm.

109 *Actually, as long as the Dalai Lama:* The full text of this press conference is available at https://china.usc.edu/president-clinton-and-president-jiang-zemin-%E6%B1%9F%E6%B3%BD%E6%B0%91-news-conference-beijing-1998.

## Chapter 12: The Final Series of Dialogues

113 *On March 18, 2008, the leader of the Communist Party in Tibet:* This was reported in Christopher Bodeen, "Dalai Lama 'a Wolf in Monk's robes': China," *Toronto Star*, March 19, 2008, citing the *Tibet Daily* newspaper.

115 *invited to speak at the US Congressional Gold Medal Ceremony:* The full text of the Dalai Lama's speech at the US Congressional Gold Medal Ceremony is found at https://www.dalailama.com/messages/acceptance-speeches/u-s-congressional-gold-medal/congressional-gold-medal.

115 *I emphasized that the Chinese and Tibetan people share a common spiritual heritage:* The full texts of these appeals from the Dalai Lama can found at https://www.dalailama.com/messages/tibet.

116 *While our position had been clear for years:* The full text of this "Memorandum on Genuine Autonomy for the Tibetan People" is contained in appendix D and can also be found at https://tibet.net/important-issues/sino-tibetan-dialogue/memorandum-on-geniune-autonomy-for-the-tibetan-people/.

117 *This same line of criticism was repeated later in China's white paper:* The full text is available at http://un.china-mission.gov.cn/eng/gyzg/xizang/200903/t20090303_8410897.htm.

118 *Confronted with such unreasonable and excessively negative responses:* The full text of the Dalai Lama's address to the plenary session of the European Parliament can be found at https://tibet.net/address-to-the-plenary-session-of-the-european-parliament/.

118 *Despite their immediate and willful attack on our proposal:* The full text of this note on the memorandum is presented in appendix E and can also be found at https://tibet.net/important-issues/sino-tibetan-dialogue/note-on-the-memorandum-on-genuine-autonomy-for-the-tibetan-people/.

118 *On March 19, 2011, when I was seventy-five years old:* The full text of the Dalai Lama's remarks on retirement can be found at https://www.dalailama.com/messages/retirement-and-reincarnation/retirement-remarks.

## Chapter 13: Taking Stock

123 *One explicit response from Beijing:* https://www.chinadaily.com.cn/kindle/2013-10/23/content_17052580.htm.

## Chapter 14: What Gives Me Hope

132 *I also said that the Beijing government keeps stressing stability:* The full English translation of this live internet Q and A with the Dalai Lama can be found at https://www.nybooks.com/online/2010/05/24/talking-about-tibet/?printpage=true.

## Chapter 15: Situation Today and the Path Forward

135 *according to some sources:* One such source is https://www.ohchr.org/en/press-releases/2023/02/china-un-experts-alarmed-separation-1-million-tibetan-children-families-and.

139 *In particular, in 2011, I convened a gathering:* The full text of this statement (in English translation) can be found at https://www.dalailama.com/news/2011

/statement-of-his-holiness-the-fourteenth-dalai-lama-tenzin-gyatso-on-the-issue-of-his-reincarnation.

## Chapter 16: Appeal

145 *The sages who have contemplated:* These verses are from Śāntideva, *Bodhicaryāvatāra* (*A Guide to the Bodhisattva Way*), 1.7–8, 3.17, 21–22, and 10:55. Translated by the editor of this book.

## Appendix A: Tibet: A Historical Overview

150 *Both Tibet and China shall keep the country:* The source for this English translation: H. E. Richardson, "The Sino-Tibetan Treaty Inscription of AD 821–823 at Lhasa," *Journal of the Royal Asiatic Society* 2 (1978): 153–54.

154 *He said that he was at the time writing a book:* Hon-Shiang Lau was a chair professor at the City University of Hong Kong and his book in Chinese, *Tibet Was Never Part of China Since Antiquity*, was later published in Taiwan in 2019.

## Appendix D: Memorandum on Genuine Autonomy for the Tibetan People

182 *Memorandum on Genuine Autonomy for the Tibetan People:* Presented by the Dalai Lama's delegation to their Chinese counterparts on October 31, 2008, at the eighth round of talks of the second cycle of formal dialogues, 2002–2010. English translation: https://tibet.net/important-issues/sino-tibetan-dialogue/memorandum-on-geniune-autonomy-for-the-tibetan-people/.

## Appendix E: A Note on the "Memorandum on Genuine Autonomy for the Tibetan People"

200 *A Note on the "Memorandum on Genuine Autonomy for the Tibetan People":* This note was formally presented by the envoys of His Holiness the Dalai Lama to their Chinese counterparts during the ninth round of dialogues in Beijing. English translation: https://tibet.net/important-issues/sino-tibetan-dialogue/note-on-the-memorandum-on-genuine-autonomy-for-the-tibetan-people/.

# Selected Bibliography


*A Poisoned Arrow: The Secret Report of the 10th Panchen Lama*. London: Tibetan Information Network, 1997.

Avedon, John F. *In Exile from the Land of Snows*. New York: Vintage Books, 1986.

Barnett, Robert, ed. *Cutting Off the Serpent's Head*. London: Human Rights Watch, Tibet Information Network, 1996.

Barnett, Robert, and Shirin Akiner, eds. *Resistance and Reform in Tibet*. London: C. Hearst & Co., 1994.

Brook, Timothy, Michael van Walt van Praag, and Miek Boltjes, eds. *Sacred Mandates: Asian International Relations Since Chinggis Khan*. Chicago: University of Chicago Press, 2018.

Buckley, Michael. *Meltdown in Tibet: China's Reckless Destruction of Ecosystems from the Highlands of Tibet to the Delta of Asia*. New York: Palgrave Macmillan, 2014.

Dalai Lama, the. *Freedom in Exile*. London: Hodder & Stoughton, 1990.

Dalai Lama, the. *My Land and My People*. New York: Grand Central, 1997; first published in 1962 by Weidenfield & Nicolson.

Franke, Herbert. "Tibetans in Yuan China." In *China Under Mongol Rule*, edited by John D. Langlois. Princeton: Princeton University Press, 1981.

Goldstein, Melvyn C. *A History of Modern Tibet*. Vol. 1, *The Demise of Lamaist State, 1913–1951*. Berkeley: University of California Press, 1989.

Goldstein, Melvyn C. *A History of Modern Tibet*. Vol. 4, *In the Eye of the Storm: 1957–1959*. Berkeley: University of California Press, 2019.

Gyari, Lodi Gyaltsen. *The Dalai Lama's Special Envoy: Memoirs of a Lifetime in Pursuit of a Reunited Tibet*. New York: Columbia University Press, 2022.

International Commission of Jurists. *The Question of Tibet and the Rule of Law*. Geneva: International Commission of Jurists, 1959.

International Commission of Jurists. *Tibet and the Chinese People's Republic: A Report to the International Commission of Jurists by Its Legal Inquiry Committee on Tibet*. Geneva: International Commission of Jurists, 1960.

Knaus, John Kenneth. *Orphans of the Cold War: America and the Tibetan Struggle for Survival*. New York: Public Affairs, 1999.

Laird, Thomas, with the Dalai Lama. *The Story of Tibet: Conversations with the Dalai Lama*. New York: Atlantic Books, 2006.

Li, Jianglin. *Agony in Tibet: Lhasa 1959*. Translated by Susan Wilf. Cambridge: Harvard University Press, 2016.

Li, Jianglin. *When the Iron Bird Flies: China's Secret War in Tibet*. Translated by Stacy Masher. California: Stanford University Press, 2022.

McCorquodale, Robert, and Nicholas Orosz, eds. *Tibet: The Position in International Law*. Report of the Conference of International Lawyers on Issues Relating to Self-Determination and Independence for Tibet. London: Serindia, 1994.

Schwartz, Ronald D. *Circle of Protest: Political Ritual in the Tibetan Uprising, 1987–1992*. New York: Columbia University Press, 1995.

Shakabpa, W. D. *Tibet: A Political History*. New Haven: Yale University Press, 1967. Reprinted by Potala Publications in 1984.

Shakya, Tsering. *The Dragon in the Land of Snows*. London: Pimlico, 1999.

Smith, Warren. *Tibetan Nation*. Boulder: Westview Press, 1996.

Thondup, Gyalo, and Anne F. Thurston. *The Noodle Maker of Kalimpong*. New York: Public Affairs, 2015.

van Schaik, Sam. *Tibet: A History*. New Haven: Yale University Press, 2011.

van Walt van Praag, Michael C. *The Status of Tibet: History, Rights, and Prospects in International Law*. Boulder: Westview Press, 1987.

van Walt van Praag, Michael C., and Miek Boltjes. *Tibet Brief 20/20*. Outskirts Press, 2020.

Woeser, Tsering. *Tibet on Fire: Self-Immolations Against Chinese Rule*. Translated by Kevin Carrico. New York: Verso, 2016.

# Index

# About the Author

One of the best-known global figures, **His Holiness the Dalai Lama** is the spiritual leader of Tibetan Buddhism and a powerful symbol of Tibet and its unique civilization. He is an important voice for compassion, and in recognition of his advocacy for world peace and environmental concerns, he was awarded the Nobel Peace Prize in 1989. He has received numerous other international awards, including the highest civilian honor in the United States, the US Congressional Gold Medal. Since being called upon to assume the leadership of Tibet, he has worked tirelessly for the freedom and dignity of his people. After fleeing into exile in 1959, the Dalai Lama has lived as a stateless Tibetan in India, a country he calls his second home.

CHRISTMAS 1972 (AUSTRA
PETER & LILIAN

# AUSTRALIAN WOMEN'S WEEKLY
# COOKBOOK

Golden Press
Sydney

The Australian Women's Weekly presents this book for your pleasure and practical use.

Here you will find many favourite recipes from our weekly features, as well as new and exciting dishes.

Our Leila Howard Test Kitchen has been proud to help readers not only with planning important family occasions, but also with preparing the daily meal; we are proud that our recipes have become so much a part of Australian home life.

In this cook book, we believe you will find something of interest on every page—dishes you will love to make over and over again.

Ellen Sinclair
*Food Editor*
*The Australian Women's Weekly*

First published 1970
by Golden Press Pty Ltd
10–16 Dowling Street,
Potts Point, Sydney, Australia
Set and designed in Australia
Printed in Hong Kong



ISBN 0 85558 200 6

Pictures in this book by
staff photographers:
Kevin Brown, Bill Payne,
Ron Berg, Keith Barlow,
Bob Clark.
Designed with line drawings
by John Sayers

**Jacket Illustration**

Savoury Lamb. See recipe on page 62.

**Rear Jacket Illustration**

Mocha Torte. See recipe on page 155.
**Frontispiece** Apple Charlotte.
See recipe on page 215. Apple Pie
(at rear). See recipe on page 212.

# CONTENTS

# APPETISERS

In this section we give a tempting selection of hors d'oeuvre, canapes, savouries and dips.

*Hors d'oeuvre* make a tasty, colourful meal beginning. They should have a distinct, sharp taste to clear the palate for the next course. They should be light, so that the appetite for the next course is not dulled.

*Canapes* are savoury pieces, generally bite-sized, to offer with drinks. They are small rounds, squares, triangles or fingers of fresh bread, toast or crisply fried bread, or savoury biscuits. They're topped, simply, with a pate or spread, or they can have an irresistible selection of good things to top them. The word 'canapes' is derived from the French, meaning 'sofa'; it was considered the small bases acted as a 'seat' for the delicacies which topped them.

*Savouries* are another popular accompaniment to party drinks; these are savoury bites such as Angels on Horseback

## Hors d'Oeuvre

A selection of any of the following would look appetising and colourful.

□ Sliced continental sausages: salami, cabanossi, etc.
□ Vegetables, both fresh and canned: artichoke hearts, kidney beans, asparagus, tiny champignons (mushrooms), mixed vegetables, cauliflower, carrot, broccoli, beetroot, etc. When using fresh vegetables, cook them lightly, drain well, toss in a little french dressing.
□ Fish of all types: smoked salmon, herrings made into roll mops, oysters—fresh and smoked—crab, prawns, lobster, etc.
□ Salads of various types: potato, mushroom, etc.

## Chicken Liver Pâté

¾ cup chicken stock
1½ teaspoons gelatine
2 tablespoons cold water
2 tablespoons brandy
1 lb. chicken livers
2 oz. butter
4 rashers bacon
2 small onions
¼ teaspoon thyme
1 bayleaf
2 tablespoons dry sherry
4 tablespoons cream
2 tablespoons chopped parsley
salt, pepper
3 oz. butter, extra

Soften gelatine in cold water, add to boiling stock, stir until dissolved. Pour into base of greased mould, refrigerate until set.

Chop chicken livers roughly, place in basin with brandy and marinate $1\frac{1}{2}$ hours. Drain livers, heat 1 oz. butter in frying pan, add livers and saute just long enough to brown on all sides.

In separate pan, melt remaining 1 oz. butter and cook the combined chopped onion, chopped bacon, thyme, and bayleaf. Add the semi-cooked chicken livers, cook further 5 minutes. Remove from heat, remove bayleaf.

Blend mixture until smooth in electric blender or pound to a paste, then push through sieve. Stir in sherry, cream, parsley, and salt and pepper to taste. Melt extra butter and fold through. Spread over gelatine in mould, pressing mixture in gently and evenly; refrigerate until firm. Unmould on to serving plate. Serve with triangles of toast.

For a large-size party pate, as shown in picture, quantities can be doubled.

## Smoked Haddock Pâté

¼ lb. cooked smoked haddock
4 oz. butter
1 teaspoon lemon juice
¼ teaspoon freshly ground pepper
¼ teaspoon curry powder
1½ tablespoons finely chopped onions or shallots
chopped parsley

Skin and bone fish. Pound butter and fish together until well blended. Add onions or shallots, pepper, lemon juice and seasoning, beat well. Sprinkle with a little chopped parsley.

Makes approx. $1\frac{1}{4}$ cups

This superb Chicken Liver Pâté makes the perfect first-course for a dinner party; or use it as a spread, on small toast squares, to serve with drinks

## Brandied Liver Pâté

1 lb. liverwurst
2 oz. butter
¼ cup chopped parsley
½ teaspoon dried thyme
pinch nutmeg
2 teaspoons grated onion
2 tablespoons cream
2 tablespoons brandy

Beat together butter and liverwurst until smooth. Add remaining ingredients, beat again. Place in a greased mould, refrigerate several hours or overnight.

Makes approx. 1½ cups

## Indonesian Prawn Puffs

1 lb. prawns
1 small onion
1 clove garlic
1 cup instant potato flakes
1 tablespoon cornflour
2 tablespoons chopped celery
salt, pepper
1 egg, separated
oil for frying

**Peanut Butter Sauce**

5 tablespoons peanut butter
1 clove garlic
1 cup coconut milk
1 dessertspoon brown sugar
1 tablespoon lemon juice
pinch salt

Make up potato according to directions on packet, omitting milk. Stir in chopped prawns, chopped onion, crushed garlic, cornflour, celery, salt, pepper and egg-yolk; mix thoroughly. Form into small balls. Beat egg-white lightly, coat prawn balls thoroughly with egg-white; fry in deep hot oil until golden. Drain on absorbent paper. Serve with Peanut Butter Sauce.

*Peanut Butter Sauce* Combine in saucepan the peanut butter, crushed garlic, brown sugar, coconut milk, lemon juice and salt. Bring to boil, reduce heat, simmer 2 minutes.

*To Make Coconut Milk:* Combine 1 cup water and ¼ cup coconut in saucepan; bring slowly to boil. Remove from heat, allow to stand 10 minutes. Then strain, pushing coconut with a spoon to get as much flavour as possible into the coconut milk.

## Savoury Pancakes

2 cups plain flour
salt, pepper
1 oz. butter
1 teaspoon dry mustard
2 eggs
approx. 1 pint milk
1½ cups grated cheese
parsley

Separate eggs, melt butter. Sift together dry ingredients. Make well in centre, add egg-yolks and melted butter to flour mixture. Gradually add milk, stirring constantly until mixture is smooth. Lastly fold in stiffly beaten egg-whites.

Heat and lightly oil frying pan. Pour sufficient batter into frying pan to make thin pancakes, cook over medium heat until lightly browned, turn and cook other side. While hot, spread desired filling evenly over pancakes. Roll each up separately, place on entree dish. Sprinkle with cheese, grill or bake in moderately hot oven until cheese melts or browns. Serve on individual dishes garnished with parsley.

Makes 10 to 12 pancakes.

A choice of 3 fillings is given below. If the main course is to be fish, meat, or poultry, you can choose a filling for the pancake entree that will contrast with the main dish.

**Red Salmon**

8 oz. can red salmon
2 dessertspoons chopped mint
4 oz. cream cheese
2 oz. cheese
1 teaspoon curry powder
½ teaspoon sugar
2 dessertspoons lemon juice
salt, pepper

Drain salmon and remove bones. Combine salmon with remaining ingredients; mix well. Season to taste with salt and pepper.

**Asparagus**

2 oz. butter
½ cup flour
1 lb. can green asparagus tips
2 oz. cheese
2 egg-yolks
⅔ cup finely chopped celery
4 rashers bacon
salt, pepper

Drain asparagus, make liquid up to ¾ pint with water. Melt butter in saucepan, stir in flour, cook few minutes. Gradually add reserved liquid. Bring to boil, stirring; simmer 3 minutes. Remove from heat, add egg-yolks, celery, grated cheese and asparagus.

Chop bacon, cook in frying pan until crisp, add to asparagus mixture. Season to taste.

**Chicken**

2 cups cooked chicken
1 stick celery
2 medium potatoes
½ cup milk
1 oz. butter
3 oz. mushrooms
2 chopped shallots
2 egg-yolks
1½ teaspoons salt
2 teaspoons curry powder
pinch pepper
½ teaspoon nutmeg
2 tablespoons port wine

Finely chop chicken meat, mushrooms and celery. Push peeled boiled potatoes through sieve.

Melt butter in saucepan, saute mushrooms until soft. Add sieved potato and milk, stir over low heat until mixture is heated and thoroughly combined. Remove from heat, add chopped shallots, celery, egg-yolks and chicken. Stir in curry powder and wine. Season to taste with salt, pepper and nutmeg; mix well.

## Dutch Bitterballs

| | |
|---|---|
| 1 oz. butter | 1 teaspoon chopped parsley |
| 1 teaspoon gelatine | salt, pepper |
| 1 oz. cheese | nutmeg |
| 2 tablespoons flour | 1 egg |
| 3 oz. chopped raw veal | oil |
| 3 oz. chopped ham | dried breadcrumbs |

Cover veal with water and simmer until tender. Drain, reserve $\frac{1}{2}$ pint stock. Dissolve gelatine in hot veal stock.

Melt butter, add flour, cook 1 minute. Remove from heat. Gradually add stock. Return to heat, bring to boil, simmer until smooth and thickened, stirring constantly. Add chopped veal and ham, grated cheese, and parsley. Season well, turn into bowl, refrigerate overnight.

Using teaspoon, form mixture into small balls. Roll in dried breadcrumbs, dip in beaten egg, roll again in breadcrumbs to give firm coating. Deep fry in hot oil until golden, drain on absorbent paper.

These are the famous Dutch savoury snack and drink accompaniment. They are traditionally served with a mild mustard, into which the balls are dipped before eating. It is the mustard accompaniment which gives them their name.

Makes approx. 2 dozen

## Grilled Chicken Livers

| | |
|---|---|
| 1 lb. chicken livers | ⅔ cup fine dry breadcrumbs |
| 2 oz. butter | |

**Sauce**

| | |
|---|---|
| 1 oz. butter | 1 dessertspoon grated onion |
| 1 tablespoon prepared mustard | pinch cayenne |
| 2 tablespoons tomato paste | 2 teaspoons worcestershire sauce |
| 2 tablespoons water | |

Melt butter, dip cleaned chicken livers into butter, then coat firmly with breadcrumbs. Thread on to 3 or 4 skewers. Place on greased grilling tray and grill about 3 minutes on each side or until chicken livers are tender. Serve with sauce for spooning over or dipping.

Serves 3 to 4.

*Sauce* Melt butter in saucepan, add remaining ingredients, stir over heat until boiling.

NOTE: In their uncooked state, chicken livers are very tender; if too thick skewers are used, the livers may break. The fine bamboo skewers are ideal. They can be bought in some specialty shops, or shops which sell oriental goods.

## Crunchy Cheese Croutons

| | |
|---|---|
| 2 oz. cheddar cheese | salt, pepper |
| ¼ cup chopped parsley | french bread |
| 1½ oz. butter | |

Combine butter, grated cheese and parsley in bowl; blend well until creamy and smooth. Season to taste Place slices of french bread on baking tray; cover surface with cheese mixture. Bake in very hot oven 8 to 10 minutes or until lightly golden brown and crisp.

Sufficient covering for approx. 12 slices of french bread.

NOTE: For a more crunchy top, press tops of croutons in finely chopped nuts before baking.

These are a quick-and-easy, delightfully savoury snack to eat just as they are, hot from the oven. Or serve them as an accompaniment to soup or grills.

## Cheese Twists

| | |
|---|---|
| 4 oz. butter | 1 egg |
| 1½ cups plain flour | salt |
| 7 oz. grated cheddar cheese | |

Rub butter into sifted flour. Add 5 oz. grated cheese, stir in egg; mix well. Roll out dough to $\frac{1}{8}$ in. thickness on floured board. Cut out $\frac{1}{4}$ in. x $4\frac{1}{2}$ in. strips. Twist 2 strips together, place on greased oven tray, sprinkle with remaining cheese. Bake in hot oven 10 to 12 minutes or until golden brown. Sprinkle with salt while still hot. Loosen and allow to cool on trays.

Makes approx. 5 dozen

## Savoury Bread Cases

| | |
|---|---|
| sliced bread | melted butter |

*To Make Cases* Remove crust from bread slices. If using one-day-old bread, brush slices lightly with melted butter; for fresh bread, this is not necessary. Press into deep, greased patty pans. Bake in moderate oven approximately 20 minutes or until golden and crisp.

☛

Spoon hot filling in just before serving, or they can be filled 30 minutes ahead, then reheated in moderate oven 5 to 7 minutes; they can also be made days ahead and stored, unfilled, in air-tight tin.

#### Fillings

#### Basic Sauce

| | |
|---|---|
| 1 oz. butter | ½ pint milk |
| 2 tablespoons flour | salt, pepper |

Melt butter in saucepan, stir in flour, cook 1 minute. Remove from heat, gradually add milk, blend well. Return to heat, bring to boil, reduce heat, simmer until smooth and thickened, stirring constantly. Season well.

Canned salmon, seasoned with lemon juice, with chopped parsley added, can be mixed into the basic sauce; or stir in drained asparagus pieces with chopped hard-boiled eggs and a little curry powder; or drained whole kernel corn, little grated cheese, chopped parsley makes a good combination.

Makes enough filling for approx. 12

## Ham Savouries

| | |
|---|---|
| 2 oz. butter | 1½ tablespoons water |
| ½ cup flour | salt, pepper |
| ½ pint milk | pinch nutmeg |
| 8 oz. cooked ham | pinch dry mustard |
| 1½ tablespoons chopped parsley | beaten egg |
| 3 teaspoons gelatine | breadcrumbs |

Soften gelatine in the water. Mince or chop ham finely. Melt butter, add flour and cook, stirring, 1 minute. Remove from heat, gradually add milk. Return to heat, cook until thickened, stirring constantly.

Dissolve gelatine over hot water. Add ham, parsley and gelatine to sauce, add mustard and nutmeg; season to taste. Spread on tray, refrigerate until set.

Form into balls, about the size of large walnut. Dip in beaten egg, then in breadcrumbs; do this twice. Deep fry until golden brown.

Makes approx. 3½ dozen

## Little Italian Pizzas

#### Quick Pizza Dough

| | |
|---|---|
| 2 cups self-raising flour | 1 oz. butter |
| pinch salt | oil |
| ¾ cup milk | |

Sift dry ingredients into basin, rub in butter. Add liquid nearly all at once, keeping a little back to be used only if dough seems too dry. Knead lightly on floured board and roll out thinly. Cut into squares or rounds, place on oiled tray. Brush dough over lightly with oil. Bake in hot oven 5 to 8 minutes. Remove from oven.

Arrange toppings on partly cooked scone dough, return to oven and continue cooking until golden brown (approximately further 10 to 15 minutes). For flavour and colour sprinkle a little chopped parsley on top of each pizza after cooking.

#### Ideas for Toppings

1. Rounds of salami, slices of tomato, salt, pepper, cheese slices, and, if desired, sliced stuffed olives.
2. Bacon and onion chopped finely and cooked lightly, slices of tomato, salt, pepper, grated cheese.

## Stuffed Eggs

Eggs, hard-boiled and halved, with yolks removed and combined with savoury ingredients, make a delicious hot weather snack. Serve on a bed of crisp lettuce, or with sticks of young celery or asparagus spears.

To make stuffed eggs, hard-boil eggs, cool and shell. Cut in halves length wise, remove yolks. Rub yolks through sieve, using wooden spoon, then mix in any of the following well-blended combinations and spoon or pipe back into egg-halves. Quantities given are sufficient for 6 eggs.

- □ 1 small jar black caviar, ½ cup cream, salt, pepper, juice ½ lemon.
- □ 2 tablespoons finely chopped ham, 2 chopped gherkins, salt, pepper. Add sufficient mayonnaise to make a creamy mixture.
- □ 2 tablespoons pate, 1 tablespoon chopped parsley, salt and pepper.
- □ 2 tablespoons cream cheese, 1 teaspoon anchovy paste, salt, and pepper. Add mayonnaise to make a creamy mixture.
- □ ¼ cup canned tuna, 1 teaspoon prepared mustard, salt and pepper, mayonnaise to bind. Decorate platter with black olives.
- □ 1 small can anchovies. Chop finely, add to eggs with sufficient mayonnaise to bind.

A tempting selection of canapés; use any of these toppings: smoked salmon with scrambled eggs; lettuce, camembert cheese, sliced radish; asparagus and rare roast beef; prawns, lettuce, mayonnaise; lettuce, sardines, lemon; creamed blue cheese with stuffed olives; smoked salmon, asparagus, cucumber; liver pâté, beetroot, gherkins; egg slices with anchovies; cucumber, prawns, mayonnaise; black caviar, lemon; cucumber, rare roast beef, cocktail onions

## Devils on Horseback

prunes
port wine
short ends of bacon rashers
small rounds of bread
oil

Stone prunes, soak overnight in port wine. Prunes can be stuffed with a little chutney. Roll each prune in slice of bacon, secure with small wooden stick. Grill gently, turning once. Serve on round of bread which has been fried in oil or hot bacon fat until crisp.

*Angels on Horseback:* Substitute plump oysters, dipped in lemon juice, for prunes; wrap and grill.

## Hot Crab Savouries

½ oz. butter
1½ tablespoons flour
½ cup chicken stock
6¾ oz. can crab meat
2 tablespoons chopped mushrooms
¼ cup mayonnaise
¼ cup cream
1 dessertspoon chopped parsley
salt, pepper
seasoned flour
oil for deep frying

Melt butter, blend in flour, cook 1 minute. Remove from heat, blend in chicken stock; return to heat and cook, stirring, until sauce boils and thickens. Drain crab well, saute mushrooms in a little butter, add to sauce with mayonnaise, cream, parsley, salt and pepper. Refrigerate mixture until firm; roll into balls, toss in seasoned flour.

Fry in hot deep oil until golden brown.

Makes approx. 1½ dozen

## Hot Steak Titbits

1 lb. rump steak
½ cup oil
½ cup wine vinegar or white vinegar
1 cup water
1 onion
2 cloves garlic
1 green pepper
1 cup red wine
1 teaspoon salt
½ teaspoon mixed spice
2 oz. butter

Cut steak into 1 in. squares. Combine in a bowl sliced pepper and onion, and crushed garlic with remaining ingredients, except butter. Marinate steak in mixture. Leave in refrigerator several hours or overnight. Drain, reserve liquid and vegetables.

Melt butter in frying pan, add meat. Saute quickly until well done. Add onions, green pepper, and ½ cup of reserved liquid. Saute further 2 to 3 minutes.

Serve hot, in a bowl, accompanied by cocktail sticks and toast squares.

## Garlic Crisps

12 slices bread
3 oz. butter
2 cloves garlic
3 to 4 oz. grated parmesan cheese

Place butter and crushed garlic in saucepan; heat gently, stirring, until butter has melted. Remove from heat, let stand several hours so butter absorbs the full garlic flavour. Remove crusts from bread. Brush bread slices generously with garlic butter on one side, sprinkle generously with grated cheese. Cut bread into fingers or triangles (or, with sharp cutter, cut out 2 in. rounds of bread before brushing with butter). Place on lightly greased baking tray, bake in moderate oven 15 to 20 minutes.

Makes approx. 12 circles or approx. 4 dozen triangles or fingers.

## Savoury Celery Sticks

celery sticks, approx. 2½ in. long
4 oz. packet cream cheese
salt, pepper
1 tablespoon chopped gherkin
2 slices ham (about 3 oz.)

Wash celery sticks, cut into required length. Beat cheese in bowl until smooth. Stir in chopped gherkin and finely chopped ham; blend well. Season to taste with salt and pepper. Fill cheese mixture into celery sticks.

Two ounces blue cheese can replace 2 oz. of the cream cheese in above ingredients.

## Crab Tartlets

8 oz. shortcrust pastry
2 oz. gruyere cheese
4 oz. can crab meat
½ cup sour cream
1 tablespoon mayonnaise
approx. ½ cup cream
1 egg
1 tablespoon finely chopped parsley
½ teaspoon salt
pepper

Roll out pastry to ¼ in. thickness, cut into rounds with 2½ in. cutter; line 24 tartlet tins. Dice cheese very finely, flake crab meat. Put into pastry cases.

Combine sour cream with mayonnaise, add cream to measure 1 cup of liquid. Blend in lightly beaten egg, chopped parsley and seasoning. Pour into pastry shells. Bake in moderately hot oven 25 minutes.

Makes 2 dozen tartlets

## Dips

Creamy mixtures, almost endless in their variety. Serve them with a surround of small cracker biscuits; or have crisp sticks of celery or young carrot, or potato chips for dunking. Dips can also be used as savoury spreads for canapes

### French Onion Dip

8 oz. packet cream cheese
½ cup water
1 packet french onion soup

Soften cream cheese in a bowl; gradually beat in water. Add onion soup, beat well. (Best if made the day before for full flavour).

Makes approx. 1½ cups.

For another delicious onion dip, blend 1 packet of french onion soup into 1 cup of sour cream.

### Asparagus Dip

4 oz. packet cream cheese
salt, pepper
1 small can asparagus pieces
lemon juice

Drain asparagus, reserve liquid, mash asparagus pieces with a fork. Place cream cheese in a basin, beat until smooth and softened, then gradually beat in asparagus pulp, mixing to a soft consistency; add a little asparagus liquid, if necessary. Season with salt, pepper, flavour with lemon juice.

Makes approx. 1 cup

### Brandied Blue Dip

4 oz. blue cheese
½ oz. butter
2 tablespoons mayonnaise
1 egg-yolk
1 tablespoon brandy
1 tablespoon cream or milk
½ clove garlic

Cream cheese and butter in bowl until smooth. Add mayonnaise, egg-yolk, brandy and cream or milk. Blend well to make a soft consistency. Add crushed garlic.

Makes approx. 1½ cups

### Devilled Ham Dip

1 teaspoon gelatine
½ cup tomato juice
6 oz. liverwurst
1 small can devilled ham paste
1 very small onion
1 teaspoon lemon juice
salt, pepper

Soften gelatine in tomato juice, stir over very low heat until gelatine dissolves. Blend liverwurst, ham paste, finely chopped onion, lemon juice, salt and pepper together in a basin; gradually stir in tomato juice mixture. Spoon into small bowl, refrigerate until required.

Serve with triangles of toast.

Makes approx. 1½ cups

### Tuna Dip

7 oz. can tuna
2 hard boiled eggs
2 oz. softened butter
1 dessertspoon chopped parsley
1 teaspoon chopped chives or shallots
salt, pepper
lemon juice

Drain tuna, push through fine sieve or blend in electric blender with eggs until well combined and smooth. Add softened butter, chives or shallots, and parsley, blend on low speed or mix until well combined. Season to taste with salt, pepper and a little lemon juice.

Makes approx. 1 cup

### Cheese and Cucumber Dip

4 oz. packet cream cheese
1½ tablespoons sour cream
1½ tablespoons grated onion
3 tablespoons finely chopped cucumber
¼ teaspoon salt
pinch pepper

Blend all ingredients in a small bowl.

Makes approx. 1½ cups

### Avocado dip

1 large, ripe avocado
4 oz. packaged cream cheese
1 tablespoon lemon juice
1 tablespoon mayonnaise
salt, pepper
1 teaspoon grated onion

Cut avocado in half, remove stone, scoop all the flesh into a bowl, add the softened cheese and mayonnaise. Blend together well. Add lemon juice, salt, pepper and grated onion, mix well. Use as a dip or savoury spread for toast and biscuits.

# SOUPS

## Hot Sou[illegible]

The family [illegible] hurry [illegible] these hot, hearty soups. A small bowl or cup of soup is a good start to a meal; a [illegible] mug of soup, served with hot cheese or bacon sandwiches, is a satisfying meal in [illegible]lf

### French Onion Soup

| | |
|---|---|
| 1 oz. butter | 3 pint[illegible] |
| 2 large onions | chicken s[illegible] |
| pinch sugar | salt, pepp[illegible] |
| 1 dessertspoon flour | |

Peel onions, cut into thick slices. Heat butter in pan (you may need a little more butter); add onions and sugar and cook, stirring, until golden and transparent; they should not be dark in colour. Stir in flour, gradually stir in stock. Season to taste with salt and pepper. Cover, cook gently 20 minutes. Spoon into hot bowls.

Take some slices of french bread, toast them, and sprinkle well with grated cheese. Place under griller until cheese melts and is golden. Put one toasted cheese slice on top of each bowl of steaming soup.

Or place a toasted round of french bread in base of soup plate, sprinkle with grated cheese, and gradually pour in soup. As toast floats to top, sprinkle with extra grated cheese.

(For easier eating, some people prefer to cut the crusts from toast before putting into bowl.)

On a cold winter's night, put 1 dessertspoon of brandy into each bowl before pouring in the hot onion soup.

Serves 6 to 8

### Scotch Broth

| | |
|---|---|
| 1½ lb. neck of mutton | 4 oz. barley |
| 2 carrots | salt, pepper |
| 2 onions | bouquet garni |
| 2 leeks | 2 quarts water or stock |
| 3 sticks celery | chopped parsley |

Prepare vegetables, chop finely. Wash barley, put into pot with vegetables, bouquet garni, meat, and stock or water. Bring slowly to the boil, skim well, then reduce heat, simmer, covered, 2 to 3 hours. Remove bones from meat, chop meat, return t[illegible] saucepan, add chopped parsley; season to taste.

Serves 8

### [illegible]y Soup with Rice

| | |
|---|---|
| [illegible] | 2 tablespoons rice |
| [illegible] | 3 pints water |
| [illegible] butter | 4 chicken stock cubes |
| [illegible] finely chopped | salt, pepper |
| cel[illegible] | chopped parsley |

Cut ham [illegible], finely chop onion. Melt butter, fry ham and [illegible] 2 minutes. Add celery and rice, fry further 2 minutes. [illegible] water, crumbled stock cubes and seasoning [illegible]. Cover, cook approximately 20 min[illegible], [illegible] occasionally. Serve sprinkled with c[illegible]

Serves 6 to 8.

### Lentil Soup

| | |
|---|---|
| 6 oz. dried lentils | [illegible] oz. [illegible] |
| 2½ pints beef stock | 1 tablespoon [illegible] |
| ham or bacon bones | freshly ground black pepper |
| 2 potatoes | |

Wash lentils and drain. Cover with cold water a[illegible] leave to stand at least 2 hours. Strain. Place in a lar[illegible] saucepan, with stock and bones, cover, bring to bo[illegible] reduce heat and simmer for half an hour, or u[illegible] lentils are tender. Add potatoes and simmer further 20 minutes. Cream together butter and fl[illegible] and gradually mix into soup, then cook for a f[illegible] minutes longer. Add pepper to taste. Serve w[illegible] lots of hot buttered toast, or hot rolls.

Serves 6

French Onion Soup—so easy to make, so very good to eat, [illegible] cheese-toast can top each serving

## Pea Soup

½ lb. split peas
1 chopped onion
1 carrot
few bacon pieces and bones
2½ pints stock or water
salt, pepper

Wash peas well. Put into saucepan with onion, carrot, bacon bones and pieces and stock or water. Bring slowly to boil, skim well. Cover, cook gently until peas are tender (about 2 hours). Push through coarse sieve, return to saucepan; taste, and season if necessary. A little finely chopped mint can be added to the soup before serving.

Top with small croutons or sippets made by sauteing small cubes of bread in bacon fat, butter or hot oil until golden; drain well before using.

Serves 6

## Curried Pea Soup

1 lb. quick-frozen peas
hot water
2 oz. butter
2 tablespoons flour
3 chicken stock cubes
2 pints water
1 to 2 dessertspoons curry powder
1 cup milk
salt, pepper

Cover peas with hot water, bring to boil, boil until tender. Drain. Push through a fine sieve or puree in electric blender.

Melt butter in saucepan, stir in flour, mix well. Cook over low heat 2 minutes. Remove from heat, gradually add chicken stock (made with stock cubes and water). Return to heat, simmer 2 minutes, stirring constantly.

Stir pureed peas, curry powder, and milk into sauce. Season with salt and pepper. Bring to boil, stirring, reduce heat, simmer 2 minutes.

Serves 6 to 8

## Minestrone

½ lb. haricot beans
1 dessertspoon oil
1 clove garlic
1 onion
1 teaspoon chopped parsley
¾ teaspoon basil
6 shallots
1 tablespoon tomato paste
3 tomatoes
3 sticks celery
2 carrots
2 potatoes
2 pints chicken stock
salt, pepper
1 cup elbow macaroni
extra parsley
grated parmesan cheese

Soak beans overnight in cold water; drain. Boil in salted water about 1 hour or until tender; drain and reserve.

Prepare vegetables: crush garlic, chop onion and shallots, peel, seed, and chop tomatoes, chop celery and 1 carrot, slice the other carrot, peel and chop potatoes.

Heat oil in large saucepan, saute garlic, onion, shallots, parsley and basil until lightly browned. Add tomato paste and cook, stirring, 5 minutes. Add tomatoes, celery, carrots, potatoes and stock. Bring to the boil; reduce heat, simmer gently 45 minutes to 1 hour or until vegetables are tender; add the beans. Add macaroni and cook 10 minutes or until tender.

Season to taste with salt and pepper. Serve sprinkled with chopped parsley and grated parmesan.

Serves 6 to 8

## Chinese Long Soup

½ lb. lean pork
8 shallots
¼ head cabbage
1 tablespoon oil
3 pints chicken stock
1½ tablespoons soy sauce
salt
4 oz. egg noodles
½ cup finely chopped shallots

Cut pork in shreds. Wash shallots and cabbage, slice finely. Heat oil in large saucepan, add pork and cabbage, fry quickly a few minutes, stirring constantly. Add stock and seasonings. Bring slowly to boil, reduce heat, add shallots, simmer 10 to 15 minutes.

Meanwhile, cook noodles until tender in boiling salted water (5 to 6 minutes); drain well. To serve, place a spoonful of noodles in the base of each soup bowl. Pour over the hot soup, sprinkle a few extra chopped shallots on top.

Serves 8

## Cream of Cauliflower Soup

¼ cauliflower
2¼ cups milk
2¼ cups water
2 oz. butter
⅓ cup flour
1 chicken stock cube
½ teaspoon nutmeg
salt, pepper
¼ cup cream

Trim cauliflower, cut into large flowerets. Wash well. Place in saucepan with milk and water. Bring to boil, reduce heat, simmer slowly, covered, until just tender. Remove from heat; drain, reserve liquid. Melt butter in saucepan, stir in flour, cook 1 minute. Remove from heat, gradually stir in reserved liquid. Return to heat, bring to boil, stirring; stir until smooth and thickened. Reduce heat, stir in crumbled stock cube, nutmeg, and salt and pepper to taste. Stir in cream. Cut cauliflower into small flowerets, return to soup. Heat through gently.

Serves 4 to 6

## Crab Chowder

1 pint fish or chicken stock
8 oz. can crab meat
½ pint milk
½ oz. butter
1 large chopped onion
2 oz. bacon
1 large potato
1½ tablespoons flour
1 teaspoon worcestershire sauce
salt, pepper
½ pint cream
3 oz. grated cheese
chopped parsley

Combine in saucepan the stock, juice from can of crab, and milk. Bring to boil; remove from heat. Melt butter in separate saucepan; add onion and chopped bacon, brown lightly. Stir in flour, cook 1 minute. Gradually add hot stock. Bring to boil, stirring; simmer 5 minutes. Add potato, cut into small cubes; cover and simmer further 20 minutes.

Season to taste with worcestershire sauce, salt and pepper. Add crab meat, flaked into large pieces. Just before serving, pour in cream, heat through gently. Top each serving with grated cheese and parsley.

Serves 4 to 6

## Cream of Asparagus

2 oz. butter
1 medium onion
2 sticks celery
⅓ cup flour
4 cups boiling water
3 chicken stock cubes
1 lb. can asparagus spears
salt, pepper
¼ pint cream

Melt butter in pan, fry chopped onion and celery until soft but not brown. Stir in flour, cook 1 minute. Remove from heat, gradually stir in water, in which stock cubes have been dissolved. Return to heat, bring to boil, stirring. Add asparagus and juice from can. Simmer for 30 to 40 minutes.

Puree in blender or rub through a sieve, return to pan, reheat gently. Add cream; season with salt and pepper, if necessary.

Serves 4 to 6

## Avgolemono (Egg-Lemon Soup)

3 pints chicken stock
⅓ cup rice
2 eggs
juice 1 lemon
salt, pepper

Put the stock in saucepan, add the washed rice, boil ten to 15 minutes until rice is cooked. In basin, beat the eggs and add the lemon juice. Add boiling broth to eggs in basin, spoon by spoon, stirring constantly. Return mixture to saucepan and stir a few minutes over very low heat; season to taste.

Serves 6 to 8

## Mulligatawny Soup

3 oz. butter
1 onion
2 teaspoons garam masala
2 cloves
2 bayleaves
2 teaspoons curry powder
1 lb. uncooked chicken
4 oz. lentils
2 tablespoons flour
½ cup tomato purée
4 pints stock
1 cup cooked rice

Melt butter, fry chopped onion until golden, add spices and cook 1 minute. Add chicken, fry 5 minutes. Add remaining ingredients, bring to boil, reduce heat and simmer, covered 1½ to 2 hours. After 30 minutes of cooking remove chicken, allow to cool, cut meat into dice. Set aside.

At serving time, strain soup through a sieve, reheat. Put a little diced chicken and a little boiled rice in base of each serving dish, pour over the hot soup.

Serves 6

## Oyster Soup

2 to 3 dozen oysters
2½ cups milk
1 cup cream
2 oz. butter
½ cup plain flour
salt, pepper
chopped parsley
paprika

Melt butter in pan, add flour; cook, stirring, 1 minute. Remove from heat, gradually stir in milk and any oyster liquor. Return to heat, cook, stirring constantly until mixture boils and thickens. Add cream and oysters, heat through but do not allow to boil. Add salt and pepper. Serve sprinkled with chopped parsley and paprika.

Serves 6 to 8

## Potato and Marjoram Soup

2 potatoes
½ pint water
½ pint milk
1 oz. butter
1 tablespoon flour
salt
chopped marjoram
¼ pint water, extra
¼ pint milk, extra

Peel potatoes, cut into small pieces. Simmer uncovered in combined water and milk until soft. When completely soft, puree or rub through a sieve with the liquid.

In another pan, melt butter, stir in flour, cook 1 minute. Remove from heat. Gradually add ¼ pint milk and ¼ pint water. Return to heat. Bring to boil, simmer until smooth and thickened, stirring constantly. Add potato puree and finely chopped marjoram. Reheat gently.

Serves 4

# Cold Soups

These are superb soups you'll be proud to serve. They're light, subtly flavoured—the perfect start to a summer meal.

## Tomato Soup

16 oz. can condensed tomato soup
1½ cups chicken stock
1 medium onion
pinch of dill or oregano
1 dessertspoon tomato paste
¼ pint cream
chopped parsley

Place tomato soup, chicken stock, chopped onion, dill and tomato paste into saucepan, heat gently, stirring constantly, until soup begins to boil; remove from heat, strain through sieve; stir in cream. Refrigerate. Serve garnished with chopped parsley.

Serves 4 to 6

## Cold Pumpkin Soup

2 lb. pumpkin
1½ lb. tomatoes
1 lb. onions
pepper and salt
water
2 chicken stock cubes

Peel pumpkin and cut into pieces; skin tomatoes; peel and chop onions. Put all vegetables in pan. Add water to cover, stir in crumbled stock cubes.

Bring to boil; reduce heat, simmer until pumpkin is tender. Puree or rub through a sieve. Season to taste. Refrigerate. Garnish with a little sour cream and chopped chives.

Serves 6 to 8

## Cold Curry Soup

6 shallots
1 oz. butter
2 teaspoons curry powder
2 tablespoons flour
2 pints vegetable or chicken stock
1 piece lemon rind
1 egg-yolk
2 tablespoons cream
salt, pepper
chopped chives

Chop shallots, cook gently in butter until golden brown; add curry powder, cook another 5 minutes. Stir in flour; add stock and lemon rind. Bring to the boil, reduce heat, simmer 15 minutes, stirring occasionally.

Puree or rub through a sieve. Return to saucepan, season to taste. Add 2 tablespoons of hot soup to egg-yolk and cream combined, then add this slowly to the soup, beating constantly. Reheat without boiling until soup thickens. Cool, then refrigerate. Serve topped with chopped chives.

Serves 4

## Iced Avocado Soup

2 large ripe avocados
little lemon juice
2 large cans beef consommé or consommé madrilene
1 cup sour cream
salt, pepper
1 teaspoon grated onion
chopped parsley

Halve avocados, scoop out flesh. Mash with lemon juice, or puree in electric blender approximately 12 seconds on low speed. Warm soup slightly, remove from heat, combine with avocado and sour cream. Season with salt, pepper, and onion; refrigerate.

Top each serving with a little parsley.

Serves 6 to 8

## Cream of Carrot Soup

4 carrots
1 onion
1 stick celery
4 cups chicken stock
salt, pepper
½ cup cooked rice
¼ pint cream

Slice carrots, onion and celery; place in saucepan with 2 cups of stock. Bring to boil; reduce heat, cover, simmer 15 minutes. Remove from heat, add salt, pepper, and rice. Puree in electric blender or rub through a fine sieve. Beat in remaining stock and cream; chill. Garnish each serving with a little chopped parsley.

Serves 4 to 6

## Cold Borsch

1 lb. fresh beetroot
1 small onion
4 cups chicken stock
1 tablespoon sugar
1 teaspoon salt
1 tablespoon lemon juice
sour cream

Peel beetroot and onion, cut into ½ in. dice; cover and cook in chicken stock until tender. Drain the vegetables, reserving the liquid. Cool a little. Place vegetables with a little liquid into electric blender, or rub through a fine sieve. Add remaining liquid, sugar, salt and lemon juice to the vegetable puree. Refrigerate until well chilled. Top each serving with a spoonful of sour cream.

Serves 6 to 8

Superbly flavoured cold soups for hot days. 1, Tomato Soup; 2, Borsch; 3, Vichyssoise; 4, Cream of Broccoli (also in tureen); 5, Pumpkin; 6, Curry

## Iced Cucumber Soup

3 cucumbers
1 oz. butter
1 leek (white part only)
1 bayleaf
1 dessertspoon flour
1 teaspoon salt
2 cups chicken stock
1 cup cream
juice ½ lemon
1 teaspoon finely chopped mint
salt, pepper

Peel and halve 2 cucumbers, remove seeds, cut into ½in. dice, slice leek. Melt butter in saucepan, add cucumber, leek, and bayleaf; saute 10 minutes until tender but not brown. Stir in flour, cook over low heat 1 minute; gradually add chicken stock. Cook, stirring constantly until thickened. Add salt, simmer gently 30 minutes. Remove from heat, cool.

Push through fine sieve or blend in electric blender; refrigerate. Peel, seed and grate remaining cucumber, add to soup with cream and lemon juice, mix well. Adjust seasoning with salt and pepper, stir in mint; refrigerate. Serve icy cold, topped with a spoonful of sour cream or whipped cream.

Serves 6 to 8

## Consommé with Caviar

2 cans consommé madrilene or beef consommé
1 cup sour cream
two 3½ oz. jars black caviar

Chill 4 soup bowls well. Place ½ can well-chilled consomme into each bowl. Place 1 or 2 tablespoons of sour cream on top of each, cover this with a generous tablespoon of caviar.

Serves 4

## Vichyssoise

4 leeks
1 medium onion
2 oz. butter
5 medium potatoes
2 pints chicken stock
1 tablespoon salt
2 cups milk
½ pint cream

Slice leeks and onions and fry in butter until just turning golden. Add sliced potatoes, chicken stock and salt. Bring to boil; reduce heat, cook 35 to 40 minutes; cool. Place about half the cooled mixture in blender, blend on high speed 1 minute, repeat with remaining half. Pour mixture back into saucepan, add milk and ¼ pint cream.

Season to taste, bring to boil; cool. Put quarter of mixture into blender. Blend on high speed 30 seconds. Repeat until all mixture is blended. When cold, stir in remaining ¼ pint cream; refrigerate.

Serve sprinkled with chopped chives or parsley.

Serves 8

## Green Vichyssoise

1 cup chopped raw potato
4 chopped shallots (green tops included)
2 cups chicken stock
½ cup fresh or frozen green peas
salt
1 cup cream
extra cream for topping

Simmer vegetables with stock and salt for 10 minutes, or until barely tender. Rub through sieve or puree in electric blender. Return to saucepan, add cream, heat gently without boiling. Cool, then refrigerate. Top each serving with a spoonful of whipped cream.

Serves 4

## Gazpacho

¾ lb. ripe tomatoes
1 small cucumber
1 small onion
½ green pepper
2 sticks celery
1 small clove garlic
1½ cups tomato juice
2½ tablespoons oil
1½ tablespoons wine vinegar
salt, pepper
few drops tabasco sauce

Peel and coarsely cube all vegetables; reserve about ¼ of vegetable mixture to use for garnish. Place remaining vegetables in blender with tomato juice, oil, vinegar, salt, pepper and tabasco sauce; blend 40 seconds on high speed. Pour into bowl, refrigerate. Place vegetable mixture reserved for garnish into blender. Blend 10 seconds on low speed. Spoon into soup bowls, pour chilled pureed mixture on top.

Serves 6

## Cream of Broccoli Soup

1 onion
1 carrot
1 stick celery
1 clove garlic
boiling water
10 oz. packet frozen broccoli
salt, pepper
1 cup chicken stock
¼ pint cream

Peel and chop onion, carrot and celery, place in small saucepan, add ½ cup boiling water and a good pinch of salt. Cover, cook until tender; set aside. Cook frozen broccoli in boiling water until tender. Drain and cool.

Puree drained broccoli with vegetables and liquid in which vegetables were cooked, crushed garlic and chicken stock in electric blender, or rub through a fine sieve. Stir in cream, season to taste. Refrigerate until well chilled. If desired, top each serving with a little whipped cream.

Serves 6

# EGGS

Eggs are one of the few foods we can eat, in one form or the other, each day—and enjoy them every time. Omelets, souffles, vegetarian curries—eggs play an essential part in all types of sweet and savoury dishes

When buying eggs it is obviously wise to obtain the freshest possible. The water trial is a reliable test for freshness. To make this test, place the egg in sufficient cold water to cover it. Fresh eggs will lie flat in water. Slightly stale eggs will tilt a little. They can be used for frying or scrambling without ill effect. Stale eggs will sit upright in water.

Eggs should be stored in refrigerator or cool cupboard, with ends pointing down; when the yolk rises, the air space protects it from touching the shell. If storing in cupboard, ensure there is good circulation of air. Eggshells are porous and should not be washed before storing, because this removes the fine covering film. They tend to absorb strong odours, and should not be stored near strong-smelling foods.

## Storage of left-over eggs

*Yolks* Store in refrigerator, covered with cold water.

*Whites* or *Whole Eggs out of shell* Store in covered container in refrigerator.

## Basic Cooking Methods

Eggs are coagulated by heat, and are best cooked slowly at low temperature. High cooking temperatures toughen coagulated protein contained in eggs, and over-cooking results in a tough, dry dish or, if any liquid has been added, curdling.

There are five basic ways of cooking eggs—boiling, poaching, steaming, baking, frying.

## Boiled Eggs

There are several methods of boiling eggs—we set them out below. You might like to try each method to see which one gives the best result for your family's taste.

In each case, choose a saucepan of suitable size. Don't have a big saucepan if you're cooking only one or two eggs, don't overcrowd a number of eggs into a small saucepan.

1 Place eggs in saucepan, add cold water to cover them by 1 in. Bring rapidly to boil. Start timing from when water boils. (Cooking times are given below.) Once water boils, reduce heat to simmering, cook for required time.

2 Bring to the boil sufficient water to cover eggs. Gently spoon eggs into saucepan. Keep at full heat until water boils again and start timing from this moment. Reduce heat to simmering for rest of cooking.

For this method it is important the eggs should be at room temperature before lowering into water, otherwise the shell could crack. A simple way to bring them quickly to room temperature is to hold eggs for a few minutes under warm running water.

3 For hard-boiled eggs use Methods 1 or 2. Cook eggs for 8 to 10 minutes. Do not over-cook eggs or the smell can be unpleasant. When eggs are cooked, run cold water over them. Crack each shell gently. Eggs will shell easier if cracked and peeled from broad end.

### Cooking Times

Times given are for a standard-sized 2 to $2\frac{1}{2}$ oz. egg. Adjust cooking times slightly for smaller or larger eggs.
Soft—3 minutes.
Medium—4 minutes.
Hard—8 to 10 minutes.

## Coddled Eggs

This cooks the eggs with a soft white, and is the method recommended for young children or invalids. Lower eggs into boiling water, as for Boiled Eggs, Method 2. Remove saucepan from heat, cover, and allow eggs to stand in hot water for 8 to 10 minutes. If a slightly firmer white is required, let egg boil for 1 minute only before removing from heat and covering to let stand.

## Fried Eggs

Butter or bacon fat adds a rich flavour when used to fry eggs, or they can be cooked without fat in non-stick pans. Here's how to get best results from both methods.

1 Melt small amount of butter or bacon fat in frying pan. Break eggs into pan one at a time—or break into saucer first, then slip into the melted butter. Cook slowly, basting yolk occasionally with the butter. Remove from pan with egg-slice.

If you like fried eggs to be perfectly round use egg-rings. These are quite cheap from hardware stores or kitchen sections of departmental stores.

Place egg-rings in hot butter, then turn over so that both sides are well greased—this will keep eggs from sticking to the rings. Use tongs or a fork for turning rings. Or use rings with non-stick coating.

Break an egg carefully into each ring. Baste the yolk occasionally until cooked. Remove rings before lifting eggs from pan with egg-slice. If rings stick, run a knife carefully around inside of ring to separate it from egg.

2 For health reasons—or because it saves time in the busy breakfast period—many people prefer to fry eggs in a non-stick pan, without butter. Just brushing the pan with butter will make all the difference to flavour and finished result. Without butter the white is apt to cook long before the yolk, and the white of the finished egg can be tough and somewhat indigestible.

However, if you prefer to fry eggs without fat, here's how to get the best results. Break eggs into pan, then quickly sprinkle about 3 tablespoons of hot water around eggs. Cover with lid. Cook gently about 3 minutes. This will partially steam the egg-yolk and hasten cooking time.

## Poached Eggs

Place approximately 1 in. of water in frying pan of suitable size. Add ½ teaspoon salt or 1 dessertspoon lemon juice to help eggs set and add flavour. Bring water to simmering point only; fast-boiling water tends to break up egg-whites.

Gently break in eggs. Hold eggs as close as possible to surface of water; this will help prevent them breaking, as they might if dropped from a height of a few inches. Occasionally, spoon some of the hot water over yolks. Simmer gently until cooked.

Cooking time will vary according to whether you like a soft or firmly poached egg, but it is around 3 to 5 minutes. Lift egg carefully with egg-slice, hold above pan for a few seconds to drain well.

*Steamed Eggs* This is a variation of the poached egg. Take a shallow pan with lid. Half-fill it with water, bring to the boil. Break eggs into the boiling water. Then place close-fitting lid on top, remove pan from heat. Let stand for 3½ to 4 minutes.

## Baked Eggs

Also known as 'Eggs en Cocotte'. Grease one small ramekin or 'cocotte' dish per person. Break an egg into each dish, season with salt and pepper; spoon cream over to cover egg. Bake in moderate oven 15 minutes, or until egg has set.

Some finely chopped cheese can be sprinkled into the dish before adding the egg and cream, and extra grated cheese sprinkled on the cream before baking.

## Scrambled Eggs

Allow 2 to 3 eggs per person. Add 1 tablespoon of water or milk or cream for each egg; water will make the scrambled eggs lighter in texture but milk or cream gives more flavour. Season with salt and pepper. Beat together lightly.

Melt ½ oz. butter in pan, add egg mixture; cook, stirring, until eggs are just set; don't have the heat too high, or eggs will be tough. Spoon on to hot toast.

Some grated cheese, chopped chives or shallots, curry powder, chopped parsley, canned whole kernel corn can be mixed in with the beaten eggs.

## Creamy Scrambled Eggs

2 oz. packaged cream cheese
1 oz. butter
⅓ cup cream
3 eggs
salt, pepper
½ cup finely chopped shallots

Combine cream cheese, butter and cream in frying pan, stir over low heat until creamy. Break eggs into mixture, cook gently until egg whites are barely set, add salt, pepper and shallots, stir mixture well with a fork until eggs are cooked. Serve on hot buttered toast.

Serves 2

Omelets — mixed and cooked in minutes — make a delicious, light meal

Citron = Omelette
10 Æggeblommer røres hvide med ½ Pd. hvidt
og med Saft af 3 Citroner, reven Skal af 2 og
røres de pidskede hvider i.

## Omelets

An omelet is quick to make, inexpensive, and most versatile. Plain, or with varying fillings, it can be served for breakfast, lunch, or a light main course for dinner. And sweet dessert omelets make a perfect light ending to a meal.

Flavourings, such as those for scrambled eggs, can be mixed into the savoury omelet. Asparagus; chopped, cooked bacon; fried tomato slices; chopped, cooked chicken; sauteed mushrooms, are other popular fillings or additions.

Serve omelets as soon as they are made; if left to stand, they become hard and tough.

### The Omelet Pan

It is best to keep a special pan just for omelets. A new omelet pan should be 'seasoned' before use. To do this, pour oil into the pan to cover the base and come a little way up sides. Warm this slowly over heat, and turn or gently shake pan occasionally so that the oil coats the sides. When the pan and oil are hot, remove from heat and allow to cool. Do this once more, and let the oil stand in the pan overnight. Next day, warm the pan and oil again, pour off the oil and wipe the pan dry. The pan is now ready for the cooking of omelets.

If possible, do not wash the omelet pan after use. Simply rub it clean with paper towelling or a clean cloth. This helps prevent omelets sticking to the pan. If you have to wash the pan, then season it again with oil, as above, before using it again.

### Types of Omelet

There are three basic types of omelets—the classic French omelet, the Spanish omelet and the Souffle, or 'puffy' omelet.

### French Omelet

3 eggs
salt, pepper
1 dessertspoon water
½ oz. butter

Break eggs into bowl, season with salt and pepper; add water. Beat eggs briskly with fork until well mixed. Heat pan, add butter; it should sizzle and foam almost immediately. Pour in egg mixture, and, using a fork, draw the eggs from the side of the pan into the centre; do this quickly, shaking the pan constantly. Continue lifting the eggs with a fork until all the liquid is cooked. With spatula or fork fold omelet and roll on to warmed serving plate. Serve immediately.

Serves 1

### Spanish Omelet

Unlike the French or Souffle omelet, the Spanish omelet is not folded or rolled, but is served flat. When the omelet is golden brown underneath, turn with spatula and cook the other side until just set, or place under griller to set the top; do not over-cook, or the omelet will toughen.

4 eggs
½ cup finely diced mixed vegetables
2 oz. butter
salt, pepper

Heat 1 oz. butter in saucepan, add vegetables, saute over gentle heat until tender but not brown. Break eggs into bowl, beat lightly with fork, season with salt and pepper, add cooked vegetables. Melt remaining butter in large omelet pan, when sizzling pour in egg mixture. Stir gently to distribute mixture evenly, then allow to set over low heat. When golden underneath, turn with spatula and allow to set on other side, or place under griller to set top. Serve immediately.

Serves 2.

Vegetables can include chopped onions, tomatoes; a light touch of crushed garlic and chopped parsley can also be added.

### Soufflé Omelet

The souffle (or 'puffy') omelet, as its name indicates, puffs up like a small souffle while cooking. After base of omelet is cooked, the pan is placed under griller or into moderate oven for a few minutes to set top lightly.

4 eggs
½ teaspoon salt
pinch pepper
1 tablespoon milk
½ oz. butter

Separate eggs, beat yolks until thick. Add salt, pepper and milk. Beat egg-whites until soft peaks form. Fold whites into yolks.

Heat pan, add butter, turn pan to allow butter to flow evenly over base and around sides of pan. Spread egg mixture evenly into pan, cook over medium heat until omelet puffs and under-part is lightly golden. Bake in moderate oven 5 minutes, or place under hot griller until top is firm and springs back when pressed lightly with fingertips. Fold over, serve immediately.

Serves 2.

For a savoury topping, sprinkle finely grated cheese over before placing under griller.

## Dessert Omelets

These are a version of the souffle omelet; omit salt and pepper from the souffle omelet recipe, add $\frac{1}{4}$ teaspoon sugar per egg before mixing omelet.

Individual dessert omelets can be made with 2 eggs in 6 in. pan.

Here are some suggested fillings:

*Apricot*: Spoon hot, sieved apricot jam over half of omelet, turn on to warm serving plate. A spoonful of rum can be added to the jam when heating, or a little rum can be warmed in a separate saucepan, poured over the omelet and set aflame. Serve a bowl of whipped cream separately.

*Strawberries and Cream*: Sweeten sliced fresh strawberries to taste, or use warmed canned strawberries. Fill omelet with 1 dessertspoon berries for each egg used. Fold over, decorate with whole fresh strawberries, or another spoonful of the canned strawberries. Serve with cream.

*Caramel Cream*: Do not fold omelet. Spread with fresh or canned peach slices marinaded in brandy or rum. Spread sour cream over, sprinkle with castor sugar. Place, unfolded, under griller just long enough to set cream and lightly caramelise the sugar.

*Sweet French Omelet*: For a sweet French omelet, add a small pinch salt and 1 dessertspoon sugar to the eggs before beating together; omit the pepper. Make the omelet, and after folding sprinkle with an extra dessertspoon of sugar; place under very hot griller for a few minutes or until sugar melts and glazes the omelet. Place on warmed serving plate. Or fill with a sweet filling as for Souffle Omelet.

## Egg and Bacon Pie

### Cheese Pastry

1½ cups plain flour
½ teaspoon salt
1 teaspoon baking powder
3 oz. butter
3 oz. tasty cheese
approx. 1 tablespoon water

### Filling

1 oz. butter
3 onions
4 to 6 rashers bacon
1 teaspoon salt
¼ teaspoon pepper
½ teaspoon dry mustard
3 eggs
1 pint milk
1 dessertspoon chopped parsley

*Pastry*: Sift flour, salt and baking powder into basin. Rub in butter, add grated cheese. Mix to dry dough with a little water. Knead lightly on floured board. Roll pastry out to line base and sides of 11 in. x 7 in. or deep 8 in. pie plate.

*Filling* Melt butter in saucepan, add sliced onions and chopped bacon; fry 4 minutes. Add salt, pepper and mustard, mix thoroughly. Beat eggs in basin, add warmed milk, drained onion-and-bacon mixture, and parsley. Spoon mixture into pastry case. Bake in moderate oven 35 to 40 minutes or until pie has set and browned.

Serves 6

## Quiche Lorraine

### Pastry

4 oz. butter
4 oz. packaged cream cheese
1 cup plain flour

### Filling

6 oz. gruyere cheese
4 rashers bacon
3 eggs
¾ cup cream
1 small onion
¼ teaspoon nutmeg
salt, pepper

*Pastry* Cream butter and cheese together. Add sifted flour, and blend with a fork. Wrap in waxed paper, refrigerate for 1 hour. Roll out to fit 8 or 9 in. pie plate. Refrigerate while preparing filling.

*Filling* Slice cheese thinly (or use packaged cheese slices), cut into 2 in. strips. Cut bacon into small pieces, fry until crisp, drain. Arrange alternate layers of bacon and cheese in pie case; sprinkle with chopped onion. Beat eggs lightly, combine with cream and seasonings, pour over bacon and cheese.

Bake in hot oven for 10 minutes, reduce heat to moderate, cook further 30 minutes or until set.

Serves 6

## Malayan Egg Curry

1½ lb. onions
1 or 2 small green chillies
1 clove garlic
2 cups chicken stock
2 teaspoons turmeric
1 tablespoon curry powder
1 teaspoon salt
6 hard boiled eggs

Slice onions, green chillies and garlic. Combine all ingredients except salt and eggs in saucepan, simmer uncovered 30 minutes. Halve eggs, add with salt to curry mixture, heat well, serve over hot boiled rice.

Serves 4.

NOTE: ½ cup coconut may be added with all ingredients, increase stock to 1½ cups.

## Indian Egg Curry

4 medium onions
2 cloves garlic
4 medium tomatoes
4 oz. butter
2 teaspoons coriander
1 teaspoon turmeric
1 teaspoon ground ginger
2 teaspoons cumin
2 teaspoons paprika
1 teaspoon salt
¼ teaspoon chilli powder
2 teaspoons garam masala
6 hard boiled eggs

Slice two onions, finely chop remaining onions and garlic. Peel and chop tomatoes. Heat butter in a saucepan, add sliced onion, saute until golden brown, add remaining onion, garlic and tomatoes, saute 3 minutes. Add remaining ingredients, except garam masala and eggs, simmer uncovered, until some of the liquid has evaporated (approximately 30 minutes), stir occasionally.

Halve eggs, add with garam masala to curry mixture, heat well, serve over hot boiled rice.

Serves 4

## Eggs Benedict

Saute a slice of ham in butter until hot. Lift on to hot buttered toast, top with a poached egg. Spoon over hollandaise sauce.

For a quick hollandaise, warm ½ cup mayonnaise in top of double saucepan over hot water, combine with ½ cup whipped cream.

## Egg Nog

1 egg
1 tablespoon sugar
1 tablespoon brandy
1 tablespoon rum
½ pint milk
grated nutmeg

Whisk all ingredients together, except nutmeg, until well blended. Pour into glass and sprinkle top with nutmeg. Serves 1

Cheese Soufflé — tall, tempting, feather-light in texture. The soufflé mixture can be refrigerated — even frozen — in advance

## Soufflés

In the past, souffles have been temperamental—you had to mix, cook, serve them without a moment's delay. But these special recipes allow you to prepare the mixture well ahead of time, refrigerate it overnight—or even freeze it for up to five days—and when baked it will rise as tall and as tempting as ever before

### Preparing the Dish

Each recipe in this section will make one large or four individual souffles. For large souffle, 7 in. (approximately 2½ pint capacity) souffle dish is used; individual souffle dishes have about ½ pint capacity. Grease dish or dishes; tie collar of greased greaseproof paper or aluminium foil round top of dish; this will help souffle to rise straight.

### Cheese Soufflé

4 eggs
4 oz. butter
4 tablespoons plain flour
1 teaspoon salt
pepper
¼ teaspoon dry mustard
1 cup milk
4 oz. cheddar cheese

Separate eggs; allow to stand, covered, while preparing sauce. Melt butter in top part of double saucepan over hot water; remove from heat, stir in flour and seasonings, stirring until smooth and free from lumps. Stir in milk all at once, return to heat; stir over hot water until smooth and thick. Remove from heat; stir in grated cheese while still hot, stirring until melted. Allow to cool slightly. Beat egg-yolks until pale and fluffy, gradually stir into cheese mixture, using thin-edged metal spoon or rubber spatula.

Using clean bowl and beaters, beat egg-whites until short, moist peaks form. Add half the whites to sauce, folding through carefully with flat spatula; then fold in remaining whites. (Adding whites in two portions like this makes it easier to fold them through the mixture; it also makes sure you do not over-beat mixture, thus breaking down the aeration). Pour souffle mixture over back of spoon or over spatula into prepared dish. This prevents mixture dropping hard on to base of dish, so bursting some of the air bubbles. Fill souffle dish to within ½ in. of top. Place on oven tray.

Serve cooked souffle with a green salad.

### Directions for Baking

*To Bake at Once* Bake in moderate oven. Allow 40 to 45 minutes for one large souffle; 25 to 30 minutes for individual souffles.

*To Refrigerate Overnight (or up to 24 hours)* Refrigerate uncovered. Next day, place in moderate oven. Allow 55 to 60 minutes cooking time for large souffle; 30 minutes for individual souffles.

*To Freeze* Cover top of souffle dish, or dishes, with plastic food wrap or aluminium foil; this will prevent hard skin forming on top of mixture during freezing time. When ready to bake, remove plastic wrap or foil. Souffles can go direct from freezer to oven; do it this way. Place souffles in cold, unlit oven; then light oven and set temperature at moderate. Allow approximately 60 minutes cooking time for large souffles; approximately 40 minutes cooking time for individual souffles.

### Crab and Chive Soufflé

4 eggs
4 oz. butter
4 tablespoons plain flour
1 teaspoon salt
¼ teaspoon mustard
1 cup milk
8 oz. can crab meat
½ cup chopped chives or shallots (including green tops)

Separate eggs; allow to stand, covered, while preparing sauce. Melt butter in top part of double saucepan over hot water; remove from heat, stir in flour and seasonings, stirring until smooth and free from lumps. Stir in milk all at once, return to heat; stir over hot water until smooth and thick. Remove from heat; stir in crab and chives. Allow to cool slightly.

Then proceed as for Cheese Souffle. Baking times are the same as for Cheese Souffle.

### Vanilla Soufflé

4 eggs
4 oz. butter
4 tablespoons plain flour
1 tablespoon castor sugar
½ teaspoon salt
1 cup milk
1 teaspoon vanilla

Separate eggs, allow to stand, covered, while preparing sauce. Melt butter in top part of double saucepan over hot water; remove from heat, stir in flour and salt, stirring until smooth and free from lumps. Stir in milk, all at once, add sugar; return to heat; stir over hot water until smooth and thick. Remove from heat, allow to cool slightly, stir in vanilla.

Then proceed as for Cheese Souffle. Baking times are the same as for Cheese Souffle.

## Chocolate Soufflé

| | |
|---|---|
| 4 eggs | 1 cup milk |
| 4 oz. butter | ¼ cup castor sugar |
| 4 tablespoons plain flour | 6 oz. dark chocolate |
| ½ teaspoon salt | |

Separate eggs; allow to stand, covered, while preparing sauce. Melt butter in top part of double saucepan over hot water; remove from heat, stir in flour and salt, stirring until smooth and free from lumps. Stir in milk all at once, return to heat; stir over hot water until smooth and thick. Remove from heat; stir in grated chocolate and sugar while still hot, stirring until dissolved.

Then proceed as for Cheese Souffle. Baking times are the same as for Cheese Souffle.

## Other Hot Soufflés

The following two souffles–Chestnut and Apricot cannot be refrigerated or frozen. They should be mixed, baked and served at once.

## Apricot Soufflé

| | |
|---|---|
| 4 egg-whites | 4 oz. dried apricots |
| ¼ cup castor sugar | extra castor sugar |

Place apricots in bowl, cover with hot water, leave until well plumped; then puree in electric blender or rub through sieve. Place egg-whites and 1 tablespoon of the sugar in large mixing bowl, beat until thick and of meringue consistency. Gradually beat in remaining sugar and apricot puree. Grease souffle or ovenproof dish, dust lightly with extra castor sugar. Pour in souffle mixture gently so air bubbles will not be broken down (a good way to do this is to pour it over back of spoon). Bake in moderate oven 30 minutes.

## Chestnut Soufflé

| | |
|---|---|
| 1 lb. can unsweetened chestnut pureé | 1 teaspoon vanilla |
| 6 oz. butter | 8 egg-yolks |
| ⅔ cup castor sugar | 6 egg-whites |
| | extra castor sugar |

Prepare 8 in. souffle dish, by greasing and dusting lightly with extra castor sugar; place a greased paper collar around top edge of dish, secure firmly with string.

Rub chestnut puree through sieve, place in saucepan with butter and sugar. Stir constantly over low heat until butter is melted and sugar dissolved; add vanilla. Remove from heat, cool slightly. Beat egg-yolks until thick and creamy, gradually add chestnut mixture, beating constantly. Beat egg-whites until soft peaks form. Lightly fold half the egg-whites into chestnut mixture, then remaining egg-whites. Pour mixture carefully into prepared dish, sprinkle top lightly with extra castor sugar. Bake in moderate oven 50 to 60 minutes. Serve at once with cream.

NOTE: There are two types of canned chestnuts; one is pureed chestnuts flavoured with sugar, glucose and vanilla. The other is pure chestnuts pureed; this is the type to use for this recipe. Check ingredients on can.

## Cold Soufflés

The cold souffle can be made in endless variations. Simply prepared, it stands above the rim of the dish in distinguished imitation of the baked souffle.

## Lemon Soufflé

| | |
|---|---|
| ½ cup castor sugar | ½ pint cream |
| 3 eggs | grated rind and juice 3 lemons |
| 1½ dessertspoons gelatine | ⅓ cup water |

Prepare a 6 in. souffle dish or straight-sided container, by tying double band of greased greaseproof paper round dish on the outside with string, extending paper 2 in. above the edge.

Separate eggs. Place yolks, sugar, lemon juice and rind in the top of double saucepan, cook over hot water, stirring constantly, until mixture thickens slightly, approximately 10 minutes.

Soak gelatine in the ⅓ cup water, dissolve over hot water, add to slightly cooled custard mixture. Allow to cool, stirring occasionally to prevent mixture setting at the bottom. When mixture is beginning to set, fold in gently the whipped cream and stiffly beaten egg-whites. Pour into prepared souffle dish, refrigerate until set. Decorate with whipped cream and a sprinkling of grated lemon rind.

## Orange Soufflé

As for Lemon Souffle, but substitute the grated rind of 2 oranges and the juice of 1 orange for the lemon rind and juice.

# CHEESE

There are so many varieties in cheeses, it is difficult to imagine that they all begin in much the same fashion. Most cheese is made from cows' milk, although cheese can be made from the milk of any milk-giving animal. Simply defined, cheese is the solid portion of milk separated from the whey. The many different cheeses which result from this similar beginning are the product of variations in the manufacture and curing of each variety

Almost all countries produce an individual type of cheese. Previously, it was not possible in Australia to taste all these international cheeses because they were not imported; cheese is a perishable food, and many varieties do not travel well.

But almost all famous cheese types are now produced in Australia. All the characteristics of the individual cheeses have been retained with the flavour that made them famous, and, because they are now locally produced, they come to us beautifully fresh—we can enjoy them at their best.

Cheese can be broadly divided into these categories: firm cheeses (such as Cheddar); semi-soft (such as Mozzarella); soft-ripening (such as Camembert or Brie); blue-veined cheese; hard, grating cheeses (such as Parmesan); cream types (such as cream, cottage, or Ricotta).

In addition to these, there is the wide range of processed cheeses. These are natural cheeses, and the flavour and texture remain uniform. They are pasteurised to give excellent keeping qualities in all conditions; there is no rind and no wastage.

Below is a list of the popular cheeses now produced in Australia. The original country of origin of each cheese type is indicated.

**Blue Vein** (France) Available in bulk, or in 4 oz. wedges. Has distinctive blue marbling; excellent dessert cheese.

**Cheddar** (England) Almost 70 types of natural cheddar are manufactured in Australia.

**Cheshire** (England) Available in 6 oz. packaged form.

**Cream, Cottage, and Creamed Cottage** (Most countries have these cheeses, although the Creamed Cottage Cheese is American in origin) Available in bulk. Cream cheese also available in 4 oz. and 8 oz. packets.

**Edam** (Holland) Mild flavour, excellent dessert cheese; has distinctive red rind.

**Feta** (Greece) Moist, white, traditionally made from ewes' or goats' milk. Good for snacks with brown bread, black olives.

**Gouda** (Holland) Rather similar to Cheddar.

**Gruyere** (Switzerland) Available in 8 oz. packets. Small quantity of bulk type also manufactured, but not available in all States. Has characteristic holes; sweet, nutlike flavour.

**Mozzarella** (Italy) Mild flavour, usually sold in pear shapes. Soft-melting cheese, good topping for pizzas, etc.

**Parmesan** (Italy) Available in bulk, also grated, in 4 oz. and 2 oz. packs. Age is determined by colour; the more mature, the whiter it becomes. Add to soups, pastas, etc.

**Pecorino Romano** (Italy) A good grating cheese.

**Pepato** (Italy) Pepato is Italian for pepper. The black peppercorns dispersed throughout the cheese impart spicy flavour.

**Provolone** (Italy) Robust, flavour good for canapes. When more matured, good for grating.

**Ricotta** (Italy) Fine curded cream cheese; the only cream cheese made from whey.

**Romano** (Italy) Also available, grated, in 8 oz. packs. Milder flavour than Parmesan.

Neapolitan Pizza has a topping of quick-melting Mozzarella cheese; it's an excellent supper dish, and popular with all teen-agers

**Samsoe** (Denmark) Sweet, nutty flavour, similar to Gruyere.

**Swiss** (Switzerland) Available in bulk, or sliced and packaged; 8 oz. packs and 4 oz. packs. Similar to Gruyere.

Some cheeses are still imported from Europe. These include English Wensleydale (mild, with white, creamy texture) and the famous English Stilton; Danish Port Salut; Dutch smoked cheese; Brie and Camembert, from France or Denmark; and others.

So there's a wide and wonderful world of cheese from which to choose—for good cooking, for excellent eating.

## Cooking with Cheese

When cheese is to be melted during the cooking process, make sure it is grated, or the pieces cut in similar size, so they will melt evenly at the same time. In all cheese cookery, it is important to remember cheese must be cooked slowly, over gentle heat. If cooked too quickly, the protein in cheese toughens, and the cheese becomes stringy.

## Keeping Qualities and Storage

The moisture content of cheese—whether it is a hard cheese or soft—is a guide to its keeping quality. Very hard cheeses, such as parmesan or romano, have excellent keeping quality. Parmesan can be bought grated in packets. If this is to be kept, once the packet has been opened, transfer it to a screw-top jar; this will ensure that it keeps fresh and retains its flavour. Wrap firm cheeses, such as cheddar, in plastic food wrap or aluminium foil, and store in a cool place, or refrigerate. For best flavour, let cheese return to room temperature before using.

Soft cheeses, such as cream or cottage cheese, have a high moisture content. Wrap them well in plastic food wrap or aluminium foil, or place in plastic food container, and keep refrigerated. They should be used within three or four days of purchase.

## Welsh Rarebit

½ oz. butter
8 oz. cheddar cheese
1 egg
2 tablespoons beer or milk
1 teaspoon dry mustard
½ teaspoon worcestershire sauce
½ teaspoon salt
4 slices hot buttered toast
pepper

Melt butter in top of double saucepan or in basin over hot water. Stir in the grated cheese until melted and smooth.

Beat the egg and beer together with fork and add slowly to the cheese, stirring constantly over low heat. Add dry mustard, worcestershire sauce and salt and mix well. Serve on hot buttered toast. Sprinkle with pepper. Serves 4

## Swiss Cheese Tart

**Pastry**

1¾ cups plain flour
4 oz. grated cheese (preferably parmesan and gruyere mixed)
pinch salt
pinch paprika
5 oz. butter
1 egg
egg-white for glazing

**Filling**

1 cup milk
½ cup sour cream
1 teaspoon cornflour
1 teaspoon flour
2 egg-yolks
4 oz. grated cheese (preferably parmesan and gruyere mixed)
salt
paprika

*Pastry:* Sift dry ingredients, rub in the butter. Add grated cheese, mix to a dry dough with beaten egg; chill 30 minutes.

Roll out, line 8 in. pie plate. Brush surface of pastry with a little beaten egg-white.

*Filling:* Blend flours with cold milk. Add cheese, egg-yolks, cream, salt and paprika. Beat together, spoon into pie case. Bake in moderate oven 40 to 50 minutes.

## Cheese-Topped Vegetable Pie

**Rice Pie Shell**

1 oz. butter
1 small onion
2 cups cooked rice
1 egg

**Filling**

1 oz. butter
4 small zucchini
2 onions
3 sticks celery
¼ lb. mushrooms
1 carrot
1 teaspoon salt
¼ teaspoon pepper
1 teaspoon curry powder

**Cheese Sauce**

2 oz. butter
4 tablespoons flour
½ teaspoon salt
pinch pepper
½ teaspoon dry mustard
1 cup milk
4 oz. tasty cheese
2 tablespoons cream
1 dessertspoon chopped parsley

*Pie Case:* Melt butter in saucepan, saute chopped onion. Add to rice; mix well. Beat egg, stir into rice mixture. Press into 8 in. pie plate, covering base and sides.

*Filling*: Melt butter in saucepan, add sliced zucchini,

chopped onion, sliced celery, halved mushrooms and thinly sliced carrot; saute 3 minutes. Add salt, pepper and curry powder; mix thoroughly. Place vegetables into rice case. Pour sauce over vegetables, bake in moderate oven 35 to 40 minutes.

*Cheese Sauce:* Melt butter in saucepan, stir in flour, and cook 1 minute; remove from heat. Add salt, pepper, mustard and milk; blend well. Return to heat, stirring constantly until mixture boils and thickens. Stir in grated cheese, cream and parsley.

## Ham and Cheese Squares

**Pastry**

2 cups self-raising flour
½ teaspoon salt
2 oz. butter
½ cup milk
¼ cup mayonnaise

**Filling**

½ lb. smoked ham sausage
1 cup chopped onion
4 oz. grated cheddar cheese
salt, pepper
¼ teaspoon dry mustard
2 tablespoons chopped parsley
milk
extra grated cheese

Sift flour and salt into basin, rub in butter. Combine milk and mayonnaise, cut into dry ingredients with knife until all liquid is absorbed. Turn on to floured board and knead lightly. Divide in half, roll out one portion to fit base of greased 11 in. x 7 in. lamington tin.

Sprinkle over chopped ham sausage. Combine onion, cheese, mustard, and parsley, season to taste and sprinkle over ham. Roll out remaining pastry and place over filling. Glaze with milk and sprinkle with extra grated cheese. Bake in very hot oven 20 minutes. Cut into squares while still warm.

Makes approx. 15 squares

## Neapolitan Pizza

**Yeast Dough**

½ oz. compressed yeast
¼ cup milk
1 egg
1½ cups plain flour
½ teaspoon salt
½ teaspoon sugar
1 oz. butter

**Filling**

15 oz. can tomatoes
1 dessertspoon oil
1 clove garlic
5 oz. can tomato paste
1 teaspoon sugar
salt, pepper
2 oz. salami
8 oz. Mozzarella cheese
sliced olives
1 teaspoon basil or oregano
chopped parsley

*Yeast Dough:* Warm milk, add crumbled yeast, stir until dissolved, add beaten egg. Add yeast mixture to well in centre of sifted dry ingredients, blend well. Cream butter, work into the dough. Cover bowl, stand in warm place 40 minutes, or until doubled in bulk.

Press dough into oiled 9 in. pie plate, or pizza pan, brush dough lightly with oil. Arrange filling ingredients except olives over dough, and bake in hot oven 15 to 20 minutes, or until golden brown. Sprinkle with sliced black or green olives.

*Filling:* Heat oil in saucepan, add undrained can of tomatoes, crushed garlic, tomato paste, sugar, salt and pepper, simmer uncovered until mixture is thick, and some of the liquid has evaporated; cool.

Spread tomato paste over dough, top with slices of salami and Mozzarella cheese. Sprinkle with basil or oregano.

## Wine and Cheese Party

A wine and cheese party is elegant, and easy on the hostess. It needs very little pre-planning; just a prettily decorated table with a selection of wine, cheese and simple foods.

Good, crusty breads are best with cheese. Buy several varieties—the long French loaf, the well-crusted Italian loaf, golden twists—there are so many delicious breads available. Include breadsticks of the Italian grissini type.

Also add some small biscuits. Don't choose biscuits with cheese flavours; the plain cracker-type of biscuit is best.

Have small bowls of savoury nibbles, such as olives, gherkins, celery curls, radishes, cucumber chunks, small pickled onions. Savoury dips, with small biscuits or crisp potato chips to use as 'dunkers' are also good.

*The Cheese*: Have at least four types of cheese available; a firm cheese, such as gruyere, edam, cheddar; a soft cheese, such as camembert or brie; a blue cheese; some cream cheese. Add any other favourite or unusual cheeses. Allow approximately 6 to 8 oz. cheese for each guest.

*The Wine*: Have an assortment of red wines and white. Allow approximately ½ bottle—or more—per guest.

# FISH

There's a wonderful variety of local fish available to us, and some of the best shell fish in the world.
Fish should be a permanent part of the weekly family menu, not only for its high protein value, but for its good taste and the interesting variety it can add to family and party meals

## Sole Véronique

1½ to 2 lb. sole or flounder fillets
½ small onion
1 bayleaf
few peppercorns
juice ½ lemon
water
½ lb. white grapes
1½ oz. butter
⅓ cup flour
1 pint milk
salt, pepper

Fold fillets or roll up and secure with small wooden sticks. Place fillets in greased ovenproof dish. Put in sliced onion, bayleaf, peppercorns and lemon juice, add sufficient water to half-cover fillets. Cover with greased paper, poach in moderate oven 15 to 20 minutes or until cooked.

Transfer fish to hot serving dish; keep warm. Reserve ½ cup liquid in which fish was cooked. Melt butter in saucepan, add flour, cook 1 minute. Remove from heat, gradually add milk and reserved liquid which has been reduced to ¼ cup by fast boiling. Return to heat, bring to boil, simmer until smooth and thickened, stirring constantly. Season to taste with salt and pepper; spoon over fish. Simmer peeled grapes in a little boiling water few minutes; drain. Arrange grapes at side of dish. Serve immediately.

Serves 4

## Sole and Asparagus with Wine Sauce

1 lb. sole fillets
1 cup white wine
1 small can asparagus tips

**Sauce**

1½ oz. butter
2 tablespoons flour
¾ cup milk
salt, pepper

Place skinned and boned fillets in ovenproof dish. Pour wine over, poach in moderately hot oven 20 minutes. Drain, reserve liquid for sauce. Place poached fillets on to warm individual dishes, arrange on top few drained asparagus tips, which have heated in their own liquor. Spoon sauce over.

*Sauce:* Melt butter in saucepan. Stir in flour, cook 1 minute. Remove from heat, gradually add milk and 1 cup of reserved liquid from fish. Return to heat, bring to boil; reduce heat, simmer until smooth and thickened, stirring constantly. Season to taste with salt and pepper.

Serves 4 as an entree

## Trout in Butter Sauce with Almonds

4 cleaned trout
salt
flour
4 oz. butter
1 teaspoon lemon juice
freshly ground pepper
⅓ cup toasted almonds
parsley
lemon slices

Select trout from 8 in. to 10 in. long; sprinkle inside and outside with salt, toss in flour. Heat half the butter in heavy frying pan, put in fish, cook until dark brown on both sides.

Transfer to hot serving dish; keep warm. Add remaining butter to pan with lemon juice, pepper and toasted almonds; simmer a few minutes; pour over fish.

Serve immediately, garnished with lemon slices and parsley.

Serves 4

## Bream Meunière

1½ lb. bream fillets (or other fillets)
seasoned flour
4 oz. butter
1½ tablespoons lemon juice
chopped parsley

Skin and bone fillets. Cut fillets into serving-size pieces, toss lightly in seasoned flour. Melt 3 oz. butter in pan, fry fillets until brown on both sides; remove. Melt remaining butter in pan; add lemon juice, spoon over fish, sprinkle with parsley.

Serves 4

Trout with Almonds is served with lemon-flavoured hot butter sauce. This method of cooking can also be used for other fish, in place of trout

## Bream Bonne Femme

1½ lb. bream fillets
1 large onion
4 oz. mushrooms
2 oz. butter
salt, pepper
¼ cup chopped parsley
1¼ cups dry white wine

**Sauce**

2 oz. butter
¼ cup flour
1 egg-yolk
½ cup cream
salt, pepper

Melt butter in shallow pan. Add chopped onion and half the sliced mushrooms. Arrange fish fillets over vegetables, season with salt and pepper. Spread remaining sliced mushrooms over fish, sprinkle with parsley; pour wine over. Cover fillets with piece of greaseproof paper the size of pan, with small hole in centre. Bring to boil, cover pan, reduce heat, simmer 10 to 15 minutes. Using large spatula, remove fish and vegetables to warm serving dish, reserving liquid. Keep fish warm.

*Sauce:* Melt butter in saucepan. Stir in flour, cook 1 minute. Remove from heat, gradually stir in reserved liquid; return to heat. Bring to boil, stirring; reduce heat, simmer until smooth and thickened, stirring constantly. Combine beaten egg-yolk and cream, stir into sauce; simmer few seconds, stirring, season to taste with salt and pepper, if necessary. Spoon over fish.

Serves 4.

## Fish Fillets Florentine

1 large bunch spinach
1 to 1½ lb. fresh or quick-frozen flounder fillets
1 oz. butter
2 tablespoons water
salt, pepper
nutmeg
1 tablespoon lemon juice
lemon slices
chopped parsley

**Mornay Sauce**

1 oz. butter
2 tablespoons flour
½ pint milk
2 oz. cheese
salt, pepper
nutmeg

Wash spinach, chop, and place in saucepan with butter and water. Steam gently over low heat until spinach is just wilted (approximately 2 minutes). Place drained spinach in greased, shallow oven-proof dish. Arrange thawed fish fillets on top, sprinkle with salt, pepper and nutmeg, pour over lemon juice. Cover with greased aluminium foil and bake in moderate oven 20 to 30 minutes or until fish is tender.

Remove foil and spoon over hot Mornay Sauce. Serve as entree or main course, garnish with lemon slices and chopped parsley.

*Mornay Sauce:* Melt bu[illegible]cep[illegible] cook 1 minute. Remove[illegible]heat[illegible] milk. Return to heat, bring to boi[illegible] until smooth and thickene[illegible] consta[illegible]y.

Remove from heat, add[illegible]d che[illegible]se[illegible] seasonings, stir until cheese has comple[illegible]

Serves 4 to 6

## Butter-Fried Bream

6 bream fillets (or other fish)
seasoned flour
butter

**Egg Butter**

3 oz. butter
2 hard boiled eggs
parsley

**Lemony Butter**

3 oz. butter
lemon juice to taste
parsley

Skin and bone fillets, dip in seasoned flour. Melt butter in frying pan; fry fillets until cooked on one side, turn and cook on the other side. Serve with Egg Butter or Lemony Butter, or with Sauce Remoulade.

Serves 6.

*Egg Butter:* Melt butter in pan. Add finely chopped eggs. Pour over fish and garnish with parsley.

*Lemony Butter:* Melt butter in pan, add lemon juice to taste. Pour over fish, garnish with lemon slices, and fried parsley sprigs. Or lemon slices can be sauteed in the hot butter and used as garnish.

## Sautéed Mullet with Capers

1 lb. mullet (filleted)
salt, pepper
lemon juice
flour
2 oz. butter
2 tablespoons capers, drained
1 tablespoon lemon juice, extra
1 dessertspoon grated lemon rind
1 tablespoon chopped parsley

Rub fillets with salt and pepper, sprinkle with lemon juice; roll in flour. Melt half the butter in frying-pan, add fish, fry until golden brown on both sides.

Transfer cooked fillets to hot dish. Wipe out pan, add remaining butter. Cook until light brown, add extra lemon juice and rind, capers and parsley. Pour over fish.

Serves 2

## Grilled Mullet

1 medium sized mullet
1 lem[illegible]
salt, pepper
1 to 2 oz. melted butter

[illegible]is qu[illegible] for each serving.

Wash and dry mullet, make several slashes across each side. Rub well with salt and pepper, sprinkle with lemon juice, insert slices of lemon in slashes on one side. Brush with melted butter, cook under pre-heated griller, allowing 7 to 10 minutes for each side, depending on size of fish. Turn fish once, brush liberally with melted butter.

Serve at once with lemon wedges.

## Baked Minted Mullet

1 medium sized mullet
2 or 3 sprigs of mint
salt, pepper
1 lemon
butter
lemon juice

NOTE: Use this quantity for each serving.

Wash and dry mullet. Rub body cavity with lemon, sprinkle with salt and pepper; place mint sprigs inside. Cut 3 gashes on each side of fish, insert small slices of lemon. Sprinkle over a little more lemon juice and about 1 teaspoon of grated lemon rind. Sprinkle with salt and pepper, dot with butter, wrap in greased aluminium foil.

Bake in moderate oven 30 minutes; serve with lemon slices.

## Sole Bercy

1½ lb. sole fillets (or other fillets)
½ pint fish stock
½ cup chopped shallots
½ pint white wine
3 oz. butter
salt, pepper
juice ½ lemon
¼ cup chopped parsley
1 cup cream
1 tablespoon dry breadcrumbs

Skin and bone fillets. Place fillets in buttered, shallow ovenproof dish, add stock; cover with sheet of greaseproof paper, poach in moderate oven 10 to 15 minutes or until tender. Saute shallots in ½ oz. butter. Add wine, bring to boil; boil over high heat until liquid is reduced by half. Strain liquid from fish into saucepan with shallots and wine; add salt, pepper, lemon juice and chopped parsley. Bring to boil, add remainder of butter, stir until melted.

Remove from heat, stir in cream. Spoon sauce over fish fillets, sprinkle with breadcrumbs. Place under hot griller or in hot oven until top is lightly brown.

Serves 4

## Baked Snapper

1 snapper (3½ to 4 lb.)
1 lemon
1½ cups cooked rice
1 stick celery, chopped
1 onion
½ chopped green pepper
½ teaspoon sage
salt, pepper
butter
1 large onion, sliced
2 tomatoes, skinned
1 tablespoon chopped parsley

Remove eyes from fish. Rub fish inside and outside with cut lemon. Combine in bowl rice, celery, chopped onion, green pepper, sage, salt and pepper. Mix well. Stuff fish firmly with rice mixture.

Place in greased baking-dish. Brush well with melted butter. Arrange onion and tomato slices alternately over fish, season well. Dot with butter. Bake in moderate oven 40 to 50 minutes. Serve with lemon slices, garnish with chopped parsley.

Serves 4 to 6

## Fish Mornay

1 lb. snapper fillets
½ lb. small prawns
1 cup milk
1 cup water
1 small onion
1 bayleaf
1½ oz. butter
2 tablespoons flour
½ cup grated cheese
salt, pepper
2 tablespoons breadcrumbs
1 oz. butter, extra

Remove bones and skin from fish. Combine milk, water, bayleaf and half the chopped onion in saucepan. Poach fish in this liquid until tender, drain, reserving liquid. Flake fish coarsely. Remove bayleaf from liquid. Combine fish and peeled prawns.

Melt butter in saucepan, saute remaining chopped onion for 1 minute, stir in flour, cook 1 minute. Remove from heat. Gradually add reserved liquid. Return to heat, stir until sauce boils and thickens; cook 5 minutes, stirring constantly. Season to taste, stir in cheese, leaving approximately 2 tablespoons for topping. Fold in fish mixture, spoon mixture into greased ovenproof dish. Sprinkle with mixture of breadcrumbs and remaining cheese. Dot with extra butter; brown under hot griller or in hot oven. Serve with hot rice.

Serves 6 as an entree or 3 as a main dish.

*Salmon Mornay:* Make up Mornay Sauce, as for Fish Mornay, omitting the fish and prawns. Add 16 oz. can salmon, with bones removed, to the sauce, stir in 1 teaspoon lemon juice. Then spoon into casserole, top with breadcrumbs and cheese, dot with butter and brown.

## Escabache

1½ to 2 lb. fish fillets
seasoned flour
1 egg
2 tablespoons milk
oil for frying

### Sauce

⅔ cup dry white wine
⅔ cup white wine vinegar
⅔ cup oil
1 dessertspoon dry mustard
salt, pepper

### Vegetable Pickles

½ lb. small carrots
½ lb. turnips or parsnips
½ lb. small onions
1 red pepper
1 green pepper
2 sticks celery
approx. 1½ pints white wine vinegar
¼ cup sugar
1 dessertspoon mustard seeds
1 teaspoon celery seeds

Skin and bone fillets. Toss fillets in seasoned flour, then in combined egg and milk mixture, then in flour again. Fry in hot oil until golden brown on both sides. Drain well on absorbent paper, cool. Break fillets up into large bite-size pieces and place in deep serving dish. Pour over the sauce and vegetables.

This is an excellent hot-weather dish; good, also, on a buffet table.

*Sauce:* Combine all ingredients, mix well. Add drained pickles.

*Vegetable Pickles:* Scrape carrots, peel onions. Wash peppers, celery, and turnips. Leave onions whole, cut carrots into 2 in. lengths. Cut celery and turnips into 2 in. lengths; dice peppers, removing pith and seeds.

Place onions, turnips, and carrots in saucepan, add sufficient vinegar to cover. Add mustard and celery seeds and sugar. Bring to boil; reduce heat, simmer 15 minutes. Add remaining vegetables with additional vinegar to cover, cook 3 minutes, drain.

Serves 6

## Gefilte Fish

1 lb. jewfish
1 lb. snapper
2 medium onions
3 eggs
2 teaspoons salt
¼ teaspoon white pepper
1 teaspoon sugar
3 tablespoons dry breadcrumbs
4 pints water
1 teaspoon salt, extra
½ teaspoon white pepper, extra
pinch sugar, extra
1 carrot
dill or parsley

Fillet fish, reserving heads, skins and bones. Put fish and 1 onion through mincer twice. Place in wooden bowl, stir in well-beaten eggs, salt, pepper and sugar. Mix well, gradually adding sufficient water, approximately ⅓ cup, to make a soft mixture. Lastly stir in breadcrumbs, mix thoroughly.

Place fish heads, skins and bones in saucepan. Add water and the extra salt, pepper and sugar. Bring to boil, skim well; reduce heat, simmer 20 minutes, strain.

Form fish mixture into balls, the size of small apples, using wet hands. Carefully place fish balls in stock. Add remaining chopped onion, adding more water if necessary to cover the fish balls. Cover, bring to rapid boil. Uncover, reduce heat and simmer gently 2 to 2½ hours or until stock has been reduced by half, add sliced carrot to stock 30 minutes before end of cooking time.

Remove fish balls and place on deep serving dish. Strain stock again and pour over as much as dish will hold. Arrange carrot and dill or parsley around fish as garnish. Cool and refrigerate until stock has jellied. Serve with horseradish sauce.

Serves 4

## Salmon Mousse

1 tablespoon gelatine
2 tablespoons water
3 8 oz. cans red salmon
4 oz. softened butter
1 tablespoon lemon juice
1 egg-white
salt, pepper
1 tablespoon french dressing
½ cup diced cucumber
¼ cup finely chopped shallots
¾ cup cream

### Cucumber Sauce

2 teaspoons finely chopped chives
¼ cup finely diced cucumber
1 cup sour cream
2 shallots, finely chopped
salt, pepper

Soften gelatine in the water, dissolve over boiling water. Remove skin and bones, place salmon in bowl with liquid from cans, and beat well. Salmon can be beaten on an electric mixer. Gradually beat in softened butter. Then add egg-white, lemon juice, pepper, salt and dressing; beat thoroughly.

Fold in dissolved gelatine, cucumber, and shallots. Whip cream until thick, and fold into salmon mixture. Pour mixture into oiled mould, refrigerate until firm. Unmould; serve with Cucumber Sauce and a green salad.

Serves 6.

*Cucumber Sauce:* Combine all ingredients, mix thoroughly.

Escabache — golden-fried fish pieces topped with a colourful vegetable pickle — makes an excellent buffet or barbecue dish; nice, too, for a light summer meal

## Salmon Croquettes

8 oz. can salmon
1 egg-yolk
1½ cups mashed potato
1 teaspoon curry powder
1 small onion
1 dessertspoon chopped parsley
1 dessertspoon lemon juice
salt, pepper
2 eggs for glazing
dry breadcrumbs
oil for frying

Drain salmon, remove bones and flake; chop onion finely. In a bowl combine salmon, potato, curry powder, onion, parsley and lemon juice; add egg-yolk, salt and pepper, mix thoroughly. Refrigerate until firm. Mould mixture into croquette shapes approximately 1 in. thick by 2 in. long.

Dip in beaten eggs, press breadcrumbs on firmly. Refrigerate 1 hour. Fry in hot oil until golden brown, drain on absorbent paper.

Makes approx. 1 dozen

## Grilled Tuna

6 fresh tuna steaks (about 1 in. thick)
salt, pepper
1 onion
few parsley stalks
1 bayleaf
dry white wine
oil

**Parsley Butter**

2 oz. butter
salt, pepper
squeeze lemon juice
1 tablespoon finely chopped parsley

Wash steaks thoroughly, season with salt and pepper, place in shallow dish. Add chopped onion, parsley stalks and bayleaf. Pour over sufficient white wine to half-cover fish; marinate about 1 hour, turning from time to time. Drain, dry, and brush with oil.

Cook under preheated griller, allowing about 5 minutes cooking time for each side, turning once. Brush several times with oil while cooking. Transfer to hot serving dish, season well with salt and pepper. Top each fish steak with a little parsley butter; serve at once.

*Parsley Butter:* Soften butter in small bowl, then beat in salt, pepper and parsley. Lastly add lemon juice; refrigerate.

Serves 6

## Haddock Kedgeree

1 lb. smoked haddock
2 hard-boiled eggs
½ cup rice
3 oz. butter
salt, pepper
⅓ cup chopped parsley
1 dessertspoon lemon juice

Cook rice in large quantity of boiling water until tender, 12 to 15 minutes; drain. Poach fish until tender. Shell and chop eggs.

Melt butter in saucepan, add boned, flaked fish and rice. Season to taste with salt and pepper. Stir in chopped eggs, heat thoroughly. Add lemon juice and half the parsley; reserve remainder for garnish.

Serves 4 as an entree, or 3 as main dish.

*Salmon Kedgeree:* Substitute 8 oz. can of salmon for the haddock; drain and add with rice, to melted butter in pan, as above.

## Sweet and Sour Fish

2 lb. cod or other thick fish fillets
1 lb. prawns
4 sticks celery
2 onions
1 red pepper
½ bunch shallots
cornflour
oil for frying

**Sauce**

1 cup chicken stock
1 tablespoon tomato paste
1 tablespoon soy sauce
1 teaspoon ginger
3 tablespoons white wine or water
1 dessertspoon cornflour
salt, pepper

Cut fish into bite-size pieces. Mix together ½ cup stock, tomato paste, soy sauce, wine and ginger. Place fish and shelled prawns in this mixture, marinate 1 hour.

Peel and slice onions. Wash celery and shallots, cut into diagonal pieces. Remove seeds from pepper, cut into thin strips.

Drain fish, reserve marinade, toss fish in cornflour to coat well. Fry in hot oil until golden brown, remove from pan, keep hot. Fry onions in a little hot oil until transparent, add celery, pepper and shallots. Cook further 3 to 4 minutes. Add fish, pour over prepared sauce. Bring to boil, stirring constantly. Serve with hot fluffy rice.

*Sauce:* Blend 1 dessertspoon cornflour with remaining stock, add to reserved marinade. Place over low heat, bring to boil, stirring. Season to taste.

Serves 6

## Indian Curried Fish

2 lb. fish fillets
juice 1 large lemon
salt, pepper
1 teaspoon turmeric
2 teaspoons curry powder
oil for deep frying

Wash fish fillets, dry well. Cut into 2 or 3 pieces, according to size. Sprinkle on both sides with lemon juice, salt and pepper, place into a dish with remaining lemon juice. Allow to stand for a few minutes, then sprinkle with turmeric and curry powder. Move fish around in this mixture to coat well.

Fry in hot, deep oil a few minutes until cooked. Delicious with fried rice.

Serves 4.

## Fish Cocktail

1 lb. fish fillets
juice 2 lemons
white vinegar
1 large onion
½ to ¾ cup mayonnaise
salt, pepper
½ cup cooked green peas
¼ red pepper
¼ green pepper

Skin and bone fish, cut into small pieces. Peel onion, cut into thin slices. Put fish and onion into glass or china bowl, pour over enough white vinegar to cover, stir in lemon juice. Cover, let stand to marinate overnight. Next day drain liquid from fish.

Combine fish and onion with peas and enough mayonnaise to hold mixture together; season to taste. Place spoonfuls of fish cocktail into lettuce cups in cocktail glasses. Sprinkle over the finely chopped or sliced peppers.

Serves 4

NOTE: The fish in this cocktail is not actually cooked; the acid action of the vinegar and lemon juice, as the fish stands overnight, simulates the cooking process.

## Poisson Cru

4 lb. fish fillets
1 tablespoon salt
1 cup lemon juice
6 small onions
1 cup fresh or desiccated coconut
2 cups boiling water
2 large tomatoes

Remove skin and bones from fillets. Cut fish into bite-size pieces, sprinkle with salt, cover with lemon juice. Cover, and refrigerate at least 4 hours. Drain, add finely chopped onion; mix well. Mix coconut with boiling water, allow to cool, then drain, pressing as much liquid from coconut as possible.

Pour coconut milk over fish; refrigerate. Skin and seed tomatoes, chop flesh into cubes and fold into fish mixture.

Serves 8.

NOTE: This is the authentic Tahitian Poisson Cru. However, for extra flavour, you might like to add a little crushed garlic and some finely chopped cucumber.

## Fish Roe

Fish roe, both smoked and fresh, is becoming increasingly popular in Australia. Fresh roe is in season from February until September, and is available at most city fish shops during that time. Most of the roe sold in Australia comes from mullet. Fresh roe is delicious if dipped in egg and breadcrumbs and deep fried. It can also be steamed and served with a melted butter sauce. Smoked roe is available all the year round. Just slice thinly and serve on toast or biscuits. It makes excellent canapes and savouries.

## Herring in Sherry Pickle

1½ lb. salted herring
3 onions
dill

**Marinade**

1 cup dry sherry
½ cup water
¾ cup white vinegar
⅔ cup sugar
½ teaspoon ground allspice

Fillet herring, soak in cold water overnight; drain. Peel onions, slice thinly. Place herring fillets and onions in bowl, pour marinade over; leave 24 hours.

Drain, reserving liquid; cut fillets into 1 in. strips. Arrange in bowl with onions, pour a little of reserved liquid over. Garnish with fresh dill. Delicious as an hors d'oeuvre, or as a savoury snack with fresh bread and butter.

*Marinade* Combine all ingredients in bowl. Stir until sugar is dissolved.

## Ragout of Octopus

1½ lb. octopus
boiling water
3 oz. butter
3 large onions
1 clove garlic
pinch dried thyme
salt, pepper
dry red wine
2 tablespoons tomato paste
chopped parsley

Clean octopus by turning inside out and removing black from suckers on base of tentacles and ink sack. Wash well, beat gently with steak mallet. Cut tentacles and body into even-sized strips; place in boiling water for 3 minutes; drain.

Melt butter in saucepan, add peeled and coarsely chopped onions, and crushed garlic, cook gently until transparent. Add octopus, cook further 5 minutes. Then add thyme, salt, pepper and tomato paste. Lastly add enough red wine to cover. Cover, simmer very gently 1½ hours or until octopus is tender. Sprinkle with parsley, serve with hot rice.

Serves 4

## Shellfish

Of all types of food, shellfish is amongst the most popular with Australians. Because of its light, subtle flavour, freshly-caught shellfish is best prepared in the simplest fashion, but shellfish are versatile—they can be prepared in many ways, some are world-renowned classic recipes

### To Cook Fresh Lobster

First, drown lobster in the most humane way. Place it in a bucket of fresh water, preferably tepid, as the warmth acts as an anaesthetic. Thirty minutes should be sufficient to drown it, depending on size. Bring a large saucepan of salted water or sea water to the boil, drop lobster in, reduce heat, simmer until cooked. Allow about 20 minutes cooking time, again depending on size. When it is cooked, drop the lobster into cold water immediately to cool quickly and remove any scum on shell.

### Lobster Mayonnaise

2 small lobsters, cooked
1½ cups mayonnaise
¼ cup cream
salt, pepper
2 tablespoons finely chopped parsley
juice ½ lemon
lemon wedges

Split lobsters in half. Remove meat from lobster shells, cut in large dice. Combine mayonnaise, whipped cream, salt, pepper, parsley and lemon juice; mix well. Take 1 cup of mayonnaise mixture, combine with the diced lobster. Mix thoroughly, fill into lobster shells. Spoon over remaining mayonnaise mixture. Serve with lemon wedges.

Serves 4

### Lobster Thermidor

two 1½ lb. lobsters, cooked
½ pint milk
1 small onion
few cloves
1 bayleaf
1 oz. butter
2 tablespoons plain flour
extra 1 oz. butter
2 shallots
½ cup white wine
½ pint cream
salt, pepper
½ teaspoon prepared mustard
4 oz. gruyere cheese

Cut lobsters in half; remove meat, reserve shells. combine milk with sliced onion, cloves, and bayleaf. Bring to boil; strain, reserve liquid. Melt butter in pan, stir in flour and cook a few minutes without browning. Gradually stir in hot milk. Cook, stirring, until mixture boils and thickens; set aside. Melt extra butter in pan, add shallots, and cook a few minutes. Add wine, reduce over high heat to half quantity; add the white sauce and cream. Season to taste with salt, pepper and mustard. Cook gently, stirring, about 5 to 8 minutes.

Stir in 3 oz. of the grated cheese. Stir until melted, add chopped lobster meat. Fill mixture into lobster shells, sprinkle with remaining cheese, and brown under hot griller, or in hot oven.

Serves 4

### Lobster Newburg

two 1½ lb. lobsters, cooked
2 oz. butter
¼ cup brandy
½ cup madeira
¼ pint cream
2 egg-yolks
salt, pepper

Cut lobsters in half; remove flesh, cut into pieces. Melt butter in pan, add lobster meat, and saute a few minutes; add brandy, set alight. Allow flame to die out, add madeira. Simmer a few minutes, then add cream, reserving 2 tablespoons. Simmer until reduced slightly. Season with salt and pepper, remove from heat and add beaten egg-yolks mixed with reserved cream. Heat gently, stirring, until mixture thickens slightly (do not allow to boil). Serve with triangles of hot buttered toast.

Serves 4

### Prawn Cocktail

1½ lb. prawns
lettuce
lemon slices

**Cocktail Sauce**

2 tablespoons tomato sauce
1 dessertspoon worcestershire sauce
1 dessertspoon white vinegar
few drops tabasco sauce
salt to taste
½ teaspoon mustard
2 tablespoons lightly whipped cream

Shell prawns, reserving 6 large ones for garnishing. Shred lettuce; arrange layer of lettuce in each serving dish. Top with prawns, spoon over cocktail sauce. Garnish side of each dish with lemon slice and reserved prawns.

*Cocktail Sauce*: Combine all ingredients except whipped cream, mix well. Fold in whipped cream.

Serves 6

Prawn Cocktail, topped with a well-seasoned sauce, makes an excellent first course.

## To Cook Prawns

Drop green (uncooked) prawns into boiling salted water; they will turn pink and float to the surface when cooked. If catching them fresh, drop into fresh water first for 15 minutes so that all sand in the prawns is disgorged.

Green prawns can also be sauteed, braised, fried, and used in many Chinese or continental recipes.

## Curried Prawns

1 lb. prawns
1½ cups chicken stock
½ cup white wine
4 oz. coconut
3 onions
1 apple
4 sticks celery
2 tablespoons oil
½ teaspoon ground ginger
½ teaspoon turmeric
1 tablespoon curry powder
¼ teaspoon cayenne pepper
½ teaspoon salt
pinch cinnamon
3 tomatoes
6 peppercorns
2 bayleaves
juice ½ lemon
1 tablespoon red currant jelly
1 dessertspoon cornflour
3 tablespoons water

Bring stock to boil, pour over coconut, cover, and stand 15 minutes. Then drain, reserving liquid. Slice onions and celery, dice apple, chop tomatoes.

Heat oil, fry onions until lightly brown. Add celery, apple, and tomatoes, cook further 5 minutes. Add curry powder, spices, salt, peppercorns and bayleaves. Pour on reserved coconut stock and wine. Cover, simmer 45 minutes. Sieve curry sauce, pressing as much of the vegetables through as possible. Add lemon juice and red currant jelly.

Blend cornflour with water, add to sauce. Bring to boil, stirring constantly; boil 2 minutes. Add shelled prawns, heat through. Serve with hot rice.

Serves 4

## Garlic Prawns

5 green king prawns
4 cloves garlic
1 small chilli
2 tablespoons olive oil or butter

NOTE: Use this quantity for each serving.
Shell prawns and place in small ovenproof dish. Add crushed or chopped garlic, chopped chilli, butter or oil. Bake in moderately hot oven until prawns are cooked. Serve at once.

## Oysters Natural

Arrange oysters on the shell on bed of lettuce or ice, with small individual servings of cocktail sauce (see Oyster Cocktail). Serve with lemon wedges and small triangles of buttered brown bread.

## Oysters Bordelaise

Moisten the oysters on the half-shell with a little red wine, flavoured with salt, paprika, and chopped shallots. Then sprinkle with fine breadcrumbs and melted butter; bake in hot oven.

## Fried Oysters

2 dozen oysters
1 egg
1 dessertspoon milk
breadcrumbs
seasoned flour
oil

Beat egg with milk. Dip oysters in seasoned flour, egg mixture, then in breadcrumbs. Drop into hot oil and cook for few minutes until golden brown; drain well. Garnish with fried parsley and serve with tartare sauce.

### Fried Parsley

Choose good-sized sprigs of parsley. Wash and dry thoroughly. (If the parsley is at all damp, the oil will splutter.) Place sprigs in frying-basket, lower slowly into hot oil. When sizzling noise from parsley ceases, remove basket and drain parsley on absorbent paper. If parsley is fried too long it will lose its colour.

## Oyster Cocktail

2 dozen oysters
4 tablespoons tomato sauce
1 tablespoon lemon juice
1 dessertspoon worcestershire sauce
1 teaspoon white wine vinegar

Arrange oysters in 4 small, stemmed glasses. Combine all remaining ingredients, spoon over oysters. Serve with lemon wedges.

## Oysters Czarina

Top each oyster on the half-shell with a teaspoon of caviar and squeeze of lemon juice. Sprinkle with pepper, garnish with lemon wedges.

## Oysters Mornay

Coat oysters on the shell with Mornay Sauce, sprinkle with a little grated cheese and melted butter. Place under griller until cheese browns, or heat in hot oven.

## Oysters Rockefeller

Cover oysters on the half-shell with mixture of finely chopped, cooked spinach and onion. Top with fine breadcrumbs and grated cheese. Brown in hot oven.

## Oysters Kilpatrick

Season oysters on the half-shell with a little worcestershire sauce, salt and pepper. Cover oysters with 1 or 2 small strips of bacon. Heat in hot oven, or place under griller, until bacon is crisp.

## To Cook Scallops

Scallops must never be overcooked. Always dry scallops thoroughly before they are to be sauteed or fried. When frying or sauteing scallops, allow between 3 to 5 minutes. Never boil scallops, but poach them gently in well-flavoured stock for 4 minutes, then use as recipe requires.

## Fried Scallops

¼ cup lemon juice
1 tablespoon oil
1 teaspoon salt
½ teaspoon paprika
2 tablespoons finely chopped parsley
1½ lb. scallops
2 eggs
1 cup dry breadcrumbs
2 tablespoons grated parmesan cheese
oil for frying
lemon wedges

Combine lemon juice, oil, salt, paprika and parsley in bowl. Add scallops, let stand 1 hour; turn several times while marinating; drain. Beat eggs well. Toss breadcrumbs with grated cheese. Dip each scallop first in beaten eggs, then in crumb mixture. Deep fry in hot oil 4 minutes, or until golden brown. Drain on absorbent paper, serve immediately; garnish with lemon wedges.

Serves 4

## Scallops in Cream Sauce

1½ lb. scallops
1½ cups dry white wine
2 oz. butter
4 oz. mushrooms
6 shallots
2 tablespoons flour
1 teaspoon curry powder
2 teaspoons chopped parsley
salt, pepper
¾ cup cream
fresh breadcrumbs
extra butter

Bring wine to boil in saucepan, drop in scallops; reduce heat, simmer 3 minutes. Set aside, reserving liquid. Melt butter in separate saucepan, add chopped shallots and sliced mushrooms; saute 5 minutes. Then add parsley, salt and pepper. Remove from heat, stir in combined curry powder and flour, cook a few minutes; off heat, gradually add $1\frac{1}{2}$ cups of the liquid in which scallops were cooked. Return to heat, stir sauce until it boils and thickens. Add scallops and cream to pan.

Spoon into greased individual dishes. Melt a little butter in saucepan, add breadcrumbs, saute $\frac{1}{2}$ minute. Sprinkle breadcrumbs over filled dishes. Brown 5 to 8 minutes in moderately hot oven or under moderate griller.

Serves 5 to 6

## To Cook Mussels

Discard any mussels which have shells open. Scrape mussel shells clean with a knife. Then place on griller rack in pan and cook under a pre-heated griller. Remove mussels from heat as soon as they open. Or place the mussels in water and bring to boil, when shells should open. Use as desired.

Only mussels found at the bottom of the sea are edible, say fish experts. It is not advisable to eat mussels found on wharfs or rocks.

## Mussels Marinière

24 mussels
3 shallots
1 cup dry white wine
2 oz. butter
1½ tablespoons flour
1 tablespoon chopped parsley
salt, pepper
¼ cup cream

Scrub mussels well and wash them in running water. Place in saucepan with finely chopped shallots and white wine. Cover, boil gently 5 to 6 minutes or until mussels open; drain, reserving liquid. Remove one shell from each mussel, leaving the meat attached to the other shell. Place mussels on to serving dish.

Reduce liquid in pan by half over high heat. Cream together butter and flour, add to liquid in pan. Simmer until butter has melted, stirring constantly. Add chopped parsley; season to taste with salt and pepper. Stir in cream, heat through. Spoon over mussels.

Serves 3 to 4

## To Cook Abalone

Abalone, when removed from its shell, resembles a large oyster. It is very tough and rubbery, and must be thoroughly pounded before cooking. Take a rolling pin, pound around the tough outer edge of abalone. The hard centre core—which resists even the toughest pounding—can be cut out.

Then cut abalone into slices, cook in hot butter about 3 minutes on one side, turn and cook other side for the same time. Add a squeeze of lemon juice to the pan.

# MEAT

## Beef

Rare, medium or well-done—whichever way you like your beef cooked, there's an art in cooking it to perfection. There are recipes here for many of the classic beef dishes of the world—each with its own individual, superb taste.

Set out below is an informative list of all the beef cuts, with suggested methods of cooking

### Cuts of Beef

**Aitch-Bone** Piece cut from butt or thigh of beef animal. Can be bought pickled or fresh. 3 to 4 lb. Very little fat, full and meaty; if pickled, fresh-cut surface is bright pink. Simmer (if pickled), pot-roast (if fresh), roast (if yearling beef).

**Barbecue Steak** Good-quality steak cut from middle portion of beef carcass. 2 to 4 slices per lb. Selvedge (edge) fat about $\frac{1}{4}$ in. thick, creamy-yellow colour; specks of fat scattered throughout flesh. Barbecue, grill.

**Bladebone Steak** Cut from shoulder of beef animal. 2 slices per lb. Meat should be red in colour, with fine grain; fat creamy-white, firm, not oily. Grill, fry (yearling beef), otherwise casserole, braise.

**Bolar Blade** Piece cut from shoulder of beef animal, sold fresh or pickled. 3 to 4 lb. See Bladebone Steak. Pot-roast (if fresh), simmer (if pickled), roast (yearling beef).

**Braising Steak** Steaks cut from fore or hind end of beef animal. $1\frac{1}{2}$ to 2 slices per lb. See Bladebone Steak. Braise.

**Breakfast Steak** (Sold packaged in some States.) Small, thin pieces of steak cut from hind part (rump) of beef animal. 2 to 4 slices per lb. See Barbecue Steak. Fry, grill.

**Brisket** (corn roll) Breast portion cut from beef animal; usually pickled and rolled. 3 to 4 lb. Outer surface is moist; not too much fat; when freshly cut, meat is bright red. Simmer.

**Buttock** Cut from thigh of beef animal; sold in the piece or as steaks. 3 to 4 lb. or $1\frac{1}{2}$ to 2 slices per lb. See Bladebone Steak. Fry, barbecue, grill (yearling beef); otherwise braise, casserole; pot-roast (in the piece).

**Carpetbag Steak** Seen on restaurant menus, is not used in butchers' shops. Can be thick piece of rump, fillet, boned sirloin, or scotch fillet steak, into which pocket is cut; oysters are filled into pocket. Grill or pan-fry.

**Chuck Steak** Cut from neck of beef animal. 1 to 2 slices per lb. Flesh is firm, with coarse grain; red colour, little fat. Braise, stew.

**Club Steak** (Sold in some States.) Cut from loin or adjacent ribs of beef animal; may or may not contain bone. 1 lb. each. See Barbecue Steak. Grill.

**Corned Beef** See Silverside and Brisket.

**Corner Cut** (topside). Firm, meaty piece cut from thigh of beef animal. 3 to 4 lb. Flesh is firm with coarse grain; some surrounding fat. Roast or pot-roast.

**Cross Cut Blade** (bone in or bone out) Steak cut from shoulder of beef animal. $1\frac{1}{2}$ to 2 slices per lb. See Bladebone Steak.

**Cube Steak** Small pieces of steak put through cubing machine; fibres are broken; steak is flattened and made thin. 4 to 6 slices per lb. Should be thin for quick cooking; red colour. Fry, grill.

**Entrecote** Seen on restaurant menus, is not used in butchers' shops. Entrecote is a boned-out sirloin steak.

**Eye Fillet Steak** Long thin piece of oval-shaped steak from inside loin of beef animal. 4 slices per lb. Small round slice of meat; little fat; very tender. Grill, pan-fry.

Boeuf à la Bourguignonne — rich-tasting beef casserole with wine and mushrooms.

**Fillet** (beef) Small, tender piece of meat, generally 2 to $3\frac{1}{2}$ lb. Roast.

**Fillet Steak** This steak, situated beneath the rump steak, is extension of eye fillet steak. 3 slices per lb. Not so small and round as eye fillet but otherwise similar. Grill, barbecue.

**Gravy Beef** (shin beef) From fore and hind leg of beef animal. Is rich in gelatine. No fat; flesh dark red, with white fibres. Simmer.

**Mignon** (or Filet Mignon) Seen on restaurant menus, it is not used in butchers' shops. Is small piece of fillet steak trimmed to round shape.

**Minute Steak** Any good grilling steak cut thinly or cubed. (See Cube Steak.) 4 to 6 slices per lb. Fry, grill. (Thinly cut, cooks quickly.)

**New York Cut** (available some States) Rump Steak with tail end trimmed off. Grill or pan-fry.

**Oxtail** From beef. $1\frac{1}{2}$ to 2 lb. Some fat. Stew.

**Oyster Blade Steak** Cut from shoulder of beef animal. 2 to 3 slices per lb. See Bladebone Steak. Grill, fry.

**Pocket Steak** Firm, meaty piece (such as corner topside) cut from fore or hind portions of beef animal; pocket is cut in steak for seasoning. 3 to 4 lb. See Corner Cut.

**Porterhouse Steak** First three to four cuts from rump end of sirloin, which contains the full eye fillet; steaks are cut very thick. Creamy-white fat; ample meat; flesh red in colour. Grill or pan-fry.

**Roast Beef** (rolled) Roll of beef from middle portion of carcass; firmly secured with skewers and/or string. Light covering of creamy-coloured fat; specks of fat in the lean of flesh; red colour. Roast. Other Beef Roasts available are:
*Wing Rib*: Cut from loin of beef, sometimes sold with bone in.
*Sirloin Roast*: Very tender.
*Standing Rib Roast*: Meaty piece cut from ribs; has bone in.
*Chuck Roast*: Boned and rolled piece cut from beneath blade or shoulder of yearling beef animal. 3 to 4 lb. Flesh firm, pinkish colour, very little fat. Pot-roast.

**Roll of Blade** (or Blade Roll or Shepherd's Tongue) Long narrow, tapered piece of meat cut from shoulder of beef animal. Flesh firm; red colour, no fat. Grill, pan-fry, pot-roast if in the piece.

**Round Steak** Slices of steak cut from thigh of beef animal. 1 to $1\frac{1}{2}$ slices per lb. Some fat; ample meat; flesh red in colour. See Buttock.

**Rump Steak** Slices of steak cut from hind part (rump) of beef animal. 1 to $1\frac{1}{2}$ slices per lb. Even selvedge of straw-coloured fat; ample meat. Barbecue, grill, pan-fry.

**Scotch Fillet** (cube roll) Small oval slices of steak cut from 'eye' of ribs of beef animal. Approximately 2 to 3 slices per lb. No selvedge fat; marbling of fat in flesh. Grill, fry.

**Shell Blade** Tip of Oyster Blade Steak (see this). 3 to 4 slices per lb. No fat. Grill, fry.

**Silverside** (corned round) Portion of meat from thigh of beef animal; sold fresh or pickled. 3 to 5 lb. Small amount of fat. Simmer (if pickled); braise, pot-roast (if fresh).

**Sirloin Steak** Steak cut from loin, with bone in or out; creamy selvedge of fat. Grill, pan-fry. Sirloin roast also obtainable (see Roast Beef).

**Skirt Steak** (or Flank Steak) Cut from inside fore and hind parts of beef animal. No fat; flesh is firm and fibrous. Stew, casserole.

**Steakettes** Small pieces of steak put through mincer-type machine which processes and shapes them; seasoning is added. 4 to 6 per lb. Meat reddish colour. Fry.

**Stewing Steak** Cut from either hind or fore parts of beef animal. 1 to $1\frac{1}{2}$ slices per lb. Very little fat; meat has coarse grain. Stew.

**T-Bone Steak** Cut from loin of beef, bone in. Selvedge fat is straw-coloured; specks of fat in flesh; flesh red; bone T-shaped. Barbecue, grill, pan-fry. Sometimes sold complete with the fillet.

**Thick Flank Steak** See Buttock Steak.

**Topside Steak** Cut from hindquarters of beef. Use in casseroles, braise; if from yearling beef, grill or pan-fry. Also available as Corner Cut. (See this.)

**Tournedos** Seen on restaurant menus, it is not used in butchers' shops. Is small, thick piece of fillet steak trimmed to round shape.

**Tripe** (plain, honeycomb). Part of stomach of beef animal, cleaned and par-cooked. Simmer.

**Undercut of Fillet** Part of the fillet steak situated beneath rump steak. See Fillet Steak.

**Undercut of Blade** Tender slice of steak cut from beneath bladebone. Grill or pan-fry.

## Roast Beef

Remove beef from refrigerator and let it stand at room temperature an hour or two before roasting.

Grind some fresh pepper over top of roast. Dot with about 2 oz. butter. Put into baking dish with 2 oz. butter and 2 tablespoons red wine or water.

Bake in moderately hot oven 15 minutes, reduce temperature to moderate for remainder of cooking time. Turn roast over once during cooking time. Allow approximately 20 to 30 minutes per lb. cooking time, depending on thickness of roast and whether you like beef rare, medium, or well done. When roast is cooked, remove to warm serving plate; let stand 10 minutes to set juices.

Season pan juices with salt and pepper. For a greater amount of gravy, add 1 or 2 tablespoons of red wine and water. Stir over low heat to incorporate all the crusty pieces from the pan. Add the juices which run off the roast while it is standing. Strain, serve over the carved beef slices.

Some cooks add $\frac{1}{2}$ lb. skirt steak, cut very finely, to the baking dish when cooking roast beef. This steak adds excellent flavour to the pan juices.

Horseradish sauce or mustard are traditional accompaniments. So, too, is a light Yorkshire Pudding.

## Roast Fillet of Beef

| | |
|---|---|
| 1 whole fillet of beef (2 to 3 lb.) | freshly ground pepper |
| | salt |
| 4 oz. melted butter | little water |

Trim all fat from meat, sprinkle with pepper. Place in baking dish, pour over melted butter. Roast in hot oven until meat is brown and sizzling, then reduce heat to moderate, continue cooking until done to taste. Allow 10 minutes per lb. for rare meat and 20 minutes per lb. for medium; allow a little longer for well done. Remove cooked fillet to serving dish; keep warm. Boil up pan juices, adding little water, salt, and pepper. Slice meat thickly, spoon over pan juices.

Serves 4 to 6

## Beef Wellington

| | |
|---|---|
| 2½ lb. fillet of beef | ¼ lb. mushrooms |
| 4 oz. butter | 1 lb. puff pastry |
| 2 oz. pâté de foie gras | salt, pepper |
| 1 small onion | 1 egg-yolk |

Spread beef with 1 oz. of the softened butter, bake in hot oven 10 to 15 minutes, or until the fillet is browned well all over. Remove from oven, allow to cool completely; reserve pan juices.

Chop onion finely, slice mushrooms. Saute in 1 oz. butter until tender.

Combine remaining 2 oz. softened butter with the pate, season lightly with salt and pepper. Spread over top of the beef fillet, top with cooled onion and mushroom mixture.

Roll out puff pastry to $\frac{1}{8}$ in. thickness. Place beef fillet in centre and wrap pastry round it; press edges neatly and firmly together. Make sure any overlapping edges of pastry are not too thick, or pastry will not rise well and will not cook through. Place pastry-wrapped fillet in baking dish, brush with beaten egg-yolk. Bake in very hot oven 10 minutes; reduce heat to hot, cook further 10 to 15 minutes, or until pastry is rich golden brown.

To the reserved pan juices add 1 cup stock (or 1 cup water and 1 crumbled beef-stock cube) and 1 tablespoon red wine. Cook over high heat until sauce is slightly reduced; strain. Cut fillet into thick slices, spoon sauce over.

NOTE: Pate de foie gras can be bought in small cans, or loose in bulk from delicatessen counters of most large department stores.

## Steak with Red Wine

| | |
|---|---|
| 4 thick pieces fillet steak | salt, pepper |
| butter | extra 2 oz. butter |
| ½ pint red wine | juice ½ lemon |
| 4 shallots | parsley |

Saute steaks in hot butter until cooked according to taste. Meanwhile, combine in saucepan the wine and the finely chopped shallots; cook over high heat until reduced by half, add pinch salt, some freshly ground pepper, extra butter, lemon juice, finely chopped parsley, and pan juices from the steaks. Cook over high heat, whisking all the time, until the sauce is hot and bubbling. Arrange steaks on heated serving dish, pour over the wine sauce. Serve with hot baked potato and green salad.

Serves 4

## Steak Kebabs

| | |
|---|---|
| 2 lb. rump steak | 1 green pepper |
| 2 medium onions | 4 medium mushrooms |
| 1 red pepper | marinade |

Remove fat from meat, cut into $1\frac{1}{2}$ in. cubes. Combine ingredients for marinade, add steak, and stir until well mixed. Cover and refrigerate overnight; stir occasionally to mix thoroughly.

Peel onions, cut in halves; remove centre portion. Wash peppers, slice in half, remove seeds, and cut flesh into $1\frac{1}{2}$ in. squares. Remove stalks from mushrooms and peel.

Thread vegetables and meat on skewers as follows: First, onion, then meat, green pepper, meat, red pepper, meat. Lastly, top with mushroom cap. Cook under heated griller, turning frequently and brushing with remaining marinade or melted butter until done to taste. Serve on hot Saffron Rice, and accompany with broccoli or other green vegetable.

Serves 4

**Soy Sauce Marinade**

1 tablespoon oil
3 tablespoons red wine
1 tablespoon lemon juice
1 tablespoon soy sauce
1 clove crushed garlic
pinch mustard
pinch ground thyme
1 small chopped onion
salt, pepper

Combine all ingredients, add the cubed steak, cover, and let stand overnight.

## Beef Stroganoff

2 lb. rump or fillet steak
½ lb. mushrooms
1 onion
½ cup sour cream
1 teaspoon salt
pepper
1 oz. butter

Cut meat into thinnest possible strips, about ½ in. by 2 in. Melt butter in pan and fry chopped onion, add meat, and continue to cook until almost done. Add the sliced mushrooms and fry until meat is tender. Pour in sour cream, season to taste, and heat through gently.

Serves 4 to 6

## Carpetbag Steak

1 piece rump steak
1½ dozen oysters
salt, pepper
butter

Ask butcher to cut the steak about 2½ in. thick, weighing about 2 lb. Make pocket in steak with sharp knife, dust pocket with salt and pepper. Stuff oysters into the pocket (a little lemon juice can be squeezed over them first, if desired); fasten pocket together with small skewers.

Grill steak to desired doneness, or pan-fry in butter. Cut into serving pieces. Transfer to hot dish, season with salt and pepper, dot with butter.

Serves 4.

## Steak Diane

8 to 10 oz. fillet steak
3 oz. butter
1 tablespoon worcestershire sauce
freshly ground pepper
little crushed garlic
1 tablespoon chopped parsley

Ask butcher to cut steak 1 in. thick, then pound steak until it is quite thin. Season each side lightly with freshly ground pepper. Put butter into pan; when sizzling, add steak. While cooking on one side, rub garlic into top of steak with wooden spoon; turn steak over. Add worcestershire sauce to pan, swirl steak round in the pan juices. When cooked to desired doneness, sprinkle with chopped parsley, transfer to heated plate.

A tablespoon of cream can be stirred into the sauce to soften the characteristic 'sharpness' of the sauce.

Makes one serving

## Steak au Poivre

4 pieces rump, sirloin, or fillet steak
2 tablespoons black peppercorns
2 oz. butter
1 dessertspoon oil
¾ cup dry white wine
1 dessertspoon brandy or sherry
1 dessertspoon butter

Coarsely crush the peppercorns, using rolling pin or mortar and pestle. You may need more peppercorns, depending on size of steaks. Press the crushed pepper into the steak, on both sides, or pound in with flat side of cleaver. Let stand 1 hour to absorb the pepper flavour.

Heat butter and oil in pan, add steaks, cook quickly on both sides to seal in juices. Then cook to desired doneness. Remove steaks to hot serving plates. Stir into pan the wine and brandy. Bring to boil, scraping the pan. Remove from heat, stir in extra butter. Strain over steaks.

Serves 4

## Tournedos

Tournedos are small, uniform slices of fillet, about 1 to 1½ in. thick. There are nearly 500 different versions; each is named according to the individual garnishings which accompany it.

Simple rules for cooking tournedos:

□ If necessary, trim or shape tournedos into a round, then tie or secure with small cocktail stick.

□ If they are to be grilled, brush them generously with melted butter or oil.

□ If they are to be sauteed, add enough butter to cover, when melted, the base of a heavy pan; then add 1 tablespoon of oil.

□ Start cooking over high heat, then reduce heat to moderate and cook to desired degree of doneness. ☛

Tournedos are small pieces of fillet steak topped with a rich sauce; shown here are Tournedos Nicoise and, at back, Tournedos Chasseur.

Remove cocktail stick. Serve at once on hot plate, accompanied by the chosen garnishing.

The tournedos is often raised up on the plate by means of a toasted or fried bread round; or hot pilaf rice can be used beneath the steak. These are to absorb the rich steak juices.

## Tournedos Chasseur

4 thick slices fillet steak
4 thick slices white bread
oil and butter for frying

### Sauce

½ lb. mushrooms
1 oz. butter
1 tablespoon oil
2 to 3 shallots
salt, pepper
¼ pint stock
1 tablespoon tomato paste
2 tablespoons madeira
1 dessertspoon cornflour
1 tablespoon chopped parsley

Trim steaks, remove crusts from bread, and cut into rounds. Heat some oil and butter in pan, fry bread until crisp and lightly browned on both sides. Keep warm in oven.

Saute steaks in oil and butter until brown on both sides, lower heat, and continue cooking until done as desired. Remove steaks from pan, season with salt and pepper. Place on top of fried bread, keep warm in oven until sauce is made.

Pour off excess fat from frying pan, pour in stock and tomato paste. Boil rapidly, stirring in all the brownings and pan juices. In another pan heat butter and oil, saute the sliced mushrooms 5 minutes over low heat. Add finely chopped shallots, season, and cook further 1 minute; set aside. Blend cornflour with madeira, stir into sauce, boil 1 minute. Add mushroom mixture, cook a few minutes more. Taste and adjust seasonings. Pour sauce over tournedos, sprinkle with chopped parsley.

Serves 4

*Tournedos Nicoise*: Prepare and cook steaks as above, top with Tomato Concasse (see page 112).

## Chateaubriand

This is a thick slice of steak cut from choicest part of fillet of beef—the 'eye' of the fillet. It is at its best when underdone, and is cooked in one piece, then sliced for serving.

Here is a simple but delicious way to serve Chateaubriand.

Chateaubriand steak
1 cup dry white wine
2 oz. butter
pepper
Sauce Chateaubriand

Steak should weigh about $1\frac{1}{2}$ to 2 lb. Heat butter in pan. Season meat with pepper, add to pan and brown quickly on all sides. Allow approximately 10 minutes cooking time per pound for rare meat, slightly more for medium-rare. Cooking time, of course, depends on thickness of steak.

When done, remove from pan, keep warm. Drain butter from pan, pour in the wine. Boil rapidly until reduced by two-thirds, stirring to collect any pan juices. Also add any juice which may have run from the fillet while being kept hot. This liquid forms the basis of the Sauce Chateaubriand.

*To serve*: Slice Chateaubriand thickly, place on hot serving dish. Spoon prepared Sauce Chateaubriand over. Serve with Pommes Parisienne.

### Sauce Chateaubriand

2 shallots
1 teaspoon chopped parsley
1 oz. butter
1 teaspoon chopped fresh tarragon
prepared pan juices

Chop shallots finely. Melt half the butter in small saucepan, add shallots. Cook until softened, then add prepared pan juices. Cook few minutes, remove from heat, swirl in remaining butter. Stir gently; as butter melts, the sauce will thicken. Add tarragon and parsley.

### Pommes Parisienne

Press potato baller into raw potato, twist, turn, scoop out potato ball. Parboil 3 minutes, drain well. Fry in hot butter, shaking pan occasionally, until golden. Alternatively, the parboiled potato balls can be deep-fried.

## Beef Goulash

1½ lb. round steak
1 onion
½ red pepper
3 tomatoes
1 tablespoon oil
½ cup seasoned flour
3 teaspoons paprika
2 cups water
2 beef stock cubes
salt, pepper

Trim meat, cut into 1 in. cubes, chop onion, seed and slice pepper, peel and chop tomatoes.

Heat oil in large saucepan, add onion and pepper, saute until tender, add paprika. Toss meat in seasoned flour, add gradually to pan, cook until well browned. Drain off any surplus fat. Add tomatoes and water in which stock cubes have been dissolved, season with salt and pepper, bring to boil, cover, reduce heat, simmer $1\frac{1}{2}$ hours, or until meat is tender.

Serves 4

## Steak Sate

2 lb. rump steak
½ cup oil
¼ cup soy sauce
2 large onions
1 clove garlic
1 dessertspoon lemon juice
1 teaspoon cumin
1 tablespoon sesame seeds

In bowl combine oil, soy sauce, grated onion, crushed garlic, lemon juice and cumin. Cut steak into 1 in. cubes and add to marinade; stir well and marinate approximately 1 hour. Using rolling pin, crush sesame seeds to a pulp; add to meat and marinade, leave to stand further 1 hour. Thread meat on skewers and grill lightly, turning occasionally and brushing with marinade.

Serves 4 to 6

## Beef Steak Tartar

4 to 6 oz. fillet steak
1 egg-yolk
1 dessertspoon finely chopped or grated onion
1 dessertspoon capers

Scrape or mince meat, removing any fat. Shape into patty shape, top with egg-yolk. Place onion and capers at side of steak (or they can be mixed into the meat). Have a pepper grinder so that fresh pepper can be ground over the meat. Serve with hot buttered toast or pumpernickel bread.

Gherkins, anchovy fillets, horseradish can be additional seasonings.

Serves 1.

NOTE: Steak Tartar also makes a good, unusual appetiser. Combine all the ingredients, spread on buttered toast, top with a little caviar.

## Steak Normandy

2 lb. chuck steak
3 onions
1 clove garlic
2 to 3 rashers bacon
2 tablespoons flour
1 tablespoon worcestershire sauce
1 dessertspoon sugar
2 tablespoons tomato sauce or purée
2 tablespoons vinegar
bouquet garni
½ cup stock
salt, pepper

Cut steak into 1 in. squares, coat with mixture of combined sugar and flour. Line ovenproof dish with 2 of the peeled and sliced onions, sprinkle with finely chopped garlic. Place meat on top, pour sauces, vinegar and stock over. Let stand several hours. Top with bacon strips (with rind removed) and remaining onion cut into rings. Season with salt and pepper, add bouquet garni. Cover, bake in moderate oven 2 to $2\frac{1}{2}$ hours. Remove cover for last 20 minutes of cooking time to crisp bacon and onion topping.

Serves 4 to 6

## Boeuf à la Bourguignonne

2 to 3 lb. topside or round steak
2 oz. butter
12 baby onions
2 oz. bacon
¼ lb. mushrooms
pinch sugar
2 teaspoons flour
1 cup dry red wine
stock
salt, freshly ground black pepper
bouquet garni
chopped parsley

Cut meat into large cubes, brown on all sides in heated butter. Remove meat, add onions, diced bacon and quartered mushrooms to remaining fat together with sugar, brown slowly. Remove vegetables and bacon, sprinkle in flour, cook slowly until brown. Pour wine into flour mixture, bring to boil, stirring constantly. Put in browned meat; add sufficient stock to cover. Season to taste, add bouquet garni.

Cover tightly, cook in slow oven or on top of stove approximately 1 hour. Then add onions, mushrooms, and bacon, continue cooking until meat is tender. Thicken, if necessary with a little blended flour. Sprinkle with chopped parsley before serving.

Serves 6 to 8

## Steak and Kidney Pie

2 sheep's kidneys or piece of ox kidney
2 lb. round or topside steak
2 onions
1¾ pints beef stock or water
½ bayleaf
1 lb. flaky or puff pastry
egg-yolk for glazing

Skin core, and dice kidneys, cut steak into 1 in. cubes. Put into saucepan. Add stock, bayleaf and chopped onions, and simmer, covered, 1 to $1\frac{1}{2}$ hours or until meat is tender. Adjust seasoning. Thicken with a little blended flour. Pour into pie dish.

If you want a rich dark colour in the gravy, add 1 dessertspoon soy sauce.

Roll out pastry to an oblong just larger than pie dish. Cut thin strips from ends and fit round moistened edge of dish. Brush pastry rim with water and place remaining pastry on top of pie. Press edges together, trim off excess pastry, using sharp knife. Make 2 slits in centre to allow steam to escape. Glaze with beaten egg-yolk. Stand dish on baking tray, bake in hot oven 20 to 25 minutes. Reduce heat to moderately hot, bake further 25 to 30 minutes or until pastry is golden brown.

Serves 6

## Carbonnade of Beef

3 lb. chuck or round steak
2 oz. butter
2 large onions
2 tablespoons flour
1 clove garlic
1 pint beer
1 pint hot water
bouquet garni
salt, pepper
pinch each nutmeg and sugar
6 to 8 pieces bread about 2 in. square (crusts removed) or use slices french bread
french mustard

Cut meat into large cubes, brown in butter. Set aside; brown sliced onions in pan. Add flour, cook slowly until brown; then add crushed garlic, beer and water. Bring to the boil, add seasonings and herbs. Put in meat, turn into ovenproof casserole. Cover, cook in moderate oven until meat is tender, about 2 hours. Skim off surface fat. Spread bread squares lightly with french mustard and place on top of casserole, pushing bread down to ensure it is well soaked with gravy. Return to oven and cook, uncovered, further 10 to 15 minutes or until bread crisps on top.

Serves 6 to 8

## Corned Beef

If meat is very salty, wash well, then soak in cold water 2 to 3 hours. Then place in large saucepan with sufficient hot water to cover. Add onion stuck with cloves, few peppercorns, bayleaf, and quartered carrot. A little brown sugar and dash of vinegar can also be added. Bring slowly to boiling point, then reduce heat until liquid is simmering. Skim well, cover, simmer until tender, allowing approximately 40 minutes per lb.

Serve hot with potatoes, baby carrots, and a green vegetable. Spoon Onion or Parsley Sauce over beef slices.

## Tangy Sweet Curry

2 lb. chuck steak
2 large carrots
4 sticks celery
1 large onion
1 teaspoon salt
1 dessertspoon curry powder
1 tablespoon golden syrup
juice ½ lemon
2 tablespoons flour
1 cooking apple
10 oz. can tomato soup
1 cup water

Trim steak and cut into 1 in. pieces, place in a large saucepan. Dice celery, peel and chop onion, carrot and apple, add to meat. Blend flour, curry powder and salt with golden syrup and lemon juice. Add to meat and vegetables with tomato soup and water; mix well. Cover, simmer gently 2 hours or until meat is tender. Serve with hot rice.

Serves 6

## Easy Sukiyaki

1½ lb. round steak
½ cup beef stock
1 teaspoon sugar
1 tablespoon soy sauce
2 tablespoons sherry
½ teaspoon salt
pepper to taste
2 tablespoons oil
1 onion
4 oz. mushrooms
½ cup sliced beans
½ bunch spinach
3 sticks celery
1 teaspoon arrowroot

Cut steak into very thin strips. In bowl, combine stock, sugar, soy sauce, sherry, salt and pepper, add meat; marinate 1 hour. Drain well, reserving marinade.

Slice beans, mushrooms, celery and spinach. Heat oil in large deep pan, saute meat and sliced onion 10 minutes, stirring occasionally. Add prepared vegetables, cook 5 minutes. Blend arrowroot in a little water; add reserved marinade and arrowroot to meat and vegetables, stir well, bring to boil, cook further 3 minutes.

Serves 4

## Kofta Curry

### Kofta Meat Balls

1½ lb. lean minced beef
½ cup shredded cabbage
pinch ground ginger
1 large onion
1 clove garlic
pinch ground cloves
1 green pepper
2 teaspoons curry powder
1 teaspoon lemon juice
salt
seasoned flour
oil for frying

### Curry

2 oz. butter
2 onions
1 clove garlic
½ teaspoon ground ginger
½ teaspoon turmeric
1 tablespoon curry powder
¼ teaspoon cayenne pepper
pinch cinnamon
2 large tomatoes
1 small potato
15 oz. can pineapple pieces, drained
1½ cups coconut milk (see below)
salt

*Meat Balls*: Mince or finely chop onion, garlic and ☞

Golden-crusted Steak and Kidney Pie — an old-fashioned favourite, just as popular today.

green pepper. Mix together cabbage, ginger, cloves, curry powder and meat. Season with salt and lemon juice; add minced ingredients. Roll into balls, dust with seasoned flour. Brown balls in hot oil. Drain, put aside.

*Curry*: Skin tomatoes, slice thickly. Heat butter in pan, add sliced onions and crushed garlic, saute until light brown in colour. Add ginger, turmeric, curry powder, cayenne and cinnamon. Stir well, cook 3 minutes. Add tomatoes, peeled potato and diced pineapple pieces. Cook gently 5 minutes, stirring constantly. Add coconut milk and salt to taste.

Add meat balls to sauce. Cover, simmer gently 15 to 20 minutes. Do not stir but shake pan lightly from time to time. Serve with hot fluffy rice.

*Coconut Milk*: Combine ⅓ cup coconut and 1½ cups water in saucepan. Bring slowly to boil. Remove from heat, let stand 10 minutes. Strain; pressing coconut with spoon to get as much flavour as possible into the liquid. Discard coconut.

## Stuffed Vine Leaves

15 oz. can vine leaves (or use fresh cabbage leaves)
1 lb. minced steak
½ cup rice
2 onions
¼ cup chopped parsley
2 teaspoons salt
pepper
15 oz. can mushroom soup

Rinse and drain the vine leaves (or blanch the cabbage leaves by cooking gently in boiling water 5 minutes). Combine the meat, rice, parsley, chopped onions, salt and pepper. Place a little in the centre of each leaf and fold into a neat parcel. If the leaves are small, put 2 together.

Arrange in casserole, pour over the mushroom soup. Bake, covered, in moderately slow oven 1½ to 2 hours. Add a little water or stock to casserole, if necessary, during cooking.

Serves 4.

In place of the mushroom soup, a lightly lemon-flavoured tomato sauce can be poured over the stuffed leaves before baking. Then bake, covered, as above.

**Lemon-Flavoured Tomato Sauce**

1 dessertspoon oil
1 large onion
1 clove garlic
3 tomatoes
salt, pepper
2 teaspoons lemon juice
1 cup stock

Heat oil, saute chopped onion and crushed garlic. Add skinned, chopped tomatoes, salt, pepper, lemon juice, and stock; simmer gently 10 minutes.

## Chilli Con Carne

2 tablespoons oil
1 large onion
1 large clove garlic
1 lb. minced steak
1 green pepper
15 oz. can whole tomatoes
2 cups water
1 bayleaf
½ teaspoon chilli powder
good pinch ground basil
1½ teaspoons salt
pepper
10 oz. can kidney beans

Heat the oil in large saucepan, add chopped onion and crushed garlic, saute until golden brown. Add minced steak and chopped green pepper, continue cooking until meat changes colour. Add tomatoes, water, bayleaf, chilli powder, basil, salt and pepper, bring to boil; reduce heat, and simmer gently, uncovered, until sauce thickens (approximately 1½ hours). Add undrained kidney beans and reheat.

Serves 4.

NOTE: The strength of chilli powders varies greatly. With some brands, ½ teaspoon will be sufficient; with others, which may be milder, slightly more chilli powder can be used. Taste after an hour's cooking; add more chilli powder then, if necessary. Of course, a lot depends on how hot you like your Chilli.

## Savoury Meatloaf

2 lb. minced hamburger steak
2 eggs
2 medium onions
½ cup tomato sauce
1 teaspoon oregano
1 tablespoon salt
½ teaspoon pepper

**Brown Sauce:**

2 oz. butter
¼ cup plain flour
¾ pint boiling water
1 chicken stock cube
¼ cup tomato sauce
salt, pepper

Combine minced steak, eggs, chopped onions, tomato sauce, oregano, salt and pepper in mixing bowl. Blend well on electric mixer (this gives very fine texture to the meatloaf) or by hand. Form meat mixture into loaf shape. Place in greased shallow baking dish. Bake in moderately hot oven 50 minutes, brushing occasionally with pan drippings. Serve hot, sliced, with brown sauce spooned over.

Serves 6.

*Brown Sauce*: Melt butter in pan, stir in flour; cook until brown, stirring occasionally; do not allow flour to burn. Remove from heat, add boiling water in which stock cube has been dissolved, blend well. Return to heat, bring to boil, stirring; reduce heat, cook until smooth and thickened, stirring constantly. Stir in tomato sauce; season to taste with salt and pepper.

## Indonesian Meatballs

1 lb. potatoes
1 lb. minced steak
1 small onion
2 cloves garlic
4 shallots
¼ teaspoon pepper
1 oz. butter
2 eggs, separated
¼ teaspoon nutmeg
1½ teaspoons salt
oil for deep frying

Cook, drain, and mash potatoes. Melt butter in frying pan. Add finely chopped onion and crushed garlic. Simmer 3 to 4 minutes, then add minced steak, season with salt, pepper and nutmeg. Cook, stirring constantly. When meat is half cooked, add finely chopped shallots, including green tops. Remove from heat when meat is cooked.

In a bowl combine mashed potatoes with meat mixture and egg-yolks. Form mixture into small balls. Refrigerate 1 hour to firm. Beat egg-whites very lightly with fork in small bowl. Dip meat balls one at a time in egg-whites. Deep-fry in hot oil until golden brown. These can be prepared in advance and reheated for 10 minutes in moderate oven.

Makes approx. 4 dozen

## Garlic Sausage

¼ lb. lean bacon pieces
½ lb. minced steak
¾ lb. sausage meat
2 cloves crushed garlic
2 beaten eggs
2 cups soft breadcrumbs
1 teaspoon salt
¼ teaspoon pepper

Put bacon pieces through mincer, or chop finely. Combine with remaining ingredients, mix well. Form mixture into thick sausage roll, approximately 8 in. long. Tie firmly in well-floured pudding cloth. Lower carefully into saucepan of boiling water, making sure sausage is well covered. Boil steadily, covered, 2½ hours. Remove from water, drain, and leave in cloth to cool. Refrigerate several hours or overnight. Remove cloth.

Makes approx. 2 lb. sausage

## Savoury-Glazed Meatloaf

1½ lb. minced steak
1 cup soft breadcrumbs
1 teaspoon salt
pepper
1 medium onion, chopped
1 egg, beaten
1 tablespoon worcestershire sauce
2 tablespoons tomato sauce
6 oz. can evaporated milk
1 dessertspoon dry mustard

**Glaze**

½ teaspoon dry mustard
¼ cup tomato sauce
1 tablespoon brown sugar

Combine ingredients for glaze, set aside. Mix together all remaining ingredients (mixture will be rather moist); press into greased 8 in. x 4 in. loaf tin, then turn upside down on to aluminium foil-lined oven tray, leaving tin still over loaf. Bake in moderate oven 15 minutes. Remove from oven, remove loaf tin. Brush meat-loaf well with glaze. (Do not replace loaf tin.) Return to oven, cook further 50 to 60 minutes.

Equally nice served hot with vegetables or cold with salads; good for sandwiches, too.

Serves 4

## Beef Olives

2 lb. skirt steak
1 small, finely chopped onion
3 oz. butter
3 oz. fresh breadcrumbs
2 tablespoons chopped parsley
½ teaspoon dried thyme
salt, pepper
little milk
3 diced onions
3 diced carrots
1 small diced turnip
1 diced stick of celery
¾ pint beef stock
bouquet garni
1 dessertspoon flour
1 dessertspoon butter, extra

Cut steak into thin slices about 2½ in. x 5 in.; mince or finely chop the trimmings. Heat 2 oz. butter in saucepan, saute chopped onions until transparent, without allowing them to brown.

Mix together the breadcrumbs, herbs, seasonings, minced or chopped meat, and sauteed onion, bind with a little milk. Spread layer of this mixture over each slice of meat. Roll up; tie with thin string. Heat 1 oz. butter or substitute in pan, add diced vegetables, cook till golden in colour. Pour over stock; return meat to pan with bouquet garni. Bring to boil, cover. Reduce heat.

Cook gently 1½ to 2 hours or until meat is tender. (Or place in casserole and cook, covered, in moderate oven.) Place meat on serving dish, remove string. Mix flour with the extra butter, pour gravy from pan over this mixture, blend together. Return to pan and bring to the boil, stirring. Adjust seasoning, remove bouquet garni. Pour gravy over meat.

Serves 4

## Lamb

We're proud of the quality of our Australian lamb; young, tender, full of flavour. Here we tell you how to roast it to perfection, and use it in many different recipes.

Set out below are the various cuts of lamb

### Cuts of Lamb and Veal

**Barbecue Chops** Thinly cut chops from forequarter of lamb. 3 to 4 chops per lb. Not over-fat; bone has pinkish tinge. Barbecue, grill.

**Braising Chops** Cut from forequarter or hind end of loin (chump), from young mutton or heavy lamb. 2 to 3 chops per lb. Should not be over-fat; flesh firm and pale red in colour; touch of pink colour in bone. Braise.

**Breast or Forequarter Chops** Cut from forequarter of lamb or young mutton. 2 to 3 per lb. Very meaty, some white fat, small round bone in each chop. Fry, grill, barbecue (lamb), braise, casserole (mutton).

**Chump Chops** (lamb, mutton). Cut from leg end of loin. 3 to 4 per lb. Very meaty, flesh pink, fat white and dry, small amount of bone. Grill, fry, barbecue.

**Crown Roast** Cut from rib ends of loin of lamb; formed into shape like a crown. Roast.

**Cutlets** (lamb, mutton) Rib chops with rib bones trimmed. 4 to 6 per lb. Bones pink, fat white, flesh red and firm. Grill, fry (after crumbing).

**Cutlets** (veal) In some States these are thin slices of veal cut from leg or shoulder of calf; no bone. 6 to 8 slices per lb. In other States they are veal chops, trimmed, cut from loin or rib.

**Fillet** (lamb, mutton, pork, veal) This is a half leg (chump or thick end). Approximate weight: Lamb 2 lb., mutton 3 lb., pork 4 lb., veal 3 lb.

**Flap or Breast** (lamb, mutton, veal) Piece cut from breast and flank of these carcasses. Roast or stew.

**Forequarter** (lamb, mutton) Cut from fore part of lamb or mutton. 3 to 5 lb. Flesh firm, bones pink. Can be sold boned and rolled. Roast.

**Forequarter Chops** (lamb, mutton) Cut from forequarters. 2 to 3 per lb. See Forequarter. Grill, barbecue, fry (lamb); stew, braise, casserole (mutton).

**French Cutlets** From lamb; all the backbone is removed. 6 per lb. See Cutlets.

**Grilling Chops** Best chops cut from loin of lamb or young mutton. 4 per lb. Flesh and bone pink in colour; fat firm and white; 'tail' of chop not too long. Grill, barbecue, pan-fry.

**Haricot or Scrag Neck Chops** Cut from neck of mutton or lamb. Not over-fat; ample meat. Stew.

**Knuckle of Veal** Part of the leg from forequarter of veal. Flesh pink colour. Simmer.

**Lamb's Fry** Liver from a lamb. 1 lb. or less. Firm; brown shiny surface. Fry, stew, braise.

**Lamb Ham** Leg of lamb which has been pickled and smoked. 4 to 5 lb. Not over-fat; brownish-yellow colour; smoky aroma. Simmer.

**Leg Chops** Large oval chops cut directly from leg (lamb and mutton). 2 per lb. White selvedge fat; meat pink to red in colour; small bone. Grill, fry.

**Leg** (lamb, mutton, pork, veal) Hind leg from one of these carcasses (for pork) 3 to 9 lb. Plump, little fat (lamb and mutton); no fat (veal); some fat, skin clean (pork). Roast if fresh; simmer if pickled.

**Loin** (lamb, mutton, pork, veal). This is cut from middle of carcass. (Chops come from here.) Roast.

**Neck** (lamb, mutton). A neck cut from these carcasses. Some fat; ample meat. Simmer, stew.

**Rack of Lamb** Two ribs of lamb joined (not cut through centre). Roast.

**Rosettes of Lamb** Chops cut from full neck of lamb. See Haricot Chops.

**Saddle of Lamb** Two loins of lamb joined (not cut through centre). Roast.

**Shank** Part of front leg from lamb or mutton. Simmer, roast.

**Side of Lamb or Mutton** A full side; two are obtained when carcass is split through backbone. Lamb 15 to 20 lb., mutton 20 to 25 lb. Lamb not over-fat; bones pink and soft. 'Lamb' strip branded down full side. Mutton (young), similar features of quality but not so pronounced; no strip brand.

**Stewing Chops** Mutton chops cut from forequarter or perhaps leg; ample meat. Stew.

Savoury Lamb — a colourful combination of vegetable and simple but subtle seasonings makes this the perfect family or party casserole.

## Roast Lamb

Leg, forequarter, or shoulder of lamb, when roasted, gives substantial helpings for family meals. You can add subtle flavour by scoring the skin lightly in several places and inserting small slivers of garlic, sprigs of rosemary, or pieces of bayleaf. Or rub lamb well, before cooking, with a cut clove of garlic; mix 1 teaspoon of rosemary into 3 tablespoons of softened butter and rub over joint.

To give a delightfully sweet flavour to meat, baste with orange or pineapple juice while cooking—you will need about $\frac{1}{2}$ cup. The Greeks use lemon and marjoram to flavour their lamb dishes.

Moderate heat is best for lamb; it ensures thorough, gentle cooking with a minimum of shrinkage. For joints, allow approximately 25 minutes per lb. Joints which have a stuffing will take a little longer.

Some cooks like to stand lamb on a rack in baking dish to cook; some prefer to put directly into the dish, without a rack. If cooking without the rack, make sure any surplus fat is poured off during the cooking—otherwise the meat will 'stew' in the fat instead of being beautifully crisp-skinned.

When meat is cooked, remove from baking dish; pour off fat, leaving about 2 tablespoons in dish; stir in $1\frac{1}{2}$ tablespoons flour. Cook, stirring, until mixture 'bubbles' and browns—do not let it burn. Gradually stir in 1 pint stock; cook, stirring, until gravy boils and thickens. Season to taste.

## Mint Sauce

- 2 tablespoons chopped fresh mint
- 1 tablespoon sugar
- 1 tablespoon boiling water
- 2 tablespoons vinegar

Wash and dry mint, remove stalks, chop finely. Boil sugar and water 1 minute, add vinegar, pour over mint; stand 15 minutes. Stir well before serving.

## Savoury Lamb

- 2 lb. lean lamb
- 4 small onions
- seasoned flour
- 3 tablespoons oil
- 15 oz. can tomato soup
- 2 cups stock
- 2 tablespoons sherry
- 1 tablespoon brown sugar
- 1 tablespoon lemon juice
- 1 tablespoon worcestershire sauce
- 1 dessertspoon dry mustard
- salt, pepper
- 2 carrots
- 1 swede or turnip
- 4 sticks celery
- 1 red pepper
- 1 green pepper

Trim lamb, cut into large pieces; peel and halve onions. Toss lamb in seasoned flour. Heat oil in large saucepan, gradually add lamb, brown well; add onions, saute until transparent. Add remaining ingredients, except for vegetables; cover, simmer 1 hour.

Peel and slice carrots and swede, chop celery into large pieces, seed peppers, chop into 1 in. squares. Add prepared vegetables to lamb mixture, cover, simmer further $\frac{1}{2}$ to 1 hour, or until lamb and vegetables are tender.

Serves 4

NOTE: 1 cup cooked haricot beans may be added when stew is cooked, if desired.

## Crumbed Cutlets

Remove skin and excess fat from each cutlet. Dip in flour, which has been seasoned with salt and pepper; shake off excess flour.

Dip cutlets in egg beaten with a little oil (to help hold crumbs firmly), or brush over with a pastry brush. Then press firmly into breadcrumbs. Repeat process if you like a crisp coating. Refrigerate 1 hour to firm crumbs.

Shallow-fry in hot oil, turning occasionally, until crumbs are golden brown and cutlets cooked through. Make sure oil is hot before adding cutlets, otherwise crumbs will not hold firm but will drop off.

## Devilled Wine Chops

- 1½ lb. best end lamb neck chops
- ¼ cup finely chopped celery
- 1 onion
- 1 dessertspoon prepared mustard
- 1 tablespoon brown sugar
- 1 clove garlic
- 1 tablespoon worcestershire sauce
- 1 tablespoon lemon juice
- 2 tablespoons sherry
- 10 oz. can tomato soup undiluted

Arrange chops in well-greased casserole, cover, and bake $\frac{3}{4}$ hour in moderate oven. Remove all excess fat. Chop onion finely and crush garlic. Heat together remaining ingredients, add onion and garlic, pour over chops; bake, covered, $\frac{3}{4}$ hour, basting occasionally.

Serves 4

## Mock Ham

- 1 pumped, corned leg of lamb
- 2 bacon bones
- 1 onion studded with cloves
- 1 dessertspoon brown sugar
- few sprigs parsley
- 1 tablespoon vinegar
- ½ cup canned pineapple syrup or juice
- warm water

**Glazing**

½ cup canned pineapple syrup or juice
3 tablespoons brown sugar

Place meat in large saucepan, cover with warm water. Add bacon bones, onion, brown sugar, pineapple syrup, parsley and vinegar. Cover, simmer gently until cooked, allowing approximately 40 minutes per lb. Test through thickest part of leg with fine skewer; allow to cool in the cooking water. Remove from pan, brush generously several times with pineapple glaze.

Pineapple rice salad and salad vegetables are good accompaniments.

Serves 6 to 8

*Glaze*: Heat pineapple juice and brown sugar in saucepan, bring to the boil; reduce heat, simmer 10 to 15 minutes.

## Italian Lamb Shanks

6 lamb shanks
seasoned flour
2 tablespoons oil
1 clove garlic
2 onions
1 cup chopped celery
1 teaspoon salt
1 teaspoon sugar
½ pint stock or water
1 cup tomato purée
¼ pint white wine
¼ teaspoon rosemary
¼ lb. mushrooms
parsley

Dredge shank pieces in seasoned flour. Slice onions. Heat oil in pan and saute shanks, crushed garlic, onions and celery until meat is well browned. Add salt, sugar, boiling stock, tomato puree, white wine and rosemary.

Bring to boil, cover, reduce heat, simmer $1\frac{1}{4}$ to $1\frac{1}{2}$ hours or until shanks are tender. Add sliced mushrooms and cook further 10 minutes. Serve hot, sprinkled with chopped parsley.

Serves 6

## Delicious Lamb Stew

2 lb. lamb neck chops
seasoned flour
2 tablespoons oil
2 onions
2 carrots
1 parsnip
1 stick celery
1 large cooking apple
3 cups stock
1 tablespoon plum jam

Dredge chops in flour and brown in heated oil. Chop onions, slice carrots, parsnip, celery and peeled apple. Add vegetables and apple to frying pan and saute a few minutes. Stir in plum jam and stock, bring to boil, reduce heat; simmer for $1\frac{1}{4}$ hours or until tender.

If extra thickening is required, blend a little seasoned flour with water and add to stew, stirring.

Serves 6

## Sweet Curry

2 lb. boned shoulder of lamb
1 cup sour cream
2 teaspoons garam masala
1 tablespoon curry powder
4 oz. butter
2 tablespoons slivered blanched almonds
¼ cup sultanas
½ cup thinly sliced dried apricots
4 cloves garlic
2 in. piece finely chopped green ginger
2 large onions
salt
lemon juice

Cut meat into 1 in. cubes. Place in bowl with sour cream, garam masala, curry powder; stir well, leave to marinate several hours.

Heat butter in saucepan, fry almonds until golden, remove, and drain. Fry sultanas and apricots until plumped, remove and drain. Fry sliced garlic, ginger, and sliced onions until golden. Add meat and marinade, cook 5 minutes on medium heat. Add sultanas and apricots, cover, and simmer 45 to 60 minutes, until meat is tender; add salt and lemon juice to taste. Garnish with the almonds.

Serves 4

## Shaslik

2 lb. lamb leg chops
2 small onions
1 green pepper
2 medium tomatoes
8 mushrooms
bayleaves
marinade

**Marinade**

1 crushed clove garlic
⅓ cup oil
2 tablespoons lemon juice
salt, pepper
2 tablespoons finely chopped onion

Remove fat from meat, cut into $1\frac{1}{2}$ in. cubes. Combine ingredients for marinade, add lamb, and stir until well mixed. Cover and refrigerate several hours; stir occasionally to mix.

Peel onions, cut in halves, remove centre portion. Wash pepper, slice in half, remove seeds, and cut flesh in $1\frac{1}{2}$ in. squares. Wash tomatoes and cut in quarters. Remove stalks from mushrooms, if desired, or leave whole.

Thread meat on to skewers, brush with marinade and, if desired, place a bayleaf at end of skewer. Thread alternate vegetables on separate skewers, brush with marinade. Cook under heated griller, turning frequently and brushing with remaining marinade or melted butter until done to taste.

Pilav is a good accompaniment for Shaslik.

Serves 2

## Hot Curry

2 lb. boned shoulder of lamb or mutton
1 teaspoon ground coriander
1 teaspoon ground cardamom
1 teaspoon poppy seeds
1 teaspoon ground cinnamon
1 teaspoon ground cloves
1 teaspoon ground black pepper
½ teaspoon salt
2 in. piece green ginger
4 cloves garlic
1 finely chopped onion
½ cup yoghurt
2 oz. butter
1 sliced onion
¼ cup slivered almonds

Cut lamb into 1 in. cubes. Combine all spices, seasonings, finely chopped onion, finely chopped ginger, crushed garlic and yoghurt. Place meat in this marinade, leave several hours.

Heat butter, fry sliced onion until golden; remove, reserve for garnish. Fry almonds, remove, reserve for garnish. Add meat and marinade to pan, stir well. Cover, and simmer 45 minutes or until meat is tender. Garnish with reserved fried onion rings and almonds.

Serves 4

## Moussaka

3 medium eggplants
salt
2 lb. lamb leg chops
1 large onion
1 clove garlic, crushed
3 oz. butter
15 oz. can tomatoes
1 cup white wine
½ teaspoon nutmeg
salt, pepper
8 oz. grated cheese
½ cup soft breadcrumbs
melted butter, extra
oil for frying

**Sauce**

2 oz. butter
⅓ cup flour
½ teaspoon nutmeg
salt, pepper
1 pint milk
1 egg

Cut eggplant into ½ in. slices, sprinkle lightly with salt, stand 20 minutes. Finely chop or mince chops, finely chop onion. Combine cheese with bread-crumbs.

Heat butter, add meat, onion and garlic, saute until meat changes colour; add drained tomatoes, wine, nutmeg, salt and pepper, cover, simmer 15 minutes, or until meat is tender.

Drain eggplant, pat dry with absorbent paper, deep fry in hot oil until golden brown; drain.

Arrange fried eggplant in base of large greased casserole dish, sprinkle with ⅓ of cheese mixture, top with meat sauce, then white sauce. Sprinkle with remaining cheese mixture, drizzle over extra melted butter. Bake in hot oven 20 minutes, or until golden brown.

Serves 4 to 6

*Sauce*: Melt butter in saucepan, remove from heat, stir in flour, nutmeg, salt and pepper, stir until smooth, return to heat, cook 1 minute. Remove from heat, gradually add milk, return to heat, stir until sauce boils and thickens. Add beaten egg, beat until smooth.

*To serve as an entree*: Cut 3 small egg plants in half lengthways, scoop out centres, leaving ½ in. shell. Sprinkle inside with salt, stand until liquid appears on surface; drain. Brush egg plants inside and out with melted butter, stand on tray in ½ in. cold water. Bake in moderate oven 8 to 10 minutes.

Layer meat sauce, cheese mixture and white sauce into eggplant shells, finish with cheese mixture, drizzle with extra melted butter. Bake in hot oven 20 minutes, or until golden brown.

Serves 6

## Savoury Lamb Stew with Parsley Dumplings

1½ lb. scrag-end neck of lamb
2 pints water
3 carrots
2 onions
4 potatoes
salt, pepper
1 bayleaf
½ cup tomato sauce
1 tablespoon finely chopped parsley
2 tablespoons flour

**Parsley Dumplings**

1 cup self-raising flour
1 teaspoon butter
½ teaspoon salt
1 tablespoon finely chopped parsley
½ cup milk

Remove meat from bones, cut into approximately 1 in. cubes, discarding any fat. Place in saucepan with bones, cover with water, bring to boil. Reduce heat, cover, and simmer 1 hour. Add peeled and diced carrots and potatoes, chopped onions, salt, pepper, bayleaf, tomato sauce, and parsley. Bring to boil; reduce heat, simmer further 10 minutes. Remove bones, skim off any surplus fat.

Blend flour with little water, add to saucepan, and cook, stirring, until liquid thickens. Drop dumpling dough by heaped dessertspoonfuls on top of hot bubbling stew. Cover tightly; cook 15 to 20 minutes.

Serves 4

*Parsley Dumplings*: Sift together flour and salt. Rub in butter, stir in parsley. Add milk all at once, stirring quickly to make a soft, sticky dough.

Moussaka can be cooked in a casserole or cooked in the delightfully unusual way shown above, and served as an entrée.

## Veal

Veal cooks so quickly, to delicious tenderness, it's a boon to the busy housewife or business woman. And it is versatile—equally good pan-fried, as for schnitzel, or made into a rich-tasting casserole.

Cuts of veal are similar to those of Lamb; see under 'Lamb' for listing of the various veal cuts

### Schnitzels

*To prepare*: Trim schnitzels carefully, then place between several thicknesses of greaseproof paper and pound with a mallet or flat blade of heavy knife. Continue pounding until schnitzels are about ⅛ in. thick. This breaks down the fibres of the meat, making it deliciously tender. Place schnitzels on flat dish and squeeze over a little lemon juice; let stand about 1 hour, turning frequently. The schnitzels are now ready for cooking.

### Schnitzels Naturel

1½ lb. prepared schnitzels
salt, pepper
flour
2 oz. butter
juice ½ lemon

Sprinkle each schnitzel with a little salt and pepper; dip in flour, shake off excess. Saute in heated butter, allowing 4 to 5 minutes for each side, or longer, depending on thickness. Arrange drained schnitzels on hot serving dish. Add lemon juice to remaining butter, spoon over schnitzels.

Serves 4 to 6

### Wiener Schnitzel

1½ lb. prepared schnitzels
seasoned flour
beaten egg
fine dry breadcrumbs
2 oz. melted butter
1 tablespoon oil
slices of hard boiled egg
rolled anchovy fillets
lemon wedges

Toss schnitzels in seasoned flour, shake off excess, and dip in beaten egg. Then roll in crumbs, pressing these on firmly; refrigerate 30 minutes to set crumbs.

Heat oil and butter in heavy frying pan, put in schnitzels and cook until golden brown on both sides. Allow 4 to 5 minutes cooking time for each side. Drain schnitzels well, arrange on serving dish. Top each with slice of hardboiled egg and rolled anchovy fillet. Serve with lemon wedges.

Serves 4 to 6

### Schnitzels with Cream

1½ lb. prepared schnitzels
seasoned flour
⅔ cup cream
salt, pepper
chopped parsley
2 oz. butter
a little oil

Dip schnitzels in seasoned flour; saute in heated butter and oil, allowing 4 to 5 minutes cooking time for each side. Transfer to serving dish; keep warm.

Add cream to pan juices; simmer until mixture is slightly reduced and well blended. Season with salt and pepper. Spoon over schnitzels; sprinkle with chopped parsley.

Serves 4 to 6

### Veal with Blue Cheese

1½ lb. veal steaks (cut thin as for schnitzel)
4 oz. butter
2 oz. blue cheese
seasoned flour
1 egg
soft breadcrumbs
4 tablespoons oil
lemon wedges

Pound veal, if necessary, until very thin. Cream together butter and blue cheese in warmed basin. Spread some of this mixture on one side of each steak; dip steaks in seasoned flour, then beaten egg; press on breadcrumbs. Refrigerate 1 hour.

Heat oil in large frying pan, cook steaks until well browned and cooked through. Dust with chopped parsley, garnish with lemon wedges.

Serves 4 to 6

### Dutch Veal Croquettes

1 lb. veal steak
2½ oz. butter
water
¼ cup flour
1 dessertspoon worcestershire sauce
salt
freshly ground pepper
1 egg
breadcrumbs
oil for frying

Cover veal steak with water, add salt, simmer veal until tender. Drain, reserve 1 pint of stock.

Melt butter in saucepan, stir in flour; cook 1 minute. Remove from heat, gradually add reserved stock. Return to heat, bring to boil, simmer until smooth and thickened, stirring constantly; simmer 2 minutes. Remove from heat, add salt, pepper and worcestershire sauce.

Cut veal into $\frac{1}{4}$ in. cubes and mix into sauce; refrigerate. Then form into croquette shapes approximately 3 in. in length, using floured hands.

Dip croquettes in lightly beaten egg, then roll in breadcrumbs. Refrigerate 1 hour. Deep-fry in hot oil. When gold in colour, remove from oil and drain on absorbent paper.

Makes approx. 1 dozen

## Veal Parmesan

- 1½ lb. veal steaks (cut thin as for schnitzel)
- 1 cup fresh breadcrumbs
- ¾ cup grated parmesan cheese
- seasoned flour
- 1 egg
- 2 oz. butter
- 2 tablespoons oil

### Mushroom Sauce

- 1 tablespoon oil
- 1 large onion
- 1½ cups tomato purée
- ¼ lb. mushrooms
- ⅓ cup dry sherry
- salt, pepper

Combine breadcrumbs, lemon rind and parmesan cheese. Pound steaks, if necessary, until thin. Dip in seasoned flour, then beaten egg; press on crumb mixture. Refrigerate 1 hour.

Heat butter and oil in large frying pan, cook steaks until golden on each side and cooked through. Remove to hot serving plates. Serve Mushroom Sauce separately. Serves 4

*Mushroom Sauce*: Chop onion and mushrooms, saute in hot oil until tender; add tomato puree, sherry, season with salt and pepper. Simmer, uncovered 5 minutes.

## Veal Marengo

- 2 lb. veal steak
- 1 oz. butter
- 1 tablespoon oil
- ½ cup seasoned flour
- 1 clove garlic
- ¼ pint white wine
- 1 pint boiling water
- 2 chicken stock cubes
- 1 tablespoon tomato paste
- 2 tomatoes
- 12 small onions
- ½ lb. button mushrooms
- chopped parsley

Trim and cut steak into serving-size pieces, toss in seasoned flour. Heat butter and oil in large frying pan, fry meat until golden; remove, place in casserole. Fry crushed garlic a few minutes, add remaining flour; cook, stirring occasionally, until lightly browned. Gradually add wine and boiling water, in which chicken stock cubes have been dissolved, bring to boil, stirring; add tomato paste. Reduce heat, simmer gently until reduced by half. Pour over meat, cover, bake in moderate oven 1 hour.

Meanwhile, parboil onions 5 minutes; remove skin from tomatoes and chop coarsely. When meat is tender, add onions, sliced mushrooms, and tomatoes; cook further 15 to 20 minutes. Sprinkle with chopped parsley.

Serves 6

## Veal and Mushroom Ragout

- 1½ lb. veal steak
- 2 onions
- 2 oz. butter
- 15 oz. can cream of mushroom or cream of tomato soup
- 2 cups boiling water
- 2 chicken stock cubes
- 1 tablespoon paprika
- 2 green peppers
- 4 oz. small mushrooms
- salt, pepper

Cut veal into 1 in. cubes. Melt butter in frying pan, saute sliced onions and veal until onions are transparent; stir in paprika.

Combine soup and boiling water, in which chicken stock cubes have been dissolved; stir into veal, season to taste; cover, simmer gently approximately 1 hour or until veal is tender.

Add sliced peppers and whole mushrooms, cook gently until mushrooms are tender, about 7 minutes.

Serves 4.

## Veal Cordon Bleu

- 6 veal steaks (cut thin as for schnitzel)
- 6 thin slices ham
- 6 thin slices gruyere cheese
- seasoned flour
- 1 egg
- fine dry breadcrumbs
- 2 oz. butter
- 2 tablespoons oil

Pound steaks, if necessary, until very thin. Top each steak with slice of ham and slice of gruyere cheese. Fold steaks in half, secure with small wooden stick. Dip in seasoned flour and beaten egg, then press on fine dry breadcrumbs. Refrigerate 1 hour.

Heat butter and oil in large frying pan. Cook steaks, turning occasionally, until cooked through. Drain well, remove small wooden sticks.

Serves 3

## Gourmet Veal

- 1½ lb. veal steaks (cut very thin as for schnitzel)
- ½ lb. mushrooms
- 6 to 8 shallots
- salt, pepper
- 2 oz. butter
- 2 tablespoons oil
- ¼ pint cream
- parsley

Pound steaks until very thin, if necessary. Slice mushrooms, chop shallots. Heat butter and oil in large frying pan, fry steaks quickly. Remove from pan and keep warm.

Add mushrooms to pan and saute until tender, add the chopped shallots, cook a few minutes. Add cream and allow to heat through (do not boil). Season to taste. Pour over the cooked veal steaks. Sprinkle with chopped parsley.

Serves 4 to 6

## Veal Chops à la Crème

6 veal chops
6 oz. small mushrooms
boiling salted water
4 oz. butter
12 small onions
½ cup cream
1 cup dry white wine
chopped parsley
salt, pepper

Peel the onions, keeping them whole; cook in boiling salted water 10 minutes.

Heat butter in pan, add chops, and cook until golden brown on one side. Turn and cook on other side. When done, remove and keep warm on serving dish. Add the small whole mushrooms and par-boiled onions to pan, season, cook until tender, and golden brown in colour. Stir in white wine, then add cream. Cook a few minutes, stirring frequently (do not allow to boil). Taste, and correct seasonings. Pour sauce over chops, sprinkle with parsley.

Serves 3

## Osso Buco

3 or 4 veal shanks sawn into 3 in. pieces
¼ cup oil
¼ pint white wine
¼ pint stock
seasoning
flour
2 carrots
3 onions
3 sticks celery
1 bayleaf
2 cloves garlic
pinch each basil and thyme
piece lemon rind
1 small can tomato paste
2 tablespoons finely chopped celery, extra
1 tablespoon grated lemon rind

Heat oil in pan, fry sliced onions gently until soft and turning golden, place in large saucepan. Gently saute sliced carrots and chopped celery, add to onions. Roll veal shanks in seasoned flour and brown in oil.

Arrange pieces on top of vegetables, standing upright so that marrow won't fall out during cooking. Add bayleaf, crushed garlic, thyme, basil, and lemon rind. Mix tomato paste into combined white wine and stock, add seasonings and pour over. Add more stock, if necessary. Bring to boil, cover, and simmer gently for approximately 4 hours or until meat is almost falling off bones. Ten minutes before serving, sprinkle with finely chopped celery and lemon rind. Serve with risotto.

Serves 4 to 6

## Herbed Shoulder of Veal

1 boned shoulder of veal
salt, pepper
1 cup chicken stock
1 oz. butter

**Stuffing**

3 cups fresh breadcrumbs
2 tablespoons finely chopped parsley
finely grated rind 1 lemon
pinch salt
pepper
1 teaspoon mixed herbs
1 egg
1 oz. butter
1 small onion

Fill shoulder with herbed breadcrumb stuffing; tie firmly into shape. Place in baking dish with stock, salt, pepper, and butter. Bake in moderate oven, basting frequently, allowing 30 minutes per lb.

Serves 6 to 8

*Stuffing*: Saute chopped onion in melted butter; mix with breadcrumbs, parsley, grated lemon rind, herbs, salt and pepper. Beat egg, add to the mixture, and stir until it binds together.

## Caraway Veal Paprika

1 lb. mushrooms
6 medium onions
6 oz. butter
4 lb. veal steak
8 oz. can tomato paste
2 pints water
2 chicken stock cubes
2 tablespoons paprika
2 bayleaves
salt, pepper
1 teaspoon caraway seeds
1 cup sour cream

Cut veal into ¾ in. cubes, slice mushrooms and onions. Heat butter in large saucepan, add mush-rooms and onions, saute 5 minutes. Add veal gradually, brown well. Add tomato paste, bayleaves, water in which stock cubes have been dissolved, and seasonings. Bring to boil, cover, reduce heat, simmer 1½ hours, or until veal is tender. Just before serving, stir in sour cream.

Serves 8

Wiener Schnitzel — golden-crumbed veal slices, seasoned lightly with lemon, are served with traditional topping of egg and anchovy.

# Pork, Ham and Bacon

For most families, there's nothing nicer than a roasted leg of pork—the crackling crisp and golden; or slices from a pink, juicy, succulent ham. In this section are the cooking methods and recipes which present pork, in its various forms, at its most appetising best

## Cuts of Pork

**Bacon** Slices cut from side or middle of pork which has been pickled and smoked. ½ lb. and 1 lb. packs, 6 to 8 slices per lb. Not over-fat, smoky aroma. Simmer, grill, fry.

**Belly Pork** Flap of pork which has been pickled and rolled, sometimes sold fresh. 3 to 4 lb. Skin is white and moist; flesh when cut has pink colour. Simmer (if pickled), roast (if fresh).

**Fillet** (see Lamb, also Pork Fillet).

**Ham** Leg of pork which has been trimmed, then pickled and smoked; whole, sliced, or canned. (Canned hams are usually made from shoulder end of loin.) 12 to 15 lb. (whole ham); 1½ lb. to 4 lb. (canned).

**Hand of Pork** Breast portion and front leg cut from carcass of pork; usually pickled, although sometimes sold fresh. Simmer (if pickled); roast (if fresh).

**Hock or Fore-Hock** Part of foreleg cut from carcass of pork. 1 to 2 per lb. Simmer.

**Leg and Loin** (See Lamb.)

**Pickled Pork** Belly pork or hand of pork which has been pickled. (Legs of pork are occasionally pickled.) 3 to 6 lb. See Belly Pork. Simmer.

**Pig's Cheek** A pig's head is split into two cheeks; these are usually pickled. Simmer.

**Pork Chops** Cut from loin or foreloin. Grill or pan-fry. Loin, in one piece, can also be roasted.

**Pork Cutlets** (Available as pork slices in some States). Thin slices cut from fresh belly of pork. Good distribution of meat. Fry.

**Pork Fillet** Long, tender portion of meat taken from inside loin of pork. Very little fat. Roast. NOTE: Fillet of Pork is quite different; it is a half-leg of pork, taken from chump end; can be sold with bone in or out.

**Pork Sausages** Made from fresh pork pieces with cereal and seasoning added. 6 per lb. Pinkish colour; moist, shiny surface. Grill, fry.

**Shoulder or Foreloin of Pork** Cut taken from shoulder of a pig. 3 to 4 lb. Small amount of fat; skin should be free from blemishes. Roast or cut into foreloin chops.

**Spareribs** (or Short Ribs). Rib bones (in the piece; meat still between the bones) taken from fresh belly of pork. Braise, simmer.

**Trotters** Pig's feet. Pickled. Simmer.

## Roast Pork

1 small leg of pork or fillet cut from leg (4 to 5 lb.)
salt
ground ginger
oil

Ask your butcher to score the pork rind well. Place roast in well-oiled baking dish. Rub skin with generous amount of salt and a little ground ginger. (The salt will ensure crisp crackling.) Roast in hot oven 20 minutes, then reduce heat to moderate; continue cooking until meat is well browned and tender, allowing 25 to 30 minutes per lb. cooking time. Make a thin gravy from the pan drippings; serve with gravy and baked apples or apple sauce.

Serves 4 to 6

## Apple Sauce

Peel, core and slice 3 tart apples. Cook until soft with 1 tablespoon sugar, 2 tablespoons water, pinch salt, squeeze lemon juice and 1 teaspoon of butter. Beat until smooth, serve hot.

## Sweet and Sour Pork

1 tablespoon soy sauce
3 dessertspoons sugar
½ teaspoon salt
1 tablespoon dry sherry
1 egg-yolk
2 to 2½ lb. lean pork
2 onions
½ bunch shallots
1 red pepper
4 oz. mushrooms
1 medium cucumber
15 oz. can pineapple pieces
cornflour
¼ cup vinegar
1 dessertspoon tomato sauce
salt, pepper

Mix together sugar, soy sauce, salt, sherry and egg-yolk; stir well. Cut meat into 1 in. cubes, place in soy sauce mixture. Stir until well coated with marinade. Cover, leave 1 hour; stir occasionally.

Drain pineapple, reserve the liquid. Slice onions, chop shallots diagonally. Remove seeds from pepper; cut into thin strips. Slice mushrooms and cucumber into chunky strips. Fry onion in a little hot oil until transparent. Add pepper and shallots, cook further 3 to 4 minutes. Add mushrooms, cook until softened. Stir in pineapple pieces and cucumber. Remove from heat, keep hot.

Drain meat from marinade, reserve liquid. Toss meat lightly in cornflour. Heat oil, cook meat until golden brown and cooked through; drain well. Add meat to vegetables, keep hot.

Blend 1 dessertspoon cornflour with reserved pineapple liquid. Add vinegar and tomato sauce, stir into remaining marinade. Bring to boil, stirring continually; season to taste. Pour sauce over meat and vegetables, stir to coat evenly. Serve with hot boiled rice.

Serves 6

## Ginger Pork Spareribs

4 lb. pork spareribs
½ cup soy sauce
¾ cup water
¾ cup orange marmalade
1 clove garlic
pepper
juice ½ lemon
½ teaspoon ground ginger
1 dessertspoon grated fresh ginger

Place spareribs, meaty side down, in well-greased, shallow baking dish. Roast in hot oven 30 minutes. Turn spareribs over, lower temperature to moderate, continue cooking further 30 minutes. Pour off excess fat from pan.

Combine soy sauce, water, marmalade, crushed garlic, lemon juice, pepper and gingers: blend thoroughly. Pour this sauce over spareribs, cook further ¾ hour, basting frequently with sauce.

Serves 6

## Chinese Barbecued Pork

1 lb. pork fillets or leg chops
1 dessertspoon sugar
1 tablespoon honey
3 tablespoons soy sauce
1 teaspoon oil
2 tablespoons dry sherry
1 clove garlic, crushed
½ teaspoon mixed spice
1 tablespoon Hoy Sin sauce
1 teaspoon salt

Trim pork, removing surplus fat. Combine remaining ingredients in large mixing bowl, mix well. Add pork, allow to marinate a few hours or overnight, turning occasionally. Drain pork, place on wire rack. Stand rack in shallow baking tray. Bake in hot oven approximately 30 minutes or until meat is tender, basting frequently with remaining marinade. Turn pork once during cooking. (Place a small amount of water in baking tray to prevent juices from burning.)

Alternatively, meat can be grilled under hot griller until tender, turning and basting often. Serve either hot or cold, cut into slices.

NOTE: Hoy Sin sauce is available at food halls of large department stores, or at Chinese food stores.

## Brawn

½ pig's head
1 lb. lean pork
1 lb. veal shoulder
salt
5 whole allspice
5 peppercorns
2 cloves
1 small onion, sliced
1 bayleaf
1 small carrot

Clean pig's head, soak in cold water 6 to 12 hours; change water once. Place with other meat in large saucepan, cover with boiling water. Bring to boil again, skim well; add remaining ingredients. Reduce heat; simmer covered, 1½ to 2 hours or until meat is very tender. Remove meat from bones, cut into small pieces. Measure liquid, return liquid to saucepan, continue boiling until liquid is reduced to half quantity; strain. Replace strained liquid and meat in saucepan, bring to boil, season to taste.

Pour into lightly oiled 9 x 5 in. loaf tin; cool, then refrigerate until set.

Serves 4 to 6

## Chinese Braised Spareribs

2 lb. pork spareribs
1 dessertspoon black beans
1 clove garlic
1 slice green ginger
oil for frying
1 tablespoon dry sherry
1½ tablespoons soy sauce
2 cups water
salt to taste
1 tablespoon cornflour

Chop spareribs into 2 in. pieces. Wash black beans, mash well. Crush garlic, chop ginger finely. Heat approximately 2 tablespoons oil in large saucepan. Add black beans, garlic and ginger: cook, stirring, few seconds. Add pork pieces and cook until brown on all sides. Add sherry, soy sauce and water; bring to boil. Reduce heat, cover, simmer until pork is tender (approximately 1 hour).

Add salt to taste. Mix cornflour to smooth paste with a little cold water. Add to pork; cook, stirring, until mixture boils and thickens slightly. Serve with boiled rice.

Serves 4

## Hawaiian Ham

4 thick ham steaks
4 oz. butter
2 tablespoons brown sugar
1 cup pineapple juice

Marinate ham steaks in combined pineapple juice and brown sugar for 3 hours. Drain well. (We found the meatiest ham steaks came from the shoulder. Cut about 1 in. thick, they kept their shape during cooking and remained beautifully moist and juicy.)

Heat butter, fry steaks until golden brown on both sides; turn constantly during cooking. Canned pineapple rings, sauteed in hot butter, can be served as an accompaniment.

Serves 4

## Ham-Asparagus Rolls

ham slices
canned asparagus spears
½ pint mornay sauce

Drain asparagus spears well. Take 4 or 5 spears and roll these inside a slice of ham. Arrange neatly on serving plate. Pour sauce over ham-asparagus rolls. Half-pint of sauce will cover approximately 6 ham-asparagus rolls.

## Boiled Ham

Soak ham for several hours in cold water, then drain and dry. Place in large vessel with enough tepid water to cover. Add a little parsley and thyme and 4 peppercorns. Bring slowly to boil, taking at least 1½ hours. Simmer gently (never boil) for time required, according to size.

To test whether ham is cooked, pull the small bone at the shank end that lies alongside the large one; when it is loose and slips out easily, then ham is done.

Allow to cool in liquid, then peel off skin, and glaze as desired. If boiled ham is to be eaten cold, remove skin, then return to water in which it was cooked and leave until quite cold. This helps to keep it juicy.

*Cooking Time per Pound*: Up to 12 lb. 20 minutes.
12 lb. and over 15 minutes.

## To Glaze the Ham

If baking a ham that has been already cooked (by boiling), simply peel off skin; score fat into squares or diamonds with sharp knife. Place ham in large baking dish, glaze with any of the following suggested glazes; bake in moderate oven 45 minutes.

□ Spread 3/4 cup orange marmalade over scored ham. Bake, baste with pan drippings.

□ Arrange pineapple rings and glace cherries on ham, secure with whole cloves or cocktail sticks. Sprinkle with brown sugar; bake.

□ Blend together 1 cup brown sugar, 1 tablespoon dry mustard; mix to a thick paste with dry sherry. Spread over scored ham; bake.

## Pork Loin with Prunes

4 lb. loin pork, boned
1 large cooking apple
4 oz. prunes
salt, pepper
2 oz. butter

Make a pocket in the loin by cutting, with a sharp knife, to within ½ in. of both ends; sprinkle with salt and pepper. Pit prunes; peel and dice apple, sprinkle with lemon juice. Stuff pocket with prunes and apple. Roll meat firmly around filling, secure with string. Rub scored crackling around loin lightly with salt.

Melt butter in baking dish; add pork. Cook in moderate oven approximately 1½ to 2 hours. Make thin gravy from pan juices. Red cabbage makes a good accompaniment.

Serves 6

## Boiled Bacon

Cuts available for boiling are from the shoulder: they are called cushion, blade, and hand of shoulder. The cushion is available in pieces of 3 to 4 lb. and upward; the other cuts weigh from 4 to 5 lb. upward. A 4 lb. piece should serve 6.

Perhaps 'simmering' would be a better word than boiling for this cooking process, because rapid boiling, over a period, will cause shrinkage and will affect the meat texture and the fat structure. Slow, careful cooking is necessary for best results.

Put bacon into saucepan, cover with cold water, and let stand 24 hours; drain. Cover with fresh cold water, bring slowly to boil, then reduce heat until water is just simmering. Cover, cook until bacon is tender. Allow 20 to 25 minutes per lb.

When the bacon has been cooked it can be glazed and baked as a ham. Remove rind while hot, spread with some melted red currant jelly or honey, or spread with a paste of brown sugar, mustard, and sherry. The fat can be cut in criss-cross squares and each square studded with a clove. Bake in moderate oven 20 minutes to melt glaze. Apple sauce, spiced lightly with cinnamon, is a nice accompaniment.

Chinese Sweet and Sour Pork combines — deliciously! — tender pieces of pork with pineapple and a rich sauce.

## The Variety Meats

Simple recipes suit the variety meats best, so that their full, delicate flavour is retained. They are easily prepared and, with just a few exceptions, can be cooked in minutes. Serve them often; in addition to their good taste, they are a rich source of nourishment at a low price

### Lamb's Fry

*To prepare*: Soak in cold water at least 1 hour before cooking. Drain well, remove outside skin. Slice fairly thinly for cooking.

### Lamb's Fry and Bacon

1 lamb's fry
seasoned flour
butter for frying
4 rashers bacon
1 onion
1 tablespoon flour
1½ cups boiling water
1 chicken or beef stock cube
salt, pepper
chopped parsley

Cut prepared lamb's fry into ½ in. slices; toss in seasoned flour. Heat butter in pan, add thinly sliced onion, saute until lightly golden; remove from pan. Add the lamb's fry, cook for about 3 minutes each side; add extra butter to pan, if necessary. Remove from pan.

Add flour to pan drippings, cook 1 minute, stirring. Stir in boiling water in which stock cube has been dissolved; bring to boil, stirring. Season to taste with salt and pepper; add a few drops of worcestershire sauce, if desired.

Strain sauce into saucepan, add lamb's fry and onions, heat through gently. Top each serving with a rasher of grilled bacon. Sprinkle with parsley.

Serves 4

### Savoury Lamb's Fry

1 lamb's fry
juice 2 lemons
cold water
seasoned flour
butter for frying
5 oz. can tomato paste
1½ cups boiling water
1 chicken stock cube
1 cup milk
¼ lb. button mushrooms
salt, pepper

Wash lamb's fry. Place in bowl with lemon juice and sufficient cold water to cover; leave 1 hour. Drain well, remove outside skin. Cut lamb's fry into ½ in. slices, drain. Toss in seasoned flour.

Heat butter in large pan, cook lamb's fry quickly on both sides. Add tomato paste, boiling water, chicken stock cube, mushrooms and milk, blend well. Bring to boil, reduce heat, simmer 15 minutes. Season to taste with salt and pepper.

Serves 4

### Brains

*To prepare*: Soak brains in cold water several hours. Then place in saucepan with 1 dessertspoon vinegar, a little salt, 1 small sliced onion, 1 small bayleaf and water to cover. Bring slowly just to boiling point. Poach gently for 10 minutes, without allowing water to boil. Drain, cover with cold water to firm; remove membranes.

### Brains in Cream Sauce

4 sets brains
2 oz. butter
1 small onion
1 tablespoon flour
2 cups boiling water
2 chicken stock cubes
2 egg-yolks
½ green pepper
1 teaspoon lemon juice
1 medium tomato
salt, pepper

Cut prepared brains into slices or cubes. Melt butter in saucepan, add finely chopped onion, cook 1 minute. Stir in flour, cook further 1 minute. Remove from heat, gradually stir in boiling water, in which chicken stock cubes have been dissolved. Return to heat, bring to boil, stirring; reduce heat, simmer until thickened, stirring constantly.

Stir 2 tablespoons of this mixture into beaten egg-yolks, gradually add to remaining sauce, stirring constantly. Simmer 5 minutes without boiling. Add brains, chopped pepper, lemon juice, peeled and chopped tomato, salt and pepper. Place in top of double saucepan over hot water, simmer 15 minutes.

Serves 4

### Brains in Black Butter

4 sets brains
seasoned flour
butter for frying
4 oz. butter, extra
juice 1 lemon
1 teaspoon capers
chopped parsley

Toss prepared brains in seasoned flour. Saute in heated butter until golden brown, remove to hot serving dish. Add extra butter to pan, cook until it turns brown. Remove from heat, add lemon juice and capers. Pour the sizzling butter over brains, sprinkle with chopped parsley.

Serves 3 to 4

## Sweetbreads

*To prepare*: Wash sweetbreads well, soak in cold water 3 to 4 hours, changing water several times. Drain, place in saucepan with sufficient cold water to cover. Bring water slowly to boil, simmer 3 to 5 minutes, according to size. Drain, plunge at once into cold water. Remove as much skin and membrane as possible; dry well.

If desired, they can be spread out on a plate and weighed down by pressing another plate on top of them. In this way, they flatten as they cool. The sweetbreads are now ready to cook in a variety of ways. They can be crumbed and fried, or served in a cream sauce.

## Sweetbreads à la King

1 lb. sweetbreads
3 oz. butter
4 oz. mushrooms
1 green pepper
1 red pepper
¼ cup dry sherry
1 cup cream
1 tablespoon flour
1 cup milk
salt, pepper
toast slices or pastry-cases

Cut prepared sweetbreads into cubes. Melt half the butter in saucepan, add sliced mushrooms, and diced peppers; cook gently 2 minutes, then add half the sherry and cream. Simmer sauce until reduced by half, then add sweetbreads.

Melt remaining butter in separate saucepan, stir in flour, cook 1 minute. Remove from heat, gradually add milk. Return to heat, bring to boil, stirring; reduce heat, simmer until thick and smooth, stirring constantly. Add sweetbread mixture, season to taste with salt and pepper. Stir in remaining sherry and cream, reheat without boiling. Spoon mixture into heated pastry cases or serve on slices of hot toast.

Serves 4

## Tripe

*To prepare*: Tripe should be absolutely fresh; if possible, cook and serve it on the day it is bought. Although tripe, when bought, has already been par-boiled in processing, a preliminary blanching before cooking is necessary.

Place tripe in large saucepan with sufficient cold water to cover; add squeeze of lemon juice. Bring slowly to the boil, simmer 5 minutes. Drain well, then prepare as desired.

## Tripe in Parsley Sauce

1½ lb. tripe
water
2 oz. butter
2 onions
¼ cup flour
1 cup milk
⅓ cup chopped parsley
salt, pepper

Cut blanched tripe into strips. Place in saucepan with sufficient cold water to cover. Bring to boil, cover, simmer approximately 2 hours or until tender; drain, reserving 1½ cups stock.

Melt butter in saucepan, add chopped onions, cook until transparent. Stir in flour, cook 1 minute. Remove from heat, gradually add reserved stock and milk. Return to heat, bring to boil stirring; reduce heat, simmer until thickened, stirring constantly. Add tripe and chopped parsley; heat through. Season to taste with salt and pepper.

Serves 4

## Tripe Bordelaise

1½ lb. tripe
2 onions
1 oz. butter
1 clove garlic
3 medium tomatoes
1 tablespoon tomato paste
1½ cups boiling water
2 chicken stock cubes
salt, pepper
bouquet garni
chopped parsley

Cut blanched tripe into strips. Saute chopped onions in butter until golden. Add crushed garlic, peeled and chopped tomatoes, tomato paste, boiling water (in which chicken stock cubes have been dissolved), seasoning and bouquet garni. Bring to boil, add tripe, reduce heat; cover and simmer slowly until tripe is tender, approximately 2 to 2½ hours. Remove bouquet garni. Correct seasonings. Transfer to serving dish, sprinkle with chopped parsley.

Serves 4

## Ox Tongue

*To prepare*: Wash the tongue. If it is highly salted, it should be soaked in water for approximately 24 hours. (If fresh, unsalted tongue is used, add some salt to water when cooking.) Place tongue in large saucepan with sufficient cold water to cover. Add a few peppercorns, 1 bayleaf, 1 sliced onion and 1 small carrot. Bring to boil, cover, reduce heat and simmer approximately 3 hours, depending on size of tongue, allowing 45 to 60 minutes cooking time per lb. Remove skin from tongue while still hot.

Allow pickled tongue, which is served cold, to cool in the cooking liquid.

## Glazed Ox Tongue

1 cooked ox tongue
1 tablespoon gelatine
1½ cups cold water
¼ cup hot water
1 tablespoon white vinegar
3 cloves
3 thin strips lemon rind
1 dessertspoon lemon juice
2 thin slices onion
2 sprigs parsley
1 teaspoon salt

Pack cooked tongue into tongue presser or basin. (If tongue is not too large, $\frac{1}{2}$ gallon ice-cream can makes a good tongue press). Pour in just enough aspic to cover tongue. Place saucer or plate and a weight on top. Leave to cool, then refrigerate overnight.

*Aspic Jelly*: Soak gelatine in hot water. Place all other ingredients into saucepan, stir lightly with fork until boiling, add soaked gelatine. Cool and strain through fine strainer lined with clean cloth. Pour over tongue (you may not need all the aspic).

## Kidneys

*To prepare*: Wash kidneys, remove skin. Cut lamb's kidneys in half. Remove hard core and any fat or gristle. When frying halved kidneys, place them cut side down in pan and press lightly. This will seal the cut edge, thus retaining all juices.

Ox kidney should not be fried; it needs long, gentle simmering to soften it, as in the filling for Steak and Kidney Pie.

## Kidneys Chasseur

8 lamb's kidneys
salt, pepper
4 oz. butter
1 tablespoon finely chopped shallots
1 dessertspoon plain flour
½ cup madeira or port wine
½ cup dry white wine
4 oz. mushrooms
parsley
triangles of fried bread

Soak kidneys in salted water for 15 minutes. Remove outer skin and fat from kidneys, cut into slices. Sprinkle with salt and pepper. Melt half the butter in frying pan, add kidneys, cook quickly until just beginning to brown; remove from pan.

Add shallots and flour to pan drippings, cook 2 minutes. Add madeira and white wine; return kidneys. Bring just to boil, simmer 5 minutes. In separate pan, saute sliced mushrooms a few minutes in remaining butter. Spoon kidney mixture on serving dish, top with mushrooms. Serve with triangles of fried bread. Garnish with parsley.

Serves 4

## Devilled Kidneys

8 lamb's kidneys
3 oz. butter
½ cup finely chopped parsley
1 small onion
1 clove garlic
1 tablespoon worcestershire sauce
1 tablespoon dry sherry
salt, pepper

Wash kidneys, remove skin, fat and hard core; slice kidneys. Melt butter in pan, add crushed garlic, finely chopped onion, salt and pepper, cook a few minutes. Add kidneys, cook quickly on both sides. Add worcestershire sauce, sherry and parsley to pan, blend well. Spoon on to slices of hot buttered toast—delicious as a supper dish; or serve with hot rice, into which some finely chopped parsley has been tossed.

Serves 4

## Oxtail Casserole

1 oz. butter
2 large onions
2 large carrots
4 oxtails
1 dessertspoon brown sugar
4 tablespoons flour
6 tomatoes
3 cloves garlic, crushed
few sprigs parsley
1 bayleaf
½ teaspoon thyme
3 pints beef stock
1 pint red wine
salt, pepper
1 large can cream of tomato soup
4 oz. haricot beans

Slice onions, dice carrots, cut oxtails into 2 in. sections. Heat butter, gradually add onions, carrots and oxtail pieces, saute, stirring constantly until well browned. Drain off any surplus fat during cooking.

Place browned meat and vegetables into a large casserole dish, sprinkle with brown sugar and flour. Peel tomatoes and chop finely, add with remaining ingredients (except haricot beans) to casserole, cover, bake in slow oven 4 hours. Cool, refrigerate overnight.

Cover haricot beans well with water, stand overnight. Next day, drain, place beans in salted water, boil 1 hour, or until tender.

Remove fat from top of casserole, remove bayleaf. Reheat casserole in slow oven for approximately 1 hour; stir in beans during last 15 minutes. Adjust seasoning, serve sprinkled with parsley.

Serves 6 to 8

A wonderful meal for men — subtle blending of hearty flavours makes this Oxtail Casserole the perfect dish for cold-weather entertaining.

# POULTRY

Chicken, so easily available at an economical price, is becoming almost a standard feature on weekly menus, either for family meals or for entertaining. Turkey, too, now available in small sizes, from around $4\frac{1}{2}$ lb, gives lots of good eating when you have a number of people to entertain.

In this section are all the basic ways of cooking the various birds, plus a wide selection of the world's most popular ways with poultry, plus stuffings and accompaniments.

## Chicken Sizes

Packaged chickens are available in a number of unit sizes, determined by weight. These sizes are given below, and are uniform throughout Australia.

| Unit Size | Weight |
|---|---|
| 1 | 1½ lb. |
| 2 | 1¾ lb. |
| 3 | 2 lb. |
| 4 | 2¼ lb. |
| 5 | 2½ lb. |
| 6 | 2¾ lb. |
| 7 | 3 lb. |
| 8 | 3¼ lb. |
| 9 | 3½ lb. |
| 10 | 3¾ lb. |
| 11 | 4 lb. |

Chicken pieces are a useful buy; they allow you to choose the cut of chicken best suited for any particular dish. Pieces usually available are breasts and half-breasts, cutlets or thighs, Maryland (combination of thigh and leg), legs, breastwing (combination of breast and wings), wings, and backs (good for soup).

## Roasting Times for Chicken

Allow approximately 25 minutes per lb. in moderate oven. For the French method of roasting, stock is added and a moderately hot oven is used for cooking.

When cooking chicken pieces, the thicker parts take more time to cook. So that they will all finish cooking at the same time, add them to pan in this order: drumsticks, thighs, wings, breast.

## How to Joint a Chicken

Many chicken recipes call for the chicken to be jointed, or cut into sections. Here's how to do it. You'll need a good sharp knife and a pair of poultry shears or a strong pair of kitchen scissors.

A chicken will joint into 8 sections: 2 legs, 2 wings, 2 breast portions, and the backbone, which is split into 2 pieces.

*To remove legs* Cut through skin connecting leg to body; bend leg out, away from body, find the joint where leg hinges, cut through this (there is no need to cut any bone).

*To remove wings* Cut a slice of breast meat with the wing to make a better serving portion, then bend wing away from body to find joint where wing joins body; cut through this. Fold wing into a neat shape with breast meat tucked under.

*To remove breast* Separate breast and back by cutting through rib-bones along each side of body. Cut down centre of breastbone to divide breast in 2; trim away excess skin and fat. (These breast portions, when removed from the bone, are called the supremes).

*The backbone* Break back in 2 where ribs end. These back portions are generally not considered as individual serving portions, but can be served to accompany another portion such as a wing, or they can be used to make soup, etc.

For many recipes—particularly those to be served with a white or cream sauce—some cooks prefer to remove the skin of the chicken before cooking. However, for those recipes where the chicken pieces are browned before cooking, the skin browns more easily and gives protection to the juicy meat beneath.

## Roast Chicken

3 lb. chicken
prepared stuffing
salt, pepper
1 cup chicken stock
butter

Fill chicken with prepared stuffing; place in baking dish. Rub breast and legs well with butter. Roast in moderate oven $1\frac{1}{2}$ hours or until bird is tender.

When bird is tender, transfer to warm serving dish, keep hot. Remove fat from pan drippings; add stock to baking dish and cook, stirring, 2 to 3 minutes. Season, strain into sauce boat.

Serves 4

*To test if chicken is cooked* the leg will move easily when moved to and fro gently with the fingers; the skin will start to shrink from the bones slightly; when the chicken leg is pierced with a skewer at the second joint, the juices will be clear, not pink.

## French Roast Chicken

1 chicken
giblets
prepared stuffing
4 oz. softened butter
½ pint stock or water
salt, pepper

Fill chicken with prepared stuffing, spread legs and breast with softened butter. Place in baking dish with giblets and stock or water. Roast in moderately hot oven until chicken is well browned and tender, basting and turning frequently, and adding extra water or stock if this reduces too much.

Transfer cooked bird to hot serving platter. Strain pan juices into saucepan, skim well, bring to the boil, cook 1 or 2 minutes, season to taste, strain; serve with chicken.

Serves 4

## Accompaniments to Roast Chicken

*Bread Sauce* Peel an onion and stud with 2 or 3 cloves. Put into saucepan with $\frac{1}{2}$ bayleaf and 2 cups milk. Bring slowly to boil, cover, simmer 5 minutes; strain, retaining liquid and discarding onion. Return liquid to rinsed-out saucepan, add $1\frac{1}{2}$ cups fresh breadcrumbs, season to taste. Simmer, stirring, 2 or 3 minutes. Stir in a little butter or cream before serving.

*Giblet Gravy* Melt 1 tablespoon butter in small saucepan, stir in $1\frac{1}{2}$ dessertspoons flour; cook, stirring, few minutes. Gradually stir in $\frac{1}{2}$ pint hot giblet stock (made by cooking giblets in water with a little onion and celery) season to taste. A few of the finely chopped giblets can also be added.

Or stir some flour into pan drippings, pour in the strained giblet stock; cook, stirring, until sauce boils and thickens slightly; season.

## Chicken in a Basket

This is one of the most popular chicken dishes, particularly for a small, informal party.

Allow one small chicken (about $1\frac{1}{2}$ lb.) for each person; roast in usual way. Serve in small basket, lined with paper napkin. Packaged potato crisps (heat them in oven first) and fried onion rings are the correct accompaniments.

Chicken in the Basket is finger food, so serve finger bowls filled with warm water, with a slice of lemon floating in the water. As the water cools, the lemon can be used to remove any grease from fingers.

There's a correct way to eat this dish: Break off one leg first. Eat this before breaking off any further pieces. In this way the chicken retains its heat.

One hand only should be used to convey the food to the mouth. Rinse fingers often in the finger bowl. Make sure the dinner napkins are a good big size.

## Coq au Vin

2 2½ lb. chickens
2 oz. butter
¼ lb. lean salt pork
12 tiny onions
salt, pepper
½ lb. mushrooms
1 to 2 cloves garlic
⅓ cup brandy
2 cups dry red wine
1 cup stock
bouquet garni
1 oz. butter, extra
2 tablespoons flour

Joint the chickens. Heat butter in heavy saucepan, add diced pork and peeled, blanched, and drained onions. Cook a few minutes, then add chicken joints; brown well, season. Add sliced mushrooms and crushed garlic, cook 5 minutes. Strain off all excess fat, add brandy. Add red wine, stock and bouquet garni.

Transfer to casserole, cover; cook in moderate oven 40 minutes or until chicken is tender. (Or cook in saucepan on top of stove.) Mix extra butter with flour and add gradually to sauce to thicken it. Stir over heat a few minutes. Check seasoning. Serve with hot garlic bread and a tossed green salad.

Serves 6

## Chicken Tetrazzini

3 lb. chicken
1 cup water or chicken stock
1 cup dry white wine
1 onion
1 bayleaf
pinch thyme
a few bacon rinds
salt, pepper
2 oz. butter
3 tablespoons flour
¾ lb. spaghetti
½ lb. mushrooms
2 oz. butter, extra
1 cup cream
1 tablespoon sherry

Gently poach chicken in combined wine and water, with chopped onion, bayleaf, thyme, bacon rinds, salt and pepper. When tender, cool, drain, strain the stock, and reserve.

Remove the flesh from the chicken bones and cut into thin pieces. Melt the butter, stir in the flour, and cook over gentle heat 2 minutes. Gradually add the reserved stock, stirring continually until mixture boils and thickens. Cook a few minutes, then set aside.

Cook spaghetti in plenty of boiling salted water until tender; drain thoroughly, place in deep, hot serving bowl. Finely slice the mushrooms, melt extra butter in frying pan, and saute the mushrooms gently until tender. Drain the mushrooms and add to the sauce with the sliced chicken and seasoning to taste. Reheat until nearly boiling.

Stir in the cream and sherry and stir over heat until heated thoroughly. Pour over spaghetti.

Serves 4 to 6

## Chicken Chow Mein

3 lb. chicken
½ lb. lean pork
½ cabbage
3 shallots
2 to 3 sticks celery
1 green pepper
1½ teaspoons soy sauce
½ lb. prawns
1 teaspoon brandy or dry sherry
1 dessertspoon cornflour
1 clove garlic
4 tablespoons oil
½ cup water
salt, pepper

Remove meat from uncooked chicken. Cut chicken meat and pork into fine shreds, place in bowl, sprinkle with salt. Add soy sauce, brandy, ½ teaspoon of the cornflour, and 1 teaspoon of oil; mix well.

Wash vegetables, cut into thin strips. Heat remaining oil in pan, add crushed garlic and chicken and pork mixture. Cook quickly 3 minutes, stirring constantly, sprinkle with pepper. Add prepared vegetables, fry until vegetables are tender, but still slightly crisp. Add shelled prawns. Mix remaining cornflour with water, add to pan, bring to boil, stirring gently. Serve on top of crisp fried noodles.

Serves 4 to 6

### Crisp Fried Noodles

Drop ½ lb. fine dried egg noodles into large saucepan of rapidly boiling salted water; stir with fork to separate, cook 3 to 4 minutes; drain well. Arrange on a clean teatowel over wire cake cooler, spread noodles over this to drain. Leave at least 6 hours.

When ready to serve, drop noodles, a few at a time, into shallow hot oil. (To ensure thorough cooking, it is best to fry the noodles in 3 or 4 lots.) They cook in seconds; turn once during cooking.

## Chicken Paprika

3 lb. chicken pieces
lard or oil for frying
2 onions
¾ pint stock
2 tomatoes
salt, pepper
1 tablespoon paprika
¼ pint sour cream

Heat lard or oil in large frying pan, add chopped onions, saute until tender. Add chicken pieces to pan, cook until brown. Add paprika, then peeled, chopped tomatoes, stock, salt and pepper. Cover, simmer over gentle heat 1 hour or until chicken is tender.

Remove chicken from sauce, stir in sour cream, return chicken; stir over low heat until well blended and hot.

Serves 4

## Paella

½ cup oil
½ lb. onions
2 red and 2 green peppers
1 lb. rice
2 cloves garlic
1 lb. tomatoes
salt, pepper
2 pints chicken stock
½ teaspoon saffron
3 lb. chicken, steamed
1 lb. prawns
½ lb. scallops

Heat oil in large pan, add sliced onions, cook slowly until golden. Add sliced peppers and rice, stir until well combined with onions; cook few minutes, stirring. Add crushed garlic, skinned chopped tomatoes, and salt and pepper. Add boiling stock in which saffron has been dissolved. Cook 10 minutes, stirring occasionally.

Cut hot cooked chicken into serving pieces and arrange over top of paella. Add shelled prawns and scallops. Cook a further 10 minutes, or until all liquid is absorbed.

Serves 6

Chicken in a Basket — a good dish for an informal luncheon or dinner. Serve the small, golden chickens with fried onion rings, potato chips

## Chicken Casserole

1 onion
4 chicken breasts
1 teaspoon salt
4 oz. butter
2 teaspoons paprika
3 tablespoons flour
½ cup water
1 chicken stock cube
½ cup sour cream
1 cup white wine
14 oz. can artichoke hearts

Chop onion finely, sprinkle chicken breasts with salt. Heat butter in frying pan, add chicken breasts, fry until golden brown; drain on absorbent paper. Add onion and paprika to remaining melted butter, saute until onion is soft. Remove pan from heat, stir in flour, return to heat, cook 1 minute. Gradually add water in which stock cube has been dissolved; stir until mixture boils and thickens. Add cream and wine, stir well, heat gently; do not boil.

Place chicken and drained artichoke hearts in ovenproof dish, top with sauce. Cover, bake in moderate oven 1 hour. If desired, before serving, garnish with crisp fried bacon and toasted slivered almonds.

Serves 4

## Burmese Chicken Curry

½ lb. coconut
2 cups chicken stock
3 lb. chicken
2 medium onions
¼ cup oil
3 cloves garlic
1 teaspoon ground ginger
1 dessertspoon curry powder
½ cup boiling water
1 teaspoon salt
2 tablespoons cornflour
3 tablespoons cold water
1 lb. broad noodles, cooked
1 red chilli
2 hard-boiled eggs
3 shallots

Combine coconut and chicken stock in saucepan, bring to the boil, stirring constantly; remove from heat, let stand 15 minutes, stirring occasionally.

Strain mixture, pressing coconut well with wooden spoon, to extract as much flavour as possible. Reserve liquid, discard coconut.

Remove meat from chicken, cut into bite-sized pieces, chop onions.

Heat oil in large saucepan, add onions, crushed garlic and ginger, saute 10 minutes; add curry powder, saute further 2 minutes. Add chicken, cover, simmer 15 minutes. Stir in 1 cup of the coconut liquid, boiling water and salt; simmer, uncovered, 30 minutes.

Blend cornflour with cold water, add to chicken mixture, stir until mixture boils and thickens, add further 1 cup coconut liquid, bring back to boil, remove from heat. Arrange hot noodles on serving plate, sprinkle with finely chopped chilli, chopped eggs and sliced shallots, top with chicken mixture.

Serves 4

## Chicken à la King

3 to 4 lb. chicken
1 small green pepper
1 oz. butter
¼ lb. sliced mushrooms
1 dessertspoon grated onion
1 tablespoon flour
salt
½ pint milk or cream
½ pint chicken stock
3 egg-yolks
1 dessertspoon lemon juice
½ teaspoon paprika
½ teaspoon celery salt
2 tablespoons dry sherry

Steam chicken until tender; remove meat from bones and cut into large dice or pieces.

Remove pith and seeds from green pepper; blanch in boiling water 5 minutes. Drain and chop finely.

Heat butter in saucepan, add green pepper, mushrooms and grated onion; saute a few minutes. Sprinkle in flour and salt, cook, stirring, 2 minutes. Gradually blend in milk or cream and stock; add chicken. Stir over gentle heat until sauce thickens, simmer 3 minutes.

Stir a little of sauce into beaten egg-yolks, return to saucepan. Add lemon juice, paprika and celery salt. Reheat very gently, stirring, but do not allow to boil. Just before serving, stir in sherry.

Serves 4 to 6

## Chicken Maryland

3 lb. chicken
½ cup seasoned flour
1 egg
1 tablespoon milk
dry breadcrumbs
2 oz. butter
¼ cup oil

Beat egg and milk together. Cut chicken into joints, roll in seasoned flour, dip in the beaten egg, then coat with crumbs. Heat butter and oil in heatproof casserole, add chicken pieces, saute until golden on all sides. Drain off excess oil, cover casserole, cook in moderate oven until tender (about 30 to 45 minutes).

Serve with fried bananas, corn fritters, bacon rolls, and grilled tomato halves.

Serves 4.

*Corn Fritters:* Sift 1 cup plain flour with 1 teaspoon baking powder and ¾ teaspoon salt. Beat the yolk of 1 egg and ¼ cup of milk; mix with 1 cup canned whole kernel corn, add to dry ingredients; mix thoroughly. Beat egg-white until stiff, fold in. Deep-fry dessertspoonfuls of mixture in hot oil until golden. Drain well.

*Fried Bananas:* Peel bananas, cut in halves crosswise, dip in beaten egg, then breadcrumbs. Fry in butter until golden. Drain well.

## Chicken Fricassée

3 lb. chicken
2 oz. butter
1 clove garlic
1 cup dry white wine
1½ cups chicken stock
3 shallots
salt, pepper
4 oz. mushrooms
1 oz. butter, extra
½ cup milk
2 tablespoons flour
2 tablespoons cream

Cut chicken into serving pieces, season with salt and pepper. Melt butter in large pan, add chicken joints, and cook until a light brown on all sides. Add crushed garlic, wine, chicken stock, chopped shallots, salt and pepper, cover and cook gently until chicken is tender.

Melt extra butter in separate pan and saute sliced mushrooms for 5 minutes, drain.

When chicken is tender, remove joints from pan, blend flour with the milk, add gradually to pan, stir over gentle heat until sauce thickens. Return chicken pieces to pan, add mushrooms, reheat, and adjust seasoning, if necessary. Just before serving, add cream, keep hot but do not boil.

Serves 4

## Chicken Croquettes

1 cup milk
few peppercorns
1 onion, sliced
1 carrot, sliced
1½ oz. butter
⅓ cup plain flour
1 lb. chopped cooked chicken
½ lb. mushrooms
2 egg-yolks
salt, pepper
1 egg
dry breadcrumbs
oil for frying

Combine milk, peppercorns, onion and carrot in saucepan. Bring to boil, simmer 5 minutes; strain.

Melt butter in separate saucepan. Stir in flour, cook 1 minute. Remove from heat. Gradually stir in hot milk, blend well. Return to heat. Bring to boil, then reduce heat and simmer until thickened, stirring constantly. Remove from heat.

Add finely chopped chicken, egg-yolks, and finely chopped mushrooms which have been sauteed in a little butter. Season to taste with salt and pepper. Blend well together.

Spread mixture on greased tray, cover with greased paper. Refrigerate until cold and set. Divide mixture into 16 pieces and mould each into croquette shape approximately $2\frac{1}{2}$ in. long. Dip in lightly beaten egg, then in breadcrumbs. Refrigerate 1 hour. Fry in hot oil until brown.

Makes 16 croquettes

## Chicken Chausseur

3 lb. chicken
1 oz. butter
3 shallots
½ lb. mushrooms
2 large tomatoes
½ cup dry white wine
1 cup chicken stock
salt, pepper
flour

Joint the chicken, chop the shallots, slice the mushrooms, peel and chop the tomatoes. Dredge the chicken pieces in flour seasoned with salt and pepper. Heat butter in frying pan, saute chicken pieces gently, browning lightly on all sides.

Remove chicken pieces from pan. Add shallots and mushrooms, cook a few minutes, then add tomatoes, wine and stock. Return chicken to the pan, bring to boil, then reduce heat, cover pan, and simmer until chicken is tender. Taste and adjust seasoning.

Serves 4

## Chicken Marengo

3 lb. chicken
2 tablespoons oil
2 cloves garlic
2 tablespoons flour
1½ cups dry white wine
1 cup chicken stock
salt, pepper
pinch mixed herbs
½ lb. sliced mushrooms
½ cup chopped shallots
3 tomatoes

Cut chicken into serving pieces. Heat oil in pan, add crushed garlic and chicken pieces, brown chicken on all sides; remove from pan.

Stir flour into oil, cook a few minutes, then add wine and stock gradually, stirring, until mixture boils and thickens. Season with pepper, salt and mixed herbs, add sliced mushrooms, chopped shallots and peeled, chopped tomatoes. Cook about 5 minutes, then return chicken to the pan, cover, and simmer 45 minutes or until chicken is tender.

Serves 4

## Chicken Cacciatore

3 lb. chicken
2 tablespoons oil
2 cloves garlic
salt, pepper
½ teaspoon oregano
½ lb. mushrooms
2 large onions
1 lb. tomatoes
½ cup red wine

Cut the chicken into serving pieces. Heat the oil in a pan and add the crushed garlic, sliced onions, and mushrooms; brown lightly. Remove and reserve.

Add the chicken pieces and brown on all sides. Return the onions and mushrooms to the pan. Peel and chop the tomatoes and add with the salt, pepper, and oregano. Pour in the red wine, bring to boil; reduce heat, cover, and simmer for $\frac{1}{2}$ hour.

Uncover and simmer for 15 to 20 minutes longer or until sauce is reduced and chicken very tender. Sprinkle with chopped parsley, if desired.

Serve with noodles or hot fluffy rice.

Serves 4

## Chicken in Aspic

3 lb. chicken
1 carrot
1 stick celery
1 medium onion
1 clove garlic
1 bayleaf
piece of lemon rind
salt, pepper
2 dessertspoons gelatine
2 tablespoons chopped parsley

Place chicken in a pan with sliced carrot, sliced celery, sliced onion, crushed garlic, bayleaf, lemon rind and a sprinkling of salt and pepper. Cover with water and bring to the boil; reduce heat and simmer until chicken is cooked.

Lift out chicken, remove meat from bone, return bones and skin to pan and allow to boil a further 10 minutes. Cut meat into small pieces, chop parsley; soften gelatine in a little water.

Strain bones and vegetables from stock, then strain again through muslin.

Take 2 cups of this stock and add the gelatine, add salt to taste. Mix together chicken, parsley and stock, pour into oiled mould. Refrigerate until set, stirring occasionally to distribute meat evenly.

Serves 4

## Assamee Chicken Curry

3 lb. chicken
2 oz. butter
salt
1 teaspoon ground black pepper
2 to 3 bayleaves
1 tablespoon turmeric
pinch chilli powder
½ teaspoon cloves
¾ teaspoon cardamom
½ teaspoon cumin
½ teaspoon coriander
¾ teaspoon ground ginger
2 1 in. pieces cinnamon
6 to 8 cloves crushed garlic
1 in. piece green ginger
2 onions
1 cup chicken stock
2 tablespoons cornflour
water

Joint chicken. Heat butter in saucepan, add all ingredients except chicken, chopped onions, cornflour, and stock; fry 5 minutes. Add chicken joints, brown well on all sides. Add chopped onions and cook gently, stirring occasionally, 25 to 30 minutes. Gradually add stock, simmer 1 hour, or until chicken is tender.

Blend cornflour with a little water, add to pan, simmer further 3 minutes. Allow to cool, refrigerate overnight. Remove any excess fat, reheat gently.

Serves 4

## Chicken Liver Risotto

1 lb. chicken livers
2 onions
4 oz. butter
1 lb. long grain rice
3 sticks celery
4½ cups chicken stock
salt, pepper
½ cup grated parmesan cheese

Heat half the butter in large saucepan. Add finely chopped onions and sliced celery, saute 10 minutes, stirring occasionally.

Cut cleaned chicken livers into quarters. Add to pan, cook further 5 minutes. Stir in well-rinsed rice and remaining butter, and cook further 5 minutes. Add stock, bring to the boil; reduce heat and simmer, covered, until rice is tender and liquid absorbed (about 20 to 25 minutes). Stir in parmesan cheese, adjust seasoning.

Serves 6

## Chicken Chop Suey

3 lb. chicken (or chicken pieces)
1 small green cabbage
16 oz. can bean sprouts
½ small bunch celery
1 onion
¼ lb. carrots
¼ lb. green beans
oil
chicken stock
salt
1 dessertspoon cornflour

Steam chicken until tender, cool; remove meat from bones, cut into large dice.

Shred cabbage, slice celery, carrots, beans diagonally, chop onion. Heat oil in large pan, add vegetables, saute until just tender but still crisp, season with salt. Add chicken pieces and chicken stock to cover, add drained bean sprouts. Reheat gently, then thicken with cornflour which has been blended with a little water; stir until thickened.

Serves 4

## Honeyed Chicken

3 lb. chicken
3 oz. butter

**Sauce**

4 shallots
1 teaspoon finely chopped green ginger
1 tablespoon honey
1 tablespoon soy sauce
½ teaspoon salt
½ cup sherry

Melt butter in baking dish, add chicken, brush well with butter, bake in moderately hot oven 45 minutes; baste frequently with the butter. Pour sauce over chicken, continue cooking for further 30 minutes,

Chicken Casserole combines tender chickens with artichoke hearts, wine, paprika; a perfect dish for a small dinner party

DO NOT LOCK OR CLAMP
THIS HANDLE BUT TURN THE LID

or until tender and golden brown. Baste chicken frequently with sauce during last 30 minutes.

*Sauce*: Chop shallots finely, combine with remaining ingredients.

Serves 4

## Roast Duck

1 duckling
prepared stuffing
melted butter
1 tablespoon flour
½ pint chicken stock
salt, pepper

Fill duck with prepared stuffing; place in baking dish, brush well with melted butter. Roast in hot oven 15 minutes, then reduce heat to moderate and cook until tender. During cooking, baste and turn bird occasionally. Allow 25 to 30 minutes per lb. Remove duck to a warm serving dish, keep hot.

Pour excess fat from baking dish, sprinkle in flour, stir over gentle heat until brown. Stir in stock, simmer, stirring, 3 or 4 minutes. Strain.

Serves 4.

NOTE: If desired, towards end of cooking time duck can be brushed with a little honey; this helps to crisp the skin. Don't use too much or skin will become too brown. For a Chinese flavour, a little crushed green ginger can be mixed into the honey.

## Orange Roast Duckling

2 small ducklings
1 stick celery
1 carrot
1 small onion
3 oranges
1 tablespoon sugar
1 dessertspoon vinegar
2 cups chicken stock
1 dessertspoon lemon juice
3 teaspoons arrowroot
½ cup sweet sherry
¼ cup Grand Marnier or other orange liqueur
salt, pepper
2 oz. butter

Remove rind from 2 oranges, cut into thin strips; squeeze juice from the 3 oranges. Set aside for sauce.

Cut ducklings in half lengthwise. Place chopped celery, carrot, and onion into baking dish, add butter; place ducklings on top. Roast in hot oven 15 minutes reduce heat to moderate, continue cooking until ducklings are tender, allowing approximately 20 minutes per lb.; baste occasionally with pan juices. Remove from pan, keep warm.

*Orange Sauce*: Skim off fat from pan, strain pan juices. Add sugar and vinegar to pan, cook over gentle heat until sugar caramelises slightly. Add strained pan juices, stock, orange juice and rind, and lemon juice. Cook rapidly until sauce is reduced in quantity by half. Blend arrowroot and sherry, stir gradually into sauce; cook, stirring, 6 to 8 minutes over gentle heat; season to taste. Just before serving, stir in orange liqueur.

Spoon the hot Orange Sauce over each serving of duckling, or pass sauce separately.

Serves 4

## Chinese Braised Duck

1 plump young duck (3½ to 4 lb.)
6 dried mushrooms
1 dessertspoon soy sauce
1 tablespoon dry sherry
1 teaspoon very finely chopped green ginger
water
1½ dessertspoons cornflour
½ teaspoon sugar
pepper
1 teaspoon soy sauce, extra
1 tablespoon oil
½ teaspoon salt
2 cloves garlic
1 small can bamboo shoots
1 small can water chestnuts
2 cups stock or water

Wash mushrooms, soak in hot water 20 minutes. Rinse, squeeze dry, cut in halves. Wash duck, cut into joints.

Combine dessertspoon of soy sauce, the sherry and ginger; add 1 dessertspoon water. Mix together the cornflour, sugar, pepper and extra soy sauce; stir in $\frac{3}{4}$ cup water.

Heat oil with salt and crushed garlic, add duck pieces, and fry, stirring until well browned. Add mushrooms, sliced bamboo shoots, and sliced water chestnuts; cook further 2 minutes. Stir in soy sauce mixture; cook 2 minutes, stirring. Add stock, cover, bring to boil. Reduce heat, simmer until duck is tender. Stir in cornflour mixture and cook, stirring, until sauce thickens. Transfer duck to serving dish, spoon sauce over.

Serve with hot, fluffy rice.

Serves 4

## Roast Turkey

1 turkey
softened butter
salt, pepper
prepared stuffing
extra butter (melted)
1 pint chicken stock
1 teaspoon flour

### Cooking times for turkey

For birds up to 12 lb., allow 25 minutes per lb. For birds over 12 lb., allow 20 minutes per lb.

*Method 1:* Stuff turkey with desired filling, truss, sprinkle with pepper. Spread the softened butter over breast and legs of bird, then cover it with piece of well-buttered greaseproof paper. Place in baking dish with the stock, cook in moderate oven, basting frequently. Remove paper halfway through cooking to allow bird to brown.

When turkey is thoroughly browned and cooked, transfer to heated serving dish. Strain pan juices into saucepan. Skim off a little of the fat, mix to paste with the flour. Add this gradually to gravy and bring to boil, stirring. Simmer a few minutes, adjust seasoning, and serve with the turkey.

*Method* 2: (Under a cloth.)
Take large piece of cheesecloth or muslin, dip in mixture of melted butter and water. Fold to double thickness, drape over breast of bird. Baste occasionally, because cloth dries out.

*Method* 3: (Wrapped in aluminium foil.)
Use heavy foil. Butter turkey and wrap in well-buttered foil. Turn up ends securely to prevent juices escaping. Cook in hot oven for first hour. Reduce to moderate. Thirty minutes before end of cooking time, turn back foil; baste.

*Method* 4: (In paper bag.)
Rub inside of large, heavy paper bag with softened butter. (You may need to slit one side of bag.) Carefully place turkey inside bag, fold ends up securely. Place in baking dish, brush outside of bag with melted butter or oil. Roast in moderate oven. Thirty minutes before end of cooking time, remove paper to allow bird to brown, baste.

Chickens, ducklings, and geese can also be cooked successfully by methods 3 and 4.

NOTE: Turkey is generally a firm bird with little surplus fat. It needs to be watched carefully through cooking time and basted often (except when cooked in foil).

Allow 1 cup stuffing to every pound of turkey.

## Roast Goose

1 goose (9 to 10 lb.)
prepared stuffing
1 cooking apple
flour
melted butter

Stuff goose with prepared stuffing. Place in baking dish with quartered apple, brush with little melted butter. Put little extra melted butter in base of baking dish. Roast in hot oven 15 to 20 minutes, reduce to moderate and allow 20 to 25 minutes per lb. If bird appears to be browning too rapidly, cover with piece of well-greased paper.

When almost cooked, prick skin of bird lightly with fine-pronged fork or skewer; this will allow excess fat to run off. Do not prick flesh of bird, or juices will run out. Dredge breast lightly with flour, baste with hot fat, and continue cooking until tender.

Transfer cooked goose to serving dish, serve with well-seasoned gravy made from pan drippings.

## Stuffings for Poultry

### Chestnut Stuffing (for Turkey)

16 oz. can unsweetened chestnut purée
4 cups fresh breadcrumbs
1 finely chopped onion
1 tablespoon chopped parsley
1½ oz. melted butter
salt, pepper
beaten egg to bind

Sieve chestnut puree into bowl. Blend with remaining ingredients.

### Sage and Onion Stuffing (for Duck and Goose)

2 chopped onions
2 cups fresh breadcrumbs
1½ teaspoons dried sage
1 oz. melted butter
salt, pepper
pinch nutmeg
½ teaspoon sugar

Place onions in saucepan. Add cold water to cover, and salt. Bring to boil; reduce heat and simmer until almost tender. Combine drained onion with remaining ingredients. Add sufficient onion water to bind, about 1 tablespoon.

### Simple Herb Stuffing (for Chicken)

2 cups fresh breadcrumbs
1 oz. softened butter
2 tablespoons chopped parsley
1 teaspoon grated lemon rind
1 teaspoon mixed dried herbs
1 small chopped onion
salt, pepper
beaten egg to bind

Mix together all ingredients, except egg. Add sufficient beaten egg to bind.

## Forcemeat (for Turkey)

1 small onion
2 oz. ham or bacon
1 oz. butter
½ lb. lean minced veal or sausage mince
3 cups fresh breadcrumbs
pinch grated lemon rind
1 dessertspoon chopped parsley
½ teaspoon mixed herbs
pinch nutmeg
salt, pepper
1 egg
milk

Chop onion and bacon finely, saute in heated butter until onion is transparent. Add minced meat, breadcrumbs and seasonings; bind with beaten egg; add a little milk if mixture seems too dry.

# FONDUES

Cheese fondue has been adopted enthusiastically in this country as a different and delightful dish for entertaining. And the other fondues—tomato (a variation of the cheese fondue), beef, fish, and even a dessert fondue—are equally popular.

For cheese fondue, a thick earthenware pot called a 'caquelon' is used; this gives the gentle heat necessary for cheese cookery. If cooked too quickly, or overheated, cheese would become stringy. For Beef Fondue (or Fondue Bourguignonne, as it is sometimes called), a cast-iron (as shown in the picture), copper, or enamel fondue pot is used. Any small heatproof bowl or casserole can be used for the dessert fondue. For all fondues, a spirit lamp with an adjustable flame is necessary. Special fondue forks, with long handles and prongs, are available

## Cheese Fondue

1 clove garlic
¾ lb. gruyere cheese
¾ lb. cheddar cheese
¾ pint white burgundy
2 tablespoons cornflour
3 tablespoons kirsch
crusty french bread

Cut bread into cubes; each cube should have some crust on it. Push the fondue fork through the crust; this will hold the bread firmly on the fork and help prevent it dropping into the fondue.

*To prepare the fondue:* Rub round inside of fondue dish with cut garlic clove. Add wine, heat to boiling point. Add the grated cheeses gradually, stirring continually, until cheese melts and mixes with wine. Add the kirsch, blended with cornflour. Continue to cook until mixture thickens (about 3 to 4 minutes) stirring all the time in the form of a figure eight.

Some like to add a light sprinkling of nutmeg or paprika, or both, to the fondue; add these with the cheese.

One after another, the guests take up a piece of bread on the prong of the fork and dip it in the thick, creamy fondue.

There's no need for hurry with fondue, but it must be stirred so it remains evenly thick. The swirling of the bread in the fondue is generally sufficient for this.

Slowly, the 'Grillon,' or rich brown crust, forms at the bottom of the fondue dish. Some consider this the best part of fondue; everybody should share in this delicacy.

A crisp green salad is a good accompaniment to cheese fondue. And don't forget to have the pepper mill on the table.

If serving wine, it should be the same as used in the fondue.

NOTE: If kirsch is not available, brandy or gin can be substituted. The fondue will not have the traditional taste, but it will be very good.

There's a traditional forfeit paid by those who drop their bread in the fondue—a kiss, if it's a lady; a bottle of wine, if it's a man.

## Tomato Fondue

1 clove garlic
1⅓ cups white burgundy
1½ lb. cheddar cheese
⅔ cup tomato purée
2 tablespoons cornflour
salt, pepper
paprika

Rub round inside of fondue dish with cut garlic clove. Add wine, heat to boiling point. Add grated cheese gradually, stirring constantly until cheese melts and mixes with wine. Add tomato puree blended with cornflour. Continue cooking until mixture thickens, approximately 3 to 4 minutes, stirring constantly. Season to taste with salt, pepper and paprika.

## Beef Fondue

Allow about ¾ lb. steak per person. Any tender steak can be used. Remove all fat, cut steak into 1in. cubes. Add equal quantities of oil and butter to fondue pot. The melted butter, combined with the oil, should

Beef Fondue (or Fondue Bourguignonne), wonderful for a party, is served with a variety of sauces and accompaniments. In smaller pictures, popular Cheese Fondue and Chocolate Dessert Fondue

USTARD

fill fondue pot to a depth of 3 ins. A clove of garlic can be added to the oil for flavour.

To save time, the oil and butter mixture can be heated on the stove and transferred to the fondue pot, then placed over spirit lamp.

Each guest spears a morsel of beef on a fondue fork and cooks it in the hot oil and butter, then slides it on to the plate with another fork. (The fork which has been in the fondue pot would be too hot to use for eating.) Another piece of beef can be cooking while the first is being eaten.

Have a selection of sauces and condiments. Offer at least two of the following: Bearnaise sauce, chilli sauce, mustard, bottled horseradish sauce, caper sauce, any savoury steak butter. Accompaniments can be simple—a good green salad, asparagus spears, onion rings, a baked potato or heated potato crisps, etc. Serve with hot crusty bread and a good red wine or beer.

*Steaks to use* Any tender steak can be used; rump will have best flavour, but there will be less wastage with fillet because of its lack of fat.

Round steak can be used, but will need to be marinated first to make it tender.

*Marinade* Combine ¼ cup salad oil, ½ cup red wine, 1 dessertspoon chopped onion. Let meat pieces marinate in this several hours, turning occasionally. Drain well, pat dry.

Here are two variations of the classic beef fondue.

□ Add other meats—kidney, veal, chicken—to the beef. Put first on the fork or skewer the meat that needs least cooking; put on last the meat that needs the most cooking. If using foregoing combination, you would put the square of kidney on first, then veal, then chicken, and finally the cube of beef, which will be immersed in the hot oil.

□ Use boiling beef bouillon in place of oil in fondue dish. Cut the steak into wafer-thin strips, wrap round the prongs of fondue forks. The steak cooks very quickly in the hot bouillon. And, when the meal is finished, don't discard the bouillon; enriched by the steak cooked in it, it makes an excellent soup for the following day.

## Fish Fondue

A fish fondue can be prepared in two ways: with an oil and butter mixture (as for Beef Fondue); for shellfish; or with fish stock to cook fish fillets.

*For Shellfish* Prepare oil and butter mixture as for Beef Fondue. Prawn Fondue makes an excellent supper dish, but prawns must be green; cooked prawns fried in this way would be very hard and tough.

*For Chinese style Prawns* Shell prawns, cut deep slit down back of each prawn, taking care not to cut through completely. Coat prawns in cornflour, shaking off excess. Dip in eggs which have been beaten lightly with soy sauce (you will need 2 eggs and 1 teaspoon soy sauce for 2 lb. prawns). Coat prawns well in breadcrumbs, pressing down prawns with palm of hand to flatten.

Prawns can be prepared in this way several hours in advance, and refrigerated until guests arrive. Guests spear a prawn on fondue fork, lower in to the hot oil and butter for few minutes; prawns cook quickly. Serve with Hoi Sin Sauce (obtainable from Chinese food stores) or with Chinese Plum Sauce (see page 147) for dipping.

*For Fish Fillets* Make a good fish broth. Place fish trimming and bones into saucepan (snapper or flathead give rich flavour), add 1 chopped onion, 1 or 2 chopped sticks celery, 1 chopped carrot, a bayleaf and few parsley sprigs. Add water to cover; about 2 pints water should be sufficient. Bring to boil, skim well, reduce heat, simmer 20 minutes; strain. Add salt and pepper to taste.

Pour this liquid into fondue pot, add 1 cup dry white wine and, if desired, three slices fresh green ginger and 1 or 2 teaspoons soy sauce. Bring to boil.

Have fish cut into 1 or 1½ in. squares. Spear fish on fondue fork, dip into broth; it will cook very quickly. Serve with small dishes of soy sauce and chopped cucumber.

Fish fillets can also be cooked in the butter and oil mixture. Cut fillets into 1½ in. pieces, put piece on fondue fork, and dip into hot oil; it cooks quickly. Serve with mustard or tartare sauce.

## Chocolate Dessert Fondue

2 14½ oz. cans evaporated milk
2 teaspoons instant coffee powder
¼ cup sugar
8 oz. dark chocolate
1 dessertspoon rum

Place milk, sugar, grated chocolate, and coffee powder in fondue dish. Heat to boiling point, stirring, then lower heat and simmer gently 5 minutes, stirring constantly. Stir in rum. A small fondue dish is used for this rich dessert sauce. Pineapple, pears, bananas—in fair-sized pieces—go well with the chocolate flavour. Or any other fresh or canned fruits can be used.

# RICE

Rice is one of the most versatile of all grains; it can be used for sweet and savoury dishes with equal success.

In this section we give the various methods of cooking rice; all work well, it's just a matter of choosing the method which suits you best

## Hints for Cooking Rice

Add a good squeeze of lemon juice to the rice when cooking; this will whiten and flavour the grains. Some cooks also like to throw in the half or quarter of lemon from which the juice was squeezed. For additional flavour, 1 or 2 small stock cubes can be crumbled into the water.

Boiled or steamed rice can have many flavourful additions lightly forked through, such as finely chopped chives, parsley, or mint; grated carrot with finely chopped shallots; raisins, toasted halved or slivered almonds; diced, cooked vegetables; chopped hard boiled eggs. The choice is as wide as the imaginative cook cares to make it.

Rice almost triples in bulk during cooking. Allow approximately ¾ cup cooked rice for each main dish serving. In other words, 1 lb. of rice, when cooked, will give 8 to 10 servings.

## Fluffy Boiled Rice

Put 3½ pints water into large saucepan, bring water to rapid boil, add 1 dessertspoon salt. Then, gradually letting it dribble through your fingers so the water does not go off the boil, add 1 cup rice. Boil rapidly, uncovered, 12 to 15 minutes. Cooking time depends on the type of rice used and also on the way you like your rice—tender, or still with a slight firmness left in the grain. Start testing at the end of 12 minutes. Lift a few grains from the pan with a fork and bite into the grain. When cooked to your liking, drain at once in a colander.

## Steamed 'Pearly' Rice

Put rice into saucepan, add water to come 1 in. above level of rice. Add salt to taste. Bring water rapidly to boil, then cover tightly, reduce heat to the lowest simmer and cook further 20 minutes. For a firmer grain, many cooks prefer to simmer the rice 15 minutes only; then remove from heat, let stand —still tightly covered—for 5 to 10 minutes.

This method applies to any amount of rice.

## Oven-Steamed Rice

Place ½ lb. rice into casserole dish, sprinkle lightly with salt. Pour over 2¾ cups boiling water, cover tightly. Cook in moderately hot oven 20 to 25 minutes.

## Reheating Rice

Rice which you have cooked in advance and stored in the refrigerator can be reheated in any of the following ways:

*To reheat with steam* Place cooked rice in colander, stand over saucepan of simmering water. Cover colander with lid, steam until rice is heated through. Another method of steaming cooked rice is to pour just enough water into saucepan to cover the base of pan. When boiling, add rice, cover, steam 5 minutes or until water is absorbed and rice is hot. The size of saucepan will depend on the amount of rice to be reheated; use a large saucepan for a large amount of rice so the steam can penetrate the grains.

*To reheat in oven* Spread rice in greased, shallow ovenproof dish, sprinkle with little water or milk, dot with butter. Cover dish with lid or aluminium foil. Place in moderate oven until heated through.

*To reheat in frypan* Melt a little butter in frypan, add rice; stir with fork until heated through.

## Pilaf

1 tablespoon butter or oil
1 small onion
12 oz. long grain rice
4 cups chicken stock
1 tablespoon melted butter, extra
3 oz. raisins
2 oz. blanched slivered toasted almonds

Heat butter or oil in pan that can be covered tightly. Add finely chopped onion, cook gently until it is soft but not brown. Add rice, stir well over gentle heat a few minutes; add boiling chicken stock.

Cover tightly, cook in moderately hot oven 25 to 30 minutes, or until liquid is absorbed and rice is tender. Turn rice on to heated serving dish, separate grains with fork, stir in melted butter, raisins, and almonds.

## Nasi Goreng

½ lb. long grain rice
boiling salted water
½ lb. prawns
1 lb. fillet steak or pork
3 cabbage leaves
2 red peppers
2 medium onions
4 shallots
3 oz. butter
2 cloves garlic, crushed
salt, pepper
2 tablespoons soy sauce
1 small can bean sprouts
1 small cucumber
thin omelets

Add rice gradually to large quantity of boiling salted water, boil rapidly for approximately 15 minutes, or until tender; drain, keep hot. Shell prawns, saute in 1 oz. of the butter, set aside.

Thinly slice steak or pork, cabbage, red peppers and omelets. Chop onions, cut shallots into 1 in. pieces. Peel and thinly slice cucumber.

Heat remaining butter in a large pan, add onion and garlic saute, 1 minute or until onion is transparent. Add steak or pork, saute until tender, season with salt and pepper. Add cabbage, peppers, shallots and hot rice, toss with a fork to mix well; add half the omelet strips, sauteed prawns, soy sauce and bean sprouts. Heat thoroughly, stirring continually.

Add a little more butter if mixture appears too dry; season to taste. Serve on hot platter, garnish with remaining omelet strips and sliced cucumber.

Serves 4 to 6

### Thin Omelets

5 eggs
3 tablespoons milk
salt, pepper
butter

Beat eggs lightly with milk, season to taste with salt and pepper. Grease pan with butter, when hot, pour in enough of the egg mixture to make 1 very thin omelet. When cooked, roll, slice into thin strips. Repeat with remaining egg mixture.

## Risotto

1 oz. butter
1 onion
12 oz. long grain rice
5 or 6 cups chicken stock
1 dessertspoon melted butter, extra
1 tablespoon grated parmesan cheese

Melt butter in large saucepan, saute finely chopped onion until it starts to turn golden. Add rice, mix well. Gradually add boiling stock, about 1 cup at a time; wait until liquid has been absorbed before adding next cup. Stir at each addition.

Cover pan and cook for remainder of cooking time. The rice should cook about 20 minutes from time first cup of stock is added. The rice should be very tender, liquid all absorbed, and mixture creamy at the end of this time.

Add melted butter and parmesan cheese, mix in carefully with fork. Serve immediately, topped, if desired, with extra parmesan cheese.

## Chinese Fried Rice

Among English speaking people, this is one of the most popular of Chinese dishes. Boil or steam rice the day before you want to fry it; it then has time to dry out completely so that it will fry with every grain separate.

Rice is fried in a small quantity of hot oil, and a variety of good tasting, colourful ingredients are added.

1 tablespoon oil
¼ lb. cooked pork
½ lb. long grain rice, cooked
salt
¼ lb. prawns
1 egg
1 teaspoon soy sauce
1 teaspoon water
2 shallots
2 oz. ham

Heat oil in frying pan, add chopped pork. Fry 1 or 2 minutes, then add rice and salt. Cook 10 minutes, stirring to prevent rice sticking, Add shelled prawns, mix well, then clear small space in rice and drop in egg, breaking yolk. When nearly cooked, stir and mix through rice.

Add soy sauce mixed with the water, and finely chopped shallots. Mix well, sprinkle with finely chopped ham.

Fried Rice, traditional accompaniment to many Chinese dishes, is also a colourful, good-tasting dish for a buffet party

# PASTAS

Finding your way among the different macaroni foods—or pastas, as they are called—can be a little puzzling at first because of the varying names. But it is a treasure hunt that will reward you with good food for all the family

Many nations have claimed to have invented macaroni (the generic term which is applied to all shapes and flavours of pasta), but it is in Italy that pasta-making was perfected. As a result, most of the macaronis bear Italian names. When these names are translated, they describe the shape or type of pasta.

Spaghetti, the long, tube-like strands, means 'little string,' lasagne means 'broad-leafed,' farfalle is 'butterfly,' and so on.

Macaroni products can be divided into four basic groups—cords, tubes, ribbons, and special shapes such as shells, crests, etc. There is a wide range of sizes and shapes within each of these groups.

Different shapes have evolved for different dishes. Generally, very small shapes—such as alphabet or animal noodles (these are really just for fun, and children love them!) or tubettini—are cooked in clear broths. Cut macaroni or shells are used in heartier soups or in salads. Wide ribbon shapes are for casserole use layered with sauces.

Spaghetti is available in two forms; thin spaghetti and thicker, or 'tubular' spaghetti. Cooking time is approximately the same for both.

Some of the macaronis—spaghetti, shells, elbows, noodles, crests, gnocchi, spirali, alphabets, animals, etc.—are sold in packages and are easily available. For the more unusual types you might need to shop at an Italian or Continental food store.

Green noodles—coloured with spinach juice—can also be purchased.

Oriental noodles, from China or Japan, are much finer than Italian pasta, and they are in plainer form —cords or ribbons of varying degrees of fineness. They are used in three ways: in soup, cooked noodles, drained and mixed with seasonings, or they can be fried.

1 Gemelli
2 Spinach Noodles
3 Fine Noodles
4 Medium Noodles
5 Wide Noodles
6 Spirali
7 Farfalle
8 Gnocchi
9 Animals

## How To Cook Pasta

Cook all forms of pasta in plenty of boiling water; a gallon of water to 1 lb. of pasta is not too much. Use large saucepan and bring water to a fast, rolling boil; add sprinkling of salt.

Add pasta gradually so water does not go off the boil.

When cooking spaghetti, vermicelli, or any of the 'long goods,' as they are called, hold long strands at one end and place other ends into the boiling water. The pasta will begin to soften in the hot water and it is then simple to lower strands into saucepan, coiling them neatly inside pan.

## Approximate Cooking Times

Spaghetti, 12 to 20 minutes; vermicelli (resembles very fine spaghetti), 6 to 10 minutes; macaroni, 12 to 20 minutes; noodles, 10 to 20 minutes, depending on width.

Cooking time of pasta varies according to individual manufacturers; freshness of the product, too, will affect cooking time. Pasta should not be overcooked; it should be tender but firm.

Start testing at the minimum cooking time given above and, when the pasta is cooked just to your liking, add a cup of cold water to the pan to stop the cooking instantly. Pour pasta into colander, drain well. If you wish, mix a knob of butter or a little oil through the pasta to prevent it sticking together.

Provided sufficient water has been used in cooking, there will be no starch adhering to the pasta, so do not rinse it under cold water; this will only cause the tender pasta to become hardened.

Spaghetti and macaroni almost double in volume during cooking; noodles remain the same in volume.

10 Rigatoni
11 Large Shells
12 Small Shells
13 Alphabets
14 Spaghetti
15 Crests
16 Tubettini
17 Elbows
18 Macaroni
19 Lasagne

1
2
3
4
5
6
7
8
9
10
11
12
13
14
15
16
17
18
19

## Baked Rigatoni

½ lb. rigatoni noodles
grated parmesan cheese

**Filling**

2 onions, chopped
1 crushed clove garlic
1 tablespoon oil
1½ lb. minced steak
1 cup fresh breadcrumbs
1 egg
1½ teaspoons salt
pepper

**Sauce**

1 onion, chopped
1 crushed clove garlic
15 oz. can drained, peeled tomatoes
1 cup juice from can (made up to 1 cup with water if necessary)
1 bayleaf
salt, pepper
oil for frying

Cook rigatoni in boiling salted water until just softened (about 5 minutes); drain and, for this dish, rinse under cold water because they must be cool enough to handle immediately.

*Filling:* Heat oil, brown onions and garlic lightly. Combine with all remaining ingredients.

Using small teaspoon, stuff rigatoni with filling mixture. Arrange stuffed rigatoni in casserole, spoon sauce over. Top with sprinkling of grated parmesan cheese. Bake in moderate oven 30 min.

*Sauce:* Heat a little oil in saucepan, add onion and garlic; saute until onion is transparent. Add all remaining ingredients (crush tomatoes well), simmer uncovered until sauce has thickened.

Serves 4 to 6

## Spaghetti Bolognese

1 large onion
1 lb. minced steak
8 oz. can tomato paste
1 pint water
salt, pepper
2 beef stock cubes
¼ teaspoon oregano
¼ teaspoon thyme
2 tablespoons oil
¾ lb. spaghetti
grated parmesan cheese

Saute the finely chopped onion in the heated oil until golden, add minced steak; cook very well, stirring with fork all the time, until steak browns well. Pour off any surplus fat. Add water, tomato paste, crumbled stock cubes, salt and pepper to taste, and herbs.

When sauce comes to the boil, reduce heat, cook gently 1 to 1½ hours, uncovered, adding a little more water if sauce becomes thick too quickly. The longer this sauce is cooked the better it is.

Arrange hot, well-drained spaghetti in individual bowls, making a slight well in the centre. Spoon in the sauce. Top with grated parmesan cheese.

Serves 4 to 6

## Spaghetti alla Carbonara

1 lb. spaghetti
boiling salted water
¾ lb. bacon
½ cup white wine
2 eggs
½ cup grated parmesan cheese
freshly ground pepper
chopped parsley
extra grated parmesan cheese

Cook spaghetti in large saucepan of salted boiling water 10 to 12 minutes or until tender but still firm. While spaghetti is cooking, remove rind from bacon, cut into ½ in. squares. Saute in pan until cooked through but not crisp.

Add wine, simmer gently 3 minutes. Drain spaghetti well, return to saucepan. Immediately add bacon and wine. Blend together, then add well-beaten eggs and cheese. Toss together over low heat. Add a little freshly ground pepper. Make sure spaghetti is well coated with egg-and-cheese mixture. Serve in individual dishes sprinkled with parsley and extra grated cheese.

Serves 6

NOTE: If completed spaghetti is a little dry, add a little extra white wine to moisten.

## Meatballs in Tomato Sauce

1 medium onion
1 lb. hamburger mince
1 egg
¼ cup dry breadcrumbs
1½ tablespoons grated parmesan cheese
1 tablespoon chopped parsley
salt, pepper
oil for frying

**Tomato Sauce**

1 small onion
1½ tablespoons oil
5 oz. can tomato paste
1 pint water
salt, pepper

Finely chop onion, combine with remaining ingredients, mix well. Shape mixture into balls approximately the size of an egg. Fry in hot oil until evenly browned.

Remove from pan, drain well, place in prepared sauce, bring to boil; reduce heat, simmer, uncovered, for approximately 1 hour or until tender. Spoon meatballs and sauce over hot spaghetti.

Serves 4

*Tomato Sauce:* Finely chop onion, saute in heated oil until soft, add remaining ingredients, stir well to combine. Bring to boil, stirring constantly.

Meatballs in Tomato Sauce have the good, rich flavour of Italian-style cooking. Spoon them over piping hot spaghetti

## Spaghetti Marinara

1 dozen oysters
1 lb. prawns
1 lb. scallops
2 oz. butter
1 clove garlic
2 tablespoons finely chopped parsley
6 large tomatoes
salt, pepper
1 lb. spaghetti

Melt butter in saucepan, add crushed garlic, parsley, and peeled, chopped tomatoes. Simmer until mixture is well blended and soft; mix in oysters, shelled prawns, scallops, cook gently 5 to 7 minutes. Season to taste.
Drain hot cooked spaghetti. Return to saucepan, stir the sauce through. Or, alternatively, spoon sauce over individual servings of spaghetti.

Serves 6

## Lasagne

¼ lb. lasagne noodles

**Meat Sauce**

1 lb. minced steak
1 tablespoon oil
1½ lb. tomatoes
6 oz. can tomato juice
1 tablespoon finely chopped onion
3 oz. can mushrooms
½ clove crushed garlic
1 teaspoon oregano
¼ teaspoon basil
¼ teaspoon rosemary
1 teaspoon salt
½ teaspoon sugar

**Topping**

½ cup grated parmesan cheese
½ cup cream

**Cheese Sauce**

2 oz. butter
3 tablespoons flour
1 pint milk
4 oz. grated processed cheese

Cook lasagne noodles in boiling, salted water until tender, 15 to 20 minutes. Drain well. Peel and chop tomatoes. Heat oil, add steak, cook, stirring, until browned. Add all other ingredients, cook until meat is tender. Place half the noodles in ovenproof dish, spread with half the meat sauce, then half the cheese sauce. Repeat layers.

Sprinkle top with grated parmesan cheese. Cook in moderate oven 15 minutes. Five minutes before end of cooking time, pour cream over top of cheese.

*Cheese Sauce:* Melt butter in saucepan, stir in flour, cook gently for 2 minutes. Gradually add milk, stir over low heat until boiling. Stir in grated cheese, stir until cheese has melted.

Serves 4 to 6

## Macaroni Cheese

6 oz. macaroni
3 oz. butter
¼ cup flour
salt, pepper
1 teaspoon dry mustard
¼ teaspoon paprika
½ pint milk
6 oz. cheese
10 oz. can tomato soup
¼ lb. bacon
1 onion
1 small green pepper
1 teaspoon worcestershire sauce
extra grated cheese

Cook macaroni in boiling salted water 12 to 15 minutes or until tender; drain.

Melt butter in saucepan, remove from heat, stir in flour and seasonings. Return to heat and cook 1 minute. Add milk gradually, stirring until sauce boils and thickens, remove from heat. Add grated cheese and tomato soup, mix well. Gently heat sauce, do not boil.

Fry lightly, chopped bacon, chopped onion, and chopped pepper, add to sauce. Add macaroni and worcestershire sauce, mix thoroughly. Place mixture into casserole dish, sprinkle with extra grated cheese. Bake in moderate oven 25 to 30 minutes.

Serves 4 to 6

## Tuna Spaghetti Casserole

¼ lb. spaghetti
boiling salted water
2 oz. butter
1 small green pepper
1 medium onion
4 oz. mushrooms
⅓ cup flour
1 teaspoon salt
¼ teaspoon pepper
½ teaspoon dry mustard
3 cups milk
6 oz. grated cheese
8 oz. can tuna
extra 1 oz. butter
¾ cup soft breadcrumbs

Add spaghetti gradually to large quantity of boiling salted water, boil rapidly for 15 minutes, or until tender; drain.

Melt butter in saucepan, add sliced green pepper, finely chopped onion and sliced mushrooms, saute 3 to 4 minutes, or until onion is transparent. Remove pan from heat, add flour, salt, pepper and mustard, stir until smooth, cook 2 minutes. Gradually add milk, stir until mixture boils and thickens. Add cheese, stir until melted.

Mix cheese sauce and drained tuna through spaghetti, pour into greased casserole dish. Melt extra butter, add breadcrumbs, cook few minutes; sprinkle over casserole. Bake in moderate oven 20 to 25 minutes or until casserole is well heated and breadcrumbs browned.

Serves 4 to 6

# VEGETABLES

Vegetables are an important part of our daily diet. We use them in salads, as colourful, good-tasting accompaniments to main meals, or they can be a complete meal in themselves.

To cover or not to cover vegetables when cooking them on top of the stove is a question often debated; as with most forms of cookery, everybody has a favourite method. But experts agree on this —vegetables should be cooked as quickly as possible, so they are crisp, full of flavour, and retain as much of their vitamin content as possible.

Seasonal times may vary slightly from State to State. Where seasonal times are not indicated, the vegetable is generally available throughout the year

## Artichoke

Seasonal: February to July.

There are two types of artichokes—the jerusalem and the globe. Many people consider the globe artichoke to be the most delicately flavoured and refined of all vegetables.

*Globe Artichokes:* Wash artichokes, then cut off stem at base. Remove any old outside leaves, shorten the tips with scissors. Plunge into large saucepan of boiling salted water; add juice of ½ lemon, cover, and cook 30 to 40 minutes, according to size. Artichokes are cooked when leaves come away easily when pulled gently. Drain well, place on individual serving dishes. Serve with bowl of melted butter, with juice of lemon and salt and pepper added.

Each diner pulls off the leaves, dips them in melted butter, and eats fleshy end. Remove central hairy "choke," when reached, and eat base.

Artichokes cooked in this way can also be served cold, with a vinaigrette sauce.

### *Jerusalem Artichokes*

Seasonal: January to September.

Is not really an artichoke but a member of sunflower family. Does not look or taste like the globe artichoke, but resembles a knotty potato. Has a sweet nutty flavour.

The tubers are small and irregular in size and shape. Scrub them well, soak in slightly salted cold water 30 minutes, then drain and rinse well. Cover with cold salted water, cook 20 to 30 minutes until tender, depending on size.

Some cooks prefer to peel the artichokes before cooking; small, sharp-pointed knife should be used for this.

However, it is much easier to peel the skins off after cooking. They are now ready to be used in a variety of ways, or they can be served topped with butter.

## Asparagus

Seasonal: August to November.

Cut off tough ends of asparagus, scrape spears a few inches up from end, tie in a bunch. Stand in deep, tall saucepan (top of double boiler or a billy-can are suitable), and add boiling salted water to come half way up spears. Cover tightly, bring to boil, reduce heat and simmer until asparagus is tender (about 20 minutes, although very young tender asparagus will take only 10 to 15 minutes). Drain asparagus well. Serve with melted butter.

## Aubergine

*See Eggplant*

## Beans

There are many varieties of this popular vegetable—some available only when in season at various times of the year. But throughout the year green beans or french beans, as they are sometimes called, are generally procurable.

*Broad Beans:* Available in eastern States from September to mid December. Very young broad beans (fresh from the garden) can be cooked whole. But usually they should be shelled, as for peas, and the pods discarded. Cook beans in boiling salted water until tender

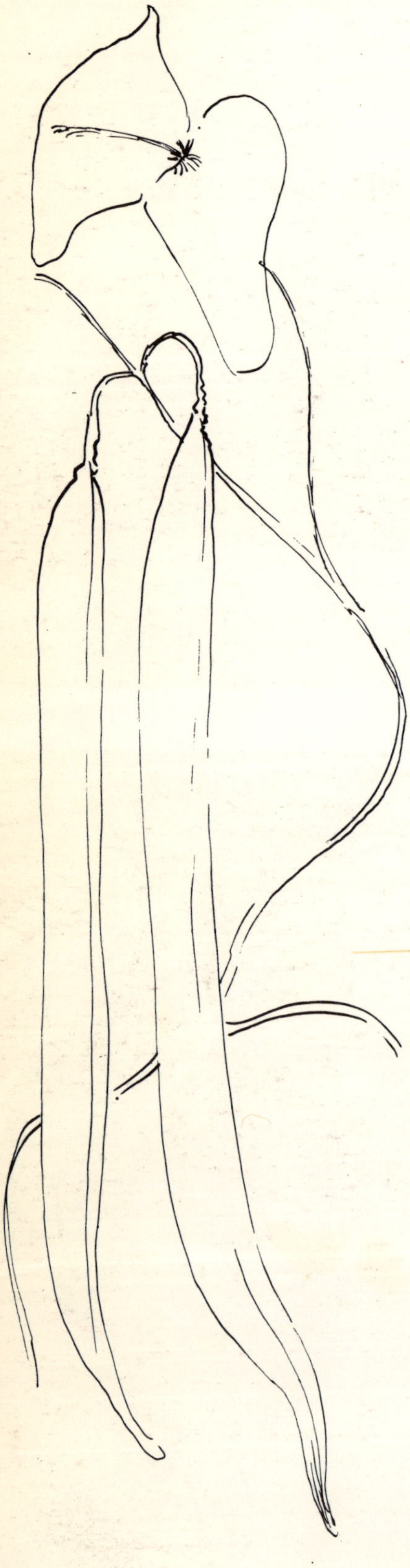

(15 to 20 minutes). Top with butter and sprinkling of finely chopped parsley.

*Continental Beans:* Available in eastern States from February to March. Have purple-coloured pod, white bean inside.

Shell like broad beans. Cook in small amount of boiling salted water until tender (approximately 20 minutes). Season with salt and pepper, toss in butter.

Another type of Continental bean, available in January and February, has white pods marbled with pink. These are cooked in exactly the same way.

*Green or French Beans:* Wash beans, then top and tail, remove strings. Young beans can be left whole for cooking, but older beans should be sliced. Cook in small amount of boiling salted water until tender (10 to 15 minutes). Drain well, season with salt and pepper, top with pat of butter. Serve at once.

*Snake Beans:* Available in eastern States from January to March. A long, slender, green-grey bean. Top and tail, cut in half or into manageable lengths. Cook in boiling salted water until barely tender (approximately 10 minutes). Drain, toss in little butter.

*Yellow Wax or Butter Beans:* Have yellow pod; available in eastern States from January to March.

Top and tail, as for green beans. They are better if cooked whole; if sliced, are inclined to break up. Cook in boiling salted water approximately 10 to 15 minutes. Have a delightful fresh-bean taste, although they lack the crispness of green beans.

### Green Beans Almondine

1 lb. green beans
2 oz. butter
pinch salt
1 oz. blanched slivered almonds
1 dessertspoon lemon juice

Top and tail beans. Cook whole, or sliced, in little boiling salted water until tender; drain. Melt butter over low heat, add almonds, saute a few minutes. Stir in salt and lemon juice. Pour over hot beans.

Serves 6.

## Beetroot

Scrub well. Leave on 1 in. or more of stems and root end. If cut too near stem the bright colour will leak into water, leaving cooked beetroot a pale pink instead of its bright natural colour. Cook, covered, in boiling salted water to cover until tender when tested with fork. Small young beetroot will take 30 to 40 minutes, older beetroot up to 1½ hours. When tender, drain and slip off skins, root, and stems.

## Broccoli

Seasonal: May to August.

Wash broccoli, trim off ends of stalks and coarse leaves. Cut deep cross in base of extra thick stalks to facilitate cooking. Place in saucepan with small amount of boiling salted water; boil until tender (10 to 15 minutes). Drain, add salt, pepper, pat of butter, and squeeze of lemon juice. Serve at once.

For additional flavour, add ½ clove garlic to cooking water. Remove garlic before serving.

### Broccoli with Lemon-Cream Sauce

1 lb. cooked broccoli spears (or use quick-frozen broccoli)
1½ oz. butter
1 dessertspoon flour
salt, pepper
1¼ cups evaporated milk or cream
2 egg-yolks
1½ tablespoons lemon juice
¼ cup blanched, slivered almonds

Melt ½ oz. butter in a saucepan, add flour and seasonings, stir until smooth. Cook 1 minute. Gradually add the evaporated milk. Bring to the boil, stirring constantly. Remove from heat. Beat egg-yolks, slowly beat a little hot sauce into the eggs, return to sauce in the pan, stir in remaining butter and lemon juice carefully.

Place the cooked broccoli spears in a shallow dish, pour over the hot sauce and garnish with almonds.

Serves 4.

## Brussels Sprouts

Seasonal: May to September.

Remove any wilted outer leaves from sprouts, remove hard end of stem; cut a cross in base of stems to ensure even cooking. Wash thoroughly. Cook in little boiling salted water until tender (10 to 15 minutes depending on size). Drain well, dot with butter, sprinkle with salt and pepper. Serve at once.

At top, from left, Zucchini, Eggplant. Below, Snake Beans, so easy to cook; just top and tail them; they do not need stringing.

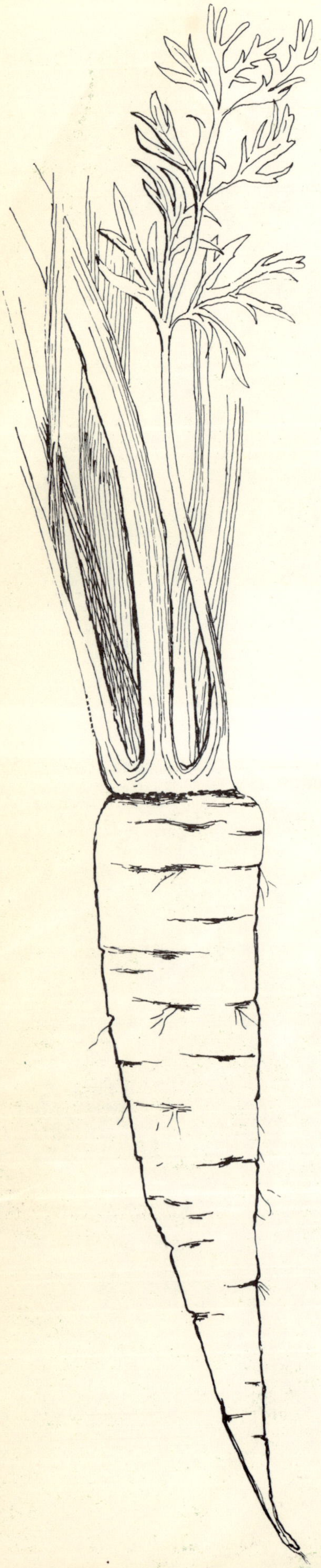

## Cabbage

Remove coarse outer leaves from cabbage, cut out hard core. Wash thoroughly, cut into fine shreds. Place in saucepan, add little salt, lump of butter, and squeeze of lemon juice. Add minimum amount of boiling water, let water come again to boil, then stir cabbage well. Boil rapidly, covered, until tender.

Alternatively, put cabbage into saucepan with salt, add boiling water to cover: bring water rapidly again to boil, boil 3 minutes, then drain. Season with freshly ground pepper, top with knob of butter. This gives a very crisp vegetable, in the Chinese style.

Half a cup of chopped celery added to cabbage when cooking gives a new and delightfully fresh flavour.

*Red Cabbage:* This, unlike green cabbage, is never boiled in water. It should be finely shredded or grated and then cooked slowly, covered, with butter or lard and vinegar; water may then be added. This initial cooking with butter and vinegar ensures a rich purple colour to the cabbage; if cooked with water, the cabbage will "bleed" and become pale pink.

## Red Cabbage

½ red cabbage
3 tablespoons sugar
½ cup white vinegar
1 medium onion
1 oz. lard
2 oz. bacon
1 apple
¾ cup water
6 peppercorns
1 bayleaf
4 whole cloves
1 teaspoon salt

Finely shred cabbage, discarding any coarse leaves. Melt lard in large saucepan, add chopped bacon and onion, saute until onion is golden. Add sugar, cook over medium heat 1 minute. Add shredded cabbage, vinegar, peeled and chopped apple; cover, simmer gently 10 minutes, turning occasionally. Stir in water and seasonings, cover; simmer gently further 1½ hours. Serve as accompaniment to any meats.

Serves 4.

## Capsicums

*See Peppers*

## Carrots

One of the most popular root vegetables. Their bright colour adds appetite appeal to many dishes, especially when served raw in salads; their sweet fresh taste teams well with many foods. Carrots are rich in vitamins.

## Carrots Vichy

1 lb. young carrots
2 oz. butter
1 teaspoon sugar
salt, pepper
water
chopped parsley

Scrape carrots and cut into slices about ½in. thick. Put in pan with the sugar, seasoning, and butter, barely cover with water. Cook quickly, turning occasionally, until all the water has evaporated and the carrots are tender, and lightly coated in butter. Sprinkle with parsley.

Serves 4.

## Cauliflower

Seasonal: March to September.

Trim cauliflower, removing outer green leaves and part of core. Make several deep cuts in core to facilitate cooking. Place in saucepan, add boiling water almost to cover cauliflower. Add salt to flavour, and a teaspoon of lemon juice or little milk; this will help keep cauliflower white. Cook gently 20 to 30 minutes or until tender (do not overcook); drain.

Alternatively, the cauliflower can be broken into flowerets and cooked for a shorter time.

## Cauliflower au Gratin

1 cauliflower
mornay sauce
grated cheese
fresh breadcrumbs
melted butter

Cook cauliflower until tender, drain well. Spread about 1 cup Mornay Sauce in ovenproof dish, place drained cauliflower on top of this. Spoon over 1 cup of Mornay Sauce, or more, if necessary, to cover. Sprinkle with grated cheese and fine, fresh breadcrumbs. Spoon over little melted butter. Cook in hot oven until top is lightly brown.

### Mornay Sauce

2 egg-yolks
1 tablespoon cream
1 pint hot white sauce
1 dessertspoon butter
2 tablespoons finely grated cheese

Mix egg yolks and cream into hot white sauce. Cook, stirring constantly, until mixture just reaches boiling point; remove from heat. Stir in butter and grated cheese.

## Cauliflower Polonaise

1 cauliflower
boiling salted water
squeeze of lemon juice
2 oz. butter
1 tablespoon grated onion
1 dessertspoon chopped parsley
2 tablespoons breadcrumbs
salt, pepper
3 hard boiled eggs
pinch nutmeg

Trim cauliflower, cook in boiling salted water, with squeeze of lemon juice added, until just tender. Drain, transfer to serving platter, keep warm.

Melt butter in saucepan, add onion, parsley, crumbs, salt and pepper. Cook slowly until onion is soft, and butter browned. Finally add chopped eggs and nutmeg; mix gently, spoon over cauliflower.

Serves 4 to 6.

## Celery

Seasonal: Some celery generally available throughout year in eastern States; local celery from November to March, South Australian celery available in winter months.

Trim heads thoroughly—for best results for cooked celery, only the tender inner stalks should be used. Scrub these, plunge into boiling water; cook 10 minutes. Then drain, dry, and tie tops of heads together; cook as desired.

The simplest way to cook celery is to blanch it as above, then continue cooking in boiling salted water until tender (about 20 minutes). Drain, serve with a well-seasoned white sauce.

Don't throw away the discarded leaves and outer stalks—these are a wonderful addition to the stock or soup pot, and young, fresh celery is delicious, of course, to eat fresh or use as a salad ingredient.

## Celery Victor

1 head celery
stock
well-seasoned french dressing
freshly ground black pepper
tomato wedges
few strips anchovy
shredded lettuce
ripe olives

Clean celery, cut head in halves lengthwise. Trim off top and if head is large, cut in half again crosswise. Place in saucepan with hot stock to cover, cook until tender. Drain well, place in shallow dish to cool. Pour over sufficient french dressing to moisten well. Refrigerate, turning pieces occasionally. At serving time, arrange on platter on bed of shredded lettuce. Sprinkle with pepper, lay few strips of anchovy over each piece. Decorate with tomato wedges, black olives.

Serves 4 to 6.

## Braised Celery

2 small heads celery
1 cup chicken stock
1 tablespoon butter
1 small onion
1 tablespoon flour
paprika
salt, pepper

Trim and blanch celery as directed, drain and tie up. Place in saucepan with chicken stock, cover, bring to boil; simmer until tender. Drain, remove string, keep warm; reserve cooking liquid. Heat butter in saucepan, add finely chopped onion, saute until golden. Blend in flour, gradually add cooking liquid. Cook, stirring, until mixture boils and thickens, adding little extra stock if sauce seems too thick. Season to taste. Spoon sauce over celery, sprinkle with paprika.

Serves 4.

## Chilli

*See Peppers*

## Chokoes

Seasonal: Supplies from Queensland available December to February; local chokoes; February to June in eastern States.

Small, young chokoes can be cooked whole, unpeeled, in boiling salted water until tender; do not overcook. Split them, season with salt and pepper, top with knob of butter. Bigger, older chokoes should be peeled, halved, or quartered, the seeds removed; cook and season as above.

Or they can be topped with well-seasoned white or parsley sauce; cheese sauce is also good. Or simply cook them until tender, drain well, sprinkle generously with grated cheese and put them under griller or into hot oven until cheese has melted.

Chokoes can also be cooked in a sugar syrup for dessert. Cooked this way, they very much resemble pears. Peel, halve, and remove seeds. Put into saucepan with water to cover, add few cloves, sugar to taste, and juice of lemon. Cook until tender, then drain and refrigerate. They can be filled into a baked pie shell and the juice, thickened with little arrowroot, poured over.

Chokoes for dessert can also be cooked in pineapple juice with squeeze of lemon added.

Young chokoes can be served as a most unusual and appetising first course at a dinner-party. Peel, cut into halves or

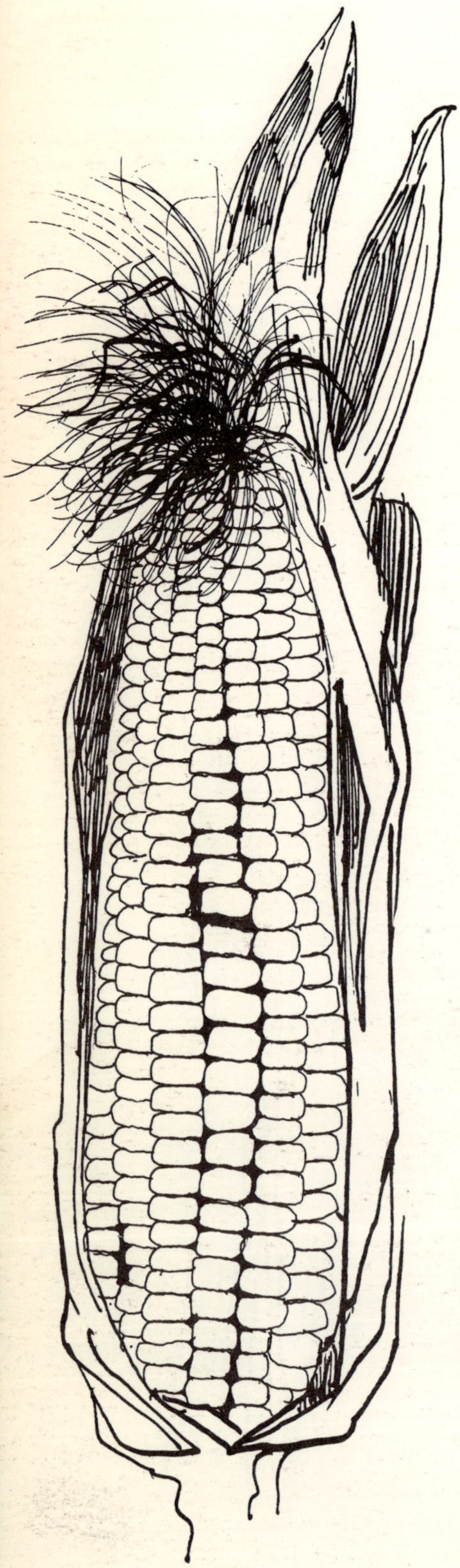

quarters, cook until just tender. Drain, toss in butter, sprinkle with parsley. Serve piping hot.

Or cook as above and, while still hot, toss in well-flavoured french dressing. Cool, then refrigerate. Serve cold, with a little of the dressing spooned over; top with a little finely chopped parsley or chives.

## Corn

Seasonal: December to April.

Corn deteriorates more rapidly after picking than any other vegetable. The sugar in the corn rapidly converts to starch. Freshly picked young corn is sweet to taste; corn which has been picked for some time develops a floury taste. Ideally, corn should be cooked as soon as possible after picking. Look for corn with dark green, fresh husks, with plump, well-filled kernels. Fresh corn looks moist and juicy; if you scratched a grain with your fingertips it would be soft. Old corn looks hard and dull. Do not buy corn that has had the husks removed.

Do not remove husks until ready to cook the corn. Have ready a deep saucepan filled with boiling water; water should be deep enough to cover cobs when they are in saucepan. Salt can be added to the water, but some cooks believe this tends to toughen the kernels; instead, they add a little sugar. Remove green leaves and the silky 'hair' from cobs, drop cobs into the boiling water, let water return to the boil, then cook for 20 minutes. Overcooking will toughen the kernels; the corn becomes harder, not softer, through longer boiling.

Lift cobs from water with tongs. Serve with butter and pepper.

Corn is also good for a barbecue. Remove husk and silk from corn. Spread cobs generously with softened butter, season well with salt and pepper. Wrap each cob in a double thickness of aluminium foil, twisting or folding ends to make a seal. Place on grill of barbecue over hot coals. Cook, turning often, 15 to 20 minutes, depending on heat of fire.

Or cobs can be boiled for 10 minutes, removed from the water, and brushed generously with melted butter; then barbecued on grill over hot coals for 10 minutes, and brushed occasionally with melted butter.

## Cucumbers

Although generally used as a salad vegetable, cucumbers are excellent when cooked and served hot.

### Buttered Cucumbers

2 to 3 cucumbers
boiling salted water
2 tablespoons melted butter
salt, pepper
lemon juice
2 tablespoons chopped parsley

Peel cucumbers, score them with fork. Cut into quarters, lengthwise, or into ½ inch slices. Drop into boiling salted water, simmer 2 minutes, drain.

Melt butter in frying pan, add well-drained cucumber, sprinkle with salt and pepper. Cook, turning once, until cucumbers are lightly golden; do not overcook. Add a good squeeze of lemon juice, stir this lightly through cucumbers. Sprinkle with parsley.

This is a delicious accompaniment to fish.

### Cucumbers in Sour Cream

2 medium cucumbers
1 tablespoon salt
1 tablespoon vinegar
1 cup sour cream
2 tablespoons chopped chives
salt, pepper to taste
pinch cayenne

Peel cucumbers and slice thinly. Sprinkle slices with salt and vinegar, let stand 30 minutes. Drain off liquid, and mix cucumber with sour cream, chives and seasonings to taste. Serve well chilled. Excellent as a curry accompaniment.

Serves 4 to 6.

## Eggplant

Seasonal: December to June for local product; some supplies from Queensland throughout year.

Also known as aubergine. To prepare for cooking, simply wipe with damp cloth and remove stem and calyx. Can be peeled or left unpeeled. Eggplant is a watery vegetable; if cut into thick slices, salted, and covered with plate with weight on top, some of the excess moisture will drain away.

When frying eggplant, do not cover pan—the slices should be crisp.

Cut unpeeled eggplant crosswise in thin slices. Coat lightly with seasoned flour, fry in hot butter until pale golden brown. Serve piping hot as vegetable accompaniment with meat, fish, etc.

Mild, sweet peppers (or capsicums) come in a variety of plain and variegated colours —red, green, yellow; shown, also, is the rarer creamy-white pepper. Yellow-green Banana Chillies (mild as peppers) and the small, hot red chilli are also shown

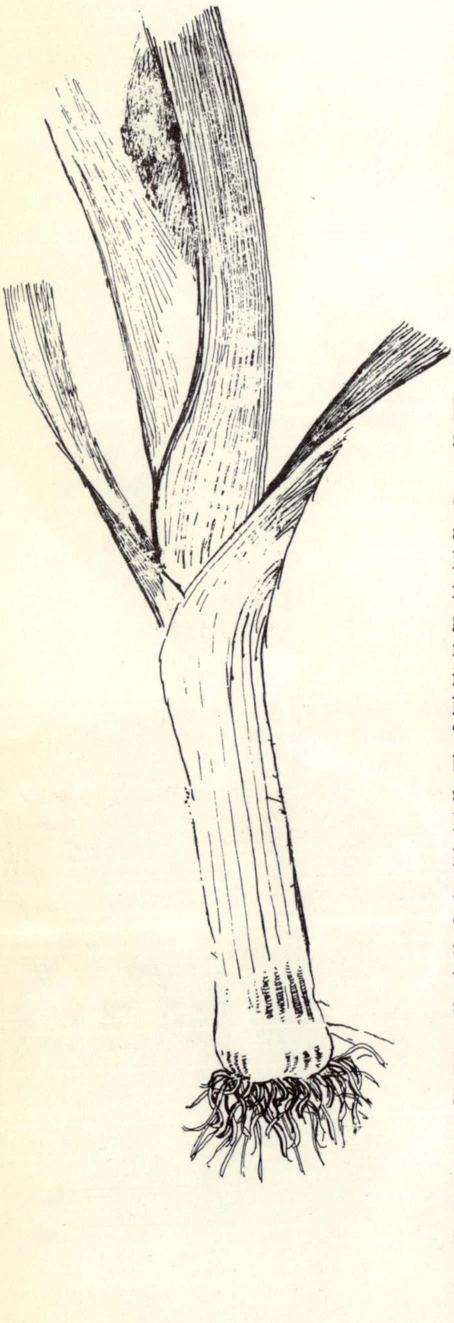

## Kale

Seasonal: Available in Eastern States March to May.

This is a vegetable of the cabbage family. The leaves are closely curled, prettily variegated in colours of green, white, and mauve.

Cut leaves from heavy stems, wash well. Cook as for spinach over gentle heat, but allow slightly longer cooking time. Drain, season with a little grated nutmeg, top with butter.

Kale can also be substituted in any recipe that calls for spinach.

## Kohlrabi

Seasonal: Winter months, May to August.

Looks like a turnip and has similar taste, but more delicate grain. Actually, is a member of the cabbage family. Select leaves that are pale green and crisp, roots about the size of medium-sized onion. Trim off leaves, peel roots, slice. Cook in boiling salted water to cover until tender, about 25 minutes. Drain, season with salt, pepper, melted butter, or serve with a medium white sauce.

## Leeks

Seasonal: January to August.

Cut off roots, trim green tops, leaving about 3 in. of green part. Peel off outside layer, then make 2 cuts, about 2 in. long, first one way and then the other, on top of green parts of leek. This makes it easy to ruffle back the tops when washing. (This is essential because all particles of grit lying between leaves must be removed.) Then place leeks in saucepan with little boiling salted water. Cover, bring to boil, simmer until tender (40 to 50 minutes). Drain well, season with salt and pepepr, pour over little melted butter.

*Leeks Vinaigrette:* Cook leeks as directed, drain and cool. Serve with vinaigrette sauce (three parts oil mixed with one part vinegar, with salt and pepper to taste), sprinkle with chopped parsley or chives.

### Braised Leeks

8 small leeks
1 tablespoon butter
1 small onion
1 cup chicken stock
salt, pepper
slices of buttered toast

Wash leeks thoroughly and trim. Melt butter in wide shallow saucepan, add chopped onion, saute until soft and golden. Add leeks, pour in stock; add salt and pepper. Cover, simmer until leeks are just tender. Serve on slices of buttered toast.

Serves 4.

## Lettuce

Widely used as a salad vegetable, lettuce can also be cooked to serve as a green vegetable. Remove wilted leaves, wash lettuce under running water. Cut heads into quarters. Put into saucepan with a little chicken stock (about 2 tablespoons for each medium-size lettuce). Cover, cook until tender, about 5 to 10 minutes. Drain, season with salt and pepper, pour over a little melted butter.

### Steamed Lettuce with Blue Cheese

2 small lettuce
3 oz. butter
1½ oz. blue cheese
boiling salted water
salt, pepper

Remove outer leaves and core from lettuce, run water through lettuce until thoroughly washed. Cut in halves, keeping leaves intact. Place in large saucepan with approximately $\frac{1}{2}$ in. boiling salted water. Steam, covered, for 2 minutes. Carefully drain, place on shallow serving plate, keep warm. Melt butter in saucepan, add crumbled cheese, season with pepper. Cook gently just until cheese melts. Add a little salt, if necessary. Pour over lettuce.

Serves 4.

## Marrow

Peel marrow, cut into neat pieces, cook in boiling salted water until just tender. Or steam over boiling water. Serve topped with butter or parsley sauce. Marrows can also be filled with a savoury stuffing and baked in the oven.

### Stuffed Vegetable Marrow

1 medium vegetable marrow
1½ cups cold cooked meat
½ cup diced cooked vegetables
1 tomato
1 cup white sauce
salt, pepper
1 dessertspoon chopped parsley
¼ cup grated cheese
¼ cup soft breadcrumbs
1 dessertspoon butter

Cut marrow in half lengthwise, do not

peel, remove seeds. Mince or dice meat finely, skin and chop tomato. Combine meat, vegetables, tomato, white sauce, salt, pepper and parsley; fill into each half of marrow. Sprinkle tops with combined cheese and breadcrumbs, dot with butter. Place marrow in baking dish with small quantity of water in bottom of dish, bake in moderate oven for approximately 45 minutes or until tender.

Serves 4.

## Mushrooms

Classified as a fungus rather than a vegetable, but used as a vegetable they are delicious! Two kinds of mushrooms are generally available — the cultivated mushroom, pink-brown underneath with creamy-white top; and the darker, generally larger and more open-capped field mushroom, which grows wild.

Mushrooms should be used when they are fresh. From the time they are picked, they gradually lose weight by dehydration; they contain 75 percent of water.

To help cut down evaporation, if they are to be kept, store in plastic bag, or well wrapped in plastic food wrap or waxed paper, in refrigerator. Don't try to keep them too long—a week is maximum, if they are to have any flavour.

Before cooking, wash mushrooms lightly. Don't let them soak in water, because this dilutes their flavour. For cultivated mushrooms, a wiping with clean, damp cloth is generally sufficient.

To prepare, slice off dry end of stem. It is not necessary to peel the cultivated mushrooms, but you might like to remove darker skin of field mushroom before cooking. They can be sliced, if large, or left whole.

Here is a simple way of cooking mushrooms.

Prepare as directed above. Saute in heated butter until barely tender (about 5 minutes). Add squeeze of lemon juice to pan, with a small clove of crushed garlic, some chopped parsley, salt and pepper. Cook a further moment or two. Nice with grills.

### Stuffed Mushrooms

½ lb. small mushrooms
2 oz. butter
1 small clove garlic
salt, pepper
1 dessertspoon chopped parsley
3 shallots
2 tablespoons soft breadcrumbs, approx.
oil

Wash and stem mushrooms; chop stems finely. Melt butter in frying pan, add stems and crushed garlic, saute 2 minutes. Add salt and pepper to taste, parsley, and chopped shallots; cook gently 1 minute. Remove from heat and add enough breadcrumbs to mix to a light stuffing.

Fill mushroom caps with this mixture, spreading evenly. Place in shallow well-greased ovenproof dish, pour 1 teaspoon oil over each mushroom. Bake in moderate oven 10 to 15 minutes. The mushrooms should not be over-cooked.

Serve as a first course or as an accompaniment to meat.

### Mushrooms à la Greque

½ cup olive oil
½ cup vinegar
½ lb. mushrooms
salt, pepper
1 bayleaf
2 cloves garlic
chopped parsley

Slice mushrooms thickly, fry in hot oil. Add vinegar and seasonings. Simmer, uncovered, 15 minutes. Cool. Serve as an hors d'oeuvre, with a little of the liquor poured over; sprinkle with chopped parsley.

## Okra

Seasonal: Available in eastern States in January and February.

Also known as Gumbo, Ladies' Fingers, or Bunya Bean. A glutinous vegetable, popular in America, okra is said to have been brought in slave boats from the Congo to the West Indies, thence to America.

Select fresh young pods that are crisp to the touch and break easily. Wash, remove stems carefully. Slice ½ in. thick, or leave young pods whole. Cook in boiling salted water just to cover, 15 to 20 minutes, or until tender. Drain; return to saucepan and swirl in knob of butter; season with salt, pepper, squeeze of lemon juice.

Young okra pods can also be steamed. Place in colander over boiling water. Cover, steam until tender. Serve hot with melted butter.

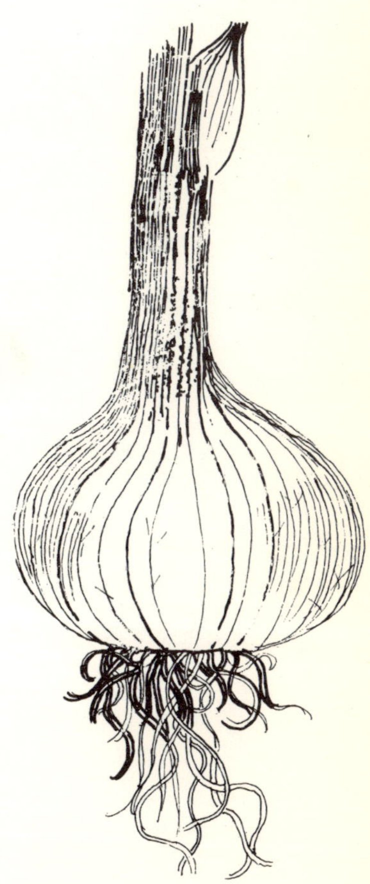

## Onions

A versatile vegetable, they adapt themselves well to almost all ways of cooking. Can be sliced and fried to top a succulent grill; baked whole with the joint; boiled and served with parsley sauce; or can be chopped, boiled, and added to a savoury white sauce to top corned beef.

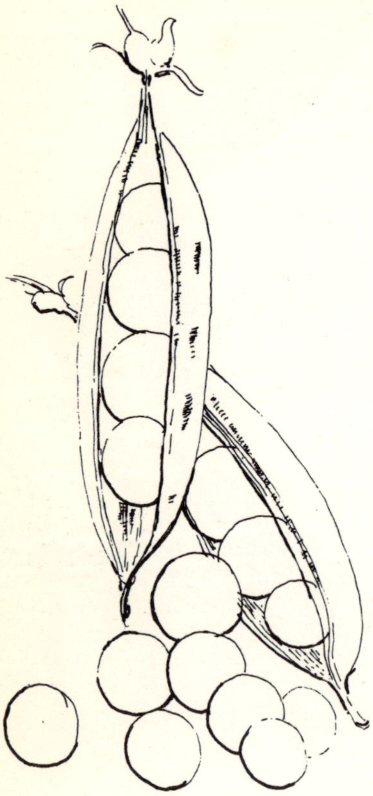

## Fried Onion Rings

4 onions
1 cup plain flour
1 cup milk
1 egg
¼ teaspoon salt
oil for frying

Skin onions, slice thinly, separate into rings. Put into bowl, add the milk, let stand 1 hour. Drain, reserve milk. Beat egg well, beat in reserved milk, salt and sifted flour. Dip each onion ring into batter, drop into hot oil a few rings at a time so heat of oil does not decrease. Fry until golden brown. Drain well, sprinkle with salt.

## Stuffed Onions

4 large onions
1 clove garlic
1 stick celery
1½ teaspoons oil
1 teaspoon thyme
½ cup dried breadcrumbs
2 tablespoons grated parmesan cheese
salt, pepper
2 tablespoons melted butter

Peel onions, cut off top ¾ of the way up onion. Cut out enough of the inside to leave a shell about ¾ in. thick. Salt the cavities well and let the onions stand while making the stuffing. Chop onion pulp finely with crushed garlic and celery. Fry slowly in oil for 5 minutes, then add thyme, breadcrumbs, cheese, salt and pepper to taste. Mix thoroughly, fill the onions; stand them flat in an ovenproof dish in which there is the melted butter and a little salt and pepper. Cover and bake in moderate oven 1 hour, or until onions are tender.

Spoon over the juices in base of the casserole.

## Parsnips

Wash, trim, and peel. Slice, if desired, or leave whole. Cook in small amount of boiling salted water until tender (about 25 to 30 minutes for whole parsnips—sliced parsnips will not take as long). Drain, season with salt and pepper, pour over little melted butter.

Parsnips are also delicious if baked around a roast. Peel parsnips and cut in halves, lengthwise. Place in baking dish with meat, spooning little of hot fat from pan over each. Bake about 45 minutes or until tender and browned.

## Parsnip Croquettes

1 lb. parsnips
¾ cup milk
1 oz. butter
2 to 3 tablespoons finely chopped chives or shallots
1 small egg
2 rashers bacon
2 tablespoons plain flour
salt, pepper
seasoned flour
egg glazing
dried breadcrumbs
oil for frying

Remove rind from bacon, cut bacon into small pieces. Fry until crisp, drain, set aside. Peel parsnips, cut into small pieces; put into saucepan with milk. Simmer, covered, until parsnips are tender and liquid is almost absorbed; mash. Add butter, chopped shallots, egg, plain flour, and bacon. Season with salt and pepper, mix well. Drop tablespoonfuls of mixture into seasoned flour, shape into croquettes; roll in flour, dip in beaten egg, toss in dry breadcrumbs. Press crumbs firmly on to croquettes. Refrigerate 1 hour. Deep fry in hot oil until golden brown.

Makes approx. 1½ dozen small croquettes.

## Peas

Shell peas just before cooking, place in saucepan with small amount of boiling salted water. Add salt, little sugar, and sprig of mint; cook until peas are tender. Cooking time will depend on age of peas, but is usually from 15 to 20 minutes. Drain, season with salt and pepper; add nut of butter; serve at once.

## Peas Bonne Femme

1 heart of lettuce
1½ to 2 lb. peas
1½ oz. butter
2 rashers bacon
6 shallots
1 dessertspoon flour
1½ cups chicken or vegetable stock
bouquet garni
salt, pepper

Shred lettuce finely, shell peas. Melt butter in saucepan, add sliced shallots and chopped bacon, shake over heat until shallots are wilted. Stir in flour, cook 2 to 3 minutes, then add lettuce. Pour on stock, bring mixture to boil, add peas, bouquet garni, salt and pepper. Cover, cook gently 20 to 30 minutes, stirring frequently. Remove bouquet garni.

Serves 6 to 8.

At top, Butter Nut Pumpkin; below, Squash. These are two of the more unusual vegetables which you may not have tried. You'll like their good flavour.

## Peppers

Generally available all year round; more expensive in winter months.

Size of pepper usually indicates how to use it in cooking. Small pointed varieties (chillies) are very hot. Like garlic, a small amount goes a long way in seasoning casseroles, pickles, relishes etc. Banana chillies are long, pale greenish-yellow in colour, are mild in flavour, like the big red and green peppers (or capsicums). Peppers can be used in many dishes; they add flavour to casseroles, and are a popular, colourful addition to salads.

To prepare peppers for cooking, remove slice from stalk end, scoop out seeds and membranes. Young, tender peppers can be used fresh, but older peppers should be blanched in hot water for 2 to 3 minutes to soften.

Perhaps the most popular way of using peppers is to stuff them with a savoury mixture and bake them; they make an easy, economical dish.

### Stuffed Peppers

4 green peppers
1 tablespoon oil
2 oz. butter
salt, pepper
1 small onion
½ cup chopped celery
1 lb. hamburger mince
1 cup cooked rice

Cut tops from peppers, or cut peppers in half lengthwise; remove seeds and membranes. Place peppers in boiling water with oil, boil 5 minutes; drain well. Season inside of peppers with salt and pepper. Heat butter, add finely chopped onion and celery, saute until tender; add meat and rice, season with salt and pepper. Cook, stirring constantly, until meat changes colour.

Place meat mixture into pepper halves, place in shallow baking dish, cover. Bake in moderate oven 30 to 40 minutes, serve at once.

Serves 4.

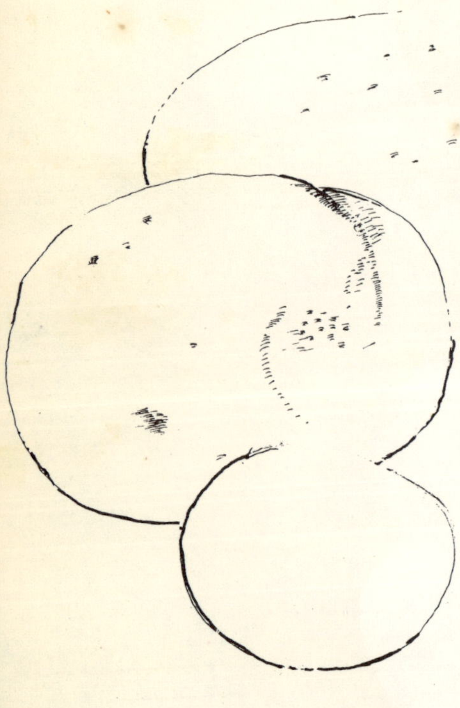

## Potatoes

A staple in the diet of most Australians, and a source of substantial nourishment. They are eaten boiled, baked, roasted and fried—there are a hundred different methods of cooking them.

*New Potatoes:* Scrub well before cooking. Cook in boiling salted water to which a sprig of mint has been added until tender, 15 minutes or a little longer, depending on size. (Don't add too much mint, this darkens the potatoes.) Drain, peel potatoes, return to pan, toss in butter, sprinkle with a little finely chopped mint. Or, as the skins on new potatoes are very thin, some cooks prefer to serve them unpeeled; just cut them in half for serving, top with a little butter and mint.

*Baked Potatoes:* Choose potatoes of uniform size so they will finish cooking at the same time; scrub skins well, prick several times with a fine-tined fork. Rub over well with oil (this will ensure a crisp skin), sprinkle with salt. Bake in moderately hot oven 45 minutes to one hour, depending on size of potatoes; the skins should be crisply brown.

Remove from oven, make 2 cuts in top of each potato, forming a cross. Press sides of each potato so it opens out. Top each with knob of butter and sprinkling of salt and freshly ground pepper.

If desired, add sprinkling of chopped chives or parsley, spoonful of thick sour cream or sprinkling of grated parmesan cheese.

Alternatively (and this is a delicious first course at a dinner party) scoop out inside of cooked potato carefully, mash well, mix with some caviar and enough sour cream to give a firm but rather creamy consistency. Spoon back into potato jacket.

### Pommes Dauphinoise

2 lb. potatoes
salt, pepper
nutmeg
1 egg
1 cup milk
few onion slices
1 cut clove garlic
4 tablespoons grated gruyere cheese
butter

Peel potatoes, slice thinly. Arrange in ovenproof casserole, sprinkle with salt, pepper, grated nutmeg. Heat milk with onion slices and garlic, strain, combine with beaten egg; pour over potatoes. Sprinkle with cheese, dot with butter. Bake in moderate oven 45 to 50 minutes, or until potatoes are soft when tested with skewer.

Serves 4 to 6.

### Paprika Potatoes

3 oz. lard or butter
3 shallots
2 lb. potatoes
salt, pepper
2 tablespoons milk
1 cup sour cream
1½ teaspoons paprika

Peel and wash potatoes, cut into 1in. cubes. Heat lard in large frying pan, add potatoes; cover and cook over low heat, stirring occasionally, until potatoes are tender and lightly golden brown. Add chopped shallots, cook few minutes longer; season with salt and pepper. Mix together sour cream, milk, and paprika, add to potatoes. Heat slowly over low heat (do not boil). Serve immediately.

Serves 4.

## Potato Scallops

1 lb. potatoes
boiling water
2 cups plain flour
1 egg
1 tablespoon oil
1 to 1¼ cups hot water
½ teaspoon salt

Peel potatoes, wash well. Cut into slices ¼ in. thick. Place in heatproof basin, cover with boiling water, let stand 1 hour.

Meanwhile, prepare batter. Sift flour and salt into basin. Make a well in centre, add beaten egg and oil; beat in enough hot water to make a fairly thick coating batter. Beat until smooth.

Drain potatoes, pat dry. Coat each slice well with batter, deep-fry in hot oil, a few at a time, until batter is golden brown and crisp. Drain on kitchen paper, sprinkle with salt.

## Potatoes Anna

2 lb. potatoes
water
salt, pepper
approx. 4 oz. butter
parsley

Peel potatoes, slice as thinly as possible. Drop them into iced water, let them stand 30 minutes. Drain, dry well. Take round mould or small baking dish, butter generously. Place layer of potatoes in base, spread over some softened butter. Repeat layers of potatoes and butter, ending with butter; sprinkle each layer with salt and pepper. Bake in hot oven 45 to 55 minutes, or until potatoes are soft when tested with thin skewer. To serve, invert on to serving dish. Garnish with parsley.

Serves 4.

## Brandied Potatoes

1 lb. potatoes
½ cup brandy
1 teaspoon salt
2 oz. butter
1 large onion
chopped parsley
salt, pepper

Peel potatoes, cut into ¼ in. slices. Place in large frying pan and pour brandy over. Cook over medium heat, uncovered, until all liquid has been absorbed, turning once. Sprinkle with salt, add butter, then saute potatoes until golden brown on both sides. Add chopped onion halfway through the browning process; drain well. Serve seasoned with salt and pepper and topped generously with parsley.

Serves 2 to 3.

## Duchesse Potatoes

3 lb. potatoes
4 egg-yolks
2 oz. butter
salt, pepper
nutmeg
melted butter

Peel potatoes, boil in salted water until tender, then drain well, mash or push through strainer. Place in bowl, season with salt, pepper and nutmeg; add yolks and softened butter, work to smooth paste. Place in piping bag with star tube, pipe small pyramids on greased baking sheets. Brush with little melted butter. Bake in hot oven until tipped with brown.

Serves 6 to 8.

## Pumpkin

Although pumpkin is readily available in most countries, Australia is one of the few to consider it seriously as a vegetable. Correctly prepared, pumpkin is a perfect accompaniment to roast lamb and other meats.

To save time and effort—as well as to retain nutriment and flavour, cook pumpkin with skin on. Then, before serving, remove the fine green skin layer.

Several varieties of pumpkin are available; one becoming increasingly popular is the Butter Nut or Butter Pumpkin, available around January/February. Peel, cut in half, remove seeds; cut into smaller pieces if the pumpkin is large. Boil or bake in usual way for pumpkin.

## Spinach

Should be thoroughly washed before cooking and every speck of dirt removed. Can be cooked in either of the following ways:

Wash spinach thoroughly. One popular variety of spinach has rather coarse white stems; these should be cut out before cooking. Place spinach in saucepan with only the water clinging to leaves. Cover tightly, cook until tender. Drain, pressing out all moisture, return to pan with salt, pepper, and squeeze of lemon juice. Shake over heat 2 or 3 minutes before serving.

*Alternative Method:*
Wash spinach thoroughly as directed above; remove white stems. Cook in plenty of boiling salted water until tender (10 to 12 minutes). Drain, press out all water, chop finely. Season with salt and pepper, then return to pan, with little butter, shake over heat 2 or 3 minutes.

Unless water is pressed out of spinach after cooking, it will have a dark colour.

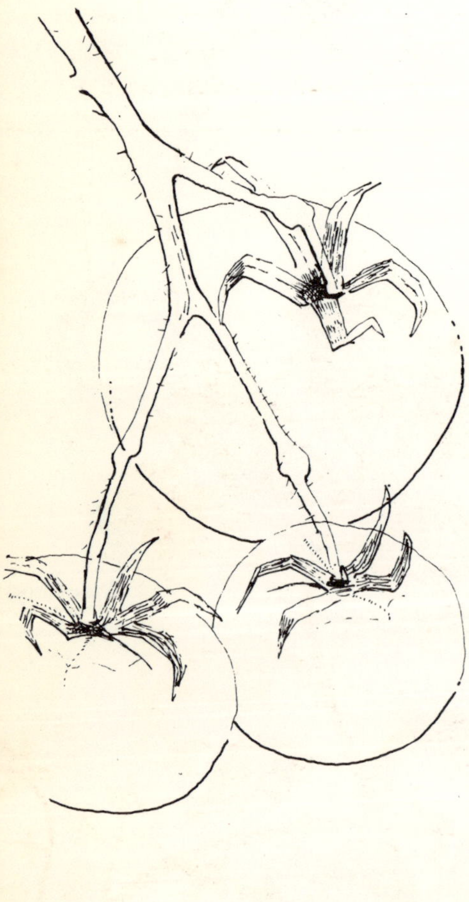

## Squash

Cook like marrow. Or the round, white-skinned squash can have the centre cut out, filled with savory stuffing, and baked.

*Acorn or Baby Squash:* A vegetable with delicious fresh flavour, should be more widely enjoyed. Trim stems, do not peel. Cook whole, in boiling salted water to cover, 15 to 20 minutes, depending on size. Split in half if desired or serve whole; season with salt, pepper, top with knob of butter.

*Butter Squash:* With deep yellow or green or brown striped skin—is cooked in similar way; slightly sweeter in flavour.

## Sweet Potato

This is an edible tuber resembling an ordinary potato in appearance but with a sweetish flavour. Sweet potatoes are also known as yams. They can be boiled or baked, and are delicious if simply scrubbed and baked in their jackets; this wili take 1 to $1\frac{1}{2}$ hours, depending on size. When cooked, serve them split open and topped with a pat of butter.

They can also be peeled, quartered, or halved and cooked with roast meat in the same way as ordinary potatoes.

Peel them just before cooking; if left to stand after peeling, their colour rapidly darkens.

## Tomatoes

Should be washed thoroughly before use. Some recipes require peeled tomatoes. This is quite simple; place tomatoes in bowl, pour over sufficient boiling water to cover. Leave a moment, then drain and plunge into cold water. Skins will slip off easily.

Other recipes require juices and seeds to be discarded and only firm flesh of tomato used. To remove juices and seeds, halve tomatoes, squeeze out seeds and juice into basin. Strain juice, if desired, and use in place of some of liquid in recipe.

### Baked Tomatoes

| | |
|---|---|
| 6 large tomatoes | 2 to 3 tablespoons chopped parsley |
| 1 onion | soft white breadcrumbs |
| salt, pepper | 1 oz. butter |
| 1 teaspoon sugar | |

Peel tomatoes, cut into firm slices. Arrange layer of tomatoes in greased ovenproof dish. Sprinkle with salt, pepper, finely chopped or grated onion and parsley. Top with another layer of tomatoes, sprinkle over any remaining onion, parsley etc. Top with layer of breadcrumbs, dot with butter. Bake in moderately hot oven about 20 minutes. Delicious with roast meats.

Serves 4 to 6.

### Tomato Concassé

| | |
|---|---|
| 1 lb. tomatoes | 1 clove garlic crushed |
| 2 shallots or 1 small onion | butter |
| | salt, pepper |

Plunge tomatoes into boiling water, then into cold water. Skin, seed and chop. Chop shallots or onion finely. Saute shallots in little hot butter until softened, but not browned. Add tomatoes, garlic, salt and pepper to taste. Simmer gently, pressing mixture with fork occasionally.

Serve over chops, steaks or sausages; delicious as filling for omelets.

## Turnips

Young, small turnips can be washed, peeled, and cooked whole in boiling salted water to cover until soft (about 30 minutes). Bigger turnips can be cut into large dice or halved. Drain them well, toss in a little butter and serve sprinkled with chopped parsley.

*Swede Turnips:* Peel, dice or cut into quarters and cook as above. They are best served mashed with salt, pepper, and a little butter.

## Zucchini

Seasonal: October to May.

Small Italian marrows; French name is courgettes. Delicately and delightfully flavoured. To prepare, trim stems. Young, small zucchini can be cooked whole and unpeeled in boiling salted water until just tender. Serve with butter. Or, when cooked, slice and mix with some finely chopped mushrooms which have been sauteed until tender in a little butter.

### Zucchini with Mushrooms

| | |
|---|---|
| 1 lb. zucchini | 1 clove garlic |
| 4 oz. mushrooms | 2 oz. butter |
| 1 large onion | salt, pepper |
| 2 tablespoons chopped parsley | |

Cut zucchini diagonally into 1in. slices, crush garlic, slice mushrooms, chop onion. Melt butter in large frying pan, add vegetables, saute until golden brown and tender. Season with salt and pepper. Sprinkle with chopped parsley and serve

# SEASONINGS FOR VEGETABLES

| Vegetable | Seasonings | Vegetable | Seasonings |
|---|---|---|---|
| **Aubergine** | Basil, dill, garlic, marjoram, oregano, rosemary. | **Celery** | Basil, onion, parsley, tarragon. |
| **Beetroot** | Celery or caraway seeds, dill, mustard, tarragon, thyme. | **Green Beans** | Basil, chilli powder, garlic, nutmeg, onion, tarragon, thyme. |
| **Broccoli** | Basil, garlic, lemon, mustard, nutmeg, onion, oregano. | **Mushrooms** | Basil, chives, garlic, parsley. |
| **Brussels Sprouts** | Basil, celery seed, curry powder, lemon, mustard, oregano. | **Peas** | Chives, mint, garlic, onion. |
| **Cabbage** | Dill, onion, nutmeg, chives, parsley, tarragon. | **Peppers** | Basil, garlic, onion, oregano. |
| **Carrots** | Bayleaf, basil, curry powder, garlic, ginger, mint, nutmeg, onion, parsley, rosemary, thyme. | **Spinach** | Basil, garlic, lemon, nutmeg, onion, rosemary. |
| **Cauliflower** | Basil, caraway seed, chives, mace, lemon, oregano, parsley, rosemary. | **Tomatoes** | Celery salt, chives, garlic, onion, oregano, parsley, tarragon, basil. |

# SALADS

Salads can be a light, colourful accompaniment to a main meal, or substantial enough to be a main meal in themselves. All types of salad recipes are given here—old favourites, such as coleslaw, rice, potato—as well as wonderful new salads. And we've given a selection of good-tasting salad dressings

## Classic Green Salad

1 lettuce
salt, pepper
french dressing

Wash lettuce, dry thoroughly; place in plastic bag in refrigerator to crisp. At serving time, tear into small pieces; place in salad bowl. Sprinkle with salt and pepper; pour over sufficient dressing to moisten, then toss lightly.

There should be just enough dressing to lightly coat each leaf.

The classic green salad uses lettuce only; however, other greens—endive, young spinach, etc.—can be added for contrasting colours of green.

## Prawn and Rice Salad

2 medium onions
1 oz. butter
4 oz. mushrooms
extra 2 oz. butter
½ lb. long grain rice, cooked
1 cup cooked peas
1 green pepper
2 tablespoons chopped parsley
4 oz. ham
1 lb. prawns
french dressing
shredded lettuce
sliced tomatoes and cucumber

Saute finely chopped onions in heated butter until lightly browned; remove from pan. Add extra butter to pan. Fry sliced mushrooms in this until tender (about 3 minutes). Spoon onion and mushroom mixture into rice, adding pan juices as well. Mix in peas, chopped green pepper, parsley, chopped ham and shelled prawns (reserving about 1 dozen with tails still on for garnishing).

Mix together lightly, pour over enough french dressing to moisten; mix lightly. Arrange rice in ring on large platter. Surround with shredded lettuce and alternate slices of tomato and cucumber. Fill centre of ring with shredded lettuce, arrange reserved prawns in crown shape on top of rice ring.

Serves 4 to 6

## Creamy Potato Salad

2 lb. potatoes
¾ cup french dressing
¾ cup sliced celery
few chopped green shallots
1 cup mayonnaise
½ cup sour cream
1½ teaspoons prepared mustard
salt
¾ cup diced cucumber

If using old potatoes, peel and cook until tender but still firm; if new potatoes, cook in their jackets and peel when cooked. Slice potatoes or cut into large dice while still warm. Put into bowl, pour over the french dressing, toss gently to coat potato pieces. Let stand 1 hour. Add celery and shallots. Combine mayonnaise, sour cream, and mustard, blend well; mix into potato, together with salt to taste; refrigerate. Just before serving, mix in the cucumber.

Serves 4 to 6

## Indian Curry Salad

½ cup french dressing
½ teaspoon worcestershire sauce
salt, pepper
1½ teaspoons curry powder
1 green pepper
½ small cauliflower
¼ lb. long grain rice, cooked
2 lb. prawns
2 cups sliced celery
2 small onions, finely sliced

In basin combine french dressing, worcestershire sauce, salt, pepper and curry powder. Cut cauliflower into small flowerets (there should be enough to make 2 cups), mix with cooked, drained rice; pour the combined dressing over and marinate $1\frac{1}{2}$ hours, stirring occasionally. Shell prawns, cut into $\frac{1}{2}$ inch pieces. Cut green pepper into thin 2 in. strips. Stir remaining vegetables and prawns into rice. Refrigerate until required.

Serves 6 to 8

## Delicious Garden Salad

½ small cauliflower
1 large onion
1 cucumber
1 large green pepper
1 large red pepper
1 teaspoon paprika
2 teaspoons sugar
½ bunch young spinach
1 teaspoon thyme
½ cup french dressing
salt, pepper

Soak cauliflower in salted water 30 minutes, wash, and drain, trim off leaves and stems leaving small flowerets. Dice onion and unpeeled cucumber; cut green and red peppers into thin strips. Wash and dry spinach, remove stalks, roughly chop leaves (this should give 2 cups). Combine prepared vegetables with remaining ingredients, toss lightly with fork. Refrigerate well before serving.

Serves 6 to 8

## Haricot Bean Salad

1 lb. haricot beans
boiling salted water
2 oz. green olives
1 clove garlic, crushed
½ cup french dressing
½ cup chopped parsley
salt, pepper
2 oz. black olives

Cover beans well with water, allow to stand overnight. Drain, add to boiling salted water, boil 1 to 1½ hours or until tender, drain well; allow to become cold. Pit and slice green olives, add to beans with garlic, dressing and parsley. Season with salt and pepper, toss lightly to combine. Garnish with black olives. Refrigerate before serving.

Serves 6

## Chicken Salad with Lychees

3½ lb. chicken, steamed
1 cup chopped celery
1 cup chopped green pepper
20 oz. can lychee nuts
¾ cup french dressing
salt, pepper
salad greens

**Mayonnaise Dressing**

¾ cup mayonnaise
¼ cup sour cream
2 teaspoons curry powder
2 tablespoons grated onion
2 tablespoons chopped parsley

Remove meat from chicken, chop into cubes. Add celery and green pepper, season with salt and pepper. Add french dressing, toss until all ingredients are lightly coated. Refrigerate ½ hour, tossing occasionally.

Heap chicken salad on to serving platter. Drain lychees, arrange on top of salad. If desired, some canned mandarin segments can be used for garnish; slip one segment into each lychee nut. Serve with salad greens. Serve the mayonnaise dressing separately to spoon over individual servings.

*Mayonnaise Dressing:* Blend together all ingredients. Refrigerate until well chilled.

Serves 6

## Home-Style Potato Salad

2 lb. potatoes
2 medium carrots
1 dessertspoon finely chopped onion
¾ cup cooked peas
1 teaspoon finely chopped mint
½ cup mayonnaise
pinch cayenne pepper

Peel and dice potatoes and carrots. Cook in boiling salted water until tender; drain and allow to cool. In a basin combine onion, mint, cayenne, and mayonnaise, mix well; fold in potatoes, carrots, and cooked peas. Refrigerate before serving. Spoon servings into crisp lettuce leaves.

Serves 6

## Party Chicken Salad

¼ lb. mushrooms
½ cup french dressing
2 small lettuce
1 steamed chicken (3½ lb.)
1 small can artichoke hearts
1 small red pepper
½ lb. sliced cooked green beans
salt, pepper
2 oz. slivered almonds

Slice mushrooms thinly, place in shallow dish. Pour french dressing over, stand 1 hour, stirring occasionally. Wash and drain whole lettuce, discarding outer leaves. Cut each lettuce crossways into 6 wedges, arrange in base of large deep salad bowl. Discard bones and skin of chicken, chop meat roughly. Drain and lightly wash artichoke hearts, slice pepper into thin strips.

In separate basin, combine chicken meat, artichoke hearts, cooked beans, strips of pepper, mushrooms and dressing. Toss lightly, adding salt and pepper to taste. Refrigerate until ready to serve. Toast almond slivers under griller until lightly brown, remove from heat. To serve, spoon chicken mixture over lettuce in large salad bowl, toss lightly. Sprinkle over toasted almonds.

Serves 6

## Waldorf Salad

3 red skinned eating apples
juice of 2 lemons
6 sticks celery
2 oz. chopped walnuts
lettuce leaves
mayonnaise

Core and dice unpeeled apples, sprinkle with lemon juice. Add sliced celery and walnuts. Toss together with enough mayonnaise to moisten thoroughly. Pile into salad bowl lined with lettuce leaves.
Serves 4 to 6

## Caesar Salad

2 small lettuce
1 oz. butter
1 clove garlic, crushed
2 slices bread
2 rashers bacon
grated parmesan cheese
chopped parsley

**Dressing**

⅔ cup french dressing
1 teaspoon salt
1 coddled egg
1 teaspoon prepared mustard

Wash lettuce well, discard tough outer leaves. Tear leaves into pieces, mix with dressing. Cut bread into $\frac{1}{2}$ in. cubes. Brown cubes with garlic in hot butter. Cook chopped bacon separately until crisp. Drain on absorbent paper.

Scatter bread croutons over salad with bacon pieces, chopped parsley and grated cheese.

*Dressing:* To coddle egg, gently lower egg into boiling water, boil 1 minute. Remove egg from shell; combine with remaining ingredients. Blend well.
Serves 4 to 6

## Oregano-Tomato Salad

1 lb. firm tomatoes
1 teaspoon ground oregano
1 teaspoon sugar
1 teaspoon salt
freshly ground pepper
2 white onions
2 tablespoons dry white wine
2 tablespoons oil
chopped parsley

Wash, dry and slice tomatoes; peel and thinly slice onions. Layer tomatoes and onions in bowl. In another bowl mix together seasonings, add oil and wine; stir until well mixed. Pour over tomatoes and onions, refrigerate several hours. Serve sprinkled with chopped parsley. Garnish, if desired, with black olives.
Serves 6

## Prawn and Green Bean Salad

1 lb. green beans
salted water
2 tablespoons french dressing
½ lb. shelled prawns
little extra french dressing
2 hard-boiled eggs

Top, tail and string beans, cook in boiling salted water until tender. Drain, pour the 2 tablespoons french dressing over. Toss lightly, arrange on platter.

Top with shelled prawns and sprinkle these with a little additional french dressing. Garnish with the eggs cut into quarters.
Serves 6

## Ratatouille

2 large onions
2 cloves garlic
⅓ cup oil
2 small eggplants
4 zucchini
2 green peppers
1 small head celery
1 lb. ripe tomatoes
1 teaspoon dried basil
1½ teaspoons salt
pepper

Heat oil in shallow pan, add sliced onions and crushed garlic; cook slowly until soft. Add the eggplant, cut into cubes, sliced zucchini, peppers cut into strips and sliced celery. Mix well, cook quickly 5 minutes. Add peeled, chopped tomatoes and seasonings, cover and simmer about 1 hour, stirring occasionally. Then remove cover and allow mixture to cook down until most of liquid has evaporated and mixture is thick. Serve cold.
Serves 4 to 6

## Asparagus Rice Salad

½ lb. long grain rice
boiling salted water
1 large onion
1 oz. butter
10 oz. can asparagus tips
2 tablespoons chopped parsley
2 tablespoons french dressing
salt, pepper

Add rice gradually to large quantity of boiling salted water, boil rapidly 10 minutes or until tender. Drain, allow to cool. Dice onion, saute in butter 2 to 3 minutes until tender (do not brown). Drain asparagus well, discard liquid.

Add onion mixture, asparagus, parsley and french dressing to rice, season with salt and pepper, toss lightly.
Serves 6

Chicken Salad with Lychees—perfect for a summer luncheon, is shown with Oregano-Tomato Salad and classic Green Salad

## Almond Coleslaw

½ medium cabbage
2 sticks celery
½ cucumber
½ green pepper
¼ cup toasted flaked almonds
1 large onion
⅔ cup mayonnaise
1 tablespoon vinegar
salt, pepper

Wash cabbage; discard outer leaves and hard central stalk. Shred finely. Chop celery, slice cucumber; thinly slice pepper, finely chop onion. Combine prepared vegetables in bowl.

Mix together mayonnaise and vinegar; season to taste with salt and pepper. Add mayonnaise mixture to vegetables, and mix with two forks until evenly coated. Top salad with almonds.

Serves 4 to 6

## Coleslaw

½ medium cabbage
2 carrots
½ bunch shallots
4 sticks celery
1 red skinned apple

**Dressing**

1 tablespoon lemon juice
¾ cup mayonnaise
½ teaspoon dry mustard
good pinch cayenne
½ teaspoon salt
freshly ground black pepper
3 tablespoons cream

Remove stalk and shred cabbage very finely; grate carrots. Cut celery and shallots, including green parts, into diagonal pieces. Wash, but do not peel apple, core, and cut into dice. Mix together all prepared vegetables and apple and add enough dressing to give even coating. Mix well.

*Dressing:* Place all dressing ingredients in small basin, mix well.

Serves 4 to 6

## Rice Coleslaw

4 cups finely shredded cabbage (about ½ medium cabbage)
¾ cup long grain rice
½ cup chopped red and green peppers
1 cup sliced radishes
1 teaspoon salt
1 medium sized onion
10 oz. can whole kernel corn
½ cup french dressing
½ teaspoon dry mustard
pinch pepper
1 dessertspoon sugar
1 clove garlic, crushed

Cook rice in usual way, drain well. Place cabbage into large bowl. Add rice, red and green peppers, radishes, grated onion and drained corn. Place remaining ingredients into screwtop jar, shake well. Pour over rice and vegetables, toss thoroughly.

Serves 6

## Smoked Oyster Salad

½ lb. long grain rice
¾ cup french dressing
1 teaspoon curry powder
4 sticks celery
2 cans smoked oysters
6 shallots
1 red or green pepper

Cook rice in usual way, drain well. Combine french dressing and curry powder in small jar, shake well.

Arrange rice in serving dish, pour dressing over; fork dressing lightly through rice. Cool.

Chop celery, shallots and pepper. Add to rice with the drained smoked oysters, toss lightly.

Serves 4 to 6

## Mushroom Salad

1 lb. very fresh mushrooms
salt
garlic
oil
chopped parsley
juice of ½ lemon
freshly ground pepper
lettuce leaves

Wipe mushrooms, slice finely. Place little salt in bowl, rub bowl with garlic. Add mushrooms, pour over sufficient oil to moisten. Mix lightly, set aside until mushrooms have absorbed most of oil (about 5 minutes).

Sprinkle with lots of chopped parsley, add lemon juice and pepper. Taste mixture, add a little more salt, pepper, lemon juice if needed. Serve on lettuce.

Serves 4

## Warm Zucchini Salad

6 zucchini
2 oz. butter
4 sticks celery
¼ cup french dressing

Slice unpeeled zucchini thinly, chop celery. Heat butter, add vegetables, and saute 2 minutes. Add french dressing, mix well; serve warm.

Serves 4

## Egg and Bacon Salad

1 lettuce
¼ lb. bacon
¼ cup chopped shallots
½ cup sliced celery
2 tomatoes
4 quartered hard boiled eggs
⅓ cup french dressing
1 clove garlic, crushed

Cook bacon until crisp, crumble into pieces. Tear lettuce into bite-sized pieces, place in salad bowl. Add half the crumbled bacon, with shallots and celery. Add garlic to french dressing, shake well, pour over salad. Toss. Garnish with tomatoes and eggs cut into wedges. Top with remaining bacon.

Serves 4

# Salad Dressings

A simple salad can become something really special when you add a well-flavoured dressing

## Mayonnaise

2 egg-yolks
½ teaspoon salt
½ teaspoon dry mustard
1½ teaspoons vinegar
1 cup olive or salad oil
½ teaspoon lemon juice

Rinse bowl with hot water; dry well. Put in egg-yolks, salt, mustard and 1 teaspoon vinegar. Beat vigorously with beater or at low speed with electric mixer; add oil, drop by drop, until a little more than ¼ cup of oil has been added. Add ½ teaspoon vinegar, still beating, then very slowly pour in remainder of oil in thin stream, beating continually. When all oil has been added, add lemon juice.

## Cooked Mayonnaise

2 tablespoons vinegar
2 tablespoons water
2 tablespoons sugar
½ oz. butter
½ teaspoon salt
½ to 1 teaspoon dry mustard
1 beaten egg

Combine all ingredients in saucepan, stir over low heat until butter melts and mixture thickens slightly. Remove from heat, cool.

## French Dressing

3 parts olive or salad oil
1 part white vinegar
½ teaspoon salt
½ teaspoon freshly ground pepper

Place all ingredients in screw-top jar, shake thoroughly before pouring over salad.

NOTE: Crushed garlic, dry or prepared mustard or chopped herbs can be added, if desired. The garlic, salt, pepper, and mustard are first mixed with the oil, then the vinegar is added. Herbs are added last.

The above are the classic proportions for french dressing. In other words, if you wanted to make 1 cup of dressing, you would use ⅔ cup of oil, ⅓ cup vinegar, plus seasonings. However, equal parts of oil and vinegar can be used, if you like a less oily dressing.

## Russian Dressing (1)

1 cup mayonnaise
1½ tablespoons chilli sauce
1 to 2 teaspoons chopped chives

Blend chilli sauce and chives into mayonnaise; a little chopped red pepper or canned pimento can also be added. Use with egg or vegetable salads or with fish.

NOTE: Strength of chilli sauce varies greatly. With a mild, American chilli sauce, the above quantity is correct. If using a hot chilli sauce, add only ½ teaspoon at first; then taste, and add a little more if desired.

## Russian Dressing (2)

1 cup mayonnaise
¼ cup finely chopped cooked beetroot
1 to 2 teaspoons bottled horseradish sauce

Combine mayonnaise and beetroot, blend in bottled horseradish sauce or relish.

## Thousand Island Dressing

1 cup mayonnaise
1 tablespoon chilli sauce
1 tablespoon finely chopped green olives
1 dessertspoon finely chopped chives

Combine all ingredients, mix well. Good with meat or fish salads. See Russian Dressing for note on chilli sauce.

## Aioli

2 egg-yolks
2 cloves garlic
1 cup oil
3 teaspoons lemon juice
salt, pepper

Beat egg-yolks in bowl with crushed garlic. Add oil, drop by drop. When half the oil has been used, add half the lemon juice, then beat in remaining oil, drop by drop. Season with salt and pepper and add remaining lemon juice.

## Green Goddess Dressing

1 clove garlic
½ cup parsley
2 tablespoons chopped chives
1 cup mayonnaise
2 tablespoons cream
3 dessertspoons tarragon vinegar
1 dessertspoon anchovy paste

Crush garlic; finely chop parsley. Combine all ingredients and stir until dressing is smooth. Serve with seafood salads.

# INTERNATIONAL COOKERY

Each year, as a nation, our food tastes are changing, becoming enriched by the national cuisine of migrants from other countries who have now settled in Australia.

Restaurants of many nationalities flourish; we've found that Chinese, Italian, Indian dishes—as well as the food of many other countries—each have their own subtle blending of flavours.

Because Australian housewives are always interested in new ways with foods, new, delicious tastes, dinner parties with an international flavour have become popular.

Here we present some of the interesting recipes of other countries; the food of each country can be presented as a complete menu. Quantities given will serve 4 to 6. The Hawaiian menu is suggested as an outdoor party; a wider range of dishes is given and quantities will serve 8

## Germany

German cooking varies from district to district and, as with Switzerland, the cooking in the various sections is influenced by the other countries on the borders. Recipes given here are representative of Bavaria, Southern Germany.

German food is hearty, and not highly spiced. Black and rye breads are popular; potato and cabbage are part of every-day meals. Beer, wine and Schnapps are the popular drinks. Kirsch and Kummel are famous German liqueurs

### Roast Pork

1 leg or loin of pork
salt, pepper
1 large onion
1 large carrot
approx. 1 pint boiling water

Wipe meat with clean cloth, score skin into small squares with sharp knife (or have butcher do this for you). Sprinkle over plenty of salt and pepper. Place meat skin-side down in large, greased baking dish. Add peeled and sliced onion and carrot, carefully pour over boiling water. Bake in hot oven until meat is tender (allow approximately 30 to 35 minutes per lb.). You may need to add more boiling water during cooking. Halfway through cooking time turn meat so that skin is uppermost.

Serve with potato balls and sauerkraut.

### Potato Balls

1 lb. potatoes
2 cups plain flour
1 teaspoon salt
1 large or two small eggs

Steam potatoes in their jackets over boiling water until cooked. Cool, refrigerate overnight. Next day, peel and mash well.

Sift together flour and salt, add alternately to potato with lightly beaten egg. Knead well. Mixture should not be sticky. Roll mixture into small balls, and drop gently into large saucepan of boiling salted water. Boil steadily, uncovered, 15 minutes. Drain, serve immediately.

### Sauerkraut

2 15 oz. cans sauerkraut
2 tablespoons oil
6 oz. fat pork in one piece
1 medium onion
½ teaspoon whole peppercorns
1 dessertspoon flour
1 pint water
1 large potato

Drain sauerkraut, wash lightly under cold running water. Heat oil in large saucepan, add pork, cook few minutes on both sides. Add chopped onion; cook, covered, over low heat until soft but not brown. Lightly mix in sauerkraut, peppercorns, and flour; add 1 pint water. Bring to boil; cover, cook ☛

Flamed Caramel Pineapple — delightfully informal dessert; guests cook their own. It's a perfect dessert for a summer barbecue

for 30 minutes, stirring occasionally. Peel potato, grate finely, stir into mixture. Continue cooking, stirring occasionally, further 30 minutes, adding little more water if necessary. Remove pork; discard.

Serve sauerkraut hot or cold.

NOTE: To keep sauerkraut a good colour, place a sheet of plain white paper on top of mixture, under lid, during boiling.

## Apple Strudel

**Pastry**

2 cups plain flour
½ teaspoon salt
2 oz. butter
approx. ¼ pint warm water

Sift flour and salt into bowl, rub in softened butter. Add little warm water gradually, kneading to soft dough. Turn out on lightly floured surface, continue kneading and adding water until mixture is smooth and shiny. This should take about 15 minutes. Hit dough a few times with a heavy wooden spoon during kneading. Form dough into a ball, place in warmed bowl or saucepan. Cover and stand in warm place 1 hour.

**Filling**

4 or 5 green apples
4 tablespoons sugar
finely grated rind 1 small lemon
2 teaspoons cinnamon
⅓ cup sultanas
extra sugar
extra cinnamon
½ pint sour cream
melted butter
icing sugar

*Filling*: Peel, core, and slice apples very thinly, stir in sugar, lemon rind, and cinnamon, mix well. Place sultanas in small bowl, add enough hot water to cover, set aside.

Divide pastry into thirds; roll each piece out very thinly on floured surface. Spread ⅓ apple mixture in centre of dough, sprinkle over a little extra sugar and cinnamon. Drain sultanas, pat dry; sprinkle a few over apples. Lightly spread ⅓ of sour cream over mixture. Roll up pastry into a long shape and seal edges.

Prepare remaining two rolls in the same way. Grease a deep 8 in. round tin. Place rolls side by side in tin, curving them carefully to fit. Bake in moderately slow oven approximately 1¾ hours. Brush a little melted butter over strudel several times during cooking.

When golden brown and crisp, remove from oven, glaze again with melted butter. Leave in tin 15 minutes before turning out on to serving plate. Sift over a little icing sugar. Serve warm with whipped cream.

# Hawaii

Hawaiian food is very similar to that of other islands of the South Pacific. All types of fish are easily available; pork is popular—particularly for a luau, or feast, when it is cooked in a pit, under the ground. Bananas, baked, are eaten as a vegetable, in addition to sweet potatoes or yams

## Tropical Dip

¾ cup mayonnaise
½ cup cream
1 tablespoon bottled horseradish relish
1½ teaspoons dry mustard
lemon juice
salt, pepper

Combine whipped cream, mayonnaise, horseradish relish and dry mustard; blend well. Season to taste with lemon juice, salt and pepper. Refrigerate. Place into serving bowl. Place all kinds of interesting titbits in sauce, such as shelled prawns, oysters, ripe olives, water chestnuts, raw vegetables, etc. Each guest arms himself with a cocktail stick and 'fishes' in the sauce.

Makes approx. 1½ cups

## Avocado Chicken Salad

3 avocados
juice 1 lemon
3 to 4 lb. steamed chicken
4 sticks celery
1 cucumber
¼ pint cream
2 tablespoons mayonnaise
¼ cup blanched slivered almonds
½ green pepper
1 teaspoon paprika
½ teaspoon nutmeg
1 teaspoon salt
½ teaspoon pepper

Peel, seed and slice avocados. Remove chicken meat from bones. Cut meat into 1 in. cubes. Slice cucumber, celery and green pepper and layer in dish or bowl with toasted almonds, chicken and half the avocado slices.

Blend paprika, nutmeg, salt and pepper with cream, mayonnaise and lemon juice; pour over chicken and vegetables. Decorate with remaining avocado slices, sprinkle with extra paprika.

NOTE: If preparing this dish in advance, dip avocado slices in lemon juice so they will keep their fresh colour.

## Baked Honeyed Pork

1 leg pork
2 tablespoons oil
2 teaspoons ground ginger
2 teaspoons salt
¼ cup honey
2 tablespoons grated green ginger

Get the butcher to score the pork thoroughly. Run knife between the skin and meat to form a pocket. Using long-bladed knife, spread grated green ginger into pocket. In basin mix oil, ground ginger and salt. Place pork in baking dish, brush leg with oil and ginger mixture. Bake in moderate oven, allowing 30 minutes per lb.; brush occasionally with remaining oil and ginger mixture. Fifteen minutes before the end of cooking time, brush leg completely with honey. Serve hot or cold.

## Hawaiian Chicken

4 lb. chicken pieces
¼ cup soy sauce
½ cup white wine
juice 1 lemon
1 clove garlic
½ teaspoon curry powder
½ teaspoon ground ginger
¼ teaspoon pepper
4 oz. butter
2 onions
seasoned flour
¾ lb. rice
3C oz. can pineapple slices
1 oz. butter, extra
½ cup toasted slivered almonds
1 red pepper

Mix together soy sauce, $\frac{1}{4}$ cup white wine, lemon juice, crushed garlic, curry powder, ginger and pepper. Pour over chicken, marinate several hours, turning occasionally. Melt butter in frying pan, add sliced onions, cook until golden brown, remove onions. Dry chicken, coat with seasoned flour. Cook in frying pan until brown. Add onions and marinade, cover, and simmer gently 45 minutes or until tender, uncovering pan for the last 15 minutes.

Meanwhile, cook and drain rice and keep hot. Cut pineapple slices in half and brown in extra butter, also fry chopped pepper until tender.

To serve, mix rice, toasted almonds, and pepper. Heap on large serving platter, arrange chicken pieces and pineapple slices round edge. Add remaining $\frac{1}{4}$ cup wh'te wine to pan drippings, heat well, and pour over.

## Flamed Caramel Pineapple

Take a ripe pineapple, cut into 4 pieces, cutting carefully through the green top. With sharp knife, slice off the hard core. Cut pineapple down into wedges, then run a knife along base of wedges, releasing them from the shell.

(If the pineapples are not too large, allow one pineapple for 4 persons.)

Take another pineapple, cut off top about quarter-way down. Hollow out inside of pineapple to take a small metal bowl. (The hollowed-out pineapple pieces can be reserved and used to replenish the pineapple quarters as they empty.)

Place metal bowl in position. Place hollowed-out pineapple in centre of heat-proof dish (a large wooden plate is good), arrange pineapple quarters decoratively around.

Arrange small bowls of rum or brandy, brown sugar, and whipped cream round dish. Have a small fork and plate for each guest.

When ready to serve the dessert, three-quarters fill metal bowl with methylated spirit and set aflame.

Guests use fork to spear a juicy piece of pineapple, dip it in the rum, roll it in brown sugar, then hold it over the flame until the sugar caramelises—it will take about a second. Then dip in the whipped cream—and eat!

Strawberries are delicious served this way, too, but have more flavour if allowed to stand in rum 10 to 15 minutes. Serve small bowls of rum-soaked strawberries round the pineapple.

NOTE: When lit, methylated spirit will burn for some time. If necessary to use more spirit, put it in another perfectly clean bowl; do not add more spirit to that already burning; do not pour fresh spirit into a hot bowl.

## Papaw Ice-Cream

1 small ripe papaw
½ cup orange juice
3 tablespoons lemon juice
½ pint cream
½ cup sugar

Peel papaw, remove seeds, chop coarsely; blend in blender or push through sieve to make a fine puree. Measure $1\frac{1}{2}$ cups of puree, mix in fruit juices. Combine cream and sugar, refrigerate 15 to 30 minutes, stirring occasionally to dissolve sugar. Gradually stir in fruit mixture. Pour into 2 freezer trays. Freeze until firm.

## China

The Oriental, it is said, 'eats with his tongue'—flavour is all-important. And Chinese food, with its subtle, well-balanced blending of flavours, has become Australia's most popular foreign food when eating out or at home.

---

There are five main schools of Chinese cooking, named after the areas in which they originated. They are:

**Canton** Has succulent pork, chicken, and duck dishes, delicious soups. Quick-frying is the favourite method of cooking; fried rice and crisp noodles are popular. Cantonese dishes, served with a variety of sauces, are delicately flavoured, not highly seasoned. Because the majority of Chinese restaurants outside China are owned or operated by Southern Chinese, Cantonese food has become better known throughout the world than the other styles of Chinese cooking.

**Fukien** Sucking pig is a favourite dish; soups of many varieties are served between courses. Popular Spring Roll is from this school.

**Szechuen** Also famous for soups. Foods, generally, are hot and highly spiced.

**Shanghai** Concentrates on steamed, rather than fried foods. More highly spiced than Cantonese, but less than Szechuenese.

**Peking** Peking-Duck is a world-renowned dish; so is Bird's-Nest Soup. Food is well spiced, of great variety.

### Crab and Sweet Corn Soup

¼ clove garlic
1 thin slice green ginger
8 oz. can crab meat
1 dessertspoon dry sherry
1 small can cream-style sweet corn
1 dessertspoon oil
3 cups chicken stock
1 egg-white
1 tablespoon cornflour
salt, pepper

Heat oil in large heavy saucepan, add crushed garlic, finely chopped ginger, and crab meat which has been drained and shredded. Fry quickly 1 minute, stirring constantly. Add sherry, corn and stock. Bring to boil, reduce heat and simmer 5 minutes. Whisk egg-white lightly, stir into soup with fork. Mix cornflour with a little cold water; add to soup, stirring constantly until mixture thickens. Add salt and pepper to taste. Mix well, serve immediately.

### Prawn Omelets

8 eggs
1 lb. prawns
6 shallots
2 sticks celery
2 oz. mushrooms
10 oz. can bean sprouts
salt, pepper
oil

**Sauce**

1 cup chicken stock
1 teaspoon sugar
1 tablespoon soy sauce
1 dessertspoon cornflour
¼ cup cold water
salt

Chop mushrooms, cook in a little hot oil until tender; drain, set aside. Chop shallots and celery finely; chop shelled prawns, if large. Beat eggs lightly, as for omelet. Add prawns, shallots, celery, mushrooms, and drained bean sprouts. Add seasonings and mix lightly. Heat a little oil in fry-pan, pour in enough omelet mixture to make small omelets about 5 in. in diameter. (Several can cook at the same time.) When firm on one side, turn, cook other side. Stack on warm plate while cooking remainder of omelets; keep warm. To serve, stack 3 omelets on top of each other; for each serving spoon sauce over.

*Sauce*: Blend cornflour with cold water. Place remaining ingredients in small saucepan, bring to boil. Stir in blended cornflour. Cook, stirring, until sauce boils and thickens.

### Chicken and Almonds

4 chicken breasts
1½ teaspoons salt
1 tablespoon cornflour
1 egg-white
1½ tablespoons sherry
1½ cups oil
4 oz. green beans
2 sticks celery
½ red pepper
4 oz. mushrooms
½ 10 oz. can water chestnuts
2 tablespoons chopped shallots
¼ cup toasted almonds

**Sauce**

½ pint water
1 tablespoon soy sauce
1 tablespoon cornflour
1 chicken stock cube

Bone chicken breasts, cut meat into ½ in. cubes. Combine chicken pieces, salt, cornflour, egg-white and sherry in bowl. Heat oil in frypan. Deep-fry

Cheeseboard has pride of place on a Smorgasbord. Offer a variety of cheeses. Shown here are, from back, Cheddar, Danish Tilsit, Edam, Blue Cheese

chicken until just changing colour; drain. String beans (or use quick-frozen beans). Cut beans, celery and pepper into 1 in. strips; par-boil 5 minutes. Slice mushrooms. Drain water chestnuts, cut in half. Pour off excess liquid from pan and leave enough to saute all vegetables together. Add prepared vegetables, and return chicken to pan. Season to taste, heat through thoroughly. Pour sauce over chicken mixture. Arrange on warm serving dish, sprinkle with toasted almonds.

*Sauce*: Combine water, crumbled chicken stock cube, soy sauce and cornflour in saucepan; blend well. Stir over low heat until sauce boils and thickens, simmer 2 minutes.

## Almond Junket

1½ dessertspoons gelatine
¾ cup cold water
1¼ cups evaporated milk
½ cup sugar
¾ cup boiling water
few drops almond essence

Soften gelatine in cold water, add sugar. Pour boiling water over and stir until sugar and gelatine have dissolved. Add milk and almond essence, stir well. Pour mixture into four individual serving dishes, set aside until cool, then refrigerate until firm. Top with sliced preserved ginger, with a little of the ginger syrup poured over.

## Scandinavia

The smorgasbord—or 'cold table'—is part of the hospitality of all Scandinavian countries. Norway, Denmark, Sweden, all have their own individual versions—but, basically, the cold table of each country offers a selection of hot and cold dishes, as set out below.

Scandinavian cooking is simple. Fish of all types is widely used; potatoes, beetroot, cucumber are favourite vegetables; dill is used often for seasoning

## Smorgasbord

The Smorgasbord is said to have originated long ago at Swedish country parties, to which each housewife brought the specialty of her own kitchen. All these dishes were arranged on a long table round which the guests walked, filling their plates several times.

A Smorgasbord can be as comprehensive and varied as desired, with rich and inviting delicacies; or it can be a simple, well-chosen and well-prepared selection, comprising only a few dishes.

There is a definite rule in the procedure of dishes. Fish dishes begin the meal; favourites are pickled herrings, anchovies, herring salad—with them might be served potatoes flavoured with dill. A hot, baked fish dish might also be offered.

Then come the meats; meatballs—very important to a Smorgasbord—smoked sausages, ham, roasted pork with apple sauce and prunes. And so it goes on . . . ending with cheese.

A typical Smorgasbord might comprise a wide variety of fish dishes such as herrings, sardines, anchovies; small meat-balls, sliced ham, pate and other meats; lobster or potato salad, cucumber, radishes, pickled beetroot, mushrooms; egg dishes, tiny omelets with assorted fillings; plain boiled potatoes, cheese, and assorted breads and crisp-breads with butter.

A simple Smorgasbord can be prepared by choosing a selection from any of these dishes.

A whole ham, sliced, or a sliced canned ham; herrings (from the delicatessen) with pickled onion and chopped gherkin; potato salad; smoked oysters; canned salmon with white onion rings, chopped shallots, and a light vinegar dressing; smoked tuna; slices of cold roast beef, pork, lamb, or seasoned veal; sliced pickled beetroot; salami or other Continental sausage; canned sardines; condiments, such as chutney, etc; smoked salmon with scrambled eggs; cheese board.

## Lamb in Cabbage

3 lb. leg of lamb
½ large cabbage
2 medium carrots
1 oz. butter
2 teaspoons peppercorns
½ cup flour
salt
1½ pints water or stock
1 tablespoon finely chopped parsley

Trim meat, cut into large cubes; do not remove

bones, these add extra flavour to the stock. Remove coarse outer leaves from cabbage. Cut cabbage into thick segments, removing centre core. Melt butter in large saucepan. Place alternate layers of meat and cabbage in pan, starting with meat and finishing with cabbage. Sprinkle flour, salt and peppercorns between each layer. Place peeled, sliced carrots on top. Pour water or stock down side of saucepan. Bring to boil, cover, reduce heat and simmer $1\frac{1}{2}$ to 2 hours or until meat is tender. Shake pan occasionally; do not stir during cooking to avoid disturbing the arranged layers. Season to taste; sprinkle with chopped parsley. Serve with boiled potatoes.

NOTE: Peppercorns can be tied in muslin bag for easy removal after cooking.

## Strawberry Mousse

1 punnet strawberries
1 dessertspoon water
1 teaspoon gelatine
2 egg-whites
½ cup castor sugar
1½ cups cream
1 tablespoon lemon juice

Wash and hull strawberries, mash well, (1 punnet should give approximately $1\frac{1}{4}$ cups pulp). Add gelatine to water, stand 5 minutes, dissolve over hot water. Beat egg-whites until soft peaks form, gradually add sugar, beating until dissolved. Whip cream until soft peaks form; fold into egg-white mixture. Add strawberries, lemon juice and gelatine, fold in lightly. Pour into wetted mould, or into individual serving dishes. Refrigerate until set.

---

# Italy

Like most European countries, Italy draws heavily on the natural products of her provinces—the luscious fruits and olives, the wonderful seafood which abounds in the waters bordering her shores.

Antipasto—the equivalent of the French hors d'oeuvre—is a pleasant start to any meal and, with a bowl of soup to follow, can be a complete meal in itself. Pasta is used in many forms.

Italian wines are very cheap in their own country, and very pleasant; the Chianti is world-famous. Wine is drunk with all main meals, and the meals are usually preceded by a glass of sweet or dry vermouth or Campari, the latter, a deep red and tangy bitters, and one of the most famous Italian aperitifs

---

## Antipasto

8 oz. can tuna
mayonnaise
1 tablespoon capers
thinly sliced celery
sliced peeled tomatoes
sliced salami
thinly sliced ham
black and green olives
anchovy fillets
quarters of hard boiled eggs
canned artichoke hearts

Arrange drained tuna (in one piece) in centre of large, round platter. Coat with mayonnaise, sprinkle with capers. Arrange remaining ingredients in decorative pattern round tuna.

## Cannelloni

**Batter**

1 cup plain flour
pinch salt
1 egg
½ pint milk

**Filling**

1 lb. minced steak
1 onion
1 clove garlic
pinch mixed herbs
salt, pepper
½ cup red wine
1 dessertspoon tomato paste
1 tablespoon flour
1 teaspoon paprika
oil for frying

**Bechamel Sauce**

½ oz. butter
1 tablespoon flour
½ pint milk
1 bayleaf
1 slice onion
4 peppercorns
parsley stalks
sprig thyme or parsley
salt, pepper

**Tomato Sauce**

1 dessertspoon oil
1 onion
1 clove garlic
2 large ripe tomatoes
2 tablespoons tomato paste
salt, pepper
bayleaf

*Batter*: Sift flour and salt into bowl. Make well in centre, add egg. Mix with wooden spoon, blending in a little of the flour from the side. When mixture begins to thicken, gradually begin to add the milk, blending thoroughly. Heat a little oil in small frying pan. Pour in enough batter to cover base. Tilt pan until batter spreads. Keep pancake as thin as possible. When cooked on one side, turn and cook the other side. Remove from pan, cook the next pancake, stacking them as you cook.

*Filling*: Put a little oil in saucepan; when hot gently saute chopped onion and crushed garlic. When tender add the meat, cook until brown, stirring occasionally with fork. Add the flour blended with the wine, stir well. Add remaining ingredients, simmer gently ½ to ¾ hour until liquid is absorbed.

Divide mixture between pancakes, roll up. Arrange in casserole.

*Bechamel Sauce*: Place bayleaf, parsley stalks, onion slice, peppercorns and thyme in saucepan, add milk. Bring slowly to boiling point, remove from heat, stand 5 minutes. Melt butter in saucepan, remove from heat, add flour, stir until smooth, gradually add strained milk, stirring constantly. Return to heat, stir until sauce boils and thickens. Season to taste with salt and pepper. Pour over pancakes.

*Tomato Sauce*: Heat oil, fry chopped onion and crushed garlic until tender but not brown. Add skinned, chopped tomatoes, tomato paste, salt, pepper and bayleaf. Simmer gently 20 minutes. Spoon carefully over the white sauce.

If desired, sprinkle with a little grated cheese. Bake pancakes in hot oven 10 to 15 minutes.

## Zabaglione

5 egg-yolks
¼ cup sugar
½ cup marsala

Beat egg yolks and sugar in top of double boiler. Add the marsala, and cook, beating constantly, until thick and foamy, approximately 10 minutes. Serve warm. Sponge fingers are a good accompaniment.

## India

Through the centuries, Arabia, Persia, Central Asia and Mongolia have all contributed toward the unique cuisine of India. The success of Indian cookery rests on the subtle use of a variety of spices. The art of curry-making lies not in hot spicing but in the delicacy of flavour blending.

In such a vast country, with varying climatic and agricultural conditions, it is natural to expect a great variation in curries, also. In the north, curries are mild—like those of Pakistan. The farther south you travel, the hotter the curries become. In Madras, chillies grow abundantly and are used generously; Madras curries, therefore, are much hotter than those of the north.

Rice is the traditional accompaniment to curry. A choice of side dishes or sambals can also be served; choose from coconut, plumped raisins, crumbled bacon, chopped hard-boiled eggs, cucumber in yoghurt, wedges of lemon, bananas dipped in lemon juice, chopped dried apricots, peanuts

## Beef Vindaloo

2 lb. topside or round steak
2 large onions
3 cloves garlic
2 red chillies or ¼ teaspoon cayenne pepper
1 teaspoon turmeric
2 tablespoons curry powder
1 teaspoon ground ginger
¼ teaspoon dry mustard
3 cardamom seeds (crushed)
1 tablespoon vinegar
1 teaspoon chopped mint
salt
1 dessertspoon butter
hot water

Place 1 chopped onion, 1 crushed clove garlic, 1 finely chopped chilli, ginger, 1 tablespoon curry powder, vinegar and salt into a bowl. Mix well together. Cut beef into 1 in. cubes, add to mixture in bowl. Mix thoroughly and allow to stand at least 3 hours.

Melt butter in frying pan and fry the remaining chopped onion, crushed garlic and chopped chilli until light brown. Add turmeric, remaining curry powder, mustard, cardamom, and meat mixture. Cook 5 minutes, reduce heat to simmer, add sufficient hot water just to cover the meat; add salt to taste. Cook gently, covered, until meat is tender, approximately 1 hour 20 minutes; add a little extra water, if necessary, during cooking time. Lastly add mint. Serve with hot rice.

Canneloni — pancakes filled with a savoury mixture, topped with sauces, baked until piping hot

## Chicken Tandoori

1 chicken
2 oz. butter

**Marinade**

1 cup yoghurt
1 teaspoon ground ginger
1 clove garlic
1 teaspoon garam masala
1 teaspoon salt

Crush garlic and mix into the yoghurt with spices and salt. Joint chicken and marinate in yoghurt mixture for 6 hours or overnight. Melt butter in baking dish, add chicken pieces. Bake uncovered in moderate oven 45 minutes to 1 hour, basting frequently.

Serve with chopped onion and lemon wedges.

## Fruit Taj

2 large oranges
2 large bananas
lemon juice
1 tablespoon slivered dates
1 egg-yolk
½ cup softened vanilla ice-cream
½ cup whipped cream
½ to 1 tablespoon rum

Peel and section oranges; arrange sections in serving bowls or glasses. Peel and slice bananas and place over oranges, sprinkle with lemon juice. Stir together softened ice-cream, beaten egg-yolk, whipped cream, and rum; spoon over fruit, garnish with dates.

---

## Indonesia

Spices are an integral part of Indonesian cookery, for these are the Spice Islands of history. Many countries have had an effect on the history of Indonesia—India, China, Arabia, Portugal, Holland; the influence of these countries is reflected in Indonesian recipes.

Sambal Oelek, mentioned in some of the recipes on this page, is obtainable in jars from most large food stores; it is made up of finely minced red chillies, seasoned with salt. If unobtainable, use same amount of finely crushed chillies; season well with salt.

See page 92 for Nasi Goreng—Indonesia's famous version of Fried Rice.

---

## Sate Kambing

Cut $1\frac{1}{2}$ lb. lean lamb into $\frac{3}{4}$ in. cubes, thread on to thin bamboo skewers. Place 4 or 6 cubes on each skewer. There should be enough meat cubes for about 15 skewers. Grill until meat is done, turning several times. Serve hot with either of these Sate sauces.

**Soy Sauce**

4 tablespoons soy sauce
3 shallots
1 teaspoon sambal oelek
2 tablespoons lemon juice

Slice shallots thinly crosswise; combine with remaining ingredients in oblong dish. This shape makes it easy to dip the sate sticks.

**Peanut Sauce**

¼ cup peanut butter
1 cup water
½ teaspoon sugar
1 tablespoon lemon juice
1 small onion
2 cloves garlic
1 tablespoon butter
1 teaspoon sambal oelek
1½ tablespoons soy sauce

Thinly slice onion. Saute onion and garlic in butter until transparent, add sambal oelek. Reduce heat, stir well. Add water, then peanut butter, bring slowly to boil. Continue stirring until mixture becomes smooth. Season with soy sauce, sugar and lemon. Taste; add a little salt if necessary.

## Serundeng

½ lb. desiccated coconut
1 teaspoon sugar
2 teaspoons coriander
1 medium onion
2 cloves garlic
1 bayleaf
¼ cup hot water
1 beef stock cube
salt, pepper
1 cup oil
½ lb. raw peanuts

Wash and dry peanuts, deep-fry in hot oil until crisp. Dissolve beef stock cube in hot water, pour over coconut, season with sugar. Add grated onion, grated garlic, coriander and bayleaf, all of which have been sauteed in little hot butter. Add salt and pepper to taste. Mix thoroughly by hand so all spices blend with the coconut.

Put into small baking dish or ovenproof dish,

pour over the oil. Cook in moderately slow oven, 30 minutes, stirring occasionally to keep from burning. Reduce heat to low, cook until coconut is golden brown. Remove from oven, stir in peanuts. Put in colander to drain and cool.

NOTE: Serundeng will keep in airtight jar about 2 weeks. It is very tasty if sprinkled on individual helpings of vegetables.

## Gado-Gado

3 medium potatoes
½ lb. green beans
3 to 4 hard-boiled eggs
2 to 3 carrots
¼ cabbage
2 medium tomatoes
1 tablespoon crisp fried onion flakes
1 lettuce

Boil potatoes in their jackets; skin and dice. Cut beans into thin, diagonal slices; boil and drain. Scrape carrots, cut into matchstick-sized strips; boil and drain. Shred cabbage very finely. Put into boiling water, bring to boil again (don't overcook); drain. Arrange vegetables on a platter as follows:

First, the washed, well-crisped lettuce, then potatoes, cabbage, beans, carrots, sliced or quartered tomatoes, sliced or quartered eggs. This gives a nice contrast of colours.

Pour over the Peanut Sauce just before serving; sprinkle with onion flakes, see Goreng Bawang.

This goes very well with a grill, or serve it as a barbecue salad. For a quick, tasty salad, pour the sauce over hard-boiled eggs, lettuce and tomatoes.

### Peanut Sauce

1 medium onion
2 teaspoons sambal oelek
½ cup peanut butter
2 cups water
1 teaspoon sugar
1 tablespoon white vinegar
1 oz. butter
1 teaspoon salt, or to taste

Saute chopped onion in butter until transparent. Add sambal oelek, reduce heat; cook few minutes, stirring constantly. Add water, then peanut butter. Bring to boil on medium heat. Continue stirring until mixture becomes smooth. Season to taste with salt, vinegar and sugar.

This sauce is nice to serve hot in winter and at room temperature in summer.

## Goreng Bawang

These fried onion flakes are widely used as a garnish for Indonesian dishes. They also give an interesting flavour when sprinkled over European-style soups just before serving; nice with chicken, beef, or vegetable soups.

Skin, wash, and slice onions; cut them into very thin and even slices. Heat a little oil in frypan, fry the onions, stirring evenly, When partly cooked, reduce heat to very low; turn onions frequently so they become evenly browned without burning. If it seems they might burn, remove from heat before they are fully browned and keep stirring. The heat of the oil should be sufficient to complete the cooking.

When cooked pour onions and oil quickly into strainer over basin. This is to avoid some of the flakes becoming over-brown and ensures the onion flakes will be left crisp and dry.

## Sambal Goreng Udang

2 lb. green prawns
1 onion, chopped
2 teaspoons sambal oelek (or 4 or 5 chillies)
1 firm tomato
2 cups coconut milk
1 lb. green beans
1 bunch shallots
2 cloves garlic, crushed
3 or 4 pieces green ginger, about 1 in. thick
1 to 2 tablespoons butter

Heat butter, stir-fry onion and garlic until they change colour. Add shelled, deveined prawns, stir constantly. When half-cooked, add sambal oelek, ginger, and beans, which have been sliced diagonally, thinly, and evenly. Cook about 3 minutes; add coconut milk. Stir continually to avoid curdling; bring to boil. Add peeled, chopped tomato, shallots cut into 2 in. lengths, including green tops. Stir constantly. When beans are tender, remove from heat.

This dish goes very well with Serundeng.

## Telur Balado

6 hard-boiled eggs
2 tablespoons sambal oelek
1 medium onion
2 tomatoes
1 chicken stock cube
salt to taste
⅓ cup oil

Fry thinly sliced onion in hot oil. When onion changes colour, reduce heat to low. Add sambal oelek, peeled, chopped tomatoes, crumbled chicken cube, salt to taste; simmer 5 minutes, stirring continuously. Add shelled eggs, simmer another 5 minutes. Turn eggs and chilli occasionally. Remove pan from heat.

Cut the eggs neatly in halves with sharp knife, arrange on platter, pour over the chilli sauce.

# BARBECUES

A barbecue is a happy, relaxed way to cook for the family or entertain a crowd, so don't try anything elaborate. Keep the food simple, but have plenty.

A barbecue notebook is very useful to keep a record of recipes, hints and ideas. You'll be surprised how often you'll refer to it during the summer months; and when next year's barbecue time comes round you'll be ready with a file of favourite recipes.

## Barbecued Sausages

2 lb. pork sausages
butter
½ cup chopped celery
2 large onions
¼ cup vinegar
¾ cup tomato sauce
¼ cup water
1 dessertspoon brown sugar
1 dessertspoon prepared mustard
1 teaspoon worcestershire sauce

Cook sausages until well browned, pricking several times. (This can be done in pan over barbecue.) Melt a little butter in saucepan, add celery and chopped onions, saute until tender. Add remaining ingredients, stir well; add sausages. Simmer 10 to 15 minutes.

Serves 4 to 6.

NOTE: To hasten cooking time, put sausages into saucepan of cold water, bring slowly to boil, simmer 5 minutes; drain. This can be done some hours beforehand. Then brown or barbecue, and add to sauce, as above.

## Barbecued Corn

Remove husk and silk from corn. Spread cobs generously with softened butter, season well with salt and pepper. Wrap each cob in double thickness of aluminium foil, twisting or folding ends to make a seal. Place on grill of barbecue over hot coals. Cook, turning often, 15 to 20 minutes, depending on heat of fire. Or cobs can be boiled for 10 minutes, removed from water, and brushed generously with melted butter, then barbecued on grill over hot coals for 10 minutes, brushing occasionally with melted butter.

NOTE: Quick-frozen corn can be used in either of the above ways, too; because it has gone through preliminary processing, cooking time is much shorter. Specific cooking times are given on packet.

## Barbecue Chicken

1 small chicken
oil
salt, pepper

NOTE: This quantity makes 2 servings.

Split chicken in half lengthwise. Break drumstick, wing joints and hip so chicken stays flat during cooking. Brush joints with oil and season well with salt and pepper. Place on grill with bone side nearest fire. When one side is well browned, turn and brown skin side, brushing with oil.

## Salad Kebabs

8 oz. processed cheese
4 oz. grapes or pitted black olives
1 bunch radishes
2 slices pineapple
1 small cucumber
lettuce
french dressing

Cut cheese into 1 in. cubes. Wash grapes and radishes, and cut pineapple into pieces. Wash lettuce and place in plastic container in refrigerator until crisp: tear into neat pieces. Cut thick slices of cucumber in half. Thread pieces of cheese alternately with the other ingredients on to individual skewers with lettuce between. Dip each skewer into dressing before serving or serve dressing separately.

Makes 4 to 6

## Foil Baked Potatoes

potatoes
oil
salt

Scrub potatoes well, dry. Brush generously with oil, sprinkle with salt; wrap in foil. Roast in the coals 35 to 40 minutes. Or place on barbecue grill; allow about 1 hour for cooking, turning frequently. Split open, top with butter or sour cream.

Well-chilled melon slices make a wonderful dessert at the barbecue.

## Seekh Kabab

2 lb. lean minced lamb or beef
1 small onion
2 tablespoons finely chopped spinach
pinch chilli powder
½ teaspoon salt
½ teaspoon cardamom
½ teaspoon cinnamon
½ teaspoon ground cloves

Pound the meat well in a basin and mix it thoroughly with grated onion, spinach, chilli powder and spices. Let stand for 10 minutes. Then lightly grease skewers and form meat firmly around skewers in $3\frac{1}{2}$ in. long kababs. Cook over the barbecue until brown, turning occasionally.

Serves 4 to 6

## Hamburgers

3 lb. minced steak
½ cup chopped parsley
1 tablespoon worcestershire sauce
1 teaspoon allspice
1 small onion, finely chopped
salt, pepper

Blend all ingredients together as lightly as possible. Form into flat cakes. The less handling the uncooked mixture receives, the more tender the hamburgers will be. Grill slowly, allowing 5 to 10 minutes for each side.

Makes approx. 1 dozen large hamburgers

## Red Cabbage Salad

1 small red cabbage
2 red apples
1 cup white vinegar
½ cup sugar
1 clove garlic
2 bayleaves
1 tablespoon salt
12 peppercorns

Place vinegar, sugar, crushed garlic, bayleaves, salt and peppercorns into saucepan, slowly bring to boil, simmer 5 minutes. In bowl, mix together finely shredded cabbage and unpeeled, grated apples, strain over hot liquid; stir, refrigerate. Can be bottled in sterilised jars and kept 1 to 2 weeks in refrigerator.

## Parsley Salad

1 very big bunch parsley
4 shallots
1 lb. tomatoes
leaves from 5 or 6 mint sprigs
1 cucumber
½ lb. bourghol (cracked wheat)
juice 6 large lemons
1 cup oil
pinch chilli powder
salt

Wash parsley, shallots, tomatoes and mint; dry. Chop parsley, shallots (including green tops), and mint very finely. Peel and chop tomatoes and cucumber very finely. Combine prepared vegetables, bourghol, lemon juice, oil, chilli powder and salt in bowl; mix well.

Serve garnished with slices of lemon, cucumber and tomato. A bowl of crisp lettuce leaves is the correct accompaniment to this salad. Some of the salad is spooned into the centre of lettuce leaf, which is rolled round filling and eaten in this way. The crispness of the lettuce makes a good contrast with the flavour of this wonderful salad.

NOTE: Cracked wheat is available at some health-food shops, or at Continental food stores or delicatessens.

## Barbecued Fish

1 small whole fish per person
salt, pepper
butter
lemon juice

Mullet, barbecued this way, is delicious. Clean and scale fish; if using mullet, make sure all black lining of fish is removed. Sprinkle inside of fish with salt and pepper and squeeze of lemon juice. Arrange each fish on square of well-greased aluminium foil, sprinkle top of fish with salt and pepper, add small knob of butter. Wrap fish neatly and securely in foil. Place on barbecue; cook, turning occasionally, approximately 20 minutes.

Serve in the foil. Serve with chopped parsley and lemon wedges.

## Barbecue Sauce

1 onion
1 tablespoon oil
½ cup tomato purée
¾ cup water
2 tablespoons vinegar
1 tablespoon worcestershire sauce
1 teaspoon salt
1 teaspoon paprika
¼ teaspoon black pepper
1 teaspoon curry powder
1 tablespoon brown sugar

Heat oil in saucepan, add finely chopped onion, and cook until brown. Add remaining ingredients and simmer, stirring for 5 minutes. Strain through fine strainer. Serve with chops, steaks or sausages.

Makes approx. $1\frac{1}{2}$ cups

## Garlic Bread

1 long loaf crusty french bread
4 oz. butter
2 cloves garlic
salt, pepper

Slice loaf, cutting just to bottom crust but not right through. Melt butter and add salt, pepper and crushed garlic. Fan slices of bread apart, and pour a little garlic butter between each slice. Brush top with any remaining butter. Wrap in aluminium foil, heat on barbecue.

Or salt, pepper and garlic can be blended into softened butter and spread on the cut slices. Spread any remaining butter over top of loaf before wrapping in foil.

NOTE: If desired, $\frac{1}{2}$ cup chopped parsley and $\frac{1}{4}$ cup chopped chives, can be added to softened butter and crushed garlic, then spread on both sides of each slice.

## Cabbage Relish

1 small cabbage
3 carrots
4 green peppers
1 lb. white onions
¼ cup salt
2¼ cups sugar
1½ dessertspoons mustard seeds
pinch cayenne pepper
4 cups white vinegar
1½ dessertspoons celery seeds
bayleaves

Wash cabbage and shred finely; slice carrots thinly; chop onion and peppers into small dice. Place all vegetables into large earthenware bowl, sprinkle salt over, mix well. Cover, stand overnight.

Next day drain vegetables well, discard liquid. Pack vegetables firmly into hot, sterilised jars, placing a bayleaf in each jar. Combine all remaining ingredients in saucepan, stir over heat until sugar dissolves. Bring to boil, reduce heat, simmer 5 minutes. Cover vegetables with hot vinegar. Seal when cold.

Makes approx. 6 pints.

Delicious with any hot or cold meats served at the barbecue.

## Barbecued Mushrooms and Bacon

bacon rashers
mushrooms
chicken livers

Wash, trim and dry chicken livers; cut in half. Cut mushrooms in half or leave button mushrooms whole. Cut bacon rashers into three if large, or two pieces if small. Roll half a mushroom and half a chicken liver into each piece of bacon. Thread bacon rolls on to skewers. Place on barbecue until bacon is crisp, turning occasionally.

## Grilled Pineapple

1 large ripe pineapple
melted butter

Cut unpeeled pineapple into 6 or 8 wedges. Remove core from each wedge. Brush generously with melted butter, grill on barbecue until lightly browned. Serve as is, warm, with cream. The skin will come away easily as the slices are eaten.

## Melons

On a hot day, there's nothing nicer to serve for a barbecue dessert than a slice of well-chilled melon. Or, for a more formal type of dessert, melons can be cut into balls or dice and refrigerated. At serving time, spoon into individual glasses or serving dishes, spoon over a little well-chilled sweet white wine.

A ripe watermelon can be made into a basket to hold fresh fruit salad. Choose a medium-sized, ripe watermelon, cut 2 sections from the upper half to leave an arched piece resembling handle of a basket. Carefully cut away melon flesh from under handle and from inside of basket; cut into cubes, drain, removing seeds, then refrigerate. Pile the melon back into the shell, together with any other fresh fruit, cut to similar size. Sprinkle with sugar, a little lemon juice and, if desired, some sweet white wine. Decorate basket with grape or other leaves.

There are many varieties of melon to choose from: watermelon, rockmelon, honeydew, the yellow-skinned Casaba melon and the dark green, almost black-skinned Spanish melon. Both the Casaba and Spanish have pale-green flesh, rather similar to a honeydew.

## Barbecued Bananas

Choose firm ripe bananas. Place on barbecue, cook until skins turn black, turning occasionally. Remove from heat with tongs, peel back top layer of skin. If serving as an accompaniment to savoury dishes, season with salt and pepper; if serving as a dessert, sprinkle with equal amounts of cinnamon and sugar, serve with whipped cream.

A Dictionary of

# HERBS & SPICES

The correct use of herbs, spices and aromatic seeds gives flavour and appetising fragrance to even the most simple foods. The herbs and spices listed here are those most commonly used in cookery; many are easy to grow in the home garden

## Herbs

Fresh herbs from the home garden or dried herbs bought at a food store add new flavour interest to familiar dishes; if substituting dried herbs for fresh in a recipe, use less of the dried variety.

Herbs should enhance, not dominate, the food's natural flavour

*Chives*

### Balm

Balm, or lemon balm as it is frequently called, is not widely used in the kitchen, although it can be added to salads, mushroom dishes, and sweet jellies. The crushed leaves give off a pleasant lemon scent, and a few, added to a teapot with tealeaves, will produce a refreshing drink. Balm is an important ingredient in potpourri, where its tang helps to offset the sweetness of the flower scents.

Variegated balm is another variety of the plant, but is grown more for ornamental than practical purposes.

### Basil

There are more than 40 varieties of this sharp, piquant herb, but the best known are the sweet, bush, and purple basils. Purple basil has deep purple-greenish leaves; its flavour is inferior to the bush and sweet types. Sweet basil is particularly suitable for drying and therefore the easiest to obtain in dried form.

Basil is traditionally teamed with tomatoes, but its flavour also adds interest to pasta dishes, and combines well with rice, liver, kidneys and fish. Try a little in omelets and with scrambled eggs; if available, use the chopped fresh leaves sprinkled on a green salad. Generally, $\frac{1}{4}$ teaspoon of dried basil with eggs, and $\frac{1}{2}$ teaspoon in a meat recipe is quite sufficient.

### Bayleaves

The bay tree is a member of the laurel family. Planted in a pot and clipped to a pleasing shape, this tree can be both attractive and useful. Bayleaves are always an ingredient of bouquet garni; they can also be used by themselves to enhance the flavour of soups, stews, stock, fish, meat and poultry. Whether used fresh or dried, bayleaves are strong, and $\frac{1}{2}$ to 1 leaf is ample in most recipes.

### Bouquet Garni

A bouquet garni, or faggot as it is sometimes called, generally consists of a bayleaf, a sprig of fresh thyme, and several parsley sprigs. These are tied together at the stems with cotton or thin string to make removal easier at the end of cooking time. When dried herbs are used it is best to tie them in a piece of muslin.

Use a bouquet garni to flavour stock, soups, stews, and fish dishes.

### Chervil

Chervil has a serrated and fernlike leaf, with a flavour reminiscent of aniseed. It is difficult to obtain fresh, but fortunately chervil dries most successfully, retaining both its colour and aroma.

Use dried chervil with discretion in soups, stews, sauces, gravies, and with fish and meat. Fresh, the leaves can be chopped and sprinkled fairly liberally on salads and cooked vegetables.

### Chives

Chives are easy to grow. Stemming from a small bulb, this member of the lily family seems to thrive in the garden or in

Parsley, sage
rosemary
& thyme
NUTMEG
CLOVES
PEPPER
GINGER
bouquets

a pot; however, if it is impossible to grow your own, bunches can usually be bought. The onion-like leaves, believed to stimulate the appetite, have a mild onion flavour.

Chopped chives add interest to cream cheese, scrambled egg, and mashed potato. Try them as a garnish for some soups or sprinkled over a green salad.

*Fennel*

## Dill

Dill—a favourite herb in Scandinavian and Russian cooking—has a flavour reminiscent of fennel, but milder. Either chopped, fresh leaves or seeds can be used.

In dill pickles the herb helps to make the cucumber more digestible. Flavours of fish and dill combine well—add a few dill seeds to the poaching liquid. Try the chopped, fresh leaves in salads, dressings, sauces, or with coleslaw. If fresh dill is difficult to obtain, the dried and powdered variety can be used in recipes where the herb is cooked with other ingredients.

## Fennel

Perennial fennel and annual Florence fennel are the two best-known varieties. Seeds of both can be used in cooking, but leaves and stems of Florence fennel have a more pleasant flavour than those of the perennial; leaves, stems, roots, and seeds all have an aniseed taste.

Try the raw stems stuffed with cream cheese and cut into 1in. slices or use to make a delicious salad. Cook the seeds with fish or add to bread and pastries; for a change, use them as a flavouring with apple. Chop the fresh leaves and add to soups and sauces.

*Mint*

## Fenugreek

Fenugreek is grown extensively in India, where the leaves are used for fodder. The seeds, which form in long, thin pods, are sold in ground form and are a component of curry powder. Fenugreek can be used in some pickles and with dried beans; also in soups and casseroles.

## Fines Herbes

The 'fines herbes' are a combination of parsley, chervil, chives, and tarragon. Finely chopped, their most frequent use is in Omelet Fines Herbes, but this combination is also called for in some French recipes for meat, chicken, and fish.

## Garlic

Garlic is the bulb of a plant belonging to the lily family. In appearance it resembles an irregular-shaped white onion. This is composed of several 'cloves' or segments, each one encased in flaky, white skin. Generally a recipe incorporating garlic will specify one clove to be used, but the strength will depend on the age of the root (young garlic is less pungent than an older bulb) and also the method of cooking.

Garlic is used extensively in Spanish, Italian, and French cooking. It can be added to very many savoury dishes, including soups, stews, roasts, poultry, steaks, stuffings, salad dressings and salads, pickles, and chutneys.

Before being added to a dish, the garlic clove is peeled, then chopped or crushed. To peel and crush, bring down the flat side of a knife blade sharply on to the clove—the skin can be lifted off quite easily. Add a little salt to the garlic and mash, again using the flat of a knife. Alternatively, peel garlic and crush in a garlic crusher.

## Marjoram

There are many varieties of marjoram. In addition to oregano (wild marjoram), knotted (or sweet) is the type most widely used in cooking. The plant grows to about 2ft. in height and its grey green leaves have a spicy, mint flavour. This herb is sometimes included in a bouquet garni.

Use marjoram mixed with other herbs in stuffings, but try it by itself with eggs, beef, pork, lamb, mutton, and in soups, sauces, cheese and fish dishes. Available in powdered form.

## Mint

Fresh mint can usually be bought, but it is easy to grow in the home garden; it prefers a sunny position. The most common variety, also best for drying, is spearmint, but there are many others.

Cook several sprigs of fresh mint, or a teaspoon of dried mint, with vegetables, especially peas and new potatoes. Serve some in iced tea and summer fruit drinks. Mint sauce or mint jelly is, of course, the traditional accompaniment to roast mutton or lamb.

## Oregano

Oregano, the wild marjoram of Italy and Spain, is prominent in the cooking of these two countries. Available in powdered form, oregano has a strong, pungent flavour and is one of the ingredients in chilli powder.

This herb gives a piquant flavour to such dishes as pizza and chilli con carne, and combines well with tomatoes. Try a little in scrambled eggs and omelets or with pork, veal, beef, and fish dishes; add a pinch to french dressing.

## Parsley

One of the most widely used and versatile of all herbs, parsley is rich in vitamin C and also contains iron, calcium, and vitamin A.

Unlike other herbs, which should be used with discretion, a liberal amount of chopped parsley can be added to many kinds of dishes. Use fresh or fried sprigs as a garnish; add chopped or dried parsley to soups, stews, mashed potatoes, egg dishes, dumplings, sauces.

## Pot-Herbs

In cooking terminology pot-herbs are plants, such as celery and watercress, which can be used either as vegetables or flavouring agents.

The plants become pot-herbs when grown in small pots.

## Rosemary

The variety of rosemary generally cultivated today grows to about 3 ft. in height and is a straight-branched bush with grey-green, spiny leaves. It is the leaves that are used in cooking—either fresh or dried and crumbled.

Rosemary has a slight pine flavour that is particularly good with lamb, but it can also be combined with chicken, veal, and pork, in soups, sauces, stuffings, or chopped and scattered on salads. Try a little in minestrone or pea soup. Rosemary can often be substituted for thyme in a recipe.

## Sage

There are many varieties of this particularly pungent herb, but the grey-leafed type with purple flowers is the most popular and is available whole, crushed, or ground.

Use as a seasoning for rissoles, meat loaves, cheese, and egg dishes or with fish —and, of course, in sage and onion stuffing. Try rubbing a joint with sage before roasting—but remember its strength, so use sparingly.

## Savory

The two best known types of savory are the annual summer and perennial winter varieties—they are similar in flavour and resemble a mild form of sage. Winter savory makes an attractive hedge to a herb garden.

Traditionally associated with beans, savory can be used also with lamb, pork, and veal, or combined with other herbs in stuffings, omelets, and salads. It is available in dried, powdered form.

*Sage*

## Tarragon

There are two varieties of tarragon—French and Russian—but the French, with its superior flavour, is used most in cooking.

Tarragon is an essential ingredient in bearnaise sauce. Its sharp taste blends well with fish and shellfish; for an interesting result, try a little in a chicken stuffing. Mayonnaise, hollandaise sauce, and french dressing benefit from a pinch of tarragon and, fresh and chopped, it is delicious sprinkled over salads.

## Thyme

Of the many varieties of thyme, lemon-scented and garden thyme are the best known and most often used in the kitchen —both are available in dried-leaf form.

A sprig of thyme is one of the bouquet garni ingredients. Use it also to season meats, soups, stuffings and forcemeat, and vegetables—especially aubergines (egg-plants), mushrooms, onions, beetroot, zucchini and marrows.

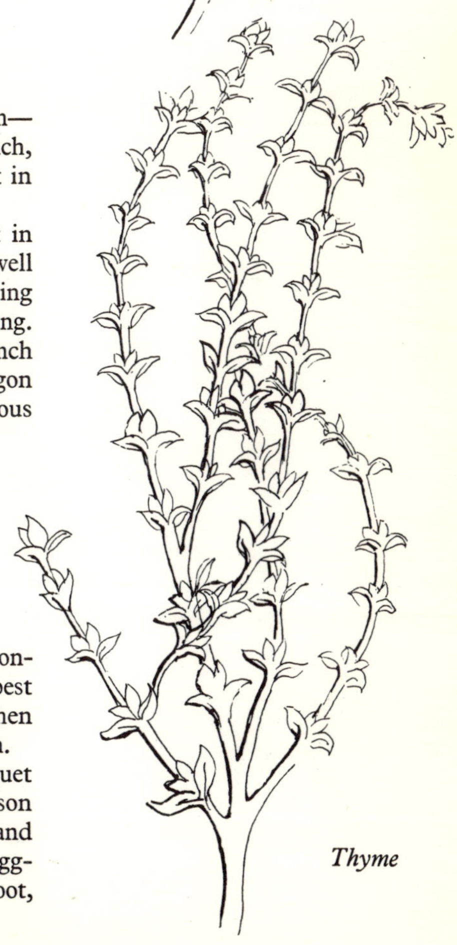

*Thyme*

## Spices

Spices have little or no food value, but the volatile oils which give them their aroma and distinctive flavour help to make simple foods appetising and interesting.

Most spices are imported and therefore are relatively expensive. For home use buy in small quantities and retain maximum freshness and flavour by storing in airtight containers in a dark, dry, cool place

*Ginger*

### Allspice

Allspice (also known as Jamaican Pepper) is the dried fruit of the pimento tree—and no relation to the pepper of that name. It is so named because of its resemblance to the combined flavours of nutmeg, cloves, and cinnamon.

Available whole or ground, allspice is used for pickling, fruit preserving, soups, gravies, cakes, puddings, boiled meats.

### Cayenne

Cayenne pepper is made from the ground, brilliant red, whole pods of the chilli or capsicum. The plant is ornamental, and is grown in many parts of the world, but chiefly in the East Indies and Africa. Depending on its country of origin, cayenne varies in pungency, but all types are very hot and should be used with discretion. It is an important ingredient in curry powder.

Add a little cayenne to meat, fish, and egg dishes, to savory batters, sauces, and salad dressings, in cheese dishes and with shellfish.

### Cinnamon

The cinnamon tree is an evergreen laurel. The thin bark is peeled from the tree and rolled into sticks as it dries, forming stick cinnamon. True cinnamon grows in Ceylon and India; cassia, a member of the same family, comes from South-East Asia, and is almost identical in flavour. The Saigon variety is recognised as being the best-quality ground cinnamon.

Cinnamon has a mellow, slightly sweet flavour that blends with both sweet and savoury foods. When a recipe calls for stick cinnamon, it will usually give the amount to be used in inches, for example, 'a 2 in. stick cinnamon.'

Use ground cinnamon in cakes, milk, and fruit puddings or with grilled or stewed meats. Add a cinnamon stick to hot drinks such as mulled wine, use in pickles and chutneys with boiled meats and when stewing fruits.

### Cloves

Cloves are the buds of an evergreen tree. Used extensively in cookery, they are available whole or ground. Their penetrating, aromatic flavour makes careful use essential—2 or 3 cloves are generally sufficient for most dishes.

Use cloves in some soups, with eggs, fish, meat, stuffings, sauces and gravies, pickles and chutneys. Try a clove-studded orange added to boiling ham or bacon, and an onion stuck with cloves, cooked with boiled chicken. A traditional use is in apple pie; ground cloves are added to cakes and biscuits.

### Ginger

Ginger, the root of the plant, can be obtained in four different forms—green (fresh root); ground (dried and powdered root); preserved (cooked in syrup and bottled); crystallised (cooked, drained, and rolled in sugar).

Green ginger is used with savoury foods (if substituting ground ginger, use only $\frac{1}{4}$ amount specified for green ginger in recipe). Ground ginger is used in savoury and sweet recipes. Preserved and crystallised gingers are interchangeable in recipes, but if no sugar is used in the recipe, rinse sugar coating off the crystallised ginger.

### Mace

Mace, the fleshy covering of nutmeg, with a similar but stronger flavour, is available in 'blade' and powdered form, although blade mace is more difficult to obtain. Use it in preserving, flavouring fish, fish sauces, and stuffings. Try a pinch of mace on grilled lamb or veal chops. A little added to whipped cream makes an interesting variation—so does a pinch in pie pastry.

### Mixed Spice

Mixed spice, as the name implies, is a

blend of certain spices in finely ground form. Generally these will be caraway, allspice, coriander, cumin, nutmeg, and ginger, but other spices, such as cinnamon, may be included.

Mixed spice is used in cakes, puddings, and with fruit.

## Nutmeg

From the same tree as mace, nutmeg is the kernel of the fruit; available in whole nut and ground form, the nuts should be grated before use. One nutmeg will generally produce 3 teaspoonfuls when grated, but, for full flavour, prepare only as much as needed at the time, then store remainder of nut until required again.

Although generally included in sweet recipes, nutmeg is also used with meats and poultry, such as chicken, and in sauces.

## Paprika

Best quality paprika is made from the dried, ground pods of a variety of sweet red pepper or capsicum imported from Hungary. Has a mild, slightly sweet flavour.

Paprika brightens otherwise insipid-looking dishes when used as a garnish. It can be mixed with breadcrumbs to use as topping for dishes such as macaroni au gratin, or used with breadcrumbs for coating chicken joints for frying.

## Pepper

Black and white pepper both come from the berry of a perennial vine. Black pepper is the whole peppercorn, white the inner seed with black outer covering removed. Whole peppercorns keep their flavour better than ground pepper; grind in a peppermill as needed.

Pepper is almost indispensable in savoury cooking. Usually, black is preferable, although it is better to use white in pale coloured foods or cream sauces.

## Saffron

Saffron is obtained from the dried stigmas of a type of crocus grown in Europe, mostly in Spain. Since it takes 225,000 stigmas to make one pound of saffron, and each one is hand picked, it is not surprising that this is the world's most expensive spice.

Saffron is used widely in Spanish cooking to impart yellow colour and subtle flavour; available in stigma or powdered form, it should be used very sparingly.

Steep saffron in a little warm water before use. Meat and poultry dishes generally incorporating rice, fish soups such as bouillabaisse, and some traditional breads and cakes include this spice.

## Turmeric

Turmeric is the root of a plant of the ginger family. It originated in China and Indonesia, is now produced in India, Haiti, and Jamaica.

Deep yellow in colour, it is often a curry ingredient and is used commercially in mustard, curry powder, and some pickles. At home, use it in sauces and dressings, marinades for chicken and shellfish, and in some pickles and chutneys.

*Saffron*

## Aromatic seeds

The seeds listed below can be used in sweet or savoury dishes; most can be obtained in whole seed or ground form

## Anise

Anise is an annual plant growing to 18 in. in height and producing flat-topped bunches of white flowers. The seeds and fresh leaves are used in cooking, and its sharp, distinctive aroma is unmistakable in the liqueur Anisette.

If you have anise in the garden, chop the fresh leaves and sprinkle them over salads. Use the seeds as a flavouring with shellfish, meat, and stuffings. In scones, rolls, bread, and biscuits the seeds can be included in the dough or sprinkled on top.

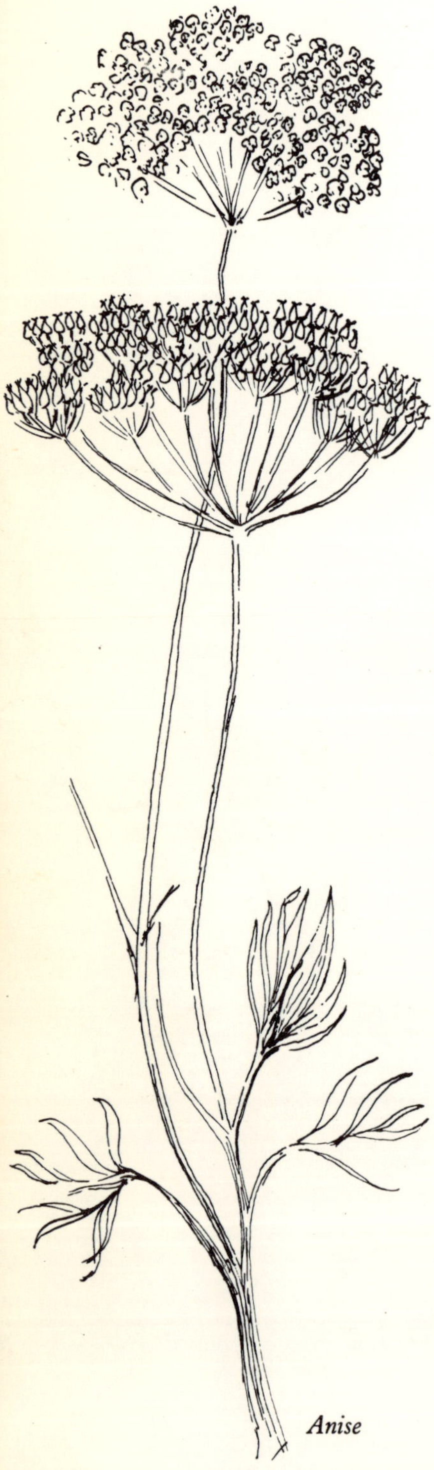

*Anise*

## Caraway

Caraway is the aromatic seed of a biennial member of the parsley family.

Most widely used in seed cake and bread, caraway can be cooked with meat, some vegetables, and cheese. Add a pinch to stews and marinades, sprinkle a little on pork before roasting; use as a flavouring in cheese dishes or crushed with cottage cheese.

## Cardamom

Cardamom is an Indian native plant used extensively in Indian cookery. Cardamom pods or the whole or ground seeds can be bought in Australia. The off-white pods are about ½in. in length and contain about 12 to 16 seeds. The seeds are very hard, so they should be crushed before use to release their pungent flavour.

Whole cardamom seeds are used in fruit punches, pickles, and marinades. In their ground form they are included in bread and cakes, meat balls, and roast pork. The flavour of cardamom combines very well with coffee and, in its ground form, is a component of curry powder.

## Celery Seed

Celery seeds do not come from the well-known vegetable, but from a plant related to the parsley family. They are available whole or ground. Sprinkle whole seeds on herb breads or include in the dough; scatter on canapes; add to marinades for beef or sprinkle on roast veal; include in pickles.

Use ground celery seeds with eggs, cheese, in salads and salad dressings, and with vegetables such as potatoes, aubergines, tomatoes, peppers.

## Coriander

Coriander is available in whole seed or ground form. It is a comparatively mild spice, has a flavour similar to nutmeg. The longer the seeds are kept (they should be stored in a dry place) the more pronounced the flavour becomes. Seeds can be left whole in cooking but it is usual to crush them first.

Use with dried pea and bean soups, spicy sauces, roast or stewed meat, some fish dishes, omelets, baked eggs, and some cakes and pies such as coffee cake, Danish pastries, and apple pie. When using coriander to flavour custards or milk puddings, include a small piece of lemon or orange rind; the two flavours blend well.

## Cumin Seed

Cumin, a low-growing annual from the Mediterranean, is used in Near and Middle Eastern cookery, and is a basic ingredient of curries. The dried ripe fruit of the plant forms the spice. With its pungent aroma, cumin is used by the Dutch and Swiss to flavour cheese, by the Germans in sauerkraut, and by the Hebrews in unleavened bread. It is available ground or in whole seed form.

Use cumin in rye bread, pickles, chutney, rice, cabbage and bean dishes with pork and lamb.

## Mustard

The hardy annual mustard plant will grow in almost any temperate area of the world. There are two main varieties, both native to Europe and producing seeds that vary in strength and flavour. Ready-mixed mustards are becoming more and more popular.

Use mustard seed in casseroles, pickles, salads, dressings, and vegetable dishes. Prepared mustards, traditional accompaniment of beef, steak, and ham, can be added to cheese dishes, sauces and dressings.

## Poppy Seeds

Grown mainly in Holland, poppy seeds are the non-narcotic seeds of the poppy. They can be used whole or ground. For best flavour bake in moderate oven approximately 10 minutes, or toast in dry frying pan over low heat. Sprinkle whole on breads, pastries, salads, pasta, baked or grilled fish, buttered new potatoes, and cauliflower. Use ground in cakes or strudel fillings. Purists, however, believe in using poppy seeds only in sweet foods.

## Sesame Seeds

Sesame seeds are small, flat, and round—and light brown, high in mineral and protein content. In many parts of the world, oil extracted from the seeds is used for cooking. The faintly nutty flavour of the seeds is brought out by baking 20 minutes in moderate oven.

Sesame seeds are sprinkled on breads, buns, cakes and pastries. They can also be added to cheese mixtures and fish dishes, sprinkled on canapes, added to salad dressings.

## Miscellaneous

Below we list a variety of ingredients which add zest to your cooking.

### Capers

The floral bud of the caper bush, that grows along the Mediterranean shores of southern Europe. Once picked, the buds are dried and pickled in vinegar.

Capers add a sharp and piquant flavour to sauces accompanying boiled meat and fish, particularly caper sauce served with boiled mutton. Try them also in salads, or as a garnish.

### Curry Powder

Curry powder is a blend of at least 6 spices which may include cumin, coriander, fenugreek, turmeric, ginger, pepper, mace, cardamom and cloves.

In addition to curries, use curry powder with eggs, in marinades, sprinkled on grilled fish, or to flavour sauces and butters. Amount used will vary according to the brand of curry powder and strength desired. Curry powder should be fried at start of making a curry—this releases its full flavour and also cooks the spices.

### Garam Masala

Garam Masala is the mixed spice of India; it is a combination of ground coriander seeds, cumin seeds, cloves, cinnamon, peppercorns, nutmeg and cardamom seeds. Unlike curry powder, it should be added to a dish at the end of cooking time so its delicate flavour is retained. The spices included in the mixture and quantities used are variable. Garam Masala is used extensively in Indian cooking.

### Horseradish

Horseradish is the root of a perennial plant, a member of the mustard family. It can be bought in jars, blended in a creamy sauce.

Horseradish, the traditional accompaniment to roast beef, can be combined with mayonnaise to give a sharp and piquant dressing. The young and tender leaves of the plant can be chopped and used in salads.

### Monosodium Glutamate

Monosodium Glutamate or MSG, as it is commonly known, is widely used in Chinese cookery. It is the sodium salt of glutamic acid present in nearly all animal and vegetable protein, and is used in cookery to give accent to flavour.

It is used in some savoury foods only and should not be added to sweet foods, fruits or dairy products.

### Salt

Salt, or sodium chloride as it is scientifically known, is a mineral mined in many parts of the world; it is also contained naturally in most foods. Salt added to food during cooking will help to bring out the flavour, and will also stimulate the appetite. A certain amount of salt in the diet is essential for health, while too much can be harmful. Salt also acts as a preservative.

### Vanilla

The vanilla bean is the seed pod of a yellow-flowered orchid native to Central America; the pods are odourless and flavourless. Over a period of six months, they are subjected to alternate heat and darkness to induce fermentation. When almost black in colour, the vanilla bean, as we know it, emerges.

Vanilla extract is produced by steeping the cured pods in a mixture of alcohol and water.

Keep a vanilla bean in a jar containing sugar—the flavour is imparted to the sugar to be used in cakes and custards. Heat the whole pod, or a small piece, in milk for any sweet dish requiring these two ingredients. The bean can be washed and dried afterwards to be stored and used again. An alternative method is to split the bean and remove the seeds. Store the bean in a sugar jar and use the seeds—the part with the strongest flavour—for heating with milk.

Vanilla flavour is popular for many sweet recipes, including custards, ice-cream, cakes, puddings, confectionery.

*Nutmeg*

# SAUCES

Basically, there are two types of savoury sauces—brown and white; nearly all sauces are variations of these. In addition, there are the butter sauces—Hollandaise and Bearnaise, and the compound sauces, Mayonnaise (see page 119) and its variations. All the favourite savoury sauce recipes are given here. See Desserts section, page 220, for a selection of delicious dessert sauces

## Basic White Sauce

1 oz. butter
2 tablespoons flour
1 pint hot milk
salt, pepper

Melt butter over low heat, remove from heat, stir in flour, working until smooth. Return to heat, cook few minutes, remove from heat. Gradually stir in heated milk, return to heat; cook, stirring constantly until boiling point is reached. Reduce heat, simmer further 3 minutes, season to taste.

The amount of flour and butter used in sauces depends on the consistency desired.

*Thin Sauce*: Use 1 oz. butter and 2 tablespoons (approximately 1 oz.) flour to 1 pint liquid.

*Medium Sauce*: Use $1\frac{1}{2}$ oz. butter and 3 tablespoons (approximately $1\frac{1}{2}$ oz.) to 1 pint liquid.

*Thick Sauce*: Use 2 oz. butter and 4 tablespoons (approximately 2 oz.) flour to 1 pint liquid.

*Parsley Sauce:* Stir $\frac{1}{4}$ cup finely chopped parsley and a squeeze of lemon juice into 1 pint medium-thickness white sauce.

*Onion Sauce:* Chop 2 onions finely, cook in boiling salted water until tender, drain. Add onions, a squeeze of lemon juice and 1 teaspoon finely chopped parsley to 1 pint medium-thickness white sauce. (Cooking liquid from onions can be used as part of liquid in making the white sauce.)

*Mornay Sauce:* Make up thick white sauce, remove from heat, stir in 4 oz. grated cheese; add a sprinkling of nutmeg. Stir, off heat, until cheese melts completely.

## Mushroom Cream Sauce

½ lb. mushrooms
1 oz. butter
1 cup cream
¼ cup medium white sauce
salt, pepper

Chop mushrooms very finely, saute in hot butter until lightly browned. Add cream, cook over low heat 5 minutes. Stir in white sauce, season to taste; heat through gently.

## Bechamel Sauce

½ oz. butter
1 tablespoon flour
½ pint milk
bayleaf
slice of onion
4 peppercorns
parsley stalks
sprig thyme
salt, pepper

Place bayleaf, parsley stalks, onion slice, peppercorns and thyme into milk in small saucepan over low heat. Gradually bring to boiling point, remove from heat, let stand 5 minutes. Melt butter in saucepan, add flour, stir until smooth; remove pan from heat, gradually add the strained milk, stirring constantly. When thoroughly blended, return to heat and stir until sauce boils and thickens. Season to taste with salt and pepper.

## Brown Sauce

3 tablespoons oil
1 carrot
1 medium onion
1 stick celery
1 clove garlic
2 tablespoons flour
1 pint boiling water
2 beef stock cubes
1 tablespoon tomato puree
bayleaf
parsley stalks
sprig of thyme

Coarsely chop carrot, onion and celery; crush garlic. Heat oil in saucepan. Saute carrot, onion, celery and garlic until lightly browned. Stir in flour and cook until well browned; do not allow to burn. Dissolve stock cubes in boiling water. Add to pan with tomato puree and herbs. Simmer, uncovered, 30 minutes. Strain, adjust seasoning

A well-flavoured sauce can transform simple grilled or roasted meats into gourmet dishes

## Quick Sauce Bordelaise

2 small onions
6 mushrooms
butter
1 cup dry white wine
1 cup stock
salt, pepper
1 tablespoon tomato purée or paste

Chop onions very finely, slice mushrooms. Saute in a little butter until lightly browned. Add wine and stock and simmer until reduced to $1\frac{1}{4}$ cups of liquid. Stir in tomato puree or paste; season to taste.

## Oyster Sauce

1 bottle of oysters (10 to 12 oysters)
½ pint milk
¼ pint water
½ carrot
1 slice of onion
few peppercorns
parsley sprig
1 small bayleaf
1 oz. butter
2 tablespoons flour
1 dessertspoon lemon juice
salt, pepper
¼ cup cream

Place milk, water, diced carrot, onion slice, peppercorns, parsley and bayleaf in saucepan. Bring to boil; reduce heat, simmer very slowly, uncovered, 5 minutes. Strain, reserve stock. Melt butter in saucepan, stir in flour, cook 1 minute, remove from heat. Gradually add strained stock. Return to heat, simmer until smooth and thickened, stirring constantly.

Add lemon juice, season to taste. Add drained, chopped oysters, simmer very slowly further 5 minutes. Stir in cream. Reheat gently, do not boil. Serve over grilled steaks or steamed or poached fish (delicious over snapper).

## Bercy Sauce

¼ cup very finely chopped shallots
1 cup dry white wine
1½ oz. butter
1 dessertspoon lemon juice
1 tablespoon finely chopped parsley
salt, pepper

Combine shallots and wine, simmer until liquid is reduced to about $\frac{1}{2}$ cup. Remove from heat, stir in butter, lemon juice and parsley; reheat without boiling. Season to taste.

## Mustard Sauce

1 oz. butter
1½ tablespoons flour
1 cup stock
salt, pepper
1 teaspoon dry mustard
½ teaspoon vinegar
1 tablespoon cream
1 egg-yolk

Melt butter in saucepan. Stir in flour, cook until lightly brown; remove from heat. Gradually add stock, blend well. Return to heat, bring to boil; reduce heat, simmer until smooth and thickened, stirring constantly. Season to taste with salt and pepper.

Blend mustard and vinegar with a little of the sauce until smooth. Add to sauce, blend well. Remove from heat, stir in cream and beaten egg-yolk.

## Stroganoff Sauce

1 oz. butter
1 large onion
½ lb. mushrooms
salt, pepper
½ teaspoon dry mustard
½ pint sour cream

Melt butter in pan, add finely chopped onion, saute gently until onion is tender. Add sliced mushrooms, cook until mushrooms are well softened. Add mustard, salt, pepper to taste, then stir in sour cream; heat together gently, simmer 5 minutes.

This sauce is equally good spooned over grilled or pan-fried steaks, or over thick slices of roasted beef fillet.

## Mushroom Sauce

½ oz. butter
2 oz. mushrooms
1 small onion
1 cup milk
¼ cup white wine
1 tablespoon cornflour
salt, pepper
1 to 2 tablespoons cream

Melt butter, fry the chopped onion and sliced mushrooms, but do not brown. Add wine, cook gently for 1 minute. Blend the cornflour with the milk, add to pan. Bring to boil, stirring continually, and cook 1 minute. Remove from heat, season to taste, stir in the cream.

## Madeira Sauce

½ oz. butter
3 shallots
1 rasher bacon
1 dessertspoon flour
1 teaspoon tomato paste
4 mushrooms
2 cups boiling water
2 beef stock cubes
salt, pepper
pinch mixed herbs
½ cup madeira

Heat butter in pan, add finely chopped bacon and shallots, cook over low heat until lightly browned. Stir in flour, add paste, finely chopped mushrooms, Gradually stir in boiling water, in which stock cubes have been dissolved. Season, bring to boil. Reduce heat, simmer 20 minutes. Add herbs, bring to boil again further 5 minutes; strain.

Let sauce simmer over low heat until reduced to half quantity. Add madeira, reboil gently until sauce thickens.

## Chinese Plum Sauce

3 oz. butter
1 onion
1 cup plum jam
2 tablespoons soy sauce
1 tablespoon wine vinegar
½ teaspoon ginger
¼ teaspoon dry mustard

Melt butter in saucepan and saute chopped onion until tender. Remove pan from heat, add remaining ingredients; heat gently, stirring, until well combined.

Serve with pork or veal

## Bearnaise Sauce

4 tablespoons tarragon vinegar
1 shallot
1 bayleaf
6 peppercorns, crushed
3 egg-yolks
4 oz. butter
salt, pepper

Boil vinegar, peppercorns, chopped shallot and bayleaf together until liquid is reduced to 2 tablespoons, strain. Beat egg-yolks lightly in top of double boiler and stir in strained liquid. Gradually beat in cooled melted butter and stir continuously over simmering water until thickened. Season with salt and pepper.

## Hollandaise Sauce

3 tablespoons wine vinegar
6 peppercorns
½ bayleaf
2 egg-yolks
4 oz. butter
salt and pepper
few drops lemon juice

Simmer vinegar, peppercorns and bayleaf gently together until liquid is reduced to half the quantity, strain. Work butter until slightly soft. Cream egg-yolks with a little of the butter and a pinch of salt in the top of a double saucepan; stir in strained liquid. Stir over gentle heat until just beginning to thicken. Add remaining butter in small pieces, stirring continually. When all the butter has been added, add lemon juice to taste.

## Black Bean Sauce

1 tablespoon black beans
1 slice green ginger
1 small clove garlic
1 dessertspoon dry sherry
½ teaspoon sugar
1 dessertspoon soy sauce
1 cup water
1 dessertspoon cornflour

Wash black beans, mash well; finely chop ginger, crush garlic. Heat pan, add beans, garlic and ginger, fry quickly 1 minute. Add sherry, sugar, soy sauce and water. Mix well, bring to boil. Blend cornflour with a little extra water, add to pan; stir until mixture boils and thickens slightly. Two or three finely chopped shallots can also be added.

This well-flavoured Chinese sauce is delicious spooned over cooked whole fish, or with crab.

The black soy beans can be bought in small cans, or in 1 lb. packets from Chinese food stores. They are salty; wash well before using.

## Cucumber-Mayonnaise Sauce

1 large cucumber
½ cup mayonnaise
¼ cup sour cream
1½ tablespoons milk
1½ tablespoons chopped parsley
4 stuffed olives
1 tablespoon lemon juice
salt

Peel, seed, grate and drain cucumber, chop olives. Heat mayonnaise and cucumber in small saucepan over low heat. Combine remaining ingredients in bowl, stir into cucumber mixture. Keep over low heat a few seconds, stirring constantly. Serve with fish.

## Tartare Sauce

¾ cup mayonnaise
2 tablespoons capers
2 tablespoons chopped gherkins
½ teaspoon chopped chives
1 tablespoon chopped parsley

In bowl combine mayonnaise, finely chopped capers, gherkins, chives and parsley. Serve with fish.

## Sauce Remoulade

1 cup mayonnaise
2 tablespoons finely chopped dill pickle or gherkin
1 dessertspoon finely chopped capers
1 teaspoon prepared mustard
1 dessertspoon finely chopped parsley
dash of worcestershire or anchovy sauce
2 tablespoons whipped cream

Combine all ingredients except cream, mix well. Stir in cream. Serve with any seafood.

## Caper Sauce

½ cup mayonnaise
1 tablespoon chopped, drained capers
1 teaspoon vinegar from capers
1 tablespoon finely chopped parsley

Combine all ingredients, mix well to blend.

# CAKES

Tea cakes, coffee cakes, small cakes, butter cakes, fruit cakes, a superb torte and gateau—there's an irresistible selection of cakes to choose from, for every occasion

## Butterscotch Teacake

4 oz. butter
1 cup brown sugar, lightly packed
2 cups plain flour
3 teaspoons baking powder
1 large egg
½ cup milk

### Butterscotch Icing

¾ cup brown sugar, lightly packed
4 dessertspoons milk
pinch salt
1 oz. butter
½ cup icing sugar
chopped almonds

Cream butter and sugar until light and fluffy. Add egg, beat well. Fold in sifted flour and baking powder alternately with the milk. Turn mixture into greased 8 in. sandwich tin. Bake in moderate oven 40 to 45 minutes, or until cake is cooked. Turn cake on to a cake cooler. When cold, top with Butterscotch Icing.

*Icing:* Place all ingredients except icing sugar in a saucepan and cook, stirring constantly, until mixture begins to boil. Boil steadily, without stirring, 4 to 5 minutes. Allow to cool until warm, beat in sifted icing sugar, adding more icing sugar, if necessary, to give a spreading consistency. Spread over cake, sprinkle with chopped almonds.

## Apple Teacake

1½ cups self-raising flour
pinch salt
½ cup castor sugar
2 oz. butter
1 egg
½ cup milk
1 to 2 apples
2 teaspoons cinnamon
extra ¼ cup sugar

Peel and core apples, cut into thin slices, cut each slice in half.

Cream butter, add sugar and beat until light and fluffy; beat in egg. Fold in sifted flour and salt alternately with milk, mix well. Spread mixture into well-greased 8 in. sandwich tin, arrange a whirl of apple slices on top, sprinkle with combined cinnamon and extra sugar. Bake in moderate oven approximately 45 minutes.

## Streusel Coffee Cake

6 oz. butter
1 cup sugar
1 teaspoon vanilla
3 eggs
1¼ cups self-raising flour
¾ cup plain flour
3 tablespoons milk

### Topping

1 cup plain flour
1 tablespoon cinnamon
½ cup brown sugar, lightly packed
3 oz. butter

Cream together butter and sugar until light and fluffy, add vanilla. Add eggs one at a time, beating well after each addition. Sift flours, add alternately with milk, mix thoroughly. Spread into greased 9 in. square cake tin. Grate topping over cake. Bake in moderately hot oven, 35 to 40 minutes, or until cooked when tested with a skewer.

*Topping*: Sift together dry ingredients. Rub in butter thoroughly, roll into a ball. Refrigerate until firm.

## Orange Loaf Cake

½ cup castor sugar
½ cup milk
4 oz. butter
1 dessertspoon grated orange rind
2 eggs
2 cups self-raising flour

Dissolve sugar in $\frac{1}{4}$ cup of milk in a small mixing bowl. Add butter and orange rind and cream well. Add beaten eggs a little at a time. Sift flour, fold in alternately with remaining milk. Spoon mixture into greased and lined 9 in. x 5 in. loaf tin. Bake in moderate oven 40 minutes.

Butterscotch Teacake, Chelsea Butter Bun and Almond Meringue Cake—full-of-flavour cakes that go equally well with tea or coffee

## Patty Cakes

4 oz. butter
½ cup castor sugar
2 eggs
½ cup milk
½ teaspoon vanilla
2 cups self-raising flour

Cream butter and sugar together until light and fluffy. Add vanilla, then gradually beat in the lightly beaten eggs. Fold in the sifted flour alternately with the milk; mix well. Drop dessertspoonfuls of mixture into well greased, deep patty tins. Bake in moderately hot oven 10 to 15 minutes.

Makes 2 dozen.

*Butterfly Cakes:* Cut a slice from top of cooled patty cake, then cut this slice in half to form two wings. Pipe or spoon whipped cream across top of cake, set the wings in position. Dust with sifted icing sugar; top, if desired, with a halved strawberry.

## Ginger Cake

4 cups (1 lb.) plain flour
½ teaspoon salt
2 dessertspoons baking powder
3 dessertspoons ground ginger
1 teaspoon bicarbonate of soda
1 cup treacle
6 oz. butter
2 cups brown sugar, lightly packed
1 egg
½ pint milk

**Lemon Icing**

2 cups icing sugar
½ oz. butter
lemon juice

Sift flour, salt, baking powder, ginger and bicarbonate of soda into a basin. Place treacle, butter and brown sugar into a saucepan, stir over a low heat until sugar dissolves. Cool. Add to dry ingredients; mix in egg and warmed milk. Pour into greased and paper-lined 10 in. square or large oblong cake tin.

Bake in moderately hot oven 1 hour. Cool slightly before turning out on to a cake cooler. When cold, top with lemon icing.

*Lemon Icing:* Sift icing sugar. Soften butter with a wooden spoon, then gradually add icing sugar, working well in, until the mixture is crumbly. Add sufficient lemon juice, a little at a time, to make a smooth spreading consistency.

## Basic Butter Cake

4 oz. butter
¾ cup castor sugar
1 teaspoon vanilla
2 eggs
2 cups self-raising flour
pinch salt
½ cup milk

Cream butter, sugar and vanilla together until light and fluffy. Add eggs one at a time, beat well. Fold in sifted dry ingredients alternately with the milk. Spoon into a greased and lined 7 in. or 8 in. cake tin. Bake in a moderate oven 50 to 60 minutes.

### Variations

**Light Fruit Cake**

Add 6oz. mixed fruit and ½ teaspoon each of mixed spice, nutmeg, and grated lemon or orange rind.

**Marble Cake**

Divide mixture into three portions. Colour one portion pink; to second portion add 3 dessertspoons cocoa blended smoothly with 3 dessertspoons warm milk; leave third portion plain. Spoon mixtures into tin in alternate spoonfuls. Cut through two or three times with knife blade or skewer, to give pattern.

**Lamingtons**

Pour cake mixture into a well-greased 7 in. x 11 in. lamington tin. Bake in moderate oven 30 to 40 minutes. Allow to stand in the tin for a few minutes before turning out on to cake cooler.

It is best to make the cake the day before you want to cut and ice the lamingtons, as fresh cake will usually crumble.

Cut cake into squares. Dip in chocolate icing, then toss in coconut.

*Chocolate Icing for Lamingtons:* Sift 1 lb. icing sugar and 4 dessertspoons cocoa into a basin. Add 1 dessertspoon melted butter to ½ cup warmed milk. Add sufficient milk mixture to icing sugar mixture to make a smooth coating consistency; beat well.

## One-Egg Butter Cake

2 cups plain flour
pinch salt
2½ teaspoons baking powder
3 oz. butter
1 cup castor sugar
1 egg
1 teaspoon vanilla
⅔ cup milk

Sift together flour, salt and baking powder. Cream butter until soft, gradually add sugar and beaten egg, beat well until light and fluffy; add vanilla. Add dry ingredients alternately with the milk. Spoon into a well-greased 7 in. cake tin. Bake in moderate oven, approximately 55 minutes.

## Two-Egg Butter Cake

4 oz. butter
1½ cups castor sugar
2 large eggs, or
3 smaller eggs
3 cups plain flour
4 teaspoons baking powder
pinch salt
1 cup milk
1 teaspoon vanilla

Cream butter, add sugar and 1 egg; beat until light and fluffy. Add remaining egg, beat well. Sift together dry ingredients; add alternately with milk to creamed mixture; add vanilla. Pour into well-greased 8 in. cake tin.

Bake in moderately slow oven, approximately $1\frac{1}{4}$ to $1\frac{1}{2}$ hours. Let cake cool in tin 5 to 10 minutes before turning out.

## Cherry Cake

4 oz. glacé cherries
6 oz. butter
¾ cup castor sugar
3 eggs
¾ cup plain flour
¾ cup self-raising flour
3 dessertspoons milk

**Snow Glaze**

1¼ cups icing sugar
1 teaspoon softened butter
¼ teaspoon vanilla
1 to 2 dessertspoons milk

Cut cherries into thirds. Cream butter and sugar until light and fluffy. Gradually add well-beaten eggs. Fold in sifted flours alternately with milk; lastly fold in cut cherries. Place mixture into a large, well-greased baba mould, or greased 8 in. round cake tin.

Bake in moderate oven approximately 1 hour, or until golden brown and cooked when tested with a skewer. Allow to stand 10 minutes before turning out; cool.

When cold, ice with Snow Glaze and decorate with glace cherry halves, if desired.

*Snow Glaze:* Combine sifted icing sugar, butter and vanilla in small basin. Gradually beat in milk until mixture is smooth and of a coating consistency; a little more milk may be necessary. Spread over cake; or warm over low heat and allow to trickle over top of cake and down the sides.

## Madeira Cake

6 oz. butter
⅔ cup castor sugar
grated rind medium size lemon
3 large eggs
2 cups plain flour
2 teaspoons baking powder
candied peel

Cream butter until light and fluffy, gradually beat in sugar. Add grated lemon rind, mix well. Beat eggs lightly, add gradually to mixture, beat well. Sift flour with baking powder; lightly fold into beaten mixture. No extra liquid should be added. Turn mixture into greased, lined 7 in. cake tin. Bake in moderate oven approximately 1 hour. Place small pieces of candied peel on top, decoratively, after $\frac{3}{4}$ hour of cooking time.

## Apple Shortcake

4 oz. butter
½ cup castor sugar
1 egg
1 cup self-raising flour
1 cup plain flour
¼ teaspoon salt
pulp of 1 passionfruit
3 peeled, coarsely grated apples
grated rind and juice ½ lemon
extra castor sugar

Cream butter and sugar lightly, add egg, beat well; mix in sifted flours and salt. Divide mixture into two, roll each piece into a round; place one round in base of 8 in. greased sandwich tin, cover with grated apple, and passionfruit pulp. Sprinkle with grated lemon rind and juice, then with 1 tablespoon extra sugar. Cover with second round of dough, pressing well at sides. Brush with water, sprinkle evenly with extra castor sugar. Bake in moderate oven 35 to 40 minutes.

## Chelsea Butter Bun

3 cups self-raising flour
½ teaspoon salt
1½ oz. butter
1 cup milk

**Filling**

2 oz. butter
⅓ cup brown sugar, lightly packed
2 oz. sultanas
2 oz. currants
2 oz. chopped glacé cherries
2 oz. mixed peel
1 teaspoon cinnamon

**Glaze**

2 dessertspoons water
2 dessertspoons sugar
1 teaspoon gelatine

Sift flour and salt into a basin, rub in butter lightly. Mix to a firm dough with milk. Roll dough into oblong shape, $\frac{1}{4}$ in. in thickness.

*Filling:* Cream butter and brown sugar together. Spread over dough; sprinkle with fruit and cinnamon. Roll up lengthwise; cut roll into 14 thick slices. Pack into a greased 8 in. sandwich tin, cut side down. Bake in a moderate oven 25 to 30 minutes.

Brush bun with glaze, while still hot.

*Glaze:* Place ingredients into a small bowl, stir over hot water until gelatine and sugar dissolve.

## Festive Fruit Cake

8 oz. dessert dates
8 oz. glacé pineapple
4 oz. glacé apricots
4 oz. green glacé cherries
4 oz. red glacé cherries
8 oz. brazil nuts
2 eggs
½ cup brown sugar, lightly packed
1 teaspoon vanilla
1 tablespoon rum
3 oz. softened butter
½ cup plain flour
½ teaspoon baking powder
pinch salt
1 to 2 tablespoons rum or brandy, extra

Stone dates, chop pineapple and apricots into fairly large pieces (leave remaining fruit and nuts whole); mix well together. Beat eggs until light and fluffy, add sugar, vanilla, rum and softened butter. Continue beating until well blended. Sift flour with baking powder and salt, add to creamed mixture with fruit and nuts. Mix well.

Spoon into greased, lined 9 in. x 5 in. loaf tin. Bake in a slow oven approximately 1½ hours or until cake is firm to touch and a skewer, when inserted in centre, comes out clean; cake may have a surface layer of melted butter; on cooling, this will settle and moisten cake. Remove from oven and, while still hot, pour extra rum or brandy over.

Cool in tin standing on wire rack. This cake keeps well. To store, remove from tin when cold, wrap cake in foil, or a clean teatowel, and store in a reasonably cool place.

## Chocolate Fruit Cake

1 lb. sultanas
8 oz. raisins
4 oz. currants
4 oz. glacé cherries
3 oz. mixed peel
2 oz. glacé pineapple
2 oz. glacé apricots
2 oz. glacé figs
2 oz. prunes or dates
1 oz. dried apricots
½ cup brandy
8 oz. butter
1½ cups brown sugar, firmly packed
1 teaspoon grated orange rind
1 teaspoon grated lemon rind
1 teaspoon vanilla
¼ teaspoon almond essence
2 tablespoons marmalade
4 oz. dark chocolate
4 eggs
2½ cups plain flour
1 teaspoon mixed spice
¼ teaspoon nutmeg
1 teaspoon cinnamon
pinch salt

Chop fruit and place in a basin, pour over brandy, mix well, cover and stand overnight. Cream butter with sugar, add grated fruit rinds, essences, marmalade and melted chocolate; mix thoroughly. Drop in the eggs one at a time, beating well after each addition. Fold in sifted dry ingredients alternately with the prepared fruits; mix well. Place mixture into deep 9 in. cake tin, which has been lined with 1 thickness white paper and 2 thicknesses brown paper. Bake in slow oven approximately 4 hours, or until cooked, when a skewer, inserted, comes out clean. Allow to cool completely in tin. Then remove from tin, peel off brown paper layers. Wrap in clean towel or aluminium foil, store in a reasonably cool place until required.

## Easy Dundee Cake

8 oz. currants
8 oz. sultanas
8 oz. raisins
2 oz. mixed peel
2 oz. cherries
⅓ cup milk
1 teaspoon baking powder
½ teaspoon mixed spice
2½ cups plain flour
6 oz. softened butter
¾ cup castor sugar
5 eggs
1 oz. blanched almonds

Chop peel and raisins, sift dry ingredients. Place softened butter in a large bowl, add all remaining ingredients with the exception of the almonds; beat together until smooth and thoroughly mixed (this is best done on an electric mixer). Place in an 8 in. round deep cake tin that has been lined with 2 layers of greaseproof paper. Decorate top with almonds and, if desired, glace cherries.

Bake in a moderately slow oven 2½ to 3 hours.

When cake is cooked, cover with a clean teatowel and leave to cool in tin.

## Sultana Cake

8 oz. butter
1 cup castor sugar
2½ cups plain flour
¼ cup self-raising flour
5 eggs
1½ lb. sultanas
4 oz. blanched almonds
¼ cup brandy
pinch salt
½ teaspoon vanilla

Cover sultanas with warm water, soak for 2 hours. Drain, let dry at least 24 hours.

Cream butter and sugar together until light and fluffy. Add eggs one at a time, beating well after each addition. If necessary, add a little flour toward the end of the egg additions, to prevent curdling. Add sifted flours and salt alternately with the sultanas, then add almonds, reserving a few almonds to decorate the top of cake. Fold in brandy and vanilla. Place mixture into a greased and paper lined 8 in. or 9 in. square cake tin. Bake in moderately slow oven, approximately 1¾ hours.

At top, from left, Madeira Cake, Chocolate Fruit Cake topped with Marzipan Fruits, Cherry Cake; below, Ginger Cake, Patty Cakes, Easy Dundee Cake

## Strawberry Hazelnut Gateau

4 egg whites
pinch salt
1¼ cups castor sugar
4½ oz. ground hazelnuts
1 teaspoon vinegar
½ teaspoon vanilla
4 dessertspoons black coffee

**Filling**

1 punnet strawberries
1 pint whipped cream
6 oz. dark chocolate
¼ cup water

Beat egg-whites with salt until stiff; gradually add sugar; beat until mixture is of meringue consistency. Fold in remaining ingredients. Spread in 2 greased and floured 8 in. springform pans. Bake in moderate oven approximately 35 minutes; release sides of pans. Cool on base of pan.

Remove from base, place a layer of meringue on serving plate. Spread with thin layer of chocolate, which has been melted with the water. Spread $\frac{3}{4}$ in. layer of cream over chocolate. Top with layer of sliced strawberries; reserve remainder for decoration.

Spread second layer of meringue with remaining chocolate mixture, place on strawberry layer, chocolate-side up. Cover sides and top with remaining cream.

Refrigerate several hours, or preferably overnight. serve decorated with reserved strawberries.

## Chocolate Roll

4 eggs
1 cup castor sugar
4 oz. dark chocolate
3 dessertspoons water
¾ cup cream
½ teaspoon vanilla
2 dessertspoons icing sugar
2 dessertspoons cocoa
little extra cocoa

Separate eggs. Beat yolks and sugar until very pale and fluffy. Melt chopped chocolate with water, stirring with a wooden spoon until chocolate has melted. Cool. Mix gently through the egg-yolk mixture. Beat egg-whites till soft peaks form. Do not overbeat. Fold the chocolate mixture into the egg-white mixture very carefully until evenly distributed.

Grease and line with greased paper a $10\frac{1}{2}$ in. x 12 in. swiss roll tin. Carefully spoon in the mixture, spread evenly. Bake in moderate oven 17 minutes. Remove from oven, cover cake with 2 layers of paper towelling rung out in cold water and 1 layer of dry paper towelling. Refrigerate for 20 minutes.

Peel off paper towels carefully. Loosen cake along the long sides, using a sharp knife. Dust top with sifted cocoa. Carefully tip out on to greased paper. Remove lining paper. Spread cake with cream mixture, roll up, and dust with extra cocoa.

NOTE: This beautifully textured chocolate cake contains no flour.

*Cream Mixture:* Whip cold cream till thick. Beat in vanilla and icing sugar.

## Dark Chocolate Cake

¾ cup hot coffee
½ cup cocoa
1¼ cups sugar
4 oz. butter
3 eggs, separated
1 teaspoon salt
1 teaspoon vanilla
1 teaspoon bicarbonate of soda
½ cup sour cream
2 cups plain flour
½ cup sugar, extra
whipped cream

**Sour Cream Frosting**

4 oz. dark chocolate
½ cup sour cream
pinch salt
4 dessertspoons icing sugar

Stir hot coffee gradually into cocoa. Combine $1\frac{1}{4}$ cups sugar with butter, egg yolks, salt, vanilla and half the cocoa mixture. Beat until light and creamy. Mix bicarbonate of soda and sour cream together. To butter and sugar mixture add sour cream and cocoa-coffee alternately with sifted flour. Beat egg whites until stiff, gradually add the $\frac{1}{2}$ cup sugar, beat until meringue stands in stiff peaks. Fold into chocolate mixture. Pour into 9 in. or 10 in. greased and paper-lined deep cake tin. Bake in moderate oven 1 to $1\frac{1}{4}$ hours.

Cool completely on cake cooler, then cut into 2 layers and join with whipped cream. Spread frosting in a thin layer over top and sides of cake, decorate with walnut halves and cherries if desired.

Refrigerate until Sour Cream Frosting is firm.

*Sour Cream Frosting:* Melt chopped chocolate over hot water. Remove from heat, allow to cool slightly, then stir in sour cream and salt. Add sifted icing sugar and beat until a spreading consistency.

## Pineapple Fruit Cake

1 cup sugar
15 oz. can crushed pineapple
1 lb. mixed fruit
1 teaspoon bicarbonate of soda
1 teaspoon mixed spice
4 oz. butter
1 cup plain flour
1 cup self-raising flour
2 eggs

Place sugar, contents of can of pineapple, chopped mixed fruit, bicarbonate of soda, spice and butter into a saucepan. Bring to boil, boil 3 minutes; remove from heat, cool completely.

Sift flours together, mix into cold fruit mixture with well-beaten eggs. Place mixture into greased and lined 8 in. cake tin.

Bake in moderate oven approximately 1½ hours, reduce heat to moderately slow, bake further 20 to 30 minutes or until a skewer, inserted, comes out clean.

## Mocha Torte

6 eggs, separated
½ cup castor sugar
4 oz. dark chocolate
2 dessertspoons plain flour
4 dessertspoons water
1 teaspoon instant coffee powder

**Coffee Cream**

1 dessertspoon instant coffee powder
½ pint cream
¼ cup castor sugar

Beat egg-yolks and sugar until pale and creamy. Melt chopped chocolate over hot water, allow to cool slightly; add to egg-yolk mixture, mixing well. Stir coffee into water, add to chocolate mixture. Gently fold in sifted flour and lightly beaten egg-whites. It is important not to overmix.

Pour mixture into 3 greased and lined 8 in. sandwich tins, bake in moderately slow oven 30 to 35 minutes; cool on wire rack.

When cold, join together with Coffee Cream. Cover top and sides of cake with remaining Coffee Cream, decorate with toasted almonds; drizzle a little melted chocolate over, if desired. Refrigerate.

*Coffee Cream:* Combine all ingredients in mixing bowl, refrigerate at least 1 hour. When ready to use, beat until thick.

## Orange Date Cake

1 lb. dates
½ cup orange juice
4½ cups self-raising flour
pinch salt
8 oz. butter
2 cups castor sugar
½ cup mixed peel
3 eggs
1½ cups warm milk
½ teaspoon vanilla

Pour orange juice over chopped dates, cover, leave overnight.

Next day sift flour and salt into bowl. Rub in butter until mixture resembles fine breadcrumbs; mix in castor sugar. Add mixed peel, dates and orange juice, rub through lightly, separating the pieces. Make well in centre of dry ingredients. Add beaten eggs alternately with milk to which vanilla has been added, stirring until all dry ingredients are well mixed. Place mixture into greased and paper lined 10 in. square cake tin. Bake in moderate oven 30 minutes, reduce heat to moderately slow, and continue cooking further 1½ hours. Leave in tin on cake cooler to cool.

## Pineapple Teacake

1½ cups self-raising flour
½ cup sugar
pinch salt
1 egg
½ cup milk
4 oz. butter
⅓ cup honey
15 oz. can crushed pineapple
¼ cup coconut

Drain pineapple (the juice is not needed for this recipe). Melt 2 oz. butter and allow it to cool slightly.

Sift flour and salt, add sugar. Combine beaten egg, milk and melted butter, add to dry ingredients; mix well. Pour into a greased, deep 8 in. round cake tin, spread pineapple over the batter. Cream remaining butter and honey well, spoon over pineapple; sprinkle with coconut. Bake in moderately hot oven 35 to 40 minutes.

When cool, sprinkle top with sifted icing sugar.

## Chocolate Orange Cake

6 oz. butter
¾ cup castor sugar
3 eggs
1½ cups self-raising flour
2 tablespoons milk
grated rind 2 oranges

**Chocolate Icing**

1 cup icing sugar
½ teaspoon butter
1 tablespoon cocoa
water to mix

Cream butter and sugar until light and fluffy, beat in eggs one at a time, beating well after each addition. Sift flour, fold in alternately with milk; add grated orange rind. Place mixture in greased and paper lined 9 in. x 5 in. loaf tin. Bake in moderate oven approximately 1 hour or until skewer inserted in centre comes out clean. Leave in tin a few minutes before turning out on to cake cooler. When cold, top with chocolate icing.

*Chocolate Icing*: Sift icing sugar and cocoa into bowl, add butter, then mix to a stiff consistency with a little cold water. Place over hot water and stir until a pouring consistency; this will take only a minute or two. Pour on top of cake and spread with spatula, swirling icing with tip of spatula.

## Almond Meringue Cake

4 oz. butter
½ cup castor sugar
pinch salt
4 egg-yolks
1 teaspoon vanilla
⅓ cup milk
1 cup self-raising flour

**Topping**

4 egg-whites
¾ cup castor sugar
2 dessertspoons castor sugar, extra
½ teaspoon cinnamon
1 oz. blanched, slivered almonds

Cream butter and sugar until light and fluffy. Beat in yolks and vanilla. Sift flour and salt; add alternately with milk. Spread mixture into a greased 8 in. springform pan.

*Topping:* Beat egg-whites until stiff, gradually add sugar, beating well. Spread this meringue over mixture in pan. Mix together the extra sugar and cinnamon, sprinkle over meringue. Sprinkle with almonds. Bake in moderate oven 60 to 65 minutes, or until cake is cooked when tested with a skewer. Leave in pan 10 minutes before turning out.

## Date and Walnut Loaf

1 cup self-raising flour
½ cup sugar
½ teaspoon bicarbonate of soda
2 teaspoons cinnamon
½ cup chopped dates
½ cup chopped walnuts
1 oz. butter
⅔ cup water

Sift flour, sugar, bicarbonate of soda and cinnamon into a basin. Add the chopped dates and walnuts, mix well. Heat butter and water in a saucepan until water just comes to the boil. Make a well in the centre of the dry ingredients, add hot liquid and mix thoroughly. Spoon into greased 10 in. x 3 in. bar tin. Bake in a moderate oven approximately 40 minutes. Serve with butter.

## Chocolate Loaf Cake

4 oz. butter
½ cup castor sugar
2 tablespoons sifted cocoa
2 eggs
1¾ cups self-raising flour
2½ tablespoons cornflour
¼ pint milk

**Chocolate Icing**

1 cup icing sugar
1 dessertspoon cocoa
1 teaspoon softened butter
little warmed milk

Cream butter, gradually add sugar and cocoa; beat well. Add beaten eggs a little at a time, beat well. Stir in sifted flours alternately with the milk. Spoon mixture into greased and lined 9 in. x 5 in. loaf tin. Bake in moderate oven 45 minutes. When cool top with chocolate icing.

*Chocolate Icing:* Sift icing sugar and cocoa into a basin, add softened butter and mix through icing sugar mixture. Add sufficient warmed milk to mix to a smooth spreading consistency.

## Fresh Lemon Loaf

4 oz. butter
1 cup castor sugar
2 eggs
1 cup self-raising flour
½ cup plain flour
½ cup milk
½ teaspoon salt
¼ cup chopped nuts
grated rind and juice 1 large lemon
¼ cup castor sugar, extra

Cream butter well, add sugar and beat again. Add eggs one at a time, beat well after each addition. Sift flour and salt, add alternately with milk. Add nuts and lemon rind. Pour into greased 9 in. x 5 in. loaf tin, bake in moderate oven 40 to 45 minutes.

Mix lemon juice with extra sugar; stir until sugar dissolves. When cake is cooked and hot from oven, pour over the lemon mixture. Leave to cool in tin.

## Rock Cakes

2 cups self-raising flour
⅓ cup sugar
3 oz. butter
3 oz. sultanas or currants
1 oz. mixed peel
1 egg
pinch salt
¼ teaspoon cinnamon
⅓ cup milk (approx.)
extra sugar

Sift dry ingredients into a bowl. Add butter, and, using fingertips rub in until mixture resembles fine breadcrumbs. Add fruit and peel, mix well. Beat egg and add to mixture, then add sufficient milk to make a moist but still stiff consistency. If mixture is too soft, cakes will spread widely during cooking instead of retaining shape. Use teaspoons or dessertspoons, depending on size of cake required, to spoon mixture out in rough heaps on to greased trays. Leave space between each to allow for slight spreading. Sprinkle cakes with extra sugar. Bake in a moderately hot oven 10 to 20 minutes, depending on size of cake. Loosen on trays while hot; allow to cool on trays.

Strawberry Hazelnut Gateau—thin wafers of hazelnut cake are sandwiched together with whipped cream and chocolate and red, ripe strawberries in this delicious dessert cake

## Slices

Everyone loves the sweet taste of a luscious slice, and there's a wonderful variety of fillings and toppings to choose from.

### Fruit Slice

4 oz. butter
1½ cups self-raising flour
⅓ cup ground rice
¼ cup castor sugar
2½ tablespoons cornflour
1 egg

**Filling**

½ lb. dates
grated rind and juice 1 lemon
4 oz. sultanas
4 oz. raisins
1 oz. mixed peel
2 oz. glacé cherries
1 dessertspoon sugar
1 oz. butter
1 teaspoon mixed spice
¾ cup water
1 tablespoon arrowroot
1 tablespoon rum or orange juice

Sift flour, ground rice, cornflour into basin, rub in butter until mixture resembles fine breadcrumbs. Stir in sugar and beaten egg. Knead lightly on floured board, roll out half the pastry, fit into greased and lined 11 in. x 7 in. lamington tin.

Cover with prepared filling. Roll out remaining pastry; cover filling.

Glaze with little cold water, sprinkle with extra castor sugar. Bake in hot oven 25 to 30 minutes. Cool; cut into slices.

*Filling:* Place in saucepan chopped fruit and all ingredients except arrowroot and rum; place over low heat, stirring continually, until thick. Blend arrowroot with rum or orange juice, stir into fruit mixture; return to heat, stirring, 3 minutes. Remove, cool completely.

### Chocolate Rough Slice

4 oz. butter
⅓rd cup castor sugar
¼ cup coconut
1 cup self-raising flour
1 dessertspoon cocoa
pinch salt

**Topping**

3 tablespoons condensed milk
1 tablespoon cocoa
1 cup sifted icing sugar
1 oz. butter
1 cup coconut
1 teaspoon vanilla

Sift dry ingredients into basin, add sugar and coconut; stir in melted butter, mixing well. Press into greased and lined 11 in. x 7 in. lamington tin. Bake in moderate oven 25 minutes.

Cool slightly; cover with Chocolate Rough Topping while still warm. Cut into slices when cold.

*Chocolate Rough Topping:* Combine all ingredients in basin, mix well.

### Raspberry Coconut Slice

1 cup self-raising flour
½ cup sugar
1 tablespoon butter
2 eggs
raspberry jam
½ cup castor sugar
1 cup coconut
few drops almond essence
extra coconut

Sift flour and sugar into basin, rub in butter until mixture resembles fine breadcrumbs. Mix to stiff dough with 1 beaten egg. Knead lightly, roll out to 8 in. square. Place on base of greased and lined shallow 8 in. square tin. Spread with little raspberry jam.

Beat remaining egg and castor sugar together until pale and thick, carefully fold in coconut and almond essence; spread over jam. Sprinkle with little extra coconut. Bake in moderate oven 30 to 35 minutes or until golden. Cut into slices while still warm.

### Passionfruit Cheese Slice

**Crumb Crust**

6 oz. coconut biscuits
3 oz. butter

**Topping**

8 oz. cottage cheese
8 oz. cream cheese
14 oz. can condensed milk
1 dessertspoon gelatine
¼ cup water
4 passionfruit
¼ cup lemon juice
1 teaspoon lemon rind
2 teaspoons vinegar
¾ cup cream

*Crumb Crust:* Crush biscuits. Combine crumbs with melted butter. Press mixture on to base of 7 in. x 11 in. lamington tin, lined with aluminium foil (lightly grease foil and bring it up and over sides of tin, to enable slice to be removed easily after it has set). Refrigerate until firm.

*Topping:* Sieve cheeses and beat together until light and creamy. Soften gelatine in water and dissolve over boiling water; allow to cool slightly. Add condensed milk, gelatine, lemon juice, lemon rind and vinegar to cheese mixture. Beat until creamy; fold in whipped cream. Carefully fold in pulp of 2 passionfruit. Pour mixture on to crumb crust, spread smoothly. Spread remaining passionfruit pulp on top. Refrigerate until set. Cut into slices.

## Apple Slice

4 oz. butter
½ cup castor sugar
1 egg
1 cup plain flour
1 teaspoon cinnamon
1 teaspoon mixed spice
1½ cups stewed apple, well drained

Cream butter and sugar together until light and fluffy, add egg and beat well. Sift flour with spices, fold lightly into creamed mixture. Spread half mixture on base of a greased 8 in. square cake tin, cover with well drained apples, spread remaining cake mixture on top. Bake in moderate oven approximately 45 minutes, or until golden brown. Serve hot or cold, cut into squares, sprinkled with sifted icing sugar.

## Peanut Slice

8 oz. shortcrust pastry
raspberry jam
1 egg white
¾ cup castor sugar
½ cup cake crumbs
1 dessertspoon cocoa
½ teaspoon vanilla
½ lb. roasted peanuts
water

Roll out pastry, line greased 7 in. x 11 in. lamington tin, bake in moderately hot oven 15 minutes; cool. Spread with jam.

Beat egg-white until stiff, gradually beat in sugar. Lightly fold in cake crumbs, cocoa, peanuts; flavour with vanilla. Spread over raspberry jam, brush with water. Bake in moderate oven approximately 25 minutes. Cut into slices.

## Vanilla Custard Slice

10 oz. puff pastry
1¾ pints milk
¾ cup sugar
2 oz. butter
½ cup cornflour
4 tablespoons custard powder
¼ pint milk, extra
1 egg
1 dessertspoon vanilla

Roll out pastry thinly, cut out two 10 in. squares; place on ungreased oven tray, bake in very hot oven approximately 15 minutes. Cool, trim to make two 8 in. squares. Place one layer on base of ungreased 8 in. square cake tin.

Place milk, sugar, butter in large saucepan. Blend cornflour and custard powder with extra milk; add to saucepan, bring to boil, stirring until smooth and thick. Remove from heat, beat in vanilla and egg. While still hot, pour over layer of pastry in tin; top with second square of pastry, pressing down firmly. Cool, top with passionfruit icing. Refrigerate until firm; cut into slices.

## Spicy Apple Slice

**Pastry**

1½ cups plain flour
3 oz. butter
¼ cup castor sugar
1 egg-yolk
1 teaspoon water
½ teaspoon baking powder

**Filling**

4 large apples
½ cup sugar
2 tablespoons water
little lemon rind

**Spicy Topping**

¾ cup plain flour
3 teaspoons cinnamon
2½ tablespoons sugar
2 oz. butter

Cream butter and sugar until light and fluffy, beat in egg-yolk and water. Knead in sifted dry ingredients until mixture comes together in a ball. Roll out on lightly floured board, line a greased 7 in. x 11 in. lamington tin.

*Filling:* Peel, core, and slice apples thinly. Place in saucepan with sugar, water and lemon rind, cook gently until apples are tender, cool. Place cold apple mixture in uncooked pastry shell.

*Spicy Topping:* Sift dry ingredients into bowl, rub in butter using fingertips, shape into a ball, chill until firm. Press ball of topping through colander or grate on to apples.

Bake in moderately hot oven, 35 to 40 minutes. Cool, cut into slices.

## Jelly and Pineapple Slice

1 packet plain sponge mix
15 oz. can pineapple pieces
2 packets raspberry jelly crystals
3 cups hot water

Make up sponge according to directions on packet. Pour half of this mixture into a greased and paper lined 7 in. x 11 in. lamington tin; bake in moderate oven approximately 35 minutes or until cooked when tested with a fine skewer. (Bake remainder of mixture in 6 in. square cake tin; use as cake). Remove from tins, allow to cool on wire rack. When cold return large sponge to lamington tin, sprinkle with a little pineapple juice. Cover with drained pineapple pieces. Make up 2 packets of jelly using 3 cups hot water; allow to set until egg-white consistency. Carefully spoon over pineapple pieces.

Refrigerate until set. Cut into slices. Serve with whipped cream.

# SPONGE CAKES

Everybody loves the light, airy, melt-in-the-mouth goodness of a sponge cake. Filled with cream and fruit, they make a delicious dessert; and they're ideal for a child's birthday cake. They're not difficult to make; here we give you all the hints you need to turn out perfect sponge cakes

The lightness of a sponge depends upon the amount of air incorporated during the mixing.

□ Sift dry ingredients well so mixture is aerated. Some champion spongemakers sift dry ingredients seven times!

□ Beat eggs with sugar until sugar is dissolved; this could take 10 to 15 minutes. Castor sugar is best to use for sponge cakes; it is finer than ordinary sugar, dissolves more easily, gives a more even texture to finished cake. Some recipes require the eggs to be separated. If so, the whites are whipped until stiff, sugar being added gradually. This is important: if the sugar was added all at once it would deflate the delicate egg-white mixture.

□ Once yolks are added, beat only until mixture is thick and of creamy consistency. Do not over-beat or mixture will become thin; the air beaten into egg-whites would be broken down.

□ Sift dry ingredients evenly over surface of batter and fold in. A large metal spoon is good for this. Dip spoon right to bottom of basin, turn spoon over gently to bring it out, so flour is 'folded' inside egg mixture. Do this lightly, smoothly, until all traces of flour have disappeared.

□ Dissolve the butter in hot water and fold in all at once, carefully and quickly. Hot water is absorbed into mixture more quickly than cold; therefore, less folding-in, which disturbs the air, is necessary.

□ Grease tins lightly; sprinkle lightly with flour or, for a sugary crust, castor sugar. Shake to cover inside surface, turn over, tap out any surplus.

Do not line tins with paper. Sponge cakes do not contain fat in any quantity and, if bottom of tin was protected with paper, the cakes would have a moist, crustless appearance when paper was removed—instead of the delightful, golden colour.

The exception to this is the Swiss Roll, which has the tin lined with greased paper.

□ To test if cake is cooked, press top lightly with fingertip; if no impression is left and cake springs back lightly it is ready to take from oven. It will also shrink away a little from sides of tin.

□ Immediately turn out on to wire cooling tray covered with teatowel; this will prevent wire marking top of cake; carefully invert so top of cake is uppermost. (Be careful not to apply pressure or cake will be squeezed between trays.) Remove top tray and teatowel. Let cake stand until quite cool. Make sure it does not stand in a draught while cooling; this will cause it to shrivel slightly.

## Sponge Cake

4 eggs
¾ cup castor sugar
1¼ cups self-raising flour
1 teaspoon butter
3 tablespoons hot water

Beat whole eggs until light. Gradually beat in sugar; continue beating until mixture is thick and sugar is completely dissolved (approximately 10 to 15 minutes). Sift flour several times; melt butter in hot water. Sift dry ingredients over egg mixture, fold in; then, working quickly, fold in the hot water and butter. Pour into greased deep 8 in. cake tin, bake in moderate oven approximately 25 minutes or until cake is elastic to touch and shrinking slightly from sides of tin. Turn out at once on to cake cooler. When quite cold, spread top of cake with lemon butter, spoon over a tablespoon or more of fresh or canned passionfruit pulp. With piping bag and star pipe, decorate round top edge of cake with whipped cream.

## Sponge Sandwich

3 large eggs
½ cup castor sugar
1 cup self-raising flour
3 tablespoons hot water
1 teaspoon butter

Separate eggs; beat whites stiffly, gradually beat in sugar, beating well after each addition to dissolve sugar thoroughly. Add yolks all at once, beat only

Deliciously light, delicate in texture, Sponge Cake is everybody's favourite. Filling can be whipped cream, jam, lemon butter

until colour is evenly mixed through. Sift flour several times, then sift over egg mixture; fold in carefully. Combine hot water and butter, stir until butter melts (or heat together a few minutes to dissolve butter); pour all at once into mixture, fold through quickly, thoroughly.

Pour into 2 deep 7 in. greased and lightly floured sandwich tins, bake in moderate oven approximately 20 minutes or until lightly browned and elastic to the touch. Turn immediately on to cake cooler. When cold, join with whipped cream.

## Honey Sponge

3 eggs
½ cup castor sugar
½ teaspoon vanilla
¾ cup self-raising flour
3 dessertspoons arrowroot
pinch salt
1 dessertspoon honey
1 dessertspoon butter
3 dessertspoons hot milk

Separate eggs, beat whites stiffly, gradually add sugar, beating well after each addition. Add vanilla, beat well; add yolks all at once, beat again. Sift dry ingredients several times, fold gently into egg mixture. Add honey and the butter, which has been melted in the milk. Pour into 2 greased and lightly floured 7 in. sandwich tins, bake in moderate oven approximately 20 to 25 minutes. When cooked, turn immediately on to cake cooler. When cold, join cakes together with whipped sweetened cream.

## Swiss Roll

For Swiss Roll, make up the Sponge Sandwich recipe on page 160 and mix as directed. Pour mixture into greased, greaseproof paper lined swiss roll tin, approximately 10 in. x 14 in.; spread mixture out lightly. Bake in moderate oven approximately 12 to 15 minutes, or until lightly coloured and elastic to touch. Be careful not to over-cook, or sponge will become dry and crack when rolled.

While sponge is cooking, prepare for the rolling. Place sheet of greaseproof paper on slightly dampened teatowel; dust paper with castor sugar.

When sponge is cooked, turn immediately from tin on to greaseproof paper; peel off lining paper; with sharp knife trim off crisp edge from long sides of cake. Gently roll up sponge, rolling the greaseproof inside as you go. Cover sponge with clean teatowel, let stand 1 minute. Unroll, remove paper, re-roll, let stand until quite cold before filling. When cold, gently unroll, spread with jam or whipped cream (or both), roll up again. Dust top with extra castor sugar, if desired.

## Chocolate Sponge

4 eggs
1 cup castor sugar
1½ tablespoons butter
2½ tablespoons cocoa
4 tablespoons boiling water
1¼ cups self-raising flour

Beat eggs together in basin, gradually add sugar; beat 15 minutes. Combine butter, cocoa, and boiling water, fold into egg mixture. Sift flour several times, sift over egg mixture, fold in, making sure no streaks of colour remain. Fill into 2 greased 7 in. sandwich tins; bake in moderate oven 20 to 25 minutes, or until elastic to touch and shrinking slightly from sides of tin. Remove from tins, cool. When cold, join together with whipped cream; top, if desired, with chocolate icing.

## Ginger Fluff Sponge

4 eggs
½ cup castor sugar
½ cup arrowroot
2 tablespoons plain flour
2 teaspoons ginger
2 teaspoons cinnamon
2 teaspoons cocoa
2 teaspoons cream of tartar
1 teaspoon bicarb. soda
1 dessertspoon golden syrup

Separate eggs; beat whites stiffly, gradually add sugar, beating well after each addition to dissolve sugar thoroughly. Add yolks all at once, beat only until colour is evenly mixed through. Sift dry ingredients at least four times to combine thoroughly. Sift on to egg mixture, fold through gently until colour is even and dry ingredients are mixed in. Pour in warmed golden syrup, fold through gently. Pour into 2 greased deep 7 in. sandwich tins, bake in moderate oven approximately 15 to 20 minutes or until elastic to touch and shrinking slightly from sides of tin. Turn on to cake cooler. When cold, join with whipped cream.

## Honey Roll

3 eggs
¼ cup castor sugar
2 tablespoons honey
1 cup plain flour
1 teaspoon cinnamon
½ teaspoon bicarbonate of soda
1 dessertspoon hot water
whipped cream
extra castor sugar

Beat eggs 3 minutes, or until light in colour. Gradually add sugar, beat until dissolved. Add honey, beat until mixture resembles thick cream. Add bicarbonate of soda dissolved in hot water. Lightly fold in sifted flour and cinnamon. Pour mixture into greased paper-lined 12½ in. x 10½ in. swiss roll tin. Bake in moderately hot oven 12 to 15 minutes.

Follow method for Swiss Roll; spread with whipped cream.

# CHEESECAKES

Cheesecake is among the most popular of all desserts. It's so rich, so luscious, you need to serve it only in small slices. One cheesecake will go a long way; in an 8 or 9-inch size, it will give up to 12 servings. They're best made the day before they're to be served, so can be made ahead for a party.

Cheesecakes can be baked in the oven, or unbaked (set in the refrigerator); there's a wide variety of both types of recipes here and everyone delicious!

## To Make Cheesecakes

When making baked cheesecakes, cooking times should be followed carefully. Don't overcook them. At the end of the specified cooking time, the cheesecake might still appear soft in the centre; but it becomes firmer as it stands.

An overbaked cheesecake develops grainy texture; it is inclined to shrink, crack, and become dry as it cools. If you cool the cheesecake by the following method you'll find there is very little shrinking, and the cheesecake does not fall in the centre.

When baking time is over, turn off the oven heat, leave the oven door ajar, and let the cheesecake stand undisturbed in the oven until it is quite cool. This helps to set the soft centre and prevent it falling. It will not cause overbaking. When the cheesecake is cool, refrigerate until it has set firmly.

Large cheesecakes are best if made the day before they are to be served, then refrigerated overnight; the filling sets firmly and they're easier to cut.

For a crumb crust that will hold its shape without crumbling, and cut well, the ideal proportions are half the amount of butter to the weight of biscuit crumbs. For example, a crumb crust which used 8 oz. biscuit crumbs will hold together well with 4 oz. melted butter.

The exception to this is when a biscuit which has a good proportion of butter added to it during the manufacturing process (such as shortbread biscuits) is used for the crumb crust. This type of crust needs slightly less melted butter added. Specific quantities are given in individual recipes in this book.

The recipes which use a crumb crust specify them in a particular size to hold the quantity of filling: for example, '8 in. crumb crust,' '9 in. crumb crust.'

As a general guide, we give below the various proportions of biscuit crumbs and butter needed for each size. To this can be added a little cinnamon, nutmeg, etc.

For 7 in. sandwich tin with removable base: use 6 oz. plain sweet biscuit crumbs and 3 oz. butter.

For 8 in. springform pan: use 8 oz. plain sweet biscuit crumbs and 4 oz. butter.

For 9 in. springform pan: use 12 oz. plain sweet biscuit crumbs and 6 oz. butter.

For 10 in.–11 in. springform pan: use 1 lb. plain sweet biscuit crumbs and 8 oz. butter.

For 8 in.–9 in. pie plate: use 6 oz. plain sweet biscuit crumbs and 3 oz. butter.

## Wonderful Basic Cheesecake

1½ lb. cream cheese
1 teaspoon vanilla
4 eggs
1 cup sugar
grated rind 1 lemon
1 dessertspoon lemon juice
8 in. crumb crust

Press cream cheese through strainer, blend with vanilla. Beat eggs until thick, beat in sugar gradually. Continue beating while adding cheese mixture in small portions, mixing each time until smooth. Mix in lemon rind and juice. Spread into crumb crust, bake in moderate oven 25 to 30 minutes. Cool, then refrigerate. Just before serving, top with whipped cream, sprinkle with cinnamon or nutmeg.

## Superb Sour Cream Cheesecake

8 oz. packaged cream cheese
8 oz. cottage cheese
3 eggs
1 cup sugar
4 dessertspoons cornflour
½ cup milk
1 cup sour cream
grated rind 2 lemons
1 teaspoon lemon juice
8 in. crumb crust

Beat cheeses together until smooth. Add eggs, one at a time, beating well after each addition. Add cornflour and sugar, mix well. Blend in milk, sour cream, lemon rind and juice. Pour mixture into crumb crust. Stand pan on oven tray. Bake in moderately slow oven 50 to 60 minutes; cool in oven. Refrigerate several hours before serving.

## Minted Cheesecake

**Crumb Crust**

5 oz. shortbread biscuits
2 oz. butter

**Topping**

1 dessertspoon gelatine
¼ cup cold water
¼ cup boiling water
8 oz. packaged cream cheese
½ cup sugar
½ teaspoon vanilla
1 teaspoon peppermint essence
2 dessertspoons lemon juice
6 oz. can evaporated milk, chilled

*Crumb Crust:* Crush biscuits. Combine crumbs and melted butter in a mixing bowl; reserve $\frac{1}{4}$ cup crumbs for topping. Press remaining mixture on to base of greased 7 in. springform pan. Refrigerate until firm.

*Topping:* Soak gelatine in cold water 5 minutes, then dissolve in boiling water; cool. Cream together cheese and sugar until smooth and fluffy. Add vanilla, peppermint essence and lemon juice; beat well. Blend in cooled gelatine and chilled evaporated milk; beat well again. Pour cheese mixture onto prepared crumb crust, sprinkle with remaining crumbs. Refrigerate several hours or overnight.

## Strawberry-Glazed Cheesecake

**Crumb Crust**

6 oz. plain sweet biscuits
3 oz. butter

**Filling**

1½ lb. cream cheese
¼ cup self-raising flour
rind ½ large lemon
¼ pint sour cream
2 eggs
¾ cup sugar
¾ cup milk

**Strawberry Glaze**

1 punnet strawberries
½ cup water
3 dessertspoons cornflour
¼ cup sugar

*Crumb Crust:* Crush biscuits finely, add melted butter and combine well. Press over base only of 8 in. springform pan.

*Filling:* Beat together sieved cream cheese, sifted flour, grated rind, and sour cream. Beat eggs and sugar together until light and fluffy, add milk. Gradually beat into cheese mixture. Pour mixture on to crumb crust. Bake in a moderately slow oven $1\frac{1}{2}$ hours.

*Strawberry Glaze:* Crush half of the strawberries, add the water and cook 2 minutes; strain. Mix cornflour with sugar, stir into strained strawberry liquid. Cook gently, stirring constantly until liquid is clear, approximately 3 minutes. (A few drops of red colouring can be added.) Cool slightly. Cut remaining strawberries in half and arrange on top of cooled cheesecake; spoon glaze over. Refrigerate.

## Luscious Gourmet Cheesecake

1 lb. cream cheese
1 cup castor sugar
2 dessertspoons plain flour
pinch salt
4 eggs, separated
1 whole egg, extra
1 cup sour cream
juice of 1 lemon
2 dessertspoons castor sugar, extra
10 in. crumb crust

Beat cream cheese until softened, combine with sugar, flour and salt, beat well. Beat in the whole egg plus the 4 egg-yolks, sour cream and lemon juice. Beat egg-whites until stiff but not dry, beat in extra sugar, fold into cream cheese mixture. Pour into prepared crumb crust. Bake in a moderately slow oven, $1\frac{1}{4}$ to $1\frac{1}{2}$ hours. Allow to cool in oven. Refrigerate until firm.

## Continental Cream Cheese Slice

**Pastry**

1½ cups plain flour
½ cup custard powder
4 dessertspoons icing sugar
½ teaspoon baking powder
4 oz. butter
milk

**Filling**

10 oz. cream cheese
2 oz. butter
2 eggs
¼ cup sugar
2 oz. sultanas
grated rind of 1 lemon
2 dessertspoons lemon juice

*Pastry:* Sift into basin the flour, custard powder, icing sugar and baking powder. Rub in butter, add sufficient milk to make into a stiff dough (approximately 4 to 6 dessertspoons of milk). Roll out $\frac{2}{3}$ of the pastry and line 7 in. x 11 in. greased lamington tin, bringing pastry $\frac{1}{2}$ inch up the sides. Prick base and bake in moderate oven 10 minutes; cool.

Strawberry-Glazed Cheesecake — light, lovely texture and flavour, with a beautiful glaze of crushed fresh strawberries

**Step 1**
Put biscuits into a plastic bag, crush finely with rolling-pin, then put through fine sieve to separate any large lumps. Larger lumps can be rubbed through sieve with fingers. Or, if using an electric blender, break up biscuits roughly, drop into blender a few at a time

**Step 2**
Add to crumbs the melted butter, sugar, any flavourings; mix to combine well. Mixture should cling together when pressed between fingers. Grease inside of pan lightly, scatter mixture across base, then press on firmly with dessertspoon

## Step by Step to Perfect Crumb Crust

*Filling:* Cream butter with cream cheese until soft and creamy. Beat eggs and sugar until light and fluffy. Gradually add to cream cheese mixture, beat until smooth. Fold in sultanas, lemon rind and juice. Smooth filling over cooked pastry shell. Cut remaining pastry into long strips and place diagonally over filling in lattice form. Brush pastry with milk. Bake in moderate oven 35 to 45 minutes; while still warm, cut into slices; leave in tin until cool, then refrigerate.

## Chocolate-Cream Cheesecake

3 oz. dark chocolate
3 eggs
¾ cup sugar
8 oz. cream cheese
¾ cup cream
⅓ cup plain flour
pinch bicarbonate of soda
pinch salt
1 teaspoon vanilla
2 dessertspoons rum
extra whipped cream
extra melted chocolate
8 in. crumb crust

Chop chocolate, melt over hot water, set aside. Beat eggs until thick and fluffy. Add sugar gradually, beating well until thick and lemon-coloured. Beat together cream cheese and cream until smooth and thickened. Add melted chocolate, stir until well blended. Fold egg mixture into chocolate cream mixture with rum and vanilla. Sift together flour, salt, and bicarbonate of soda; add to creamed mixture. Pour into crumb crust. Bake in slow oven 55 to 60 minutes. Allow to cool, then refrigerate until well firmed.

Top with whipped sweetened cream, drizzle melted chocolate over.

## Strawberry Cheesecake

**Filling**

8 oz. packaged cream cheese
½ cup sugar
3 egg-yolks
3 dessertspoons plain flour
1 teaspoon vanilla
pinch salt
½ pint scalded cream
2 egg-whites

**Topping**

fresh strawberries
½ cup red currant jelly
3 dessertspoons sweet sherry

*Crumb Crust:* Crush 4 oz. coconut biscuits and combine with 2 oz. melted butter. Press mixture on to base only of greased 8 in. springform pan. Refrigerate until firm.

*Filling:* Beat together cheese and sugar until smooth and fluffy, approximately 8 minutes. Add egg-yolks, beat well. Add sifted flour, vanilla and salt, beating continually. Gradually pour in hot

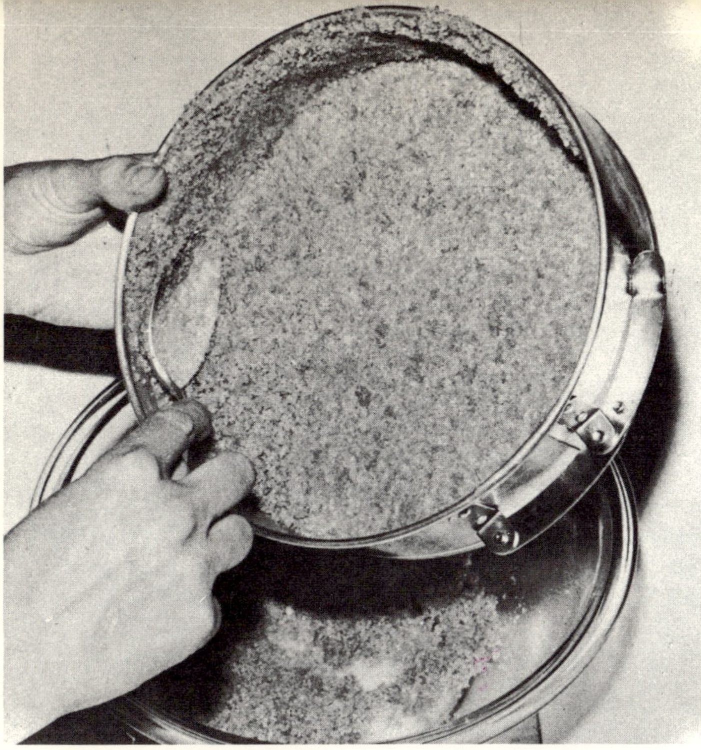

**Step 3**
Now turn pan on its side and put large spoonfuls of crumbs in place on side; press on with back of spoon. Continue until all sides of pan are coated with a firm, even layer of crumbs. You can relax while doing this. Sit down with the pan on your lap

**Step 4**
Stand pan firmly on table, take smooth-sided glass or jar, work it smoothly over base and sides of pan until crust is even. Hold thumb on top of crust as you press to keep top even. Refrigerate 1 hour or bake 10 minutes to set crumbs

**Step 5**
Do not remove filled crumb crust from pan until well refrigerated, preferably overnight. Then release catch at side of pan, loosen gently round top with knife. Stand on top of glass or jar, slide side of pan down; make sure cake doesn't slip off jar

**Step 6**
When the cheesecake has been removed from the pan, neaten the edge of crumb crust by pressing a sharp knife across, as shown above; work carefully to avoid cracking the crust. Use a pastry brush to brush off gently any crumbs on the top

scalded cream, beating all the time. Lastly fold in stiffly beaten egg-whites. Pour cheese mixture on to crumb crust. Stand pan on oven tray, bake in slow oven $1\frac{1}{2}$ hours. Cool, then refrigerate.

*Topping:* Place jelly and sherry in a saucepan. Dissolve over low heat, stirring with a wooden spoon. Refrigerate until commencing to set. Decorate cake when cold with strawberries cut into quarters. Spoon jelly mixture over, refrigerate until set.

## Cheesecake Squares

1 cup plain flour
1 cup self-raising flour
½ cup cornflour
¼ cup custard powder
¼ cup icing sugar
6 oz. butter
⅓ cup water
1 teaspoon lemon juice
½ cup apricot jam
egg glazing
icing sugar

**Filling**

3 oz. butter
2 eggs
¼ cup sugar
⅓ cup raisins
½ teaspoon grated lemon rind
10 oz. cottage cheese
¼ cup sour cream

Sift dry ingredients into basin, rub in butter until mixture resembles fine breadcrumbs. Mix to dry dough with water and lemon juice. Turn out on to floured board and knead lightly. Divide in half, roll out one half to fit base of greased lamington tin, spread with apricot jam, then spread cheese filling over evenly.

*Filling:* Separate eggs. Cream butter, add egg-yolks, sugar, raisins, lemon rind, cottage cheese and sour cream; mix well. Fold in stiffly beaten egg-whites, spread over pastry. Roll out remaining pastry, place on top of cream mixture. Trim edges, brush with beaten egg. Bake in moderate oven 30 to 40 minutes; cool. Cut into squares to serve. Sprinkle with sifted icing sugar.

## Chocolate Cheesecake

**Crumb Crust**

4 oz. plain chocolate biscuits
1½ oz. melted butter

**Filling**

8 oz. packaged cream cheese
½ cup sugar
1 teaspoon vanilla
2 eggs, separated
1 cup cream
4 oz. dark chocolate
pinch salt
2 dessertspoons finely chopped walnuts

*Crumb Crust:* Combine crushed biscuit crumbs and melted butter, mix well. Press mixture on to base of 8 in. springform pan. Bake in moderately slow oven 8 minutes; cool.

*Filling:* Beat cheese until smooth, add $\frac{1}{4}$ cup sugar and the vanilla, beat well. Add lightly beaten egg-yolks and chocolate, which has been melted over hot water. Beat egg-whites and salt until peaks form, gradually beat in remaining sugar; fold into chocolate mixture. Finally, fold through whipped cream and the walnuts. Pour into prepared crumb crust. Refrigerate until set.

To serve, decorate with extra whipped cream and grated chocolate.

## Coffee-Cream Cheesecake

4 oz. cottage cheese
12 oz. cream cheese
2 dessertspoons gelatine
4 dessertspoons cold water
4 dessertspoons boiling water
½ pint cream
2 dessertspoons grated lemon rind
2 dessertspoons lemon juice
4 dessertspoons coffee essence
1 egg-white
¾ cup sugar
8 in. crumb crust

Sieve cheeses into a bowl, beat well. Soften gelatine in cold water, add boiling water, stir until dissolved. Add to cheese mixture with lemon rind and juice, continue beating until smooth. Whip cream until stiff, fold in coffee essence. Beat egg-white, gradually add sugar, continue beating until of meringue consistency. Fold whipped cream, then egg-white, carefully into cheese mixture. Pour into prepared crumb crust. Refrigerate several hours or until set. If desired, decorate top, just before serving, with grated chocolate.

## Lemon Jelly Cheesecake

½ cup boiling water
1 pkt. lemon jelly crystals
½ cup lemon juice
1 teaspoon lemon rind
14 oz. can condensed milk
8 oz. cream cheese
1 teaspoon vanilla
8 in. crumb crust

Pour boiling water over jelly and stir until dissolved; strain. Add lemon juice and rind; cool. Whip chilled condensed milk until thick. Beat cream cheese until soft, add milk, vanilla and jelly, mix well. Pour into crumb crust, refrigerate until set.

Cheesecake Squares — one of the most popular of all cheesecakes. A delicious pastry holds a filling of cream cheese, sour cream, raisins, apricot jam

# PAVLOVAS

Here are recipes for pavlovas using one, two, three, or four egg-whites; ingredients and method for each are slightly different. It's just a matter of choosing which type you like the best

## The ingredients

There are several different types of pavlova: recipes can vary in ingredients and in method. Below are the ingredients used and the reasons for their use.

*Egg-whites* Eggs a few days old are best for making pavlovas; when very fresh, straight from the nest, the egg-white is thin and does not beat up to great volume. Egg-whites should be firm, jelly-like in consistency; they should be at room temperature before beating.

Frozen egg-whites, brought back to room temperature, can be used.

In methods where whites are beaten first and sugar added gradually, beat whites until firm before adding sugar.

Once meringue is made, quickly add other ingredients; if left to stand, beaten egg-whites will lose their volume as the tiny air-bubbles collapse; once collapsed, they will not beat up again.

For the same reason, when the complete pavlova mixture is made, it should be handled quickly and baked as soon as possible.

*Cream of tartar and salt* Used to strengthen and stabilise egg-whites, helping them hold their aerated volume.

*Sugar* In some recipes castor sugar is used for quick dissolving; for others, granulated sugar gives a firmer result.

It is important, when beating sugar into egg-whites, to make sure all sugar is dissolved—otherwise, the undissolved sugar will melt during cooking, and give a 'weepy,' sticky pavlova.

Where sugar is added gradually, make sure each addition of sugar is dissolved before any more sugar is added; otherwise, the weight of undissolved sugar will break down egg-white aeration and mixture will collapse.

To test if sugar is dissolved, rub a little of the mixture between two fingers; any undissolved sugar crystals can be quickly detected.

If using electric mixer, make sure the bowl is continually rotating and evenly dissolving sugar; it may be necessary to assist the bowl gently round with your fingers—mixing may slow down as egg-whites whip up firmly and mixture becomes thick.

Like all rules, there are exceptions to it; the exception to the firm beating of sugar to dissolve all crystals completely, is the Classic Pavlova (see recipe overleaf).

In this recipe, the last quantity of sugar is mixed with cornflour and just lightly folded in at the last minute. The cornflour prevents sugar 'weeping.' This method gives a very characteristic pavlova—crisp and crunchy on outside, with soft, marshmallowy centre.

*Cornflour* Helps to dry out pavlova; the more cornflour used, the drier will be the pavlova.

*Vinegar and lemon juice* This combination helps to form the marshmallowy centre; also whitens the pavlova.

## The equipment

*Bowls* A bowl with small rounded base and deep, gently sloping sides is considered best. The small bowl of electric mixer can be used in mixtures with up to 3 egg-whites.

It is most important that all equipment—bowls, beaters, etc.—be clean, dry, free from any dust, moisture, or fat (this includes egg-yolk). These could prevent egg-whites whipping up to good volume.

## Preparation of trays

There are several different methods of preparing trays; each is effective, the pavlova does not stick. They are:

*Cornfloured* Cover that part of baking tray on which you are going to spoon pavlova mixture with a thick, even layer of sifted cornflour. Suitable for large or small pavlovas.

*Greased and Cornfloured* Brush tray lightly with melted butter, dust with sifted cornflour; shake off excess cornflour. Best suited to small individual pavlovas.

*Lined, Greased, and Cornfloured* Place sheet of greaseproof paper, trimmed to size of tray, on greased baking tray; brush paper lightly with melted butter, dust with sifted cornflour. Shake off excess cornflour. Suitable for all types of pavlova.

*Aluminium Foil* Cover tray with layer of aluminium foil—there is no need to grease. Place pavlova mixture directly on foil. When pavlova has cooked and cooled, it is easy to peel off foil gently. Suitable for all types of pavlovas—particularly good for large pavlovas.

## Removing from trays

Allow pavlova to cool completely on its tray, then loosen with spatula or broad, flat-bladed knife. Make sure spatula or knife blade is kept flat on tray —do not try to lever pavlova up, or it will break.

If syrup from undissolved sugar has 'weeped' out during cooking, thus making pavlova difficult to remove, place tray over low heat for a second to melt greasing, then loosen again carefully, as above.

## How to bake

Baking times and temperatures vary, according to the varying recipes, and also type of oven—gas or electric.

Place baking tray with pavlova in low position in oven, leave for stipulated cooking time, then turn off heat and, if possible, allow pavlova to remain in oven, with door ajar, until it has completely cooled. This dries it out and makes it crisp.

This method has been used for all recipes in this section.

If you are making pavlova in a hurry, and cannot wait for it to cool in oven, allow a little longer cooking time than given in individual recipe. Remove from oven, cool on tray. Pavlovas should be light, dry, pale in colour.

## How to store

Provided pavlovas have been cooked to correct dryness, we recommend the following keeping times for recipes in this section. Keep pavlovas in air-tight tin.

*One-Egg Pavlova* 1 to 2 weeks

*Easy Two-Egg Pavlova* 2 to 3 weeks

*Classic Pavlova* 10 days

*Stored Heat Pavlova* 1 week

*Marshmallow Pavlova* 2 days

Marshmallow Pavlova is best stored in air-tight tin in refrigerator; the others can be stored in dark cupboard.

The Easy Two-Egg Pavlova, because it is a dry mixture, can be wrapped and frozen; keeps 2 months frozen.

## One-Egg Pavlova

1 egg-white
2 tablespoons boiling water
pinch salt
good pinch cream of tartar
⅞ cup granulated sugar

Place all ingredients in small, deep, heat-proof basin. Stand basin over saucepan of boiling water; reduce heat, beat with electric mixer or rotary beater until mixture is stiff and glossy, approximately 7 minutes. (Do not allow water to boil; there should be just enough heat to keep water hot.) Remove immediately from hot water and spread quickly on prepared trays. This mixture makes one 8 in. pavlova or 4 small individual pavlova shells.

*Baking in Electric Oven* Large pavlova; bake in very slow oven 1½ to 2 hours, cool in oven. Individual pavlovas; bake in very slow oven 30 to 45 minutes, cool in oven.

*Baking in Gas Oven* Large pavlova; bake in slow oven 1 hour, reduce heat to very slow, bake further 1 hour, cool in oven. Small individual pavlovas; bake in slow oven 45 to 60 minutes, cool in oven.

## Easy Two-Egg Pavlova

2 egg-whites
1½ cups castor sugar
½ teaspoon vanilla
1 teaspoon vinegar
1 teaspoon cornflour
4 tablespoons boiling water

Place all ingredients into small bowl of electric mixer, beat on high speed until mixture is very stiff (approximately 15 minutes). Spread on to prepared trays. This mixture makes one 11in. pavlova or 15 small shells.

*Baking in Electric Oven* Large pavlova; bake in moderate oven 10 minutes, reduce heat to slow, bake further 45 minutes, cool in oven. Small individual pavlovas; bake in moderate oven 10 minutes, reduce heat to slow, bake further 30 minutes, cool in oven.

*Baking in Gas Oven* Large pavlova; bake in moderate oven 10 minutes, reduce heat to slow, bake further 1 to 1½ hours, cool in oven. Small individual pavlovas, bake in moderate oven 10 minutes, reduce heat to slow, bake further 40 to 50 minutes, cool in oven.

## Classic Pavlova

3 egg-whites
pinch salt
¾ cup castor sugar
¼ cup granulated sugar
1 tablespoon cornflour
1 teaspoon lemon juice

Beat egg-whites and salt until stiff and dry; add castor sugar gradually, beating well between each addition. Make sure sugar is completely dissolved. Mix together granulated sugar and cornflour, lightly fold into meringue with lemon juice. This mixture will make one large pavlova. It can also be used for 2 pavlovas, and they can be arranged in tiers, as shown in colour picture. To do this, mark prepared tray with 5 in. circle and another prepared tray with 7 in. circle. Spread approximately ¼ in. layer of mixture to fit each circle. With remainder of mixture, pipe or spoon swirls round edges to form shell. Baking times are as for large pavlova (see below).

To assemble the 2-tiered pavlova (as shown in picture), when completely cooled, place larger shell on serving dish. Spread over generous layer of whipped cream, then any fresh fruit or well-drained canned fruit. Place smaller shell on top, fill centre with fresh or canned fruit.

*Baking in Electric Oven* Large pavlova; bake in slow oven 30 to 40 minutes, cool in oven. Small individual pavlovas; bake as for large pavlova.

*Baking in Gas Oven* Large pavlova; bake in very slow oven 1 hour or until pavlova is dry to touch, cool in oven. Small individual pavlovas; bake in very slow oven 45 minutes, cool in oven.

## Stored heat Pavlova

(Cooks in oven overnight)

4 egg-whites
1¼ cups granulated sugar
½ teaspoon cream of tartar
1 teaspoon lemon juice
1 teaspoon vanilla
¼ teaspoon salt

Beat egg-whites until foamy, add cream of tartar and salt; beat until stiff. Gradually add sugar, a tablespoon at a time, beating well until all sugar is dissolved. Continue beating until all sugar is added and mixture is thick and glossy. Stir in lemon juice and vanilla. Spread or pipe mixture on to prepared trays, making two 8 in. shells, or 15 small individual shells.

*Baking in Electric Oven* Large pavlova; place in very hot oven, close door, turn off heat, leave in oven overnight. Small individual pavlovas; preheat oven to hot, place pavlovas in oven. Turn off heat, leave pavlovas in oven overnight.

*Baking in Gas Oven* Large pavlova; preheat oven to very hot, place pavlova in oven, reduce heat to hot, bake 5 minutes. Turn off heat, leave pavlova in oven overnight. Small individual pavlovas; preheat oven to hot, bake 5 minutes. Turn off heat, leave pavlovas in oven overnight.

NOTE: It is important not to open door until it is time to take baked pavlova from oven—otherwise stored heat will be lost and pavlova will not crisp correctly.

## Marshmallow Pavlova

4 egg-whites
1 cup castor sugar
1 dessertspoon cornflour
1 teaspoon vinegar

Beat egg-whites, until stiff, add ½ cup castor sugar, beat thoroughly until sugar is dissolved (approx. 5 minutes). Add remaining sugar, a tablespoon at a time, beating well after each addition. Lightly fold in sifted cornflour, then vinegar. Take 30 in. length of aluminium foil, fold in half lengthwise. Make circle of foil and secure. Place on thickly cornfloured tray, fill pavlova mixture into foil; level off top (do not make into a shell). This mixture will make one deep 9 in. pavlova. Do not use this mixture to make small individual pavlovas.

*Baking in Electric Oven* Preheat oven to moderate, reduce heat to slow, bake 1¼ hours, cool in oven.

*Baking in Gas Oven* Preheat oven to moderate, reduce heat to slow, bake 1¼ to 1½ hours, cool in oven.

Be very careful when peeling off collar, so as not to break crisp coating.

NOTE: This is a favourite type of pavlova—with its deep, soft, marshmallowy centre and crisp, slightly chewy coating. It has, when cooked, a rather 'untidy' appearance, compared with other mixtures —but the taste, texture, and flavour are delightful. In the preliminary cooking, this mixture rises very high; toward end of cooking time, the centre falls, leaving a high, crisp shell around. (It will fall a little more as pavlova cools.) The filling or topping is put inside the high, crisp shell.

Fresh fruit salad or strawberries make a colourful topping, spread whipped cream over. Or fill with whipped cream and spread fruit over top. Do this as near to serving time as possible.

Classic Pavlova has the traditional crisp shell with the soft, marshmallow centre. Fill with whipped cream and any fresh or canned fruit; we've used strawberries and colourful Chinese gooseberries

# Fillings for Pavlovas

Whipped cream, or ice-cream, with fresh or canned fruit are favourite fillings for pavlovas. But they can be made even more special with any of the luscious fillings given here

## Frozen Fruit Cream

20 oz. block vanilla ice-cream
orange segments
grated rind 2 oranges
15 oz. can crushed pineapple
1 tablespoon marsala

Drain pineapple. Mix drained pineapple with grated orange rind and marsala. Fold in vanilla ice-cream, pour into freezer trays, allow to set slightly. Just before serving, arrange layer of orange segments on base of pavlova. Spoon over partially frozen pineapple cream. Decorate with extra orange segments. Serve at once.

## Chestnut Cream

½ pint cream
1 tablespoon brandy
9 oz. can cream of chestnuts (in vanilla-flavoured syrup)

Beat chestnuts until soft, add brandy, stir in whipped cream. Fill into 8 in. pavlova shell and refrigerate.

NOTE: There are two types of canned chestnuts; one is pure chestnuts pureed, with no sweetening added. The second has sugar, glucose, and vanilla added; this is the best for above filling. Check ingredients on can.

## Brandy Bavarian Cream

2 egg-yolks
¼ cup sugar
½ pint hot milk
1 tablespoon water
1½ teaspoons gelatine
1 tablespoon brandy
½ cup cream

Soften gelatine in cold water. Beat egg-yolks and sugar until thick and light in colour, stir in hot milk gradually. Stir over boiling water until mixture coats back of spoon. Add softened gelatine, stirring until dissolved; cool, stirring occasionally to prevent skin forming. Whip cream and brandy together, fold into cooled custard. Pour into pavlova case, refrigerate until set. Delicious topped with brandied strawberries.

## Rich Chocolate Custard

2 egg-yolks
3 tablespoons cocoa
2 tablespoons cornflour
½ cup sugar
2 cups milk
¼ pint cream

Place egg-yolks, cocoa, cornflour and sugar into saucepan; gradually add milk, stirring until well blended. Stir over medium heat until mixture boils and thickens; cool. Whip cream and fold into cooled chocolate custard. Pour into pavlova case, refrigerate. Serve decorated with whipped cream and almond slivers.

## Lemon Chiffon

2 eggs, separated
¼ cup castor sugar
¼ pint cream
¼ cup cold water
1 dessertspoon gelatine
juice and rind 2 lemons

Soak gelatine in cold water. Beat egg-yolks, sugar and lemon rind over boiling water until thick, creamy, and pale in colour. Dissolve gelatine over boiling water, add lemon juice. Add gelatine mixture to cooled egg mixture, off heat, and continue beating until mixture begins to thicken. Beat egg-whites until stiff, and whip cream; gently fold into lemon mixture. When starting to set, spoon into pavlova case, refrigerate until firm. Decorate with extra whipped cream.

## Mocha Chiffon

1 tablespoon gelatine
½ cup water
½ cup sugar
2 tablespoons cornflour
2 eggs, separated
2 cups milk
2 oz. grated chocolate
1 dessertspoon instant coffee powder
2 tablespoons sugar, extra
¼ teaspoon cream of tartar
vanilla

Soak gelatine in cold water. In saucepan, blend cornflour, egg-yolks and sugar with a little of the milk, add remaining milk, stir over low heat until custard boils and thickens. Flavour with vanilla. Measure out 1 cup of this custard mixture, reserve. To remaining custard add chocolate and instant coffee; stir until melted and well blended. Cool, spread over base of pavlova. Dissolve soaked gelatine over boiling water, stir into reserved custard; cool. Beat egg-whites and cream of tartar until stiff, gradually beat in extra sugar. Lightly whisk in cooled custard. When starting to set, spoon over mocha layer. Refrigerate until firm. Serve topped with whipped cream and chocolate shavings.

# WEDDING CAKES

A good, rich fruit cake is the basis for the traditional wedding cake. Fruit cake recipes given on these pages also make excellent Christmas cakes; they have rich flavour, keep well, cut well.

The cakes are named according to the amount of butter and sugar used in each. For example, Quarter-pound Cake uses $\frac{1}{4}$ lb. of butter; Half-pound Cake uses $\frac{1}{2}$ lb., and so on

## Method for Fruit Cakes

The method of preparing the four cakes is the same:

NOTE: See the four fruit cake recipes that follow for the quantities of ingredients required.

Prepare fruits by washing, drying, and removing stems. Chop and place in basin, pour over spirits, and mix well. Cover, stand overnight. Cream butter with brown sugar, grated fruit rinds, and essences, add marmalade and caramel or parisian essence. Drop in eggs one at a time, beating well after each addition. Fold in prepared fruit alternately with sifted dry ingredients, mix well.

Fill into lined tin (see page 177), smooth top. Bake as directed in individual recipes. When cooked, cake should feel firm, and a thin-bladed knife, when inserted into centre of cake, should come out clean.

Immediately cake is removed from oven, wrap in clean towel, or aluminium foil, to ensure soft surface on top of cake.

Cake can be stored in tin until required. Store in a reasonably cool place.

## Quarter-Pound Cake

¾ lb. sultanas
¼ lb. raisins
2 oz. currants
2 oz. glacé cherries
2 oz. mixed peel
¼ cup rum, brandy, or sherry
4 oz. butter
¾ cup brown sugar, firmly packed
½ teaspoon grated orange rind
½ teaspoon grated lemon rind
few drops almond essence
½ teaspoon vanilla
1 tablespoon marmalade
½ teaspoon caramel or parisian essence
2 eggs
1¼ cups plain flour
pinch salt
½ teaspoon mixed spice
⅛ teaspoon cinnamon
⅛ teaspoon nutmeg

Prepare and mix ingredients as directed in Method for Fruit Cakes on this page. Fill into 6 in. round or square cake tin lined with 1 thickness of white paper and 1 thickness of brown paper.

Bake in slow oven approx. $2\frac{1}{2}$ hours.

## Half-Pound Cake

1½ lb. sultanas
½ lb. raisins
4 oz. currants
4 oz. glacé cherries
4 oz. mixed peel
½ cup rum, brandy, or sherry
8 oz. butter
1½ cups brown sugar, firmly packed
1 teaspoon grated orange rind
1 teaspoon grated lemon rind
few drops almond essence
1 teaspoon vanilla
2 tablespoons marmalade
1 teaspoon caramel or parisian essence
4 eggs
2½ cups plain flour
pinch salt
1 teaspoon mixed spice
¼ teaspoon cinnamon
¼ teaspoon nutmeg

Prepare and mix ingredients as in Method for Fruit Cakes. Fill into 8 in. round or square cake tin lined with 1 thickness white paper and 2 thicknesses brown.

Bake in slow oven approx. 4 hours.

## One-Pound Cake

3 lb. sultanas
1 lb. raisins
½ lb. currants
½ lb. glacé cherries
½ lb. mixed peel
1 cup rum, brandy, or sherry
1 lb. butter
1 lb. brown sugar
2 teaspoons grated lemon rind
½ teaspoon almond essence
2 teaspoons grated orange rind
2 teaspoons vanilla
4 tablespoons marmalade
1 dessertspoon caramel or parisian essence
8 eggs
5 cups plain flour
pinch salt
2 teaspoons spice
½ teaspoon cinnamon
½ teaspoon nutmeg

Prepare and mix ingredients as in Method for Fruit

Tins in which rich fruit cakes are to be baked need linings to protect the mixture during the long cooking time. Line tin with two layers of brown paper, then one of greaseproof paper; this is the inside layer next to cake

*For square tin:* Cut 3 pieces of lining paper the width of tin, and to come 1½ in. higher than the sides. Fit them into tin, overlapping them in opposite directions. Corners must be even

*For round tin:* Stand tin on paper, trace circle around with pencil, then cut out the circle. Cut out strip 3 in. higher than depth of tin, fold over 1½ in. of strip and cut diagonally into the fold at 1 in. intervals.

## Preparing the cake tin

Cakes. Fill into 10 in. cake tin lined with 1 thickness white paper and 2 thicknesses brown.

Bake in slow oven approx. 6 hours.

## One-and-a-Half-Pound Cake

- 4½ lb. sultanas
- 1½ lb. raisins
- ¾ lb. currants
- ¾ lb. glacé cherries
- ¾ lb. mixed peel
- 1½ cups rum, brandy, or sherry
- 1½ lb. butter
- 1½ lb. brown sugar
- 3 teaspoons grated lemon rind
- 3 teaspoons grated orange rind
- 1 teaspoon almond essence
- 3 teaspoons vanilla
- 6 tablespoons marmalade
- 1 tablespoon caramel or parisian essence
- 12 eggs
- 7½ cups plain flour (1 lb. 14 oz.)
- ½ teaspoon salt
- 3 teaspoons spice
- ¾ teaspoon cinnamon
- ¾ teaspoon nutmeg

Prepare and mix ingredients according to Method for Fruit Cakes on previous page. Fill mixture into round or square 12 in. cake tin lined with one thickness white paper and two thicknesses brown paper.

Bake in slow oven about 7 to 8 hours.

NOTE: Mixed fruit can be used in place of the sultanas, raisins, currants, cherries, and peel listed in the ingredients in the four cake recipes named according to butter content, which appear above and on previous page.

These substitutions are as follows:

Quarter-Pound Cake: Use 1 lb. 6 oz. mixed fruit.
Half-Pound Cake: Use 2¾ lb. mixed fruit.
One-Pound Cake: Use 5½ lb. mixed fruit.
One-and-a-Half-Pound Cake: Use 8¼ lb. mixed fruit.

## Covering the Cakes

Brush cake with lightly beaten egg-white or sieved apricot jam, apply almond paste.

After applying almond paste, let cake stand for at least 24 hours. Then take a little lightly beaten egg white and brush evenly over cake. Now apply the fondant.

## Almond Paste

- 2 lb. pure icing sugar
- 8 oz. marzipan meal or ground almonds
- 4 egg-yolks
- good squeeze lemon or orange juice
- almond essence
- 4 tablespoons sherry

Sift icing sugar into basin, add marzipan meal, mix

*Fit strips of paper* round sides of tin, pressing the cut edges flat at the base of tin. Then take the paper circle previously cut out and fit it into base of tin to cover cut-out side sections; press paper out evenly

*Settle mixture into tin* by lifting tin up about 12 in. and letting it drop sharply on a firm, hard surface. This ensures that the mixture settles into tin, resulting in a good shape for cake; this also breaks up any air bubbles that may form in mixture.

*For smooth top to cake,* wet your hand and smooth the surface of the raw mixture before putting cake in oven to cook. This will ensure a flat even top and give a nice gloss to finished cake

---

well. Beat egg-yolks with sherry and fruit juice, mix into dry ingredients. Turn on to board lightly dusted with extra icing sugar; knead well. Flavour with a little almond essence.

If too dry, add more fruit juice.

## Fondant

2 lb. pure icing sugar
2 egg-whites
4 tablespoons liquid glucose
1 tablespoon glycerine

Sift icing sugar into bowl. Remove about 1 cup icing sugar, put aside. Make well in centre of icing sugar in basin, add egg-whites, cover lightly with icing sugar from sides. Add glycerine and warmed glucose, mix well. Sprinkle reserved icing sugar on to board; turn fondant on to this, knead well, working in reserved icing sugar, until mixture is of correct consistency. Extra icing sugar may be needed.

Flavour and colour as desired.

## Wedding Cakes

When assembling wedding cakes, it is very important to have good balance in the height of cakes that will form the tiers.

If cake for top tier is deeper than bottom tier, the complete cake will look top-heavy.

Average height for a wedding cake tier is 3 in. to $3\frac{1}{2}$ in. deep.

Tier heights can be graduated; for example, base cake, 4 in. deep; the middle cake, $3\frac{1}{2}$ in. deep; top tier, 3 in. deep.

## Wedding-Cake Sizes

*Large Wedding Cakes* Three-tier, bake base in 12 in. tin; middle cake in 9 in. tin; top cake, 6 in. tin.

Two-tier: Base cake, 12 in. tin; top cake, 6 in. tin.

*Small to Average Cakes* Three-tier, base cake, 10 in. tin; middle cake, 8 in. tin; top cake, 6 in. tin.

Two-tier: Base cake, 10 in. tin; top cake, 6 in. tin.

*Single-tiers* Bake in 10 in. or 12 in. tin.

# BATTERS

Pancakes, pikelets, waffles, sweet or savoury fritters—these are just some of the good things which can be made with a versatile batter, which can be mixed in minutes.

The basic recipes for many types of batters are given here, together with delightful variations

## Pikelets

1 cup self-raising flour
pinch salt
¼ teaspoon bicarbonate of soda
½ cup sour milk
3 tablespoons sugar
1 egg
1 dessertspoon melted butter

NOTE: Fresh milk soured with 1 teaspoon vinegar or lemon juice can be used in place of the ½ cup of sour milk listed above.

Sift dry ingredients, add sugar. Mix to a smooth batter with beaten egg and milk, add melted butter. Heat and grease pan, drop batter by dessertspoonfuls on to pan, cook until bubbly on top, light brown underneath. Turn, cook other side.

*Fruit Pikelets* Add 2 tablespoons sultanas to batter.

## Orange Pikelets

1 cup milk
juice ½ lemon
2 eggs
3 tablespoons sugar
pinch salt
1½ cups self-raising flour
grated rind and juice 1 orange
butter

Combine milk and lemon juice, stand aside in warm place to turn sour. Separate eggs. Place egg-yolks in basin, add 1 tablespoon of the sugar and beat well. Beat egg-whites in separate basin until stiff, gradually beat in remaining sugar. Combine with egg-yolk mixture, and fold in sifted flour and salt, sour milk, juice and rind of orange. Mix to smooth batter. Heat frypan, grease lightly with butter. Drop dessertspoonfuls of batter on to pan, cook until bubbles appear on top of pikelets. Turn and cook other side.

*Lemon Pikelets* Substitute grated rind and juice of 1 lemon for the orange juice and rind in the above recipe.

## Cream Pikelets

1 cup self-raising flour
2½ teaspoons baking powder
½ teaspoon salt
1 egg
1 tablespoon sugar
1 oz. melted butter
½ cup milk
2 tablespoons cream

Sift together flour, baking powder, and salt; stir in sugar. Beat egg lightly, add milk, butter, and cream. Beat liquid into flour mixture until smooth. Heat frying pan or griddle; spoon 1 tablespoon mixture on to greased heated griddle. Cook until bubbly and browned at edges, turn and cook on other side. Serve warm, buttered, with honey or lemon juice.

Makes 1 dozen.

## Yoghurt Pikelets

3 eggs
3 dessertspoons sugar
½ cup plain flour
1 tablespoon cornflour
2 teaspoons baking powder
¼ teaspoon salt
½ cup milk
½ cup yoghurt

Separate eggs. Beat together egg-yolks and sugar. Sift flour with cornflour, baking powder and salt. Combine with egg-mixture, then add milk and yoghurt; mix well. Beat egg-whites until stiff and fold into mixture. Drop by dessertspoonfuls on to well-greased frypan, cook until golden brown on both sides, turning once. Serve hot with butter.

NOTE: Sour cream can be substituted for yoghurt in recipe above.

## Yorkshire Pudding

1 cup plain flour
pinch salt
½ pint milk
1 egg
1 to 2 tablespoons drippings from roast

Sift flour and salt into basin. Make a well in the centre, add egg. Beat into flour, then gradually add ½ milk, beating constantly and incorporating flour from sides of bowl. When a thick batter consistency has formed, beat well about 5 minutes. Stir in remaining milk, cover, refrigerate 30 minutes. Place the dripping from the roasting meat in small baking dish and heat. When very hot, add the batter and bake in hot oven until well browned (20 to 25 minutes). Serve with roast beef.

## Basic Waffles

2 eggs
1 dessertspoon sugar
¾ cup milk
½ cup water
1 teaspoon vanilla
pinch salt
2 cups self-raising flour
2 tablespoons cornflour
4 oz. butter

Separate eggs. Beat egg-yolks and sugar together, add milk, water, vanilla; beat again. Add to sifted dry ingredients. Pour in melted butter; beat well. Finally fold in stiffly beaten egg-whites. Allow batter to stand 10 minutes. Spoon into hot, greased waffle iron, cook approximately 5 minutes or until golden brown and crisp.

## Crisp Golden Waffles

1 cup self-raising flour
1 dessertspoon sugar
½ teaspoon salt
2 eggs
1 cup cream
1 tablespoon melted butter

Sift flour, sugar and salt. Separate eggs, beat egg-yolks until thick. Add cream and mix lightly. Stir in sifted dry ingredients all at once, and stir only until smooth. Stir in melted butter. Beat egg-whites until stiff and fold into mixture. Cook in hot, greased waffle iron until golden brown.

## Fritter Batter 1

2 cups plain flour
1 teaspoon salt
1 egg
1 tablespoon oil
1 to 1¼ cups hot water

Sift flour and salt into basin. Make a well in centre, add beaten egg and oil. Add enough water to make a coating batter. Beat until smooth. Use to coat fish, meat, etc.

## Fritter Batter 2

½ cup plain flour
1 tablespoon oil
1 egg
pinch salt
approx. ⅓ cup tepid water

Separate egg. Mix sifted flour and salt gradually with water. Beat in egg-yolk and oil until batter is smooth. Leave to stand at room temperature 2 hours. Then whisk egg-white and fold into batter. Use to coat fruit, such as apple slices, pineapple, bananas, etc.

## Fritter Binding Batter

1¾ cups self-raising flour
½ teaspoon salt
2 eggs
1 cup milk
1 dessertspoon melted butter

Sift flour and salt. Combine lightly beaten eggs, milk, and melted butter, stir into dry ingredients and beat until smooth. Use to bind 1 to 2 cups of filling. Drop by spoonfuls into hot oil, cook until brown all over. Drain well on absorbent paper.

NOTE: Finely chopped, cooked meat, chicken, etc., can be used with this batter; it's an excellent way to use up small quantities of leftover meat or fish.

## Brandied Prune Fritters

12 large prunes
1 cup white wine
12 blanched almonds
⅓ cup self-raising flour
pinch salt
1 tablespoon brandy
water
oil for frying
2 oz. grated chocolate
3 tablespoons brown sugar

Place prunes with wine in saucepan, simmer slowly 10 minutes. Drain, cool, stone, and replace each prune stone with an almond. Sift flour, add salt and brandy and a little water to make a smooth batter. Dip prunes in batter, fry until golden in hot oil. Drain and roll in mixed chocolate and brown sugar.

## Chinese Fried Prawns

1 lb. prawns, shelled and cleaned
1 tablespoon brandy or lemon juice
oil for deep frying
½ teaspoon soy or worcestershire sauce
mayonnaise seasoned with horseradish or capers

**Frying Batter**

½ cup plain flour
pinch salt
1 dessertspoon melted butter
1 egg, beaten
½ cup beer
1 egg-white, extra

Marinate prawns in brandy and sauce. Meanwhile, make the frying batter; sift flour and salt into bowl, stir in butter and egg. Add beer gradually, stirring only until mixture is smooth. Let batter stand in warm place for 1 hour, then fold in stiffly beaten egg-white. Drain prawns, then dip into the batter and fry, a few at a time, in deep, hot oil until golden brown. Drain and serve with mayonnaise.

## Pancakes

1 cup plain flour
pinch salt
1 egg
½ pint milk

Sift flour and salt into bowl, make well in centre.

Add whole egg, work flour in from sides, add milk a little at a time. Beat well until bubbles rise to surface; stand 1 hour. Heat pan, grease lightly. From small jug pour 2 to 3 tablespoons batter into pan, cook slowly, loosening edges with knife until set and lightly browned underneath. Toss or turn, brown on other side. Lift on to kitchen paper, sprinkle with lemon juice and sugar. Roll up and serve.

## French Crêpes

⅓ cup plain flour
1 egg
1 egg-yolk, extra
1 tablespoon oil
pinch salt
1 cup milk

Sift flour into bowl, add egg, egg-yolk, oil, salt and 2 tablespoons milk. Beat until smooth with small whisk. Mix in remainder of milk; refrigerate ½ hour. Heat heavy pan, grease with butter. Pour thin layer of pancake batter into pan, brown on one side. Turn, brown other side. Turn out on to plate. Repeat until all batter is used; keep warm. These can be filled with any savoury or sweet filling; seafood or chicken in a well-flavoured white sauce is good—and, for a sweet filling, try spreading pancakes with warmed apricot jam mixed with a little brandy, roll up, spoon lightly whipped cream over.

## Crepes Suzette

2 tablespoons sugar
1 orange
1 lemon
2 oz. butter
⅓ cup Grand Marnier
French Crepes, see above

Squeeze orange and lemon, set aside ½ cup orange juice and 1 dessertspoon lemon juice to add to the sauce. Melt butter in pan, add sugar. Continue cooking over low heat until sugar melts and begins to caramelise. Pour in fruit juices. Cook rapidly over high heat until liquid reduces slightly and the caramelised sugar dissolves. Reduce heat, add the pancakes, one at a time, swirling them around in the sauce. Then, using fork and spoon, fold them in half, then in quarters. Allow pancakes to cook for a few minutes to soak up sauce, turning them once. Pour over the grand marnier; when warm, set aflame. Arrange pancakes on warmed plates (allow 2 to a serving). Spoon the hot sauce over.

## Cream Cheese Blintzes

2 cups plain flour
1 tablespoon sugar
3 cups milk
½ teaspoon salt
1 egg
oil for deep frying
sour cream

**Cream Cheese Filling**

½ lb. cream cheese
½ lb. cottage cheese
yolk of 1 egg
little grated lemon rind
1 tablespoon melted butter
½ cup sugar
pinch salt
½ cup raisins, plumped in warm water
little chopped preserved ginger

Break egg in bowl, add 1 tablespoon of sugar, the salt, 1 cup of milk, and mix. Then gradually stir in the sifted flour and remainder of milk. Heat the pan, grease with butter, pour in just enough batter to cover bottom of pan. As soon as one side is done, take the pancake out and continue to cook remainder. Cook on one side only. (The pancakes must be very thin; add more milk to the batter if necessary.) Put a tablespoon of filling on to cooked side of each pancake, fold into envelope shape, brushing the last fold with some of the batter to hold it. Just before serving, drop pancakes, one or two at a time, into deep, hot oil. Cook a few minutes until crisp and golden; drain well. Serve topped with sour cream.

*Filling* Sieve the cheeses, add egg-yolk, sugar, salt, lemon rind, butter, and mix thoroughly. Stir in the raisins and ginger.

## German Potato Pancakes

¼ cup plain flour
1½ teaspoons salt
¼ teaspoon baking powder
pinch pepper
2 eggs
1 tablespoon chopped onion
1 tablespoon chopped parsley
2 lb. potatoes
2 oz. butter

Sift dry ingredients into bowl. Beat eggs well, add to dry ingredients with chopped onion and parsley; blend well. Wash, peel, and grate potatoes. Place in cloth and squeeze out excess liquid, add potatoes to egg mixture. Beat thoroughly with wooden spoon. Heat 2 oz. butter in frying pan. Spoon about 2 tablespoons batter into pan, flatten slightly with spoon. Cook over medium heat until golden brown and crisp on one side. Turn carefully, brown other side. Drain on absorbent paper. Add more butter to pan for remainder of pancakes, if necessary.

Pikelets are mixed and cooked in minutes. Serve them hot, well-buttered — they're good, light eating at any time

# MADE WITHOUT BAKING

There's no need to light the oven in hot weather to make pies, biscuits and cakes. There are recipes for all types — all delicious! — including some special-occasion biscuits to serve with after-dinner coffee

## Coffee Cream Roll

½ lb. plain sweet biscuits
¾ cup icing sugar
3 oz. ground almonds
½ cup hot black coffee
½ teaspoon vanilla
extra icing sugar

**Butter-Cream Filling**

4 oz. butter
¾ cup sugar
⅓ cup water
1 to 2 teaspoons rum

**Cream Filling**

1 cup cream
¼ cup icing sugar
1 to 2 teaspoons rum

Crush biscuits very finely; place in mixing bowl with sifted icing sugar and ground almonds. Mix well, make a well in centre, stir in coffee and vanilla. Mix together well to form a soft dough. Sift a little extra icing sugar on to a large sheet of greaseproof paper. Roll out mixture on greaseproof paper to rectangular shape approximately 9 in. x 12 in. Spread filling over evenly. Holding paper with both hands, gently roll into swiss roll shape. Roll in greaseproof paper, refrigerate until firm.

We've given a choice of two fillings for the roll— cream or butter-cream. If you want to make the Coffee Cream Roll several days in advance, use the butter-cream filling; the whipped cream filling will soften the biscuit crumbs if kept for more than 1 day. However, if making the roll to use the same day the whipped cream filling is delicious.

*Butter-Cream Filling* Place sugar and water in saucepan, place over low heat, stirring, until sugar dissolves. Bring to the boil, boil 5 minutes. Remove from heat, cool. Beat butter until creamy, gradually add cold syrup, beating well after each addition. Add rum to taste, beat well.

*Cream Filling* Beat cream until stiff, gradually adding sifted icing sugar and rum.

## Chocolate Caramel Crisps

8 oz. dark chocolate
4 oz. butter
½ cup sugar
1 cup chopped dates
3 cups rice bubbles

Melt half chopped chocolate over hot water, spread over base of well-greased lamington tin; refrigerate.

Put butter, sugar and dates in saucepan; cook, stirring, until dates are soft. Stir in rice bubbles, spread mixture over chilled chocolate.

Melt remaining chocolate, spread over as a topping; refrigerate until firm. Cut into small squares.

Makes approx. 2 dozen

## Continental Chocolate Slice

4 oz. butter
½ cup sugar
3 dessertspoons cocoa
1 egg
1 teaspoon vanilla
2 cups crushed wheatmeal biscuits
¾ cup coconut
½ cup chopped walnuts

**Topping**

2 oz. butter
2 cups icing sugar
2 dessertspoons custard powder
4 dessertspoons hot water
4 oz. dark chocolate

Combine butter, sugar, and cocoa in saucepan. Stir over low heat until well blended. Stir in beaten egg and vanilla. Cook, stirring, 1 minute. Remove from heat, stir in biscuit crumbs, coconut and walnuts, mix well. Press mixture into greased lamington tin, refrigerate until set.

*Topping* Cream butter well. Sift together icing sugar and custard powder, add to butter alternately with hot water. Beat until light and fluffy. Spread over biscuit base, refrigerate.

Melt chopped chocolate over hot water, spread evenly over topping, refrigerate. Cut into small squares to serve.

Makes approx. 2 dozen

## Chocolate Fruit Squares

¼ cup drinking chocolate
1 cup coconut
⅓ cup sultanas
½ cup crushed cornflakes
3 oz. dark chocolate
¼ cup chopped walnuts
1 teaspoon sherry or fruit juice
2 tablespoons crushed sweet biscuit crumbs
4 tablespoons condensed milk

Place all ingredients except chocolate into mixing bowl; mix well together. Press mixture into lightly greased 7 in. square tin, smooth the surface. Melt chocolate over hot water, spread evenly over surface of mixture; mark with fork. Refrigerate; when set and firm, cut into small bars or squares.

Makes approx. 1½ dozen

## Mocha Rum Torte

2 lb. stale sponge cake
2 cups milk
4 dessertspoons instant coffee powder
½ cup rum
1¼ cups sugar
8 oz. butter
1 dessertspoon gelatine
4 dessertspoons water

**Icing**

4 oz. chocolate
½ oz. solid white vegetable shortening
1 teaspoon rum

**Rum Balls**

chocolate sprinkles
extra cake crumbs
egg-white

Crumble cake into crumbs. Place sugar, butter, and milk in saucepan. Stir over low heat until sugar dissolves and butter melts. Bring to boiling point, stir in instant coffee. Pour on to cake crumbs.

Soak gelatine in water, then place over hot water to dissolve. Stir into cake mixture with rum. Take out 4 tablespoons of mixture and reserve for rum balls.

Turn remaining mixture into a well-greased, 8 in. spring form pan. Refrigerate overnight.

*Rum Balls* To reserved mixture add enough extra cake crumbs to make firm dough. Roll mixture to make balls the size of golf balls. Refrigerate. Cut firmed balls into halves, brush with lightly beaten egg-white or warmed jam. Toss in chocolate sprinkles.

*Icing* Mix together chopped chocolate, vegetable shortening and rum. Place over hot water until chocolate melts. Stir well until smooth.

Pour icing over cake while still in tin. Refrigerate at least 2 hours until firm. Before removing cake from tin, slip point of very sharp knife round chocolate to release from tin. (To make icing easier to cut, mark it lightly into wedges with a knife before chocolate is quite set.)

*To assemble* Place cake on serving dish. Using a little egg-white, press rum balls in position, circling top of cake.

## Chocolate Peppermint Squares

**Base**

4 oz. butter
3 dessertspoons cocoa
½ cup castor sugar
1 egg
few drops vanilla
1 cup coconut
½ cup walnuts
2 cups wheatmeal biscuit crumbs

**Filling**

1 oz. solid white vegetable shortening
3 dessertspoons milk
1 cup icing sugar
½ teaspoon peppermint essence

**Topping**

1 oz. butter
6 oz. dark chocolate

Combine butter, cocoa and sugar in saucepan, stir over low heat until well blended. Remove from heat, add beaten egg and vanilla. Stir in coconut, chopped walnuts, and biscuit crumbs; mix well. Press into greased 13 in. x 10 in. slab tin. Refrigerate until set. Spread with peppermint filling and return to refrigerator to firm. Smooth chocolate topping over, refrigerate. When set, cut into squares.

*Filling* Sift icing sugar, add melted shortening, milk and essence; mix well.

*Topping* Coarsely chop chocolate, place in basin with butter. Stand basin in saucepan of boiling water until chocolate and butter are melted, stirring occasionally.

Makes approx. 3 dozen

## Hazelnut Truffles

1 cup icing sugar
4 oz. ground hazelnuts
12 oz. dark chocolate
1 egg-white
¼ cup cream
1 teaspoon rum
chocolate sprinkles

Sift icing sugar into bowl, mix with hazelnuts. Stir in just enough egg-white to make a firm paste; add cream. Chop chocolate, place in top of double saucepan, stir over hot water until melted. Blend into hazelnut mixture, stirring with wooden spoon; add rum. Turn mixture into shallow tin lined with greased greaseproof paper; refrigerate until set.

When firm, cut into small squares, then roll into balls between palms of hands; roll in sprinkles. Refrigerate.

Makes approx. 2½ dozen

## Rum Balls

9 oz. (approx. 3 cups) cake crumbs
3 tablespoons apricot jam
3 tablespoons cocoa
1 tablespoon rum
2 tablespoons water
2 tablespoons apricot jam, extra
chocolate sprinkles

Mix together cake crumbs, cocoa, 3 tablespoons of sieved apricot jam, and rum until a stiff paste is formed. Make into approximately 24 balls. Warm 2 tablespoons of sieved jam with water; dip the balls in this jam mixture, then coat with chocolate sprinkles. Place in paper patty cases.

Makes approx. 2 dozen

# Summer Pies

A simple crumb crust is used in place of pastry base for these pies, and there's a delightful selection of fillings; all can be made without lighting the oven

## Crumb Crust

8 oz. plain sweet biscuits
4 oz. butter
½ teaspoon nutmeg

Crush biscuits into fine crumbs, place in bowl with nutmeg. Melt butter, add enough to crumbs so a tablespoon of mixture squeezed in the hand forms firm ball. Press this mixture firmly round sides and base of well-greased 7 in. sandwich tin with removable base or 9 in. pie plate. Refrigerate while preparing filling.

## Lemon Cream Pie

1 teaspoon gelatine
¾ cup lemon spread or lemon butter
1 cup cream
4 dessertspoons hot water
crumb crust

Dissolve gelatine in hot water. Add lemon spread or lemon butter, stir until smooth. Fold whipped cream into lemon mixture. Pour into prepared pie case. Refrigerate several hours or, preferably, overnight.

## Chocolate Rum Pie

1 dessertspoon gelatine
2 cups milk
½ cup sugar
2½ dessertspoons cornflour
4 eggs
3 dessertspoons rum
4 oz. dark chocolate
¼ pint cream
chocolate shavings
crumb crust

Soften gelatine in ¼ cup of the milk; scald remaining milk. Blend sugar with cornflour, stir in hot milk. Separate eggs. Beat yolks, add cornflour mixture. Cook in top of double saucepan over simmering water, stirring until mixture thickens. Add softened gelatine and chopped chocolate, stir until gelatine dissolves and chocolate melts; add rum. Allow to cool slightly. Beat egg whites until soft peaks form; fold into chocolate mixture. Pour into prepared crumb crust. Refrigerate until set. Whip cream. Sweeten, if desired, with little sugar and vanilla. Spread evenly over chocolate filling. Decorate with chocolate shavings.

## Apricot Cheese Pie

8 oz. cream cheese
½ cup sweetened condensed milk
4 dessertspoons lemon juice
¼ pint cream
9 in. crumb crust

**Topping**

1 cup apricot jam
4 dessertspoons sugar
4 dessertspoons water
1 teaspoon gelatine

Sieve cream cheese, add condensed milk and lemon juice; beat until smooth. Fold in whipped cream. Pour into prepared crumb crust. Refrigerate while preparing topping.

*Topping* Soften gelatine in 2 dessertspoons of the water. Sieve apricot jam. Add sugar and remaining water. Cook until sugar dissolves, bring up to boil. Boil, without stirring, 2 minutes. Remove from heat, add softened gelatine, stir until dissolved. Allow to cool slightly, spoon over cream cheese filling. Refrigerate well before serving.

Coffee Cream Roll and, at back, Continental Chocolate Slice—two of the delicious cakes and biscuits which can be made without lighting the oven. See page 182

# BISCUITS

There are biscuits here to suit every taste, and every occasion—from wholesome biscuits for the children, to pack into their lunches, or for when they come home from school—or just for any time good eating, to luxurious little mouthfuls for special afternoon-teas, or to serve with coffee

## Butter Oat Biscuits

4 oz. butter
½ cup castor sugar
1 dessertspoon treacle or golden syrup
1 cup self-raising flour
2 cups rolled oats
1 teaspoon bicarbonate of soda
¼ cup boiling water

Cream butter and sugar, add treacle, and cream well. Blend in sifted flour and oats. Dissolve soda in boiling water and add to mixture while still hot. Mix to a stiff dough. Roll teaspoonfuls of mixture into balls; place on greased slides, allowing room for spreading; press flat. Bake in moderate oven approximately 15 minutes. Cool on slides.

Makes approx. 4 dozen

NOTE: 3 oz. flaked almonds can be added with the oats.

## Chocolate Mint Slices

**Biscuit Layer**

1½ cups self-raising flour
½ cup brown sugar
1 cup desiccated coconut
6 oz. butter

**Peppermint Icing**

1 cup icing sugar
1 oz. solid white vegetable shortening
3 dessertspoons milk
½ teaspoon peppermint essence

**Chocolate Icing**

3 oz. solid white vegetable shortening
½ cup drinking chocolate

*Biscuit Layer* Sift flour, mix dry ingredients together, melt butter and pour over dry ingredients; mix well. Press into greased and lined 12 x 18 in. swiss roll tin, bake in moderate oven 20 minutes. While still warm, top with Peppermint Icing.

*Peppermint Icing* Melt chopped shortening over gentle heat. Sift icing sugar into basin, add melted shortening, milk, and essence. Mix well, spread over biscuit layer. When cold top with Chocolate Icing.

*Chocolate Icing* Pour melted white shortening over drinking chocolate and mix well. Cool slightly, then pour evenly on top of Peppermint Icing. Leave to set, then cut into slices to serve.

Makes approx. 3 dozen

## Almond Fingers

**Pastry**

5 oz. butter
⅓ cup sugar
1½ cups plain flour

**Filling**

½ cup cream
⅓ cup brown sugar
1 egg-yolk
½ cup ground almonds or marzipan meal
1 teaspoon cinnamon

**Icing**

½ cup icing sugar
lemon juice

*Pastry* Cream together butter and sugar in bowl until light and fluffy. Stir in sifted flour. Press dough, with lightly floured hand, into greased 11 in. x 7 in. lamington tin. Bake in moderately slow oven 20 minutes. Remove from oven, cool slightly.

*Filling* Whip the cream and add almonds, sugar and cinnamon. Mix in lightly beaten egg-yolk. Spread cream mixture over cooled pastry. Bake in moderately slow oven further 40 minutes. Remove from oven, cool, then refrigerate several hours. Spread icing over top. Refrigerate until icing is firm. Cut into fingers.

*Icing* Sift icing sugar into bowl. Add enough lemon juice to make spreading consistency. Blend until smooth; spread evenly over filling.

Makes approx. 2 dozen

## Hazelnut Chocolate Biscuits

6 oz. butter
1 cup castor sugar
1 egg
½ teaspoon vanilla
2 cups self-raising flour
2 oz. ground or chopped hazelnuts
2 oz. dark chocolate or chocolate pieces
½ cup desiccated coconut
melted chocolate

Cream together butter and sugar until light and fluffy. Beat in egg and vanilla, beat well. Beat in sifted flour, blending thoroughly. Stir in hazelnuts, chopped chocolate and coconut, mix well. Roll into small balls about the size of a walnut; place on greased oven tray, allowing room to spread. Bake in moderate oven 15 minutes or until golden. Leave plain or dip half the biscuit in melted chocolate or drizzle chocolate over top.

Makes approx. 4½ dozen

## Easy Florentines

¾ cup sultanas
2 cups crushed cornflakes
¾ cup raw peanuts
½ cup chopped cherries
½ can condensed milk
3 oz. dark chocolate

Combine all ingredients except chocolate in mixing bowl; mix well. Grease flat baking trays, line with greaseproof paper; grease paper, then dust lightly with cornflour. Shake trays to remove any excess cornflour. Place dessertspoonfuls of mixture in small heaps on trays. Bake in moderate oven 15 to 20 minutes. Leave on trays to cool before lifting off carefully with spatula. Melt chopped chocolate over hot water, remove from heat, and stir until thickened slightly. Spread chocolate over flat side of biscuit, mark with fork. Allow chocolate to set before storing in airtight tins.

Makes approx. 2½ dozen

## Lunch-Box Cookies

3 oz. butter
½ cup brown sugar
½ cup castor sugar
1 teaspoon vanilla
1 egg
1½ cups plain flour
½ teaspoon baking powder
½ teaspoon bicarbonate of soda
½ teaspoon salt
½ teaspoon ginger
½ teaspoon cinnamon
1¼ cups rolled oats
¼ cup marmalade
1 cup chopped raisins

Cream butter and sugars, beat in egg and vanilla. Sift dry ingredients together, add to creamed mixture, then fold in oats, marmalade, and raisins. Drop by teaspoonfuls on to greased oven trays. Bake in moderately hot oven approximately 15 minutes or until evenly browned.

Makes approx. 3½ dozen

## Anzac Biscuits

1 cup rolled oats
¾ cup desiccated coconut
1 cup plain flour
1½ teaspoons bicarbonate of soda
2 tablespoons boiling water
1 cup sugar
4 oz. butter
1 tablespoon golden syrup

Combine rolled oats, sifted flour, sugar, and coconut. Combine butter and golden syrup, stir over gentle heat until melted. Mix soda with boiling water, add to melted butter mixture, stir into dry ingredients. Spoon dessertspoonfuls of mixture on to greased oven trays; allow room for spreading. Bake in slow oven 20 minutes. Cool on trays.

Makes approx. 3 dozen

## Viennese Biscuits

8 oz. butter
¼ cup castor sugar
½ teaspoon vanilla
2 cups plain flour
pinch salt
melted chocolate

Cream together butter and sugar until light and fluffy. Add vanilla and carefully fold in sifted flour and salt. Fill into piping bag fitted with large star pipe. Pipe into finger lengths on lightly greased oven tray. Bake in moderately hot oven 15 to 20 minutes. Cool on tray. Leave plain, or dip one end in melted chocolate for pretty effect.

Makes approx. 3 dozen

## Brandy Snaps

2 tablespoons golden syrup
2 oz. butter
⅓ cup brown sugar
½ cup plain flour
2 teaspoons ground ginger
pinch salt

Place syrup, butter and brown sugar into saucepan, heat slowly until butter has melted, stirring occasionally. Sift flour, ginger, and salt into a bowl, stir in syrup and butter mixture; mix well. Drop dessertspoonfuls of mixture on to greased trays, allowing room for spreading. Bake in moderate oven 5 to 7 minutes, or until golden brown. Remove from oven, cool 1 minute. With knife, lift brandy snap from tray. Roll immediately around the handle of a wooden spoon. Allow to firm and cool on spoon handle. Just before serving, fill with whipped cream.

Makes 6 to 8 brandy snaps.

NOTE: Two brandy snaps will fit comfortably on to a baking tray. It is a good idea to bake only two at a time. If they firm up before you have time to mould them into shape, return to the oven for a few minutes to soften again.

## Sunflower Honey Chews

4 oz. butter
¾ cup honey
4½ cups cornflakes
⅔ cup sunflower seed kernels
⅓ cup desiccated coconut
2 oz. glacé cherries

Melt butter and honey in saucepan and boil gently 5 minutes. Crush cornflakes, place in large bowl with sunflower seed kernels, coconut, and chopped cherries. Stir in boiling butter and honey mixture, mix well. Press firmly into 11 in. x 7 in. greased lamington tin. Refrigerate until set. Best if left overnight or for a day or two, to allow flavours to blend. Cut into squares or fingers.

Makes approx. 16

## Ginger Crunch Biscuits

4 oz. butter
¼ cup sugar
1 cup plain flour
1 teaspoon baking powder
1 teaspoon ground ginger

**Topping**

⅓ cup icing sugar
2 oz. butter
1 teaspoon ground ginger
3 teaspoons golden syrup

Cream butter and sugar together. Add sifted dry ingredients, mix well until thoroughly absorbed. Spread into greased 11 in. x 7 in. lamington tin and bake in moderate oven until lightly browned, approximately 15 to 20 minutes.

*Topping* Place all ingredients in saucepan, stir over gentle heat until butter is melted and ingredients well mixed. Pour over biscuit layer while both are still warm. Cut into squares or fingers when cold.

Makes approx. 1½ dozen

## Chocolate Cherry Bars

8 oz. dark chocolate
2 small eggs
½ cup castor sugar
1 cup coconut
2 to 3 oz. glacé cherries
icing sugar

Chop chocolate roughly. Place in top of double saucepan over hot water; heat gently, stirring, until melted and smooth. Spread chocolate over base of well greased 11 in. x 7 in. lamington tin. Refrigerate until firm. Beat together eggs and sugar until light and frothy; gently fold in coconut and chopped cherries. Spread over firm chocolate. Bake in moderate oven 10 to 15 minutes until topping is lightly golden and firm to the touch. Cool, then refrigerate. Before serving, sprinkle with sifted icing sugar, cut into small fingers.

Makes approx. 2 dozen

## Ginger Nuts

2 cups plain flour
1 cup castor sugar
½ teaspoon bicarbonate of soda
1 teaspoon cinnamon
pinch salt
2 teaspoons ground ginger
4 oz. butter
1 very small egg
1 teaspoon golden syrup

Sift into basin the flour, sugar, soda, cinnamon, salt and ginger. Rub in butter until mixture is of very fine crumb consistency. Beat egg with golden syrup, add to dry ingredients. Work into a firm dough with hands. Roll into small balls about size of half a walnut, place on greased oven slides, about 2 in. apart. Bake in moderately slow oven approximately 15 minutes. Loosen, cool on oven slide.

Makes approx. 3½ dozen

## Meringues

2 egg-whites
1½ cups castor sugar
1 teaspoon vinegar
1 teaspoon cornflour
½ teaspoon vanilla
4 tablespoons boiling water

Place all ingredients in basin, beat until mixture is of thick, satiny meringue consistency (10 to 15 minutes). Spoon mixture into piping bag; using large star tube, pipe meringues on to lightly greased baking trays. Bake in moderate oven 10 minutes, then reduce heat to slow, bake further 50 minutes.

Allow to cool in oven.

Makes approx. 3 dozen

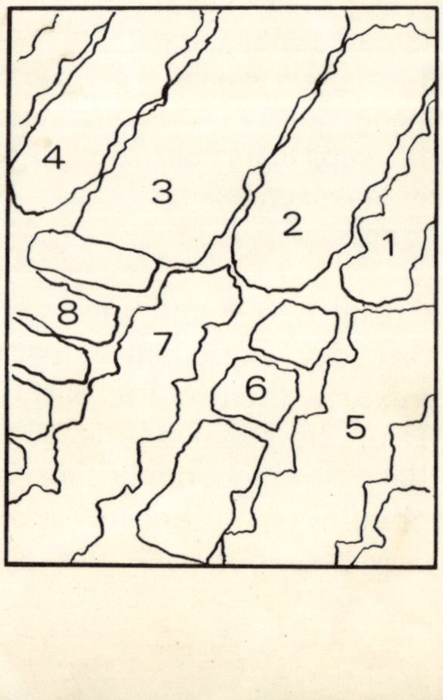


1 Macaroons
2 Butter Coconut Crisps
3 Almond Bread
4 Butter Oat Biscuits
5 Chocolate Cherry Bars
6 Chocolate Mint Slices
7 Easy Florentines
8 Viennese Biscuits

## Macaroons

2 egg-whites
¾ cup castor sugar
3½ oz. ground almonds or marzipan meal
grated rind 1 lemon

Beat egg-whites until peaks form. Gradually beat in sugar, beat until sugar is dissolved; mixture should be of meringue consistency. Fold in ground almonds and grated lemon rind. Using 2 teaspoons, spoon mixture on to greased and cornfloured oven trays, allowing room for spreading. Bake in moderate oven approximately 15 to 20 minutes or until firm.

Makes approx. 3 dozen

## Butter Coconut Crisps

4 oz. butter
1¼ cups self-raising flour
1 cup sugar
1 egg
desiccated coconut

Melt butter. Sift flour and sugar into bowl, add beaten egg and melted butter, mix thoroughly. Form into small balls the size of a walnut, roll in coconut, and place on greased trays, allowing room to spread. Bake in moderate oven 10 to 15 minutes. Loosen and leave until cold on tray.

Makes approx. 2½ dozen

## Crisp Coconut Biscuits

4 oz. butter
1 cup castor sugar
1 egg
2 cups self-raising flour
pinch salt
1 cup desiccated coconut
extra sugar

Cream butter and sugar, beat in egg, add sifted flour, salt and coconut. Roll into balls and press flat between the hands. Dip the top side into extra sugar. Place on greased baking trays, allow for spreading. Bake in moderately hot oven 10 to 15 minutes.

Makes approx. 2 dozen

## Shortbread

2 cups plain flour
¼ cup icing sugar
1 tablespoon ground rice
6 oz. butter

Sift flour, sugar and ground rice into bowl. Rub in butter and knead until mixture is smooth. Roll mixture out to ¼ in. thickness on lightly-floured board; cut into 2 in. rounds with cutter. Place on ungreased trays, bake in moderate oven 15 to 20 minutes or until pale golden.

Makes approx. 2½ dozen.

Mixture can also be pressed into ungreased 7 in x 11 in. lamington tin. Cut with knife into finger shapes, bake as above.

Makes approx. 2 dozen

## Easy Ratafias

2 egg-whites
pinch salt
1 cup sugar
1 cup desiccated coconut
½ cup instant mashed potato flakes (dry)
few drops almond essence
almond flakes to decorate

Beat egg-whites with salt until very stiff. Gradually add sugar, beat until thick and sugar is dissolved. Fold in potato flakes, coconut, and essence. Place teaspoonfuls of mixture on greased baking tray, top with almond flake. Bake in moderate oven 15 to 20 minutes.

Makes approx. 3 dozen

## Peanut Crisps

4 oz. butter
1 cup sugar
1 egg
1 cup plain flour
pinch salt
½ teaspoon bicarbonate soda
½ teaspoon baking powder
1 cup rolled oats
½ cup chopped salted peanuts
1 cup cornflakes

Cream together butter and sugar, add egg; beat well. Fold in sifted flour, salt, bicarbonate soda and baking powder. Work in the rolled oats, peanuts and cornflakes, blend well.

Place teaspoonfuls on greased baking trays, leaving room for spreading. Bake in hot oven 10 minutes. Cool on trays, then store in airtight tins.

Makes approx. 4½ dozen

## Caramel Shortbread Squares

1 cup plain flour
pinch salt
½ cup icing sugar
4 oz. butter

**Caramel**

4 oz. butter
¼ cup golden syrup
½ cup brown sugar
1 teaspoon gelatine
⅔ cup condensed milk

Sift flour, salt and icing sugar into bowl. Rub in butter. Press into greased 8 in. square shallow tin. Bake in moderate oven 20 to 25 minutes. Leave to cool in tin, then pour caramel over. Refrigerate several hours or overnight until topping is quite firm.

Carefully turn biscuit over on to plastic food-wrap and, with biscuit base uppermost, cut into small squares. (It is easier to cut biscuit this way.)

Makes approx. 25.

*Caramel* Melt butter and syrup in saucepan over low heat; add sugar, gelatine and condensed milk;

beat thoroughly. Continue stirring over low heat until sugar dissolves, then bring to boil and boil 4 minutes, stirring constantly. Remove from heat, beat well with wooden spoon. Pour over biscuit.

## Almond Bread

3 egg-whites
½ cup castor sugar
1 cup plain flour
4 oz. whole unblanched almonds

Beat egg-whites until stiff, gradually beat in castor sugar until mixture is of good meringue consistency, forming thick peaks. Fold in sifted flour and whole almonds. Fill into very lightly greased 8 in. x 4 in. loaf tin. Bake in moderate oven 30 to 40 minutes. Leave in tin until completely cold. Wrap in aluminium foil, put aside for one or two days. Using very sharp knife, cut into wafer thin slices. Place slices on oven tray, put into slow oven 45 minutes to dry out completely.

Serve just one slice with after dinner coffee. Or serve as a delightfully crisp biscuit with ice-cream.

## Butterscotch Bars

**Base:**

1 cup plain flour
3 oz. butter
pinch salt
½ cup firmly packed brown sugar

**Topping**

6 oz. butterscotch toffees
1 tablespoon golden syrup
1 tablespoon water
1 oz. butter
pinch salt
4 oz. walnuts

*Base:* Combine ingredients in small bowl of electric mixer; blend at low speed until well combined and particles are small (or rub butter into sifted dry ingredients until mixture resembles fine breadcrumbs).

Press mixture into paper-lined 8 in. square shallow tin. Bake in moderately hot oven 10 to 12 minutes. Remove from oven, spread topping over. Return to moderately hot oven 8 to 10 minutes. Cool on wire rack; when cold cut into small squares.

*Topping* Combine all ingredients except walnuts in small saucepan, stir over low heat until butterscotch has dissolved. Stir in chopped walnuts. Spread evenly over hot partially baked base.

Makes approx. 16

## Flaky Cheese Biscuits

2 oz. butter
2 oz. cheddar cheese
½ egg-yolk
salt
good pinch paprika
½ cup plain flour

Beat butter until creamy, gradually add finely grated cheese, egg-yolk, salt and paprika. Work in sifted flour. When well blended, refrigerate 1 hour. Knead lightly, roll out on floured board to ¼ in. thickness. Cut out in 1 in. rounds; place on lightly greased oven trays, bake in hot oven 10 minutes.

Make approx. 2½ dozen

## Cheese and Sesame Wafers

1 cup plain flour
½ teaspoon salt
pinch cayenne pepper
½ teaspoon dry mustard
½ teaspoon ground ginger
½ teaspoon sugar
2 oz. grated cheese
⅓ cup toasted sesame seeds
1 egg-yolk
2 oz. butter
1 tablespoon water

Sift together dry ingredients into bowl. Stir in cheese and toasted sesame seeds. Combine lightly beaten egg-yolk, melted butter and water. Stir into dry ingredients; form into a ball. Wrap in greaseproof paper; refrigerate 30 minutes. Roll out to ⅛ in. thickness on lightly floured board. Cut into 1 in. x 2 in. strips or 2 in. squares. Place on ungreased oven tray, bake in moderate oven 15 minutes. Cool on tray.

Makes approx. 4½ dozen.

*To toast sesame seeds* Place seeds on baking tray, bake in moderate oven 15 minutes, shaking tray occasionally.

## Paprika Biscuits

3 oz. butter
3 oz. cheese
1 cup plain flour
1 teaspoon paprika
½ teaspoon salt
½ teaspoon dry mustard
1 dessertspoon poppy seeds

Beat together butter and grated cheese until soft and creamy. Sift together dry ingredients, add to cheese mixture, beat until well blended. Take dessertspoonfuls of mixture and roll into small balls, using floured hands. Place on greased oven tray, flatten slightly, sprinkle poppy seeds lightly over each biscuit. Bake in moderate oven 15 to 20 minutes or until lightly golden brown. Loosen and cool on tray.

Makes approx. 1½ dozen

# SCONES

It's easy to whip up a batch of feather-light scones and, in this section, we give a wide variety of recipes for plain and sweet scones.

To make sure they turn out perfect every time, it is important they be mixed and baked correctly—and we show how to do this in step by step pictures.

Here is a list of the basic ingredients used in scone making, and the reasons for their use

## Basic Ingredients

*Self-raising flour* Should be as fresh as possible, to guarantee maximum rising power. Stale flour will give poor results.

*Salt* Used to accent flavour.

*Sugar* Small amount used adds flavour, but does not sweeten. For a sweet scone, perhaps with sultanas, use 1 tablespoon sugar.

*Butter* Scones are best eaten the day they're made. Small amount of butter used does not give keeping quality, but adds flavour and colour.

*Milk and water* Combination of equal quantities of milk and water will produce a lighter scone than all milk.

## Scones

2 cups self-raising flour
½ teaspoon salt
1 teaspoon sugar
1 oz. butter
approx. ¾ cup milk and water

Sift flour and salt into basin, stir in sugar. Rub in butter until mixture resembles fine breadcrumbs. Pour nearly all the liquid in at once and mix to a soft dough. (Flours vary in the way they absorb liquid; if mixture is not soft enough, add remaining liquid.) Place on floured surface and knead lightly. Pat dough out to approximately ¾ in. in thickness, and, using a 2 in. cutter, cut into rounds. Place on to a greased baking tray or into a lightly greased 11 in. x 7 in. lamington tin, glaze with a little milk. Bake in a very hot oven for 10 minutes or until golden brown.

Makes approx. 1 dozen

## Cream Scones

2 cups self-raising flour
1 egg
2 dessertspoons sugar
½ cup cream
½ cup milk

Beat egg and sugar together until light and creamy. Add cream and milk, mix thoroughly. Add sifted flour and mix to soft dough. Turn on to floured surface and knead lightly. Pat dough to ¾ inch in thickness, cut into rounds with 2 inch cutter. Place scones into greased lamington tin; glaze with a little milk. Bake in very hot oven 10 to 12 minutes.

Makes 1 dozen

## Cheese-Topped Scones

3 cups self-raising flour
½ teaspoon salt
1½ oz. butter
1 cup milk

**Cheese Topping**

3 oz. butter
3 oz. tasty cheese
pinch pepper
pinch salt
½ teaspoon dry mustard

Sift flour and salt into basin. Rub in butter until mixture resembles fine breadcrumbs. Pour nearly all the milk in at once and mix to a soft dough; add remainder of milk, if necessary. Place dough on a floured surface and knead lightly. Pat out to approximately ¾ in. in thickness, and, using a 2 in. cutter, cut into rounds. Place into greased 11 in x 7 in. lamington tin, place a teaspoon of cheese topping on to each scone. Bake in a very hot oven 10 to 15 minutes, or until golden brown.

*Cheese Topping* Melt butter in a small saucepan, allow to cool slightly. Add grated cheese, pepper, salt and mustard; mix thoroughly.

Makes approx. 15

So easily and quickly made, scones are everybody's favourite. Serve them hot with strawberry jam or honey

**Step 1**
*Rub in butter correctly:* Sift dry ingredients, then rub in butter. Use tips of fingers only for rubbing in; these are the coolest part of the hand, and butter will not be softened or melted during rubbing in process. To rub in, rub thumbs over fingertips in circular motion, lifting hands above bowl so flour falls through fingers to bowl beneath; this aerates and lightens the mixture.

Some prize-winning cooks heat a little of the milk and melt the butter in it before adding it, with the rest of the milk, to the flour mixture. This gives even distribution throughout the scone and prevents any uneven butter-patches

**Step 2**
*Mix lightly:* Add the liquid to rubbed in mixture almost all at once (this is important to avoid over mixing), then lightly stir and cut liquid through mixture, adding remainder of liquid, if required. Dough should be soft, sticking to sides of bowl. Use a knife for mixing; it is light, functional, makes it easier to avoid over-mixing dough

# Step by Step Perfect Scones

## Sultana Scones

3 cups self-raising flour
½ teaspoon salt
2 oz. butter
¼ cup sugar
1 cup sultanas
1 egg
approx. 1 cup milk

Sift flour and salt, rub in butter until mixture resembles fine breadcrumbs. Stir in sugar and sultanas. Beat egg and add to dry ingredients with sufficient milk to give a soft dough. Place on floured surface and knead lightly. Pat out to approximately $\frac{3}{4}$ in. in thickness, and cut into 2 in. rounds. Place into greased 11 in. x 7 in. lamington tin. Glaze with milk. Bake in a very hot oven 12 to 15 minutes.

Makes approx. 15.

## Date Scones

2 cups self-raising flour
½ teaspoon salt
2 oz. butter
¼ cup sugar
¾ cup finely chopped dates
1 egg
approx. ½ cup milk

Sift flour and salt, rub in butter until mixture resembles fine breadcrumbs. Stir in dates and sugar. Beat egg and add to dry ingredients with sufficient milk to give a soft dough. Place on floured surface and knead lightly. Pat out to approximately $\frac{1}{2}$ in. thickness, and, using a 2 in. floured cutter, cut into rounds. Place into a greased 11 in. x 7 in. lamington tin. Glaze tops with milk. Bake in very hot oven 12 to 15 minutes.

Makes approx. 1 dozen.

## Feather-Light Scones

1 egg
1 dessertspoon sugar
1 oz. melted butter
¾ cup milk
2 cups self-raising flour
½ teaspoon salt
milk for glazing

Beat egg and sugar together until thick; add melted butter to milk. Sift together flour and salt into a bowl, make a well in centre. Stir in egg mixture, then milk mixture; mix to a soft dough. Turn out on to a floured surface, knead lightly. Pat or roll to $\frac{1}{2}$ in. in thickness, cut out with a floured 2 in. cutter. Place on a lightly greased scone tray, brush tops with a little cold milk. Bake in a hot oven 10 to 12 minutes.

Makes approx. 1 dozen.

**Step 3**
*Knead briefly, gently:* Turn mixture out from bowl on to lightly floured board; using fingertips, knead gently by turning outside edge of dough into centre, turning dough round, then turning edges in again. Repeat until dough is smooth, free from creases underneath, elastic to the touch. This kneading should be thorough, but as brief and gentle as possible, otherwise scones will be toughened

**Step 4**
*Cut sharply, evenly:* Turn smooth side of dough uppermost, shape into round; using palms of hands, press out lightly to approximately $\frac{3}{4}$ inch high. Use as little flour on board as possible, to avoid floury base on scones. (Rolling pin is not necessary for small amount of scone dough; also, using rolling pin you're inclined to roll out dough too thinly.) Dip plain, sharp-edged cutter in flour; press sharply and evenly into dough, without twisting cutter. (Twisting cutter would retard rising.) One, 2, or $2\frac{1}{2}$ inch diameter cutter can be used, depending on size of scone required

**Step 5**
*Arrange correctly on tray:* Cut as many scones as possible from the first rolling; each successive kneading toughens dough. Shake scones out of cutter and, to obtain even cooking, place in centre of prepared tray, close together but not touching. As scones cook and rise they will be close enough to support each other, yet still retain their individual shape. Scones baked in a lamington tin are placed close together, to fit into tin, and cling together as they rise; this gives a softer sided scone. Brush tops of scones lightly with milk; this gives a glossy golden brown finish to cooked scone

**Step 6**
*Bake in hot oven, cool correctly:* Bake scones in hot oven 10 to 15 minutes. Scones baked in lamington tin may need longer cooking time. When cooked, they should be golden brown on top, sound hollow when tapped with fingertip. Remove from tray to wire cake cooler. If you prefer scones with firm, crisp top, let them stand, uncovered, on wire tray. If you prefer soft scones, wrap them, as soon as they come from oven, in clean teatowel; the trapped steam will soften the crisp top.

And remember, never cut a scone—break it open with the fingers

## Honeyed Banana Scones

1 cup self-raising flour
1 cup wholemeal self-raising flour
½ teaspoon salt
1 oz. butter
2 bananas
2 tablespoons honey
½ cup milk

Sift flours and salt into basin, rub in butter until mixture resembles fine breadcrumbs. Mash bananas; combine milk, honey, and mashed bananas add to dry ingredients and work into soft dough. Turn on to floured surface and knead lightly. Pat out to $\frac{3}{4}$ inch in thickness, cut with floured 2 in. cutter. Place into greased lamington tin, glaze tops with a little milk. Bake in very hot oven 12 to 15 minutes.

Makes 1 dozen

## Caramel Fruit Buns

4 oz. butter
1 cup brown sugar, lightly packed
2 oz. walnuts
3 cups self-raising flour
pinch salt
¼ cup sugar
1½ oz. butter, extra
1 egg
1 cup milk, approx.
¾ cup raisins

Cream together butter and brown sugar until light and creamy. Spread half of this mixture over base of greased and greased paper lined 9 in. square slab tin. Sprinkle chopped walnuts over.

Sift flour, salt and sugar into basin. Rub in extra butter, until mixture resembles fine breadcrumbs. Beat egg lightly and add to flour mixture. Then add enough milk to mix to soft dough. Turn dough out on to floured surface and knead lightly. Roll dough into oblong 14 inches x 9 inches approximately. Spread over remaining creamed mixture, sprinkle with chopped raisins.

Roll up as for swiss roll, cut into 16 even slices. Place slices on top of walnuts, cut side up. Bake in moderately hot oven 30 to 35 minutes.

## Milk Scones

2 cups self-raising flour
4 dessertspoons powdered milk
1 teaspoon sugar
pinch salt
1½ oz. butter
¾ cup water

Sift flour, powdered milk, and salt into basin. Add sugar and rub in butter until mixture resembles fine breadcrumbs. Pour nearly all the water in at once and mix to a soft dough; add extra water if necessary. Place on floured surface and knead lightly. Pat dough out to approximately $\frac{3}{4}$ in. in thickness, and, using a 2 in. cutter, cut into rounds. Place on to a greased baking tray or into a greased 11 in. x 7 in. lamington tin, glaze with a little water or milk. Bake in a very hot oven for 12 to 15 minutes or until golden brown.

Makes approx. 1 dozen

## Pumpkin Scones

1 oz. softened butter
¼ cup castor sugar
1 cup cooked, mashed pumpkin (approx. ¾ lb.)
1 egg
2½ cups self-raising flour
pinch salt
½ teaspoon cinnamon
¼ teaspoon nutmeg
¼ to ½ cup milk, depending on dryness of pumpkin

Beat butter and sugar together, add pumpkin; mix well. Add egg and beat well. Fold in sifted dry ingredients alternately with $\frac{1}{4}$ cup milk. If necessary, add remaining milk to make a soft, but not sticky dough. Turn mixture on to a floured surface and knead lightly. Pat out to $\frac{3}{4}$ in. thickness, cut out with 2 in. floured cutter.

Place into a greased 11 in. x 7 in. lamington tin. Glaze with a little milk. Bake in hot oven 12 to 15 minutes, or until golden brown.

Makes approx. 1 dozen

## Scones in Large Quantity

6 cups (1½ lb.) self-raising flour
2 tablespoons sugar
½ teaspoon salt
3 oz. butter
1 cup milk
1 cup water
milk for glazing

Sift flour, sugar and salt into basin. Rub butter into dry ingredients. Mix to soft dough with combined milk and water, adding extra milk, if necessary. Knead dough, roll out and fit into greased 10 in. x 11 in. baking dish. With sharp knife cut dough into approximately 36 squares. Glaze with milk, bake in hot oven 15 to 20 minutes or until golden brown. Makes approx. 3 dozen

*For Sultana Scones*: Add 1 cup sultanas to dry ingredients before adding the liquid; increase sugar to half cup.

# PASTRY

If you remember the few essentials for making perfect pastry, you will have good results every time you bake. There are just five important rules to follow

*Keep everything as cold as possible*

Fat should be firm; liquid should be chilled. If time permits, place mixing bowl in refrigerator for an hour before using.

*Use only as much liquid as necessary*

Too much liquid will result in hard pastry, and will also cause pastry to shrink during baking, as the excess water evaporates in heat of oven.

If insufficient liquid is added, dough will be too crumbly for rolling.

Liquid should be added gradually, until just sufficient has been added to make pastry firm enough to be handled and rolled out without breaking.

*Sift the dry ingredients*

Sift flour and any other dry ingredients well. This sifting helps to incorporate air into pastry mixture, as well as ensuring flour is fine, without lumps.

*Fold in as much air as possible as you mix*

With shortcrust pastry, air is incorporated by lifting flour and butter mixture from bowl when rubbing in with fingertips.

With puff pastry, air is incorporated through the process of folding and rolling.

Roll pastry with short, jerky movements; lift rolling pin after each roll. This allows air to move about in dough. Heavy rolling will destroy air bubbles, resulting in heavy pastry.

*Handle the pastry lightly*

Too much handling will make pastry heavy.

When handling soft pastries, such as biscuit, roll out between lightly floured sheets of grease-proof paper; this makes them easier to handle and avoids over-working the pastry.

Never stretch pastry—it will shrink back when cooking.

When rolling out pastry on a floured board, use only enough flour to prevent pastry sticking to the surface. Excess flour will upset the balance of the ingredients, and could result in tough pastry. For this reason too, never turn pastry over during rolling.

## How Much Pastry To Use

When a recipe calls for 8 oz. pastry it means pastry made with 8 oz. (2 cups) flour (plus the corresponding ingredients).

The exception to this is where packaged puff pastry is an ingredient; when a recipe calls for 12 oz. or 1 lb. packaged puff pastry, this is the full weight of the completed pastry in its package.

Basic pastry recipes given in this book can be reduced or increased if necessary; be sure to reduce or increase all other ingredients in proportion.

The list given below is an approximate guide to help you assess the quantity of pastry you may need.

*Tarts* 6 oz. pastry will line 7 in. pie plate.

8 oz. to 10 oz. pastry will line 8 in. or 9 in. pie plate.

*Double-crust Pies* 10 oz. pastry will give bottom and top crust for 7 in. pie.

12 oz. to 14 oz. pastry will give bottom and top crust for 8 in. or 9 in. pie.

*Small Tartlets* 8 oz. pastry will make approximately 2 dozen small tartlet cases.

When large tart cases with a filling require a longer cooking time than approximately 25 minutes, a double edge of pastry will prevent edges of tart case from becoming too crisp. Cut long strips of pastry, the width of the pie plate edge, from rolled out pastry. Place strips around edge of pie plate, brush strips lightly with water, line plate with pastry in usual manner. Press edges together, trim, decorate as desired.

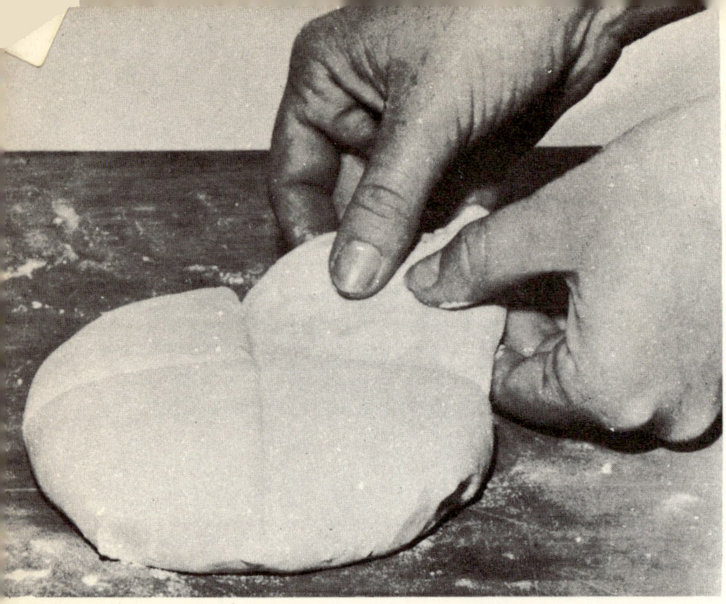

**Step 1**
Cut four divisions in dough; cut only half-way through, so it is still joined at base. Pull out centre point of each division

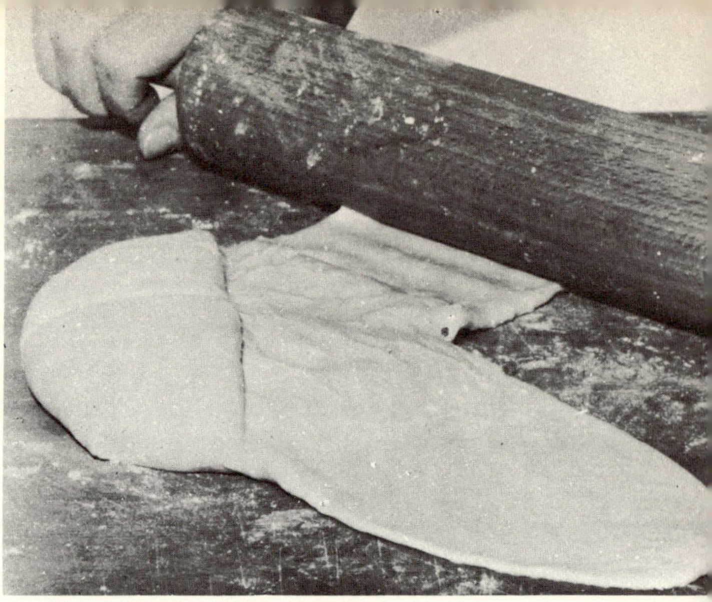

**Step 2**
Leaving uncut base part unrolled, roll out each of the points, as shown in picture above.

## Step by Step Puff Pastry

## Shortcrust Pastry

Shortcrust is probably the most widely used of all pastries, and is good for pies with sweet or savoury fillings.

Basic shortcrust uses half the amount of shortening (butter, margarine) to flour. For example, shortcrust with 8 oz. flour would use 4 oz. shortening; with 12 oz. flour, 6 oz. shortening, etc.

2 cups plain flour
½ teaspoon baking powder
pinch salt
4 oz. butter
1½ tablespoons water
1 teaspoon lemon juice

Sift dry ingredients, rub in butter until mixture resembles dry breadcrumbs. Mix to pliable dry dough with water and lemon juice.

The finished pastry, when it is mixed, should form a smooth ball, leaving the sides of the mixing bowl clean.

Turn on to lightly floured board, knead lightly. Roll to size and shape required.

*Sweet Shortcrust:* Add 1 dessertspoon castor sugar for every 2 cups flour. Dissolve sugar in the water before adding it to flour, or sift 1 dessertspoon icing sugar with dry ingredients.

## Rich Shortcrust Pastry

2 cups plain flour
½ teaspoon baking powder
4-6 oz. butter
pinch salt
1 egg-yolk
water
1 teaspoon lemon juice

Sift dry ingredients, rub in butter until mixture resembles dry breadcrumbs. Using egg-yolk, lemon juice, and little water if necessary, mix into a dry dough. Turn on to lightly floured surface and knead into a smooth round.

## Biscuit Pastry

3 oz. butter
¼ cup sugar
1 egg
1¼ cups plain flour
¼ cup self-raising flour

Beat butter until creamy, add sugar, beat until just combined. Add beaten egg gradually, beating well after each addition. Over-creaming at this stage will make pastry difficult to handle. Work in ⅔ of sifted flours with a wooden spoon, then remaining flour with the hand. Turn on to lightly floured board, knead lightly until smooth. (Heavy handling of pastry will toughen it and make it difficult to roll.) Refrigerate 30 minutes before using.

## Custard Tart

1 quantity biscuit pastry
3 eggs
1 teaspoon vanilla
2 tablespoons sugar
1 pint milk
nutmeg

Roll pastry on lightly floured board, carefully line a greased 8 in. tart plate. (Any breaks in the pastry could cause custard to seep through.) Pinch edges decoratively.

Beat eggs, vanilla and sugar together; warm milk, gradually stir into egg mixture. Carefully spoon custard into pastry case. Bake in moderate oven 30 to 35 minutes. After 15 minutes cooking time, sprinkle with nutmeg. Do not over-cook; custard will firm as it cools.

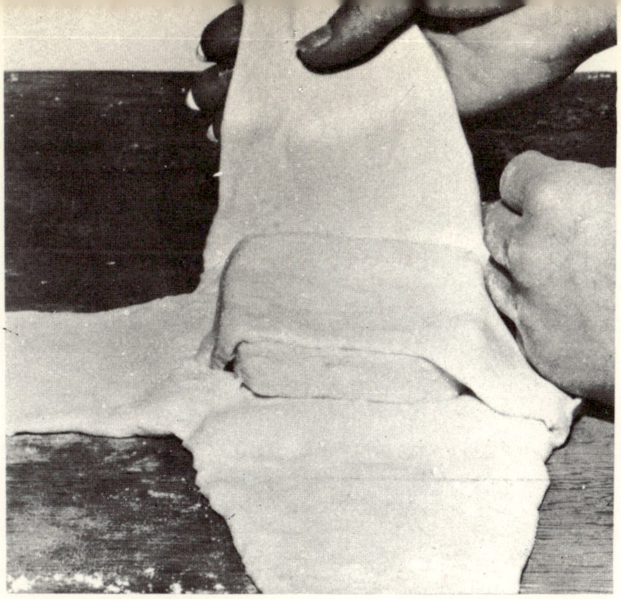

**Step 3**
Work butter well with spatula until soft, form into block shape. Place butter in centre of pastry. Take each individual long piece of dough, and fold it neatly over the butter

**Step 4**
With rolling pin, gently press out dough; this will ease the butter through evenly, forming ridges as shown. Butter must be well distributed through dough for successful result

## Puff Pastry

Puff pastry is used as a topping for savoury pies, for vol-au-vents and for sweet pastries. Good quality puff pastry can now be bought in packaged form all ready to use—and it certainly saves a lot of time. But many housewives still prefer to make their own.

Full puff pastry uses equal amounts of flour and shortening (that is, 8 oz. butter and 8 oz. flour), but the recipe below, known as three-quarter puff (it uses three-quarters the amount of shortening to flour — 8 oz. flour to 6 oz. butter) is more generally used. When cooked, it is easier to handle, less liable to break.

2 cups plain flour
¼ teaspoon salt
6 oz. butter
approx. ¼ pint iced water

Sift flour and salt. Divide butter equally into 4 portions. Rub one portion into the flour. Mix with enough water to make a soft but pliable dough. Turn on to lightly floured board, knead 1 minute. Shape into a neat square. Put remaining butter on plate, work it well with spatula until it is soft, then shape into a block.

With sharp knife, cut down and across dough to make 4 divisions; cut only half-way through, so dough is still joined at base. Pull out centre point of each division and press down. Leaving uncut base part unrolled, roll out each of the points, as shown in Step 2 of picture.

Place prepared butter in centre of what is now a star shape; fold each of the points over, tuck well round the butter. (At this stage depth of dough at base is approximately equal to quantity folded over top of butter.)

With rolling pin, gently press out dough, easing butter through evenly. Prominent ridges will result. Fold this into three.

Fold up bottom third, fold top third down. Seal and press edges together, give dough a half turn, so fold is on right hand side.

Repeat rolling and folding. Put pastry aside and allow to relax at least 30 minutes before continuing rolling. Roll and fold 6 times in all, with 30 minutes rest between each 2 roll-and-folds. Allow to rest another 30 minutes before using as required. When pastry is rolled and shaped as required, allow to rest another 10 minutes on oven slide before baking.

Puff pastry must always be baked in a very hot oven; baking times vary with individual recipes.

Small items (which cook quickly) cook for the required time in a very hot oven. Larger items (such as toppings for large pies, where cooking time is longer) bake for the first 15 minutes at very hot, then the temperature is reduced to hot or moderate for remainder of cooking time.

NOTE: In puff pastry, it is important to have a similar consistency of dough and shortening. If shortening is too soft, it will ooze out from between layers of dough; if too hard, it will break through when pastry is rolled, thus allowing the air to escape when pastry is cooked; this will prevent correct rising. It will also prevent even layers of shortening through pastry.

When rolling puff pastry, the ends are sealed with a rolling-pin between each rolling so air is trapped in and cannot escape, and shortening is sealed in. By the sequence of rolling and folding, the basic dough is layered with sheets of shortening in between. This process gives the 'puff' to puff pastry.

Correctly rolled and folded puff pastry will have almost 800 layers of shortening!

Dust pastry lightly with flour between each rolling; before folding and proceeding to roll again, brush off flour gently but thoroughly. Extra flour would prevent pastry from rising well.

Rest pastry (preferably in refrigerator) for 30 minutes between each two rollings and for 30 minutes after final rolling. This enables the shortening to become firm again, and allows the pastry to relax so it does not shrink during cooking.

Do not turn pastry over during rolling. By just turning it round on the board each time it is rolled, shortening is evenly distributed throughout dough.

When rolling is completed and pastry is "resting", cover it with a sheet of waxed paper, then a damp cloth. Waxed paper prevents pastry absorbing moisture from cloth.

Puff pastry rises considerably in baking, so roll it thinly; $\frac{1}{4}$ in. to $\frac{1}{2}$ in. is suitable for most purposes, but for large vol-au-vent cases it needs to be thicker —from $\frac{3}{4}$ in. to 1 in.

Rolled in plastic food wrap or aluminium foil, puff pastry will keep up to 4 days in refrigerator.

## Flaky Pastry

Flaky pastry is often used in place of puff pastry. It is much easier to make than puff pastry, and is delightfully light.

It is often used for Continental-type pastries—thin layers of pastry sandwiched together with jam and cream.

2 cups plain flour
½ teaspoon salt
6 oz. butter
approx. ¼ pint iced water
1 teaspoon lemon juice

Sift flour and salt. Divide butter into 4 equal portions. Take one portion and rub it into flour with fingertips. Add water and lemon juice, mix to a soft dough.

Turn out on lightly floured board, knead lightly until no cracks appear in surface. Cover, let rest 15 to 20 minutes. Roll out to rectangular shape, about $\frac{1}{4}$ in. thick; shape should be about 3 times as long as it is wide.

Take second portion of butter, dot it in small pieces evenly over top two-thirds of pastry to within $\frac{1}{2}$ in. of edge. Fold up bottom third, fold top third down. Seal open edges with rolling-pin, give dough a half turn so fold is on right-hand side. Rest 10 minutes.

Repeat rolling and dotting-with-butter procedures until all butter is used. Roll dough into rectangular shape after the last of butter has been used, fold into 3, and let rest 30 minutes. Then roll to desired shape.

## Rough Puff Pastry

Rolling and folding procedures for rough puff pastry are the same as those for puff and flaky pastries. Rough puff is not as rich as these two pastries and is easier to make.

Because all the shortening is incorporated into the dough, rough puff pastry should be kneaded very lightly.

2 cups plain flour
1 teaspoon baking powder
6 oz. butter
¼ teaspoon salt
approx. ¼ pint iced water
few drops lemon juice

Sift together dry ingredients. Cut cold, firm butter into pieces the size of a small nut and drop into the flour; stir. Mix into a fairly stiff dough with water and lemon juice, using the fingertips. Turn on to floured surface and knead very lightly.

Roll and fold as directed for puff pastry.

Although puff pastry is specified in the following recipes, rough puff or flaky pastry can be substituted with the same excellent results.

## Vol-au-Vent

1 lb. puff pastry
1 egg-yolk

Roll out pastry to $\frac{3}{4}$ in. thickness, cut out two 6 in. circles. Brush oven slide with water, lay one circle on it.

Cut 4 in. circle from centre of second round; set this aside.

Moisten edge of pastry on oven slide, place over it the cut-out rim; it should fit exactly. Press rim down lightly on circle. Score rim with a knife at $\frac{1}{2}$ in. intervals in diamond pattern. Refrigerate 15 minutes. Brush top of shell with egg-yolk, beaten with 1 teaspoon of water. Make sure this glaze does not run down sides or it will prevent pastry rising evenly. Bake in very hot oven 10 minutes, reduce heat to moderately hot, bake approximately 30 minutes longer, or until shell is well risen and brown.

Custard Tart with smooth, velvet-textured custard filling; biscuit or shortcrust pastry can be used for the pie shell

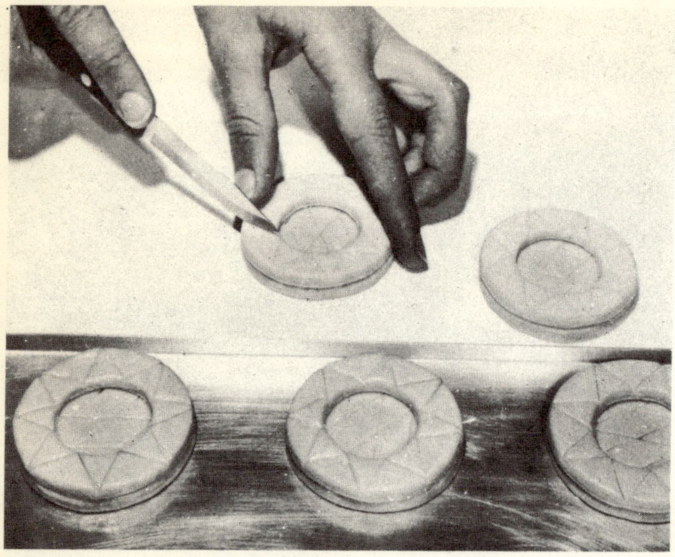

*Bouchées* with back of small knife, mark top ring of pastry in V-shape, for decorative finish

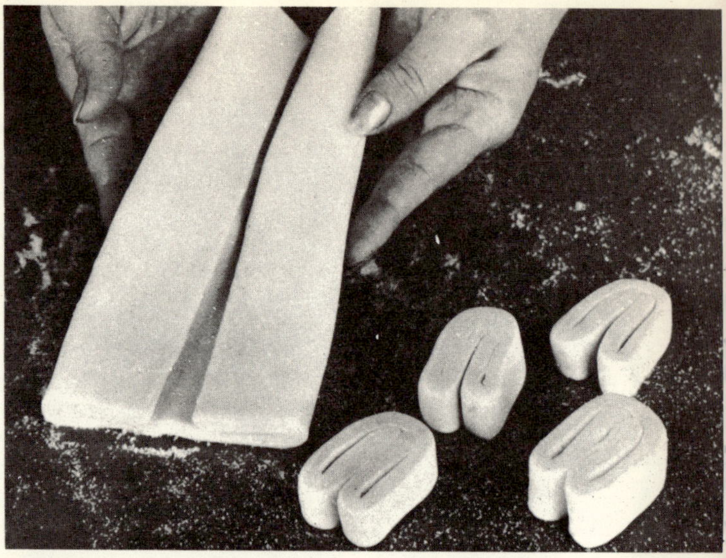

*Palmiers* fold puff, rough puff or flaky pastry as shown, cut into slices with sharp knife

The cut-out circle, which forms lid of vol-au-vent, should be baked separately, because it cooks much more quickly than the large puff shell. Score the cut-out circle in diamond shapes with sharp knife, brush with egg-glaze. Bake in hot oven approximately 10 to 15 minutes, or until well puffed and brown.

Vol-au-vents can be filled with creamy mixtures of chicken, fish, mushroom, etc.

## Bouchées

1 lb. puff pastry | beaten egg for glazing

Roll out pastry to $\frac{1}{4}$ in. thickness. Heat a 2 in. cutter in boiling water, cut four circles. Re-heat cutter as it cools. Using 1 in. cutter, also heated, cut a small round from centre of each alternate circle, thus making rings.

With back of small knife, mark centre of each whole circle with criss-cross pattern. Brush pattern only, with beaten egg. Brush outer rims with water. Carefully place rings into position on top of circles with patterned base. Do not stretch pastry. Press edges firmly without squashing. Again using back of small knife, mark the ring of pastry in V pattern, brush with egg.

Place well apart on oven slide, which has been sprinkled with cold water. Bake in hot oven 5 minutes, cover with brown paper to prevent tops burning, reduce heat to moderately hot, cook further 5 minutes.

The criss-cross part of base will rise through centre ring. When pastry cools, carefully cut out this part with a sharp knife, and use as a lid on filled bouchees.

Fill with desired filling just before serving, heat in a moderate oven until filling is piping hot. Finely chopped chicken, drained flaked salmon, oysters, chopped prawns, lobster or crab, finely chopped mushrooms, or drained chopped asparagus, can all be folded into a well-seasoned white sauce, and used as a filling.

Makes approx. $2\frac{1}{2}$ dozen

## Palmiers

On a board lightly dusted with castor sugar, roll out 12 oz. puff pastry into oblong approximately 8 in. by 14 in.; pastry should be about $\frac{1}{8}$ in. in thickness. Sprinkle lightly with castor sugar.

Fold as shown in picture, folding long sides so they meet in the centre, then bring folds over so there are four layers of pastry.

With sharp knife, cut into $\frac{1}{2}$ in. pieces. Brush cut side of each with water, sprinkle with castor sugar. Place on greased oven slide, cut side down; allow room for expanding. Spread them open at folded ends to make a small V. Refrigerate 10 minutes.

Bake in hot oven 15 minutes or until crisp and golden. Halfway through cooking time, turn them to allow second side to crisp and brown; cool.

Serve plain or dust with icing sugar.

For a delicious dessert, join two Palmiers together with whipped cream, top with passionfruit icing.

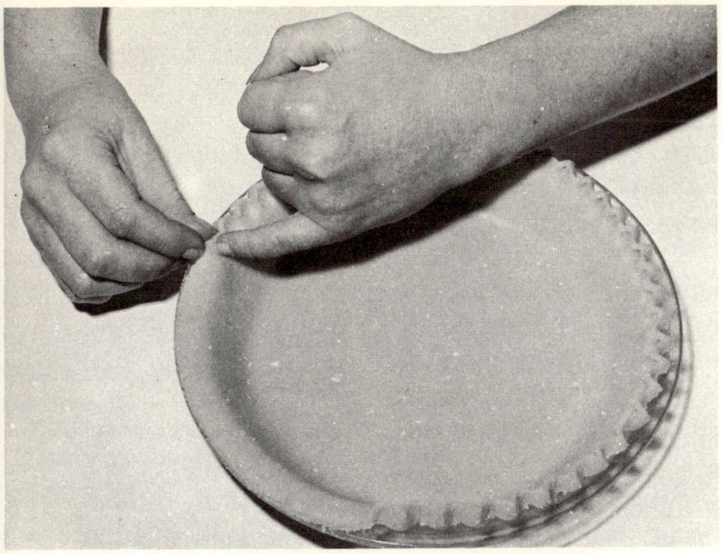

*Pie edging* pinch pastry between thumb and forefinger of left hand, pushing gently with right forefinger.

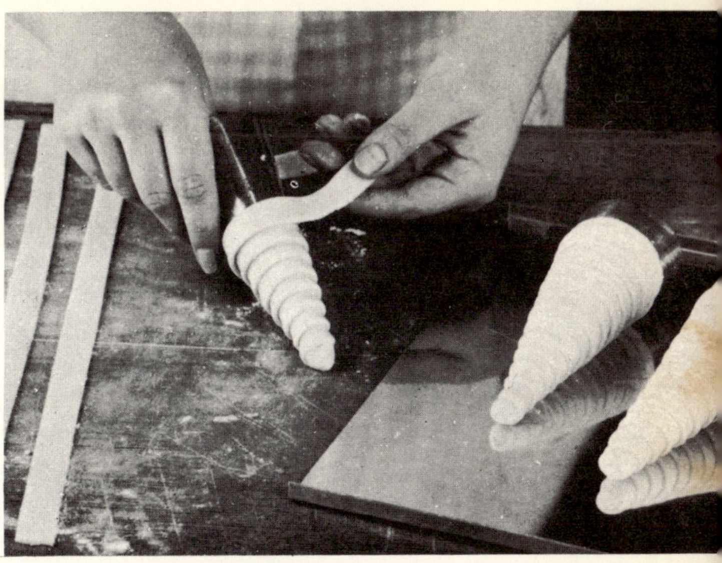

*Cream Horns* wind pastry round metal horn, overlapping dampened edge

## Cream Horns

Roll out puff pastry thinly, cut into strips approximately 18 in. long and ½ in. wide (depending on size of the conical metal moulds). Moisten one side of each pastry strip with cold water.

Start at point of metal cone, wind pastry round, overlapping the dampened edge.

It may be necessary to join one or more strips of pastry, depending on size of horns required. Brush cut ends of pastry with water to join, press firmly with the finger, but do not stretch pastry.

Do not bring pastry up to top end of cone; it will be difficult to remove from cone when baked.

Brush lightly with milk or beaten egg. Place on oven slide, allow room for expanding. Bake in hot oven 5 minutes, reduce heat to moderately hot, cook further 10 to 15 minutes. Halfway through baking time, lift out oven slide, slip the metal moulds from the pastry horn, so pastry dries and cooks through. Cool, fill with whipped cream.

NOTE: 1 lb. puff pastry will make approx. 6 large Cream Horns.

## Sausage Rolls

1 lb. puff pastry
egg-yolk for glazing

**Filling**

1½ lb. sausage meat
1 onion
salt, pepper
water
½ teaspoon mixed herbs
2 thick slices bread

Remove crusts from bread, place into basin, barely cover with hot water. Stand 10 minutes, drain, press out all surplus water. Combine bread, meat, grated onion, salt, pepper and herbs; mix with the hands to combine thoroughly.

Fill mixture into large piping bag, without nozzle. Roll pastry out into a rectangle, approximately 16 in. x 12 in., trim edges; cut lengthwise into three even strips. Pipe the filling lengthwise along each strip, fold one side of pastry over filling, glaze the the other side with egg glazing, fold over. Do not glaze cut edges of pastry as this will prevent pastry rising well. Using back of a knife, mark the roll at ½ in. intervals. Cut rolls into 2½ to 3 in. pieces. Place on to ungreased oven slides, brush with egg glazing. Bake in hot oven 10 minutes, reduce heat to moderate, bake a further 15 to 20 minutes, or until golden brown and crisp.

NOTE: Some sausage mince contains a large amount of fat; it may be necessary to drain surplus fat from the trays half-way during the cooking time, to ensure rolls are crisp on base.

## Choux Pastry

No wonder the French chose choux pastry to make many of the delicious pastries for which they are world-famous. It is delicate, crisp, light as a feather in the hand.

Choux pastry is leavened by steam that builds up in the batter under heat.

Once the pastry is in the oven resist the temptation to peep at it. The oven door should not be opened until cooking time is almost completed, otherwise the steam which has built up in the hot oven will escape and the puffs will fall.

To provide more steam, when baking choux puffs, sprinkle puffs and tray very lightly with water before putting into oven; the additional steam will provide bigger puffs.

However, if baking eclairs, do not sprinkle with water; they need a dry heat to preserve their shape.

If pastry shrinks when removed from the oven, generally, the simple explanation is that the pastry has not been cooked long enough.

Once the puffs are cooked and removed from the oven keep them out of draughts; a cold wind on the puffs when they are hot will also cause them to fall.

## Choux Pastry

1 cup water
2½ oz. butter
pinch salt
1 cup plain flour
3 large eggs

Place water, butter and salt in saucepan. Bring to boil. Add sifted flour all at once. Stir vigorously with wooden spoon over heat until mixture is thick. When mixture forms a smooth ball and leaves sides of pan remove from heat. Cool slightly. Add beaten eggs a little at a time, beating thoroughly after each addition.

Beat paste well when all egg is added until it is free of lumps. Mixture should be smooth and glossy.

If eggs are only of medium size, it may be necessary to add an extra egg, or portion of egg. Beat the egg and add it gradually to the batter, adding only enough to give you batter of the desired consistency.

Then cook as directed in the individual recipes.

NOTE: If making choux pastry for sweet puffs or eclairs, 1 teaspoon of sugar can be added to the basic recipe; stir it in with the sifted flour.

*To Store Choux Pastry:* All the soft, uncooked mixture from centre of cooked puffs or eclairs must be removed before storing, otherwise pastries will soften.

Put pastries into plastic bag, fasten loosely at top; keep in refrigerator. Kept this way, pastries will stay crisp for 3 or 4 days.

Pastries may also be stored in an air-tight container.

If pastry does soften during storage, re-crispen in a moderate oven for a few minutes.

Pastries, of course, should not be filled before storing; spoon or pipe in desired filling just before serving.

## Cream Puffs

Drop rounded spoonfuls of pastry on to greased oven slide, allowing about 2 in. space between puffs; they will spread during cooking. Bake in hot oven 10 minutes, reduce heat to moderate, bake further 20 to 30 minutes or until puffs are golden and feel light in the hand.

Cooking time will depend on size of puffs. Allow approximate overall cooking time of 25 to 30 minutes for small puffs; approximate overall cooking time of 35 to 40 minutes for large puffs.

When cooked, remove from oven, make small slit in side to allow steam to escape; return to oven a few minutes to dry out.

When cool, puffs can be filled with whipped cream or custard; fill just before serving or the filling will soften the puffs. Sift icing sugar over top of puffs.

If serving cream puffs as dessert, ice-cream makes a delightful filling; spoon it in just before serving. Top with a rich caramel sauce.

## Chocolate Eclairs

Take basic choux paste, fill into piping bag fitted with ½ in. plain tube; pipe into 2 in. lengths on very lightly greased oven-slide. Leave about 2 in. between each eclair shape.

Bake in a hot oven 10 minutes, reduce heat to moderate, bake further 20 minutes or until dry.

Slit each eclair open, remove any soft filling with a teaspoon, return to oven for a few minutes to dry out. Cool.

Fill with whipped cream and top with melted chocolate (you will need about 4 oz.).

## Savoury Puffs

Savoury puffs are generally made in small size; they are ideal party savouries. However, large-size puffs, filled with a savoury mixture, can also be an unusual first course, or light luncheon or supper dish.

Chicken stock (stock cubes can be used) can be used in place of the water in the basic recipe when making puffs which are to be filled with a savoury mixture.

A creamy, well-seasoned white sauce of fairly thick consistency can be used as a filling for savoury puffs; to this can be added some chopped chicken; smoked oysters; finely chopped shallots; chopped prawns, crab, lobster; mayonnaise or whipped cream; curry powder; etc.

Cream Puffs, light as a feather, make a superb dessert; fill them with cream and sliced strawberries

## Hot Water Pastry

Hot-water pastry is used mainly for meat or game pies, such as the traditional favourite, Melton Mowbray Pie, given below. This is a firm, strong dough, prepared in a different way from other pastries. Boiling liquid is added to flour, and dough used while warm.

| | |
|---|---|
| 2½ cups plain flour | 3 oz. lard |
| ½ teaspoon salt | ¼ pint water |
| 1 egg-yolk | |

Sift flour and salt into bowl. Make well in centre of flour, drop in egg-yolk, cover with some of the flour. Place lard and water in saucepan. Place over gentle heat until lard melts. Increase heat, bring rapidly to the boil. Pour all boiling liquid into flour.

Water must be boiling, otherwise pastry will be difficult to mould and may crack in cooking.

Mix with wooden spoon until pastry is cool enough to handle. Continue mixing and kneading until all egg streaks are gone and dough is smooth.

This is important; insufficient kneading could cause pastry to crack during cooking.

Cover and rest in warm place 20 to 30 minutes.

## Melton Mowbray Pie

1 quantity hot water pastry

**Filling**

| | |
|---|---|
| 2½ lb. lean boned shoulder of pork | 1 onion |
| 1 chopped knuckle of veal | water |
| salt, pepper | egg glaze |

*Filling:* Reserve bones from pork, and put these into large saucepan with veal knuckle, sliced onion, salt and pepper; add water to cover. Simmer mixture at least 2 hours to make a good stock that jells when cold; set aside.

Cut pork meat into ½ in. pieces, season with salt and pepper. Set aside.

Set aside ¼ of pastry for pie lid. Roll out remainder, line lightly greased 7 in. cake tin with pastry extended ½ in. above top. Place seasoned meat in pie shell, moisten with little stock. Roll out remaining pastry, place on top of pie, trim edges, pressing firmly together. Make rose and leaves from pastry trimmings, place on top of pie. Brush well with egg glaze. Place in hot oven, cook 1 hour. Reduce heat to moderate, cook approximately further 1½ hours. Brush again with glaze during cooking. Cover top with paper if too brown. Leave until cool.

Heat jelly stock. With sharp knife, carefully remove rose from centre of pie. Pour in cooled jelly, using funnel; replace decoration. Refrigerate.

The pie should be made the day before it is to be used, so jellied filling can set completely.

*Veal and ham pie:* Substitute trimmed stewing veal for pork in recipe above; add ¼ lb. bacon, diced; one or two hard-boiled eggs can be placed in centre of meat mixture before baking.

## Suet Pastry

Suet pastry—hearty, substantial, and filling—is ideal for the cold weather. It's used for old-fashioned favourite dishes, both sweet and savoury.

Be sure suet is finely chopped or grated before adding it to flour; if it tends to stick, sprinkle it with some of the measured sifted flour after grating.

Suet pastry is one of the few pastries which uses self-raising flour.

| | |
|---|---|
| 2 cups self-raising flour | ½ teaspoon salt |
| 3 to 4 oz. finely grated beef suet | water to mix, approx. ¼ pint |

Sift dry ingredients, add prepared suet, and mix well. Mix with sufficient water to give a soft but dry dough. Turn on to lightly floured board and knead well.

## Steak and Kidney Pudding

| | |
|---|---|
| 3 cups self-raising flour | 5 oz. suet |
| 1 teaspoon salt | water to mix |

**Filling**

| | |
|---|---|
| 2 lb. round steak | pepper |
| 8 oz. ox kidney | 1 large onion |
| 2 tablespoons flour | ½ cup stock |
| 2 teaspoons salt | |

Make pastry as for basic recipe.

Dice meat and kidney into 1 in. cubes, discarding any gristle or excess fat. Toss meat in seasoned flour until well coated. Dice onion finely, add to meat.

Use ⅔ of prepared pastry to line 4-pint greased pudding basin, fill with meat; add stock. Roll out remaining pastry to form a lid. Wet edges of pudding, place top in position, sealing edges.

Cover pudding with greased aluminium foil. Steam approximately 6 to 7 hours. After this time of cooking, pudding can be turned out on to serving dish.

Watch water level in saucepan carefully during cooking time; as it evaporates, replace with boiling water.

## Tartlets

Small tartlets make good eating at any time. Baked in advance, they can quickly be filled with a variety of fillings and used as a dessert or for afternoon tea. They provide a delicious treat for the family or unexpected visitors.

Biscuit or sweet shortcrust is best for tartlet cases. Four ounces of biscuit or sweet shortcrust will make 1 dozen tartlet cases. Each filling given here makes sufficient for 1 dozen tartlets.

Roll out pastry to $\frac{1}{4}$ in. thickness, cut with 3 in. floured cutter, fit into greased patty tins.

Some tartlets are baked complete with filling; some have the filling spooned into the baked, cooled cases.

When baking tartlet cases 'blind', or without a filling, prick pastry shells well with a fork, bake in moderately hot oven for approximately 10 minutes.

## Brandied Custard Tarts

1 egg
1 tablespoon sugar
⅔ cup milk
1 tablespoon brandy
nutmeg
1 dozen unbaked tartlet cases

Beat egg, sugar, milk and brandy together. Strain, spoon carefully into tartlet cases. Sprinkle with a little nutmeg. Bake in moderately hot oven for 20 minutes or until custard is set.

## Apricot Cream Tarts

1 egg-yolk
1½ tablespoons castor sugar
½ teaspoon vanilla
1 tablespoon plain flour
¼ pint milk
1 dozen baked tartlet cases

**Topping**

15 oz. can apricot halves
2 teaspoons arrowroot

Whisk egg yolk, sugar and vanilla until white, stir in flour. Warm milk, stir gradually into egg mixture. Place mixture in saucepan, stir until mixture boils and thickens. When filling is cold, spoon into pastry cases, level tops.

*Topping:* Drain apricots, reserve $\frac{1}{2}$ cup syrup. Place one apricot half, cut-side down, into each pastry case. Blend arrowroot with the reserved syrup in a saucepan, stir until mixture boils and thickens, spoon over apricot halves.

## Mushrooms

1 tablespoon jam
1 oz. butter
1 cup icing sugar
1 tablespoon milk, approx.
½ teaspoon vanilla
cinnamon
1 dozen baked tartlet cases

Retain any left-over pastry to make 'stems' for mushrooms. Bake stems in a moderate oven for approximately 5 minutes or until golden brown.

Place small amount of jam into each tartlet case. Cream butter until soft and white, gradually add sifted icing sugar, and enough milk to give a smooth consistency, flavour with vanilla. Fill tart cases with the butter cream, level the tops, dust with cinnamon, place 'stems' in position.

## Butterscotch Meringue Tartlets

⅓ cup brown sugar
¼ cup plain flour
¾ cup milk
1 oz. butter
1 egg-yolk
1 teaspoon instant coffee powder
½ teaspoon vanilla
1 dozen baked tartlet cases

**Meringue**

1 egg-white
¼ cup sugar

Blend brown sugar and flour with milk in a saucepan, stir until mixture boils and thickens, simmer 1 minute. Beat in butter, egg yolk, coffee and vanilla. When cold, spoon into pastry cases. Pipe or spoon meringue on top of each tartlet, bake in moderate oven for 5 to 10 minutes, or until meringue is set and lightly browned.

*Meringue:* Beat egg-white until foamy, gradually add sugar, beat until grains are dissolved and mixture is of meringue consistency.

## Chocolate Tarts

1 egg, separated
1 oz. dark chocolate
¼ cup cream
1 teaspoon brandy or rum
extra melted chocolate
1 dozen baked tartlet cases

Melt chocolate in top of a double saucepan, remove from heat, blend in egg-yolk, beat until smooth and thick. Whisk cream until soft peaks form, fold into mixture with brandy or rum; lastly fold in well-beaten egg-white.

Spoon mixture into pastry cases, refrigerate until firm. Drizzle with extra melted chocolate.

## Pineapple and Cream Cheese Tarts

2 oz. packaged cream cheese
2 teaspoons lemon juice
½ cup drained crushed pineapple
1 dozen baked tartlet cases

**Glaze**

1 teaspoon arrowroot
½ cup pineapple syrup
few drops yellow food colouring

Beat cream cheese until smooth, beat in lemon juice and pineapple. Spoon mixture into pastry cases, level tops. Spoon slightly cooled glaze over, refrigerate before serving.

*Glaze:* Blend arrowroot with pineapple juice in a saucepan, stir until mixture boils and thickens. Colour as desired.

## Iced Fruit Mince Tarts

1 lb. can fruit mince
2 tablespoons icing sugar
½ egg-white
few drops red food colouring
1 dozen baked tartlet cases

Fill tart cases with fruit mince, making sure the top is level. Sift icing sugar, mix with the egg white, colour pink with few drops of red food colouring. Spread icing thinly over each tartlet. Bake in moderate oven 5 to 10 minutes, or until icing sets.

## Honeyed Lemon Cheese Tartlets

2 eggs
½ cup sugar
¼ cup honey
2 oz. butter
1 dessertspoon grated lemon rind
⅓ cup lemon juice
1 dozen baked tartlet cases

Beat eggs, combine with remaining ingredients in top of a double boiler, stir constantly over hot water until thickened. Allow to become cold before spooning into tartlet cases.

## Maids of Honour

1 tablespoon raspberry jam
2 oz. butter
½ teaspoon vanilla
¼ cup sugar
1 egg
½ cup self-raising flour
1 dozen unbaked tartlet cases

Place a little jam into each pastry case. Cream butter, vanilla and sugar until light and fluffy. Add beaten egg a little at a time, beat well. Fold in sifted flour. Place a teaspoonful of mixture into each pastry case, top with a pastry cross made from small strips of remaining pastry. Bake in moderate oven for 20 to 25 minutes. When cool, dust tops with icing sugar.

## Nougat Tarts

1 tablespoon raspberry jam
1 egg-white
½ cup sugar
2 oz. ground almonds
¾ cup coconut
1 tablespoon milk
few drops almond essence
glacé cherry quarters
1 dozen unbaked tartlet cases

Place a little jam into each pastry case. Whisk egg white stiffly, fold in all remaining ingredients, except cherries. Place a teaspoonful of mixture into each pastry case, top with a piece of glace cherry. Bake in a moderate oven 20 to 25 minutes or until golden brown.

## Jam Tartlets

raspberry or other jam
sweetened whipped cream
1 dozen unbaked tartlet cases

Fill each tartlet case with jam, bake in hot oven 10 to 15 minutes. When cold, top with dot of whipped cream.

Tartlet cases may be pricked well with a fork, and baked in a moderately hot oven for 10 to 15 minutes or until crisp, then filled with jam.

## Fresh Strawberry Tarts

1 punnet strawberries
2 tablespoons sugar
½ cup water
1 teaspoon arrowroot
1 teaspoon brandy
few drops red food colouring
1 dozen baked tartlet cases

Arrange washed, hulled strawberries in pastry cases. Heat sugar and water over a low heat until sugar dissolves; remove from heat. Blend arrowroot with a little water, stir into syrup, stir over heat until mixture boils and thickens. Add brandy, colour as desired. Cool slightly, spoon over strawberries as a glaze.

Recipes for these attractive little tartlets are given on pages 207 and 208

# DESSERTS

## Hot Desserts

Here's a choice of steamed or baked puddings; some are hearty winter foods, many are light enough to serve throughout the year. And there's a selection of other popular hot puddings

### Steamed Pudding

4 oz. butter
½ cup sugar
2 eggs
2 cups self-raising flour
pinch salt
¼ pint milk
2 tablespoons jam

Beat butter and sugar together until light and fluffy; add eggs one at a time, beat well after each addition. Fold sifted dry ingredients and milk alternately into creamed mixture.

Grease 2½ pint pudding basin, line base with greased greaseproof paper, cover base with jam. Spoon in pudding mixture, cover, steam 1½ hours.

Serves 4

### Ginger Pudding

2 oz. butter
2 tablespoons golden syrup
1 teaspoon ground ginger
½ cup warm milk
½ teaspoon bicarbonate of soda
1 cup self-raising flour
pinch salt

Beat butter, golden syrup and ginger until light and fluffy; add warm milk, in which soda has been dissolved. Stir in sifted flour and salt, mix well. Place mixture into 2½-pint greased pudding basin, cover, steam 1½ hours.

Serves 4

### Steamed Date Pudding

½ lb. dates
½ oz. butter
½ cup boiling water
½ teaspoon bicarbonate of soda
½ cup milk
1 cup plain flour
½ cup sugar

Chop dates, melt butter in boiling water, dissolve soda in milk. Sift dry ingredients into basin, add dates, water and milk, stir until smooth. Pour into 2½-pint greased pudding basin, cover, steam 2 hours.

Serves 4

### Steamed Lemon Pudding

4 oz. butter
grated rind 2 lemons
½ cup sugar
2 eggs
1 cup self-raising flour
¼ cup sugar, extra
juice 2 lemons

Cream butter and lemon rind, add ½ cup sugar, beat until light and fluffy. Add eggs one at a time, beating well after each addition. Fold in sifted flour, beat lightly until smooth.

Combine ¼ cup sugar with strained lemon juice, pour into greased 2½-pint pudding basin. Spoon mixture into liquid, cover, steam 1½ hours.

Serves 4 to 6

### Christmas Pudding

¼ lb. currants
½ lb. raisins
½ lb. sultanas
¼ lb. mixed peel
6 oz. butter
½ lb. fresh breadcrumbs (approx. crumbs from 1 large loaf bread)
½ lb. brown sugar
1 dessertspoon mixed spice
juice and grated rind 1 small lemon
1 teaspoon nutmeg
2 eggs
½ cup brandy or ale

Chop fruit, pour over brandy or ale, add grated lemon rind and juice; cover, leave overnight.

Cream butter, gradually add beaten eggs and brown sugar; beat well. Add remaining ingredients; stir vigorously.

*To Steam* Pack into greased 4½-pint pudding basin; cover with greased aluminium foil. Secure with string and steam 4 hours. For a large family pudding, double the quantities above, steam 6 hours. Steam further 2 hours on day of serving.

*To Boil* Place pudding mixture in floured pudding cloth, tie securely, allowing room for pudding to expand during cooking, boil 4 hours. Reboil for 2 hours on day of serving.

NOTE: Breadcrumbs give sufficient substance to this rich pudding; flour is not used.

## Apple Sponge Dessert

4 apples
½ cup sugar
4 tablespoons water
1 teaspoon grated lemon rind
few whole cloves

**Topping:**

2 eggs
½ teaspoon vanilla
¼ cup castor sugar
½ cup self-raising flour
pinch salt
1 tablespoon sugar, extra

Peel, core and slice apples, combine in saucepan with sugar, water, lemon rind and cloves, cover, cook gently until apples are tender. Place in greased pie dish; remove cloves. Spoon topping over hot apples, sprinkle with extra sugar. Bake in moderate oven 30 to 35 minutes. Serve warm with custard.

*Topping* Beat eggs and vanilla until thick and creamy, gradually add sugar, beat until dissolved. Fold in sifted flour and salt.

Serves 4

## Lemon Delicious Pudding

3 eggs
½ cup sugar
1 cup milk
1 tablespoon self-raising flour
grated rind and juice 2 large lemons
pinch salt
1 tablespoon sugar, extra

Separate eggs; beat yolks with ½ cup sugar until light and creamy. Beat in milk, sifted flour, rind and juice of lemons, and salt. Beat egg-whites, add extra sugar gradually, continue beating until stiff but not dry. Fold into lemon mixture.

Pour into greased deep 2-pint ovenproof dish, stand in shallow pan of cold water. Bake in moderate oven 50 to 60 minutes.

Serves 4

## Baked Custard

3 eggs
2 tablespoons sugar
1 teaspoon vanilla
1 pint milk
nutmeg or cinnamon

Beat eggs, sugar and vanilla together lightly with a fork, add warm milk gradually, stir to combine evenly. Pour into shallow ovenproof dish, sprinkle with nutmeg or cinnamon. Stand dish in baking tin, with enough cold water to come halfway up sides of dish. Bake in moderate oven 30 minutes, reduce heat to moderately slow, bake further 20 to 30 minutes or until set.

Serves 4

## Steamed Fruit Pudding

2 cups plain flour
1 cup brown sugar
½ lb. sultanas
½ lb. raisins
¼ lb. currants
2 oz. glacé cherries
2 oz. mixed peel
1 teaspoon mixed spice
4 oz. butter
1 cup hot water
1 teaspoon bicarbonate of soda
½ cup cold water
½ cup brandy

Dissolve bicarbonate of soda in the cold water and brandy; melt butter in the hot water. Chop fruit. Put all dry ingredients in basin and mix with the liquid; allow to stand overnight. Mixture thickens with standing. Next day, place mixture into a greased 3 pint pudding basin, steam for 4 hours.

## Chocolate Sauce Pudding

2 oz. butter
½ cup milk
1 teaspoon vanilla
1 cup self-raising flour
¾ cup castor sugar
1 tablespoon cocoa
2 cups hot water

**Topping**

¾ cup brown sugar
1 tablespoon cocoa

Heat butter and milk in saucepan, stir until butter melts, add vanilla. Sift dry ingredients into basin, add butter mixture to well in centre, stir until smooth, pour into deep, greased 2-pint ovenproof dish. Sprinkle with topping, carefully pour over hot water. Bake in moderate oven 40 to 45 minutes.

Serves 4

*Topping*: Combine ingredients well.

## Caramel Dumplings

**Dumplings**

1¼ cups self-raising flour
pinch salt
1 oz. butter
⅓ cup sugar
1 teaspoon vanilla
⅓ cup milk

**Sauce**

1 oz. butter
1½ cups brown sugar, firmly packed
pinch salt
1½ cups water

*Dumplings:* Sift flour and salt into basin, rub in butter, add sugar. Add combined milk and vanilla, stir well.

*Sauce:* Combine all ingredients in large saucepan, stir constantly until boiling, reduce heat. Drop tablespoonfuls of dumpling dough into simmering sauce, cover, simmer 20 minutes. Serve warm with whipped cream.

Serves 4

## Rum Babas

½ oz. compressed yeast
1 dessertspoon sugar
¼ cup milk
2 cups plain flour
pinch salt
3 eggs
5 oz. butter
1 tablespoon currants
2 tablespoons sultanas

**Syrup**

30 oz. can apricot nectar
2 cups sugar
3 dessertspoons lemon juice
¼ cup rum

Cream yeast and sugar, add luke-warm milk. Sift flour and salt into basin, make well in centre, stir in yeast mixture and well-beaten eggs. Dot surface of dough with 1 oz. softened butter, cover with clean towel and set aside in warm place until doubled in bulk (about 40 minutes). When dough is well-risen, mix in the remaining softened butter and fruits. Turn out on to lightly floured board, knead well, turning edges of dough into centre. Divide mixture over eight well-greased small cups or moulds which have been stood on baking tray. Fill them not quite half-full. Cover, let rise again in warm place for 20 minutes. Bake in hot oven 15 minutes until golden. Drop Babas one at a time into the hot syrup until they are well-soaked. Babas can be made some time ahead and reheated, at serving time, in the hot syrup. Serve whipped cream separately.

*Syrup:* Combine apricot nectar and sugar in saucepan, stir until sugar dissolves. Bring to boil, boil rapidly 5 minutes. Remove from heat, stir in lemon juice and rum.

## Apple Pie

**Pastry**

2½ cups plain flour
pinch salt
8 oz. butter
2 egg-yolks
⅓ cup icing sugar
grated rind 1 lemon
1 tablespoon lemon juice

*Pastry:* Sift flour and salt into a basin, make a well in the centre. Slice butter, add with sifted icing sugar and remaining ingredients to well in centre of flour. Work centre ingredients to a paste with the hand, then gradually work in the flour. Form dough into a ball, cover, refrigerate 30 minutes.

**Filling**

5 medium cooking apples
½ cup apricot jam
milk
sugar

Peel and core apples, quarter, slice finely, sprinkle with a little sugar if desired. Roll ⅔ of the pastry on a lightly floured board, large enough to line base and sides of a lightly greased 11 in. x 7 in. lamington tin. Place apples into pastry case, dot evenly with apricot jam.

Roll remaining pastry to cover top of pie, glaze between two edges of pastry with a little milk, pinch edges together. Brush top of pie with milk, sprinkle with sugar, slit top of pie in several places, to allow steam to escape. Bake in hot oven 15 minutes, reduce heat to moderate, bake further 25 to 30 minutes.

Drizzle with glace icing. Allow to cool slightly before serving. Serve with cream.

*Glace Icing:* Sift 1 cup icing sugar into a basin, add sufficient milk, about 1 tablespoon, to give a stiff paste.

## Caramel Bananas

4 large ripe bananas
2 oz. butter
1 cup brown sugar
¼ cup cream
thin pancakes

Peel and slice bananas. Melt butter in frying pan, add sugar, stir over low heat until sugar dissolves, bring to the boil, add sliced bananas; reduce heat, simmer until tender; stir occasionally. Stir in cream, pour over pancakes. Serve with whipped cream or ice-cream.

Serves 4

## Creamed Rice

2 pints milk
⅔ cup sugar
½ teaspoon salt
½ cup rice
½ teaspoon vanilla

Combine milk, sugar and salt in saucepan, bring to boil. Gradually add rice to gently boiling milk, stirring constantly. Reduce heat, cover, simmer gently, stirring occasionally until ⅔ of liquid is absorbed and rice is tender (approx. 1¼ hours). Stir in vanilla.

Serves 4 to 6

## Baked Rice Pudding

½ cup rice
¼ cup castor sugar or brown sugar
1¼ pints milk
1 oz. butter

Place all ingredients in lightly greased ovenproof dish; stir to combine. Dot with butter. Bake in moderately slow oven 55 to 60 minutes.

Serves 4.

Pears can be cooked in red or white wine. Serve them well-chilled, with the wine syrup spooned over

## Cold Desserts

Cool, elegant, quite delicious—recipes in this section range from family desserts to many of the world's classic recipes. You'll find a dessert idea here suitable for any occasion

### Banana Cream Pie

**Pastry**

3 oz. butter
¼ cup castor sugar
1 egg
1½ cups plain flour
2 tablespoons ground rice
¼ teaspoon baking powder

**Filling**

1 oz. butter
⅔ cup brown sugar, lightly packed
¼ pint water
½ pint milk
3 to 4 bananas
1 tablespoon gelatine
2 eggs
¼ pint cream
lemon juice
extra whipped cream

*Pastry*: Cream butter and sugar, add egg, beat well. Sift flour, ground rice and baking powder, work into creamed mixture, knead well until smooth. Refrigerate 30 minutes. Roll out pastry on floured surface to fit lightly greased 9 in. pie plate. Decorate edges with trimmings, brush with water. Prick well with fork on base and round sides. Bake in hot oven approximately 15 minutes or until lightly golden; cool.

*Filling*: Combine butter, brown sugar and half the water in saucepan; cook, stirring until sugar is dissolved (approximately 2 minutes). Cool slightly, stir in milk. Soften gelatine in remaining water, dissolve over hot water; cool. Blend into milk mixture. Separate eggs, add lightly beaten egg-yolks to milk mixture.

Allow to cool; when beginning to stiffen slightly, fold in lightly whipped cream and stiffly beaten egg-whites. Slice bananas, dip into lemon juice; reserve some slices for decoration. Arrange remainder on base of cooked pie case. Pour cream mixture over carefully; refrigerate until set.

Just before serving, decorate with extra whipped cream and reserved banana slices.

### Lemon Meringue Pie

¾ cup sugar
⅓ cup cornflour
1 cup water
⅔ cup lemon juice
2 oz. butter
grated rind 2 lemons
2 egg-yolks
9 in. baked pastry case

**Meringue**

2 egg-whites
¼ cup sugar

Combine sugar and cornflour in saucepan, blend in water and lemon juice gradually, stir until smooth. Stir constantly over medium heat until mixture boils and thickens. Remove from heat, quickly stir in butter, lemon rind and egg-yolks, beat until butter has melted. When filling is cold, spread into cooled baked pastry case. Top with meringue, bake in moderate oven 5 to 10 minutes, or until meringue is set and lightly browned.

*Meringue:* Beat egg-whites until foamy, gradually add sugar, beat until sugar has dissolved and mixture is of thick meringue consistency.

### Strawberry Shortcake

2 oz. butter
4 tablespoons sugar
2 egg-yolks
¾ cup plain flour
2 punnets strawberries
1 dessertspoon gelatine
1 tablespoon water
whipped cream
red currant jelly
extra strawberries

Cream butter until soft, add 2 tablespoons sugar and egg-yolks, beat until light and fluffy. Work in sifted flour until well combined, place dough on to lightly floured board, knead until smooth. Press into lightly greased 8 in. sandwich tin, bake in moderate oven 15 to 20 minutes. Remove from tin, allow to cool slightly.

Wash and remove stems from half the strawberries, combine with remaining 2 tablespoons sugar, mash well with fork. Combine gelatine and water set aside. Place strawberry mixture into saucepan, simmer until reduced by half, add gelatine mixture, stir well.

Halve remaining strawberries, arrange strawberry halves over warm shortcake, pour over the strawberry syrup. Refrigerate until set. Decorate with whipped cream and extra strawberries, which have been brushed with warmed red currant jelly.

### Baked Alaska

1 layer sponge cake
1 large block neapolitan or other ice-cream
6 egg-whites
1½ cups castor sugar

Place sponge cake on heavy board, such as small bread board which has been covered with aluminium foil. If desired, moisten cake with a little fruit syrup or rum or brandy; some chopped sliced peaches can be arranged over cake, and pressed in gently. Place ice-cream on top, place in freezing compartment of refrigerator. Beat egg whites until stiff, gradually add sugar, beat until of meringue consistency. Cover ice-cream and cake completely with meringue; rough up meringue slightly. Bake in very hot oven 3 to 5 minutes, until meringue is lightly browned. Serve at once.

NOTE: Baked Alaska is not the tricky thing to make that people imagine. Nor does it need last minute touches. The whole Alaska can be prepared, covered with meringue, baked briefly as indicated above, then returned to the freezing compartment of the refrigerator. It will stand perfectly for several hours.

## Apple Charlotte

**Pastry**

1 cup plain flour
½ cup self-raising flour
¼ cup custard powder
¼ cup cornflour
2 tablespoons icing sugar
4 oz. butter
¼ cup water, approx.

**Filling**

30 oz. can pie apple
1 tablespoon lemon juice
½ teaspoon nutmeg

*Pastry:* Sift dry ingredients into a basin, rub in butter until mixture resembles fine breadcrumbs. Add sufficient water to make a firm, but pliable dough. Turn dough on to a lightly floured board, knead lightly until smooth, refrigerate 30 minutes.

Combine all ingredients for filling, sweeten with a little sugar, if necessary.

Roll ⅔ of pastry to line base and sides of a greased 7 in. sandwich tin with removable base. Spread apple filling into pastry case, top with remaining pastry, joining edges with a little milk. Slit top in 2 places. Glaze top of pastry with milk, bake in hot oven 10 minutes, reduce heat to moderate, bake further 20 minutes or until pastry is golden brown. Allow to cool before removing from tin, top with Passionfruit Icing.

*Passionfruit Icing:* Sift 1 cup icing sugar, beat in ½ teaspoon softened butter and pulp of 3 passionfruit; add sufficient milk to make a stiff paste. Stir icing over hot water until of a spreading consistency.

## Creamy Chocolate Mousse

4 oz. dark chocolate
4 eggs
½ pint cream
1 tablespoon brandy

Separate eggs. Chop chocolate roughly, put into top of double saucepan; stir over hot water until melted. Remove from heat, cool a little, then blend in egg-yolks, one at a time. Beat until mixture is smooth and thick.

Fold in whipped cream, brandy, then stiffly beaten egg-whites. Spoon into individual serving dishes, refrigerate until firm. To serve, top with a little whipped cream and grated chocolate.

Serves 4

## Toffee Strawberries

1 punnet strawberries
2 cups sugar
1 cup water

Wash strawberries gently, spread on absorbent paper to dry. Place sugar and water in a small saucepan and stir over a gentle heat until the sugar has dissolved. Increase heat and bring to boil. Boil syrup until it becomes a very pale gold colour. Remove from heat immediately.

Using tongs, dip strawberries by the stem into the syrup, coating the entire fruit except the stem. Place on greased baking trays and leave until toffee has hardened. Serve within an hour of making as, if kept too long, juice of the strawberries will make the toffee soft and sticky.

Toffee Grapes can be made in the same way. They're delicious to serve with after-dinner coffee.

## Grape Brulée

1½ lb. seedless white grapes
½ pint cream
3 tablespoons brown sugar

Peel grapes; drain on absorbent paper. Place in heatproof dish, spoon over cream. Leave overnight in refrigerator. Just before serving, sift sugar over surface and place under slow griller until sugar melts. Increase heat to high, continue grilling until sugar caramelises. Serve immediately.

Serves 6

When grapes are out of season, other fresh or canned fruit can be used.

## Mango Mousse

4 ripe mangoes
1 tablespoon gelatine
¼ cup cold water
1 tablespoon lemon juice
¾ cup sugar
1 pint cream

Peel mangoes, cut the flesh away from the stones and, with fork, mash to a puree. Soften gelatine in cold water, dissolve over hot water. Add to mango puree with lemon juice and sugar. For a light-textured mousse, fold in 1 stiffly beaten egg-white. Whip cream, carefully fold into mango mixture.

Spoon into individual dishes, or into one large serving dish; refrigerate until set. Decorate, if desired, with extra mango slices which have been sprinkled with sugar and rum.

Serves 8

NOTE: When mangoes are out of season, 16 oz. can of mango puree can be used in this recipe.

## Crème Caramel

**Caramel**

½ cup sugar
½ cup water

**Custard**

½ pint milk
½ pint cream
3 eggs
¼ cup castor sugar
½ teaspoon vanilla
2 egg-yolks, extra

*Caramel*: Place sugar and water in saucepan. Stir over low heat until sugar dissolves. Stop stirring, turn heat up to moderate, and boil until mixture turns a caramel colour. Pour a little caramel in the base of greased, small, individual, heatproof cups or mould.

*Custard*: Place eggs, extra yolks, vanilla and sugar in bowl. Beat lightly to combine. Combine milk and cream in a saucepan and bring to scalding point; cool slightly. Pour over egg mixture, stirring all the time. Strain into a large jug. Pour into individual moulds, over the caramel. (Makes 5 or 6, depending on size of moulds.)

Place moulds in shallow baking dish containing approximately $\frac{3}{4}$ in. of cold water. Bake in moderately slow oven for approximately 30 minutes, or until custard is set. Remove moulds from water. Cool, then refrigerate a few hours. Turn out on to individual serving plates.

## Strawberries Flambé

rind 1 lemon
rind and juice 2 oranges
½ cup sugar
2 punnets strawberries
½ cup brandy
vanilla ice-cream

Add lemon and orange rind to sugar and juice. Cook slowly in saucepan 5 minutes, pressing rind with spoon to extract all the flavour possible. Remove rind, add strawberries, which have been carefully washed and dried. Spoon syrup gently over strawberries until they are coated with it. Warm brandy, pour over strawberries, set aflame. Serve spooned over vanilla ice-cream.

Serves 6

## Strawberries Romanoff

2 punnets fresh or 2 packets quick-frozen strawberries
½ cup brandy or cointreau
1 cup cream

Wash and hull strawberries or allow to defrost. Pour brandy or cointreau over; cover until serving time. Arrange in individual serving dishes, top with whipped cream. Or blend whipped cream with 1 small block of vanilla ice cream which has been allowed to soften slightly. Spoon over strawberries.

Serves 6

## Biscotten Torte

¾ lb. plain sweet oblong biscuits (24 biscuits)
1½ tablespoons rum
½ cup milk
4 oz. butter
½ cup castor sugar
2 eggs
4 oz. ground almonds
few drops almond essence
extra ½ cup milk
½ pint cream
toasted, slivered almonds

Cream butter and sugar until light and fluffy. Separate eggs, beat yolks into creamed mixture. Add ground almonds, almond essence and the extra $\frac{1}{2}$ cup milk. Beat egg-whites stiffly, fold in. Mix rum and $\frac{1}{2}$ cup milk together.

Arrange 6 biscuits lengthwise in 2 rows (3 biscuits to a row) beside each other on a sheet of greaseproof paper. Brush liberally with the rum-milk mixture. Spread with $\frac{1}{3}$ of creamed mixture. Continue with brushed biscuits and filling, ending with row of biscuits. Wrap securely in aluminium foil, refrigerate several hours, preferably overnight.

Just before serving, arrange on serving plate, cover entire torte with whipped cream; decorate with toasted almonds. Cut in slices to serve.

## Orange Compote

6 oranges
2 cups sugar
1 cup water
2 tablespoons grand marnier or curacao

Combine sugar and water in saucepan; heat, stirring until sugar dissolves, bring to boil. Remove from heat and cool completely. Remove rind and all white pith from oranges. Cut oranges into sections, cutting between the membranes. Do this over a bowl so no juice is lost.

Pour over the cooled syrup, stir in the grand marnier. Cover, then refrigerate until serving time. Spoon into serving dishes. Delicious served just as it is or top with a scoop of ice-cream.

Biscotten Torte can be prepared the day beforehand for a wonderful party dessert

## Strawberry Bavarian Cream

1 tablespoon gelatine
½ cup cold water
½ cup boiling water
½ cup sugar
16 oz. can strawberries
2 egg-whites
1 cup cream

In a saucepan soak gelatine in cold water 5 minutes. Add boiling water and sugar, stir over heat until gelatine and sugar are dissolved. Place strawberries and syrup into blender; blend on high speed 1 minute, or press through sieve. Add pureed strawberries to gelatine mixture. Refrigerate until mixture is partially set.

Beat egg-whites until stiff, gradually add strawberry mixture, beat until thick and creamy. Lightly fold in whipped cream. Pour into lightly oiled 2½ to 3 pint mould. Refrigerate several hours or, preferably, overnight before unmoulding.

Serves 4

*Raspberry Bavarian Cream*: Proceed as for Strawberry Bavarian Cream, substituting 14 oz. can raspberries for the strawberries.

## Caramel Bavarian Cream

1½ dessertspoons gelatine
¼ cup water
¾ cup sugar
¼ cup water, extra
¾ cup milk
2 eggs, separated
¼ cup milk, extra
½ teaspoon vanilla
½ pint cream

Soften gelatine in water and dissolve over boiling water. Place sugar and extra water in saucepan, stir over low heat until sugar has dissolved. Simmer without stirring until syrup is caramel colour. Heat milk in saucepan; when hot, add hot caramel and continue stirring over low heat until caramel is dissolved. Remove from heat. Beat egg yolks with extra milk, add to caramel; mix thoroughly. Add softened gelatine and vanilla. Refrigerate until mixture begins to set.

Fold in stiffly beaten egg-whites and whipped cream. Pour into lightly oiled 2½-pint mould. Refrigerate several hours or overnight before unmoulding.

Serves 4

## Crème Brulée

1 pint cream
1 in. piece vanilla bean
6 egg-yolks
3 tablespoons sugar
½ cup brown sugar
crushed ice

Warm cream with vanilla bean in top of double boiler over hot water. Beat egg-yolks and sugar in basin until light and creamy. Remove vanilla bean; slowly stir warmed cream into the egg-yolk mixture. Return mixture to top of double boiler. Cook over hot, not boiling, water, stirring, until mixture coats a wooden spoon well. Pour custard into a heatproof serving dish, or into individual heatproof serving dishes.

Refrigerate until custard is firm, about 1 hour. Place dish in shallow tray filled with ice cubes. Sift a layer of brown sugar evenly over top. Place under griller at moderate heat until sugar caramelises; watch carefully that sugar does not burn. Refrigerate again until ready to serve.

## Pears in White Wine

6 medium pears
1 cup sugar
1 pint water
1 pint white wine
grated rind 1 lemon
1 dessertspoon lemon juice
4 whole cloves
2 in. cinnamon stick

Peel whole pears thinly, keeping a good shape and leaving stalks in place. Place pears and remaining ingredients in saucepan. Liquid should just cover pears; if necessary add more water and wine in equal proportions. Cover, simmer gently 20 minutes, (depending on ripeness of pears), or until tender. Strain syrup, pour over pears, refrigerate. Serve with syrup spooned over.

Serves 6

*Pears in Red Wine*: Substitute red wine for white in the above recipe. When pears are cooked, cool then refrigerate. For jellied glaze on pears, as shown in picture, dissolve ½ packet port wine jelly crystals in ½ cup boiling water; cool. Brush the jelly glaze over the cold pears. Repeat the brushing several times, if a rich glaze is desired. Serve with the strained syrup.

## Cherries Jubilee

16 oz. can cherries
1 tablespoon sugar
1 in. piece cinnamon stick
2 teaspoons arrowroot
water
½ cup brandy or cherry brandy
ice-cream

Drain cherries, reserving syrup. Pit cherries. Combine cherry syrup, sugar and cinnamon stick in saucepan, bring slowly to boil, simmer gently 3 minutes, strain. Blend arrowroot with a little water, stir into cherry syrup mixture, return to heat, stir until sauce boils and thickens. Add pitted cherries, heat thoroughly.

Add warmed brandy, ignite. Spoon sauce immediately over servings of vanilla ice-cream.

Serves 4

## Italian Lemon Gelato

1¼ cups sugar
¼ cup lemon juice
4¾ cups water
rind 1 lemon
½ pint cream

In large saucepan place sugar, lemon juice, water and lemon rind. Bring slowly to the boil, stirring until sugar has dissolved. Boil 15 minutes, strain, and allow to cool. When quite cold, stir in whipped cream, pour into refrigerator trays, and freeze. When the cream is added to the lemon syrup, the mixtures do not immediately combine. However, while freezing, stir the mixture with fork frequently; the two mixtures soon blend together.

Serves 6

## Lemon Water Ice

2 cups hot water
¾ cup sugar
½ cup lemon juice
1 egg-white
grated rind 1 lemon
1 tablespoon sugar, extra

Dissolve the sugar in the hot water, add lemon juice and rind; set aside to cool; strain. Pour into refrigerator trays and freeze, stirring occasionally, until mixture is mushy; remove from trays. Beat egg-white stiffly, adding the extra sugar gradually; fold in lemon mixture. Return to freezer trays, freeze until firm.

Serves 4

## Wine Trifle

1 jam filled swiss roll
30 oz. can peach halves
⅓ cup any dessert wine
or sweet sherry
⅔ cup custard powder
¾ cup sugar
1½ pints milk
3 eggs
½ teaspoon vanilla
½ pint cream
1 oz. chocolate
1 teaspoon butter

Drain peaches and reserve ½-cup of syrup. Arrange peaches on base of deep glass bowl. Slice swiss roll, stand slices round side of bowl. Dice any surplus cake, place over peaches. Combine wine and reserved peach syrup, pour over cake slices. In saucepan blend custard powder and sugar with a little milk, add remainder of milk, stir well. Cook over medium heat until mixture boils and thickens, stirring constantly. Remove from heat, add well beaten egg-yolks and vanilla; cool. Fold in stiffly beaten egg-whites. Pour over peaches, refrigerate. Before serving, spoon over whipped cream, drizzle with chocolate which has been melted with butter over boiling water.

Serves 6

## Vanilla Ice-Cream

1 dessertspoon gelatine
½ cup sugar
½ cup water
1¼ cups full cream
powdered milk
2 pints milk
1 dessertspoon vinegar
2 teaspoons vanilla

Combine gelatine, sugar and water in saucepan, stir over low heat until sugar and gelatine are dissolved; pour into large basin. Add powdered milk, whisk until smooth, gradually beat in milk. Pour mixture into two 11 in. x 7 in. lamington tins or into freezer trays; freeze until almost set. Spoon mixture into large basin, add vinegar and vanilla, beat until thick and creamy; this can be done on electric mixer. Pour mixture into lamington tins or freezer trays. Freeze until set.

This economical recipe makes approximately 5 pints of beautifully-textured ice-cream. For an even richer ice-cream, beat in ¼ pint cream with the milk.

## Cassata

½ gallon vanilla
ice-cream
1 dessertspoon sugar
juice 1 lemon
1 banana
2 oz. glacé cherries
2 glacé apricots
1 slice glacé pineapple
2 oz. dark chocolate
¼ cup cocoa
1 tablespoon sugar
1 tablespoon water
2 oz. blanched, slivered
almonds
1 teaspoon rum
1 oz. butter
almond essence

Divide ice-cream evenly into three bowls. Keep in freezer until each is required. Combine strained lemon juice and the 1 dessertspoon sugar with sliced banana and finely chopped glace fruits, stir into one bowl of slightly softened ice-cream. Pour into foil-lined aluminium 9 in. x 5 in. loaf tin; freeze until firm. Each layer must be firm before topping with the next.

Melt chocolate over hot water, blend cocoa and the 1 tablespoon sugar with water, stir into melted chocolate; add rum. Stir chocolate mixture into the second bowl of ice-cream, pour over fruit layer; freeze.

Heat butter, add almonds, stir over medium heat until golden brown, drain; cool. Add almonds to remaining ice-cream, flavour to taste with few drops of almond essence, pour over chocolate layer. Cover tin with aluminium foil, freeze 4 hours or overnight. Cut into slices to serve. A little rum or brandy can be spooned over each slice.

NOTE: If desired substitute 2 oz. mixed peel for glace apricots and pineapple.

Serves 6 to 8

# Dessert Sauces

These are easy-to-make dessert sauces, with delicious flavour. Some are to serve over hot puddings; some make a rich topping when spooned over ice-cream

## Stirred Custard

3 eggs
2 tablespoons sugar
½ teaspoon vanilla
1 pint milk

Beat eggs, sugar and vanilla together, place in top of double saucepan. Warm milk, stir into egg mixture. Stir constantly over simmering water until custard thickens slightly. Remove from heat immediately.

Makes 1 pint

## Brandy Custard

¼ cup sugar
¼ pint water
2 egg-yolks
pinch salt
2 tablespoons brandy
3 tablespoons whipped cream

Place sugar and water into saucepan; stir to dissolve sugar, bring to boil, reduce heat, simmer 10 minutes. Beat egg-yolks and salt, pour hot syrup in slowly, beating until thick and creamy. Fold in brandy and whipped cream.

Makes approx. 1½ cups

## Rich Caramel Sauce

4 oz. butter
2 cups brown sugar, lightly packed
¾ cup liquid glucose
½ pint cream

Combine butter, brown sugar and glucose in saucepan, stir over low heat until sugar dissolves; bring to boil, boil 5 minutes. Remove from heat, allow bubbles to subside, gradually add cream, stirring constantly. Serve warm or cold. This sauce will thicken on standing.

Makes 3 cups

## Butterscotch Sauce

1 oz. butter
¼ cup brown sugar
¼ cup condensed milk
1 dessertspoon golden syrup
½ cup hot milk

Combine butter, brown sugar, condensed milk and golden syrup in saucepan. Cook over low heat, stirring constantly until mixture leaves sides of saucepan and is rich golden colour. Remove from heat; gradually stir in hot milk. Return to heat, cook 1 to 2 minutes.

Makes approx. 1 cup

## Chocolate Rum Sauce

6 oz. dark chocolate
½ cup black coffee
1 tablespoon rum

Chop chocolate roughly, add to small saucepan with hot coffee, stir constantly over low heat until chocolate melts. Remove from heat, add rum to taste. Serve warm.

Makes 1 cup

## Chocolate Sauce

4 oz. dark chocolate
⅔ cup water
¼ cup sugar
1 dessertspoon cornflour
1 tablespoon water, extra
½ teaspoon vanilla

Chop chocolate roughly, combine with water and sugar in small saucepan, stir over low heat until chocolate melts and sugar is dissolved; remove from heat. Blend cornflour with extra water, stir into chocolate mixture, return to heat, stir until sauce boils and thickens, remove from heat, add vanilla. Serve warm or cold.

Makes 1 cup

*Mocha Sauce* Add 1 dessertspoon instant coffee powder to saucepan with chocolate mixture.

## Hard Sauce

4 oz. butter
2 cups icing sugar
1 tablespoon brandy

Cream butter, gradually blend in sifted icing sugar and brandy. Refrigerate until firm. Serve with Christmas pudding.

## Melba Sauce

Rub fresh, canned or thawed frozen raspberries through a sieve. If using fresh raspberries, a little icing sugar may be added.

Caramel Bavarian Cream has light, lovely texture. Serve with cream or with caramel sauce

# YEAST COOKERY

For those who haven't tried it, yeast cookery may seem involved and difficult. But, provided the simple instructions given in the recipes are followed, you'll find it easy to make beautiful bread and buns; each step of each recipe has been carefully timed

There are just a few main points to remember when cooking with yeast.

- Yeast must be fresh.
- Liquid added to yeast should be lukewarm, as individual recipes specify. If liquid is too cold, it will not have any effect on the yeast—the dough will not rise; if too hot, it will kill the action of the yeast. But liquid of the right temperature will bring the yeast to life.
- When setting the dough to prove, leave it in a warm (but not hot) place, away from draughts.

When the dough is in the oven you will have the house filled with the fragrance of yeast cookery—which Mark Twain described as 'the very breath and perfume of home'.

## Continental Cinnamon Snails

3 cups plain flour
2 tablespoons sugar
pinch salt
8 oz. butter
1 oz. compressed yeast
½ cup lukewarm milk
3 egg-yolks

### Walnut Filling

½ cup ground or finely chopped walnuts
1 cup sugar
1 tablespoon cinnamon
1 egg, beaten
2 egg-whites

Sift flour, sugar and salt into bowl. Rub in butter. Add crumbled yeast to milk, stand 5 minutes; add egg-yolks. Beat with rotary beater 3 minutes. Add to flour mixture, mix to a soft dough. Wrap in waxed paper or aluminium foil, refrigerate overnight. Remove from refrigerator ½ hour before dough is to be used. Roll out dough ¼ in. thick on lightly floured surface. Spread with stiffly beaten egg-whites then the walnut mixture. Roll up carefully, as for swiss roll. Cut into 1½ in. thick slices, place in well-greased lamington tin. Let rise in warm place 30 to 40 minutes. Bake in hot oven 20 minutes, or until browned. If browned before completely cooked, reduce temperature to moderate, cover with sheet of brown paper, and continue cooking. Remove from oven and brush with sugar glaze (see recipe for Cream Buns).

Makes approx. 1 dozen.

*Walnut Filling:* Combine walnuts, sugar, cinnamon and egg in bowl. Stiffly beat egg-whites in separate bowl.

Below is a simple, alternative filling. You might like to halve filling recipes and make half the buns with walnut filling and half with sultana filling.

### Cinnamon Sultana Filling

½ cup sultanas
1 cup brown sugar
½ cup chopped almonds
1 dessertspoon cinnamon
4 oz. butter

Combine sultanas, brown sugar, almonds and cinnamon in bowl. Melt butter. Brush rolled-out dough with melted butter, sprinkle with cinnamon mixture. Proceed with rolling, cutting, baking, and glazing as directed above.

## White Bread

1 lb. plain flour
½ oz. compressed yeast
1 teaspoon salt
1 teaspoon sugar
½ oz. butter
½ pint tepid water

Sift flour and salt into bowl. Crumble yeast into tepid water; add sugar and butter. Stir well until yeast turns liquid and sugar dissolves. Make a well in centre of flour, pour in yeast mixture. Mix centre portion only into a soft batter, leaving walls of dry flour round edges. Knock down walls of flour to cover batter mixture. Cover with dry cloth and stand in warm place for 20 minutes. Using one hand, mix dough together, adding approximately ¼ cup of extra water if dough is too dry. Beat well for 5 minutes until dough is dry and springy. Place in greased bowl, reverse dough so that upper side is coated with grease. Cover with dry cloth and stand in warm place for approximately 45 minutes, until dough has doubled in bulk. Turn on to lightly floured board. Knead for approximately 5 minutes, until bubbles of gas are evenly distributed. (Check this by cutting dough in half and looking to see if gas bubbles are small and even throughout dough.) Press dough into lightly greased 8 in. x 4 in. loaf tin. Place in warm place until dough rises well above top of tin. Bake in very hot oven for 15 minutes. Reduce heat to moderate and continue baking for further 45 minutes. For last 10 minutes of cooking time, remove loaf carefully from tin and place on dry baking sheet to brown sides.

## Health Bread

- 1½ lb. wholemeal plain flour
- 1 cup millet meal
- ¾ cup skim-milk powder
- 1⅔ cups water
- 2 cups cold milk
- 1½ oz. compressed yeast
- 1 tablespoon salt
- 3 teaspoons raw sugar
- 2 tablespoons sunflower seeds, hulled

Bring water to boil in saucepan, add to milk. Take ⅓ cup of this and put into small basin with the sugar; leave until lukewarm, then mix in yeast. Cover, let stand 20 minutes. In the meantime, sift flour, millet meal, milk powder and salt into large basin, sprinkle sunflower seeds on top. After 20 minutes, add yeast mixture to remaining milk and water mixture; it should be lukewarm (it must not be hot). Gradually add to dry ingredients, mix well to a soft dough. Beat 5 minutes with wooden spoon, until dough is smooth. Divide dough evenly into 2 greased 9 in. x 5 in. loaf tins. Smooth tops with spoon dipped in water. Cover loaves, let rise in warm place, out of draughts, 30 to 45 minutes or until dough is rounded and level with tops of tins. Bake in hot oven 40 to 45 minutes. When cooked, turn on to cooling rack.

## Rye Bread

- 2 cups rye flour
- 1 cup wholemeal plain flour
- 1 cup plain flour
- 1 teaspoon ground aniseed
- 1 teaspoon salt
- 1 dessertspoon sugar
- 1 oz. compressed yeast
- 1 dessertspoon oil
- 1 cup water
- ¾ cup milk

Combine water and milk; heat to lukewarm.

Sift dry ingredients into large basin. Make a well in centre. Dissolve crumbled yeast in a li lukewarm water and milk mixture, add r water and milk mixture and oil. Pour yeast ure into dry ingredients and beat well together. Sprinkle with a little flour, cover, and let stand in warm place until doubled in bulk. Knock down and knead a little with hand. Cover again, and let stand in warm place until doubled in bulk. Knead until smooth and elastic on floured surface. Form into bread shape and place in well-greased 8 in. x 4 in. loaf tin. Cover and leave in warm place further ½ hour or until top rises to edge of tin. Brush with a little water, in which a little sugar has been dissolved. Bake in hot oven 40 to 45 minutes. Remove from tin, cool on wire rack.

## Raisin Bread

- 1 lb. plain flour
- 1½ teaspoons ground cardamom
- 1¼ cups milk
- 4 oz. butter
- ½ cup sugar
- 1 oz. compressed yeast
- ⅔ cup raisins
- ⅓ cup dried apricots

Sift flour and cardamom into bowl. Combine milk, butter and sugar in saucepan, heat until lukewarm. Remove from heat, add yeast, stir to dissolve. Make a well in centre of flour. Pour in yeast mixture and beat well together. Cover with cloth and leave in warm place until doubled in bulk, approximately 45 minutes. Add raisins and chopped apricots, and knead on floured surface until smooth and elastic. Shape into loaf shape and place in well-greased 9 in. x 5 in. loaf tin. Cover and leave in warm place until dough has risen to just under edge of tin. Brush top with a little water, in which a little sugar has been dissolved. Bake in moderately hot oven 45 to 55 minutes. Cool on wire rack.

## Cream Buns

- 1 lb. plain flour
- 1 teaspoon salt
- 1 oz. compressed yeast
- ½ pint milk
- 1½ oz. sultanas
- 2 oz. butter
- ¼ cup sugar
- 1 egg

**Fluffy Mock Cream**

- 4 oz. butter
- 1 tablespoon boiling milk
- 1 cup castor sugar
- ½ teaspoon gelatine
- 3 tablespoons boiling water
- ½ teaspoon vanilla

Crumble yeast into basin, mix with 1 teaspoon each of flour and sugar and all the lukewarm milk. Stand basin in warm place 15 minutes or until mixture is spongy. Sift flour and salt into large basin, rub in the butter, add sugar and sultanas, mix well. Beat egg well, add to yeast mixture, add this to flour mixture and make into soft dough. Stand in warm place 40 minutes, covered with cloth without touching dough. Turn on to floured surface. Knead well until smooth and elastic. Cut into 16 even-sized pieces, knead each piece into a small ball. Place on greased baking tray. Set again in warm place 15 to 20 minutes. Bake in moderately hot oven 15 to 20 minutes or until golden brown. Remove from oven, brush glaze over. Break buns apart when glaze sets, allow to cool on wire rack. When quite cold, cut small sections about $\frac{1}{4}$ in. wide along top of each bun and pipe into this whipped fresh cream or mock cream, sprinkle with icing sugar, drop a little raspberry jam into centre of row of cream.

*Fluffy Mock Cream:* Soften butter in basin with boiling milk, add sugar, beat to a cream. When mixture is creamy, dissolve gelatine in the boiling water. Add gradually to creamed mixture, beating continuously, until sugar is completely dissolved and mixture is light and fluffy. Add vanilla, beat well.

*Sugar Glaze:* Combine 1 tablespoon gelatine, 1 tablespoon sugar and $\frac{1}{2}$ cup water; stir over gentle heat until sugar dissolves.

## Hot Cross Buns

1 lb. plain flour
1 teaspoon salt
1 oz. compressed yeast
½ pint warm milk
2 oz. sultanas
2 oz. currants
2 oz. butter
¼ cup sugar
1 egg
½ teaspoon mixed spice
½ teaspoon cinnamon

### Paste for Crosses

¼ cup plain flour
little cold water

### Glaze

1 tablespoon sugar
1 teaspoon gelatine
1 tablespoon hot water

Crumble yeast into basin, mix with 1 teaspoon each previously measured flour and sugar; mix in warm milk. Stand in warm place 15 minutes or until mixture is spongy. Sift flour, salt and spices into large basin. Rub in butter, add sugar and fruit. Beat egg well, add it to yeast and milk sponge. Add this to flour mixture, make into soft dough. Cover with clean cloth, stand in warm place 40 minutes: at the end of this time dough should have doubled in bulk. Turn on to lightly floured board. Knead well, turning outside edges of dough into centre. Knead until dough is smooth and elastic. Cut into 15 or 16 even-sized pieces, knead each piece into a round. Place in greased lamington tin, space $\frac{1}{2}$ in. apart. Set again in warm place 10 to 15 minutes. Make paste for crosses by mixing sifted flour to very soft paste with cold water. Using small plain nozzle, pipe crosses on each bun. Bake in hot oven 15 to 20 minutes. Remove from oven, brush with glaze made by dissolving sugar and gelatine in hot water. Cool on wire rack.

## Coffee Walnut Buns

2 lb. plain flour
1 oz. compressed yeast
2 oz. butter
2 eggs
¼ cup sugar
2 cups milk
pinch salt
½ cup sultanas

### Warm Coffee Icing

½ lb. icing sugar
1 teaspoon instant coffee powder
½ oz. butter
milk to mix
chopped walnuts

Place milk, sugar and butter in small saucepan, heat just to lukewarm; dissolve yeast in this mixture. Sift flour and salt, make well in centre, break in eggs. Stir in lukewarm yeast and milk mixture, beat until thoroughly combined. Mix in sultanas. Cover, stand in warm place 30 to 40 minutes to rise. Turn out on lightly floured board, knead 2 minutes; place in greased basin, stand in a warm place further 15 minutes. Turn out on floured surface, knead lightly, break off small pieces of dough about size of a lemon, roll between palms of hands to make long roll, tie this in knot. Place 1 to $1\frac{1}{2}$ in. apart on well-greased oven slide, let stand in warm place 20 to 30 minutes or until nearly double in size. Bake in moderate oven 20 to 25 minutes or until golden brown. Glaze immediately while hot with Sugar Glaze (see recipe for Cream Buns), then drizzle while still warm with warm coffee icing and sprinkle with chopped walnuts.

Makes approx. 20

*Warm Coffee Icing:* Sift icing sugar and coffee into heatproof basin, add butter and enough milk to make icing of a fairly thin consistency. Place over saucepan of boiling water, stir until mixture begins to shine and butter melts. Allow to remain over water while using.

In foreground, Continental Cinnamon Snails; Coffee Walnut Buns in basket. These are just two of the wonderful recipes you can make with yeast

# JAMS & JELLIES

## Jams

There's pride and pleasure in making your own good-tasting jams and jellies—when fresh fruit are in season and in good supply, or perhaps from fruit in your own garden

### Choice of Fruit

Fruit for jam-making is best used early in its season, freshly picked, dry, just ripe or slightly under ripe, when the pectin acid content is highest. As fruit ripens, the acid it contains changes pectin to sugar, so the jam does not set well.

The acid in just-ripe or slightly under-ripe fruit is necessary to draw out the pectin, improve flavour, and help to prevent sugar crystallising. If fruit is over-ripe jam does not set; if picked during wet weather jam may ferment or mould quickly.

### Equipment

The following equipment is necessary for making all types of jams.

1. Aluminium, enamel, or stainless steel preserving pan, boiler or large saucepan with wide top to allow evaporation and prevent jam frothing and bubbling over while boiling.
2. Long-handled spoon, preferably wooden, for stirring.
3. Jars free from chips and cracks.
4. Soup ladle or enamel mug for filling jars.
5. Waxed or parchment covers, paraffin wax and/or screwtops for coverings.

NOTE: Jars must be sterilised before bottling jam. To sterilise jars, wash in warm soapy water, rinse, stand upside down to drain; then stand on wooden board, place in slow oven until jars are completely dry.

### Pectin Content

*Rich in pectin and acid:* Cooking apples, black currants, plums, gooseberries, lemons, limes, grapefruit, seville oranges.

*Moderately rich in pectin and acid:* Apricots, blackberries, greengage plums, loganberries, raspberries, sweet oranges, mandarins.

*Poor in pectin and acid:* Late blackberries, cherries, pineapple, jam melon, pears, peaches, strawberries.

*To overcome pectin deficiency:*

1. Combine fruit deficient in pectin with pectin-rich fruit (for example, apple with blackberry).
2. Add lemon juice which is rich in pectin and contains acid.
3. Add commercial pectin, following manufacturer's directions.

*To test pectin content:* When fruit has simmered with water until soft, place 1 teaspoon of mixture into glass, add 3 teaspoons methylated spirit and leave 2 minutes to form clot.

Large, firm clot indicates fruit is rich in pectin.

Medium-size, not-so-firm clot indicates fruit moderately rich in pectin.

Weak, flabby clot indicates fruit with poor pectin content.

### Use of Sugar

Correct proportion is important. For fruit with moderate to rich pectin content use 1 lb. sugar to 1 lb. fruit; for fruit with poor pectin content use $\frac{3}{4}$ lb. sugar to 1 lb. fruit. Sugar, warmed for quicker dissolving, is added after fruit and skins have simmered until soft.

### Basic Method

1. Remove stalks, stones, any bruised parts, and skin from such ingredients as pineapple, jam melon.
2. Place fruit in preserving pan, greased to prevent burning. Make sure the preserving pan is big enough for the quantity of jam you wish to make. It should not be more than half full when the fruit and sugar are combined, otherwise the jam may boil over when boiled rapidly.

3. Pour over small quantity of water, approximately $\frac{1}{4}$ pint to 2 lb. fruit. Juicy fruits may not require any water.

4. Cook gently over low heat until fruit is soft and pulpy. Stir frequently to prevent sticking. This cooking softens the fruit and helps extract the pectin.

5. Add warmed sugar, stir over low heat until sugar has dissolved, then bring jam to boiling point as quickly as possible and boil rapidly, uncovered. Jam must not be allowed to boil until all sugar has dissolved. *Slow cooking before the addition of sugar, and rapid, short cooking afterwards is the golden rule for jam-making.*

NOTE: Sugar can be warmed in enamel or heatproof bowl in slow oven. It is not essential to heat sugar, but heated sugar dissolves more quickly.

In some whole-fruit jams, the sugar is added to the fruit and the mixture allowed to stand overnight. In this case the mixture should be heated very slowly until the sugar has dissolved.

6. Boil jam rapidly, stirring occasionally, until it jells when tested.

*To test*: Spoon a little on cold saucer (place saucer in refrigerator 30 minutes before testing), refrigerate 2 or 3 minutes. If it jells, glazes on surface, and crinkles when touched, jam is cooked. If no skin forms, further boiling is necessary to evaporate more liquid. Remove jam from heat while testing.

7. Just before bottling, skim jam well to remove any scum on top.

8. Fill into sterilised jars. (For some whole-fruit jams or marmalades, allow to cool in pan until a thin skin begins to form on top, then stir gently and pour into jars. The liquid thickens on cooling and holds the fruit in suspension—this means it will not rise to the top when put into jars.)

9. Fill jars to the brim.

10. Cover with disc of waxed paper, then with metal or plastic airtight lid.

11. Label jars, mark them with date of bottling. Store in cool, dry place.

*Covering jam:* If there is condensation between jam and its cover, mould will form on top. To avoid this, cover jam when hot or when completely cold; never cover jam when it is warm.

## Strawberry Conserve

2 cups strawberries
1 lb. sugar
finely grated rind and juice ½ lemon

Wash and hull strawberries, place in a saucepan with sugar and lemon. Stir over low heat until sugar dissolves. Increase heat, boil gently 10 minutes, or until conserve jells when tested on a cold saucer. Skim, turn on to a large plate; stand overnight, turning over several times so that berries become plump and well mixed with juice. Pack into hot sterilised jars, seal.

Makes 1 pint.

*Mulberry Conserve:* Follow directions for Strawberry Conserve, but substitute Mulberries for Strawberries.

## Blackberry Jelly Jam

2 cups blackberries (including some red ones)
1 lb. sugar
juice ½ lemon

Wash blackberries, place in large saucepan, crush well. Bring to the boil, reduce heat, simmer 30 minutes. Add lemon juice and warmed sugar, stir until dissolved, bring quickly to the boil, boil rapidly for approximately 10 minutes, or until jam jells when tested on a cold saucer. Pour into hot sterilised jars, seal.

Makes approx. 1 pint

## Bush Lemon Marmalade

8 bush lemons
water
1 oz. salt
5 pints water, extra
6 lb. sugar

Place whole lemons in a large bowl, cover well with water, add salt, cover and stand 36 hours. Drain, discard salted water.

Wash lemons well; squeeze juice and strain into a large bowl, add 4 pints of the water. Scoop pulp from the lemons and place in a separate bowl with seeds and pulp from strained juice, add remaining 1 pint water. Cover and stand a further 12 hours.

Put lemon skins through a mincer, add to the bowl containing juice and 4 pints water, cover, stand 12 hours.

Strain the 1 pint liquid from seeds and pulp, discard pulp and seeds. Add this water to juice, rind and water. Place in a large saucepan, simmer gently, uncovered, 45 minutes. Add warmed sugar, boil rapidly until jam jells when tested on a cold saucer, approximately 45 minutes.

Allow to stand 5 minutes, stir before pouring into hot sterilised jars, seal.

Makes approx. 3 pints

## Swiss Cherry Jam

2 lb. cherries
juice 2 lemons
1 cup water
1¼ lb. sugar

Wash cherries, remove stones, (stones can be removed with a special cherry pitter); tie stones in a piece of muslin. Place strained lemon juice and water in large bowl. Place layer of sugar in bowl and layer of cherries, continue until all sugar and cherries are used. Cover and stand overnight.

Next day, strain syrup into saucepan, place over medium heat, stir until sugar dissolves. When syrup is boiling, add cherries and muslin bag, boil 15 minutes. Start testing jam after first 15 minutes, or boil until jam jells when tested on a cold saucer. Remove jam from heat while testing, as it is very easy to overcook cherry jam, and spoil both flavour and colour. Discard muslin bag.

Remove any scum from jam, (but avoid stirring) before bottling into hot sterilised jars, seal.

Makes 1½ pints

## Sweet Orange Jam

2 oranges
1 lemon
2 pints water
3 lb. sugar

Wash oranges and lemon, slice very thinly, remove pips. Place fruit in a basin, add water, cover and stand 2 days.

Place fruit and water in a large saucepan; boil 1 hour. Add warmed sugar, stir until dissolved. Boil rapidly for approximately 40 to 50 minutes, or until jam jells when tested on a cold saucer. Pour into hot sterilised jars, seal.

Makes 1½ pints

## Tomato and Passionfruit Jam

2 lb. ripe tomatoes
¾ cup passionfruit pulp
(approx. 10 passionfruit)
2½ lb. sugar

Skin and chop tomatoes. Place half the skins from the passionfruit into a saucepan, cover with water. Boil rapidly until skins are soft inside, approximately 1 hour. With a spoon scoop out all the soft pulp inside skins; reserve pulp, discard skins.

Place tomatoes and passionfruit pulp in separate saucepan, add reserved pulp from skins and warmed sugar, stir over a low heat until sugar is dissolved, bring quickly to the boil, boil rapidly until jam jells when tested on a cold saucer, approximately 50 minutes. Pour into hot sterilised jars, seal.

Makes 1¼ pints

## Fig Jam

2 lb. figs
¾ cup orange juice
¼ cup lemon juice
2 tablespoons sweet sherry
2 lb. sugar

Wash figs, cut off stems, chop roughly. Place in large saucepan with orange juice, lemon juice and sherry. Bring to boil, reduce heat, simmer until figs are tender. Add warmed sugar, stir over a low heat until sugar dissolves. Increase heat, boil rapidly, uncovered, until jam jells when tested on a cold saucer, approximately 25 minutes. Pour into hot sterilised jars, seal.

Makes 2 pints

## Grape Jam

2 lb. grapes
2 cups water
¼ lb. raisins
juice 3 oranges
3 lb. sugar

Squeeze pulp from grapes, reserve skins. Add water to pulp, simmer until seeds become separate, approximately 30 minutes; strain out seeds. Combine skins with pulp and liquid in large saucepan. Add raisins and orange juice. Bring to the boil, reduce heat, simmer 15 minutes. Add sugar, stir over a low heat until sugar dissolves, increase heat, boil rapidly until jam jells when tested on a cold saucer, approximately 30 minutes. Pour into hot sterilised jars, seal.

Makes 2 pints

## Rose Petal Jam

1 lb. red rose petals
juice 2 lemons
1 pint water
3 lb. sugar

NOTE: For best flavour and results, only petals of fresh young buds should be used.

Cut petals into thin strips, arrange on plates, sprinkle over juice of 1 lemon. Stand several hours or overnight. Place petals into saucepan with water, bring just to the boil, strain, reserve half the petals. Return water to saucepan; add sugar and juice of remaining lemon. Add reserved petals, simmer gently 30 minutes. Cool for 15 minutes before pouring into hot sterilised jars, seal.

Makes approx. 1 pint

NOTE: By using commercial pectin, a smaller

Recipes in this section for jams and jellies enable you to make the most of fresh fruits in season. Even three or four pieces of fruit will give several jars of jam with orchard-fresh flavour

MULBERRY JELLY
MANDARIN JAM
SWEET ORANGE
JAM
MANDARIN JAM

amount of rose petals can be used; yield will be approximately the same.

You will need $\frac{1}{4}$ lb. rose petals, juice $1\frac{1}{2}$ lemons, $1\frac{1}{2}$ cups water, 1 lb. sugar and 2 tablespoons powdered pectin (obtainable from grocers). Proceed exactly as above, stirring in pectin at the end of cooking time, then boiling rapidly for 3 minutes.

## Plum Jam

3 lb. plums
¾ pint water
2½ lb. sugar
juice ½ lemon

Wash plums, cut in halves, remove stones. Place in large saucepan with the water and $\frac{3}{4}$lb. sugar. Cook gently until plums are tender, stirring occasionally. Add remaining sugar, stir over low heat until sugar dissolves; add lemon juice. Boil rapidly until jam jells when tested on a cold saucer, (approximately 1 hour). Pour into hot sterilised jars, seal.

Makes 4 pints

## Mandarin Jam

6 mandarins
2½ pints water
3 lb. sugar
juice 1 lemon
juice 1 orange

Slice unpeeled mandarins thinly, remove seeds. Place fruit in a bowl, add water, leave overnight. Place fruit and liquid in a large saucepan, bring to the boil, reduce heat, simmer gently until rind is tender, approximately 1 hour. Add warmed sugar, stir over a low heat until sugar dissolves, increase heat, boil rapidly until jam jells when tested on a cold saucer, approximately 30 minutes. Add lemon and orange juice after jam has been boiling 15 minutes. Pour into hot sterilised jars, seal.

Makes $3\frac{1}{2}$ pints

## Apricot and Pineapple Jam

½ lb. dried apricots
15 oz. can crushed pineapple
¾ cup grated carrot
1¾ cups water
grated rind 1 lemon
juice 2 lemons
2 lb. sugar

Combine chopped dried apricots, undrained pineapple, carrot and water in a saucepan, bring slowly to the boil, cover, simmer until apricots are tender, (approximately 20 minutes). Add sugar, lemon rind and juice, stir over a low heat until sugar dissolves. Increase heat, boil rapidly until jam jells when tested on a cold saucer; start testing after 10 minutes. Pour into hot sterilised jars, seal.

Makes approx. 3 pints

## Cumquat Marmalade

3 lb. cumquats
6 pints water
5 lb. sugar
juice 2 lemons

Wash fruit, slice finely, place seeds aside in a small basin. Place fruit in large saucepan, cover with 5 pints of the water. Cover seeds with remaining 1 pint water; leave overnight. Boil fruit and liquid with strained liquid from seeds until rind is tender, and liquid is reduced by half. Add sugar and lemon juice, stir over a low heat until sugar is dissolved, then boil rapidly for approximately $1\frac{1}{2}$ hours, or until marmalade jells when tested on a cold saucer. Pour into hot sterilised jars, seal.

Makes approx. 4 pints

## Three Fruit Marmalade

1 large orange
1 large grapefruit
1 large lemon
3¼ pints water
sugar (approx. 4½ lb.)

Wash fruit, slice orange and grapefruit finely; using skin, pith and flesh; discard seeds. Roll lemon well with the palm of the hand until skin is soft, halve lemon and extract juice, discard seeds. Place fruit (including the lemon halves) into large saucepan with the water, cover, bring to boil, add lemon juice, simmer 30 minutes, cool. Pour mixture into large crockery basin, cover, stand 36 hours. Remove lemon skins, measure fruit mixture, allow 1 cup sugar to each cup of fruit, add 1 extra cup of sugar. Heat fruit mixture, add warmed sugar, stir over low heat until sugar dissolves. Increase heat, boil rapidly until marmalade jells when tested on a cold saucer, approximately 30 minutes. Allow to stand 5 minutes before pouring into hot sterilised jars, seal.

Makes approx. 2 pints.

## Blender Marmalade

1 large carrot
1 orange
2 lemons
2 cups cold water
2 lb. sugar

Wash and coarsely chop carrot and unpeeled orange and lemons. Place in electric blender and blend on low speed until very finely chopped (about 30 seconds). Pour into large saucepan, add sugar and water. Heat gently, stirring constantly, until sugar dissolves. Bring to the boil, reduce heat, simmer 30 minutes; increase heat, boil rapidly 30 minutes, or until jam jells when tested on a cold saucer, pour into hot sterilised jars, seal. Makes $1\frac{1}{2}$ pints.

If you haven't an electric blender, wash and roughly chop carrot, orange and lemons and put through a hand mincer, or an electric mincer.

## Dundee Marmalade

4 lb. Seville oranges
4 lemons
4 quarts water
8 lb. sugar

Wash fruit, place in large saucepan with water. Bring to boil, reduce heat, simmer, uncovered, $1\frac{1}{2}$ hours. Remove fruit, cool, then slice thinly. Remove pips from fruit, add to pan with liquid, boil steadily 10 minutes; strain. Replace liquid and fruit in pan with sugar; stir until sugar dissolves, then boil rapidly without stirring for approximately 20 to 25 minutes or until marmalade jells when tested on a cold saucer. Stand 10 minutes before pouring into hot sterilised jars, seal.

Makes approx. 5 pints

## Grapefruit Jam

1 large grapefruit
2 pints boiling water
2 lb. sugar

Wash grapefruit, slice finely, removing seeds. Place in a basin, add boiling water, cover, stand overnight. Place fruit and liquid in a large saucepan, simmer over a low heat for approximately 30 minutes or until rind is tender. Add warmed sugar; stir over low heat until sugar dissolves. Bring quickly to the boil, boil rapidly until jam jells when tested on a cold saucer, approximately 40 minutes. Allow to cool for 10 minutes before pouring into hot sterilised jars, seal.

Makes $1\frac{1}{4}$ pints

## Jellies

The perfect jelly is bright, clear, and slightly a-quiver; it should have the true flavour of fruit used. Here are hints for turning out perfect jellies

### To Prepare Fruit

*Hard or firm fruits* Leave unpeeled and uncored, cut into small pieces.

*Soft fruits or berries* Wash and allow to drain.

### Basic Method

1. Place prepared fruit in greased preserving pan with water to cover. Cook gently until fruit is quite tender—usually $\frac{1}{2}$ to $\frac{3}{4}$ hour. Overcooking destroys jelling properties. It is not necessary to add water to berry fruits; they generally contain enough liquid. However, if berries are not very soft, a little water may need to be added to prevent fruit sticking to pan.
2. Test for pectin. (See Jams.)
3. Prepare quantity of sugar, amount depending on result of pectin test: For fruit rich in pectin allow 1 lb. sugar to 1 pint syrup; for fruits moderately rich in pectin allow $\frac{3}{4}$ lb. sugar to 1 pint syrup.
4. Strain fruit through layers of cheese-cloth tied to legs of stool or chair inverted on table; place basin under centre of cloth.

   Pour boiling water through cloth, then pour fruit pulp through. Leave to drip overnight. Do not squeeze bag, as it can cause cloudiness in jelly.
5. Measure syrup, place in pan with correct proportion of warmed sugar, stir until dissolved.
6. Boil rapidly until jelly sets when tested.
7. Skim; bottle immediately.

## Mulberry Jelly

3 lb. mulberries (not too ripe)
juice 1 lemon
sugar

Wash and stem mulberries, place in saucepan with lemon juice. Simmer gently for approximately 1 hour or until fruit is pulpy and the juice drawn out. Strain liquid through fine muslin; measure liquid, and to each 1 pint liquid allow $\frac{3}{4}$ lb. sugar. Place liquid and sugar in a clean saucepan, stir over a low heat until sugar dissolves, increase heat, boil rapidly until jelly jells when tested on a cold saucer. Start testing after 15 minutes of boiling. Pour into hot sterilised jars, seal.

Makes approx. 1 pint

## Crab-Apple Jelly

crab-apples
water
sugar

Remove stalks from crab-apples, wash fruit, cut in halves. Place fruit into large saucepan, cover with water. Bring to the boil, reduce heat, simmer gently 30 to 45 minutes, or until fruit is soft. Strain through cloth; measure liquid, bring to boil. For every pint of liquid allow $\frac{3}{4}$ lb. sugar; boil for approximately 45 minutes, or until mixture jells when tested on a cold saucer. Pour into hot sterilised jars, seal.

# PICKLES & CHUTNEYS

Hot or cold meals gain extra flavour when you add the zesty taste of a good pickle, or richly flavoured chutney or relish. For best results use good quality ingredients and the right equipment, as outlined below

## Ingredients

*Vegetables, Fruit* Fresh, crisp, in season, barely ripe, in good condition.

Vegetables of inferior quality do not keep; if wilted, will not absorb pickling solution well.

*Vinegar* Essential ingredient, used plain or spiced; use good-quality brewed malt vinegar; for light-coloured vegetables use white, wine, or cider vinegar.

Only the best vinegar should be used for pickling, i.e., vinegar containing an acetic acid content of at least 4 percent. Bulk vinegar usually contains less than this and is therefore not as satisfactory.

## Equipment

Aluminium or enamel-lined vessels; wooden spoon for stirring and mixing flavouring and thickening ingredients.

NOTE: Do not use unlined copper pans, metal tops for jars or bottles, or pans which are used for jam-making.

## Bottling and Sealing

Fill pickles and chutneys into clean, dry, sterilised, wide-necked jars.

Make jars completely airtight with plastic (not metal) screw-tops, wax, or use patent jars.

## Sweet Fruit Chutney

2 lb. tomatoes
3 large onions
2 large cooking apples
1½ lb. sugar
¾ cup sultanas
¾ cup currants
1 tablespoon salt
1 tablespoon whole cloves
pinch cayenne pepper
2 pints brown malt vinegar

Skin tomatoes, chop roughly. Peel and chop onions; peel, core and chop apples. Combine all ingredients in large pan, stir over low heat until sugar is dissolved. Simmer, uncovered, approximately 2½ hours or until chutney is thick. Pour into hot sterilised jars, seal.

Makes 2½ pints

## Mango Chutney

3 large ripe mangoes
1 small onion
1 chilli
1 teaspoon mustard seeds
1 teaspoon celery seeds
⅓ cup raisins
¼ cup currants
1 tablespoon chopped mixed peel
1 teaspoon finely chopped green ginger
1 clove garlic, crushed
1 teaspoon salt
½ teaspoon cinnamon
½ teaspoon nutmeg
½ teaspoon allspice
⅓ cup brown sugar
⅓ cup brown malt vinegar
⅓ cup lemon juice

Peel mangoes, roughly chop flesh, discard skin and seeds. Chop onion and chilli; tie mustard and celery seeds in a muslin bag. Combine all ingredients, cover, stand overnight. Place mixture in a large saucepan, boil steadily for 30 minutes, or until thickened. Remove muslin bag, pour chutney into hot sterilised jars, seal.

Makes approx. 1 pint

## Papaw and Mango Chutney

Prepare as for Mango Chutney; add ½ medium papaw, peeled, seeded and chopped.

Cook as above; cooking time will be approximately the same.

Bottle into hot sterilised jars, seal.

Makes approx. 1 pint

Mangoes and papaw, with ginger and spices, combine to make a delicious tropical chutney to serve with hot or cold meats; delicious with curries

## Green Tomato Pickle

2 lb. green tomatoes
½ cauliflower
1½ lb. onions
½ cup salt
water
2½ pints brown malt vinegar
2½ lb. brown sugar
1¼ cups plain flour
1 dessertspoon turmeric
1 dessertspoon dry mustard
1 dessertspoon curry powder
½ teaspoon nutmeg
½ teaspoon ground cloves
½ teaspoon ginger

Wash vegetables well, chop skinned tomatoes into small pieces, break cauliflower into small flowerets. Peel and chop onions, place all vegetables into a large bowl, sprinkle with salt, cover with water, stand overnight. Drain, rinse well in cold water. Place 2 pints of the vinegar into a large pan with brown sugar, stir over a low heat until sugar is dissolved. Bring to boil. Add vegetables, bring to boil again. Blend all dry ingredients with remaining ½ pint vinegar, gradually add to vegetable mixture, stir until mixture boils and thickens, reduce heat, simmer 10 minutes, stirring occasionally. Pour into hot sterilised jars, seal.

Makes approx. 7 pints

## Pickled Onions

4 lb. small onions
1½ lb. salt
water
2 pints white vinegar
2 dessertspoons salt
1 dessertspoon ginger
1½ teaspoons whole allspice
1½ teaspoons whole cloves
1 in. cinnamon stick
few whole peppercorns

Place unpeeled onions, 1½ lb. salt and enough water to cover in a large bowl; cover, stand 2 days, stirring occasionally. Drain liquid, peel onions. Cover onions with boiling water, stand 3 minutes, drain. Repeat this boiling water and draining process two more times. Pack onions into hot sterilised jars. Combine all remaining ingredients in a saucepan, bring slowly to boil, reduce heat, simmer 10 minutes. Cool slightly, strain, pour over onions, seal.

## Corn Relish

1¼ pints white vinegar
1 cup sugar
2 10 oz. cans whole kernel corn
1 medium onion
½ cup chopped celery
¼ cup chopped green pepper
¼ cup chopped red pepper
3 tablespoons cornflour
1 tablespoon dry mustard
1 teaspoon mustard seeds

Place 1 pint vinegar and the sugar in a large saucepan, bring to the boil. Add drained corn, chopped onion and remaining chopped vegetables. Reduce heat, simmer 20 minutes. Blend cornflour and mustard with remaining ¼ pint vinegar, add with mustard seeds to vegetable mixture. Stir until mixture boils and thickens; reduce heat, simmer further 5 minutes, stirring constantly. Pour into hot sterilised jars, seal.

Makes approx. 1½ pints

## Choko Pickle

3 lb. chokoes
1½ lb. onions
½ cup salt
water
2 pints brown malt vinegar
2 lb. brown sugar
1 dessertspoon turmeric
1 dessertspoon dry mustard
1 dessertspoon curry powder
½ teaspoon ginger
1 cup plain flour

Peel chokoes and onions, chop into small pieces; place in a large bowl, sprinkle with salt, cover with water. Cover bowl, stand overnight. Drain vegetables, rinse in cold water. Place 1½ pints vinegar and the sugar into large pan, bring to boil, add vegetables, bring back to boiling point. Mix all dry ingredients to a paste with remaining ½ pint vinegar, gradually add to vegetable mixture, stir constantly until mixture boils and thickens. Reduce heat, simmer 10 minutes. Pour into hot sterilised jars, seal.

Makes approx. 6 pints

## Mustard Pickles

Any assortment of chopped vegetables—cauliflower, green tomatoes, etc.—can be used in addition to, or in place of chokoes in above recipe.

## Pickled Beetroot

1 bunch beetroot
salt
water
½ pint brown malt vinegar
¼ pint water
½ cup sugar
¼ teaspoon cinnamon
1 bayleaf
2 whole cloves
4 peppercorns

Wash beetroot well, cook in boiling salted water until tender, or until skins are easily removed. Combine remaining ingredients in separate saucepan, bring to boil, lower heat, simmer 5 minutes. Cool.

Peel and slice beetroots, pack into hot sterilised jars. Strain vinegar, pour over beetroot, Seal.

NOTE: Beetroot, because of its high sugar content, ferments easily, so this type of pickle is best made in small quantities, and used as soon as possible.

## Bread and Butter Pickles

4 large cucumbers
salt
2 cups cider vinegar
½ cup hot water
3 dessertspoons sugar
1 dessertspoon mustard seeds
1 teaspoon salt
4 strips pimento or red pepper

Wash cucumbers well, slice very thinly. Arrange in layers in large shallow dish, sprinkling a little salt between each layer (about ¼ cup salt in all). Cover, stand overnight.

Wash cucumbers well in cold water, drain, set aside. In a large saucepan, combine vinegar, hot water, sugar, mustard seeds and salt, bring to boil; reduce heat, simmer, uncovered, 5 minutes. Add cucumbers, bring just to boiling point, remove from heat. Using tongs, and working quickly, pack cucumbers tightly into hot sterilised jars. Add a pimento strip to each jar. Fill with vinegar mixture to within ½ in. of top, seal at once.

Makes approx. 4 pints

## Crisp Cucumber Sticks

These are prepared exactly as Bread and Butter Pickles, but instead of cutting cucumbers into thin slices, cut them lengthwise into thick sticks. If cucumbers are long, cut sticks to convenient size to fit into jars. Then proceed as for Bread and Butter Pickles.

## Cucumber Relish

4 cucumbers (approx. 4 lb.)
¼ cup salt
1 red pepper
1 green pepper
½ lb. onions
3 sticks celery
½ oz. mustard seeds
¾ lb. sugar
¾ pint white vinegar

Peel and dice cucumbers, sprinkle with salt. Stand 3 hours, or overnight; drain liquid from cucumbers. Seed and dice peppers, peel and chop onion, chop celery. Chop all vegetables finely. Add cucumbers and prepared vegetables with remaining ingredients to large saucepan.

Stir over low heat until sugar dissolves, increase heat, boil 30 minutes uncovered. Pour into hot sterilised jars, seal.

Makes approx. 2½ pints

## Pimentos

2 lb. red peppers
boiling water
iced water
2 cups vinegar
2 cups oil

Wash peppers, cut in half, remove seeds and stems. Place in basin, pour over enough boiling water to cover, allow to stand 2 minutes. Drain, cover with iced water; drain again, pack firmly into hot sterilised jars.

Boil vinegar in saucepan for 2 minutes, add oil. When it boils again, pour over peppers, making sure they are covered with liquid. Seal.

Makes approx. 2 pints

## Pickled Red Cabbage

1 red cabbage
salt
4 pints white vinegar
½ oz. whole cloves
½ oz. whole allspice
½ oz. cinnamon stick
few peppercorns
¼ teaspoon nutmeg

Remove discoloured outer leaves from cabbage, cut in quarters, remove thick core. Shred cabbage finely; place in large china basin in layers, sprinkling each layer well with salt. Cover, stand overnight. Drain well. Combine remaining ingredients in heatproof basin, cover with a plate, stand over a saucepan of water; bring water slowly to boil, remove saucepan from heat. Allow vinegar and spices to steep over the warm water for 2 hours; strain through a fine cloth. Pack drained cabbage into hot sterilised jars, pour vinegar over, seal.

## Clear Mixed Pickles

1 cauliflower
1 large carrot
2 cucumbers
½ cabbage
4 green peppers
2 chillies
2½ pints white vinegar
1½ cups sugar
1 dessertspoon salt

Wash all vegetables well. Cut cauliflower into small flowerets, peel carrot, cut into thick strips. Place cauliflower and carrot in saucepan, cover with water, boil until just tender; drain. Cut cucumbers into quarters lengthwise, remove seeds, chop roughly. Cut cabbage into coarse pieces; remove seeds from peppers, cut into 1in. pieces.

Place prepared vegetables into a large bowl. Combine sugar, vinegar and salt in a saucepan, bring to the boil, pour over vegetables, cover, stand overnight. Pour into hot sterilised jars. Remove seeds from chillies, add 1 or 2 chilli strips to each jar, seal.

Makes approx. 6 pints

For a Chinese-style of mixed pickle, 4 sticks of celery, ½ bunch shallots (use white part only) and 1 in. piece of green ginger can be added. Cut celery and shallots into 2 in. pieces, peel ginger, cut into thin slices. Cook these in boiling water 2 minutes, drain then add to other vegetables.

# CONFECTIONERY

A tempting assortment of home-made sweets is irresistible and, if you have some cooking to do for a school or church fete, you'll find the sweets made from these recipes are always fast-sellers at the confectionery stall

A sweets thermometer is a good investment if you plan to make a large quantity of sweets; it helps to take the guesswork and uncertainty out of cooking times and temperatures. Some of the recipes given here use a sweets thermometer; below are directions for its correct use and care.

But if you have not got a thermometer, use the following temperature table and the cold water test as guides.

*Soft ball* 236–240 degrees Fahrenheit. A small quantity of syrup dropped into cold water moulds easily with the fingers into a soft ball.

*Firm or hard ball* 250–260 degrees F. Test as for soft ball. The syrup should mould into firm ball.

*Small crack* 265–290 degrees F. Syrup is clear, but when dropped into cold water cracks and breaks if crushed with fingers.

*Hard crack* 295–315 degrees F. Syrup is golden in colour, snaps and crackles when a little is dropped into cold water.

*The cold water test* Spoon a little syrup into cold water and mould with fingers; a shallow bowl makes it easier to see and manipulate syrup; if desired consistency is not reached, cook further and test again. Use fresh cold water for each test, because as water becomes warm the test is less accurate.

*Use and care of sweets thermometer* Do not place cold thermometer in boiling syrup. First immerse in cold water and bring to the boil, then check the reading on the thermometer for accuracy (water boils at 212 degrees F., use this reading to check accuracy). If thermometer is not the type that clings to side of pan, return to hot water after each test. When immersing in syrup, cover bulb completely and gently change position of thermometer occasionally in syrup. With thermometer upright, take reading as near eye level as possible.

## Butterscotch Popcorn

4 oz. popping corn
2 tablespoons oil
4 oz. butter
2 tablespoons honey
¾ cup sugar

In a large saucepan or frypan, heat oil until very hot. Add corn, place lid on pan, shake pan continually until popping ceases. Place popped corn in large bowl. Combine honey, sugar and butter in separate pan, slowly bring to boil; boil 5 minutes. Pour syrup over popped corn and mix till corn is well coated. Pour quickly on to well greased oven trays, cool.

## Toffees

3 cups sugar
1 cup water
¼ cup brown malt vinegar

Combine sugar, water and vinegar in saucepan, stir over a low heat until sugar has dissolved. Increase heat, boil rapidly for approximately 15 minutes, or until a small amount of mixture will crack when tested in cold water. Remove toffee from heat, allow bubbles to subside, pour into paper patty cases. Leave for 5 minutes before decorating with chopped nuts, hundreds-and-thousands, coconut etc.

Makes 1 dozen

## Honeycomb

¾ cup sugar
2 tablespoons honey
2 tablespoons golden syrup
2 tablespoons water
1½ teaspoons bicarbonate of soda

Place sugar, honey, golden syrup, and water into saucepan, dissolve over low heat, stirring occasionally. When sugar has dissolved, bring to boil,

Ever popular Toffees, with an assortment of colourful toppings, are always fast sellers at school or church fetes

then reduce heat to low; heat should be just sufficient to keep mixture gently boiling. Cook approximately 12 to 15 minutes or until syrup is brittle when a little is dropped in cold water; cooking time will vary slightly, depending on size and thickness of saucepan.

Be careful syrup does not burn. Remove from heat, stir in bicarbonate of soda quickly. Pour immediately into greased 6 in. sandwich tin. When cold, break into pieces.

## Cooked Fondant

| | |
|---|---|
| 1 lb. icing sugar | ¼ pint water |
| 2 dessertspoons liquid glucose | flavouring |
| | food colouring |

Place sugar, glucose and water in saucepan, stir over low heat until sugar has thoroughly dissolved; increase heat, bring to boil, and, using sweets thermometer, boil to 240 degrees F. Remove immediately from heat, allow bubbles to settle, then pour into basin, allow to cool.

When syrup is cool, beat with a wooden spoon until thick, then knead with hands until firm enough to handle.

If required, use a little sifted icing sugar when kneading. Colour and flavour and use as desired.

*Peppermint Creams* Colour green, flavour with peppermint essence, roll into balls, flatten slightly.

*Prune or Date Creams:* Remove stone from fruit, press into canoe-shape, fill recess with coloured and flavoured fondant.

## Coconut Ice

| | |
|---|---|
| 1 lb. icing sugar | 2 egg-whites |
| ½ lb. desiccated coconut | 4 oz. solid white vegetable shortening |
| 1 teaspoon vanilla | pink or green food colouring |
| ½ teaspoon lemon juice | |

Put sifted icing sugar, coconut, vanilla, lemon juice and slightly beaten egg-whites into large basin. Melt shortening over gentle heat. Allow to cool slightly, pour on to ingredients in basin. Combine thoroughly. Press half the mixture into greased bar tin lined with greaseproof paper. Add pink or green colouring to remaining mixture. Press firmly on top of white mixture.

NOTE: If a third layer is desired, divide mixture into three parts. Add 1 dessertspoon sifted cocoa, blended to a smooth paste with a little milk, to one part; blend well, press on top of pink or green layer in tin.

## Buttered Rum Brazil Nuts

| | |
|---|---|
| 1½ cups sugar | 2 dessertspoons liquid glucose |
| ½ cup water | 1 lb. shelled brazil nuts |
| 1 oz. butter | 4 dessertspoons rum |

Place the sugar and glucose in saucepan, add the water, stir until sugar dissolves; do not stir after mixture reaches boiling point. Boil steadily to 238 degrees F. on sweets thermometer, (or soft ball stage), then add butter and rum. Boil again until mixture is light honey colour or when a little dropped into cold water forms a hard ball and snaps and crackles. Remove from heat, drop in nuts, lift out one at a time, place on greased paper to set.

## Butterscotch

| | |
|---|---|
| 1 lb. white sugar | ¼ pint water |
| ½ cup brown sugar | 2 oz. butter |
| 4 dessertspoons liquid glucose | ½ teaspoon cream of tartar |

Place in saucepan the sugars, glucose, butter, and water in which cream of tartar, has been dissolved; stir over low heat until sugar has thoroughly dissolved. Increase heat, bring to the boil, using sweets thermometer, boil to 290 degrees F. Remove immediately from heat, allow bubbles to settle, then pour into greased tin about 8 in. square. or on to oiled slab. Mark into squares with oiled knife before it becomes cold.

## Rocky Road

| | |
|---|---|
| 2½ tablespoons gelatine | ½ cup chopped nuts |
| 1 lb. sugar | 1 cup chopped glacé cherries |
| ¾ cup cold water | 4 oz. dark chocolate |
| ½ cup boiling water | 2 oz. solid white vegetable shortening |
| 1 dessertspoon lemon juice | pink and green food colouring |
| 1 teaspoon vanilla | |

Soak gelatine in cold water, place sugar and boiling water in large saucepan, bring slowly to the boil. Add the soaked gelatine, boil steadily 10 minutes. Add lemon juice and vanilla. Pour into two large basins; cool. Colour one pink and one green. Beat each colour until very thick, then pour into greased, shallow tins. When quite cold and set, remove from tins, and cut into irregular pieces. Fill roughly into lamington tin, sprinkle nuts and cherries through marshmallows. Melt chopped chocolate and shortening together over hot water, set aside to thicken slightly. Trickle chocolate mixture thickly through and over marshmallows.

Cut into pieces when set.

## Marzipan Fruits

1 lb. icing sugar
4 oz. marzipan meal
2 egg-yolks
4 dessertspoons sherry
squeeze of orange or lemon juice
few drops almond essence, if desired

Sift icing sugar, add marzipan meal; mix well. Stir in egg-yolks beaten with sherry, fruit juice, and almond essence. Mix into stiff paste, adding a little more fruit juice, if required. Knead slightly on board.

*Apple* Shape from round of marzipan. Push clove in each end, with pointed end out for stalk and clubbed end for blossom.

*Orange* Roll a round of marzipan on fine grater to get indented skin effect. Push in clove for stalk.

*Strawberry* Roll small amount of marzipan to slight point at one end; paint with food colouring, then roll in red sugar (coloured with food colouring).

*Banana* Shape from cylinder of marzipan. Point ends and slightly curve banana.

*Pear* Shape from round of marzipan, bring one end to a point. Press clove in pointed end for stalk.

Let fruit dry 24 hours, then paint with appropriate food colouring.

## Toffee Apples

3 cups sugar
1 cup water
1 dessertspoon white vinegar
½ teaspoon cream of tartar
apples
red food colouring

Combine water, sugar, vinegar, and cream of tartar in saucepan. Heat over low heat, stirring to dissolve sugar completely. Use small brush dipped in cold water to wash down sugar grains from the sides of the saucepan. Undissolved sugar in the syrup or on sides of saucepan could cause mixture to 'candy' instead of remaining clear.

When sugar has dissolved, stop stirring. (Stirring after mixture has boiled will cause candied toffee). Bring mixture to the boil. Boil steadily approximately 5 to 8 minutes. This time will depend on degree of heat under saucepan and also on size and type of saucepan used. A small saucepan will take longer, because there will be less quick evaporation of mixture; also a heavy based saucepan will take longer to cook the mixture than a thin based one.

Begin testing syrup by dropping small teaspoons of syrup into small bowl of cold water. Use fresh water after each test. First test; the mixture will probably be like syrup and will dissolve in the cold water. A few minutes later the mixture will be thick and sticky. Then the mixture will form a soft ball when rolled between the fingers in the testing water. At this stage mixture will begin to bubble thickly. Test again; mixture should form a hard ball when rolled between fingers.

Quickly add red food colouring to give a rich colour. If obtainable, burgundy red food colouring gives best colour. Don't stir; the boiling movement will evenly mix the colouring through toffee. (Stirring the colouring in after the toffee has reached right temperature can cause candying).

Test mixture as before; it should form thin threads of toffee in the water. Test again a few minutes later. Listen carefully as toffee hits the water; it should give quite a loud, sharp crack. Remove pan from heat immediately.

Stand saucepan about 10 to 15 minutes until all bubbling has completely stopped and toffee has cooled.

Have apples prepared: Wash apples well, pat dry; do not rub or polish. Pierce each apple through centre with a butcher's wooden skewer, set aside. Do not refrigerate.

All varieties of apples can be used, but the best results are obtained by using green Granny Smith apples.

The natural oils on the skin of some varieties of red apples can affect toffee coating. The oils tend to prevent toffee clinging to apples, and as toffee drains away, bubbles form under toffee.

Tip pan on its side until there is a deep pool of toffee in the base. Gently lower apples one at a time, at a slight angle, into toffee. Slowly turn apples once round in toffee until completely coated. Lift apple from toffee. Do not hold apple upright, but keep at the angle. Twist round once or twice, allowing excess toffee to run around apple. Then stand apple upright on greased greaseproof paper to set.

If using red apples and bubbles begin to form during coating, plunge toffee coated apples in basin of cold water. This sets toffee and arrests the forming of further bubbles.

## Turkish Delight

4 dessertspoons gelatine
½ cup cold water
1 cup sugar
grated rind of 1 orange
grated rind of 1 lemon
½ cup hot water
⅓ cup orange juice
⅓ cup lemon juice
pink food colouring

Soften gelatine in cold water. Make syrup from sugar, rinds and hot water; when boiling add softened gelatine. Boil gently 20 minutes. Remove from heat, add fruit juices; strain mixture. Colour with few drops of pink food colouring.

Pour into wetted 8 in. tin, allow to set. When firm cut into squares, using knife dipped in hot water. Roll in sifted icing sugar mixed with a little cornflour.

## Marshmallows

2 oz. gelatine
2 lb. sugar
1½ cups boiling water
1 cup cold water
2 teaspoons vanilla
1 dessertspoon lemon juice

Soften gelatine in cold water. Add sugar to boiling water. Stir to dissolve sugar, bring back to the boil. Add soaked gelatine, boil steadily 20 minutes. Allow to cool to lukewarm. Flavour with vanilla and lemon juice. Beat until very thick and white. Pour into tins which have been rinsed out with cold water. Allow to set. Cut into squares, roll in icing sugar or toasted coconut.

*To Toast Coconut* Spread coconut on baking trays, bake in moderate oven 10 to 15 minutes. Shake trays occasionally. Alternatively, the coconut can be put into large, heavy frypan and toasted over moderate heat. Shake pan continually so coconut does not burn.

## Sherried Chocolate Dates

2 dozen dessert dates
rind of 1 orange
⅓ cup sweet sherry
4 oz. dark chocolate
1 oz. solid white vegetable shortening

Peel rind from orange, taking care not to remove any white pith. Place rind in saucepan, cover with water, simmer 5 minutes. Drain, chop finely.

Pit dates, fill with small amount of orange rind, press together. Place sherry in basin, add dates, cover; leave overnight or at least 1 hour.

Chop chocolate and shortening, melt in top of double saucepan over hot water. Drain dates slightly. Using tongs, dip dates in melted chocolate; place on waxed paper until chocolate has set.

## Coconut Roughs

⅓ cup hot mashed potato
1 oz. melted butter
1⅔ cups icing sugar
1¼ tablespoons cocoa
1¾ cups coconut
1 teaspoon vanilla
pinch salt

Beat butter into hot potato, gradually beat in sifted icing sugar, salt and cocoa. Add coconut and vanilla, mix well. Spoon teaspoonfuls on to greaseproof paper, refrigerate until firm.

## Chocolate Ginger Sticks

½ cup finely chopped dates
3 oz. dark chocolate
2 oz. crystallized ginger

Put ginger and dates through fine mincer or chop very finely. Shape into sticks approximately 2 in. in length and ¼ in. wide. Place chocolate in top of double boiler, melt over hot water.

Place date and ginger sticks on wire rack, spoon chocolate over. Refrigerate until set.

Makes approx. 1½ dozen

## Caramels

14 oz. can sweetened condensed milk
1 cup sugar
4 oz. butter
½ cup golden syrup

Place all ingredients into saucepan, stir over low heat until sugar has thoroughly dissolved. Bring to boil, stirring constantly; continue stirring until desired colour, the darker the colour the harder the caramel.

When desired colour, remove from heat, stop stirring, allow bubbles to settle; pour into oiled and lined 8 in. square tin or 7 in. sandwich tin. Do not scrape pan (put scrapings into another tin, as this may 'candy').

When cold, cut into sections with oiled knife.

## Old Fashioned Fudge

3 cups sugar
pinch salt
½ cup cocoa
1 cup milk
2 tablespoons liquid glucose
1½ oz. butter
1 teaspoon vanilla

The right degree of heat is essential for success in this economical delicious fudge; a sweets thermometer is necessary.

Combine sugar, salt, cocoa, milk and glucose in saucepan, stir over low heat until sugar dissolves. Increase heat, boil rapidly until mixture reaches 234 degrees F. Remove from heat, add butter, allow to cool to 110 degrees F. Add vanilla, beat until fudge loses its gloss and starts to change colour Immediately pour into greased and lined 8 in. sandwich tin, cut into squares when cold.

Sherried Chocolate Dates, with fresh orange-flavoured filling, are delicious to serve with after-dinner coffee

# DRINKS&PUNCHES

There's a selection of well-blended punch recipes here for every occasion—weddings, engagements, birthday parties; plus thirst-quenching drinks for summer, and hot drinks to warm when the weather is cold

## Iced Tea

freshly brewed tea
ice cubes
sugar
lemon slices
mint sprigs

Allow tea to cool at room temperature. (Chilling tea too rapidly will make it cloudy.) Sweeten to taste if desired, strain. Place ice cubes in glasses, add tea. Garnish each glass with lemon slice and mint sprig.

## Delicious Iced Coffee

1 cup hot water
2½ tablespoons instant coffee powder
3 cups cold water
vanilla ice-cream
whipped cream
grated chocolate
glacé cherries

Dissolve coffee in hot water, add cold water; sweeten if desired; refrigerate until ready to serve. Place a generous scoop of ice-cream into each glass, fill with iced coffee. Top with whipped cream, grated chocolate and a glace cherry.

Serves approx. 4

## Lemon Cordial

1 lb. 10 oz. sugar
1½ oz. (1½ tablespoons) tartaric acid
¼ oz. (1 dessertspoon) epsom salts
1½ pints boiling water
2 large lemons

Combine sugar, tartaric acid and epsom salts in a large bowl, add boiling water, stir until sugar is dissolved. Cool. Finely grate the rind of 2 lemons, squeeze juice, add to liquid, allow to become cold. Pour into bottles, cork, or cover with screw caps, store in refrigerator. Mixture will keep for 2 to 3 weeks.

Makes $2\frac{3}{4}$ pints of concentrated lemon cordial. To drink, dilute with iced water.

## Blender Lemonade

1 large lemon
¼ cup sugar
1 pint iced water

Wash lemon, cut off thick ends, cut lemon into 8 pieces. Place all ingredients into electric blender, blend on high speed until lemon is finely shredded. Strain. Use soon after blending.

Makes approx. 1 pint.

## Home Style Ginger Beer

**Ginger Beer Plant**

1 cup cold water
1 teaspoon ground ginger
1 teaspoon sugar
½ teaspoon instant coffee powder
1 teaspoon honey

Combine all ingredients in a screw top jar. Feed plant each day for 7 days with additional 1 teaspoon sugar, 1 teaspoon ginger, 1 teaspoon honey and $\frac{1}{2}$ teaspoon instant coffee powder.

*To Make up Ginger Beer*: Dissolve 3 cups sugar in 4 cups hot water. Add 7 pints cold water and strained juice of 3 lemons. Add to this the strained liquid from screw-top jar (strain through fine muslin cloth). Pour into clean, dry, airtight bottles; seal tops. The best bottles to use have special clamp tops. Keep 3 to 4 weeks before using.

Makes approx. 10 pints.

*To Keep Plant Alive*: Halve the residue strained into muslin, return to jar with 1 cup water; let stand 1 week, feeding each day as before.

## Irish Coffee

1 tablespoon Irish whiskey
1 teaspoon sugar
strong black coffee
unwhipped cream

Place whiskey into small, warmed goblet, add sugar. Fill to within $\frac{1}{2}$ in. of top with black coffee. Stir quickly to dissolve sugar. Top with $\frac{1}{4}$ in. layer of cream. The best way to do this is to hold a spoon over coffee, and gently pour cream over back of spoon bowl so that cream floats on top. Do not stir.

*Gaelic Coffee:* Use Scotch whisky instead of Irish whiskey.

## Mulled Wine

1 bottle claret
2 cinnamon sticks
6 cloves
1 tablespoon sugar
1 cup brandy
1 piece lemon rind
nutmeg

Combine claret, crushed cinnamon sticks, cloves, sugar, brandy and lemon rind in saucepan, heat slowly, do not boil. Strain wine through a fine strainer. Serve hot in mugs, sprinkle with a little nutmeg.

Makes approx. $1\frac{1}{2}$ pints.

## Gluehwein

1 bottle claret
6 whole cloves
1 cinnamon stick
6 lemon slices
6 orange slices
2 tablespoons sugar

Place all ingredients in saucepan, heat slowly but do not allow to boil. Strain wine through a fine strainer, serve hot. Garnish with extra lemon and orange slices.

Makes approx. $1\frac{1}{2}$ pints

NOTE: 1 tablespoon brandy may be added to each glass before adding the hot Gluehwein.

## Glogg

1 bottle port wine
1 bottle Burgundy
1 bottle Aquavit
1 cinnamon stick
1 tablespoon whole cloves
raisins
blanched almonds

Combine port, burgundy and aquavit in a saucepan, heat slowly, simmer 3 minutes. Tie cinnamon and cloves in a muslin bag, dip into simmering wine mixture for 1 minute. Place a few raisins and almonds in each glass, top with the Glogg, serve hot in coffee mugs.

Makes approx. 4 pints

## Apple Cider

4 lb. over-ripe, bruised or spotted apples
6 pints cold water
1 cup sugar

Wash and dry apples, cut into $\frac{1}{2}$ in. slices; place in large crockery basin, cover with the cold water. Cover with cloth and allow to stand 10 days, stirring daily. The mixture will ferment and bubble.

After 10 days, drain apples and discard, reserve liquid. Stir in sugar, stirring until dissolved. Strain through several thicknesses of fine muslin; do not squeeze muslin. Bottle into clean dry bottles and allow to stand, uncorked but covered with cloth, for 14 days. The cider will continue to bubble in the bottle, the bubbles becoming smaller and less frequent toward the end of this period. If necessary, re-strain into clean dry bottles to remove sediment. Cork securely, label and date. Keep for three months before using.

Makes 3 pints

## Port Sangria

1 bottle claret
½ bottle port
1 cup marsala
¼ cup orange juice
1 tablespoon lemon juice

Combine all ingredients, mix well. Passionfruit pulp, sliced strawberries can also be added. Pour into jugs. Garnish with orange and lemon slices.

Makes about $2\frac{1}{2}$ pints

## Wine Sangria

2 bottles red wine
½ cup brandy
26 oz. bottle lemonade
oranges, strawberries or other fruit

Combine wine and brandy, add a few orange or lemon slices and whole strawberries, pour over crushed ice. Just before serving add chilled lemonade. Garnish with spirals of orange rind.

Makes approx. 4 pints

## Teenagers' Punch

4 oranges
4 bananas
4 apples
4 passionfruit
30 oz. can pineapple pieces
1 cup sugar
1 bottle lemon cordial
1 bottle orange cordial
8 26 oz. bottles lemonade
3 26 oz. bottles ginger ale
6 13 oz. bottles soda water
1 punnet strawberries

Peel and chop oranges, bananas and apples, remove pulp from passionfruit. Combine in a large basin with undrained pineapple and sugar; refrigerate until ready to serve. Combine cordials and 2 bottles lemonade in punch bowl; refrigerate. Just before serving, add ginger ale, soda water and remaining lemonade; stir in fruit mixture, hulled strawberries and ice.

Makes approx. 3 gallons.

NOTE: For an adult punch, 1 or 2 bottles brandy can be added.

## Party Punch

1 cup sugar
2 pints water
¼ cup strong black tea
4 oranges
4 lemons
15 oz. can light grape juice
15 oz. can crushed pineapple
26 oz. bottle ginger ale
orange slices
maraschino cherries
strawberries

Combine sugar and water in saucepan, stir over low heat until sugar dissolves, bring to boil; reduce heat, simmer 5 minutes. Add strained tea, refrigerate. Squeeze juice from oranges and lemons. Add strained fruit juices, grape juice and undrained pineapple to syrup; refrigerate. Pour into punch bowl; just before serving, add ginger ale, garnish with orange slices, cherries and hulled and sliced strawberries.

Makes approx. 6 pints

## White Wine Punch

3 bottles white wine
1 cup brandy
juice ½ lemon
watermelon

With melon baller, cut balls from watermelon. Put into bowl, cover, refrigerate.

Have the wine well chilled; Moselle is a good wine to use for this punch.

At serving time, pour wine into punch bowl, add lemon juice, brandy and melon balls. Ice cubes can also be added.

Makes approx. 4 pints

## Champagne Fruit Punch

½ lemon
1 orange
15 oz. can pineapple pieces
½ cup brandy
2 tablespoons sugar
1 bottle Moselle
1 bottle champagne
2 13 oz. bottles soda water

Slice the lemon and orange finely, drain pineapple pieces, discard syrup. Combine fruit, brandy and sugar in punch bowl; refrigerate. Before serving, add remaining ingredients.

Makes approx. 4 pints

## Superb Party Punch

2 lb. peaches
sugar
1 flagon dry white wine
½ bottle red wine
¼ cup brandy
¼ cup Cointreau
1 bottle champagne

Peel peaches, slice into punch bowl, sprinkle lightly with sugar. Add chilled white wine, red wine, Cointreau and brandy. Just before serving, stir in chilled champagne.

Makes approx. $1\frac{1}{4}$ gallons

## Pineapple Punch

3 cups strong tea
¾ cup lemon juice
2 cups pineapple juice
1 cup fresh orange juice
1 cup sugar
2 26 oz. bottles lemonade
26 oz. bottle ginger ale
lemon slices

Strain tea, combine with fruit juices and sugar, refrigerate. Just before serving, add chilled lemonade, ginger ale and ice. Place half a lemon slice in each glass before pouring in punch.

Makes approx. 7 pints

## Tahitian Rum Punch

1 bottle white rum
½ cup canned pineapple juice
¾ cup fresh orange juice
¾ cup lime or lemon juice
2 26 oz. bottles ginger ale
sugar
fresh fruit slices

Chill all ingredients well; combine rum, strained fruit juices and sugar to taste, in a punch bowl. Just before serving, add ice and ginger ale. Garnish with fresh fruit slices.

Makes approx. 5 pints

## West Indian Punch

This is the famous rum punch of the West Indies. It is compiled in the following proportions:

1 bitter (1 measure of lemon juice)
2 sweet (2 measures of sugar syrup)
3 strong (3 measures of rum)
4 weak (4 measures of water)

With 1 bottle of rum as the base, the punch is prepared as follows:

1 cup lemon juice
2 cups sugar syrup (made from 2 cups sugar and ¾ cup water)
26 oz. bottle rum
4 cups water, extra
grated nutmeg
angostura bitters

Make syrup; combine water and sugar in saucepan. Bring to boil, stir to dissolve sugar; cool.

Mix all ingredients together lightly. Add a few drops of angostura bitters to give a light pink tint. Refrigerate until well chilled.

Put a spoonful of crushed ice in each glass, pour in punch. Top each glass with grated nutmeg. A maraschino cherry, a light dash of pineapple juice or a few pieces of pineapple can be added.

Makes 4 pints

White Wine Punch, served sparkling cold, has colourful balls of watermelon added just before serving

# MEASUREMENTS

## Recipe Measurements

### Cup Measures

The standard eight liquid ounce measuring cup is used for recipes in this book.

A standard ½ pint measuring jug has been approved by the Standards Association. As shown in the sketch, this measures up to ½ pint, or 10 fluid ounces. The 8 fluid ounce, or 1 cup measure, is clearly shown, together with fractions of cup measures. Millilitre (ml.) measures are also shown, for when the metric system comes into operation.

To measure dry ingredients with a cup, spoon ingredient lightly into cup until it reaches required mark. Hold glass measure at eye level to make sure of measurement. Never pack ingredients tightly into cup, unless recipe specifies this, as '1 cup firmly packed brown sugar.'

When measuring a liquid ingredient, the cup should be on level surface.

### Cup Measures

*(Using the eight-liquid-ounce cup)*

| | |
|---|---|
| 1 cup flour | 4 oz. |
| 1 cup sugar (crystal or castor) | 8 oz. |
| 1 cup icing sugar (free from lumps) | 5 oz. |
| 1 cup shortening (butter, margarine, etc.) | 8 oz. |
| 1 cup honey, golden syrup, treacle | 10 oz. |
| 1 cup brown sugar (lightly packed) | 4 oz. |
| 1 cup brown sugar (firmly packed) | 5 oz. |
| 1 cup soft breadcrumbs | 2 oz. |
| 1 cup dry breadcrumbs (made from fresh breadcrumbs) | 3 oz. |
| 1 cup packet dry breadcrumbs | 4 oz. |
| 1 cup rice (uncooked) | 6 oz. |
| 1 cup rice (cooked) | 5 oz. |
| 1 cup mixed fruit or individual fruit such as sultanas, etc. | 4 oz. |
| 1 cup grated cheese | 4 oz. |
| 1 cup nuts (chopped) | 4 oz. |
| 1 cup coconut | 2½ oz. |

### Liquid Measures

*(Using the eight-liquid-ounce cup measure)*

| | |
|---|---|
| 1 cup liquid | 8 oz. |
| 2½ cups liquid | 20 oz. (1 pint) |
| 1 gill liquid | 5 oz. (¼ pint) |

### Spoon Measures

Standard spoon measures have now been established by the Standards Association of Australia. These are based on metric measures.
The tablespoon measures 20 ml.;
the teaspoon, 5 ml.
Standard spoon sets, which give exact measurement, are available.

Level spoon measurements are used in all recipes in this book

NOTE: The standard measuring cup shown on this page measures up to 250 millilitres; this is equivalent to quarter of a litre.

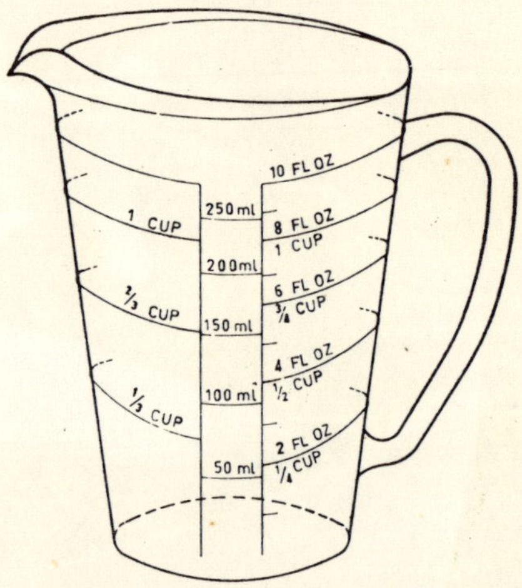


Standard ½-Pint (10 Aust. Fl. Oz.) Measure.

## English and American Measures

### English

Similar to Australian, except the term '1 cup' refers to 10 fluid oz. measuring cup, not the 8 fluid oz. measure used in Australia.

### American

The American pint is 16 fluid oz., compared with our Imperial pint measure of 20 fluid oz. The American tablespoon is equal to 14.8 ml.; the teaspoon, 4.8 ml. The American cup measure is 8 fluid oz., the same as Australian.

## Metric Measures

The metric system is scheduled to come into operation in Australia. We will measure in grams then, instead of ounces; in kilograms, instead of pounds; in millilitres and litres, instead of pints.

Set out below is a table with exact conversions. For easier working out of recipes, converting them from ounces to grammes, 30 grammes could be taken as the basic unit, instead of the exact 28.35. In England, 25 g. has been suggested as the basic unit; this multiplies easily into larger metric measures.

### Metric Weights

| | | |
|---|---|---|
| One gram | = | .035 ounce |
| 1 oz. | = | 28.35 g. |
| 2 oz. | = | 56.7 g. |
| 4 oz. | = | 113.4 g. |
| 8 oz. | = | 226.8 g. |
| 12 oz. | = | 340.2 g. |
| 16 oz. (1 lb.) | = | 453.6 g. |
| 1 kilogram | = | 2.2 lb. |

### Metric Liquid Measures

| | | |
|---|---|---|
| ¼ pint | = | 142 millilitres |
| ½ pint | = | 284 ml. |
| 1 pint | = | 568 ml. |
| ½ litre | = | 0.88 pint. |
| 1 litre | = | 1.76 pints (approx. 1¾ pints) |
| 1,000 millilitres | = | 1 litre |
| 100 centilitres | = | 1 litre |
| 10 decilitres | = | 1 litre |
| 1 decilitre | = | 1/10th litre, or 3½ fluid oz. |

## Oven Temperatures

Below is a general guide to oven heats and temperatures. Oven heats in electric ranges can vary, depending on the manufacturer; it is always wise to consult the manufacturer's booklet issued with the particular model of range.

### Gas Temperatures

| | |
|---|---|
| Slow | 250–275 deg. F. |
| Moderately slow | 300–325 deg. F. |
| Moderate | 350 deg. F. |
| Moderately hot | 375 deg. F. |
| Hot | 400–450 deg. F. |
| Very hot | 475–500 deg. F. |

### Electric Temperatures

| | |
|---|---|
| Slow | 250–300 deg. F. |
| Moderately slow | 300–325 deg. F. |
| Moderate | 350–400 deg. F. |
| Moderately hot | 425–450 deg. F. |
| Hot | 475–500 deg. F. |
| Very hot | 525–550 deg. F. |

# CALORIE COUNTER & WEIGHT TA

## FIND YOUR IDEAL WEIGHT

Find your ideal weight from the weight tables in this calorie counter. Multiply the number of pounds by 16 if your work is sedentary, by 18 if fairly active, by 20 if very active. (The average office worker should use the 16.) The result is the number of calories needed per day to MAINTAIN your weight. Reduce this number by 500 per day and you should lose at least 1 lb. per week. Reduce it by 1000 and you should lose 2 lb. per week.

EXAMPLE. You are an active housewife weighing 10 st. You are aged 28, with a light frame, 5 ft. 2 in. tall. Your ideal weight is 8 st. (i.e., 112 lb.). Multiply 112 x 20. Result, 2240 calories per day. This will keep you at your present weight. Subtract 1000 per day. On 1240 calories daily you should lose 2 lb. per week.

EXAMPLE. You are a typist, aged 33, 5 ft. 8 in tall, big frame, and weigh 12 st. 2 lb. Your ideal weight is 11 st. 8 lb. (162 lb.). Multiply 162 x 16. Result, 2592. If you eat 2592 calories a day you'll stay the same weight. Subtract 1000 per day. On 1500 calories you should lose that 6 lb. in three weeks.

## IDEAL WEIGHTS FOR MEN

Undressed. For clothing and shoes allow 8 lb
L—Light frame. A—Average frame
B—Big frame

AGE GROUPS

| HEIGHT | 25-29 | | | 30-34 | | | 35-39 | | | 40-44 | | |
|---|---|---|---|---|---|---|---|---|---|---|---|---|
| | L | A | B | L | A | B | L | A | B | L | A | B |
| 4′11″ | 110 | 116 | 138 | 112 | 118 | 140 | 112 | 118 | 140 | 112 | 117 | 139 |
| 5′ 0″ | 112 | 118 | 140 | 114 | 120 | 142 | 114 | 120 | 142 | 114 | 119 | 141 |
| 5′ 1″ | 114 | 120 | 142 | 116 | 122 | 144 | 116 | 122 | 144 | 116 | 121 | 143 |
| 5′ 2″ | 115 | 123 | 143 | 117 | 125 | 145 | 117 | 125 | 145 | 117 | 124 | 144 |
| 5′ 3″ | 118 | 126 | 146 | 120 | 128 | 148 | 120 | 128 | 148 | 120 | 127 | 147 |
| 5′ 4″ | 122 | 130 | 150 | 124 | 132 | 152 | 124 | 132 | 152 | 124 | 131 | 151 |
| 5′ 5″ | 125 | 134 | 154 | 127 | 136 | 156 | 127 | 136 | 156 | 127 | 135 | 155 |
| 5′ 6″ | 130 | 138 | 159 | 132 | 140 | 161 | 132 | 140 | 161 | 132 | 139 | 160 |
| 5′ 7″ | 133 | 142 | 163 | 135 | 144 | 165 | 135 | 144 | 165 | 135 | 143 | 164 |
| 5′ 8″ | 136 | 146 | 167 | 138 | 148 | 169 | 138 | 148 | 169 | 138 | 147 | 168 |
| 5′ 9″ | 140 | 150 | 173 | 143 | 153 | 176 | 143 | 153 | 176 | 143 | 152 | 175 |
| 5′10″ | 143 | 155 | 178 | 146 | 158 | 181 | 146 | 158 | 181 | 146 | 157 | 180 |
| 5′11″ | 149 | 161 | 185 | 152 | 164 | 188 | 152 | 164 | 188 | 152 | 163 | 187 |
| 6′ 0″ | 154 | 167 | 190 | 157 | 170 | 193 | 157 | 170 | 193 | 157 | 169 | 192 |
| 6′ 1″ | 159 | 173 | 193 | 162 | 176 | 196 | 162 | 176 | 196 | 162 | 175 | 195 |
| 6′ 2″ | 164 | 178 | 195 | 168 | 182 | 203 | 168 | 182 | 203 | 168 | 181 | 202 |

| HEIGHT | 45-49 | | | 50-54 | | | 55-59 | | | 60-64 | | |
|---|---|---|---|---|---|---|---|---|---|---|---|---|
| | L | A | B | L | A | B | L | A | B | L | A | B |
| 4′11″ | 112 | 116 | 138 | 111 | 115 | 137 | 110 | 114 | 136 | 107 | 111 | 132 |
| 5′ 0″ | 114 | 118 | 140 | 113 | 117 | 139 | 112 | 116 | 138 | 109 | 113 | 134 |
| 5′ 1″ | 116 | 120 | 142 | 115 | 119 | 141 | 114 | 118 | 140 | 111 | 115 | 136 |
| 5′ 2″ | 117 | 123 | 143 | 116 | 122 | 142 | 115 | 121 | 141 | 112 | 118 | 137 |
| 5′ 3″ | 120 | 126 | 146 | 119 | 125 | 145 | 118 | 124 | 144 | 115 | 121 | 140 |
| 5′ 4″ | 124 | 130 | 150 | 123 | 129 | 149 | 122 | 128 | 148 | 119 | 125 | 144 |
| 5′ 5″ | 127 | 134 | 154 | 126 | 133 | 153 | 125 | 132 | 152 | 122 | 129 | 148 |
| 5′ 6″ | 132 | 138 | 159 | 131 | 137 | 158 | 130 | 136 | 157 | 127 | 133 | 153 |
| 5′ 7″ | 135 | 142 | 163 | 134 | 141 | 162 | 133 | 140 | 161 | 130 | 137 | 157 |
| 5′ 8″ | 138 | 146 | 167 | 137 | 145 | 166 | 136 | 144 | 165 | 133 | 141 | 161 |
| 5′ 9″ | 143 | 151 | 174 | 142 | 150 | 173 | 141 | 149 | 172 | 138 | 146 | 168 |
| 5′10″ | 146 | 156 | 179 | 145 | 155 | 178 | 144 | 154 | 177 | 141 | 151 | 173 |
| 5′11″ | 152 | 162 | 186 | 151 | 161 | 185 | 150 | 160 | 184 | 147 | 157 | 180 |
| 6′ 0″ | 157 | 168 | 191 | 156 | 167 | 190 | 155 | 166 | 189 | 152 | 163 | 185 |
| 6′ 1″ | 162 | 174 | 194 | 161 | 173 | 193 | 160 | 172 | 192 | 157 | 169 | 188 |
| 6′ 2″ | 168 | 180 | 201 | 167 | 179 | 200 | 166 | 178 | 199 | 163 | 175 | 195 |

BLES

*A diary notebook makes a vigilant companion to your counter. During the day, list everything you eat and its calorie value, then you'll know what you can afford*

## IDEAL WEIGHTS FOR WOMEN

Undressed. For clothing and shoes allow 4 lb
L—Light frame A—Average frame
B—Big frame

AGE GROUPS

| HEIGHT | 21-24 | | | 25-29 | | | 30-34 | | | 35-39 | | | 40-44 | | |
|---|---|---|---|---|---|---|---|---|---|---|---|---|---|---|---|
| | L | A | B | L | A | B | L | A | B | L | A | B | L | A | B |
| 4′ 9″ | 99 | 108 | 121 | 101 | 110 | 123 | 103 | 112 | 125 | 103 | 112 | 125 | 103 | 111 | 124 |
| 4′10″ | 101 | 110 | 123 | 103 | 112 | 125 | 105 | 114 | 127 | 105 | 114 | 127 | 105 | 113 | 126 |
| 4′11″ | 103 | 112 | 125 | 105 | 114 | 127 | 107 | 116 | 129 | 107 | 116 | 129 | 107 | 115 | 128 |
| 5′ 0″ | 105 | 114 | 127 | 107 | 116 | 129 | 109 | 118 | 131 | 109 | 118 | 131 | 109 | 117 | 130 |
| 5′ 1″ | 107 | 116 | 128 | 109 | 118 | 130 | 111 | 120 | 132 | 111 | 120 | 132 | 111 | 119 | 131 |
| 5′ 2″ | 110 | 119 | 133 | 112 | 121 | 135 | 114 | 123 | 137 | 114 | 123 | 137 | 114 | 122 | 136 |
| 5′ 3″ | 112 | 123 | 134 | 114 | 125 | 136 | 116 | 127 | 138 | 116 | 127 | 138 | 116 | 126 | 137 |
| 5′ 4″ | 116 | 126 | 141 | 118 | 128 | 143 | 120 | 130 | 145 | 120 | 130 | 145 | 120 | 129 | 144 |
| 5′ 5″ | 119 | 130 | 142 | 121 | 132 | 144 | 123 | 134 | 146 | 123 | 134 | 146 | 123 | 133 | 145 |
| 5′ 6″ | 123 | 134 | 150 | 125 | 136 | 152 | 127 | 138 | 154 | 127 | 138 | 154 | 127 | 137 | 153 |
| 5′ 7″ | 127 | 138 | 152 | 129 | 140 | 154 | 131 | 142 | 156 | 131 | 142 | 156 | 131 | 141 | 155 |
| 5′ 8″ | 131 | 142 | 158 | 133 | 144 | 150 | 135 | 146 | 162 | 135 | 146 | 162 | 135 | 145 | 161 |
| 5′ 9″ | 134 | 146 | 161 | 136 | 148 | 163 | 138 | 150 | 165 | 138 | 150 | 165 | 138 | 149 | 164 |

| HEIGHT | 45-49 | | | 50-54 | | | 55-59 | | | 60-64 | | | 65-70 | | |
|---|---|---|---|---|---|---|---|---|---|---|---|---|---|---|---|
| | L | A | B | L | A | B | L | A | B | L | A | B | L | A | B |
| 4′ 9″ | 103 | 110 | 123 | 102 | 109 | 122 | 101 | 108 | 121 | 98 | 105 | 117 | 95 | 102 | 114 |
| 4′10″ | 105 | 112 | 125 | 104 | 111 | 124 | 103 | 110 | 123 | 100 | 107 | 119 | 97 | 104 | 116 |
| 4′11″ | 107 | 114 | 127 | 106 | 113 | 126 | 105 | 112 | 125 | 102 | 109 | 121 | 99 | 106 | 118 |
| 5′ 0″ | 109 | 116 | 129 | 108 | 115 | 128 | 107 | 114 | 127 | 104 | 111 | 123 | 101 | 108 | 120 |
| 5′ 1″ | 111 | 118 | 130 | 110 | 117 | 129 | 109 | 116 | 128 | 106 | 113 | 124 | 103 | 110 | 121 |
| 5′ 2″ | 114 | 121 | 135 | 113 | 120 | 134 | 112 | 119 | 133 | 109 | 116 | 129 | 106 | 113 | 126 |
| 5′ 3″ | 116 | 125 | 136 | 115 | 124 | 135 | 114 | 123 | 134 | 111 | 120 | 130 | 108 | 117 | 127 |
| 5′ 4″ | 120 | 128 | 143 | 119 | 127 | 142 | 118 | 126 | 141 | 115 | 123 | 137 | 112 | 120 | 134 |
| 5′ 5″ | 123 | 132 | 144 | 122 | 131 | 143 | 121 | 130 | 142 | 118 | 127 | 138 | 115 | 124 | 135 |
| 5′ 6″ | 127 | 136 | 152 | 126 | 135 | 151 | 125 | 134 | 150 | 122 | 131 | 146 | 119 | 128 | 143 |
| 5′ 7″ | 131 | 140 | 154 | 130 | 139 | 153 | 129 | 138 | 152 | 126 | 135 | 148 | 123 | 132 | 145 |
| 5′ 8″ | 135 | 144 | 160 | 134 | 143 | 159 | 133 | 142 | 158 | 130 | 139 | 154 | 127 | 136 | 151 |
| 5′ 9″ | 138 | 148 | 163 | 137 | 147 | 162 | 136 | 146 | 161 | 133 | 143 | 157 | 130 | 140 | 154 |

*Weigh yourself once a week in the same clothes at the same time. There is a normal variation of at least 2 lb. weight from day to day, so do not be disappointed if at times you register an apparent gain. If you stick faithfully to your diet you should see a result the next week*

### BUILD GUIDE FOR WOMEN

Have you a light, average, or big frame? There are seven parts of the body which vary noticeably in skeletons—shoulders, chest, pelvis, hips, wrists, knees, and ankles. If you are large in the majority of these you fit in the large-frame group. Wrists that measure 6¼ in. or less show you are in the light-frame classification

*NOTE: Almost anyone can lose weight on 1200 calories per day.*

# CALORIE COUNTER

## Batter Foods

(Calorie count does not include calories in butter, jam, sugar, or syrup served with batter foods.)

| | |
|---|---|
| 1 Pancake, 6 in. diameter | 90 |
| 1 Pikelet, 3 in. diameter | 65 |
| 1 Waffle, 5 in. diameter | 200 |
| 1 Crumpet, 3 in. diameter | 90 |

## Bread, Buns, Biscuits

| | |
|---|---|
| 1 slice Bread, 3 in. x 4 in. x ½ in. | 80 |
| 1 small Bread Roll, restaurant size | 100 |
| 1 slice Bun Loaf with sultanas | 65 |
| 1 slice Melba or Fairy Toast, 3 in. x 4 in. x ⅛ in. | 25 |
| 1 Yeast Bun, 2½ in. diameter | 140 |
| 1 Wheatmeal Biscuit | 42 |
| 1 Dry Biscuit, plain | 25 to 40 |
| 1 Sweet Biscuit, plain | 50 |

## Cakes

| | |
|---|---|
| Chocolate Eclair, cream filled | 300 |
| Chocolate Cake, 3 in. x 2 in. x ¾ in. | 300 |
| Cup Cake or Rock Cake, 1 | 105 |
| Fruit Cake, 1 small slice, 1½ oz. | 165 |
| Gingerbread, 3 in. x 2 in. x ¾ in. | 200 |
| Pastry, 3 in. square x ½ in. | 275 |
| Plain Cake, 1 small slice, 1½ oz. | 180 |
| Plain Cake, small slice, iced or filled | 300 |
| Sponge Cake, plain, 1 oz. slice | 90 |
| Sponge Cake, 1 slice, iced and filled | 300 |

## Cereals

(Calorie count does not include calories in milk and sugar used.)

| | |
|---|---|
| Breakfast cereals, 1 oz., dry (1 cup) | 105 |
| Porridge, cooked, 8 oz. cup | 200 |

## Condiments and Sauces

| | |
|---|---|
| Apple Sauce, 4 oz. | 85 |
| Chilli Sauce, 1 dessertspoon | 15 |
| Chocolate Sauce, 1 dessertspoon | 100 |
| Chutney, 2 tablespoons | 45 |
| Cream Sauce, 1 dessertspoon | 35 |
| French Dressing, 1 dessertspoon | 35 |
| Gravy (thick), 4 tablespoons | 80 |
| Hard Sauce, 1 dessertspoon | 100 |
| Hollandaise Sauce, 1 dessertspoon | 15 |
| Horseradish Sauce, 1 dessertspoon | 15 |
| Mayonnaise, 1 dessertspoon | 100 |
| Mustard, 1 teaspoon | 10 |
| Mustard Pickles, 4 dessertspoons | 15 |
| Sweet White Sauce, 1 dessertspoon | 25 |
| Tartare Sauce, 1 dessertspoon | 90 |
| Thousand Island, 1 dessertspoon | 90 |
| Melted Butter Sauce, 1 dessertspoon | 100 |
| Tomato Sauce, 1 tablespoon | 15 |
| Vinegar | 0 |
| White Sauce, medium thick, 4 tablespoons | 100 |
| Worcestershire Sauce, 1 dessertspoon | 10 |

## Dairy Products

| | |
|---|---|
| Butter, ½ oz. | 105 |
| Butter, 1 teaspoon | 25 |
| Cheese, Cheddar and Processed, 1¼ in. cube (1 oz.) | 120 |
| Cottage Cheese, made from skim milk, 1 oz. | 32 |
| Cheese (Edam), 1 oz. | 100 |
| Cheese (Gruyere), 1 oz. | 130 |
| Cheese (Gorgonzola), 1 oz. | 110 |
| Cream, 1 tablespoon (½ oz.) | 50 |
| Milk, 8 oz. glass | 150 |
| Milk (skim), 8 oz. glass | 75 |
| Yoghurt, 1 oz. | 25 |

## Desserts

PIES:

(Pie slices are one-sixth of a 9 in. diameter pie 1 in. thick).

| | |
|---|---|
| Apple, 1 slice | 330 |
| Apricot, 1 slice | 300 |
| Butterscotch, 1 slice | 350 |
| Custard, 1 slice | 270 |
| Lemon Meringue, 1 slice | 300 |
| Mince (fruit), 1 slice | 340 |
| Peach, 1 slice | 300 |
| Rhubarb, 1 slice | 330 |

PUDDINGS:

| | |
|---|---|
| Apple Dumplings, 1 oz. | 55 |
| Banana Custard, 4 oz. (av. serv.) | 120 |
| Blancmange, 4 oz. (av. serv.) | 135 |
| Custard (boiled), 5 tablespoons | 80 |
| Custard (baked), 5 oz. (av. serv.) | 150 |
| Custard (baked with bread, macaroni, rice, sago, tapioca), 5 oz. (av. serv.) | 200 |
| Fruit Salad, ½ cup sweetened | 110 |
| Fruit gelatine shape, 4 oz. | 85 |
| Ice-cream (1 small bucket or 5 tablespoons) | 70 |
| Jelly, 4 oz. | 75 |
| Junket, 4 oz. | 95 |
| Plum Pudding (no sauce), 4 oz. | 370 |
| Steamed Pudding, 2 oz., serving | 240 |

## Drinks

| | |
|---|---|
| Apple Cider, 8 oz. glass | 100 |
| Cocoa (all milk), breakfast cup, 8 oz. | 165 |
| Cocoa (half milk, half water), breakfast cup, 8 oz. | 90 |
| Coffee (black) (Add 20 calories for two tablespoons milk; add 25 calories for each teaspoon sugar) | 0 |
| Ginger Ale, 8 oz. glass | 55 |
| Lemonade, 8 oz. glass | 55 |
| Malted milk, plain (no icecream), 8 oz. glass | 180 |
| Milk, 8 oz. glass | 150 |
| Soda Water | 0 |
| Tea, black (add calories for milk and sugar as in coffee) | 0 |
| Tonic Water, 8 oz. glass | 55 |
| Water | 0 |

## Drinks (alcoholic)

| | |
|---|---|
| Beer, ½ pint | 115 |
| Brandy, 1 oz. | 55 |
| Gin, 1 oz. | 55 |
| Rum, 1 oz. | 55 |
| Stout, ½ pint | 100 |
| Whisky, 1 oz. | 55 |
| Wine, dry white, 5 oz. glass | 90 |
| Wine, sweet white, 5 oz. glass | 100 |
| Wine, dry red, 5 oz. glass | 90 |
| Wines (fortified): Dry Sherry, Dry Vermouth, 3 oz. glass | 90 |
| Muscat, Port, Sweet Sherry, Vermouth, 3 oz. glass | 115 |

## Eggs

| | |
|---|---|
| Boiled (1) | 80 |
| Fried (1) | 135 |
| Omelet (1) | 135 |
| Poached (1) | 80 |
| Scrambled (1), with milk and butter | 145 |
| White only (1) | 15 |
| Yolk only (1) | 65 |

## Fats and Cooking Oils

| | |
|---|---|
| Cooking fat, ½ oz. | 130 |
| Oil, ½ oz. | 130 |

## Fish

| | |
|---|---|
| Caviar, 1 oz. | 90 |
| Crab, Crayfish, Lobster, 4 oz. | 150 |
| Fish — non-fatty, e.g., Bream, Flathead, Whiting, Flounder, 4 oz. grilled or steamed | 115 |
| Fried in batter | 235 |
| Fish — fatty, e.g., Herring, Mullet, 4 oz. grilled or steamed | 200 |
| Fried in batter | 320 |
| Haddock, smoked, 4 oz. | 110 |
| Kipper herring, ½ large fish, grilled | 255 |
| Oysters, 8 | 100 |
| Prawns, shelled, 3 oz. | 85 |
| Salmon, canned, 2 oz. | 100 |
| Sardines, canned 2 oz. | 120 |
| Scallops, 4 oz. | 90 |
| Tuna, canned, 2 oz. | 140 |

## Flour Foods

| | |
|---|---|
| Flour, Cornflour, 1 tablespoon | 25 |
| Macaroni, cooked, 8 oz. cup | 170 |
| Macaroni Cheese, 4 oz. | 350 |
| Rice, cooked, 8 oz. cup | 200 |
| Spaghetti, cooked, 8 oz. cup | 170 |

## Fresh Fruit and Vegetable Juices

| | |
|---|---|
| Apple, 4 oz. glass | 100 |
| Apricot, 4 oz. glass | 75 |
| Carrot, 4 oz. glass | 25 |
| Grape, 4 oz. glass | 60 |
| Grapefruit, 4 oz. glass | 45 |
| Orange, 4 oz. glass | 55 |
| Pineapple, 4 oz. glass | 60 |
| Tomato, 4 oz. glass | 25 |

(Diabetic fruit juices have no extra sugar added and are equal to fresh fruit juices.)

## Fresh Fruit

| | |
|---|---|
| Apple, medium size | 80 |
| Apricot, medium size | 20 |
| Avocado, half medium size | 160 |
| Banana, medium size | 100 |
| Blackberries, 8 oz. cup | 80 |
| Cantaloupe, half medium size (5 oz.) | 30 |
| Cherries, 8 oz. cup | 60 |
| Figs, 3 medium | 60 |
| Gooseberries, 8 oz. cup | 60 |
| Grapefruit, half medium size | 70 |
| Grapes, 8 oz. cup | 100 |
| Honeydew melon, half medium size, 5 oz. | 45 |
| Lemon, medium size | 25 |
| Loganberries, 8 oz. cup | 60 |
| Mandarin, medium size | 40 |
| Mango, medium size | 90 |
| Nectarine, medium size | 25 |
| Orange, medium size | 70 |
| Papaw, 8 oz. | 100 |
| Passionfruit, 1 | 20 |
| Peach, medium size | 50 |
| Pear, medium size | 85 |
| Persimmon, medium size | 75 |
| Pineapple, 1 slice, 3 oz. | 40 |
| Plum, medium size | 30 |
| Pomegranate, medium size | 75 |
| Raspberries, 8 oz. cup | 80 |
| Rockmelon, ½ medium | 30 |
| Strawberries, 8 oz. cup | 60 |
| Watermelon, slice 10 in. x ¾ in. | 50 |

## Fruit (dried)

| | |
|---|---|
| Currants, raisins, sultanas, chopped dates, 1 oz. | 80 |
| Prunes (4 medium) | 70 |
| Dried apples, apricots, pears, peaches or nectarines, 1 oz. | 80 |

## Fruit (cooked or canned)

| | |
|---|---|
| Apples, baked, medium size | 90 |
| Apples, stewed, 8 oz. cup (sweetened) | 160 |
| Apricots, canned, no syrup, 4 halves | 100 |
| Apricots, canned, with syrup, 8 oz. cup | 200 |
| Apricots, stewed, 5 medium size | 125 |
| Blackberries, canned, with syrup, 8 oz. cup | 220 |
| Cherries, canned, with syrup, 8 oz. | 120 |
| Figs, canned, with syrup, 4 oz. cup | 150 |
| Peaches, canned, with syrup, 2 halves | 100 |
| Peaches, canned, no syrup, 2 halves | 75 |
| Prunes, cooked with sugar, 4 oz. | 130 |

(Diabetic canned fruits or fruit cooked without sugar are equal in calorie content to fresh fruit.)

## Meat

| | |
|---|---|
| Bacon, grilled, 2 strips 6 in. long | 125 |
| Beef, roast, 4 in. x 4 in. x ¼ in. | 140 |
| Beef Casserole, 4 tablespoons with gravy | 335 |
| Brains, sheep, 1 set crumbed and fried (5 oz.) | 455 |
| Corned Beef, 2 oz. | 135 |
| Devon Sausage, 2 oz. | 130 |
| Frankfurt, one | 145 |
| Ham, 2 oz. | 230 |
| Hamburger or Rissole, 1 oz. | 90 |
| Kidneys, 2 oz. | 110 |
| Lamb Chop, one grilled | 130 |
| Lamb Cutlet, one small grilled | 65 |
| Lamb, roast, 3 oz. | 300 |
| Liver, fried, 3 oz. | 175 |
| Meat Pie (2 oz. pastry, 1 oz. filling) | 350 |
| Mince Steak, 3 oz. | 300 |
| Pork Chop, one, 3 oz. | 285 |
| Pork, roast, 3 oz. | 285 |
| Rabbit, baked, 3 oz. | 160 |
| Sausage, beef, one grilled | 160 |
| Sausage, pork, one grilled | 170 |
| Sausage Roll, small | 100 |
| Steak, grilled, 3 oz. | 255 |
| Tongue, 3 oz. | 160 |
| Tripe, 4 oz. (add 100 for 4 tablespoons white sauce) | 60 |
| Veal, roast, 3 oz. | 160 |
| Veal, breaded cutlet or schnitzel, 3 oz. | 185 |

## Nuts

(Calorie counts are for 1 oz.)

| | |
|---|---|
| Almonds | 170 |
| Brazil Nuts | 170 |
| Cashew Nuts | 160 |
| Coconut, desiccated | 185 |
| Macadamia Nuts | 200 |
| Peanuts, roasted | 160 |
| Walnuts | 145 |

## Poultry

One ounce of poultry is about 1 slice, 4 in. x 2 in. x ⅞ in. thick. Allow 70 calories per oz. of duck or turkey, 55 calories per oz. of chicken; 3 oz. is a medium-size helping.

## Soups

| | |
|---|---|
| Chicken Noodle, 1 cup | 100 |
| Clear Chicken Broth, 1 cup | 20 |
| Consomme, 1 cup | 20 |
| Creamed Vegetable Soups, 1 cup | 215 |
| Pea Soup, 1 cup | 150 |
| Tomato Soup, 1 cup | 75 |
| Vegetable Soup with Barley, 1 cup | 50 |

## Vegetables

| | |
|---|---|
| Asparagus, ½ cup | 20 |
| Beetroot, ½ cup | 60 |
| Broad Beans, ½ cup | 80 |
| Beans, French, ½ cup | 20 |
| Broccoli, ½ cup | 30 |
| Brussels Sprouts, ½ cup | 30 |
| Cabbage, ½ cup | 20 |
| Carrots, ½ cup | 30 |
| Cauliflower, ½ cup | 20 |
| Celery, 6 stalks | 15 |
| Choko, ½ cup | 30 |
| Corn, sweet, ½ cup | 90 |
| Corn, sweet, 1 ear 5 in. | 145 |
| Cucumber, medium size | 10 |
| Eggplant, medium slice | 30 |
| Endive, half head | 10 |
| Kohlrabi, ½ cup | 30 |
| Leek (1) | 5 |
| Lettuce, half head | 10 |
| Marrow, ½ cup | 5 |
| Mushrooms, ½ cup | 30 |
| Onions, ½ cup | 30 |
| Parsnips, ½ cup | 50 |
| Peas, ½ cup | 50 |
| Peppers, green (capsicum) | 10 |
| Potato, boiled, 1 medium | 100 |
| Potato, mashed, ½ cup | 100 |
| Potato, baked in fat, 1 medium | 200 |
| Potato chips, fried, 8 chips, 4 in. long | 220 |
| Pumpkin, mashed, ½ cup | 50 |
| Radishes, 6 | 10 |
| Spinach, ½ cup | 20 |
| Sweet Potato, medium size, baked in fat | 250 |
| Tomato, medium | 30 |
| Turnips, white, ½ cup | 20 |
| Turnips, Swede, ½ cup | 30 |

## Miscellaneous

| | |
|---|---|
| Chocolate, 2 oz. | 300 |
| Fish and meat paste, 1 oz. | 55 |
| Honey, 1 level dessertspoon | 60 |
| Jam, 1 level dessertspoon | 55 |
| Olive, green, 1 oz. (about 5, medium size) | 35 |
| Olives, black, 1 oz. (about 5, medium size) | 30 |
| Peanut Butter, 1 level dessertspoon | 100 |
| Sugar, 1 teaspoon | 25 |
| Sugar, 1 tablespoon | 55 |

# INDEX

Figures in italics
refer to colour plate

## A



## B



## C

# D



# E

# Q



# R



# S

# T



# U



# V



# W



# Y



# Z